STEPHEN KING

STEPHEN KING

THE SHINING

CARRIE

MISERY

TED SMART

The Shining was first published in Great Britain
by New English Library Limited in 1977

Carrie was first published in Great Britain
by New English Library Limited in 1974

Misery was first published in Great Britain
by Hodder and Stoughton Limited in 1987

This edition was first published in Great Britain in 1992
by Chancellor Press
an imprint of
Reed International Books Limited
Michelin House
81 Fulham Road
London SW3 6RB

This edition produced exclusively for the Book People.
Reprinted 1992, 1993.

ISBN 1 85613 820 8

The characters and situations in this book are entirely imaginary
and bear no relation to any real person or actual happenings.

Printed in Great Britain by the Bath Press.

CONTENTS

THE SHINING

ACKNOWLEDGMENTS

From 'Call Me,' © 1973 by Jec Music Publishing Co. and Al Green Music, Inc. for the world. All rights for Canada controlled by Felsted Music of Canada Ltd. All rights for world except the United States and Canada controlled by Burlington Music Co. Ltd., London, England.

'Your Cheatin' Heart,' by Hank Williams. Copyright 1952 by Fred Rose Music, Inc. Used by permission of the publisher, Fred Rose Music, Inc., 2510 Franklin Road, Nashville, Tennessee 37204. All rights reserved.

Lyrics from 'Twenty Flight Rock' by Ned Fairchild Copyright © 1957 by Hill and Range Songs, Inc. Noma Music, Inc. and Elvis Presley Music. International Copyright Secured. ALL RIGHTS RESERVED. Used by permission of Unichappell Music, Inc.

'Bad Moon Rising' by John C. Fogerty, © 1969 Jondora Music, Berkeley, Calif. Used by permission. All rights reserved. International copyright secured.

The Shining

This is for Joe Hill King, who shines on.

My editor on this book, as on the previous two, was Mr. William G. Thompson, a man of wit and good sense. His contribution to this book has been large, and for it, my thanks.

S.K.

Some of the most beautiful resort hotels in the world are located in Colorado, but the hotel in these pages is based on none of them. The Overlook and the people associated with it exist wholly within the author's imagination.

It was in this apartment, also, that there stood . . . a gigantic clock of ebony. Its pendulum swung to and fro with a dull, heavy, monotonous clang; and when . . . the hour was to be stricken, there came from the brazen lungs of the clock a sound which was clear and loud and deep and exceedingly musical, but of so peculiar a note and emphasis that, at each lapse of an hour, the musicians of the orchestra were constrained to pause . . . to hearken to the sound; and thus the waltzers perforce ceased their evolutions; and there was a brief disconcert of the whole gay company; and, while the chimes of the clock yet rang, it was observed that the giddiest grew pale, and the more aged and sedate passed their hands over their brows as if in confused reverie or meditation. But when the echoes had fully ceased, a light laughter at once pervaded the assembly . . . and [they] smiled as if at their own nervousness . . . and made whispering vows, each to the other, that the next chiming of the clock should produce in them no similar emotion; and then, after the lapse of sixty minutes . . . there came yet another chiming of the clock, and then were the same disconcert and tremulousness and meditation as before.

But in spite of these things, it was a gay and magnificent revel . . .

—E. A. Poe

'*The Masque of the Red Death*'

The sleep of reason breeds monsters.

Goya

It'll shine when it shines.

Folk saying

BOOK ONE

PREFATORY MATTERS

Chapter One

Job interview

Jack Torrance thought: *Officious little prick.*

Ullman stood five-five, and when he moved, it was with the prissy speed that seems to be the exclusive domain of all small plump men. The part in his hair was exact, and his dark suit was sober but comforting. I am a man you can bring your problems to, that suit said to the paying customer. To the hired help it spoke more curtly: This had better be good, you. There was a red carnation in the lapel, perhaps so that no one on the street would mistake Stuart Ullman for the local undertaker.

As he listened to Ullman speak, Jack admitted to himself that he probably could not have liked any man on that side of the desk – under the circumstances.

Ullman had asked a question he hadn't caught. That was bad; Ullman was the type of man who would file such lapses away in a mental Rolodex for later consideration.

'I'm sorry?'

'I asked if your wife fully understood what you would be taking on here. And there's your son, of course.' He glanced down at the application in front of him. 'Daniel. Your wife isn't a bit intimidated by the idea?'

'Wendy is an extraordinary woman.'

'And your son is also extraordinary?'

Jack smiled, a big wide PR smile. 'We like to think so, I suppose. He's quite self-reliant for a five-year-old.'

No returning smile from Ullman. He slipped Jack's application back into the file. The file went into a drawer. The desk top was now completely bare except for a blotter, a telephone, a Tensor lamp, and an in/out basket. Both sides of the in/out were empty, too.

Ullman stood up and went to the file cabinet in the corner. 'Step around the desk, if you will, Mr Torrance. We'll look at the floor plans.'

He brought back five large sheets and set them down on the glossy walnut plain of the desk. Jack stood by his shoulder, very much aware of the scent of Ullman's cologne. *All my men wear English Leather or they wear nothing at all* came into his mind for no reason at all, and he had to clamp his tongue between his teeth to keep in a bray of laughter. Beyond the wall, faintly, came the sounds of the Overlook Hotel's kitchen, gearing down from lunch.

'Top floor,' Ullman said briskly. 'The attic. Absolutely nothing up there now but bric-a-brac. The Overlook has changed hands several times since World War II and it seems that each successive manager has put everything they don't want up in the attic. I want rattraps and poison bait sowed around in it. Some of the third-floor chambermaids say they have heard rustling noises. I don't believe it, not for a moment, but there mustn't even be that one-in-a-hundred chance that a single rat inhabits the Overlook Hotel.'

Jack, who suspected that every hotel in the world had a rat or two, held his tongue.

'Of course you wouldn't allow your son up in the attic under any circumstances.'

'No,' Jack said, and flashed the big PR smile again. Humiliating situation. Did this officious little prick actually think he would allow his son to goof around in a rattrap attic full of junk furniture and God knew what else?

Ullman whisked away the attic floor plan and put it on the bottom of the pile.

'The Overlook has one hundred and ten guest quarters,' he said in a scholarly voice. 'Thirty of them, all suites, are here on the third floor. Ten in the west wing (including the Presidential Suite), ten in the center, ten more in the east wing. All of them command magnificent views.'

Could you at least spare the salestalk?

But he kept quiet. He needed the job.

Ullman put the third floor on the bottom of the pile and they studied the second floor.

'Forty rooms,' Ullman said, 'thirty doubles and ten singles. And on the first floor, twenty of each. Plus three linen closets on each floor, and a storeroom which is at the extreme east end of the hotel on the second floor and the extreme west end on the first. Questions?'

Jack shook his head. Ullman whisked the second and first floors away.

Now. Lobby level. Here in the center is the registration desk. Behind it are the offices. The lobby runs for eighty feet in either direction from the desk. Over here in the west wing is the Overlook Dining Room and the Colorado Lounge. The banquet and ballroom facility is in the east wing. Questions?'

'Only about the basement,' Jack said. 'For the winter caretaker, that's the most important level of all. Where the action is, so to speak.'

'Watson will show you all that. The basement floor plan is on the boiler room wall.' He frowned impressively, perhaps to show that as manager, he did not concern himself with such mundane aspects of the Overlook's operation as the boiler and the plumbing. 'Might not be a bad idea to put some traps down there too. Just a minute . . .'

He scrawled a note on a pad he took from his inner coat pocket (each sheet bore the legend *From the Desk of Stuart Ullman* in bold black script), tore it off, and dropped it into the out basket. It sat there looking lonesome. The pad disappeared back into Ullman's jacket pocket like the conclusion of a magician's trick. Now you see it, Jacky-boy, now you don't. This guy is a real heavyweight.

They had resumed their original positions, Ullman behind the desk and Jack in front of it, interviewer and interviewee, supplicant and reluctant patron. Ullman folded his neat little hands on the desk blotter and looked directly at Jack, a small, balding man in a banker's suit and a quiet gray tie. The flower in his lapel was balanced off by a small lapel pin on the other side. It read simply STAFF in small gold letters.

'I'll be perfectly frank with you, Mr Torrance. Albert Shockley is a powerful man with a large interest in the Overlook, which showed a profit this season for the first time in its history. Mr Shockley also sits on the Board of Directors, but he is not a hotel man and he would be the first to admit this. But he has made his wishes in this caretaking matter quite obvious. He wants you hired. I will do so. But if I had been given a free hand in this matter, I would not have taken you on.'

Jack's hands were clenched tightly in his lap, working against each other, sweating. *Officious little prick, officious*

'I don't believe you care much for me, Mr Torrance. I *little prick, officious—*
don't care. Certainly your feelings toward me play no part in my own belief that you are not right for the job. During the season that runs from May fifteenth to September thirtieth, the Overlook employs one hundred and ten people full-time; one for every room in the hotel, you might say. I don't think many of them like me and I suspect that some of them think I'm a bit of a bastard. They would be correct in their judgment of my character. I have to be a bit of a bastard to run this hotel in the manner it deserves.'

He looked at Jack for comment, and Jack flashed the PR smile again, large and insultingly toothy.

Ullman said: 'The Overlook was built in the years 1907 to 1909. The closest town is Sidewinder, forty miles east of here over roads that are closed from sometime in late October or November until sometime in April. A man named Robert Townley Watson built it, the grandfather of our present maintenance man. Vanderbilts have stayed here, and Rockefellers, and Astors, and Du Ponts. Four Presidents have stayed in the Presidential Suite. Wilson, Harding, Roosevelt, and Nixon.'

'I wouldn't be too proud of Harding and Nixon,' Jack murmured.

Ullman frowned but went on regardless. 'It proved too much for Mr Watson, and he sold the hotel in 1915. It was sold again in 1922, in 1929, in 1936. It stood vacant until the end of World War II, when it was purchased and completely renovated by Horace Derwent, millionaire inventor, pilot, film producer, and entrepreneur.'

'I know the name,' Jack said.

'Yes. Everything he touched seemed to turn to gold . . . except the Overlook. He funneled over a million dollars into it before the first postwar guest ever stepped through its doors, turning a decrepit relic into a showplace. It was Derwent who added the roque court I saw you admiring when you arrived.'

'Roque?'

'A British forebear of our croquet, Mr Torrance. Croquet is bastardized roque. According to legend, Derwent learned the game from his social secretary and fell completely in love with it. Ours may be the finest roque court in America.'

'I wouldn't doubt it,' Jack said gravely. A roque court, a topiary full of hedge animals out front, what next? A life-sized Uncle Wiggly game behind the equipment shed? He was getting very tired of Mr Stuart Ullman, but he could see that Ullman wasn't done. Ullman was going to have his say, every last word of it.

'When he had lost three million, Derwent sold it to a group of California investors. Their experience with the Overlook was equally bad. Just not hotel people.

'In 1970, Mr Shockley and a group of his associates bought the hotel and turned its management over to me. We have also run in the red for several years, but I'm happy to say that the trust of the present owners in me has never wavered. Last year we broke even. And this year the Overlook's accounts were written in black ink for the first time in almost seven decades.'

Jack supposed that this fussy little man's pride was justified, and then his original dislike washed over him again in a wave.

He said: 'I see no connection between the Overlook's admittedly colorful history and your feeling that I'm wrong for the post, Mr Ullman.'

'One reason that the Overlook has lost so much money lies in the depreciation that occurs each winter. It shortens the profit margin a great deal more than you might believe, Mr Torrance. The winters are fantastically cruel. In order to cope with the problem, I've installed a full-time winter caretaker to run the boiler and to heat different parts of the hotel on a daily rotating basis. To repair breakage as it occurs and to do repairs, so the elements can't get a foothold. To be constantly alert to any and every contingency. During our first winter I hired a family instead of a single man. There was a tragedy. A horrible tragedy.'

Ullman looked at Jack coolly and appraisingly.

'I made a mistake. I admit it freely. The man was a drunk.'

Jack felt a slow, hot grin – the total antithesis of the toothy PR grin – stretch across his mouth. 'Is that it? I'm surprised Al didn't tell you. I've retired.'

'Yes, Mr Shockley told me you no longer drink. He also told me about your last job . . . your last position of trust, shall we say? You were teaching English in a Vermont prep school. You lost your temper, I don't believe I need to be any more specific than that. But I do happen to believe that Grady's case has a bearing, and that is why I have brought the matter of your uh, previous history into the conversation. During the winter of 1970–71, after we had refurbished the Overlook but before our first season, I hired this . . . this unfortunate named Delbert Grady. He moved into the quarters you and your wife and son will be sharing. He had a wife and two daughters. I had reservations, the main ones being the harshness of the winter season and the fact that the Gradys would be cut off from the outside world for five to six months.'

'But that's not really true, is it? There are telephones here, and probably a citizen's band radio as well. And the Rocky Mountain National Park is within helicopter range and surely a piece of ground that big must have a chopper or two.'

'I wouldn't know about that,' Ullman said. 'The hotel does have a two-way radio that Mr Watson will show you, along with a list of the correct frequencies to broadcast on if you need help. The telephone lines between here and Sidewinder are still aboveground, and they go down almost every winter at some point or other and are apt to stay down for three weeks to a month and a half. There is a snowmobile in the equipment shed also.'

'Then the place really isn't cut off.'

Mr Ullman looked pained. 'Suppose your son or your wife tripped on the stairs and fractured his or her skull, Mr Torrance. Would you think the place was cut off then?'

Jack saw the point. A snowmobile running at top speed could get you down to Sidewinder in an hour and a half . . . maybe. A helicopter from the Parks Rescue Service could get up here in three hours . . . under optimum conditions. In a blizzard it would never even be able to lift off and you couldn't hope to run a snowmobile at top speed, even if you dared take a seriously injured person out into temperatures that might be twenty-five below – or forty-five below, if you added in the wind chill factor.

'In the case of Grady,' Ullman said, 'I reasoned much as Mr Shockley seems to have done in your case. Solitude can be damaging in itself. Better for the man to have his family with him. If there was trouble, I thought, the odds were very high that it would be something less urgent than a fractured skull or an accident with one of the power tools or some sort of convulsion. A serious case of the flu, pneumonia, a broken arm, even appendicitis. Any of those things would have left enough time.

'I suspect that what happened came as a result of too much cheap whiskey, of which Grady had laid in a generous supply, unbeknownst to me, and a curious condition which the old-timers call cabin fever. Do you know the term?' Ullman offered a patronizing little smile, ready to explain as soon as Jack admitted his ignorance, and Jack was happy to respond quickly and crisply.

'It's a slang term for the claustrophobic reaction that can occur when people are shut in together over long periods of time. The feeling of claustrophobia is externalized as dislike for the people you happen to be shut in with. In extreme cases it can result in hallucinations and violence – murder has been done over such minor things as a burned meal or an argument about whose turn it is to do the dishes.'

Ullman looked rather nonplussed, which did Jack a world of good. He decided to press a little further, but silently promised Wendy he would stay cool.

'I suspect you did make a mistake at that. Did he hurt them?'

'He killed them, Mr Torrance, and then committed suicide. He murdered the little girls with a hatchet, his wife with a shotgun, and himself the same way. His leg was broken. Undoubtedly so drunk he fell downstairs.'

Ullman spread his hands and looked at Jack self-righteously.

'Was he a high school graduate?'

'As a matter of fact, he wasn't,' Ullman said a little stiffly. 'I thought a, shall we say, less imaginative individual would be less susceptible to the rigors, the loneliness—'

'That was your mistake,' Jack said. 'A stupid man is more prone to cabin fever just as he's more prone to shoot someone over a card game or commit a spur-of-the-moment robbery. He gets bored. When the snow comes, there's nothing to do but watch TV or play solitaire and cheat when he can't get all the aces out. Nothing to do but bitch at his wife and nag at the kids and drink. It gets hard to sleep because there's nothing to hear. So he drinks himself to sleep and wakes up with a hangover. He gets edgy. And maybe the telephone goes out and the TV aerial blows down and there's nothing to do but think and cheat at solitaire and get edgier and edgier. Finally . . . boom, boom, boom.'

'Whereas a more educated man, such as yourself?'

'My wife and I both like to read. I have a play to work on, as Al Shockley probably told you. Danny has his puzzles, his coloring books, and his crystal radio. I plan to teach him to read, and I also want to teach him to snowshoe. Wendy would like to learn how, too. Oh yes, I think we can keep busy and out of each other's hair if the TV goes on the fritz.' He paused. 'And Al was telling the truth when he told you I no longer drink. I did once, and it got to be serious. But I haven't had so much as a glass of beer in the last fourteen months. I don't intend to bring any alcohol up here, and I don't think there will be an opportunity to get any after the snow flies.'

'In that you would be quite correct,' Ullman said. 'But as long as the three of you are up here, the potential for problems is multiplied. I have told Mr Shockley this, and he told me he would take the responsibility. Now I've told you, and apparently you are also willing to take the responsibility—'

'I am.'

'All right. I'll accept that, since I have little choice. But I would still rather have an unattached college boy taking a year off. Well, perhaps you'll do. Now I'll turn you over to Mr Watson, who will take you through the basement and around the grounds. Unless you have further questions?'

'No. None at all.'

Ullman stood. 'I hope there are no hard feelings, Mr Torrance. There is nothing personal in the things I have said to you. I only want what's best for the Overlook. It is a great hotel. I want it to stay that way.'

'No. No hard feelings.' Jack flashed the PR grin again, but he was glad Ullman didn't offer to shake hands. There were hard feelings. All kinds of them.

Chapter Two

Boulder

She looked out the kitchen window and saw him just sitting there on the curb, not playing with his trucks or the wagon or even the balsa glider that had pleased him so much all the last week since Jack had brought it home. He was just sitting there, watching for their shopworn VW, his elbows planted on his thighs and his chin propped in his hands, a five-year-old kid waiting for his daddy.

Wendy suddenly felt bad, almost crying bad.

She hung the dish towel over the bar by the sink and went downstairs, buttoning the top two buttons of her house dress. Jack and his pride! *Hey no, Al, I don't need an advance. I'm okay for a while.* The hallway walls were gouged and marked with crayons, grease pencil, spray paint. The stairs were steep and splintery. The whole building smelled of sour age, and what sort of place was this for Danny after the small neat brick house in Stovington? The people living above them on the third floor weren't married, and while that didn't bother her, their constant, rancorous fighting did. It scared her. The guy up there was Tom, and after the bars had closed and they had returned home, the fights would start in earnest – the rest of the week was just a prelim in comparison. The Friday Night Fights, Jack called them, but it wasn't funny. The woman – her name was Elaine – would at last be reduced to tears and to repeating over and over again: 'Don't, Tom. Please don't. Please don't.' And he would shout at her. Once they had even awakened Danny, and Danny slept like a corpse. The next morning Jack caught Tom going out and had spoken to him on the sidewalk at some length. Tom had started to bluster and Jack had said something else to him, too quietly for Wendy to hear, and Tom had only shaken his head sullenly and walked away. That had been a week ago and for a few days things had been better, but since the weekend things had been working back to normal – excuse me, abnormal. It was bad for the boy.

Her sense of grief washed over her again but she was on the walk now and she smothered it. Sweeping her dress under her and sitting down on the curb beside him, she said: 'What's up, doc?'

He smiled at her but it was perfunctory. 'Hi, Mom.'

The glider was between his sneakered feet, and she saw that one of the wings had started to splinter.

'Want me to see what I can do with that, honey?'

Danny had gone back to staring up the street. 'No. Dad will fix it.'

'Your daddy may not be back until suppertime, doc. It's a long drive up into those mountains.'

'Do you think the bug will break down?'

'No, I don't think so.' But he had just given her something new to worry about. *Thanks, Danny. I needed that.*

'Dad said it might,' Danny said in a matter-of-fact, almost bored manner. 'He said the fuel pump was all shot to shit.'

'Don't say that, Danny.'

'Fuel pump?' he asked her with honest surprise.

She sighed. 'No, "All shot to shit." Don't say that.'

'Why?'

'It's vulgar.'

'What's vulgar, Mom?'

'Like when you pick your nose at the table or pee with the bathroom door open. Or saying things like "All shot to shit." Shit is a vulgar word. Nice people don't say it.'

'Dad says it. When he was looking at the bugmotor he said, "Christ this fuel pump's all shot to shit." Isn't Dad nice?'

How do you get into these things, Winifred? Do you practice?

'He's nice, but he's also grown-up. And he's very careful not to say things like that in front of people who wouldn't understand.'

'You mean like Uncle Al?'

'Yes, that's right.'

'Can I say it when I'm grown-up?'

'I suppose you will, whether I like it or not.'

'How old?'

'How does twenty sound, doc?'

'That's a long time to have to wait.'

'I guess it is, but will you try?'

'Hokay.'

He went back to staring up the street. He flexed a little, as if to rise, but the beetle coming was much newer, and much brighter red. He relaxed again. She wondered just how hard this move to Colorado had been on Danny. He was close-mouthed about it, but it bothered her to see him spending so much time by himself. In Vermont three of Jack's fellow faculty members had had children about Danny's age – and there had been the preschool – but in this neighborhood there was no one for him to play with. Most of the apartments were occupied by students attending CU, and of the few married couples here on Arapahoe Street, only a tiny percentage had children. She had spotted perhaps a dozen of high school or junior high school age, three infants, and that was all.

'Mommy, why did Daddy lose his job?'

She was jolted out of her reverie and floundering for an answer. She and Jack had discussed ways they might handle just such a question from Danny, ways that had varied from evasion to the plain truth with no varnish on it. But Danny had never asked. Not until now, when she was feeling low and least prepared for such a question. Yet he was looking at her, maybe reading the confusion on her face and forming his own ideas about that. She thought that to children adult motives and actions must seem as bulking and ominous as dangerous animals seen in the shadows of a dark forest. They were jerked about like puppets, having only the vaguest notions why. The thought brought her dangerously close to tears again, and while she fought them off she leaned over, picked up the disabled glider, and turned it over in her hands.

'Your daddy was coaching the debate team, Danny. Do you remember that?'

'Sure,' he said. 'Arguments for fun, right?'

'Right.' She turned the glider over and over, looking at the trade name (SPEEDOGLIDE) and the blue star decals on the wings, and found herself telling the exact truth to her son.

'There was a boy named George Hatfield that Daddy had to cut from the team. That means he wasn't as good as some of the others. George said your daddy cut him because he didn't like him and not because he wasn't good enough. Then George did a bad thing. I think you know about that.'

'Was he the one who put the holes in our bug's tires?'

'Yes, he was. It was after school and your daddy caught him doing it.' Now she hesitated again, but there was no question of evasion now; it was reduced to tell the truth or tell a lie.

'Your daddy . . . sometimes he does things he's sorry for later. Sometimes he doesn't think the way he should. That doesn't happen very often, but sometimes it does.'

'Did he hurt George Hatfield like the time I spilled all his papers?'

Sometimes—

(Danny with his arm in a cast)

—he does things he's sorry for later.

Wendy blinked her eyes savagely hard, driving her tears all the way back.

'Something like that, honey. Your daddy hit George to make him stop cutting the tires and George hit his head. Then the men who are in charge of the school said that George couldn't go there anymore and your daddy couldn't teach there anymore.' She stopped, out of words, and waited in dread for the deluge of questions.

'Oh,' Danny said, and went back to looking up the street. Apparently the subject was closed. If only it could be closed that easily for her—

She stood up. 'I'm going upstairs for a cup of tea, doc. Want a couple of cookies and a glass of milk?'

'I think I'll watch for Dad.'

'I don't think he'll be home much before five.'

'Maybe he'll be early.'

'Maybe,' she agreed. 'Maybe he will.'

She was halfway up the walk when he called, 'Mommy?'

'What, Danny?'

'Do you want to go and live in that hotel for the winter?'

Now, which of five thousand answers should she give to that one? The way she had felt yesterday or last night or this morning? They were all different, they crossed the spectrum from rosy pink to dead black.

She said: 'If it's what your father wants, it's what I want.' She paused. 'What about you?'

'I guess I do,' he said finally. 'Nobody much to play with around here.'

'You miss your friends, don't you?'

'Sometimes I miss Scott and Andy. That's about all.'

She went back to him and kissed him, rumpled his light colored hair that was just losing its baby-fineness. He was such a solemn little boy, and sometimes she wondered just how he was supposed to survive with her and Jack for parents. The high hopes they had begun with came down to this unpleasant apartment building in a city they didn't know. The image of Danny in his cast rose up before her again. Somebody in the Divine Placement Service had made a mistake, one she sometimes feared could never be corrected and which only the most innocent bystander could pay for.

'Stay out of the road, doc,' she said, and hugged him tight.

'Sure, Mom.'

She went upstairs and into the kitchen. She put on the teapot and laid a couple of Oreos on a plate for Danny in case he decided to come up while she was lying down. Sitting at the table with her big pottery cup in front of her, she looked out the window at him, still sitting on the curb in his bluejeans and his over-sized dark green Stovington Prep sweatshirt, the glider now lying beside him. The tears which had threatened all day now came in a cloudburst and she leaned into the fragrant, curling steam of the tea and wept. In grief and loss for the past, and terror of the future.

Chapter Three

Watson

You lost your temper, Ullman had said.

'Okay, here's your furnace,' Watson said, turning on a light in the dark, musty-smelling room. He was a beefy man with fluffy popcorn hair, white shirt, and dark green chinos. He swung open a small square grating in the furnace's belly and he and Jack peered in together. 'This here's the pilot light.' A steady blue-white jet hissing steadily upward channeled destructive force, but the key word, Jack thought, was *destructive* and not *channeled*: If you stuck your hand in there, the barbecue would happen in three quick seconds.

Lost your temper.

(Danny, are you all right?)

The furnace filled the entire room, by far the biggest and oldest Jack had ever seen.

'The pilot's got a fail-safe,' Watson told him. 'Little sensor in there measures heat. If the heat falls below a certain point, it sets off a buzzer in your quarters. Boiler's on the other side of the wall. I'll take you around.' He slammed the grating shut and led Jack behind the iron bulk of the furnace toward another door. The iron radiated a stuporous heat at them, and for some reason Jack thought of a large, dozing cat. Watson jingled his keys and whistled.

Lost your—

(When he went back into his study and saw Danny standing there, wearing nothing but his training pants and a grin, a slow, red cloud of rage had eclipsed Jack's reason. It had seemed slow subjectively, inside his head, but it must have all happened in less than a minute. It only seemed slow the way some dreams seem slow. The bad ones. Every door and drawer in his study seemed to have been ransacked in the time he had been gone. Closet, cupboards, the sliding bookcase. Every desk drawer yanked out to the stop. His manuscript, the three-act play he had been slowly developing from a novelette he had written seven years ago as an undergraduate, was scattered all over the floor. He had been drinking a beer and doing the Act II corrections when Wendy said the phone was for him, and Danny had poured the can of beer all over the pages. Probably to see it foam. *See it foam, see it foam*, the words played over and over in his mind like a single sick chord on an out-of-tune piano, completing the circuit of his rage. He stepped deliberately toward his three-year-old son, who was looking up at him with that pleased grin, his pleasure at the job of work so successfully and recently completed in Daddy's study; Danny began to say something and that was when he had grabbed Danny's hand and bent it to make him drop the typewriter eraser and the mechanical pencil he was clenching in it. Danny had cried out a little . . . no . . . no . . . tell the truth . . . he screamed. It was all hard to remember through the fog of anger, the sick single thump of that one Spike Jones chord. Wendy somewhere, asking what was wrong. Her voice faint, damped by the inner mist. This was between the two of them. He had whirled Danny around to spank him, his big adult fingers digging into the scant meat of the boy's forearm, meeting around it in a closed fist, and the snap of the breaking bone had not been loud, not loud but it had been *very* loud, *HUGE*, but not loud. Just enough of a sound to slit through the red fog like an arrow – but instead of letting in sunlight, that sound let in the dark clouds of shame and remorse, the terror, the agonizing convulsion of the spirit. A clean sound with the past on one side of it and all the future on the other, a sound like a breaking pencil lead or a small piece of kindling when you brought it down over your knee. A moment of utter silence on the other side, in respect to the beginning future maybe, all the rest of his life. Seeing Danny's face drain of color until it was like cheese, seeing his eyes, always large, grow larger still, and glassy, Jack sure the boy was going to faint dead away into the puddle of beer and papers; his own voice, weak and drunk, slurry, trying to take it all back, to find *a way* around that not too loud sound of bone cracking and into the past – is there a status quo in the house? – saying: *Danny, are you all right*? Danny's answering shriek, then Wendy's shocked gasp as she came around them and saw the peculiar angle Danny's forearm had to his elbow; no arm was meant to hang quite that way in a world of normal families. Her own scream as she swept him into her arms, and a nonsense babble: *Oh God Danny oh dear God oh sweet God your poor sweet arm*; and Jack was standing there, stunned and stupid, trying to understand how a thing like this could have happened. He was standing there and his eyes met the eyes of his wife and he saw that Wendy hated him. It did not occur to him what the hate might mean in practical terms; it was only later that he realized she might have left him that night, gone to a motel, gotten a divorce lawyer in the morning; or called the police. He saw only that his wife hated him and he felt staggered by it, all alone. He felt awful. This was what oncoming death felt like. Then she fled for the telephone and dialed the hospital with their screaming boy wedged in the crook of her arm and Jack did not go after her, he only stood in the ruins of his office, smelling beer and thinking—)

You lost your temper.

He rubbed his hand harshly across his lips and followed Watson into the boiler room. It was humid in here, but it was more than the humidity that brought the sick and slimy sweat onto his brow and stomach and legs. The remembering did that, it was a total thing that made that night two years ago seem like two hours ago. There was no lag. It brought the shame and revulsion back, the sense of having no worth at all, and that feeling always made him want to have a drink, and the wanting of a drink brought still blacker despair – would he ever have an hour, not a week or even a day, mind you, but just one waking hour when the craving for a drink wouldn't surprise him like this?

'The boiler,' Watson announced. He pulled a red and blue bandanna from his back pocket, blew his nose with a decisive honk, and thrust it back out of sight after a short peek into it to see if he had gotten anything interesting.

The boiler stood on four cement blocks, a long and cylindrical metal tank, copper-jacketed and often patched. It squatted beneath a confusion of pipes and ducts which zig-zagged upward into the high, cobweb-festooned basement ceiling. To Jack's right, two large heating pipes came through the wall from the furnace in the adjoining room.

'Pressure gauge is here.' Watson tapped it. 'Pounds per square inch, psi. I guess you'd know that. I got her up to a hundred now, and the rooms get a little chilly at night. Few guests complain, what the fuck. They're crazy to come up here in September anyway. Besides, this is an old baby. Got more patches on her than a pair of welfare overalls.' Out came the bandanna. A honk. A peek. Back it went.

'I got me a fuckin cold,' Watson said conversationally. 'I get one every September. I be tinkering down here with this old whore, then I be out cuttin the grass or rakin that roque court. Get a chill and catch a cold, my old mum used to say. God bless her, she been dead six year. The cancer got her. Once the cancer gets you, you might as well make your will.

'You'll want to keep your press up to no more than fifty, maybe sixty. Mr Ullman, he says to heat the west wing one day, central wing the next, east wing the day after that. Ain't he a crazyman? I hate that little fucker. Yap-yap-yap, all the livelong day, he's just like one of those little dogs that bites you on the ankle then run around an pee all over the rug. If brains was black powder he couldn't blow his own nose. It's a pity the things you see when you ain't got a gun.

'Look here. You open an close these ducks by pullin these rings. I got em all marked for you. The blue tags all go to the rooms in the east wing. Red tags is the middle. Yellow is the west wing. When you go to heat the west wing, you got to remember that's the side of the hotel that really catches the weather. When it whoops, those rooms get as cold as a frigid woman with an ice cube up her works. You can run your press all the way to eighty on west wing days. I would, anyway.'

'The thermostats upstairs—' Jack began.

Watson shook his head vehemently, making his fluffy hair bounce on his skull. 'They ain't hooked up. They're just there for show. Some of these people from California, they don't think things is right unless they got it hot enough to grow a palm tree in their fuckin bedroom. All the heat comes from down here. Got to watch the press, though. See her creep?'

He tapped the main dial, which had crept from a hundred pounds per square inch to a hundred and two as Watson soliloquized. Jack felt a sudden shiver cross his back in a hurry and thought: *The goose just walked over my grave.* Then Watson gave the pressure wheel a spin and dumped the boiler off. There was a great hissing, and the needle dropped back to ninety-one. Watson twisted the valve shut and the hissing died reluctantly.

'She creeps,' Watson said. 'You tell that fat little peckerwood Ullman, he drags out the account books and spends three hours showing how he can't afford a new one until 1982. I tell you, this whole place is gonna go sky-high someday, and I just hope that fat fuck's here to ride the rocket. God, I wish I could be as charitable as my mother was. She could see the good in everyone. Me, I'm just as mean as a snake with the shingles. What the fuck, a man can't help his nature.

'Now you got to remember to come down here twice a day and once at night before you rack in. You got to check the press. If you forget, it'll just creep and creep and like as not you an your fambly'll wake up on the fuckin moon. You just dump her off a little and you'll have no trouble.'

'What's top end?'

'Oh, she's rated for two-fifty, but she'd blow long before that now. You couldn't get me to come down an stand next to her when that dial was up to one hundred and eighty.'

'There's no automatic shutdown?'

'No, there ain't. This was built before such things were required. Federal government's into everything these days, ain't it? FBI openin mail, CIA buggin the goddam phones . . . and look what happened to that Nixon. Wasn't that a sorry sight?

'But if you just come down here regular an check the press you'll be fine. An remember to switch those ducks around like he wants. Won't none of the rooms get much above forty-five unless we have an amazin warm winter. And you'll have your own apartment just as warm as you like it.'

'What about the plumbing?'

'Okay, I was just getting to that. Over here through this arch.'

They walked into a long, rectangular room that seemed to stretch for miles. Watson pulled a cord and a single seventy-five-watt bulb cast a sickish, swinging glow over the area they were standing in. Straight ahead was the bottom of the elevator shaft, heavy greased cables descending to pulleys twenty feet in diameter and a huge, grease-clogged motor. Newspapers were everywhere, bundled and banded and boxed. Other cartons were marked *Records* or *Invoices* or *Receipts* – SAVE! The smell was yellow and moldy. Some of the cartons were falling apart, spilling yellow flimsy sheets that might have been twenty years old out onto the floor. Jack stared around, fascinated. The Overlook's entire history might be here, buried in these rotting cartons.

'That elevator's a bitch to keep runnin,' Watson said, jerking his thumb at it. 'I *know* Ullman's buying the state elevator inspector a few fancy dinners to keep the repairman away from that fucker.

'Now here's your central plumbin core.' In front of them five large pipes, each of them wrapped in insulation and cinched with steel bands, rose into the shadows and out of sight.

Watson pointed to a cobwebby shelf beside the utility shaft. There were a number of greasy rags on it, and a loose-leaf binder. 'That there is all your plumbin schematics,' he said. 'I don't think you'll have any trouble with leaks – never has been – but sometimes the pipes freeze up. Only way to stop that is to run the faucets a little bit durin the nights, but there's over four hundred taps in this fuckin palace. That fat fairy upstairs would scream all the way to Denver when he saw the water bill. Ain't that right?'

'I'd say that's a remarkably astute analysis.'

Watson looked at him admiringly. 'Say, you really are a college fella, aren't you? Talk just like a book. I admire that, as long as the fella ain't one of those fairy-boys. Lots of em are. You know who stirred up all those college riots a few years ago? The hommasexshuls, that's who. They get frustrated an have to cut loose. Comin out of the closet, they call it. Holy shit, I don't know what the world's comin to.

'Now, if she freezes, she most likely gonna freeze right up in this shaft.

No heat, you see. If it happens, use this.' He reached into a broken orange crate and produced a small gas torch.

'You just unstrap the insulation when you find the ice plug and put the heat right to her. Get it?'

'Yes. But what if a pipe freezes outside the utility core?'

'That won't happen if you're doin your job and keepin the place heated. You can't get to the other pipes anyway. Don't you fret about it. You'll have no trouble. Beastly place down here. Cobwebby. Gives me the horrors, it does.'

'Ullman said the first winter caretaker killed his family and himself.'

'Yeah, that guy Grady. He was a bad actor, I knew that the minute I saw him. Always grinnin like an egg-suck dog. That was when they were just startin out here and that fat fuck Ullman, he woulda hired the Boston Strangler if he'd've worked for minimum wage. Was a ranger from the National Park that found em; the phone was out. All of em up in the west wing on the third floor, froze solid. Too bad about the little girls. Eight and six, they was. Cute as cut-buttons. Oh, that was a hell of a mess. That Ullman, he manages some honky-tonky resort place down in Florida in the off-season, and he caught a plane up to Denver and hired a sleigh to take him up here from Sidewinder because the roads were closed – a *sleigh*, can you believe that? He about split a gut trying to keep it out of the papers. Did pretty well, I got to give him that. There was an item in the Denver *Post*, and of course the bituary in that pissant little rag they have down in Estes Park, but that was just about all. Pretty good, considerin the reputation this place has got. I expected some reporter would dig it all up again and just sorta put Grady in it as an excuse to rake over the scandals.'

'What scandals?'

Watson shrugged. 'Any big hotels have got scandals,' he said. 'Just like every big hotel has got a ghost. Why? Hell, people come and go. Sometimes one of em will pop off in his room, heart attack or stroke or something like that. Hotels are superstitious places. No thirteenth floor or room thirteen, no mirrors on the back of the door you come in through, stuff like that. Why, we lost a lady just this last July. Ullman had to take care of that, and you can bet your ass he did. That's what they pay him twenty-two thousand bucks a season for, and as much as I dislike the little prick, he earns it. It's like some people just come here to throw up and they hire a guy like Ullman to clean up the messes. Here's this woman, must be sixty fuckin years old – my age! – and her hair's dyed just as red as a whore's spotlight, tits saggin just about down to her belly button on account of she ain't wearin no brassy-ear, big varycoarse veins all up and down her legs so they look like a couple of goddam roadmaps, the jools drippin off her neck and arms an hangin out her ears. And she's got this kid with her, he can't be no more than seventeen, with hair down to his asshole and his crotch bulgin like he stuffed it with the funnypages. So they're here a week, ten days maybe, and every night it's the same drill. Down in the Colorado Lounge from five to seven, her suckin up singapore slings like they're gonna outlaw em tomorrow and him with just the one bottle of Olympia, suckin it, makin it last. And she'd be makin jokes and sayin all these witty things, and every time she said one he'd grin just like a fuckin ape, like she had strings tied to the corners of his mouth. Only after a few days you could see it was gettin harder and harder for him to grin, and God knows what he had to think about to get his pump primed by bedtime. Well, they'd go in for dinner, him walkin and her staggerin, drunk as a coot, you know, and he'd be pinchin the waitresses and grinnin at em when she wasn't lookin. Hell, we even had bets on how long he'd last.'

Watson shrugged.

'Then he comes down one night around ten, sayin his "wife" is "indisposed" – which meant she was passed out again like every other night they was there – and he's goin to get her some stomach medicine. So off he goes in the little Porsche they come in, and that's the last we see of him. Next morning she comes down and tries to put on this big act, but all day she's gettin paler an paler, and Mr Ullman asks her, sorta diplomatic-like, would she like him to notify the state cops, just in case maybe he had a little accident or something. She's on him like a cat. No-no-no, he's a fine driver, she isn't worried, everything's under control, he'll be back for dinner. So that afternoon she steps into the Colorado around three and never has no dinner at all. She goes up to her room around ten-thirty, and that's the last time anybody saw her alive.'

'What happened?'

'County coroner said she took about thirty sleepin pills on top of all the booze. Her husband showed up the next day, some big-shot lawyer from New York. He gave old Ullman four different shades of holy hell. I'll sue this an I'll sue that an when I'm through you won't even be able to find a clean pair of underwear, stuff like that. But Ullman's good, the sucker. Ullman got him quieted down. Probably asked that bigshot how he'd like to see his wife splashed all over the New York papers: Wife of Prominent New York Blah Blah Found Dead With Bellyful of Sleeping Pills. After playing hide-the-salami with a kid young enough to be her grandson.

'The state cops found the Porsche in the back of this all-night burger joint down in Lyons, and Ullman pulled a few strings to get it released to that lawyer. Then both of them ganged up on old Archer Houghton, which is the county coroner, and got him to change the verdict to accidental death. Heart attack. Now ole Archer's driving a Chrysler. I don't begrudge him. A man's got to take it where he finds it, especially when he starts gettin along in years.'

Out came the bandanna. Honk. Peek. Out of sight.

'So what happens? About a week later this stupid cunt of a chambermaid, Delores Vickery by name, she gives out with a helluva shriek while she's makin up the room where those two stayed, and she faints dead away. When she comes to she says she seen the dead woman in the bathroom, layin naked in the tub. "Her face was all purple an puffy," she says, "an she was grinnin at me." So Ullman gave her two weeks' worth of walking papers and told her to get lost. I figure there's maybe forty-fifty people died in this hotel since my grandfather opened it for business in 1910.'

He looked shrewdly at Jack.

'You know how most of em go? Heart attack or stroke, while they're bangin the lady they're with. That's what these resorts get a lot of, old types that want one last fling. They come up here to the mountains to pretend they're twenty again. Sometimes somethin gives, and not all the guys who ran this place was as good as Ullman is at keepin it out of the papers. So the Overlook's got a reputation, yeah. I'll bet the fuckin Biltmore in New York City has got a reputation, if you ask the right people.'

'But no ghosts?'

'Mr Torrance, I've worked here all my life. I played here when I was a kid no older'n your boy in that wallet snapshot you showed me. I never seen a ghost yet. You want to come out back with me, I'll show you the equipment shed.'

'Fine.'

As Watson reached up to turn off the light, Jack said, 'There sure are a lot of papers down here.'

'Oh, you're not kiddin. Seems like they go back a thousand years. Newspapers and old invoices and bills of lading and Christ knows what else. My dad used to keep up with them pretty good when we had the old wood-burning furnace, but now they've got all out of hand. Some year I got to get a boy to haul them down to Sidewinder and burn em. If Ullman will stand the expense. I guess he will if I holler "rat" loud enough.'

'Then there are rats?'

'Yeah, I guess there's some. I got the traps and the poison Mr Ullman wants you to use up in the attic and down here. You keep a good eye on your boy, Mr Torrance. You wouldn't want nothing to happen to him.'

'No, I sure wouldn't.' Coming from Watson the advice didn't sting.

They went to the stairs and paused there for a moment while Watson blew his nose again.

'You'll find all the tools you need out there and some you don't, I guess. And there's the shingles. Did Ullman tell you about that?'

'Yes, he wants part of the west roof reshingled.'

'He'll get all the for-free out of you that he can, the fat little prick, and then whine around in the spring about how you didn't do the job half right. I told him once right to his face, I said . . .'

Watson's words faded away to a comforting drone as they mounted the stairs. Jack Torrance looked back over his shoulder once into the impenetrable, musty-smelling darkness and thought that if there was ever a place that should have ghosts, this was it. He thought of Grady, locked in by the soft, implacable snow, going quietly berserk and committing his atrocity. Did they scream? he wondered. Poor Grady, feeling it close in on him more every day, and knowing at last that for him spring would never come. He shouldn't have been here. And he shouldn't have lost his temper.

As he followed Watson through the door, the words echoed back to him like a knell, accompanied by a sharp snap – like a breaking pencil lead. Dear God, he could use a drink. Or a thousand of them.

Chapter Four

Shadowland

Danny weakened and went up for his milk and cookies at quarter past four. He gobbled them while looking out the window, then went in to kiss his mother, who was lying down. She suggested that he stay in and watch 'Sesame Street' – the time would pass faster – but he shook his head firmly and went back to his place on the curb.

Now it was five o'clock, and although he didn't have a watch and couldn't tell time too well yet anyway, he was aware of passing time by the lengthening of the shadows, and by the golden cast that now tinged the afternoon light.

Turning the glider over in his hands, he sang under his breath: 'Skip to m Lou, n I don't care . . . skip to m Lou, n I don't care . . . my master's gone away . . . Lou, Lou, skip to m Lou . . .'

They had sung that song all together at the Jack and Jill Nursery School he had gone to back in Stovington. He didn't go to nursery school out here because Daddy couldn't afford to send him anymore. He knew his mother and father worried about that, worried that it was adding to his loneliness (and even more deeply, unspoken between them, that Danny blamed them), but he didn't really want to go to that old Jack and Jill anymore. It was for babies. He wasn't quite a big kid yet, but he wasn't a baby anymore. Big kids went to the big school and got a hot lunch. First grade. Next year. This year was someplace between being a baby and a real kid. It was all right. He did miss Scott and Andy – mostly Scott – but it was still all right. It seemed best to wait alone for whatever might happen next.

He understood a great many things about his parents, and he knew that many times they didn't like his understandings and many other times refused to believe them. But someday they would have to believe. He was content to wait.

It was too bad they couldn't believe more, though, especially at times like now. Mommy was lying on her bed in the apartment, just about crying she was so worried about Daddy. Some of the things she was worried about were too grown-up for Danny to understand – vague things that had to do with security, with Daddy's *selfimage*, feelings of guilt and anger and the fear of what was to become of them – but the two main things on her mind right now were that Daddy had had a breakdown in the mountains (*then why doesn't he call?*) or that Daddy had gone off to do the Bad Thing. Danny knew perfectly well what the Bad Thing was since Scotty Aaronson, who was six months older, had explained it to him. Scotty knew because his daddy did the Bad Thing, too. Once, Scotty told him, his daddy had punched his mom right in the eye and knocked her down. Finally, Scotty's dad and mom had gotten a DIVORCE over the Bad Thing, and when Danny had known him, Scotty lived with his mother and only saw his daddy on weekends. The greatest terror of Danny's life was DIVORCE, a word that always appeared in his mind as a sign painted in red letters which were covered with hissing, poisonous snakes. In DIVORCE, your parents no longer lived together. They had a tug of war over you in a court (tennis court? badminton court? Danny wasn't sure which or if it was some other, but Mommy and Daddy had played both tennis and badminton at Stovington, so he assumed it could be either) and you had to go with one of them and you practically never saw the other one, and the one you were with could marry somebody you didn't even know if the urge came on them. The most terrifying thing about DIVORCE was that he had sensed the word – or concept, or whatever it was that came to him in his understandings – floating around in his own parents' heads, sometimes diffuse and relatively distant, sometimes as thick and obscuring and frightening as thunderheads. It had been that way after Daddy punished him for messing the papers up in his study and the doctor had to put his arm in a cast. That memory was already faded, but the memory of the DIVORCE thoughts was clear and terrifying. It had mostly been around his mommy that time, and he had been in constant terror that she would pluck the word from her brain and drag it out of her mouth, making it real. DIVORCE. It was a constant undercurrent in their thoughts, one of the few he could always pick up, like the beat of simple music. But like a beat, the central thought formed only the spine of more complex thoughts, thoughts he could not as yet even begin to interpret. They came to him only as colors and moods. Mommy's DIVORCE thoughts centered around what Daddy had done to his arm, and what had happened at Stovington when Daddy lost his job. That boy. That George Hatfield who got pissed off at Daddy and put the holes in their bug's feet. Daddy's DIVORCE thoughts were more complex, colored dark violet and shot through with frightening veins of pure black. He seemed to think they would be better off if he left. That things would stop hurting. His daddy hurt almost all the time, mostly about the Bad Thing. Danny could almost always pick that up too: Daddy's constant craving to go into a dark place and watch a color TV and eat peanuts out of a bowl and do the Bad Thing until his brain would be quiet and leave him alone.

But this afternoon his mother had no need to worry and he wished he could go to her and tell her that. The bug had not broken down. Daddy was not off somewhere doing the Bad Thing. He was almost home now, put-putting along the highway between Lyons and Boulder. For the moment his daddy wasn't even thinking about the Bad Thing. He was thinking about . . . about . . .

Danny looked furtively behind him at the kitchen window. Sometimes thinking very hard made something happen to him. It made things – real things – go away, and then he saw things that weren't there. Once, not long after they put the cast on his arm, this had happened at the supper table. They weren't talking much to each other then. But they were thinking. Oh yes. The thoughts of DIVORCE hung over the kitchen table like a cloud full of black rain, pregnant, ready to burst. It was so bad he couldn't eat. The thought of eating with all that black DIVORCE around made him want to throw up. And because it had seemed desperately important, he had thrown himself fully into concentration and something had happened. When he came back to real things, he was lying on the floor with beans and mashed potatoes in his lap and his mommy was holding him and crying and Daddy had been on the phone. He had been frightened, had tried to explain to them that there was nothing wrong, that this sometimes happened to him when he concentrated on understanding more than what normally came to him. He tried to explain about Tony, who they called his 'invisible playmate.'

His father had said: 'He's having a Ha Loo Sin Nation. He seems okay, but I want the doctor to look at him anyway.'

After the doctor left, Mommy had made him promise to never do that again, to *never* scare them that way, and Danny had agreed. He was frightened himself. Because when he had concentrated his mind, it had flown out to his daddy, and for just a moment, before Tony had appeared (far away, as he always did, calling distantly) and the strange things had blotted out their kitchen and the carved roast on the blue plate, for just a moment his own consciousness had plunged through his daddy's darkness to an incomprehensible word much more frightening than DIVORCE, and that word was SUICIDE. Danny had never come across it again in his daddy's mind, and he had certainly not gone looking for it. He didn't care if he never found out exactly what that word meant.

But he did like to concentrate, because sometimes Tony would come. Not every time. Sometimes things just got woozy and swimmy for a minute and then cleared – most times, in fact – but at other times Tony would appear at the very limit of his vision, calling distantly and beckoning . . .

It had happened twice since they moved to Boulder, and he remembered how surprised and pleased he had been to find Tony had followed him all the way from Vermont. So all his friends hadn't been left behind after all.

The first time he had been out in the back yard and nothing much had happened. Just Tony beckoning and then darkness and a few minutes later he had come back to real things with a few vague fragments of memory, like a jumbled dream. The second time, two weeks ago, had been more interesting. Tony, beckoning, calling from four yards over: '*Danny . . . come see . . .*' It seemed that he was getting up, then falling into a deep hole, like Alice into Wonderland. Then he had been in the basement of the apartment house and Tony had been beside him, pointing into the shadows at the trunk his daddy carried all his important papers in, especially 'THE PLAY.'

'See?' Tony had said in his distant, musical voice. 'It's under the stairs. Right under the stairs. The movers put it right . . . under . . . the stairs.'

Danny had stepped forward to look more closely at this marvel and then he was falling again, this time out of the back-yard swing, where he had been sitting all along. He had gotten the wind knocked out of himself, too.

Three or four days later his daddy had been stomping around, telling Mommy furiously that he had been all over the goddam basement and the trunk wasn't there and he was going to sue the goddam movers who had left it somewhere between Vermont and Colorado. How was he supposed to be able to finish 'THE PLAY' if things like this kept cropping up?

Danny said, 'No, Daddy. It's under the stairs. The movers put it right under the stairs.'

Daddy had given him a strange look and had gone down to see. The trunk had been there, just where Tony had shown him. Daddy had taken him aside, had sat him on his lap, and had asked Danny who let him down cellar. Had it been Tom from upstairs? The cellar was dangerous, Daddy said. That was why the landlord kept it locked. If someone was leaving it unlocked, Daddy wanted to know. He was glad to have his papers and his 'PLAY' but it wouldn't be worth it to him, he said, if Danny fell down the stairs and broke his . . . his leg. Danny told his father earnestly that he hadn't been down in the cellar. That door was always locked. And Mommy agreed. Danny never went down in the back hall, she said, because it was damp and dark and spidery. And he didn't tell lies.

'Then how did you know, doc?' Daddy asked.

'Tony showed me.'

His mother and father had exchanged a look over his head. This had happened before, from time to time. Because it was frightening, they swept it quickly from their minds. But he knew they worried about Tony, Mommy especially, and he was careful about thinking the way that could make Tony come where she might see. But now he thought she was lying down, not moving about in the kitchen yet, and so he concentrated hard to see if he could understand what Daddy was thinking about.

His brow furrowed and his slightly grimy hands clenched into tight fists on his jeans. He did not close his eyes – that wasn't necessary – but he squinched them down to slits and imagined Daddy's voice, Jack's voice, John Daniel Torrance's voice, deep and steady, sometimes quirking up with amusement or deepening even more with anger or just staying steady because he was thinking. Thinking of. Thinking about. Thinking . . .

(thinking)

Danny sighed quietly and his body slumped on the curb as if all the muscles had gone out of it. He was fully conscious; he saw the street and the girl and boy walking up the sidewalk on the other side, holding hands because they were

(?in love?)

so happy about the day and themselves together in the day. He saw autumn leaves blowing along the gutter, yellow cartwheels of irregular shape. He saw the house they were passing and noticed how the roof was covered with

(*shingles. i guess it'll be no problem if the flashing's ok yeah that'll be all right. that watson. christ what a character. wish there was a place for him in 'THE PLAY.' i'll end up with the whole fucking human race in it if i don't watch out. yeah. shingles. are there nails out there? oh shit forgot to ask him well they're simple to get. sidewinder hardware store. wasps. they're nesting this time of year. i might want to get one of those bug bombs in case they're there when i rip up the old shingles. new shingles. old*)

shingles. So that's what he was thinking about. He had gotten the job and was thinking about shingles. Danny didn't know who Watson was, but everything else seemed clear enough. And he might get to see a wasps' nest. Just as sure as his name was

'*Danny . . . Dannee . . .*'

He looked up and there was Tony, far up the street, standing by a stop sign and waving. Danny, as always, felt a warm burst of pleasure at seeing his old friend, but this time he seemed to feel a prick of fear, too, as if Tony had come with some darkness hidden behind his back. A jar of wasps which when released would sting deeply.

But there was no question of not going.

He slumped further down on the curb, his hands sliding laxly from his thighs and dangling below the fork of his crotch. His chin sank onto his chest. Then there was a dim, painless tug as part of him got up and ran after Tony into funneling darkness.

'*Dannee—*'

Now the darkness was shot with swirling whiteness. A coughing, whooping sound and bending, tortured shadows that resolved themselves into fir trees at night, being pushed by a screaming gale. Snow swirled and danced. Snow everywhere.

'Too deep,' Tony said from the darkness, and there was a sadness in his voice that terrified Danny. 'To deep to get out.'

Another shape, looming, rearing. Huge and rectangular. A sloping roof. Whiteness that was blurred in the stormy darkness. Many windows. A long building with a shingled roof. Some of the shingles were greener, newer. His daddy put them on. With nails from the Sidewinder hardware store. Now the snow was covering the shingles. It was covering everything.

A green witchlight glowed into being on the front of the building, flickered, and became a giant, grinning skull over two crossed bones.

'Poison,' Tony said from the floating darkness. 'Poison.'

Other signs flickered past his eyes, some in green letters, some of them on boards stuck at leaning angles into the snowdrifts. NO SWIMMING. DANGER! LIVE WIRES. THIS PROPERTY CONDEMNED. HIGH VOLTAGE. THIRD RAIL. DANGER OF DEATH. KEEP OFF. KEEP OUT. NO TRESPASSING. VIOLATORS WILL BE SHOT ON SIGHT. He understood none of them completely – he couldn't read! – but got a sense of all, and a dreamy terror floated into the dark hollows of his body like light brown spores that would die in sunlight.

They faded. Now he was in a room filled with strange furniture, a room that was dark. Snow spattered against the windows like thrown sand. His mouth was dry, his eyes like hot marbles, his heart triphammering in his chest. Outside there was a hollow booming noise, like a dreadful door being thrown wide. Footfalls. Across the room was a mirror, and deep down in its silver bubble a single word appeared in green fire and that word was: REDRUM.

The room faded. Another room. He knew

(would know)

this one. An overturned chair. A broken window with snow swirling in; already it had frosted the edge of the rug. The drapes had been pulled free and hung on their broken rod at an angle. A low cabinet lying on its face.

More hollow booming noises, steady, rhythmic, horrible. Smashing glass. Approaching destruction. A hoarse voice, the voice of a madman, made the more terrible by its familiarity:

Come out! Come out, you little shit! Take your medicine!

Crash. Crash. Crash. Splintering wood. A bellow of rage and satisfaction. REDRUM. Coming.

Drifting across the room. Pictures torn off the walls. A record player

(?Mommy's record player?)

overturned on the floor. Her records, Grieg, Handel, the Beatles, Art Garfunkel, Bach, Liszt, thrown everywhere. Broken into jagged black pie wedges. A shaft of light coming from another room, the bathroom, harsh white light and a word flickering on and off in the medicine cabinet mirror like a red eye, REDRUM, REDRUM, REDRUM—

'No,' he whispered. 'No, Tony please—'

And, dangling over the white porcelain lip of the bathtub, a hand. Limp. A slow trickle of blood (REDRUM) trickling down one of the fingers, the third, dripping onto the tile from the carefully shaped nail—

No oh no oh no—

(oh please, Tony, you're scaring me)

REDRUM REDRUM REDRUM

(stop it, Tony, stop it)

Fading.

In the darkness the booming noises grew louder, louder still, echoing, everywhere, all around.

And now he was crouched in a dark hallway, crouched on a blue rug with a riot of twisting black shapes woven into its pile, listening to the booming noises approach, and now a Shape turned the corner and began to come toward him, lurching, smelling of blood and doom. It had a mallet in one hand and it was swinging it (REDRUM) from side to side in vicious arcs, slamming it into the walls, cutting the silk wallpaper and knocking out ghostly bursts of plasterdust:

Come on and take your medicine! Take it like a man!

The Shape advancing on him, reeking of that sweet-sour odor, gigantic, the mallet head cutting across the air with a wicked hissing whisper, then the great hollow boom as it crashed into the wall, sending the dust out in a puff you could smell, dry and itchy. Tiny red eyes glowed in the dark. The monster was upon him, it had discovered him, cowering here with a blank wall at his back. And the trapdoor in the ceiling was locked.

Darkness. Drifting.

'Tony, please take me back, please, please—'

And he *was* back, sitting on the curb of Arapahoe Street, his shirt sticking damply to his back, his body bathed in sweat. In his ears he could still hear that huge, contrapuntal booming sound and smell his own urine as he voided himself in the extremity of his terror. He could see that limp hand dangling over the edge of the tub with blood running down one finger, the third, and that inexplicable word so much more horrible than any of the others: REDRUM.

And now sunshine. Real things. Except for Tony, now six blocks up, only a speck, standing on the corner, his voice faint and high and sweet. 'Be careful, doc . . .'

Then, in the next instant, Tony was gone and Daddy's battered red bug was turning the corner and chattering up the street, farting blue smoke behind it. Danny was off the curb in a second, waving, jiving from one foot to the other, yelling: 'Daddy! Hey, Dad! Hi! Hi!'

His daddy swung the VW into the curb, killed the engine, and opened the door. Danny ran toward him and then froze, his eyes widening. His heart crawled up into the middle of his throat and froze solid. Beside his daddy, in the other front seat, was a short-handled mallet, its head clotted with blood and hair.

Then it was just a bag of groceries.

'Danny . . . you okay, doc?'

'Yeah. I'm okay.' He went to his daddy and buried his face in Daddy's sheepskin-lined denim jacket and hugged him tight tight tight. Jack hugged him back, slightly bewildered.

'Hey, you don't want to sit in the sun like that, doc. You're drippin sweat.'

'I guess I fell asleep a little. I love you, Daddy. I been waiting.'

'I love you too, Dan. I brought home some stuff. Think you're big enough to carry it upstairs?'

'Sure am!'

'Doc Torrance, the world's strongest man,' Jack said, and ruffled his hair. 'Whose hobby is falling asleep on street corners.'

Then they were walking up to the door and Mommy had come down to the porch to meet them and he stood on the second step and watched them kiss. They were glad to see each other. Love came out of them the way love had come out of the boy and girl walking up the street and holding hands. Danny was glad.

The bag of groceries – *just* a bag of groceries – crackled in his arms. Everything was all right. Daddy was home. Mommy was loving him. There were no bad things. And not everything Tony showed him always happened.

But fear had settled around his heart, deep and dreadful, around his heart and around that indecipherable word he had seen in his spirit's mirror.

Chapter Five

Phonebooth

Jack parked the VW in front of the Rexall in the Table Mesa shopping center and let the engine die. He wondered again if he shouldn't go ahead and get the fuel pump replaced, and told himself again that they couldn't afford it. If the little car could keep running until November, it could retire with full honors anyway. By November the snow up there in the mountains would be higher than the beetle's roof . . . maybe higher than three beetles stacked on top of each other.

'Want you to stay in the car, doc. I'll bring you a candy bar.'

'Why can't I come in?'

'I have to make a phone call. It's private stuff.'

'Is that why you didn't make it at home?'

'Check.'

Wendy had insisted on a phone in spite of their unraveling finances. She had argued that with a small child – especially a boy like Danny, who sometimes suffered from fainting spells – they couldn't afford not to have one. So Jack had forked over the thirty-dollar installation fee, bad enough, and a ninety-dollar security deposit, which really hurt. And so far the phone had been mute except for two wrong numbers.

'Can I have a Baby Ruth, Daddy?'

'Yes. You sit still and don't play with the gearshift, right?'

'Right. I'll look at the maps.'

'You do that.'

As Jack got out, Danny opened the bug's glovebox and took out the five battered gas station maps: Colorado, Nebraska, Utah, Wyoming, New Mexico. He loved road maps, loved to trace where the roads went with his finger. As far as he was concerned, new maps were the best part of moving West.

Jack went to the drugstore counter, got Danny's candy bar, and newspaper, and a copy of the October *Writer's Digest*. He gave the girl a five and asked for his change in quarters. With the silver in his hand he walked over to the telephone booth by the keymaking machine and slipped inside. From here he could see Danny in the bug through three sets of glass. The boy's head was bent studiously over his maps. Jack felt a wave of nearly desperate love for the boy. The emotion showed on his face as a stony grimness.

He supposed he could have made his obligatory thank-you call to Al from home; he certainly wasn't going to say anything Wendy would object to. It was his pride that said no. These days he almost always listened to what his pride told him to do, because along with his wife and son, six hundred dollars in a checking account, and one weary 1968 Volkswagen, his pride was all that was left. The only thing that was his. Even the checking account was joint. A year ago he had been teaching English in one of the finest prep schools in New England. There had been friends – although not exactly the same ones he'd had before going on the wagon – some laughs, fellow faculty members who admired his deft touch in the classroom and his private dedication to writing. Things had been very good six months ago. All at once there was enough money left over at the end of each two-week pay period to start a little savings account. In his drinking days there had never been a penny left over, even though Al Shockley had stood a great many of the rounds. He and Wendy had begun to talk cautiously about finding a house and making a down payment in a year or so. A farmhouse in the country, take six or eight years to renovate it completely, what the hell, they were young, they had time.

Then he had lost his temper.

George Hatfield.

The smell of hope had turned to the smell of old leather in Crommert's office, the whole thing like some scene from his own play: the old prints of previous Stovington headmasters on the walls, steel engravings of the school as it had been in 1879, when it was first built, and in 1895, when Vanderbilt money had enabled them to build the field house that still stood at the west end of the soccer field, squat, immense, dressed in ivy. April ivy had been rustling outside Crommert's slit window and the drowsy sound of steam heat came from the radiator. It was no set, he remembered thinking. It was real. His life. How could he have fucked it up so badly?

'This is a serious situation, Jack. Terribly serious. The Board has asked me to convey its decision to you.'

The Board wanted Jack's resignation and Jack had given it to them. Under different circumstances, he would have gotten tenure that June.

What had followed that interview in Crommert's office had been the darkest, most dreadful night of his life. The wanting, the *needing* to get drunk had never been so bad. His hands shook. He knocked things over.

And he kept wanting to take it out on Wendy and Danny. His temper was like a vicious animal on a frayed leash. He had left the house in terror that he might strike them. Had ended up outside a bar, and the only thing that had kept him from going in was the knowledge that if he did, Wendy would leave him at last, and take Danny with her. He would be dead from the day they left.

Instead of going into the bar, where dark shadows sat sampling the tasty waters of oblivion, he had gone to Al Shockley's house. The Board's vote had been six to one. Al had been the one.

Now he dialed the operator and she told him that for a dollar eighty-five he could be put in touch with Al two thousand miles away for three minutes. Time is relative, baby, he thought, and stuck in eight quarters. Faintly he could hear the electronic boops and beeps of his connection sniffing its way eastward.

Al's father had been Arthur Longley Shockley, the steel baron. He had left his only son, Albert, a fortune and a huge range of investments and directorships and chairs on various boards. One of these had been on the Board of Directors for Stovington Preparatory Academy, the old man's favorite charity. Both Arthur and Albert Shockley were alumni and Al lived in Barre, close enough to take a personal interest in the school's affairs. For several years Al had been Stovington's tennis coach.

Jack and Al had become friends in a completely natural and uncoincidental way: at the many school and faculty functions they attended together, they were always the two drunkest people there. Shockley was separated from his wife, and Jack's own marriage was skidding slowly downhill, although he still loved Wendy and had promised sincerely (and frequently) to reform, for her sake and for baby Danny's.

The two of them went on from many faculty parties, hitting the bars until they closed, then stopping at some mom 'n' pop store for a case of beer they would drink parked at the end of some back road. There were mornings when Jack would stumble into their leased house with dawn seeping into the sky and find Wendy and the baby asleep on the couch, Danny always on the inside, a tiny fist curled under the shelf of Wendy's jaw. He would look at them and the self-loathing would back up his throat in a bitter wave, even stronger than the taste of beer and cigarettes and martinis – martians, as Al called them. Those were the times that his mind would turn thoughtfully and sanely to the gun or the rope or the razor blade.

If the bender had occurred on a weeknight, he would sleep for three hours, get up, dress, chew four Excedrins, and go off to teach his nine o'clock American Poets still drunk. Good morning, kids, today the Red-Eyed Wonder is going to tell you about how Longfellow lost his wife in the big fire.

He hadn't believed he was an alcoholic, Jack thought as Al's telephone began ringing in his ear. The classes he had missed or taught unshaven, still reeking of last night's martians. Not me, I can stop anytime. The nights he and Wendy had passed in separate beds. Listen, I'm fine. Mashed fenders. Sure I'm okay to drive. The tears she always shed in the bathroom. Cautious looks from his colleagues at any party where alcohol was served, even wine. The slowly dawning realization that he was being talked about. The knowledge that he was producing nothing at his Underwood but balls of mostly blank paper that ended up in the wastebasket. He had been something of a catch for Stovington, a slowly blooming American writer perhaps, and certainly a man well qualified to teach that great mystery, creative writing. He had published two dozen short stories. He was working on a play, and thought there might be a novel incubating in some mental back room. But now he was not producing and his teaching had become erratic.

It had finally ended one night less than a month after Jack had broken his son's arm. That, it seemed to him, had ended his marriage. All that remained was for Wendy to gather her will . . . if her mother hadn't been such a grade A bitch, he knew, Wendy would have taken a bus back to New Hampshire as soon as Danny had been okay to travel. It was over.

It had been a little past midnight. Jack and Al were coming into Barre on U.S. 31, Al behind the wheel of his Jag, shifting fancily on the curves, sometimes crossing the double yellow line. They were both very drunk; the martians had landed that night in force. They came around the last curve before the bridge at seventy, and there was a kid's bike in the road, and then the sharp, hurt squealing as rubber shredded from the Jag's tires, and Jack remembered seeing Al's face looming over the steering wheel like a round white moon. Then the jingling crashing sound as they hit the bike at forty, and it had flown up like a bent and twisted bird, the handlebars striking the windshield, and then it was in the air again, leaving the starred safety glass in front of Jack's bulging eyes. A moment later he heard the final dreadful smash as it landed on the road behind them. Something thumped underneath them as the tires passed over it. The Jag drifted around broadside, Al still jockeying the wheel, and from far away Jack heard himself saying: 'Jesus, Al. We ran him down. I felt it.'

In his ear the phone kept ringing. *Come on, Al. Be home. Let me get this over with.*

Al had brought the car to a smoking halt not more than three feet from a bridge stanchion. Two of the Jag's tires were flat. They had left zigzagging loops of burned rubber for a hundred and thirty feet. They looked at each other for a moment and then ran back in the cold darkness.

The bike was completely ruined. One wheel was gone, and looking back over his shoulder Al had seen it lying in the middle of the road, half a dozen spokes sticking up like piano wire. Al had said hesitantly: 'I think that's what we ran over, Jacky-boy.'

'Then where's the kid?'

'Did you *see* a kid?'

Jack frowned. It had all happened with such crazy speed. Coming around the corner. The bike looming in the Jag's headlights. Al yelling something. Then the collision and the long skid.

They moved the bike to one shoulder of the road. Al went back to the Jag and put on its four-way flashers. For the next two hours they searched the sides of the road, using a powerful four-cell flashlight. Nothing. Although it was late, several cars passed the beached Jaguar and the two men with the bobbing flashlight. None of them stopped. Jack thought later that some queer providence, bent on giving them both a last chance, had kept the cops away, had kept any of the passers-by from calling them.

At quarter past two they returned to the Jag, sober but queasy. 'If there was nobody riding it, what was it doing in the middle of the road?' Al demanded. 'It wasn't parked on the side; it was right in the fucking *middle!*'

Jack could only shake his head.

'Your party does not answer,' the operator said. 'Would you like me to keep on trying?'

'A couple more rings, operator. Do you mind?'

'No, sir,' the voice said dutifully.

Come on, Al!

Al had hiked across the bridge to the nearest pay phone, called a bachelor friend and told him it would be worth fifty dollars if the friend would get the Jag's snow tires out of the garage and bring them down to the Highway 31 bridge outside of Barre. The friend showed up twenty minutes later, wearing a pair of jeans and his pajama top. He surveyed the scene.

'Kill anybody?' he asked.

Al was already jacking up the back of the car and Jack was loosening lug nuts. 'Providentially, no one,' Al said.

'I think I'll just head on back anyway. Pay me in the morning.'

'Fine,' Al said without looking up.

The two of them had gotten the tires on without incident, and together they drove back to Al Shockley's house. Al put the Jag in the garage and killed the motor.

In the dark quiet he said: 'I'm off drinking, Jacky-boy. It's all over. I've slain my last martian.'

And now, sweating in this phonebooth, it occurred to Jack that he had never doubted Al's ability to carry through. He had driven back to his own house in the VW with the radio turned up, and some disco group chanted over and over again, talismanic in the house before dawn: *Do it anyway . . . you wanta do it . . . do it anyway you want . . .* No matter how loud he heard the squealing tires, the crash. When he blinked his eyes shut, he saw that single crushed wheel with its broken spokes pointing at the sky.

When he got in, Wendy was asleep on the couch. He looked in Danny's room and Danny was in his crib on his back, sleeping deeply, his arm still buried in the cast. In the softly filtered glow from the streetlight outside he could see the dark lines on its plastered whiteness where all the doctors and nurses in pediatrics had signed it.

It was an accident. He fell down the stairs.

(o you dirty liar)

It was an accident. I lost my temper.

(you fucking drunken waste god wiped snot out of his nose and that was you)

Listen, hey, come on, please, just an accident—

But the last plea was driven away by the image of that bobbing flashlight as they hunted through the dry late November weeds, looking for the sprawled body that by all good rights should have been there, waiting for the police. It didn't matter that Al had been driving. There had been other nights when he had been driving.

He pulled the covers up over Danny, went into their bedroom, and took the Spanish Llama .38 down from the top shelf of the closet. It was in a shoe box. He sat on the bed with it for nearly an hour, looking at it, fascinated by its deadly shine.

It was dawn when he put it back in the box and put the box back in the closet.

That morning he had called Bruckner, the department head, and told him to please post his classes. He had the flu. Bruckner agreed, with less good grace than was common. Jack Torrance had been extremely susceptible to the flu in the last year.

Wendy made him scrambled eggs and coffee. They ate in silence. The only sound came from the back yard, where Danny was gleefully running his trucks across the sand pile with his good hand.

She went to do the dishes. Her back to him, she said: 'Jack. I've been thinking.'

'Have you?' He lit a cigarette with trembling hands. No hangover this morning, oddly enough. Only the shakes. He blinked. In the instant's darkness the bike flew up against the windshield, starring the glass. The tires shrieked. The flashlight bobbed.

'I want to talk to you about . . . about what's best for me and Danny. For you too, maybe. I don't know. We should have talked about it before, I guess.'

'Would you do something for me?' he asked, looking at the wavering tip of his cigarette. 'Would you do me a favor?'

'What?' Her voice was dull and neutral. He looked at her back.

'Let's talk about it a week from today. If you still want to.'

Now she turned to him, her hands lacy with suds, her pretty face pale and disillusioned. 'Jack, promises don't work with you. You just go right on with—'

She stopped, looking in his eyes, fascinated, suddenly uncertain.

'In a week,' he said. His voice had lost all its strength and dropped to a whisper. 'Please. I'm not promising anything. If you still want to talk then, we'll talk. About anything you want.'

They looked across the sunny kitchen at each other for a long time, and when she turned back to the dishes without saying anything more, he began to shudder. God, he needed a drink. Just a little pick-me-up to put things in their true perspective—

'Danny said he dreamed you had a car accident,' she said abruptly. 'He has funny dreams sometimes. He said it this morning, when I got him dressed. Did you, Jack? Did you have an accident?'

'No.'

By noon the craving for a drink had become a low-grade fever. He went to Al's.

'You dry?' Al asked before letting him in. Al looked horrible.

'Bone dry. You look like Lon Chaney in *Phantom of the Opera*.'

'Come on in.'

They played two-handed whist all afternoon. They didn't drink.

A week passed. He and Wendy didn't speak much. But he knew she was watching, not believing. He drank coffee black and endless cans of Coca-Cola. One night he drank a whole six-pack of Coke and then ran into the bathroom and vomited it up. The level of the bottles in the liquor cabinet did not go down. After his classes he went over to Al Shockley's – she hated Al Shockley worse than she had ever hated anyone – and when he came home she would swear she smelled scotch or gin on his breath, but he would talk lucidly to her before supper, drink coffee, play with Danny after supper, sharing a Coke with him, read him a bedtime story, then sit and correct themes with cup after cup of black coffee by his hand, and she would have to admit to herself that she had been wrong.

Weeks passed and the unspoken word retreated further from the back of her lips. Jack sensed its retirement but knew it would never retire completely. Things began to get a little easier. Then George Hatfield. He had lost his temper again, this time stone sober.

'Sir, your party still doesn't—'

'Hello?' Al's voice, out of breath.

'Go ahead,' the operator said dourly.

'Al, this is Jack Torrance.'

'Jacky-boy!' Genuine pleasure. 'How are you?'

'Good. I just called to say thanks. I got the job. It's perfect. If I can't finish that goddam play snowed in all winter, I'll never finish it.'

'You'll finish.'

'How are things?' Jack asked hesitantly.

'Dry,' Al responded. 'You?'

'As a bone.'

'Miss it much?'

'Every day.'

A! laughed. 'I know that scene. But I don't know how you stayed dry after that Hatfield thing, Jack. That was above and beyond.'

'I really bitched things up for myself,' he said evenly.

'Oh, hell. I'll have the Board around by spring. Effinger's already saying they might have been too hasty. And if that play comes to something—'

'Yes. Listen, my boy's out in the car, Al. He looks like he might be getting restless—'

'Sure. Understand. You have a good winter up there, Jack. Glad to help.'

'Thanks again, Al.' He hung up, closed his eyes in the hot booth, and again saw the crashing bike, the bobbing flashlight. There had been a squib in the paper the next day, no more than a space-filler really, but the owner had not been named. Why it had been out there in the night would always be a mystery to them, and perhaps that was as it should be.

He went back out to the car and gave Danny his slightly melted Baby Ruth.

'Daddy?'

'What, doc?'

Danny hesitated, looking at his father's abstracted face.

'When I was waiting for you to come back from that hotel, I had a bad dream. Do you remember? When I fell asleep?'

'Um-hm.'

But it was no good. Daddy's mind was someplace else, not with him. Thinking about the Bad Thing again.

(I dreamed that you hurt me, Daddy)

'What was the dream, doc?'

'Nothing,' Danny said as they pulled out into the parking lot. He put the maps back into the glove compartment.

'You sure?'

'Yes.'

Jack gave his son a faint, troubled glance, and then his mind turned to his play.

Chapter Six

Night Thoughts

Love was over, and her man was sleeping beside her.

Her man.

She smiled a little in the darkness, his seed still trickling with slow warmth from between her slightly parted thighs, and her smile was both rueful and pleased, because the phrase *her man* summoned up a hundred feelings. Each feeling examined alone was a bewilderment. Together, in this darkness floating to sleep, they were like a distant blues tune heard in an almost deserted night club, melancholy but pleasing.

Lovin' you baby, is just like rollin' off a log,
But if I can't be your woman, I sure ain't goin' to be your dog.

Had that been Billie Holiday? Or someone more prosaic like Peggy Lee? Didn't matter. It was low and torchy, and in the silence of her head it played mellowly, as if issuing from one of those old-fashioned jukeboxes, a Wurlitzer, perhaps, half an hour before closing.

Now, moving away from her consciousness, she wondered how many beds she had slept in with this man beside her. They had met in college and had first made love in his apartment . . . that had been less than three months after her mother drove her from the house, told her never to come back, that if she wanted to go somewhere she could go to her father since she had been responsible for the divorce. That had been in 1970. So long ago? A semester later they had moved in together, had found jobs for the summer, and had kept the apartment when their senior year began. She remembered that bed the most clearly, a big double that sagged in the middle. When they made love, the rusty box spring had counted the beats. That fall she had finally managed to break from her mother. Jack had helped her. She wants to keep beating you, Jack had said. The more times you phone her, the more times you crawl back begging forgiveness, the more she can beat you with your father. It's good for her, Wendy, because she can go on making believe it was your fault. But it's not good for you. They had talked it over again and again in that bed, that year.

(Jack sitting up with the covers pooled around his waist, a cigarette burning between his fingers, looking her in the eye – he had a half-humorous, half-scowling way of doing that – telling her: *She told you never to come back, right? Never to darken her door again, right? Then why doesn't she hang up the phone when she knows it's you? Why does she only tell you that you can't come in if I'm with you? Because she thinks I might cramp her style a little bit. She wants to keep putting the thumbscrews right to you, baby. You're a fool if you keep letting her do it. She told you never to come back, so why don't you take her at her word? Give it a rest.* And at last she'd seen it his way.)

It had been Jack's idea to separate for a while – to get perspective on the relationship, he said. She had been afraid he had become interested in someone else. Later she found it wasn't so. They were together again in the spring and he asked her if she had been to see her father. She had jumped as if he'd struck her with a quirt.

How did you know that?

The Shadow knows.

Have you been spying on me?

And his impatient laughter, which had always made her feel so awkward – as if she were eight and he was able to see her motivations more clearly than she.

You needed time, Wendy.

For what?

I guess . . . to see which one of us you wanted to marry.

Jack, what are you saying?

I think I'm proposing marriage.

The wedding. Her father had been there, her mother had not been. She discovered she could live with that, if she had Jack. Then Danny had come, her fine son.

That had been the best year, the best bed. After Danny was born, Jack had gotten her a job typing for half a dozen English Department profs – quizzes, exams, class syllabi, study notes, reading lists. She ended up typing a novel for one of them, a novel that never got published . . . much to Jack's very irreverent and very private glee. The job was good for forty a week, and skyrocketed all the way up to sixty during the two months she spent typing the unsuccessful novel. They had their first car, a five-year-old Buick with a baby seat in the middle. Bright, upwardly mobile young marrieds. Danny forced a reconciliation between her and her mother, a reconciliation that was always tense and never happy, but a reconciliation all the same. When she took Danny to the house, she went without Jack. And she didn't tell Jack that her mother always remade Danny's diapers, frowned over his formula, could always spot the accusatory first signs of a rash on the baby's bottom or privates. Her mother never said anything overtly, but the message came through anyway: the price she had begun to pay (and maybe always would) for the reconciliation was the feeling that she was an inadequate mother. It was her mother's way of keeping the thumbscrews handy.

During the days Wendy would stay home and housewife, feeding Danny his bottles in the sunwashed kitchen of the four-room second-story apartment, playing her records on the battered portable stereo she had had since high school. Jack would come home at three (or at two if he felt he could cut his last class), and while Danny slept he would lead her into the bedroom and fears of inadequacy would be erased.

At night while she typed, he would do his writing and his assignments. In those days she sometimes came out of the bedroom where the typewriter was to find both of them asleep on the studio couch, Jack wearing nothing but his underpants, Danny sprawled comfortably on her husband's chest with his thumb in his mouth. She would put Danny in his crib, then read whatever Jack had written that night before waking him up enough to come to bed.

The best bed, the best year.

Sun gonna shine in my backyard someday . . .

In those days, Jack's drinking had still been well in hand. On Saturday nights a bunch of his fellow students would drop over and there would be a case of beer and discussions in which she seldom took part because her field had been sociology and his was English: arguments over whether Pepys's diaries were literature or history; discussions of Charles Olson's poetry; sometimes the reading of works in progress. Those and a hundred others. No, a thousand. She felt no real urge to take part; it was enough to sit in her rocking chair beside Jack, who sat cross-legged on the floor, one hand holding a beer, the other gently cupping her calf or braceleting her ankle.

The competition at UNH had been fierce, and Jack carried an extra burden in his writing. He put in at least an hour at it every night. It was his routine. The Saturday sessions were necessary therapy. They let something out of him that might otherwise have swelled and swelled until he burst.

At the end of his grad work he had landed the job at Stovington, mostly on the strength of his stories – four of them published at that time, one of them in *Esquire*. She remembered that day clearly enough; it would take more than three years to forget it. She had almost thrown the envelope away, thinking it was a subscription offer. Opening it, she had found instead that it was a letter saying that *Esquire* would like to use Jack's story 'Concerning the Black Holes' early the following year. They would pay nine hundred dollars, not on publication but on acceptance. That was nearly half a year's take typing papers and she had flown to the telephone, leaving Danny in his high chair to goggle comically after her, his face lathered with creamed peas and beef purée.

Jack had arrived from the university forty-five minutes later, the Buick weighted down with seven friends and a keg of beer. After a ceremonial toast (Wendy also had a glass, although she ordinarily had no taste for beer), Jack had signed the acceptance letter, put it in the return envelope, and went down the block to drop it in the letter box. When he came back he stood gravely in the door and said, '*Veni, vidi, vici.*' There were cheers and applause. When the keg was empty at eleven that night, Jack and the only two others who were still ambulatory went on to hit a few bars.

She had gotten him aside in the downstairs hallway. The other two were already out in the car, drunkenly singing the New Hampshire fight song. Jack was down on one knee, owlishly fumbling with the lacings of his moccasins.

'Jack,' she said, 'you shouldn't. You can't even tie your shoes, let alone drive.'

He stood up and put his hands calmly on her shoulders. 'Tonight I could fly to the moon if I wanted to.'

'No,' she said. 'Not for all the *Esquire* stories in the world.'

'I'll be home early.'

But he hadn't been home until four in the morning, stumbling and mumbling his way up the stairs, waking Danny up when he came in. He had tried to soothe the baby and dropped him on the floor. Wendy had rushed out, thinking of what her mother would think if she saw the bruise before she thought of anything else – God help her, God help them both – and then picked Danny up, sat in the rocking chair with him, soothed him. She had been thinking of her mother for most of the five hours Jack had been gone, her mother's prophecy that Jack would never come to anything. *Big ideas,* her mother had said. *Sure. The welfare lines are full of educated fools with big ideas.* Did the *Esquire* story make her mother wrong or right? *Winnifred, you're not holding that baby right. Give him to me.* And was she not holding her husband right? Why else would he take his joy out of the house? A helpless kind of terror had risen up in her and it never occurred to her that he had gone out for reasons that had nothing to do with her.

'Congratulations,' she said, rocking Danny – he was almost asleep again. 'Maybe you gave him a concussion.'

'It's just a bruise.' He sounded sulky, wanting to be repentant: a little boy. For an instant she hated him.

'Maybe,' she said tightly. 'Maybe not.' She heard so much of her mother talking to her departed father in her own voice that she was sickened and afraid.

'Like mother like daughter,' Jack muttered.

'Go to bed!' she cried, her fear coming out sounding like anger. 'Go to bed, you're drunk!'

'Don't tell me what to do.'

'Jack . . . please, we shouldn't . . . it . . .' There were no words.

'Don't tell me what to do,' he repeated sullenly, and then went into the bedroom. She was left alone in the rocking chair with Danny, who was sleeping again. Five minutes later Jack's snores came floating out to the living room. That had been the first night she had slept on the couch.

Now she turned restlessly on the bed, already dozing. Her mind, freed of any linear order by encroaching sleep, floated past the first year at Stovington, past the steadily worsening times that had reached low ebb when her husband had broken Danny's arm, to that morning in the breakfast nook.

Danny outside playing trucks in the sandpile, his arm still in the cast. Jack sitting at the table, pallid and grizzled, a cigarette jittering between his fingers. She had decided to ask him for a divorce. She had pondered the question from a hundred different angles, had been pondering it in fact for the six months before the broken arm. She told herself she would have made the decision long ago if it hadn't been for Danny, but not even that was necessarily true. She dreamed on the long nights when Jack was out, and her dreams were always of her mother's face and of her own wedding.

(*Who giveth this woman?* Her father standing in his best suit which was none too good – he was a traveling salesman for a line of canned goods that even then was going broke – and his tired face, how old he looked, how pale: *I do.*)

Even after the accident – if you could call it an accident – she had not been able to bring it all the way out, to admit that her marriage was a lopsided defeat. She had waited, dumbly hoping that a miracle would occur and Jack would see what was happening, not only to him but to her. But there had been no slowdown. A drink before going off to the Academy. Two or three beers with lunch at the Stovington House. Three or four martinis before dinner. Five or six more while grading papers. The weekends were worse. The nights out with Al Shockley were worse still. She had never dreamed there could be so much pain in a life when there was nothing physically wrong. She hurt all the time. How much of it was her fault? That question haunted her. She felt like her mother. Like her father. Sometimes, when she felt like herself she wondered what it would be like for Danny, and she dreaded the day when he grew old enough to lay blame. And she wondered where they would go. She had no doubt her mother would take her in, and no doubt that after a year of watching her diapers remade, Danny's meals recooked and/or redistributed, of coming home to find his clothes changed or his hair cut or the books her mother found unsuitable spirited away to some limbo in the attic . . . after half a year of that, she would have a complete nervous breakdown. And her mother would pat her hand and say comfortingly, *Although it's not your fault, it's all your own fault. You were never ready. You showed your true colors when you came between your father and me.*

My father, Danny's father. Mine, his.

(*Who giveth this woman? I do.* Dead of a heart attack six months later.)

The night before that morning she had lain awake almost until he came in, thinking, coming to her decision.

The divorce was necessary, she told herself. Her mother and father didn't belong in the decision. Neither did her feelings of guilt over their marriage nor her feelings of inadequacy over her own. It was necessary for her son's sake, and for herself, if she was to salvage anything at all from her early adulthood. The handwriting on the wall was brutal but clear. Her husband was a lush. He had a bad temper, one he could no longer keep wholly under control now that he was drinking so heavily and his writing was going so badly. Accidentally or not accidentally, he had broken Danny's arm. He was going to lose his job, if not this year then the year after. Already she had noticed the sympathetic looks from the other faculty wives. She told herself that she had stuck with the messy job of her marriage for as long as she could. Now she would have to leave it. Jack could have full visitation rights, and she would want support from him only until she could find something and get on her feet – and that would have to be fairly rapidly because she didn't know how long Jack would be able to pay support money. She would do it with as little bitterness as possible. But it had to end.

So thinking, she had fallen off into her own thin and unrestful sleep, haunted by the faces of her own mother and father. *You're nothing but a home-wrecker*, her mother said. *Who giveth this woman?* the minister said. *I do*, her father said. But in the bright and sunny morning she felt the same. Her back to him, her hands plunged in warm dishwater up to the wrists, she had commenced with the unpleasantness.

'I want to talk to you about something that might be best for Danny and I. For you too, maybe. We should have talked about it before, I guess.'

And then he had said an odd thing. She had expected to discover his anger, to provoke the bitterness, the recriminations. She had expected a mad dash for the liquor cabinet. But not this soft, almost toneless reply that was so unlike him. It was almost as though the Jack she had lived with for six years had never come back last night – as if he had been replaced by some unearthly doppelgänger that she would never know or be quite sure of.

'Would you do something for me? A favor?'

'What?' She had to discipline her voice strictly to keep it from trembling.

'Let's talk about it in a week. If you still want to.'

And she had agreed. It remained unspoken between them. During that week he had seen Al Shockley more than ever, but he came home early and there was no liquor on his breath. She imagined she smelled it, but knew it wasn't so. Another week. And another.

Divorce went back to committee, unvoted on.

What had happened? She still wondered and still had not the slightest idea. The subject was taboo between them. He was like a man who had leaned around a corner and had seen an unexpected monster lying in wait, crouching among the dried bones of its old kills. The liquor remained in the cabinet, but he didn't touch it. She had considered throwing them out a dozen times but in the end always backed away from the idea, as if some unknown charm would be broken by the act.

And there was Danny's part in it to consider.

If she felt she didn't know her husband, then she was in awe of her child – awe in the strict meaning of that word: a kind of undefined superstitious dread.

Dozing lightly, the image of the instant of his birth was presented to her. She was again lying on the delivery table, bathed in sweat, her hair in strings, her feet splayed out in the stirrups

(and a little high from the gas they kept giving her whiffs of; at one point she had muttered that she felt like an advertisement for gang rape, and the nurse, an old bird who had assisted at the births of enough children to populate a high school, found that extremely funny)

the doctor between her legs, the nurse off to one side, arranging instruments and humming. The sharp, glassy pains had been coming at steadily shortening intervals, and several times she had screamed in spite of her shame.

Then the doctor told her quite sternly that she must *PUSH*, and she did, and then she felt something being taken from her. It was a clear and distinct feeling, one she would never forget – the thing *taken*. Then the doctor held her son up by the legs – she had seen his tiny sex and known he was a boy immediately – and as the doctor groped for the air-mask, she had seen something else, something so horrible that she found the strength to scream again after she had thought all screams were used up:

He has no face!

But of course there had been a face, Danny's own sweet face, and the caul that had covered it at birth now resided in a small jar which she had kept, almost shamefully. She did not hold with old superstition, but she had kept the caul nevertheless. She did not hold with wives' tales, but the boy had been unusual from the first. She did not believe in second sight but—

Did Daddy have an accident? I dreamed Daddy had an accident.

Something had changed him. She didn't believe it was just her getting ready to ask for a divorce that had done it. Something had happened before that morning. Something that had happened while she slept uneasily. Al Shockley said that nothing had happened, nothing at all, but he had averted his eyes when he said it, and if you believed faculty gossip, Al had also climbed aboard the fabled wagon.

Did Daddy have an accident?

Maybe a chance collision with fate, surely nothing much more concrete. She had read that day's paper and the next day's with a closer eye than usual, but she saw nothing she could connect with Jack. God help her, she had been looking for a hit-and-run accident or a barroom brawl that had resulted in serious injuries or . . . who knew? Who wanted to? But no policeman came to call, either to ask questions or with a warrant empowering him to take paint scrapings from the VW's bumpers. Nothing. Only her husband's one hundred and eighty degree change and her son's sleepy question on waking:

Did Daddy have an accident? I dreamed . . .

She had stuck with Jack more for Danny's sake than she would admit in her waking hours, but now, sleeping lightly, she could admit it: Danny had been Jack's for the asking, almost from the first. Just as she had been her father's, almost from the first. She couldn't remember Danny ever spitting a bottle back on Jack's shirt. Jack could get him to eat after she had given up in disgust, even when Danny was teething and it gave him visible pain to chew. When Danny had a stomachache, she would rock him for an hour before he began to quiet; Jack had only to pick him up, walk twice around the room with him, and Danny would be asleep on Jack's shoulder, his thumb securely corked in his mouth.

He hadn't minded changing diapers, even those he called the special deliveries. He sat with Danny for hours on end, bouncing him on his lap, playing finger games with him, making faces at him while Danny poked at his nose and then collapsed with the giggles. He made formulas and administered them faultlessly, getting up every last burp afterward. He would take Danny with him in the car to get the paper or a bottle of milk or nails at the hardware store even when their son was still an infant. He had taken Danny to a Stovington-Keene soccer match when Danny was only six months old, and Danny had sat motionlessly on his father's lap through the whole game, wrapped in a blanket, a small Stovington pennant clutched in one chubby fist.

He loved his mother but he was his father's boy.

And hadn't she felt, time and time again, her son's wordless opposition to the whole idea of divorce? She would be thinking about it in the kitchen, turning it over in her mind as she turned the potatoes for supper over in her hands for the peeler's blade. And she would turn around to see him sitting cross-legged in a kitchen chair, looking at her with eyes that seemed both frightened and accusatory. Walking with him in the park, he would suddenly seize both her hands and say – almost demand: 'Do you love me? Do you love daddy?' And, confused, she would nod or say, 'Of course I do, honey.' Then he would run to the duck pond, sending them squawking and scared to the other end, flapping their wings in a panic before the small ferocity of his charge, leaving her to stare after him and wonder.

There were even times when it seemed that her determination to at least discuss the matter with Jack dissolved, not out of her own weakness, but under the determination of her son's will.

I don't believe such things.

But in sleep she did believe them, and in sleep, with her husband's seed still drying on her thighs, she felt that the three of them had been permanently welded together – that if their three/oneness was to be destroyed, it would not be destroyed by any of them but from outside.

Most of what she believed centered around her love for Jack. She had never stopped loving him, except maybe for that dark period immediately following Danny's 'accident.' And she loved her son. Most of all she loved them together, walking or riding or only sitting, Jack's large head and Danny's small one poised alertly over the fans of old maid hands, sharing a bottle of Coke, looking at the funnies. She loved having them with her, and she hoped to dear God that this hotel caretaking job Al had gotten for Jack would be the beginning of good times again.

And the wind gonna rise up, baby,
and blow my blues away . . .

Soft and sweet and mellow, the song came back and lingered, following her down into a deeper sleep where thought ceased and the faces that came in dreams went unremembered.

Chapter Seven

In Another Bedroom

Danny awoke with the booming still loud in his ears, and the drunk, savagely pettish voice crying hoarsely: *Come out here and take your medicine! I'll find you! I'll find you!*

But now the booming was only his racing heart, and the only voice in the night was the faraway sound of a police siren.

He lay in bed motionlessly, looking up at the wind-stirred shadows of the leaves on his bedroom ceiling. They twined sinuously together, making shapes like the vines and creepers in a jungle, like patterns woven into the nap of a thick carpet. He was clad in Doctor Denton pajamas, but between the pajama suit and his skin he had grown a more closely fitting singlet of perspiration.

'Tony?' he whispered. 'You there?'

No answer.

He slipped out of bed and padded silently across to the window and looked out on Arapahoe Street, now still and silent. It was two in the morning. There was nothing out there but empty sidewalks drifted with fallen leaves, parked cars, and the long-necked streetlight on the corner across from the Cliff Brice gas station. With its hooded top and motionless stance, the streetlight looked like a monster in a space show.

He looked up the street both ways, straining his eyes for Tony's slight, beckoning form, but there was no one there.

The wind sighed through the trees, and the fallen leaves rattled up the deserted walks and around the hubcaps of parked cars. It was a faint and sorrowful sound, and the boy thought that he might be the only one in Boulder awake enough to hear it. The only human being, at least. There was no way of knowing what else might be out in the night, slinking hungrily through the shadows, watching and scenting the breeze.

I'll find you! I'll find you!

'Tony?' he whispered again, but without much hope.

Only the wind spoke back, gusting more strongly this time, scattering leaves across the sloping roof below his window. Some of them slipped into the raingutter and came to rest there like tired dancers.

Danny . . . Danneee . . .

He started at the sound of that familiar voice and craned out of the window, his small hands on the sill. With the sound of Tony's voice the whole night seemed to have come silently and secretly alive, whispering even when the wind quieted again and the leaves were still and the shadows had stopped moving. He thought he saw a darker shadow standing by the bus stop a block down, but it was hard to tell if it was a real thing or an eye-trick.

Don't go, Danny . . .

Then the wind gusted again, making him squint, and the shadow by the bus stop was gone . . . if it had ever been there at all. He stood by his window for

(a minute? an hour?)

some time longer, but there was no more. At last he crept back into his bed and pulled the blankets up and watched the shadows thrown by the alien streetlight turn into a sinuous jungle filled with flesh-eating plants that wanted only to slip around him, squeeze the life out of him, and drag him down into a blackness where one sinister word flashed in red:

REDRUM.

BOOK TWO

CLOSING DAY

Chapter Eight

A View of the Overlook

Mommy was worried.

She was afraid the bug wouldn't make it up and down all these mountains and that they would get stranded by the side of the road where somebody might come ripping along and hit them. Danny himself was more sanguine;

if Daddy thought the bug would make this one last trip, then probably it would.

'We're just about there,' Jack said.

Wendy brushed her hair back from her temples. 'Thank God.'

She was sitting in the right-hand bucket, a Victoria Holt paperback open but face down in her lap. She was wearing her blue dress, the one Danny thought was her prettiest. It had a sailor collar and made her look very young, like a girl just getting ready to graduate from high school. Daddy kept putting his hand high up on her leg and she kept laughing and brushing it off, saying Get away, fly.

Danny was impressed with the mountains. One day Daddy had taken them up in the ones near Boulder, the ones they called the Flatirons, but these were much bigger, and on the tallest of them you could see a fine dusting of snow, which Daddy said was often there year-round.

And they were actually *in* the mountains, no goofing around. Sheer rock faces rose all around them, so high you could barely see their tops even by craning your neck out the window. When they left Boulder, the temperature had been in the high seventies. Now, just after noon, the air up here felt crisp and cold like November back in Vermont and Daddy had the heater going . . . not that it worked all that well. They had passed several signs that said FALLING ROCK ZONE (Mommy read each one to him), and although Danny had waited anxiously to see some rock fall, none had. At least not yet.

Half an hour ago they had passed another sign that Daddy said was very important. This sign said ENTERING SIDEWINDER PASS, and Daddy said that sign was as far as the snowplows went in the wintertime. After that the road got too steep. In the winter the road was closed from the little town of Sidewinder, which they had gone through just before they got to that sign, all the way to Buckland, Utah.

Now they were passing another sign.

'What's that one, Mom?'

'That one says SLOWER VEHICLES USE RIGHT LANE. That means us.'

'The bug will make it,' Danny said.

'Please, God,' Mommy said, and crossed her fingers. Danny looked down at her open-toed sandals and saw that she had crossed her toes as well. He giggled. She smiled back, but he knew that she was still worried.

The road wound up and up in a series of slow S curves, and Jack dropped the bug's stick shift from fourth gear to third, then into second. The bug wheezed and protested, and Wendy's eye fixed on the speedometer needle, which sank from forty to thirty to twenty, where it hovered reluctantly.

'The fuel pump . . .' she began timidly.

'The fuel pump will go another three miles,' Jack said shortly.

The rock wall fell away on their right, disclosing a slash valley that seemed to go down forever, lined a dark green with Rocky Mountain pine and spruce. The pines fell away to gray cliffs of rock that dropped for hundreds of feet before smoothing out. She saw a waterfall spilling over one of them, the early afternoon sun sparkling in it like a golden fish snared in a blue net. They were beautiful mountains but they were hard. She did not think they would forgive many mistakes. An unhappy foreboding rose in her throat. Further west in the Sierra Nevada the Donner Party had become snowbound and had resorted to cannibalism to stay alive. The mountains did not forgive many mistakes.

With a punch of the clutch and a jerk, Jack shifted down to first gear and they labored upward, the bug's engine thumping gamely.

'You know,' she said, 'I don't think we've seen five cars since we came through Sidewinder. And one of them was the hotel limousine.'

Jack nodded. 'It goes right to Stapleton Airport in Denver. There's already some icy patches up beyond the hotel, Watson says, and they're forecasting more snow for tomorrow up higher. Anybody going through the mountains now wants to be on one of the main roads, just in case. That goddam Ullman better still be up there. I guess he will be.'

'You're sure the larder is fully stocked?' she asked, still thinking of the Donners.

'He said so. He wanted Hallorann to go over it with you. Hallorann's the cook.'

'Oh,' she said faintly, looking at the speedometer. It had dropped from fifteen to ten miles an hour.

'There's the top,' Jack said, pointing three hundred yards ahead. 'There's a scenic turnout and you can see the Overlook from there. I'm going to pull off the road and give the bug a chance to rest.' He craned over his shoulder at Danny, who was sitting on a pile of blankets. 'What do you think, doc? We might see some deer. Or caribou.'

'Sure, Dad.'

The VW labored up and up. The speedometer dropped to just above the five-mile-an-hour hashmark and was beginning to hitch when Jack pulled off the road

('What's that sign, Mommy?' 'SCENIC TURNOUT,' she read dutifully.)

and stepped on the emergency brake and let the VW run in neutral.

'Come on,' he said, and got out.

They walked to the guardrail together.

'That's it,' Jack said, and pointed at eleven o'clock.

For Wendy, it was discovering truth in a cliché: her breath was taken away. For a moment she was unable to breathe at all; the view had knocked the wind from her. They were standing near the top of one peak. Across from them – who knew how far? – an even taller mountain reared into the sky, its jagged tip only a silhouette that was now nimbused by the sun, which was beginning its decline. The whole valley floor was spread out below them, the slopes that they had climbed in the laboring bug falling away with such dizzying suddenness that she knew to look down there for too long would bring on nausea and eventual vomiting. The imagination seemed to spring to full life in the clear air, beyond the rein of reason, and to look was to helplessly see one's self plunging down and down and down, sky and slopes changing places in slow cartwheels, the scream drifting from your mouth like a lazy balloon as your hair and your dress billowed out . . .

She jerked her gaze away from the drop almost by force and followed Jack's finger. She could see the highway clinging to the side of this cathedral spire, switching back on itself but always tending northwest, still climbing but at a more gentle angle. Further up, seemingly set directly into the slope itself, she saw the grimly clinging pines give way to a wide square of green lawn and standing in the middle of it, overlooking all this, the hotel. The Overlook. Seeing it, she found breath and voice again.

'Oh, Jack, it's gorgeous!'

'Yes, it is,' he said. 'Ullman says he thinks it's the single most beautiful location in America. I don't care much for him, but I think he might be . . . Danny! Danny, are you all right?'

She looked around for him and her sudden fear for him blotted out everything else, stupendous or not. She darted toward him. He was holding onto the guardrail and looking up at the hotel, his face a pasty gray color. His eyes had the blank look of someone on the verge of fainting.

She knelt beside him and put steadying hands on his shoulders. 'Danny, what's—'

Jack was beside her. 'You okay, doc?' He gave Danny a brisk little shake and his eyes cleared.

'I'm okay, Daddy. I'm fine.'

'What was it, Danny?' she asked. 'Were you dizzy, honey?'

'No, I was just . . . thinking. I'm sorry. I didn't mean to scare you.' He looked at his parents, kneeling in front of him, and offered them a small puzzled smile. 'Maybe it was the sun. The sun got in my eyes.'

'We'll get you up to the hotel and give you a drink of water,' Daddy said.

'Okay.'

And in the bug, which moved upward more surely on the gentler grade, he kept looking out between them as the road unwound, affording occasional glimpses of the Overlook Hotel, its massive bank of westward-looking windows reflecting back the sun. It was the place he had seen in the midst of the blizzard, the dark and booming place where some hideously familiar figure sought him down long corridors carpeted with jungle. The place Tony had warned him against. It was here. It was here. Whatever Redrum was, it was here.

Chapter Nine

Checking It Out

Ullman was waiting for them just inside the wide, old-fashioned front doors. He shook hands with Jack and nodded coolly at Wendy, perhaps noticing the way heads turned when she came through into the lobby, her golden hair spilling across the shoulders of the simple navy dress. The hem of the dress stopped a modest two inches above the knee, but you didn't have to see more to know they were good legs.

Ullman seemed truly warm toward Danny only, but Wendy had experienced that before. Danny seemed to be a child for people who ordinarily held W. C. Fields' sentiments about children. He bent a little from the waist and offered Danny his hand. Danny shook it formally, without a smile.

'My son Danny,' Jack said. 'And my wife Winnifred.'

'I'm happy to meet you both,' Ullman said. 'How old are you, Danny?'

'Five, sir.'

'*Sir*, yet.' Ullman smiled and glanced at Jack. 'He's well mannered.'

'Of course he is,' Jack said.

'And Mrs Torrance.' He offered the same little bow, and for a bemused instant Wendy thought he would kiss her hand. She half-offered it and he did take it, but only for a moment, clasped in both of his. His hands were small and dry and smooth, and she guessed that he powdered them.

The lobby was a bustle of activity. Almost every one of the old-fashioned high-backed chairs was taken. Bellboys shuttled in and out with suitcases and there was a line at the desk, which was dominated by a huge brass cash register. The BankAmericard and Master Charge decals on it seemed jarringly anachronistic.

To their right, down toward a pair of tall double doors that were pulled closed and roped off, there was an old-fashioned fireplace now blazing with birch logs. Three nuns sat on a sofa that was drawn up almost to the hearth itself. They were talking and smiling with their bags stacked up to either side, waiting for the check-out line to thin a little. As Wendy watched them they burst into a chord of tinkling, girlish laughter. She felt a smile touch her own lips; not one of them could be under sixty.

In the background was the constant hum of conversation, the muted *ding!* of the silver-plated bell beside the cash register as one of the two clerks on duty struck it, the slightly impatient call of 'Front, please!' It brought back strong, warm memories of her honeymoon in New York with Jack, at the Beekman Tower. For the first time she let herself believe that this might be exactly what the three of them needed: a season together away from the world, a sort of family honeymoon. She smiled affectionately down at Danny, who was goggling around frankly at everything. Another limo, as gray as a banker's vest, had pulled up out front.

'The last day of the season,' Ullman was saying. 'Closing day. Always hectic. I had expected you more around three, Mr Torrance.'

'I wanted to give the Volks time for a nervous breakdown if it decided to have one,' Jack said. 'It didn't.'

'How fortunate,' Ullman said. 'I'd like to take the three of you on a tour of the place a little later, and of course Dick Hallorann wants to show Mrs Torrance the Overlook's kitchen. But I'm afraid—'

One of the clerks came over and almost tugged his forelock.

'Excuse me, Mr Ullman—'

'Well? What is it?'

'It's Mrs Brant,' the clerk said uncomfortably. 'She refuses to pay her bill with anything but her American Express card. I told her we stopped taking American Express at the end of the season last year, but she won't . . .' His eyes shifted to the Torrance family, then back to Ullman. He shrugged.

'I'll take care of it.'

'Thank you, Mr Ullman.' The clerk crossed back to the desk, where a dreadnought of a woman bundled into a long fur coat and what looked like a black feather boa was remonstrating loudly.

'I have been coming to the Overlook Hotel since 1955,' she was telling the smiling, shrugging clerk. 'I continued to come even after my second husband died of a stroke on that tiresome roque court – I told him the sun was too hot that day – and I have *never* . . . I repeat: *never* . . . paid with anything but my American Express credit card. Call the police if you like! Have them drag me away! I will still refuse to pay with anything but my American Express credit card. I repeat: . . .'

'Excuse me,' Mr Ullman said.

They watched him cross the lobby, touch Mrs Brant's elbow deferentially, and spread his hands and nod when she turned her tirade on him. He listened sympathetically, nodded again, and said something in return. Mrs Brant smiled triumphantly, turned to the unhappy desk clerk, and said loudly: 'Thank God there is one employee of this hotel who hasn't become an utter Philistine!'

She allowed Ullman, who barely came to the bulky shoulder of her fur coat, to take her arm and lead her away, presumably to his inner office.

'Whooo!' Wendy said, smiling. 'There's a dude who earns his money.'

'But he didn't like that lady,' Danny said immediately. 'He was just pretending to like her.'

Jack grinned down at him. 'I'm sure that's true, doc. But flattery is the stuff that greases the wheels of the world.'

'What's flattery?'

'Flattery,' Wendy told him, 'is when your daddy says he likes my new yellow slacks even if he doesn't or when he says I don't need to take off five pounds.'

'Oh. Is it lying for fun?'

'Something very like that.'

He had been looking at her closely and now said: 'You're pretty, Mommy.' He frowned in confusion when they exchanged a glance and then burst into laughter.

'Ullman didn't waste much flattery on me,' Jack said. 'Come on over by the window, you guys. I feel conspicuous standing out here in the middle with my denim jacket on. I honest to God didn't think there'd be anybody much here on closing day. Guess I was wrong.'

'You look very handsome,' she said, and then they laughed again, Wendy putting a hand over her mouth. Danny still didn't understand, but it was okay. They were loving each other. Danny thought this place reminded her of somewhere else

(the beak-man place)

where she had been happy. He wished he liked it as well as she did, but he kept telling himself over and over that the things Tony showed him didn't always come true. He would be careful. He would watch for something called Redrum. But he would not say anything unless he absolutely had to. Because they were happy, they had been laughing, and there were no bad thoughts.

'Look at this view,' Jack said.

'Oh, it's gorgeous! Danny, look!'

But Danny didn't think it was particularly gorgeous. He didn't like heights; they made him dizzy. Beyond the wide front porch, which ran the length of the hotel, a beautifully manicured lawn (there was a putting green on the right) sloped away to a long, rectangular swimming pool. A CLOSED sign stood on a little tripod at one end of the pool; *closed* was one sign he could read by himself, along with *Stop, Exit, Pizza*, and a few others.

Beyond the pool a graveled path wound off through baby pines and spruces and aspens. Here was a small sign he didn't know: ROQUE. There was an arrow below it.

'What's R-O-Q-U-E, Daddy?'

'A game,' Daddy said. 'It's a little bit like croquet, only you play it on a gravel court that has sides like a big billiard table instead of grass. It's a very old game, Danny. Sometimes they have tournaments here.'

'Do you play it with a croquet mallet?'

'Like that,' Jack agreed. 'Only the handle's a little shorter and the head has two sides. One side is hard rubber and the other side is wood.'

(*Come out, you little shit!*)

'It's pronounced *roke*,' Daddy was saying. 'I'll teach you how to play, if you want.'

'Maybe,' Danny said in an odd colorless little voice that made his parents exchange a puzzled look over his head. 'I might not like, it, though.'

'Well if you don't like it, doc, you don't have to play. All right?'

'Sure.'

'Do you like the animals?' Wendy asked. 'That's called a topiary.' Beyond the path leading to *roque* there were hedges clipped into the shapes of various animals. Danny, whose eyes were sharp, made out a rabbit, a dog, a horse, a cow, and a trio of bigger ones that looked like frolicking lions.

'Those animals were what made Uncle Al think of me for the job,' Jack told him. 'He knew that when I was in college I used to work for a landscaping company. That's a business that fixes people's lawns and bushes and hedges. I used to trim a lady's topiary.'

Wendy put a hand over her mouth and snickered. Looking at her, Jack said, 'Yes, I used to trim her topiary at least once a week.'

'Get away, fly,' Wendy said, and snickered again.

'Did she have nice hedges, Dad?' Danny asked, and at this they both stifled great bursts of laughter. Wendy laughed so hard that tears streamed down her cheeks and she had to get a Kleenex out of her handbag.

'They weren't animals, Danny,' Jack said when he had control of himself. 'They were playing cards. Spades and hearts and clubs and diamonds. But the hedges grow, you see—'

(*They creep*, Watson had said . . . no, not the hedges, the boiler. *You have to watch it all the time or you and your fambly will end up on the fuckin moon.*)

They looked at him, puzzled. The smile had faded off his face.

'Dad?' Danny asked.

He blinked at them, as if coming back from far away. 'They grow, Danny, and lose their shape. So I'll have to give them a haircut once or twice a week until it gets so cold they stop growing for the year.'

'And a playground, too,' Wendy said. 'My lucky boy.'

The playground was beyond the *topiary*. Two slides, a big swing set with half a dozen swings set at varying heights, a jungle gym, a tunnel made of cement rings, a sandbox, and a playhouse that was an exact replica of the Overlook itself.

'Do you like it, Danny?' Wendy asked.

'I sure do,' he said, hoping he sounded more enthused than he felt. 'It's neat.'

Beyond the playground there was an inconspicuous chain link security fence, beyond that the wide, macadamized drive that led up to the hotel, and beyond that the valley itself, dropping away into the bright blue haze of afternoon. Danny didn't know the word *isolation*, but if someone had explained it to him he would have seized on it. Far below, lying in the sun like a long black snake that had decided to snooze for a while, was the road that led back through Sidewinder Pass and eventually to Boulder. The road that would be closed all winter long. He felt a little suffocated at the thought, and almost jumped when Daddy dropped his hand on his shoulder.

'I'll get you that drink as soon as I can, doc. They're a little busy right now.'

'Sure, Dad.'

Mrs Brant came out of the inner office looking vindicated. A few moments later two bellboys, struggling with eight suitcases between them, followed her as best they could as she strode triumphantly out the door. Danny watched through the window as a man in a gray uniform and a hat like a captain in the Army brought her long silver car around to the door and got out. He tipped his cap to her and ran around to open the trunk.

And in one of those flashes that sometimes came, he got a complete thought from her, one that floated above the confused, low-pitched babble of emotions and colors that he usually got in crowded places.

(*i'd like to get into his pants*)

Danny's brow wrinkled as he watched the bellboys put her cases into the trunk. She was looking rather sharply at the man in the gray uniform, who was supervising the loading. Why would she want to get that man's pants? Was she cold, even with that long fur coat on? And if she was that cold, why hadn't she just put on some pants of her own? His mommy wore pants just about all winter.

The man in the gray uniform closed the trunk and walked back to help her into the car. Danny watched closely to see if she would say anything about his pants, but she only smiled and gave him a dollar bill – a tip. A moment later she was guiding the big silver car down the driveway.

He thought about asking his mother why Mrs Brant might want the car-man's pants, and decided against it. Sometimes questions could get you in a whole lot of trouble. If had happened to him before.

So instead he squeezed in between them on the small sofa they were sharing and watched all the people check out at the desk. He was glad his mommy and daddy were happy and loving each other, but he couldn't help being a little worried. He couldn't help it.

Chapter Ten

Hallorann

The cook didn't conform to Wendy's image of the typical resort hotel kitchen personage at all. To begin with, such a personage was called a *chef*, nothing so mundane as a cook – cooking was what she did in her apartment kitchen when she threw all the leftovers into a greased Pyrex casserole dish and added noodles. Further, the culinary wizard of such a place as the Overlook, which advertised in the resort section of the New York Sunday *Times*, should be small, rotund, and pasty-faced (rather like the Pillsbury Dough-Boy); he should have a thin pencil-line mustache like a forties musical comedy star, dark eyes, a French accent, and a detestable personality.

Hallorann had the dark eyes and that was all. He was a tall black man with a modest afro that was beginning to powder white. He had a soft southern accent and he laughed a lot, disclosing teeth too white and too even to be anything but 1950-vintage Sears and Roebuck dentures. Her own father had had a pair, which he called Roebuckers, and from time to time he would push them out at her comically at the supper table . . . always, Wendy remembered now, when her mother was out in the kitchen getting something else or on the telephone.

Danny had stared up at this black giant in blue serge, and then had smiled when Hallorann picked him up easily, set him in the crook of his elbow, and said: 'You ain't gonna stay up here all winter.'

'Yes I am,' Danny said with a shy grin.

'No, you're gonna come down to St. Pete's with me and learn to cook and go out on the beach every damn evenin watchin for crabs. Right?'

Danny giggled delightedly and shook his head no. Hallorann set him down.

'If you're gonna change your mind,' Hallorann said, bending over him gravely, 'you better do it quick. Thirty minutes from now and I'm in my car. Two and a half hours after that, I'm sitting at Gate 32, Concourse B, Stapleton International Airport, in the mile-high city of Denver, Colorado. Three hours after *that*, I'm rentin a car at the Miama Airport and on my way to sunny St. Pete's, waiting to get inta my swimtrunks and just laaafin up my sleeve at anybody stuck and caught in the snow. Can you dig it, my boy?'

'Yes, sir,' Danny said, smiling.

Hallorann turned to Jack and Wendy. 'Looks like a fine boy there.'

'We think he'll do,' Jack said, and offered his hand. Hallorann took it. 'I'm Jack Torrance. My wife Winnifred. Danny you've met.'

'And a pleasure it was. Ma'am, are you a Winnie or a Freddie?'

'I'm a Wendy,' she said, smiling.

'Okay. That's better than the other two, I think. Right this way. Mr

Ullman wants you to have the tour, the tour you'll get.' He shook his head and said under his breath: 'And won't I be glad to see the last of *him*.'

Hallorann commenced to tour them around the most immense kitchen Wendy had ever seen in her life. It was sparkling clean. Every surface was coaxed to a high gloss. It was more than just big; it was intimidating. She walked at Hallorann's side while Jack, wholly out of his element, hung back a little with Danny. A long wallboard hung with cutting instruments which went all the way from paring knives to two-handed cleavers hung beside a four-basin sink. There was a breadboard as big as their Boulder apartment's kitchen table. An amazing array of stainless-steel pots and pans hung from floor to ceiling, covering one whole wall.

'I think I'll have to leave a trail of breadcrumbs every time I come in,' she said.

'Don't let it get you down,' Hallorann said. 'It's big, but it's still only a kitchen. Most of this stuff you'll never even have to touch. Keep it clean, that's all I ask. Here's the stove I'd be using, if I was you. There are three of them in all, but this is the smallest.'

Smallest, she thought dismally, looking at it. There were twelve burners, two regular ovens and a Dutch oven, a heated well on top in which you could simmer sauces or bake beans, a broiler, and a warmer – plus a million dials and temperature gauges.

'All gas,' Hallorann said. 'You've cooked with gas before, Wendy?'

'Yes . . .'

'I love gas,' he said, and turned on one of the burners. Blue flame popped into life and he adjusted it down to a faint glow with a delicate touch. 'I like to be able to see the flame you're cookin with. You see where all the surface burner switches are?'

'Yes.'

'And the oven dials are all marked. Myself, I favor the middle one because it seems to heat the most even, but you use whichever one you like – or all three, for that matter.'

'A TV dinner in each one,' Wendy said, and laughed weakly.

Hallorann roared. 'Go right ahead, if you like. I left a list of everything edible over by the sink. You see it?'

'Here it is, Mommy!' Danny brought over two sheets of paper, written closely on both sides.

'Good boy,' Hallorann said, taking it from him and ruffling his hair. 'You sure you don't want to come to Florida with me, my boy? Learn to cook the sweetest shrimp creole this side of paradise?'

Danny put his hands over his mouth and giggled and retreated to his father's side.

'You three folks could eat up here for a year, I guess,' Hallorann said. 'We got a cold-pantry, a walk-in freezer, all sorts of vegetable bins, and two refrigerators. Come on and let me show you.'

For the next ten minutes Hallorann opened bins and doors, disclosing food in such amounts as Wendy had never seen before. The food supplies amazed her but did not reassure her as much as she might have thought: the Donner Party kept recurring to her, not with thoughts of cannibalism (with all this food it would indeed be a long time before they were reduced to such poor rations as each other), but with the reinforced idea that this was indeed a serious business: when snow fell, getting out of here would not be a matter of an hour's drive to Sidewinder but a major operation. They would sit up here in this deserted grand hotel, eating the food that had been left them like creatures in a fairy tale and listening to the bitter wind around their snowbound eaves. In Vermont, when Danny had broken his arm

(when *Jack* broke Danny's arm)

she had called the emergency Medix squad, dialing the number from the little card attached to the phone. They had been at the house only ten minutes later. There were other numbers written on that little card. You could have a police car in five minutes and a fire truck in even less time than that, because the fire station was only three blocks away and one block over. There was a man to call if the lights went out, a man to call if the shower stopped up, a man to call if the TV went on the fritz. But what would happen up here if Danny had one of his fainting spells and swallowed his tongue?

(*oh God what a thought!*)

What if the place caught on fire? If Jack fell down the elevator shaft and fractured his skull? What if—?

(*what if we have a wonderful time now* stop *it, Winnifred!*)

Hallorann showed them into the walk-in freezer first, where their breath puffed out like comic strip balloons. In the freezer it was as if winter had already come.

Hamburger in big plastic bags, ten pounds in each bag, a dozen bags. Forty whole chickens hanging from a row of hooks in the wood-planked walls. Canned hams stacked up like poker chips, a dozen of them. Below the chickens, ten roasts of beef, ten roasts of pork, and a huge leg of lamb.

'You like lamb, doc?' Hallorann asked, grinning.

'I love it,' Danny said immediately. He had never had it.

'I knew you did. There's nothin like two good slices of lamb on a cold night, with some mint jelly on the side. You got the mint jelly here, too. Lamb eases the belly. It's a non-contentious sort of meat.'

From behind them Jack said curiously: 'How did you know we called him doc?'

Hallorann turned around. 'Pardon?'

'Danny. We call him doc sometimes. Like in the Bugs Bunny cartoons.'

'Looks sort of like a doc, doesn't he?' He wrinkled his nose at Danny, smacked his lips, and said, 'Ehhhh, what's up, doc?'

Danny giggled and then Hallorann said something

(*Sure you don't want to go to Florida, doc?*)

to him, very clearly. He heard every word. He looked at Hallorann, startled and a little scared. Hallorann winked solemnly and turned back to the food.

Wendy looked from the cook's broad, serge-clad back to her son. She had the oddest feeling that something had passed between them, something she could not quite follow.

'You got twelve packages of sausage, twelve packages of bacon,' Hallorann said. 'So much for the pig. In this drawer, twenty pounds of butter.'

'*Real* butter?' Jack asked.

'The A-number-one.'

'I don't think I've had real butter since I was a kid back in Berlin, New Hampshire.'

'Well, you'll eat it up here until oleo seems a treat,' Hallorann said, and laughed. 'Over in this bin you got your bread – thirty loaves of white, twenty of dark. We try to keep racial balance at the Overlook, don't you know. Now I know fifty loaves won't take you through, but there's plenty of makings and fresh is better than frozen any day of the week.

'Down here you got your fish. Brain food, right, doc?'

'Is it, Mom?'

'If Mr Hallorann says so, honey.' She smiled.

Danny wrinkled his nose. 'I don't like fish.'

'You're dead wrong,' Hallorann said. 'You just never had any fish that liked *you*. This fish here will like you fine. Five pounds of rainbow trout, ten pounds of turbot, fifteen cans of tuna fish—'

'Oh yeah, I like tuna.'

'and five pounds of the sweetest-tasting sole that ever swam in the sea. My boy, when next spring rolls around, you're gonna thank old . . .' He snapped his fingers as if he had forgotten something. 'What's my name, now? I guess it just slipped my mind.'

'Mr Hallorann,' Danny said, grinning. 'Dick, to your friends.'

'That's right! And you bein a friend, you make it Dick.'

As he led them into the far corner, Jack and Wendy exchanged a puzzled glance, both of them trying to remember if Hallorann had told them his first name.

'And this here I put in special,' Hallorann said. 'Hope you folks enjoy it.'

'Oh really, you shouldn't have,' Wendy said, touched. It was a twenty-pound turkey wrapped in a wide scarlet ribbon with a bow on top.

'You got to have your turkey on Thanksgiving, Wendy,' Hallorann said gravely. 'I believe there's a capon back here somewhere for Christmas. Doubtless you'll stumble on it. Let's come on out of here now before we all catch the peenumonia. Right, doc?'

'Right!'

There were more wonders in the cold-pantry. A hundred boxes of dried milk (Hallorann advised her gravely to buy fresh milk for the boy in Sidewinder as long as it was feasible), five twelve-pound bags of sugar, a gallon jug of blackstrap molasses, cereals, glass jugs of rice, macaroni, spaghetti; ranked cans of fruit and fruit salad; a bushel of fresh apples that scented the whole room with autumn; dried raisins, prunes, and apricots ('You got to be regular if you want to be happy,' Hallorann said, and pealed laughter at the cold-pantry ceiling, where one old-fashioned light globe hung down on an iron chain); a deep bin filled with potatoes; and smaller caches of tomatoes, onions, turnips, squashes, and cabbages.

'My word,' Wendy said as they came out. But seeing all that fresh food after her thirty-dollar-a-week grocery budget so stunned her that she was unable to say just what her word was.

'I'm runnin a bit late,' Hallorann said, checking his watch, 'so I'll just let you go through the cabinets and the fridges as you get settled in. There's cheeses, canned milk, sweetened condensed milk, yeast, bakin soda, a whole bagful of those Table Talk pies, a few bunches of bananas that ain't even near to ripe yet—'

'Stop,' she said, holding up a hand and laughing. 'I'll never remember it all. It's super. And I promise to leave the place clean.'

'That's all I ask.' He turned to Jack. 'Did Mr Ullman give you the rundown on the rats in his belfry?'

Jack grinned. 'He said there were possibly some in the attic, and Mr Watson said there might be some more down in the basement. There must be two tons of paper down there, but I didn't see any shredded, as if they'd been using it to make nests.'

'That Watson,' Hallorann said, shaking his head in mock sorrow. 'Ain't he the foulest-talking man you ever ran on?'

'He's quite a character,' Jack agreed. His own father had been the foulest-talking man Jack had ever run on.

'It's sort of a pity,' Hallorann said, leading them back toward the wide swinging doors that gave on the Overlook dining room. 'There was money in that family, long ago. It was Watson's granddad or great-graddad – I can't remember which – that built this place.'

'So I was told,' Jack said.

'What happened?' Wendy asked.

'Well, they couldn't make it go,' Hallorann said. 'Watson will tell you the whole story – twice a day, if you let him. The old man got a bee in his bonnet about the place. He let it drag him down, I guess. He had two boys and one of them was killed in a riding accident on the grounds while the hotel was still a-building. That would have been 1908 or '09. The old man's wife died of the flu, and then it was just the old man and his youngest son. They ended up getting took back on as caretakers in the same hotel the old man had built.'

'It is sort of a pity,' Wendy said.

'What happened to him? The old man?' Jack asked.

'He plugged his finger into a light socket by mistake and that was the end of him,' Hallorann said. 'Sometime in the early thirties before the Depression closed this place down for ten years.

'Anyway, Jack, I'd appreciate it if you and your wife would keep an eye out for rats in the kitchen, as well. If you should see them . . . traps, not poison.'

Jack blinked. 'Of course. Who'd want to put rat poison in the kitchen?'

Hallorann laughed derisively. 'Mr Ullman, that's who. That was his bright idea last fall. I put it to him, I said: "What if we all get up here next May, Mr Ullman, and I serve the traditional opening night dinner" – which just happens to be salmon in a very nice sauce – "and everybody gits sick and the doctor comes and says to you, 'Ullman, what have you been doing up here? You've got eighty of the richest folks in America suffering from rat poisoning!' " '

Jack threw his head back and bellowed laughter. 'What did Ullman say?'

Hallorann tucked his tongue into his cheek as if feeling for a bit of food in there. 'He said: "Get some traps, Hallorann." '

This time they all laughed, even Danny, although he was not completely sure what the joke was, except it had something to do with Mr Ullman, who didn't know everything after all.

The four of them passed through the dining room, empty and silent now, with its fabulous western exposure on the snow-dusted peaks. Each of the white linen tablecloths had been covered with a sheet of tough clear plastic. The rug, now rolled up for the season, stood in one corner like a sentinel on guard duty.

Across the wide room was a double set of batwing doors, and over them an old-fashioned sign lettered in gilt script: *The Colorado Lounge*.

Following his gaze, Hallorann said, 'If you're a drinkin man, I hope you brought your own supplies. That place is picked clean. Employee's party last night, you know. Every maid and bellhop in the place is goin around with a headache today, me included.'

'I don't drink,' Jack said shortly. They went back to the lobby.

It had cleared greatly during the half hour they'd spent in the kitchen. The long main room was beginning to take on the quiet, deserted look that Jack supposed they would become familiar with soon enough. The high-backed chairs were empty. The nuns who had been sitting by the fire were gone, and the fire itself was down to a bed of comfortably glowing coals. Wendy glanced out into the parking lot and saw that all but a dozen cars had disappeared.

She found herself wishing they could get back in the VW and go back to Boulder . . . or anywhere else.

Jack was looking around for Ullman, but he wasn't in the lobby.

A young maid with her ash-blond hair pinned up on her neck came over. 'Your luggage is out on the porch, Dick.'

'Thank you, Sally.' He gave her a peck on the forehead. 'You have yourself a good winter. Getting married, I hear.'

He turned to the Torrances as she strolled away, backside twitching pertly. 'I've got to hurry along if I'm going to make that plane. I want to wish you all the best. Know you'll have it.'

'Thanks,' Jack said. 'You've been very kind.'

'I'll take good care of your kitchen,' Wendy promised again. 'Enjoy Florida.'

'I always do,' Hallorann said. He put his hands on his knees and bent down to Danny. 'Last chance, guy. Want to come to Florida?'

'I guess not,' Danny said, smiling.

'Okay. Like to give me a hand out to my car with my bags?'

'If my mommy says I can.'

'You can,' Wendy said, 'but you'll have to have that jacket buttoned.' She leaned forward to do it but Hallorann was ahead of her, his large brown fingers moving with smooth dexterity.

'I'll send him right back in,' Hallorann said.

'Fine,' Wendy said, and followed them to the door. Jack was still looking around for Ullman. The last of the Overlook's guests were checking out at the desk.

Chapter Eleven

The Shining

There were four bags in a pile just outside the door. Three of them were giant, battered old suitcases covered with black imitation alligator hide. The last was an oversized zipper bag with a faded tartan skin.

'Guess you can handle that one, can't you?' Hallorann asked him. He picked up two of the big cases in one hand and hoisted the other under his arm.

'Sure,' Danny said. He got a grip on it with both hands and followed the cook down the porch steps, trying manfully not to grunt and give away how heavy it was.

A sharp and cutting fall wind had come up since they had arrived; it whistled across the parking lot, making Danny wince his eyes down to slits as he carried the zipper bag in front of him, bumping on his knees. A few errant aspen leaves rattled and turned across the now mostly deserted asphalt, making Danny think momentarily of that night last week when he had wakened out of his nightmare and had heard – or thought he heard, at least – Tony telling him not to go.

Hallorann set his bags down by the trunk of a beige Plymouth Fury. 'This ain't much car,' he confided to Danny, 'just a rental job. My Bessie's on the other end. She's a car. 1950 Cadillac, and does she run sweet? I'll tell the world. I keep her in Florida because she's too old for all this mountain climbing. You need a hand with that?'

'No, sir,' Danny said. He managed to carry it the last ten or twelve steps without grunting and set it down with a large sigh of relief.

'Good boy,' Hallorann said. He produced a large key ring from the pocket of his blue serge jacket and unlocked the trunk. As he lifted the bags in he said: 'You shine on, boy. Harder than anyone I ever met in my life. And I'm sixty years old this January.'

'Huh?'

'You got a knack,' Hallorann said, turning to him. 'Me, I've always called it shining. That's what my grandmother called it, too. She had it. We used to sit in the kitchen when I was a boy no older than you and have long talks without even openin our mouths.'

'Really?'

Hallorann smiled at Danny's openmouthed, almost hungry expression and said, 'Come on up and sit in the car with me for a few minutes. Want to talk to you.' He slammed the trunk.

In the lobby of the Overlook, Wendy Torrance saw her son get into the passenger side of Hallorann's car as the big black cook slid in behind the wheel. A sharp pang of fear struck her and she opened her mouth to tell Jack that Hallorann had not been lying about taking their son to Florida

– there was a kidnaping afoot. But they were only sitting there. She could barely see the small silhouette of her son's head, turned attentively toward Hallorann's big one. Even at this distance that small head had a set to it that she recognized – it was the way her son looked when there was something on the TV that particularly fascinated him, or when he and his father were playing old maid or idiot cribbage. Jack, who was still looking around for Ullman, hadn't noticed. Wendy kept silent, watching Hallorann's car nervously, wondering what they could possibly be talking about that would make Danny cock his head that way.

In the car Hallorann was saying: 'Get you kinda lonely, thinkin you were the only one?'

Danny, who had been frightened as well as lonely sometimes, nodded. 'Am I the only one you ever met?' he asked.

Hallorann laughed and shook his head. 'No, child, no. But you shine the hardest.'

'Are there lots, then?'

'No,' Hallorann said, 'but you do run across them. A lot of folks, they got a little bit of shine to them. They don't even know it. But they always seem to show up with flowers when their wives are feelin blue with the monthlies, they do good on school tests they don't even study for, they got a good idea how people are feelin as soon as they walk into a room. I come across fifty or sixty like that. But maybe only a dozen, countin my gram, that *knew* they was shinin.'

'Wow,' Danny said, and thought about it. Then: 'Do you know Mrs Brant?'

'Her?' Hallorann asked scornfully. 'She don't shine. Just sends her supper back two-three times every night.'

'I know she doesn't,' Danny said earnestly. 'But do you know the man in the gray uniform that gets the cars?'

'Mike? Sure, I know Mike. What about him?'

'Mr Hallorann, why would she want his pants?'

'What are you talking about, boy?'

'Well, when she was watching him, she was thinking she would sure like to get into his pants and I just wondered why—'

But he got no further. Hallorann had thrown his head back, and rich, dark laughter issued from his chest, rolling around in the car like cannonfire. The seat shook with the force of it. Danny smiled, puzzled, and at last the storm subsided by fits and starts. Hallorann produced a large silk handkerchief from his breast pocket like a white flag of surrender and wiped his streaming eyes.

'Boy,' he said, still snorting a little, 'you are gonna know everything there is to know about the human condition before you make ten. I dunno if to envy you or not.'

'But Mrs Brant—'

'You never mind her,' he said. 'And don't go askin you mom, either. You'd only upset her, dig what I'm sayin?'

'Yes, sir,' Danny said. He dug it perfectly well. He had upset his mother that way in the past.

'That Mrs Brant is just a dirty old woman with an itch, that's all you have to know.' He looked at Danny speculatively. 'How hard can you hit, doc?'

'Huh?'

'Give me a blast. Think at me. I want to know if you got as much as I think you do.'

'What do you want me to think?'

'Anything. Just think it *hard*.'

'Okay,' Danny said. He considered it for a moment, then gathered his concentration and flung it out at Hallorann. He had never done anything precisely like this before, and at the last instant some instinctive part of him rose up and blunted some of the thought's raw force – he didn't want to hurt Mr Hallorann. Still the thought arrowed out of him with a force he never would have believed. It went like a Nolan Ryan fastball with a little extra on it.

(Gee I hope I don't hurt him)

And the thought was:

(*!!! HI, DICK!!!*)

Hallorann winced and jerked backward on the seat. His teeth came together with a hard click, drawing blood from his lower lip in a thin trickle. His hands flew up involuntarily from his lap to the level of his chest and then settled back again. For a moment his eyelids fluttered limply, with no conscious control, and Danny was frightened.

'Mr Hallorann? Dick? Are you okay?'

'I don't know,' Hallorann said, and laughed weakly. 'I honest to God don't. My God, boy, you're a pistol.'

'I'm sorry,' Danny said, more alarmed. 'Should I get my daddy? I'll run and get him.'

'No, here I come. I'm okay, Danny. You just sit right there. I feel a little scrambled, that's all.'

'I didn't go as hard as I could,' Danny confessed. 'I was scared to, at the last minute.'

'Probably my good luck you did . . . my brains would be leakin out my ears.' He saw the alarm on Danny's face and smiled. 'No harm done. What did it feel like to you?'

'Like I was Nolan Ryan throwing a fastball,' he replied promptly.

'You like baseball, do you?' Hallorann was rubbing his temples gingerly.

'Daddy and me like the Angels,' Danny said. 'The Red Sox in the American League East and the Angels in the West. We saw the Red Sox against Cincinnati in the World Series. I was a lot littler then. And Daddy was . . .' Danny's face went dark and troubled.

'Was what, Dan?'

'I forget,' Danny said. He started to put his thumb in his mouth to suck it, but that was a baby trick. He put his hand back in his lap.

'Can you tell what your mom and dad are thinking, Danny?' Hallorann was watching him closely.

'Most times, if I want to. But usually I don't try.'

'Why not?'

'Well . . .' he paused a moment, troubled. 'It would be like peeking into the bedroom and watching while they're doing the thing that makes babies. Do you know that thing?'

'I have had acquaintance with it,' Hallorann said gravely.

'They wouldn't like that. And they wouldn't like me peeking at their thinks. It would be dirty.'

'I see.'

'But I know how they're feeling,' Danny said. 'I can't help that. I know how you're feeling, too. I hurt you. I'm sorry.'

'It's just a headache. I've had hangovers that were worse. Can you read other people, Danny?'

'I can't read yet at all,' Danny said, 'except a few words. But Daddy's going to teach me this winter. My daddy used to teach reading and writing in a big school. Mostly writing, but he knows reading, too.'

'I mean, can you tell what anybody is thinking?'

Danny thought about it.

'I can if it's *loud*,' he said finally. 'Like Mrs Brant and the pants. Or like once, when me and Mommy were in this big store to get me some shoes, there was this big kid looking at radios, and he was thinking about taking one without buying it. Then he'd think, what if I get caught? Then he'd think, I really want it. Then he'd think about getting caught again. He was making himself sick about it, and he was making *me* sick. Mommy was talking to the man who sells the shoes so I went over and said, "Kid, don't take that radio. Go away." And he got really scared. He went away fast.'

Hallorann was grinning broadly. 'I bet he did. Can you do anything else, Danny? Is it only thoughts and feelings, or is there more?'

Cautiously: 'Is there more for you?'

'Sometimes,' Hallorann said. 'Not often. Sometimes . . . sometimes there are dreams. Do you dream, Danny?'

'Sometimes,' Danny said, 'I dream when I'm awake. After Tony comes.' His thumb wanted to go into his mouth again. He had never told anyone but Mommy and Daddy about Tony. He made his thumb-sucking hand go back into his lap.

'Who's Tony?'

And suddenly Danny had one of those flashes of understanding that frightened him most of all; it was like a sudden glimpse of some incomprehensible machine that might be safe or might be deadly dangerous. He was too young to know which. He was to young to understand.

'What's wrong?' he cried. 'You're asking me all this because you're worried, aren't you? Why are you worried about me? Why are you worried about *us*?'

Hallorann put his large dark hands on the small boy's shoulders. 'Stop,' he said. 'It's probably nothin. But if it is somethin . . . well, you've got a large thing in your head, Danny. You'll have to do a lot of growin yet before you catch up to it, I guess. You got to be brave about it.'

'But I don't *understand* things!' Danny burst out. 'I *do* but I *don't!* People . . . they feel things and I feel them, but I don't know what I'm feeling!' He looked down at his lap wretchedly. 'I wish I could read. Sometimes Tony shows me signs and I can hardly read any of them.'

'Who's Tony?' Hallorann asked again.

'Mommy and Daddy call him my "invisible playmate," ' Danny said, reciting the words carefully. 'But he's really real. At least, I think he is. Sometimes, when I try real hard to understand things, he comes. He says,

"Danny, I want to show you something." And it's like I pass out. Only . . . there are dreams, like you said.' He looked at Hallorann and swallowed. 'They used to be nice. But now . . . I can't remember the word for dreams that scare you and make you cry.'

'Nightmares?' Hallorann asked.

'Yes. That's right. Nightmares.'

'About this place? About the Overlook?'

Danny looked down at his thumb-sucking hand again. 'Yes,' he whispered. Then he spoke shrilly, looking up into Hallorann's face: 'But I can't tell my daddy, and you can't, either! He has to have this job because it's the only one Uncle Al could get for him and he has to finish his play or he might start doing the Bad Thing again and I know what that is, it's getting *drunk*, that's what it is, it's when he used to always be *drunk* and that was a Bad Thing to do!' He stopped, on the verge of tears.

'Shh,' Hallorann said, and pulled Danny's face against the rough serge of his jacket. It smelled faintly of mothballs. 'That's all right, son. And if that thumb likes your mouth, let it go where it wants.' But his face was troubled.

He said: 'What you got, son, I call it shinin on, the Bible calls it having visions, and there's scientists that call it precognition. I've read up on it, son. I've studied on it. They all mean seeing the future. Do you understand that?'

Danny nodded against Hallorann's coat.

'I remember the strongest shine I ever had that way . . . I'm not liable to forget. It was 1955. I was still in the Army then, stationed overseas in West Germany. It was an hour before supper, and I was standin by the sink, givin one of the KPs hell for takin too much of the potato along with the peel. I says, "Here, lemme show you how that's done." He held out the potato and the peeler and then the whole kitchen was gone. Bang, just like that. You say you see this guy Tony before . . . before you have dreams?'

Danny nodded.

Hallorann put an arm around him. 'With me it's smellin oranges. All that afternoon I'd been smellin them and thinkin nothin of it, because they were on the menu for that night – we had thirty crates of Valencias. Everybody in the damn kitchen was smellin oranges that night.

'For a minute it was like I had just passed out. And then I heard an explosion and saw flames. There were people screaming. Sirens. And I heard this hissin noise that could only be steam. Then it seemed like I got a little closer to whatever it was and I saw a railroad car off the tracks and laying on its side with *Georgia and South Carolina Railroad* written on it, and I knew like a flash that my brother Carl was on that train and it jumped the tracks and Carl was dead. Just like that. Then it was gone and here's this scared, stupid little KP in front of me, still holdin out that potato and the peeler. He says, "Are you okay, Sarge?" And I says, "No. My brother's just been killed down in Georgia." And when I finally got my momma on the overseas telephone, she told me how it was.

'But see, boy, I already knew how it was.'

He shook his head slowly, as if dismissing the memory, and looked down at the wide-eyed boy.

'But the thing you got to remember, my boy, is this: *Those things don't always come true*. I remember just four years ago I had a job cookin at a boys' camp up in Maine on Long Lake. So I am sittin by the boarding gate at Logan Airport in Boston, just waiting to get on my flight, and I start to smell oranges. For the first time in maybe five years. So I say to myself, "My God, what's comin on this crazy late show now?" and I got down to the bathroom and sat on one of the toilets to be private. I never did black out, but I started to get this feelin, stronger and stronger, that my plane was gonna crash. Then the feeling went away, and the smell of oranges, and I knew it was over. I went back to the Delta Airlines desk and changed my flight to one three hours later. And do you know what happened?'

'What?' Danny whispered.

'*Nothin!*' Hallorann said, and laughed. He was relieved to see the boy smile a little, too. 'Not one single thing! That old plane landed right on time and without a single bump or bruise. So you see . . . sometimes those feelins don't come to anything.'

'Oh,' Danny said.

'Or you take the race track. I go a lot, and I usually do pretty well. I stand by the rail when they go by the starting gate, and sometimes I get a little shine about this horse or that one. Usually those feelins help me get real well. I always tell myself that someday I'm gonna get three at once on three long shots and make enough on the trifecta to retire early. It ain't happened yet. But there's plenty of times I've come home from the track on shank's mare instead of in a taxicab with my wallet swollen up. Nobody shines on all the time, except maybe for God up in heaven.'

'Yes, sir,' Danny said, thinking of the time almost a year ago when Tony had showed him a new baby lying in a crib at their house in Stovington. He had been very excited about that, and had waited, knowing that it took time, but there had been no new baby.

'Now you listen,' Hallorann said, and took both of Danny's hands in his own. 'I've had some bad dreams here, and I've had some bad feelins. I've worked here two seasons now and maybe a dozen times I've had . . . well, nightmares. And maybe half a dozen times I've thought I've seen things. No, I won't say what. It ain't for a little boy like you. Just nasty things. Once it had something to do with those damn hedges clipped to look like animals. Another time there was a maid, Delores Vickery her name was, and she had a little shine to her, but I don't think she knew it. Mr Ullman fired her . . . do you know what that is, doc?'

'Yes, sir,' Danny said candidly, 'my daddy got fired from his teaching job and that's why we're in Colorado, I guess.'

'Well, Ullman fired her on account of her saying she'd seen something in one of the rooms where . . . well, where a bad thing happened. That was in Room 217, and I want you to promise me you won't go in there, Danny. Not all winter. Steer right clear.'

'All right,' Danny said. 'Did the lady – the maiden – did she ask you to go look?'

'Yes, she did. And there was a bad thing there. But . . . I don't think it was a bad thing that could *hurt* anyone, Danny, that's what I'm tryin to say. People who shine can sometimes see things that are *gonna* happen, and I think sometimes they can see things that *did* happen. But they're just like pictures in a book. Did you ever see a picture in a book that scared you, Danny?'

'Yes,' he said, thinking of the story of *Bluebeard* and the picture where *Bluebeard*'s new wife opens the door and sees all the heads.

'But you knew it couldn't hurt you, didn't you?'

'Ye–ess . . .' Danny said, a little dubious.

'Well, that's how it is in this hotel. I don't know why, but it seems that all the bad things that ever happened here, there's little pieces of those things still layin around like fingernail clippins or the boogers that somebody nasty just wiped under a chair. I don't know why it should just be here, there's bad goings-on in just about every hotel in the world, I guess, and I've worked in a lot of them and had no trouble. Only here. But Danny, I don't think those things can hurt anybody.' He emphasized each word in the sentence with a mild shake of the boy's shoulders. 'So if you should see something, in a hallway or a room or outside by those hedges . . . just look the other way and when you look back, it'll be gone. Are you diggin me?'

'Yes,' Danny said. He felt much better, soothed. He got up on his knees, kissed Hallorann's cheek, and gave him a big hard hug. Hallorann hugged him back.

When he released the boy he asked: 'Your folks, they don't shine, do they?'

'No, I don't think so.'

'I tried them like I did you,' Hallorann said. 'Your momma jumped the tiniest bit. I think all mothers shine a little, you know, at least until their kids grow up enough to watch out for themselves. Your dad . . .'

Hallorann paused momentarily. He had probed at the boy's father and he just didn't know. It wasn't like meeting someone who had the shine, or someone who definitely did not. Poking at Danny's father had been . . . strange, as if Jack Torrance had something – *something* – that he was hiding. Or something he was holding in so deeply submerged in himself that it was impossible to get to.

'I don't think he shines at all,' Hallorann finished. 'So you don't worry about them. You just take care of you. *I don't think there's anything here that can hurt you.* So just be cool, okay?'

'Okay.'

'*Danny! Hey, doc!*'

Danny looked around. 'That's Mom. She wants me. I have to go.'

'I know you do,' Hallorann said. 'You have a good time here, Danny. Best you can, anyway.'

'I will. Thanks, Mr Hallorann. I feel a lot better.'

The smiling thought came in his mind:

(Dick, to my friends)

(Yes, Dick, okay)

Their eyes met, and Dick Hallorann winked.

Danny scrambled across the seat of the car and opened the passenger side door. As he was getting out, Hallorann said, 'Danny?'

'What?'

'If there *is* trouble . . . you give a call. A big loud holler like the one you gave a few minutes ago. I might hear you even way down in Florida. And if I do, I'll come on the run.'

'Okay,' Danny said, and smiled.

'You take care, big boy.'

'I will.'

Danny slammed the door and ran across the parking lot toward the porch, where Wendy stood holding her elbows against the chill wind. Hallorann watched, the big grin slowly fading.

I don't think there's anything here that can hurt you.

I don't *think*.

But what if he was wrong? He had know that this was his last season at the Overlook ever since he had seen that thing in the bathtub of Room 217. It had been worse than any picture in any book, and from here the boy running to his mother looked so *small* . . .

'I don't *think*—

His eyes drifted down to the topiary animals.

Abruptly he started the car and put it in gear and drove away, trying not to look back. And of course he did, and of course the porch was empty. They had gone back inside. It was as if the Overlook had swallowed them.

Chapter Twelve

The Grand Tour

'What were you talking about, hon?' Wendy asked him as they went back inside.

'Oh, nothing much.'

'For nothing much it sure was a long talk.'

He shrugged and Wendy saw Danny's paternity in the gesture; Jack could hardly have done it better himself. She would get no more out of Danny. She felt strong exasperation mixed with an even stronger love: the love was helpless, the exasperation came from a feeling that she was deliberately being excluded. With the two of them around she sometimes felt like an outsider, a bit player who had accidentally wandered back onstage while the main action was taking place. Well, they wouldn't be able to exclude her this winter, her two exasperating males; quarters were going to be a little too close for that. She suddenly realized she was feeling jealous of the closeness between her husband and her son, and felt ashamed. That was too close to the way her own mother might have felt . . . too close for comfort.

The lobby was now empty except for Ullman and the head desk clerk (they were at the register, cashing up), a couple of maids who had changed to warm slacks and sweaters, standing by the front door and looking out with their luggage pooled around them, and Watson, the maintenance man. He caught her looking at him and gave her a wink . . . a decidedly lecherous one. She looked away hurriedly. Jack was over by the window just outside the restaurant, studying the view. He looked rapt and dreamy.

The cash register apparently checked out, because now Ullman ran it shut with an authoritative snap. He initialed the tape and put it in a small zipper case. Wendy silently applauded the head clerk, who looked greatly relieved. Ullman looked like the type of man who might take any shortage out of the head clerk's hide . . . without ever spilling a drop of blood. Wendy didn't much care for Ullman or his officious, ostentatiously bustling manner. He was like every boss she'd ever had, male or female. He would be saccharin sweet with the guests, a petty tyrant when he was backstage with the help. But now school was out and the head clerk's pleasure was written large on his face. It was out for everyone but she and Jack and Danny, anyway.

'Mr Torrance,' Ullman called peremptorily. 'Would you come over here, please?'

Jack walked over, nodding to Wendy and Danny that they were to come too.

The clerk, who had gone into the back, now came out again wearing an overcoat. 'Have a pleasant winter, Mr Ullman.'

'I doubt it,' Ullman said distantly. 'May twelfth, Braddock. Not a day earlier. Not a day later.'

'Yes, sir.'

Braddock walked around the desk, his face sober and dignified, as befitted his position, but when his back was entirely to Ullman, he grinned like a schoolboy. He spoke briefly to the two girls still waiting by the door for their ride, and he was followed out by a brief burst of stifled laughter.

Now Wendy began to notice the silence of the place. It had fallen over the hotel like a heavy blanket muffling everything but the faint pulse of the afternoon wind outside. From where she stood she could look through the inner office, now neat to the point of sterility with its two bare desks and two sets of gray filing cabinets. Beyond that she could see Hallorann's spotless kitchen, the big portholed double doors propped open by rubber wedges.

'I thought I would take a few extra minutes and show you through the Hotel,' Ullman said, and Wendy reflected that you could always hear that capital *H* in Ullman's voice. You were supposed to hear it. 'I'm sure your husband will get to know the ins and outs of the Overlook quite well, Mrs Torrance, but you and your son will doubtless keep more to the lobby level and the first floor, where your quarters are.'

'Doubtless,' Wendy murmured demurely, and Jack shot her a private glance.

'It's a beautiful place,' Ullman said expansively. 'I rather enjoy showing it off.'

I'll bet you do, Wendy thought.

'Let's go up to third and work our way down,' Ullman said. He sounded positively enthused.

'If we're keeping you—' Jack began.

'Not at all,' Ullman said. 'The shop is shut. *Tout fini*, for this season, at least. And I plan to overnight in Boulder – at the Boulderado, of course. Only decent hotel this side of Denver . . . except for the Overlook itself, of course. This way.'

They stepped into the elevator together. It was ornately scrolled in copper and brass, but it settled appreciably before Ullman pulled the gate across. Danny stirred a little uneasily, and Ullman smiled down at him. Danny tried to smile back without notable success.

'Don't you worry, little man,' Ullman said. 'Safe as houses.'

'So was the *Titanic*,' Jack said, looking up at the cut-glass globe in the center of the elevator ceiling. Wendy bit the inside of her cheek to keep the smile away.

Ullman was not amused. He slid the inner gate across with a rattle and a bang. 'The *Titanic* made only one voyage, Mr Torrance. This elevator has made thousands of them since it was installed in 1926.'

'That's reassuring,' Jack said. He ruffled Danny's hair. 'The plane ain't gonna crash, doc.'

Ullman threw the lever over, and for a moment there was nothing but a shuddering beneath their feet and the tortured whine of the motor below them. Wendy had a vision of the four of them being trapped between floors like flies in a bottle and found in the spring . . . with little bits and pieces gone . . . like the Donner Party . . .

(*Stop it!*)

The elevator began to rise, with some vibration and clashing and banging from below at first. Then the ride smoothed out. At the third floor Ullman brought them to a bumpy stop, retracted the gate, and opened the door. The elevator car was still six inches below floor level. Danny gazed at the difference in height between the third-floor hall and the elevator floor as if he had just sensed the universe was not as sane as he had been told. Ullman cleared his throat and raised the car a little, brought it to a stop with a jerk (still two inches low), and they all climbed out. With their weight gone the car rebounded almost to floor level, something Wendy did not find reassuring at all. Safe as houses or not, she resolved to take the stairs when she had to go up or down in this place. And under no conditions would she allow the three of them to get into the rickety thing together.

'What are you looking at, doc?' Jack inquired humorously. 'See any spots there?'

'Of course not,' Ullman said, nettled. 'All the rugs were shampooed just two days ago.'

Wendy glanced down at the hall runner herself. Pretty, but definitely not anything she would choose for her own home, if the day ever came when she had one. Deep blue pile, it was entwined with what seemed to be a surrealistic jungle scene full of ropes and vines and trees filled with exotic birds. It was hard to tell just what sort of birds, because all the interweaving was done in unshaded black, giving only silhouettes.

'Do you like the rug?' Wendy asked Danny.

'Yes, Mom,' he said colorlessly.

They walked down the hall, which was comfortably wide. The wallpaper was silk, a lighter blue to go against the rug. Electric flambeaux stood at ten-foot intervals at a height of about seven feet. Fashioned to look like London gas lamps, the bulbs were masked behind cloudy, cream-hued glass that was bound with crisscrossing iron strips.

'I like those very much,' she said.

Ullman nodded, pleased. 'Mr Derwent had those installed throughout the Hotel after the war – number Two, I mean. In fact most – although not all – of the third-floor decorating scheme was his idea. This is 300, the Presidential Suite.'

He twisted his key in the lock of the mahogany double doors and swung them wide. The sitting room's wide western exposure made them all gasp, which had probably been Ullman's intention. He smiled. 'Quite a view, isn't it?'

'It sure is,' Jack said.

The window ran nearly the length of the sitting room, and beyond it the sun was poised directly between two sawtoothed peaks, casting golden light across the rock faces and the sugared snow on the high tips. The clouds around and behind this picture-postcard view were also tinted gold, and a sunbeam glinted duskily down into the darkly pooled firs below the timberline.

Jack and Wendy were so absorbed in the view that they didn't look down at Danny, who was staring not out the window but at the red-and-white-striped silk wallpaper to the left, where a door opened into an interior bedroom. And his gasp, which had been mingled with theirs, had nothing to do with beauty.

Great splashes of dried blood, flecked with tiny bits of grayish-white tissue, clotted the wallpaper. It made Danny feel sick. It was like a crazy picture drawn in blood, a surrealistic etching of a man's face drawn back in terror and pain, the mouth yawning and half the head pulverized—

(*So if you should see something . . . just look the other way and when you look back, it'll be gone. Are you diggin me?*)

He deliberately looked out the window, being careful to show no expression on his face, and when his mommy's hand closed over his own he took it, being careful not to squeeze it or give her a signal of any kind.

The manager was saying something to his daddy about making sure to shutter that big window so a strong wind wouldn't blow it in. Jack was nodding. Danny looked cautiously back at the wall. The big dried bloodstain was gone. Those little gray-white flecks that had been scattered all through it, they were gone, too.

Then Ullman was leading them out. Mommy asked him if he thought the mountains were pretty. Danny said he did, although he didn't really care for the mountains, one way or the other. As Ullman was closing the door behind them, Danny looked back over his shoulder. The bloodstain had returned, only now it was fresh. It was running. Ullman, looking directly at it, went on with his running commentary about the famous men who had stayed here. Danny discovered that he had bitten his lip hard enough to make it bleed, and he had never even felt it. As they walked on down the corridor, he fell a little bit behind the others and wiped the blood away with the back of his hand and thought about

(blood)

(Did Mr Hallorann see blood or was it something worse?)

(*I don't think those things can hurt you.*)

There was an iron scream behind his lips, but he would not let it out. His mommy and daddy could not see such things; they never had. He would keep quiet. His mommy and daddy were loving each other, and that was a real thing. The other things were just like pictures in a book. Some pictures were scary, but they couldn't hurt you. *They . . . couldn't . . . hurt you.*

Mr Ullman showed them some other rooms on the third floor, leading them through corridors that twisted and turned like a maze. They were all sweets up here, Mr Ullman said, although Danny didn't see any candy. He showed them some rooms where a lady named Marilyn Monroe once stayed when she was married to a man named Arthur Miller (Danny got a vague understanding that Marilyn and Arthur had gotten a DIVORCE not long after they were in the Overlook Hotel).

'Mommy?'

'What, honey?'

'If they were married, why did they have different names? You and Daddy have the same names.'

'Yes, but we're not famous, Danny,' Jack said. 'Famous women keep their same names even after they get married because their names are their bread and butter.'

'Bread and butter,' Danny said, completely mystified.

'What Daddy means is that people used to like to go to the movies and see Marilyn Monroe,' Wendy said, 'but they might not like to go to see Marilyn Miller.'

'Why not? She'd still be the same lady. Wouldn't everyone know that?'

'Yes, but—' She looked at Jack helplessly.

'Truman Capote once stayed in this room,' Ullman interrupted impatiently. He opened the door. 'That was in my time. An awfully nice man. Continental manners.'

There was nothing remarkable in any of these rooms (except for the absence of sweets, which Mr Ullman kept calling them), nothing that Danny was afraid of. In fact, there was only one other thing on the third floor that bothered Danny, and he could not have said why. It was the fire extinguisher on the wall just before they turned the corner and went back to the elevator, which stood open and waiting like a mouthful of gold teeth.

It was an old-fashioned extinguisher, a flat hose folded back a dozen times upon itself, one end attached to a large red valve, the other ending in a brass nozzle. The folds of the hose were secured with a red steel slat on a hinge. In case of a fire you could knock the steel slat up and out of the way with one hard push and the hose was yours. Danny could see that much: he was good at seeing how things worked. By the time he was two and a half he had been unlocking the protective gate his father had installed at the top of the stairs in the Stovington house. He had seen how the lock worked. His daddy said it was a NACK. Some people had the NACK and some people didn't.

This fire extinguisher was a little older than others he had seen – the one in the nursery school, for instance – but that was not so unusual. Nonetheless it filled him with faint unease, curled up there against the light blue wallpaper like a sleeping snake. And he was glad when it was out of sight around the corner.

'Of course all the windows have to be shuttered,' Mr Ullman said as they stepped back into the elevator. Once again the car sank queasily beneath their feet. 'But I'm particularly concerned about the one in the Presidential Suite. The original bill on that window was four hundred and twenty dollars, and that was over thirty years ago. It would cost eight times that to replace today.'

'I'll shutter it,' Jack said.

They went down to the second floor where there were more rooms and even more twists and turns in the corridor. The light from the windows had begun to fade appreciably now as the sun went behind the mountains. Mr Ullman showed them one or two rooms and that was all. He walked past

217, the one Dick Hallorann had warned him about, without slowing. Danny looked at the bland number-plate on the door with uneasy fascination.

Then down to the first floor. Mr Ullman didn't show them into any rooms here until they had almost reached the thickly carpeted staircase that led down into the lobby again. 'Here are your quarters,' he said. 'I think you'll find them adequate.'

They went in. Danny was braced for whatever might be there. There was nothing.

Wendy Torrance felt a strong surge of relief. The Presidential Suite, with its cold elegance, had made her feel awkward and clumsy – it was all very well to visit some restored historical building with a bedroom plaque that announced Abraham Lincoln or Franklin D. Roosevelt had slept there, but another thing entirely to imagine you and your husband lying beneath acreages of linen and perhaps making love where the greatest men in the world had once lain (the most powerful, anyway, she amended). But this apartment was simpler, homier, almost inviting. She thought she could abide this place for a season with no difficulty.

'It's very pleasant,' she said to Ullman, and heard the gratitude in her voice.

Ullman nodded. 'Simple but adequate. During the season, this suite quarters the cook and his wife, or the cook and his apprentice.'

'Mr Hallorann lived here?' Danny broke in.

Mr Ullman inclined his head to Danny condescendingly. 'Quite so. He and Mr Nevers.' He turned back to Jack and Wendy. 'This is the sitting room.'

There were several chairs that looked comfortable but not expensive, a coffee table that had once been expensive but now had a long chip gone from the side, two bookcases (stuffed full of Reader's Digest Condensed Books and Detective Book Club trilogies from the forties, Wendy saw with some amusement), and an anonymous hotel TV that looked much less elegant than the buffed wood consoles in the rooms.

'No kitchen, of course,' Ullman said, 'but there is a dumb-waiter. This apartment is directly over the kitchen.' He slid aside a square of paneling and disclosed a wide, square tray. He gave it a push and it disappeared, trailing rope behind it.

'It's a secret passage?' Danny said excitedly to his mother, momentarily forgetting all fears in favor of that intoxicating shaft behind the wall. 'Just like in *Abbott and Costello Meet the Monsters!*'

Mr Ullman frowned but Wendy smiled indulgently. Danny ran over to the dumb-waiter and peered down the shaft.

'This way, please.'

He opened the door on the far side of the living room. It gave on the bedroom, which was spacious and airy. There were twin beds. Wendy looked at her husband, smiled, shrugged.

'No problem,' Jack said. 'We'll push them together.'

Mr Ullman looked over his shoulder, honestly puzzled. 'Beg pardon?'

'The beds,' Jack said pleasantly. 'We can push them together.'

'Oh, quite,' Ullman said, momentarily confused. Then his face cleared and a red flush began to creep up from the collar of his shirt. 'Whatever you like.'

He led them back into the sitting room, where a second door opened on a second bedroom, this one equipped with bunk beds. A radiator clanked in one corner, and the rug on the floor was a hideous embroidery of western sage and cactus – Danny had already fallen in love with it, Wendy saw. The walls of this smaller room were paneled in real pine.

'Think you can stand it in here, doc?' Jack asked.

'Sure I can. I'm going to sleep in the top bunk. Okay?'

'If that's what you want.'

'I like the rug, too. Mr Ullman, why don't you have all the rugs like that?'

Mr Ullman looked for a moment as if he had sunk his teeth into a lemon. Then he smiled and patted Danny's head. 'Those are your quarters,' he said, 'except for the bath, which opens off the main bedroom. It's not a huge apartment, but of course you'll have the rest of the hotel to spread out in. The lobby fireplace is in good working order, or so Watson tells me, and you must feel free to eat in the dining room if the spirit moves you to do so.' He spoke in the tone of a man conferring a great favor.

'All right,' Jack said.

'Shall we go down?' Mr Ullman asked.

'Fine,' Wendy said.

They went downstairs in the elevator, and now the lobby was wholly deserted except for Watson, who was leaning against the main doors in a rawhide jacket, a toothpick between his lips.

'I would have thought you'd be miles from here by now,' Mr Ullman said, his voice slightly chill.

'Just stuck around to remind Mr Torrance here about the boiler,' Watson said, straightening up. 'Keep your good weather eye on her, fella, and she'll be fine. Knock the press down a couple of times a day. She creeps.'

She creeps, Danny thought, and the words echoed down a long and silent corridor in his mind, a corridor lined with mirrors where people seldom looked.

'I will,' his daddy said.

'You'll be fine,' Watson said, and offered Jack his hand. Jack shook it. Watson turned to Wendy and inclined his head. 'Ma'am,' he said.

'I'm pleased,' Wendy said, and thought it would sound absurd. It didn't. She had come out here from New England, where she had spent her life, and it seemed to her that in a few short sentences this man Watson, with his fluffy fringe of hair, had epitomized what the West was supposed to be all about. And never mind the lecherous wink earlier.

'Young master Torrance,' Watson said gravely, and put out his hand. Danny, who had known all about handshaking for almost a year now, put his own hand out gingerly and felt it swallowed up. 'You take good care of em, Dan.'

'Yes, sir.'

Watson let go of Danny's hand and straightened up fully. He looked at Ullman. 'Until next year, I guess,' he said, and held his hand out.

Ullman touched it bloodlessly. His pinky ring caught the lobby's electric lights in a baleful sort of wink.

'May twelfth, Watson,' he said. 'Not a day earlier or later.'

'Yes, sir,' Watson said, and Jack could almost read the codicil in Watson's mind: . . . *you fucking little faggot.*

'Have a good winter, Mr Ullman.'

'Oh, I doubt it,' Ullman said remotely.

Watson opened one of the two big main doors; the wind whined louder and began to flutter the collar of his jacket. 'You folks take care now,' he said.

It was Danny who answered. 'Yes, sir, we will.'

Watson, whose not-so-distant ancestor had owned this place, slipped humbly through the door. It closed behind him, muffling the wind. Together they watched him clop down the porch's broad front steps in his battered black cowboy boots. Brittle yellow aspen leaves tumbled around his heels as he crossed the lot to his International Harvester pickup and climbed in. Blue smoke jetted from the rusted exhaust pipe as he started it up. The spell of silence held among them as he backed, then pulled out of the parking lot. His truck disappeared over the brow of the hill and then reappeared, smaller, on the main road, heading west.

For a moment Danny felt more lonely than he ever had in his life.

Chapter Thirteen

The Front Porch

The Torrance family stood together on the long front porch of the Overlook Hotel as if posing for a family portrait, Danny in the middle, zippered into last year's fall jacket which was now too small and starting to come out at the elbow, Wendy behind him with one hand on his shoulder, and Jack to his left, his own hand resting lightly on his son's head.

Mr Ullman was a step below them, buttoned into an expensive-looking brown mohair overcoat. The sun was entirely behind the mountains now, edging them with gold fire, making the shadows around things look long and purple. The only three vehicles left in the parking lots were the hotel truck, Ullman's Lincoln Continental, and the battered Torrance VW.

'You've got your keys, then,' Ullman said to Jack, 'and you understand fully about the furnace and the boiler?'

Jack nodded, feeling some real sympathy for Ullman. Everything was done for the season, the ball of string was neatly wrapped up until next May 12 – not a day earlier or later – and Ullman, who was responsible for all of it and who referred to the hotel in the unmistakable tones of infatuation, could not help looking for loose ends.

'I think everything is well in hand,' Jack said.

'Good. I'll be in touch.' But he still lingered for a moment, as if waiting for the wind to take a hand and perhaps gust him down to his car. He sighed. 'All right. Have a good winter, Mr Torrance, Mrs Torrance. You too, Danny.'

'Thank you, sir,' Danny said. 'I hope you do, too.'

'I doubt it,' Ullman repeated, and he sounded sad. 'The place in Florida is a dump, if the out-and-out truth is to be spoken. Busywork. The Overlook is my real job. Take good care of it for me, Mr Torrance.'

'I think it will be here when you get back next spring,' Jack said, and a thought flashed through Danny's mind

(but will we?)

and was gone.

'Of course. Of course it will.'

Ullman looked out toward the playground where the hedge animals were clattering in the wind. Then he nodded once more in a businesslike way.

'Good-by, then.'

He walked quickly and prissily across to his car – a ridiculously big one for such a little man – and tucked himself into it. The Lincoln's motor purred into life and the taillights flashed as he pulled out of his parking stall. As the car moved away, Jack could read the small sign at the head of the stall: RESERVED FOR MR ULLMAN, MGR.

'Right,' Jack said softly.

They watched until the car was out of sight, headed down the eastern slope. When it was gone, the three of them looked at each other for a silent, almost frightened moment. They were alone. Aspen leaves whirled and skittered in aimless packs across the lawn that was now neatly mowed and tended for no guest's eyes. There was no one to see the autumn leaves steal across the grass but the three of them. It gave Jack a curious shrinking feeling, as if his life force had dwindled to a mere spark while the hotel and the grounds had suddenly doubled in size and become sinister, dwarfing them with sullen, inanimate power.

Then Wendy said: 'Look at you, doc. Your nose is running like a fire hose. Let's get inside.'

And they did, closing the door firmly behind them against the restless whine of the wind.

BOOK THREE

THE WASPS' NEST

Chapter Fourteen

Up on the Roof

'*Oh you goddam fucking son of a bitch!*'

Jack Torrance cried these words out in both surprise and agony as he slapped his right hand against his blue chambray workshirt, dislodging the big, slow-moving wasp that had stung him. Then he was scrambling up the roof as fast as he could, looking back over his shoulder to see if the wasp's brothers and sisters were rising from the nest he had uncovered to do battle. If they were, it could be bad; the nest was between him and his ladder, and the trapdoor leading down into the attic was locked from the inside. The drop was seventy feet from the roof to the cement patio between the hotel and the lawn.

The clear air above the nest was still and undisturbed.

Jack whistled disgustedly between his teeth, sat straddling the peak of the roof, and examined his right index finger. It was swelling already, and he supposed he would have to try and creep past that nest to his ladder so he could go down and put some ice on it.

It was October 20. Wendy and Danny had gone down to Sidewinder in the hotel truck (an elderly, rattling Dodge that was still more trustworthy than the VW, which was now wheezing gravely and seemed terminal) to get three gallons of milk and do some Christmas shopping. It was early to shop, but there was no telling when the snow would come to stay. There had already been flurries, and in some places the road down from the Overlook was slick with patch ice.

So far the fall had been almost preternaturally beautiful. In the three weeks they had been here, golden day had followed golden day. Crisp, thirty-degree mornings gave way to afternoon temperatures in the low sixties, the perfect temperature for climbing around on the Overlook's gently sloping western roof and doing the shingling. Jack had admitted freely to Wendy that he could have finished the job four days ago, but he felt no real urge to hurry. The view from up here was spectacular, even putting the vista from the Presidential Suite in the shade. More important, the work itself was soothing. On the roof he felt himself healing from the troubled wounds of the last three years. On the roof he felt at peace. Those three years began to seem like a turbulent nightmare.

The shingles had been badly rotted, some of them blown entirely away by last winter's storms. He had ripped them all up, yelling 'Bombs away!' as he dropped them over the side, not wanting Danny to get hit in case he had wandered over. He had been pulling out bad flashing when the wasp had gotten him.

The ironic part was that he warned himself each time he climbed onto the roof to keep an eye out for nests; he had gotten that bug bomb just in case. But this morning the stillness and peace had been so complete that his watchfulness had lapsed. He had been back in the world of the play he was slowing creating, roughing out whatever scene he would be working on that evening in his head. The play was going very well, and although Wendy had said little, he knew she was pleased. He had been roadblocked on the crucial scene between Denker, the sadistic headmaster, and Gary Benson, his young hero, during the last unhappy six months at Stovington, months when the craving for a drink had been so bad that he could barely concentrate on his in-class lectures, let alone his extracurricular literary ambitions.

But in the last twelve evenings, as he actually sat down in front of the office-model Underwood he had borrowed from the main office downstairs, the roadblock had disappeared under his fingers as magically as cotton candy dissolves on the lips. He had come up almost effortlessly with the insights into Denker's character that had always been lacking, and he had rewritten most of the second act accordingly, making it revolve around the new scene. And the progress of the third act, which he had been turning over in his mind when the wasp put an end to cogitation, was coming clearer all the time. He thought he could rough it out in two weeks, and have a clean copy of the whole damned play by New Year's.

He had an agent in New York, a tough red-headed woman named Phyllis Sandler who smoked Herbert Tareytons, drank Jim Beam from a paper cup, and thought the literary sun rose and set on Sean O'Casey. She had marketed three of Jack's short stories, including the *Esquire* piece. He had written her about the play, which was called *The Little School*, describing the basic conflict between Denker, a gifted student who had failed into becoming the brutal and brutalizing headmaster of a turn-of-the-century New England prep school, and Gary Benson, the student he sees as a younger version of himself. Phyllis had written back expressing interest and admonishing him to read O'Casey before sitting down to it. She had written again earlier that year asking where the hell was the play? He had written back wryly that *The Little School* had been indefinitely – and perhaps infinitely – delayed between hand and page 'in that interesting intellectual Gobi known as the writer's block.' Now it looked as if she might actually get the play. Whether or not it was any good or if it would ever see actual production was another matter. And he didn't seem to care a great deal about those things. He felt in a way that the play itself, the whole thing, was the roadblock, a colossal symbol of the bad years at Stovington Prep, the marriage he had almost totaled like a nutty kid behind the wheel of an old jalopy, the monstrous assault on his son, the incident in the parking lot with George Hatfield, an incident he could no longer view as just another sudden and destructive flare of temper. He now thought that part of his drinking problem had stemmed from an unconscious desire to be free of Stovington and the security he felt was stifling whatever creative urge he had. He had stopped drinking, but the need to be free had been just as great. Hence

George Hatfield. Now all that remained of those days was the play on the desk in his and Wendy's bedroom, and when it was done and sent off to Phyllis's hole-in-the wall New York agency, he could turn to other things. Not a novel, he was not ready to stumble into the swamp of another three-year undertaking, but surely more short stories. Perhaps a book of them.

Moving warily, he scrambled back down the slope of the roof on his hands and knees past the line of demarcation where the fresh green Bird shingles gave way to the section of roof he had just finished clearing. He came to the edge on the left of the wasps' nest he had uncovered and moved gingerly toward it, ready to backtrack and bolt down his ladder to the ground if things looked too hot.

He leaned over the section of pulled-out flashing and looked in.

The nest was in there, tucked into the space between the old flashing and the final roof undercoating of three-by-fives. It was a damn big one. The grayish paper ball looked to Jack as if it might be nearly two feet through the center. Its shape was not perfect because the space between the flashing and the boards was too narrow, but he thought the little buggers had still done a pretty respectable job. The surface of the nest was acrawl with the lumbering, slow-moving insects. They were the big mean ones, not yellow jackets, which are smaller and calmer, but wall wasps. They had been rendered sludgy and stupid by the fall temperatures, but Jack, who knew about wasps from his childhood, counted himself lucky that he had been stung only once. And, he thought, if Ullman had hired the job done in the height of summer, the workman who tore up that particular section of the flashing would have gotten one hell of a surprise. Yes indeedy. When a dozen wall wasps land on you all at once and start stinging your face and hands and arms, stinging your legs right through your pants, it would be entirely possible to forget you were seventy feet up. You might just charge right off the edge of the roof while you were trying to get away from them. All from those little things, the biggest of them only half the length of a pencil stub.

He had read someplace – in a Sunday supplement piece or a back-of-the-book newsmagazine article – that 7 per cent of all automobile fatalities go unexplained. No mechanical failure, no excessive speed, no booze, no bad weather. Simply one-car crashes on deserted sections of road, one dead occupant, the driver, unable to explain what had happened to him. The article had included an interview with a state trooper who theorized that many of these so-called 'foo crashes' resulted from insects in the car. Wasps, a bee, possibly even a spider or moth. The driver gets panicky, tries to swat it or unroll a window to let it out. Possibly the insect stings him. Maybe the driver just loses control. Either way it's bang! . . . all over. And the insect, usually completely unharmed, would buzz merrily out of the smoking wreck, looking for greener pastures. The trooper had been in favor of having pathologists look for insect venom while autopsying such victims, Jack recalled.

Now, looking down into the nest, it seemed to him that it could serve as both a workable symbol for what he had been through (and what he had dragged his hostages to fortune through) and an omen for a better future. How else could you explain the things that had happened to him? For he still felt that the whole range of unhappy Stovington experiences had to be looked at with Jack Torrance in the passive mode. He had not done things; things had been done to him. He had known plenty of people on the Stovington faculty, two of them right in the English Department, who were hard drinkers. Zack Tunney was in the habit of picking up a full keg of beer on Saturday afternoon, plonking it in a backyard snow-bank overnight, and then killing damn near all of it on Sunday watching football games and old movies. Yet through the week Zack was as sober as a judge – a weak cocktail with lunch was an occasion.

He and Al Shockley had been alcoholics. They had sought each other out like two castoffs who were still social enough to prefer drowning together to doing it alone. The sea had been whole-grain instead of salt, that was all. Looking down at the wasps, as they slowly went about their instinctual business before winter closed down to kill all but their hibernating queen, he would go further. He was *still* an alcoholic, always would be, perhaps had been since Sophomore Class Night in high school when he had taken his first drink. It had nothing to do with willpower, or the morality of drinking, or the weakness or strength of his own character. There was a broken switch somewhere inside, or a circuit breaker that didn't work, and he had been propelled down the chute willy-nilly, slowly at first, then accelerating as Stovington applied its pressures on him. A big greased slide and at the bottom had been a shattered, ownerless bicycle and a son with a broken arm. Jack Torrance in the passive mode. And his temper, same thing. All his life he had been trying unsuccessfully to control it. He could remember himself at seven, spanked by a neighbor lady for playing with matches. He had gone out and hurled a rock at a passing car. His father had seen that, and he had descended on little Jacky, roaring. He had reddened Jack's behind . . . and then blacked his eye. And when his father had gone into the house, muttering, to see what was on television, Jack had come upon a stray dog and had kicked it into the gutter. There had been two dozen fights in grammar school, even more of them in high school, warranting two suspensions and uncounted detentions in spite of his good grades. Football had provided a partial safety valve, although he remembered perfectly well that he had spent almost every minute of every game in a state of high piss-off, taking every opposing block and tackle personally. He had been a fine player, making All-Conference in his junior and senior years, and he knew perfectly well that he had his own bad temper to thank . . . or to blame. He had not enjoyed football. Every game was a grudge match.

And yet, through it all, he hadn't *felt* like a son of a bitch. He hadn't felt mean. He had always regarded himself as Jack Torrance, a really nice guy who was just going to have to learn how to cope with his temper someday before it got him in trouble. The same way he was going to have to learn how to cope with his drinking. But he had been an emotional alcoholic just as surely as he had been a physical one – the two of them were no doubt tied together somewhere deep inside him, where you'd just as soon not look. But it didn't much matter to him if the root causes were interrelated or separate, sociological or psychological or physiological. He had had to deal with the results: the spankings, the beatings from his old man, the suspensions, with trying to explain the school clothes torn in playground brawls, and later the hangovers, the slowly dissolving glue of his marriage, the single bicycle wheel with its bent spokes pointing into the sky, Danny's broken arm. And George Hatfield, of course.

He felt that he had unwittingly stuck his hand into The Great Wasps' Nest of Life. As an image it stank. As a cameo of reality, he felt it was serviceable. He had stuck his hand through some rotted flashing in high summer and that hand and his whole arm had been consumed in holy, righteous fire, destroying conscious thought, making the concept of civilized behavior obsolete. Could you be expected to behave as a thinking human being when your hand was being impaled on red-hot darning needles? Could you be expected to live in the love of your nearest and dearest when the brown, furious cloud rose out of the hole in the fabric of things (the fabric you thought was so innocent) and arrowed straight at you? Could you be held responsible for your own actions as you ran crazily about on the sloping roof seventy feet above the ground, not knowing where you were going, not remembering that your panicky, stumbling feet could lead you crashing and blundering right over the rain gutter and down to your death on the concrete seventy feet below? Jack didn't think you could. When you unwittingly stuck your hand into the wasps' nest, you hadn't made a covenant with the devil to give up your civilized self with its trappings of love and respect and honor. It just happened to you. Passively, with no say, you ceased to be a creature of the mind and became a creature of the nerve endings; from college-educated man to wailing ape in five easy seconds.

He thought about George Hatfield.

Tall and shaggily blond, George had been an almost insolently beautiful boy. In his tight faded jeans and Stovington sweatshirt with the sleeves carelessly pushed up to the elbows to disclose his tanned forearms, he had reminded Jack of a young Robert Redford, and he doubted that George had much trouble scoring – no more than that young football-playing devil Jack Torrance had ten years earlier. He could say that he honestly didn't feel jealous of George, or envy him his good looks; in fact, he had almost unconsciously begun to visualize George as the physical incarnation of his play hero, Gary Benson – the perfect foil for the dark, slumped, and aging Denker, who grew to hate Gary so much. But he, Jack Torrance, had never felt that way about George. If he had, he would have known it. He was quite sure of that.

George had floated through his classes at Stovington. A soccer and baseball star, his academic program had been fairly undemanding and he had been content with C's and an occasional B in history or botany. He was a fierce field contender but a lackadaisical, amused sort of student in the classroom. Jack was familiar with the type, more from his own days as a high school and college student than from his teaching experience, which was at second hand. George Hatfield was a jock. He could be a calm, undemanding figure in the classroom, and when the right set of competitive stimuli was applied (like electrodes to the temples of Frankenstein's monster, Jack thought wryly), he could become a juggernaut.

In January, George had tried out with two dozen others for the debate team. He had been quite frank with Jack. His father was a corporation lawyer, and he wanted his son to follow in his footsteps. George, who felt no burning call to do anything else, was willing. His grades were not top end, but this was, after all, only prep school and it was still early times. If should be came to must be, his father could pull some strings. George's own athletic ability would open still other doors. But Brian Hatfield thought his son should get on the debate team. It was good practice, and it was something that law-school admissions boards always looked for. So George went out for debate, and in late March Jack cut him from the team.

The late winter inter-squad debates had fired George Hatfield's competitive soul. He became a grimly determined debater, prepping his pro or con position fiercely. It didn't matter if the subject was legalization of marijuana, reinstating the death penalty, or the oil-depletion allowance. George became conversant, and he was just jingoist enough to honestly not care which side he was on – a rare and valuable trait even in high-level debaters, Jack knew. The souls of a true carpetbagger and a true debater were not far removed from each other; they were both passionately interested in the main chance. So far, so good.

But George Hatfield stuttered.

This was not a handicap that had even shown up in the classroom, where George was always cool and collected (whether he had done his homework or not), and certainly not on the Stovington playing fields, where talk was not a virtue and they sometimes even threw you out of the game for too much discussion.

When George got tightly wound up in a debate, the stutter would come out. The more eager he became, the worse it was. And when he felt he had an opponent dead in his sights, an intellectual sort of buck fever seemed to take place between his speech centers and his mouth and he would freeze solid while the clock ran out. It was painful to watch.

'S-S-So I th-th-think we have to say that the fuh-fuh-facts in the c-case Mr D-D-D-Dorsky cites are ren-ren-rendered obsolete by the ruh-recent duh-duh-decision handed down in-in-in . . .'

The buzzer would go off and George would whirl around to stare furiously at Jack, who sat beside it. George's face at those moments would be flushed, his notes crumpled spasmodically in one hand.

Jack had held on to George long after he had cut most of the obvious flat tires, hoping George would work out. He remembered one late afternoon about a week before he had reluctantly dropped the ax. George had stayed after the others had filed out, and then had confronted Jack angrily.

'You s-set the timer ahead.'

Jack looked up from the papers he was putting back into his briefcase.

'George, what are you talking about?'

'I d-didn't get my whole five mih-minutes. You set it ahead. I was wuh-watching the clock.'

'The clock and the timer may keep slightly different times, George, but I never touched the dial on the damned thing. Scout's honor.'

'Yuh-yuh-you *did!*'

The belligerent, I'm-sticking-up-for-my-rights way George was looking at him had sparked Jack's own temper. He had been off the sauce for two months, two months too long, and he was ragged. He made one last effort to hold himself in. 'I assure you I did not, George. It's your stutter. Do you have any idea what causes it? You don't stutter in class.'

'*I duh-duh-don't s-s-st-st-stutter!*'

'Lower your voice.'

'*You w-want to g-get me! You duh-don't w-want me on your g-g-goddam team!*'

'Lower your voice, I said. Let's discuss this rationally.'

'F-fuh-fuck th-that!'

'George, if you control your stutter, I'd be glad to have you. You're well prepped for every practice and you're good at the background stuff, which means you're rarely surprised. But all that doesn't mean much if you can't control that—'

'I've neh-neh-never stuttered!' he cried out. 'It's yuh-you! I-i-if suh-someone else had the d-d-deb-debate t-team, I could—'

Jack's temper slipped another notch.

'George, you're never going to make much of a lawyer, corporation or otherwise, if you can't control that. Law isn't like soccer. Two hours of practice every night won't cut it. What are you going to do, stand up in front of a board meeting and say, "Nuh-nuh-now, g-gentlemen, about this t-t-tort"?'

He suddenly flushed, not with anger but with shame at his own cruelty. This was not a man in front of him but a seventeen-year-old boy who was facing the first major defeat of his life, and maybe asking in the only way he could for Jack to help him find a way to cope with it.

George gave him a final, furious glance, his lips twisting and bucking as the words bottled up behind them struggled to find their way out.

'Yuh-yuh-you s-s-set it ahead! You huh-hate me b-because you nuh-nuh-nuh-know . . . you know . . . nuh-nuh—'

With an articulate cry he had rushed out of the classroom, slamming the door hard enough to make the wire-reinforced glass rattle in its frame. Jack had stood there, feeling, rather than hearing, the echo of George's Adidas in the empty hall. Still in the grip of his temper and his shame at mocking George's stutter, his first thought had been a sick sort of exultation: For the first time in his life George Hatfield had wanted something he could not have. For the first time there was something wrong that all of Daddy's money could not fix. You couldn't bribe a speech center. You couldn't offer a tongue an extra fifty a week and a bonus at Christmas if it would agree to stop flapping like a record needle in a defective groove. Then the exultation was simply buried in shame, and he felt the way he had after he had broken Danny's arm.

Dear God, I am not a son of a bitch. Please.

That sick happiness at George's retreat was more typical of Denker in the play than of Jack Torrance the playwright.

You hate me because you know . . .

Because he knew what?

What could he possibly know about George Hatfield that would make him hate him? That his whole future lay ahead of him? That he looked a little bit like Robert Redford and all conversation among the girls stopped when he did a double gainer from the pool diving board? That he played soccer and baseball with a natural, unlearned grace?

Ridiculous. Absolutely absurd. He envied George Hatfield nothing. If the truth was known, he felt worse about George's unfortunate stutter than George himself, because George really would have made an excellent debater. And if Jack had set the timer ahead – and of course he hadn't – it would have been because both he and the other members of the squad were embarrassed for George's struggle, they had agonized over it the way you agonize when the Class Night speaker forgets some of his lines. If he had set the timer ahead, it would have been just to . . . to put George out of his misery.

But he hadn't set the timer ahead. He was quite sure of it.

A week later he had cut him, and that time he had kept his temper. The shouts and the threats had all been on George's side. A week after that he had gone out to the parking lot halfway through practice to get a pile of sourcebooks that he had left in the trunk of the VW and there had been George, down on one knee with his long blond hair swinging in his face, a hunting knife in one hand. He was sawing through the VW's right front tire. The back tires were already shredded, and the bug sat on the flats like a small, tired dog.

Jack had seen red, and remembered very little of the encounter that followed. He remembered a thick growl that seemed to issue from his own throat: 'All right, George. If that's how you want it, just come here and take your medicine.'

He remembered George looking up, startled and fearful. He had said: 'Mr Torrance—' as if to explain how all this was just a mistake, the tires had been flat when he got there and he was just cleaning dirt out of the front treads with the tip of this gutting knife he just happened to have with him and—

Jack had waded in, his fists held up in front of him, and it seemed that he had been grinning. But he wasn't sure of that.

The last thing he remembered was George holding up the knife and saying: 'You better not come any closer—'

And the next thing was Miss Strong, the French teacher, holding Jack's arms, crying, screaming: 'Stop it, Jack! Stop it! You're going to kill him!'

He had blinked around stupidly. There was the hunting knife, glittering harmlessly on the parking lot asphalt four yards away. There was his Volkswagen, his poor old battered bug, veteran of many wild midnight drunken rides, sitting on three flat shoes. There was a new dent in the right front fender, he saw, and there was something in the middle of the dent that was either red paint or blood. For a moment he had been confused, his thoughts

(jesus christ al we hit him after all)

of that other night. Then his eyes had shifted to George, George lying dazed and blinking on the asphalt. His debate group had come out and they were huddled together by the door, staring at George. There was blood on his face from a scalp laceration that looked minor, but there was also blood running out of one of George's ears and that probably meant a concussion. When George tried to get up, Jack shook free of Miss Strong and went to him. George cringed.

Jack put his hands on George's chest and pushed him back down. 'Lie still,' he said. 'Don't try to move.' He turned to Miss Strong, who was staring at them both with horror.

'Please go call the school doctor, Miss Strong,' he told her. She turned and fled toward the office. He looked at his debate class then, looked them right in the eye because he was in charge again, fully himself, and when he was himself there wasn't a nicer guy in the whole state of Vermont. Surely they knew that.

'You can go home now,' he told them quietly. 'We'll meet again tomorrow.'

But by the end of that week six of his debaters had dropped out, two of them the class of the act, but of course it didn't matter much because he had been informed by then that he would be dropping out himself.

Yet somehow he had stayed off the bottle, and he supposed that was something.

And he had not hated George Hatfield. He was sure of that. He had not acted but had been acted upon.

You hate me because you know . . .

But he had known nothing. *Nothing.* He would swear that before the Throne of Almighty God, just as he would swear that he had set the timer ahead no more than a minute. And not out of hate but out of pity.

Two wasps were crawling sluggishly about on the roof beside the hole in the flashing.

He watched them until they spread their aerodynamically unsound but strangely efficient wings and lumbered off into the October sunshine, perchance to sting someone else. God had seen fit to give them stingers and Jack supposed they had to use them on somebody.

How long had he been sitting there, looking at that hole with its unpleasant surprise down inside, raking over old coals? He looked at his watch. Almost half an hour.

He let himself down to the edge of the roof, dropped one leg over, and felt around until his foot found the top rung of the ladder just below the overhang. He would go down to the equipment shed where he had stored the bug bomb on a high shelf out of Danny's reach. He would get it, come back up, and then they would be the ones surprised. You could be stung, but you could also sting back. He believed that sincerely. Two hours from now the nest would be just so much chewed paper and Danny could have it in his room if he wanted to – Jack had had one in his room when he was just a kid, it had always smelled faintly of woodsmoke and gasoline. He could have it right by the head of his bed. It wouldn't hurt him.

'I'm getting better.'

The sound of his own voice, confident in the silent afternoon, reassured him even though he hadn't meant to speak aloud. He *was* getting better. It was possible to graduate from passive to active, to take the thing that had once driven you nearly to madness as a neutral prize of no more than occasional academic interest. And if there was a place where the thing could be done, this was surely it.

He went down the ladder to get the bug bomb. They would pay. They would pay for stinging him.

Chapter Fifteen

Down in the Front Yard

Jack had found a huge white-painted wicker chair in the back of the equipment shed two weeks ago, and had dragged it around to the porch over Wendy's objections that it was really the ugliest thing she had ever seen in her whole life. He was sitting in it now, amusing himself with a copy of E. L. Doctorow's *Welcome to Hard Times*, when his wife and son rattled up the driveway in the hotel truck.

Wendy parked it in the turn-around, raced the engine sportily, and then turned it off. The truck's single taillight died. The engine rumbled grumpily with post-ignition and finally stopped. Jack got out of his chair and ambled down to meet them.

'Hi, Dad!' Danny called, and raced up the hill. He had a box in one hand. 'Look what Mommy bought me!'

Jack picked his son up, swung him around twice, and kissed him heartily on the mouth.

'Jack Torrance, the Eugene O'Neill of his generation, the American Shakespeare!' Wendy said, smiling. 'Fancy meeting you here, so far up in the mountains.'

'The common ruck became too much for me, dear lady,' he said, and slipped his arms around her. They kissed. 'How was your trip?'

'Very good. Danny complains that I keep jerking him but I didn't stall the truck once and . . . oh, Jack, you finished it!'

She was looking at the roof, and Danny followed her gaze. A faint frown touched his face as he looked at the wide swatch of fresh shingles atop the Overlook's west wing, a lighter green than the rest of the roof. Then he looked down at the box in his hand and his face cleared again. At night the pictures Tony had showed him came back to haunt in all their original clarity, but in sunny daylight they were easier to disregard.

'Look, Daddy, look!'

Jack took the box from his son. It was a model car, one of the Big Daddy Roth caricatures that Danny had expressed an admiration for in the past. This one was the Violent Violet Volkswagen, and the picture on the box showed a huge purple VW with long '59 Cadillac Coupe de Ville taillights burning up a dirt track. The VW had a sunroof, and poking up through it, clawed hands on the wheel down below, was a gigantic warty monster with popping bloodshot eyes, a maniacal grin, and a gigantic English racing cap turned around backward.

Wendy was smiling at him, and Jack winked at her.

'That's what I like about you, doc,' Jack said, handing the box back. 'Your taste runs to the quiet, the sober, the introspective. You are definitely the child of my loins.'

'Mommy said you'd help me put it together as soon as I could read all of the first Dick and Jane.'

'That ought to be by the end of the week,' Jack said. 'What else have you got in that fine-looking truck, ma'am?'

'Uh-uh.' She grabbed his arm and pulled him back. 'No peeking. Some of that stuff is for you. Danny and I will take it in. You can get the milk. It's on the floor of the cab.'

'That's all I am to you,' Jack cried, clapping a hand to his forehead. 'Just a dray horse, a common beast of the field. Dray here, dray there, dray everywhere.'

'Just dray that milk right into the kitchen, mister.'

'It's too much!' he cried, and threw himself on the ground while Danny stood over him and giggled.

'Get up, you ox,' Wendy said, and prodded him with the toe of her sneaker.

'See?' he said to Danny. 'She called me an ox. You're a witness.'

'Witness, witness!' Danny concurred gleefully, and broad-jumped his prone father.

Jack sat up. 'That reminds me, chumly. I've got something for you, too. On the porch by my ashtray.'

'What is it?'

'Forgot. Go and see.'

Jack got up and the two of them stood together, watching Danny charge up the lawn and then take the steps to the porch two by two. He put an arm around Wendy's waist.

'You happy, babe?'

She looked up at him solemnly. 'This is the happiest I've been since we were married.'

'Is that the truth?'

'God's honest.'

He squeezed her tightly. 'I love you.'

She squeezed him back, touched. Those had never been cheap words with John Torrance; she could count the number of times he had said them to her, both before and after marriage, on both her hands.

'I love you too.'

'Mommy! Mommy!' Danny was on the porch now, shrill and excited. 'Come and see! Wow! It's neat!'

'What is it?' Wendy asked him as they walked up from the parking lot, hand in hand.

'Forgot,' Jack said.

'Oh, you'll get yours,' she said, and elbowed him. 'See if you don't.'

'I was hoping I'd get it tonight,' he remarked, and she laughed. A moment later he asked, 'Is Danny happy, do you think?'

'You ought to know. You're the one who has a long talk with him every night before bed.'

'That's usually about what he wants to be when he grows up or if Santa Claus is really real. That's getting to be a big thing with him. I think his old buddy Scott let some pennies drop on that one. No, he hasn't said much of anything about the Overlook to me.'

'Me either,' she said. They were climbing the porch steps now. 'But he's very quiet a lot of the time. And I think he's lost weight, Jack, I really do.'

'He's just getting tall.'

Danny's back was to them. He was examining something on the table by Jack's chair, but Wendy couldn't see what it was.

'He's not eating as well, either. He used to be the original steam shovel. Remember last year?'

'They taper off,' he said vaguely. 'I think I read that in Spock. He'll be using two forks again by the time he's seven.'

They had stopped on the top step.

'He's pushing awfully hard on those readers, too,' she said. 'I know he wants to learn how, to please us . . . to please you,' she added reluctantly.

'To please himself most of all,' Jack said. 'I haven't been pushing him on that at all. In fact, I do wish he wouldn't go quite so hard.'

'Would you think I was foolish if I made an appointment for him to have a physical? There's a G.P. in Sidewinder, a young man from what the checker in the market said—'

'You're a little nervous about the snow coming, aren't you?'

She shrugged. 'I suppose. If you think it's foolish—'

'I don't. In fact, you can make appointments for all three of us. We'll get our clean bills of health and then we can sleep easy at night.'

'I'll make the appointments this afternoon,' she said.

'Mom! Look, Mommy!'

He came running to her with a large gray thing in his hands, and for one comic-horrible moment Wendy thought it was a brain. She saw what it really was and recoiled instinctively.

Jack put an arm around her. 'It's all right. The tenants who didn't fly away have been shaken out. I used the bug bomb.'

She looked at the large wasps' nest her son was holding but would not touch it. 'Are you sure it's safe?'

'Positive. I had one in my room when I was a kid. My dad gave it to me. Want to put it in your room, Danny?'

'Yeah! Right now!'

He turned around and raced through the double doors. They could hear his muffled, running feet on the main stairs.

'There *were* wasps up there,' she said. 'Did you get stung?'

'Where's my purple heart?' he asked, and displayed his finger. The swelling had already begun to go down, but she ooohed over it satisfyingly and gave it a small, gentle kiss.

'Did you pull the stinger out?'

'Wasps don't leave them in. That's bees. They have barbed stingers. Wasp stingers are smooth. That's what makes them so dangerous. They can sting again and again.'

'Jack, are you sure that's safe for him to have?'

'I followed the directions on the bomb. The stuff is guaranteed to kill every single bug in two hours' time and then dissipate with no residue.'

'I hate them,' she said.

'What . . . wasps?'

'Anything that stings,' she said. Her hands went to her elbows and cupped them, her arms crossed over her breasts.

'I do too,' he said, and hugged her.

Chapter Sixteen

Danny

Down the hall, in the bedroom, Wendy could hear the typewriter Jack had carried up from downstairs burst into life for thirty seconds, fall silent for a minute or two, and then rattle briefly again. It was like listening to machine-gun fire from an isolated pillbox. The sound was music to her ears; Jack had not been writing so steadily since the second year of their marriage, when he wrote the story that *Esquire* had purchased. He said he thought the play would be done by the end of the year, for better or worse, and he would be moving on to something new. He said he didn't care if *The Little School* stirred any excitement when Phyllis showed it around, didn't care if it sank without a trace, and Wendy believed that, too. The actual act of his writing made her immensely hopeful, not because she expected great things from the play but because her husband seemed to be slowly closing a huge door on a roomful of monsters. He had had his shoulder to that door for a long time now, but at last it was swinging shut.

Every key typed closed it a little more.

'Look, Dick, look.'

Danny was hunched over the first of the five battered primers Jack had dug up by culling mercilessly through Boulder's myriad secondhand bookshops. They would take Danny right up to the second-grade reading level, a program she had told Jack she thought was much too ambitious. Their son was intelligent, they knew that, but it would be a mistake to push him too far too fast. Jack had agreed. There would be no pushing involved. But if the kid caught on fast, they would be prepared. And now she wondered if Jack hadn't been right about that, too.

Danny, prepared by four years of 'Sesame Street' and three years of 'Electric Company,' seemed to be catching on with almost scary speed. It bothered her. He hunched over the innocuous little books, his crystal radio and balsa glider on the shelf above him, as though his life depended on learning to read. His small face was more tense and paler than she liked in the close and cozy glow of the goosenecked lamp they had put in his room. He was taking it very seriously, both the reading and the workbook pages his father made up for him every afternoon. Picture of an apple and a peach. The word *apple* written beneath in Jack's large, neatly made printing. Circle the right picture, the one that went with the word. And their son would stare from the word to the pictures, his lips moving, sounding out, actually *sweating* it out. And with his double-sized red pencil curled into his pudgy right fist, he could now write about three dozen words on his own.

His finger traced slowly under the words in the reader. Above them was a picture Wendy half-remembered from her own grammar school days, nineteen years before. A laughing boy with brown curly hair. A girl in a short dress, her hair in blond ringlets, one hand holding a jump rope. A prancing dog running after a large red rubber ball. The first-grade trinity. Dick, Jane, and Jip.

'See Jip run,' Danny read slowly. 'Run, Jip, run. Run, run, run.' He paused, dropping his finger down a line. 'See the . . .' He bent closer, his nose almost touching the page now. 'See the . . .'

'Not so close, doc,' Wendy said quietly. 'You'll hurt your eyes. It's—'

'Don't tell me!' he said, sitting up with a jerk. His voice was alarmed. 'Don't tell me, Mommy, I can get it!'

'All right, honey,' she said. 'But it's not a big thing. Really it's not.'

Unheeding, Danny bent forward again. On his face was an expression that might be more commonly seen hovering over a graduate record exam in a college gym somewhere. She liked it less and less.

'See the . . . buh. Aw. El. El. See the buhaw-el-el? See the buhawl. *Ball!*' Suddenly triumphant. Fierce. The fierceness in his voice scared her. '*See the ball!*'

'That's right,' she said. 'Honey, I think that's enough for tonight.'

'A couple more pages, Mommy? Please?'

'No, doc.' She closed the red-bound book firmly. 'It's bedtime.'

'Please?'

'Don't tease me about it, Danny. Mommy's tired.'

'Okay.' But he looked longingly at the primer.

'Go kiss your father and then wash up. Don't forget to brush.'

'Yeah.'

He slouched out, a small boy in pajama bottoms with feet and a large flannel top with a football on the front and NEW ENGLAND PATRIOTS written on the back.

Jack's typewriter stopped, and she heard Danny's hearty smack. 'Night, Daddy.'

'Goodnight, doc. How'd you do?'

'Okay, I guess. Mommy made me stop.'

'Mommy was right. It's past eight-thirty. Going to the bathroom?'

'Yeah.'

'Good. There's potatoes growing out of your ears. And onions and carrots and chives and—'

Danny's giggle, fading, then cut off by the firm click of the bathroom door. He was private about his bathroom functions, while both she and Jack were pretty much catch-as-catch-can. Another sign – and they were multiplying all the time – that there was another human being in the place, not just a carbon copy of one of them or a combination of both. It made her a little sad. Someday her child would be a stranger to her, and she would be strange to him . . . but not as strange as her own mother had become to her. Please don't let it be that way, God. Let him grow up and still love his mother.

Jack's typewriter began its irregular bursts again.

Still sitting in the chair beside Danny's reading table, she let her eyes wander around her son's room. The glider's wing had been neatly mended. His desk was piled high with picture books, coloring books, old Spiderman comic books with the covers half torn off, Crayolas, and an untidy pile of

Lincoln Logs. The VW model was neatly placed above these lesser things, its shrink-wrap still undisturbed. He and his father would be putting it together tomorrow night or the night after if Danny went on at this rate, and never mind the end of the week. His pictures of Pooh and Eyore and Christopher Robin were tacked neatly to the wall, soon enough to be replaced with pin-ups and photographs of dope-smoking rock singers, she supposed. Innocence to experience. Human nature, baby. Grab it and growl. Still it made her sad. Next year he would be in school and she would lose at least half of him, maybe more, to his friends. She and Jack had tried to have another one for a while when things had seemed to be going well at Stovington, but she was on the pill again now. Things were too uncertain. God knew where they would be in nine months.

Her eyes fell on the wasps' nest.

It held the ultimate high place in Danny's room, resting on a large plastic plate on the table by his bed. She didn't like it, even if it was empty. She wondered vaguely if it might have germs, thought to ask Jack, then decided he would laugh at her. But she would ask the doctor tomorrow, if she could catch him with Jack out of the room. She didn't like the idea of that thing, constructed from the chewings and saliva of so many alien creatures, lying within a foot of her sleeping son's head.

The water in the bathroom was still running, and she got up and went into the big bedroom to make sure everything was okay. Jack didn't look up; he was lost in the world he was making, staring at the typewriter, a filter cigarette clamped in his teeth.

She knocked lightly on the closed bathroom door. 'You okay, doc? You awake?'

No answer.

'Danny?'

No answer. She tried the door. It was locked.

'Danny?' She was worried now. The lack of any sound beneath the steadily running water made her uneasy. 'Danny? Open the door, honey.'

No answer.

'Danny!'

'Jesus Christ, Wendy, I can't think if you're going to pound on the door all night.'

'Danny's locked himself in the bathroom and he doesn't answer me!'

Jack came around the desk, looking put out. He knocked on the door once, hard. 'Open up, Danny. No games.'

No answer.

Jack knocked harder. 'Stop fooling, doc. Bedtime's bedtime. Spanking if you don't open up.'

He's losing his temper, she thought, and was more afraid. He had not touched Danny in anger since that evening two years ago, but at this moment he sounded angry enough to do it.

'Danny, honey—' she began.

No answer. Only running water.

'Danny, if you make me break this lock I can guarantee you you'll spend the night sleeping on your belly,' Jack warned.

Nothing.

'Break it,' she said, and suddenly it was hard to talk. 'Quick.'

He raised one foot and brought it down hard against the door to the right of the knob. The lock was a poor thing; it gave immediately and the door shuddered open, banging the tiled bathroom wall and rebounding halfway.

'*Danny!*' she screamed.

The water was running full force in the basin. Beside it, a tube of Crest with the cap off. Danny was sitting on the rim of the bathtub across the room, his toothbrush clasped limply in his left hand, a thin foam of toothpaste around his mouth. He was staring, trancelike, into the mirror on the front of the medicine cabinet above the washbasin. The expression on his face was one of drugged horror, and her first thought was that he was having some sort of epileptic seizure, that he might have swallowed his tongue.

'*Danny!*'

Danny didn't answer. Guttural sounds came from his throat.

Then she was pushed aside so hard that she crashed into the towel rack, and Jack was kneeling in front of the boy.

'Danny,' he said. 'Danny, Danny!' He snapped his fingers in front of Danny's blank eyes.

'Ah-sure,' Danny said. 'Tournament play. Stroke. Nurrrrr . . .'

'Danny—'

'Roque!' Danny said, his voice suddenly deep, almost manlike. 'Roque. Stroke. The roque mallet . . . has two sides. *Gaaaaaa—*'

'Oh Jack my God *what's wrong with him?*'

Jack grabbed the boy's elbows and shook him hard. Danny's head rolled limply backward and then snapped forward like a balloon on a stick.

'Roque. Stroke. Redrum.'

Jack shook him again, and Danny's eyes suddenly cleared. His toothbrush fell out of his hand and onto the tiled floor with a small click.

'What?' he asked, looking around. He saw his father kneeling before him, Wendy standing by the wall. 'What?' Danny asked again, with rising alarm. 'W-W-Wuh-What's wr-r-r—'

'*Don't stutter!*' Jack suddenly screamed into his face. Danny cried out in shock, his body going tense, trying to draw away from his father, and then he collapsed into tears. Stricken, Jack pulled him close. 'Oh, honey, I'm sorry. I'm sorry, doc. Please. Don't cry. I'm sorry. Everything's okay.'

The water ran ceaselessly in the basin, and Wendy felt that she had suddenly stepped into some grinding nightmare where time ran backward, backward to the time when her drunken husband had broken her son's arm and had then mewled over him in almost the exact same words.

(*Oh honey. I'm sorry. I'm sorry, doc. Please. So sorry.*)

She ran to them both, pried Danny out of Jack's arms somehow (she saw the look of angry reproach on his face but filed it away for later consideration), and lifted him up. She walked him back into the small bedroom, Danny's arms clasped around her neck, Jack trailing them.

She sat down on Danny's bed and rocked him back and forth, soothing him with nonsensical words repeated over and over. She looked up at Jack and there was only worry in his eyes now. He raised questioning eyebrows at her. She shook her head faintly.

'Danny,' she said. 'Danny, Danny, Danny. 'S okay, doc. 'S fine.'

At last Danny was quiet, only faintly trembling in her arms. Yet it was

Jack he spoke to first, Jack who was now sitting beside them on the bed, and she felt the old faint pang

(It's him first and it's always been him first)

of jealousy. Jack had shouted at him, she had comforted him, yet it was to his father that Danny said,

'I'm sorry if I was bad.'

'Nothing to be sorry for, doc.' Jack ruffled his hair. 'What the hell happened in there?'

Danny shook his head slowly, dazedly. 'I . . . I don't know. Why did you tell me to stop stuttering, Daddy? I don't stutter.'

'Of course not,' Jack said heartily, but Wendy felt a cold finger touch her heart. Jack suddenly looked scared, as if he'd seen something that might just have been a ghost.

'Something about the timer . . .' Danny muttered.

'*What?*' Jack was leaning forward, and Danny flinched in her arms.

'Jack, you're scaring him!' she said, and her voice was high, accusatory. It suddenly came to her that they were all scared. But of what?

'I don't know, I don't know,' Danny was saying to his father. 'What . . . what did I say, Daddy?'

'Nothing,' Jack muttered. He took his handkerchief from his back pocket and wiped his mouth with it. Wendy had a moment of that sickening time-is-running-backward feeling again. It was a gesture she remembered well from his drinking days.

'Why did you lock the door, Danny?' she asked gently. 'Why did you do that?'

'Tony,' he said. 'Tony told me to.'

They exchanged a glance over the top of his head.

'Did Tony say why, son?' Jack asked quietly.

'I was brushing my teeth and I was thinking about my reading,' Danny said. 'Thinking real hard. And . . . and I saw Tony way down in the mirror. He said he had to show me again.'

'You mean he was behind you?' Wendy asked.

'No, he was *in* the mirror.' Danny was very emphatic on this point. 'Way down deep. And then I went through the mirror. The next thing I remember Daddy was shaking me and I thought I was being bad again.'

Jack winced as if struck.

'No, doc,' he said quietly.

'Tony told you to lock the door?' Wendy asked, brushing his hair.

'Yes.'

'And what did he want to show you?'

Danny tensed in her arms; it was as if the muscles in his body had turned into something like piano wire. 'I don't remember,' he said, distraught. 'I don't remember. Don't ask me. I . . . *I don't remember nothing!*'

'Shh,' Wendy said, alarmed. She began to rock him again. 'It's all right if you don't remember, hon. Sure it is.'

At last Danny began to relax again.

'Do you want me to stay a little while? Read you a story?'

'No. Just the night light.' He looked shyly at his father. 'Would you stay, Daddy? For a minute?'

'Sure, doc.'

Wendy sighed. 'I'll be in the living room, Jack.'

'Okay.'

She got up and watched as Danny slid under the covers. He seemed very small.

'Are you sure you're okay, Danny?'

'I'm okay. Just plug in Snoopy, Mom.'

'Sure.'

She plugged in the night light, which showed Snoopy lying fast asleep on top of his doghouse. He had never wanted a night light until they moved into the Overlook, and then he had specifically requested one. She turned off the lamp and the overhead and looked back at them, the small white circle of Danny's face, and Jack's above it. She hesitated a moment

(*and then I went through the mirror*)

and then left them quietly.

'You sleepy?' Jack asked, brushing Danny's hair off his forehead.

'Yeah.'

'Want a drink of water?'

'No . . .'

There was silence for five minutes. Danny was still beneath his hand. Thinking the boy had dropped off, he was about to get up and leave quietly when Danny said from the brink of sleep:

'Roque.'

Jack turned back, all zero at the bone.

'Danny—?'

'You'd never hurt Mommy, would you, Daddy?'

'No.'

'Or me?'

'No.'

Silence again, spinning out.

'Daddy?'

'What?'

'Tony came and told me about roque.'

'Did he, doc? What did he say?'

'I don't remember much. Except he said it was in innings. Like baseball. Isn't that funny?'

'Yes.' Jack's heart was thudding dully in his chest. How could the boy possibly know a thing like that? Roque was played by innings, not like baseball but like cricket.

'Daddy . . .?' He was almost asleep now.

'What?'

'What's redrum?'

'Red drum? Sounds like something an Indian might take on the warpath.'

Silence.

'Hey, doc?'

But Danny was asleep, breathing in long, slow strokes. Jack sat looking down at him for a moment, and a rush of love pushed through him like tidal water. Why had he yelled at the boy like that? It was perfectly normal for him to stutter a little. He had been coming out of a daze or some weird kind of trance, and stuttering was perfectly normal under those circumstances.

Perfectly. And he hadn't said *timer* at all. It had been something else, nonsense, gibberish.

How had he known roque was played in innings? Had someone told him? Ullman? Hallorann?

He looked down at his hands. They were made into tight, clenched fists of tension

(*god how i need a drink*)

and the nails were digging into his palms like tiny brands. Slowly he forced them to open.

'I love you, Danny,' he whispered. 'God knows I do.'

He left the room. He had lost his temper again, only a little, but enough to make him feel sick and afraid. A drink would blunt that feeling, oh yes. It would blunt that

(Something about the timer)

and everything else. There was no mistake about those words at all. None. Each had come out clear as a bell. He paused in the hallway, looking back and automatically wiped his lips with his handkerchief.

Their shapes were only dark silhouettes in the glow of the night light. Wendy, wearing only panties, went to his bed and tucked him in again; he had kicked the covers back. Jack stood in the doorway, watching as she put her inner wrist against his forehead.

'Is he feverish?'

'No.' She kissed his cheek.

'Thank God you made that appointment,' he said as she came back to the doorway. 'You think that guy know his stuff?'

'The checker said he was very good. That's all I know.'

'If there's something wrong, I'm going to send you and him to your mother's, Wendy.'

'No.'

'I know,' he said, putting an arm around her, 'how you feel.'

'You don't know how I feel at all about her.'

'Wendy, there's no place else I can send you. You know that.'

'If you came—'

'Without this job we're done,' he said simply. 'You know that.'

Her silhouette nodded slowly. She knew it.

'When I had that interview with Ullman, I thought he was just blowing off his bazoo. Now I'm not so sure. Maybe I really shouldn't have tried this with you two along. Forty miles from nowhere.'

'I love you,' she said. 'And Danny loves you even more, if that's possible. He would have been heartbroken, Jack. He will be, if you send us away.'

'Don't make it sound that way.'

'If the doctor says there's something wrong, I'll look for a job in Sidewinder,' she said. 'If I can't get one in Sidewinder, Danny and I will go to Boulder. I can't go to my mother, Jack. Not on those terms. Don't ask me. I . . . I just can't.'

'I guess I know that. Cheer up. Maybe it's nothing.'

'Maybe.'

'The appointment's at two?'

'Yes.'

'Let's leave the bedroom door open, Wendy.'

'I want to. But I think he'll sleep through now.'

But he didn't.

Boom . . . boom . . boomboomBOOMBOOM—

He fled the heavy, crashing, echoing sounds through twisting, mazelike corridors, his bare feet whispering over a deep-pile jungle of blue and black. Each time he heard the roque mallet smash into the wall somewhere behind him he wanted to scream aloud. But he mustn't. He mustn't. A scream would give him away and then

(then *REDRUM*)

(*Come out here and take your medicine, you fucking cry-baby!*)

Oh and he could hear the owner of that voice coming, coming for him, charging up the hall like a tiger in an alien blue-black jungle. A man-eater.

(*Come out here, you little son of a bitch!*)

If he could get to the stairs going down, if he could get off this third floor, he might be all right. Even the elevator. If he could remember what had been forgotten. But it was dark and in his terror he had lost his orientation. He had turned down one corridor and then another, his heart leaping into his mouth like a hot lump of ice, fearing that each turn would bring him face to face with the human tiger in these halls.

The booming was right behind him now, the awful hoarse shouting.

The whistle the head of the mallet made cutting through the air

(*roque . . . stroke . . . roque . . . stroke . . . REDRUM*)

before it crashed into the wall. The soft whisper of feet on the jungle carpet. Panic squirting in his mouth like bitter juice.

(*You will remember what was forgotten* . . . but would he? What was it?)

He fled around another corner and saw with creeping, utter horror that he was in a cul-de-sac. Locked doors frowned down at him from three sides. The west wing. He was in the west wing and outside he could hear the storm whooping and screaming, seeming to choke on its own dark throat filled with snow.

He backed up against the wall, weeping with terror now, his heart racing like the heart of a rabbit caught in a snare. When his back was against the light blue silk wallpaper with the embossed pattern of wavy lines, his legs gave way and he collapsed to the carpet, hands splayed on the jungle of woven vines and creepers, the breath whistling in and out of his throat.

Louder. Louder.

There was a tiger in the hall, and now the tiger was just around the corner, still crying out in that shrill and petulant and lunatic rage, the roque mallet slamming, because this tiger walked on two legs and it was—

He woke with a sudden indrawn gasp, sitting bolt upright in bed, eyes wide and staring into the darkness, hands crossed in front of his face.

Something on one hand. Crawling.

Wasps. Three of them.

They stung him then, seeming to needle all at once, and that was when all the images broke apart and fell on him in a dark flood and he began to shriek into the dark, the wasps clinging to his left hand, stinging again and again.

The lights went on and Daddy was standing there in his shorts, his eyes glaring. Mommy behind him, sleepy and scared.

'*Get them off me!*' Danny screamed.

'Oh my God,' Jack said. He saw.

'Jack, what's wrong with him? *What's wrong?*'

He didn't answer her. He ran to the bed, scooped up Danny's pillow, and slapped Danny's thrashing left hand with it. Again. Again. Wendy saw lumbering, insectile forms rise into the air, droning.

'Get a magazine!' he yelled over his shoulder. 'Kill them!'

'Wasps?' she said, and for a moment she was inside herself, almost detached in her realization. Then her mind crosspatched, and knowledge was connected to emotion. 'Wasps, oh Jesus, Jack, you said—'

'*Shut the fuck up and kill them!*' he roared. '*Will you do what I say!*'

One of them had landed on Danny's reading desk. She took a coloring book off his worktable and slammed it down on the wasp. It left a viscous brown smear.

'There's another one on the curtain,' he said, and ran out past her with Danny in his arms.

He took the boy into their bedroom and put him on Wendy's side of the makeshift double. 'Lie right there, Danny. Don't come back until I tell you. Understand?'

His face puffed and streaked with tears, Danny nodded.

'That's my brave boy.'

Jack ran back down the hall to the stairs. Behind him he heard the coloring book slap twice, and then his wife screamed in pain. He didn't slow but went down the stairs two by two into the darkened lobby. He went through Ullman's office into the kitchen, slamming the heavy part of his thigh into the corner of Ullman's oak desk, barely feeling it. He slapped on the kitchen overheads and crossed to the sink. The washed dishes from supper were still heaped up in the drainer, where Wendy had left them to drip-dry. He snatched the big Pyrex bowl off the top. A dish fell to the floor and exploded. Ignoring it, he turned and ran back through the office and up the stairs.

Wendy was standing outside Danny's door, breathing hard. Her face was the color of table linen. Her eyes were shiny and flat; her hair hung damply against her neck. 'I got all of them,' she said dully, 'but one stung me. Jack, you said they were all dead.' She began to cry.

He slipped past her without answering and carried the Pyrex bowl over to the nest by Danny's bed. It was still. Nothing there. On the outside, anyway. He slammed the bowl down over the nest.

'There,' he said. 'Come on.'

They went back into their bedroom.

'Where did it get you?' he asked her.

'My . . . on my wrist.'

'Let's see.'

She showed it to him. Just above the bracelet of lines between wrist and palm, there was a small circular hole. The flesh around it was puffing up.

'Are you allergic to stings?' he asked. 'Think hard! If you are, Danny might be. The fucking little bastards got him five or six times.'

'No,' she said, more calmly. 'I . . . I just hate them, that's all. *Hate* them.'

Danny was sitting on the foot of the bed, holding his left hand and looking at them. His eyes, circled with the white of shock, looked at Jack reproachfully.

'Daddy, you said you killed them all. My hand . . . it really hurts.'

'Let's see it, doc . . . no, I'm not going to touch it. That would make it hurt even more. Just hold it out.'

He did and Wendy moaned. 'Oh Danny . . . oh, your poor hand!'

Later the doctor would count eleven separate stings. Now all they saw was a dotting of small holes, as if his palm and fingers had been sprinkled with grains of red pepper. The swelling was bad. His hand had begun to look like one of those cartoon images where Bugs Bunny or Daffy Duck had just slammed himself with a hammer.

'Wendy, go get that spray stuff in the bathroom,' he said.

She went after it, and he sat down next to Danny and slipped an arm around his shoulders.

'After we spray your hand, I want to take some Polaroids of it, doc. Then you sleep the rest of the night with us, 'kay?'

'Sure,' Danny said. 'But why are you going to take pictures?'

'So maybe we can sue the ass out of some people.'

Wendy came back with a spray tube in the shape of a chemical fire extinguisher.

'This won't hurt, honey,' she said, taking off the cap.

Danny held out his hand and she sprayed both sides until it gleamed. He let out a long, shuddery sigh.

'Does it smart?' she asked.

'No. Feels better.'

'Now these. Crunch them up.' She held out five orange-flavored baby aspirin. Danny took them and popped them into his mouth one by one.

'Isn't that a lot of aspirin?' Jack asked.

'It's a lot of stings,' she snapped at him angrily. 'You go and get rid of that nest, John Torrance. Right now.'

'Just a minute.'

He went to the dresser and took his Polaroid Square Shooter out of the top drawer. He rummaged deeper and found some flashcubes.

'Jack, what are you doing?' she asked, a little hysterically.

'He's gonna take some pictures of my hand,' Danny said gravely, 'and then we're gonna sue the ass out of some people. Right, Dad?'

'Right,' Jack said grimly. He had found the flash attachment, and he jabbed it onto the camera. 'Hold it out, son. I figure about five thousand dollars a sting.'

'What are you *talking* about?' Wendy nearly screamed.

'I'll tell you what,' he said. 'I followed the directions on that fucking bug bomb. We're going to sue them. The damn thing was defective. Had to have been. How else can you explain this?'

'Oh,' she said in a small voice.

He took four pictures, pulling out each covered print for Wendy to time on the small locket watch she wore around her neck. Danny, fascinated with the idea that his stung hand might be worth thousands and thousands of dollars, began to lose some of his fright and take an active interest. The hand throbbed dully, and he had a small headache.

When Jack had put the camera away and spread the prints out on top of the dresser to dry, Wendy said: 'Should we take him to the doctor tonight?'

'Not unless he's really in pain,' Jack said. 'If a person has a strong allergy to wasp venom, it hits within thirty seconds.'

'Hits? What do you—'

'A coma. Or convulsions.'

'Oh. Oh my Jesus.' She cupped her hands over her elbows and hugged herself, looking pale and wan.

'How do you feel, son? Think you could sleep?'

Danny blinked at them. The nightmare had faded to a dull, featureless background in his mind, but he was still frightened.

'If I can sleep with you.'

'Of course,' Wendy said. 'Oh honey, I'm so sorry.'

'It's okay, Mommy.'

She began to cry again, and Jack put his hands on her shoulders. 'Wendy, I swear to you that I followed the directions.'

'Will you get rid of it in the morning? Please?'

'Of course I will.'

The three of them got in bed together, and Jack was about to snap off the light over the bed when he paused and pushed the covers back instead. 'Want a picture of the nest, too.'

'Come right back.'

'I will.'

He went to the dresser, got the camera and the last flashcube, and gave Danny a closed thumb-and-forefinger circle. Danny smiled and gave it back with his good hand.

Quite a kid, he thought as he walked down to Danny's room. *All of that and then some.*

The overhead was still on. Jack crossed to the bunk setup, and as he glanced at the table beside it, his skin crawled into goose flesh. The short hairs on his neck prickled and tried to stand erect.

He could hardly see the nest through the clear Pyrex bowl. The inside of the glass was crawling with wasps. It was hard to tell how many. Fifty at least. Maybe a hundred.

His heart thudding slowly in his chest, he took his pictures and then set the camera down to wait for them to develop. He wiped his lips with the palm of his hand. One thought played over and over in his mind, echoing with

(*You lost your temper. You lost your temper. You lost your temper.*)

an almost superstitious dread. They had come back. He had killed the wasps but they had come back.

In his mind he heard himself screaming into his frightened, crying son's face: *Don't stutter!*

He wiped his lips again.

He went to Danny's worktable, rummaged in its drawers, and came up with a big jigsaw puzzle with a fiberboard backing. He took it over to the bedtable and carefully slid the bowl and the nest onto it. The wasps buzzed angrily inside their prison. Then, putting his hand firmly on top of the bowl so it wouldn't slip, he went out into the hall.

'Coming to bed, Jack?' Wendy asked.

'Coming to bed, Daddy?'

'Have to go downstairs for a minute,' he said, making his voice light.

How had it happened? How in God's name?

The bomb sure hadn't been a dud. He had seen the thick white smoke start to puff out of it when he had pulled the ring. And when he had gone up two hours later, he had shaken a drift of small dead bodies out of the hole in the top.

Then how? Spontaneous regeneration?

That was crazy. Seventeenth-century bullshit. Insects didn't regenerate. And even if wasp eggs could mature full-grown insects in twelve hours, this wasn't the season in which the queen laid. That happened in April or May. Fall was their dying time.

A living contradiction, the wasps buzzed furiously under the bowl.

He took them downstairs and through the kitchen. In back there was a door which gave on the outside. A cold night wind blew against his nearly naked body, and his feet went numb almost instantly against the cold concrete of the platform he was standing on, the platform where milk deliveries were made during the hotel's operating season. He put the puzzle and the bowl down carefully, and when he stood up he looked at the thermometer nailed outside the door. FRESH UP WITH 7-UP, the thermometer said, and the mercury stood at an even twenty-five degrees. The cold would kill them by morning. He went in and shut the door firmly. After a moment's thought he locked it, too.

He crossed the kitchen again and shut off the lights. He stood in the darkness for a moment, thinking, wanting a drink. Suddenly the hotel seemed full of a thousand stealthy sounds: creakings and groans and the sly sniff of the wind under the eaves where more wasps' nests might be hanging like deadly fruit.

They had come back.

And suddenly he found that he didn't like the Overlook so well anymore, as if it wasn't wasps that had stung his son, wasps that had miraculously lived through the bug bomb assault, but the hotel itself.

His last thought before going upstairs to his wife and son

(*from now on you will hold your temper. No Matter What.*)

was firm and hard and sure.

As he went down the hall to them he wiped his lips with the back of his hand.

Chapter Seventeen

The Doctor's Office

Stripped to his underpants, lying on the examination table, Danny Torrance looked very small. He was looking up at Dr ('Just call me Bill') Edmonds, who was wheeling a large black machine up beside him. Danny rolled his eyes to get a better look at it.

'Don't let it scare you, guy,' Bill Edmonds said. 'It's an electroencephalograph, and it doesn't hurt.'

'Electro—'

'We call it EEG for short. I'm going to hook a bunch of wires to your head – no, not stick them in, only tape them – and the pens in this part of the gadget will record your brain waves.'

'Like on "The Six Million Dollar Man"?'

'About the same. Would you like to be like Steve Austin when you grow up?'

'No way,' Danny said as the nurse began to tape the wires to a number of tiny shaved spots on his scalp. 'My daddy says that someday he'll get a short circuit and then he'll be up sh . . . he'll be up the creek.'

'I know that creek well,' Dr Edmonds said amiably. 'I've been up it a few times myself, *sans* paddle. An EEG can tell us lots of things, Danny.'

'Like what?'

'Like for instance if you have epilepsy. That's a little problem where—'

'Yeah, I know what epilepsy is.'

'Really?'

'Sure. There was a kid in my nursery school back in Vermont – I went to nursery school when I was a little kid – and he had it. He wasn't supposed to use the flashboard.'

'What was that, Dan?' He had turned on the machine. Thin lines began to trace their way across graph paper.

'It had all these lights, all different colors. And when you turned it on, some colors would flash but not all. And you had to count the colors and if you pushed the right button, you could turn it off. Brent couldn't use that.'

'That's because bright flashing lights sometimes cause an epileptic seizure.'

'You mean using the flashboard might've made Brent pitch a fit?'

Edmonds and the nurse exchanged a brief, amused glance. 'Inelegantly but accurately put, Danny.'

'What?'

'I said you're right, except you should say "seizure" instead of "pitch a fit." That's not nice . . . okay, lie just as still as a mouse now.'

'Okay.'

'Danny, when you have these . . . whatever they ares, do you ever recall seeing bright flashing lights before?'

'No.'

'Funny noises? Ringing? Or chimes like a doorbell?'

'Huh-uh.'

'How about a funny smell, maybe like oranges or sawdust? Or a smell like something rotten?'

'No, sir.'

'Sometimes do you feel like crying before you pass out? Even though you don't feel sad?'

'No way.'

'That's fine, then.'

'Have I got epilepsy, Dr Bill?'

'I don't think so, Danny. Just lie still. Almost done.'

The machine hummed and scratched for another five minutes and then Dr Edmonds shut it off.

'All done, guy,' Edmonds said briskly. 'Let Sally get those electrodes off you and then come into the next room. I want to have a little talk with you. Okay?'

'Sure.'

'Sally, you go ahead and give him a tine test before he comes in.'

'All right.'

Edmonds ripped off the long curl of paper the machine had extruded and went into the next room, looking at it.

'I'm going to prick your arm just a little,' the nurse said after Danny had pulled up his pants. 'It's to make sure you don't have TB.'

'They gave me that at my school just last year,' Danny said without much hope.

'But that was a long time ago and you're a big boy now, right?'

'I guess so,' Danny sighed, and offered his arm up for sacrifice.

When he had his shirt and shoes on, he went through the sliding door and into Dr Edmonds's office. Edmonds was sitting on the edge of his desk, swinging his legs thoughtfully.

'Hi, Danny.'

'Hi.'

'How's that hand now?' He pointed at Danny's left hand, which was lightly bandaged.

'Pretty good.'

'Good. I looked at your EEG and its seems fine. But I'm going to send it to a friend of mine in Denver who makes his living reading those things. I just want to make sure.'

'Yes, sir.'

'Tell me about Tony, Dan.'

Danny shuffled his feet. 'He's just an invisible friend,' he said. 'I made him up. To keep me company.'

Edmonds laughed and put his hands on Danny's shoulders. 'Now that's what your Mom and Dad say. But this is just between us, guy. I'm your doctor. Tell me the truth and I'll promise not to tell them unless you say I can.'

Danny thought about it. He looked at Edmonds and then, with a small effort of concentration, he tried to catch Edmonds's thoughts or at least the color of his mood. And suddenly he got an oddly comforting image in his head: file cabinets, their doors sliding shut one after another, locking with a click. Written on the small tabs in the center of each door was: A-C, SECRET; D-G, SECRET; and so on. This made Danny feel a little easier.

Cautiously he said: 'I don't know who Tony is.'

'Is he your age?'

'No. He's at least eleven. I think he might be even older. I've never seen him right up close. He might be old enough to drive a car.'

'You just see him at a distance, huh?'

'Yes, sir.'

'And he always comes just before you pass out?'

'Well, I don't pass out. It's like I go with him. And he shows me things.'

'What kind of things?'

'Well . . .' Danny debated for a moment and then told Edmonds about Daddy's trunk with all his writing in it, and about how the movers hadn't lost it between Vermont and Colorado after all. It had been right under the stairs all along.

'And your daddy found it where Tony said he would?'

'Oh yes, sir. Only Tony didn't *tell* me. He showed me.'

'I understand. Danny, what did Tony show you last night? When you locked yourself in the bathroom?'

'I don't remember,' Danny said quickly.

'Are you sure?'

'Yes, sir.'

'A moment ago I said *you* locked the bathroom door. But that wasn't right, was it? *Tony* locked the door.'

'No, sir. Tony couldn't lock the door because he isn't real. He wanted me to do it, so I did. I locked it.'

'Does Tony always show you where lost things are?'

'No, sir. Sometimes he shows me things that are going to happen.'

'Really?'

'Sure. Like one time Tony showed me the amusements and wild animal park in Great Barrington. Tony said Daddy was going to take me there for my birthday. He did, too.'

'What else does he show you?'

Danny frowned. 'Signs. He's always showing me stupid old *signs*. And I can't read them, hardly ever.'

'Why do you suppose Tony would do that, Danny?'

'I don't know.' Danny brightened. 'But my daddy and mommy are teaching me to read, and I'm trying real hard.'

'So you can read Tony's signs.'

'Well, I really want to learn. But that too, yeah.'

'Do you like Tony, Danny?'

Danny looked at the tile floor and said nothing.

'Danny?'

'It's hard to tell,' Danny said. 'I used to. I used to hope he'd come every day, because he always showed me good things, especially since Mommy and Daddy don't think about DIVORCE anymore.' Dr Edmonds's gaze sharpened, but Danny didn't notice. He was looking hard at the floor, concentrating on expressing himself. 'But now whenever he comes he shows me bad things. *Awful* things. Like in the bathroom last night. The things he shows me, they sting me like those wasps stung me. Only Tony's things sting me up here.' He cocked a finger gravely at his temple, a small boy unconsciously burlesquing suicide.

'What things, Danny?'

'I can't remember!' Danny cried out, agonized. 'I'd tell you if I could! It's like I can't remember because it's so bad I don't *want* to remember. All I can remember when I wake up is REDRUM.'

'Red *drum* or red *rum*?'

'Rum.'

'What's that, Danny?'

'I don't know.'

'Danny?'

'Yes, sir?'

'Can you make Tony come now?'

'I don't know. He doesn't always come. I don't even know if I want him to come anymore.'

'Try, Danny. I'll be right here.'

Danny looked at Edmonds doubtfully. Edmonds nodded encouragement.

Danny let out a long, sighing breath and nodded. 'But I don't know if it will work. I never did it with anyone looking at me before. And Tony doesn't always come, anyway.'

'If he doesn't, he doesn't,' Edmonds said. 'I just want you to try.'

'Okay.'

He dropped his gaze to Edmonds's slowly swinging loafers and cast his mind outward toward his mommy and daddy. They were here someplace . . . right beyond that wall with the picture on it, as a matter of fact. In the waiting room where they had come in. Sitting side by side but not talking. Leafing through magazines. Worried. About him.

He concentrated harder, his brow furrowing, trying to get into the feeling of his mommy's thoughts. It was always harder when they weren't right there in the room with him. Then he began to get it. Mommy was thinking about a sister. Her sister. The sister was dead. His mommy was thinking that was the main thing that turned her mommy into such a

(*bitch?*)

into such an old biddy. Because her sister had died. As a little girl she was

(*hit by a car oh god i could never stand anything like that again like aileen but what if he's sick really sick cancer spinal meningitis leukemia brain tumor like john gunther's son or muscular dystrophy oh jeez kids his age get leukemia all the time radium treatments chemotherapy we couldn't afford anything like that but of course they just can't turn you out to die on the street can they and anyway he's all right all right all right you really shouldn't let yourself think*)

(*Danny—*)

(*about aileen and*)

(*Dannee—*)

(*that car*)

(*Dannee—*)

But Tony wasn't there. Only his voice. And as it faded, Danny followed it down into darkness, falling and tumbling down some magic hole between Dr Bill's swinging loafers, past a loud knocking sound, further, a bathtub cruised silently by in the darkness with some horrible thing lolling in it, past a sound like sweetly chiming church bells, past a clock under a dome of glass.

Then the dark was pierced feebly by a single light, festooned with cobwebs. The weak glow disclosed a stone floor that looked damp and unpleasant. Somewhere not far distant was a steady mechanical roaring sound, but muted, not frightening. Soporific. It was the thing that would be forgotten, Danny thought with dreamy surprise.

As his eyes adjusted to the gloom he could see Tony just ahead of him, a silhouette. Tony was looking at something and Danny strained his eyes to see what it was.

(*Your daddy. See your daddy?*)

Of course he did. How could he have missed him, even in the basement light's feeble glow? Daddy was kneeling on the floor, casting the beam of a flashlight over old cardboard boxes and wooden crates. The cardboard boxes were mushy and old; some of them had split open and spilled drifts of paper onto the floor. Newspapers, books, printed pieces of paper that looked like bills. His daddy was examining them with great interest. And then Daddy looked up and shone his flashlight in another direction. Its beam of light impaled another book, a large white one bound with gold string. The cover looked like white leather. It was a scrapbook. Danny suddenly needed to cry out to his daddy, to tell him to leave that book alone, that some books should not be opened. But his daddy was climbing toward it.

The mechanical roaring sound, which he now recognized as the boiler at the Overlook which Daddy checked three or four times every day, had developed an ominous, rhythmic hitching. It began to sound like . . . like pounding. And the smell of mildew and wet, rotting paper was changing to something else – the high, junipery smell of the Bad Stuff. It hung around his daddy like a vapor as he reached for the book . . . and grasped it.

Tony was somewhere in the darkness

(*This inhuman place makes human monsters. This inhuman place*)

repeating the same incomprehensible thing over and over.

(*makes human monsters.*)

Falling through darkness again, now accompanied by the heavy, pounding thunder was no longer the boiler but the sound of a whistling mallet striking silk-paper walls, knocking out whiffs of plaster dust. Crouching helplessly on the blue-black woven jungle rug.

(*Come out*)

(*This inhuman place*)

(*and take your medicine!*)

(*makes human monsters.*)

With a gasp that echoed in his own head he jerked himself out of the darkness. Hands were on him and at first he shrank back, thinking that the dark thing in the Overlook of Tony's world had somehow followed him back into the world of real things – and then Dr Edmonds was saying: 'You're all right, Danny. You're all right. Everything is fine.'

Danny recognized the doctor, then his surroundings in the office. He began to shudder helplessly. Edmonds held him.

When the reaction began to subside, Edmonds asked, 'You said something about monsters, Danny – what was it?'

'This inhuman place,' he said gutturally. 'Tony told me . . . this inhuman place . . . makes . . . makes . . .' He shook his head. 'Can't remember.'

'Try!'

'I can't.'

'Did Tony come?'

'Yes.'

'What did he show you?'

'Dark. Pounding. I don't remember.'

'Where were you?'

'*Leave me alone! I don't remember! Leave me alone!*' He began to sob helplessly in fear and frustration. It was all gone, dissolved into a sticky mess like a wet bundle of paper, the memory unreadable.

Edmonds went to the water cooler and got him a paper cup of water. Danny drank it and Edmonds got him another one.

'Better?'

'Yes.'

'Danny, I don't want to badger you . . . tease you about this, I mean. But can you remember anything about *before* Tony came?'

'My mommy,' Danny said slowly. 'She's worried about me.'

'Mothers always are, guy.'

'No . . . she had a sister that died when she was a little girl. Aileen. She was thinking about how Aileen got hit by a car and that made her worried about me. I don't remember anything else.'

Edmonds was looking at him sharply. 'Just now she was thinking that? Out in the waiting room?'

'Yes, sir.'

'Danny, how would you know that?'

'I don't know,' Danny said wanly. 'The shining, I guess.'

'The what?'

Danny shook his head very slowly. 'I'm awful tired. Can't I go see my mommy and daddy? I don't want to answer any more questions. I'm tired. And my stomach hurts.'

'Are you going to throw up?'

'No, sir. I just want to go see my mommy and daddy.'

'Okay, Dan.' Edmonds stood up. 'You go on out and see them for a minute, then send them in so I can talk to them. Okay?'

'Yes, sir.'

'There are books out there to look at. You like books, don't you?'

'Yes, sir,' Danny said dutifully.

'You're a good boy, Danny.'

Danny gave him a faint smile.

'I can't find a thing wrong with him,' Dr Edmonds said to the Torrances. 'Not physically. Mentally, he's bright and rather too imaginative. It happens. Children have to grow into their imaginations like a pair of oversized shoes. Danny's is still way too big for him. Ever had his IQ tested?'

'I don't believe in them,' Jack said. 'They straight-jacket the expectations of both parents and teachers.'

Dr Edmonds nodded. 'That may be. But if you did test him, I think you'd find he's right off the scale for his age group. His verbal ability, for a boy who is five going on six, is amazing.'

'We don't talk down to him,' Jack said with a trace of pride.

'I doubt if you've ever had to in order to make yourself understood.' Edmonds paused, fiddling with a pen. 'He went into a trance while I was with him. At my request. Exactly as you described him in the bathroom last night. All his muscles went lax, his body slumped, his eyeballs rotated outward. Textbook auto-hypnosis. I was amazed. I still am.'

The Torrances sat forward. 'What happened?' Wendy asked tensely, and Edmonds carefully related Danny's trance, the muttered phrase from which Edmonds had only been able to pluck the word 'monsters,' the 'dark,' the 'pounding.' The aftermath of tears, near-hysteria, and nervous stomach.

'Tony again,' Jack said.

'What does it mean?' Wendy asked. 'Have you any idea?'

'A few. You might not like them.'

'Go ahead anyway,' Jack told him.

'From what Danny told me, his "invisible friend" was truly a friend until you folks moved out here from New England. Tony has only become a threatening figure since that move. The pleasant interludes have become nightmarish, even more frightening to your son because he can't remember exactly what the nightmares are about. That's common enough. We all remember our pleasant dreams more clearly than the scary ones. There seems to be a buffer somewhere between the conscious and the subconscious, and one hell of a blue-nose lives in there. This censor only lets through a small amount, and often what does come through is only symbolic. That's oversimplified Freud, but it does pretty much describe what we know of the mind's interaction with itself.'

'You think moving has upset Danny that badly?' Wendy asked.

'It may have, if the move took place under traumatic circumstances,' Edmonds said. 'Did it?'

Wendy and Jack exchanged a glance.

'I was teaching at a prep school,' Jack said slowly. 'I lost my job.'

'I see,' Edmonds said. He put the pen he had been playing with firmly back in its holder. 'There's more here, I'm afraid. It may be painful to you. Your son seems to believe you two have seriously contemplated divorce. He spoke of it in an offhand way, but only because he believes you are no longer considering it.'

Jack's mouth dropped open, and Wendy recoiled as if slapped. The blood drained from her face.

'We never even discussed it!' she said. 'Not in front of him, not even in front of each other! We—'

'I think it's best if you understand everything, Doctor,' Jack said. 'Shortly after Danny was born, I became an alcoholic. I'd had a drinking problem all the way through college, it subsided a little after Wendy and I met, cropped up worse than ever after Danny was born and the writing I consider to be my real work was going badly. When Danny was three and a half, he spilled some beer on a bunch of papers I was working on . . . papers I was shuffling around, anyway . . . and I . . . well . . . oh shit.' His voice broke, but his eyes remained dry and unflinching. 'It sounds so goddam beastly said out loud. I broke his arm turning him around to spank him. Three months later I gave up drinking. I haven't touched it since.'

'I see,' Edmonds said neutrally. 'I knew the arm had been broken, of course. It was set well.' He pushed back from his desk a little and crossed his legs. 'If I may be frank, it's obvious that he's been in no way abused since then. Other than the stings, there's nothing on him but the normal bruises and scabs that any kid has in abundance.'

'Of course not,' Wendy said hotly. 'Jack didn't mean—'

'No, Wendy,' Jack said. 'I meant to do it. I guess someplace inside I really did mean to do that to him. Or something even worse.' He looked back at Edmonds again. 'You know something, Doctor? This is the first time the word divorce has been mentioned between us. And alcoholism. And child-beating. Three firsts in five minutes.'

'That may be at the root of the problem,' Edmonds said. 'I am not a psychiatrist. If you want Danny to see a child psychiatrist, I can recommend a good one who works out of the Mission Ridge Medical Center in Boulder. But I am fairly confident of my diagnosis. Danny is an intelligent, imaginative, perceptive boy. I don't believe he would have been as upset by your marital problems as you believed. Small children are great accepters. They don't understand shame, or the need to hide things.'

Jack was studying his hands. Wendy took one of them and squeezed it.

'But he sensed the things that were wrong. Chief among them from his point of view was not the broken arm but the broken – or breaking – link between you two. He mentioned divorce to me, but not the broken arm. When my nurse mentioned the set to him, he simply shrugged it off. It was no pressure thing. "It happened a long time ago" is what I think he said.'

'That kid,' Jack muttered. His jaws were clamped together, the muscles in the cheeks standing out. 'We don't deserve him.'

'You have him, all the same,' Edmonds said dryly. 'At any rate, he retires into a fantasy world from time to time. Nothing unusual about that; lots of kids do. As I recall, I had my own invisible friend when I was Danny's age, a talking rooster named Chug-Chug. Of course no one could see Chug-Chug but me. I had two older brothers who often left me behind, and in such a situation Chug-Chug came in mighty handy. And of course you two must understand why Danny's invisible friend is named Tony instead of Mike or Hal or Dutch.'

'Yes,' Wendy said.

'Have you ever pointed it out to him?'

'No,' Jack said. 'Should we?'

'Why bother? Let him realize it in his own time, by his own logic. You see, Danny's fantasies were considerably deeper than those that grow around the ordinary invisible friend syndrome, but he felt he needed Tony that much more. Tony would come and show him pleasant things. Sometimes amazing things. Always good things. Once Tony showed him where Daddy's lost trunk was . . . under the stairs. Another time Tony showed him that Mommy and Daddy were going to take him to an amusement park for his birthday—'

'At Great Barrington!' Wendy cried. 'But how could he *know* those things? It's eerie, the things he comes out with sometimes. Almost as if—'

'He had second sight?' Edmonds asked, smiling.

'He was born with a caul,' Wendy said weakly.

Edmonds's smile became a good, hearty laugh. Jack and Wendy exchanged a glance and then also smiled, both of them amazed at how easy it was. Danny's occasional 'lucky guesses' about things was something else they had not discussed much.

'Next you'll be telling me he can levitate,' Edmonds said, still smiling. 'No, no, no, I'm afraid not. It's not extrasensory but good old human perception, which in Danny's case is unusually keen. Mr Torrance, he knew your trunk was under the stairs because you had looked everywhere else. Process of elimination, what? It's so simple Ellery Queen would laugh at it. Sooner or later you would have thought of it yourself.

'As for the amusement park at Great Barrington, whose idea was that originally? Yours or his?'

'His, of course,' Wendy said. 'They advertised on all the morning children's programs. He was wild to go. But the thing is, Doctor, we couldn't afford to take him. And we had told him so.'

'Then a men's magazine I'd sold a story to back in 1971 sent a check for fifty dollars,' Jack said. 'They were reprinting the story in an annual, or something. So we decided to spend it on Danny.'

Edmonds shrugged. 'Wish fulfillment plus a lucky coincidence.'

'Goddammit, I bet that's just right,' Jack said.

Edmonds smiled a little. 'And Danny himself told me that Tony often showed him things that never occurred. Visions based on faulty perception, that's all. Danny is doing subconsciously what these so-called mystics and mind readers do quite consciously and cynically. I admire him for it. If life doesn't cause him to retract his antennae, I think he'll be quite a man.'

Wendy nodded – of course she thought Danny would be quite a man – but the doctor's explanation struck her as glib. It tasted more like margarine than butter. Edmonds had not lived with them. He had not been there when Danny found lost buttons, told her that maybe the *TV Guide* was under the bed, that he thought he better wear his rubbers to nursery school even though the sun was out . . . and later that day they had walked home under her umbrella through the pouring rain. Edmonds couldn't know of the curious way Danny had of preguessing them both. She would decide to have an unusual evening cup of tea, go out in the kitchen and find her cup out with a tea bag in it. She would remember that the books were due at the library and find them all neatly piled up on the hall table, her library card on top. Or Jack would take it into his head to wax the Volkswagen and find Danny already out there, listening to tinny top-forty music on his crystal radio as he sat on the curb to watch.

Aloud she said, 'Then why the nightmares now? Why did Tony tell him to lock the bathroom door?'

'I believe it's because Tony has outlived his usefulness,' Edmonds said. 'He was born – Tony, not Danny – at a time when you and your husband were straining to keep your marriage together. Your husband was drinking too much. There was the incident of the broken arm. The ominous quiet between you.'

Ominous quiet, yes, that phrase was the real thing, anyway. The stiff, tense meals where the only conversation had been please pass the butter or Danny, eat the rest of your carrots or may I be excused, please. The nights when Jack was gone and she had lain down, dry-eyed, on the couch while Danny watched TV. The morning when she and Jack had stalked around each other like two angry cats with a quivering, frightened mouse between them. It all rang true;

(dear God, do old scars ever stop hurting?)

horribly, horribly true.

Edmonds resumed, 'But things have changed. You know, schizoid behavior is a pretty common thing in children. It's accepted, because all we adults have this unspoken agreement that children are lunatics. They have invisible friends. They may go and sit in the closet when they're depressed, withdrawing from the world. They attach talismanic importance to a special blanket, or a teddy bear, or a stuffed tiger. They suck their thumbs. When an adult sees things that aren't there, we consider him ready for the rubber room. When a child says he's seen a troll in his bedroom or a vampire outside the window, we simply smile indulgently. We have a one-sentence explanation that explains the whole range of such phenomena in children—'

'He'll grow out of it,' Jack said.

Edmonds blinked. 'My very words,' he said. 'Yes. Now I would guess that Danny was in a pretty good position to develop a full-fledged psychosis. Unhappy home life, a big imagination, the invisible friend who was so real to him that he nearly became real to you. Instead of "growing out of" his childhood schizophrenia, he might well have grown into it.'

'And become autistic?' Wendy asked. She had read about autism. The word itself frightened her; it sounded like dread and white silence.

'Possible but not necessarily. He might simply have entered Tony's world someday and never come back to what he calls "real things." '

'God,' Jack said.

'But now the basic situation has changed drastically. Mr Torrance no longer drinks. You are in a new place where conditions have forced the three of you into a tighter family unit than ever before – certainly tighter than my own, where my wife and kids may see me for only two or three hours a day. To my mind, he is in the perfect healing situation. And I think the very fact that he is able to differentiate so sharply between Tony's world and "real things" says a lot about the fundamentally healthy state of his mind. He says that you two are no longer considering divorce. Is he as right as I think he is?'

'Yes,' Wendy said, and Jack squeezed her hand tightly, almost painfully. She squeezed back.

Edmonds nodded. 'He really doesn't need Tony anymore. Danny is flushing him out of his system. Tony no longer brings pleasant visions but hostile nightmares that are too frightening for him to remember except fragmentarily. He internalized Tony during a difficult – desperate – life situation, and Tony is not leaving easily. But he *is* leaving. Your son is a little like a junkie kicking the habit.'

He stood up, and the Torrances stood also.

'As I said, I'm not a psychiatrist. If the nightmares are still continuing when your job at the Overlook ends next spring, Mr Torrance, I would strongly urge you to take him to this man in Boulder.'

'I will.'

'Well, let's go out and tell him he can go home,' Edmonds said.

'I want to thank you,' Jack told him painfully. 'I feel better about all this than I have in a very long time.'

'So do I,' Wendy said.

At the door, Edmonds paused and looked at Wendy. 'Do you or did you have a sister, Mrs Torrance? Named Aileen?'

Wendy looked at him, surprised. 'Yes, I did. She was killed outside our home in Somersworth, New Hampshire, when she was six and I was ten. She chased a ball into the street and was struck by a delivery van.'

'Does Danny know that?'

'I don't know. I don't think so.'

'He says you were thinking about her in the waiting room.'

'I was,' Wendy said slowly. 'For the first time in . . . oh, I don't know how long.'

'Does the word "redrum" mean anything to either of you?'

Wendy shook her head but Jack said, 'He mentioned that word last night, just before he went to sleep. Red drum.'

'No, *rum*,' Edmonds corrected. 'He was quite emphatic about that. *Rum*. As in the drink. The alcoholic drink.'

'Oh,' Jack said. 'It fits in doesn't it?' He took his handkerchief out of his back pocket and wiped his lips with it.

'Does the phrase "the shining" mean anything to you?'

This time they both shook their heads.

'Doesn't matter, I guess,' Edmonds said. He opened the door into the waiting room. 'Anybody here named Danny Torrance that would like to go home?'

'Hi, Daddy! Hi, Mommy!' He stood up from the small table where he had been leafing slowly through a copy of *Where the Wild Things Are* and muttering the words he knew aloud.

He ran to Jack, who scooped him up. Wendy ruffled his hair.

Edmonds peered at him. 'If you don't love your mommy and daddy, you can stay with good old Bill.'

'No, sir!' Danny said emphatically. He slung one arm around Jack's neck, one arm around Wendy's, and looked radiantly happy.

'Okay,' Edmonds said, smiling. He looked at Wendy. 'You call if you have any problems.'

'Yes.'

'I don't think you will,' Edmonds said, smiling.

Chapter Eighteen

The Scrapbook

Jack found the scrapbook on the first of November, while his wife and son were hiking up the rutted old road that ran from behind the roque court to a deserted sawmill two miles further up. The fine weather still held, and all three of them had acquired improbable autumn suntans.

He had gone down in the basement to knock the press down on the boiler and then, on impulse, he had taken the flashlight from the shelf where the plumbing schematics were and decided to look at some of the old papers. He was also looking for good places to set his traps, although he didn't plan to do that for another month – I want them all to be home from vacation, he had told Wendy.

Shining the flashlight ahead of him, he stepped past the elevator shaft (at Wendy's insistence they hadn't used the elevator since they moved in) and through the small stone arch. His nose wrinkled at the smell of rotting paper. Behind him the boiler kicked on with a thundering *whoosh*, making him jump.

He flickered the light around, whistling tunelessly between his teeth. There was a scale-model Andes range down here: dozens of boxes and crates stuffed with papers, most of them white and shapeless with age and damp. Others had broken open and spilled yellowed sheaves of paper onto the stone floor. There were bales of newspaper tied up with hayrope. Some boxes contained what looked like ledgers, and others contained invoices bound with rubber bands. Jack pulled one out and put the flashlight beam on it.

ROCKY MOUNTAIN EXPRESS, INC.
To: OVERLOOK HOTEL
From: SIDEY'S WAREHOUSE, 1210 16th Street, Denver, CO.
Via: CANDIAN PACIFIC RR
Contents: 400 CASES DELSEY TOILET TISSUE, 1 GROSS/CASE
Signed *D E F*
Date *August 24, 1954*

Smiling, Jack let the paper drop back into the box.

He flashed the light above it and it speared a hanging lightbulb, almost buried in cobwebs. There was no chain pull.

He stood on tiptoe and tried screwing the bulb in. It lit weakly. He picked up the toilet-paper invoice again and used it to wipe off some of the cobwebs. The glow didn't brighten much.

Still using the flashlight, he wandered through the boxes and bales of paper, looking for rat spoor. They had been here, but not for quite a long time . . . maybe years. He found some droppings that were powdery with age, and several nests of neatly shredded paper that were old and unused.

Jack pulled a newspaper from one of the bundles and glanced down at the headline.

JOHNSON PROMISES ORDERLY TRANSITION
Says Work Begun by JFK Will Go Forward in Coming Year

The paper was the *Rocky Mountain News*, dated December 19, 1963. He dropped it back onto its pile.

He supposed he was fascinated by that commonplace sense of history that anyone can feel glancing through the fresh news of ten or twenty years ago. He found gaps in the piled newspapers and records; nothing from 1937 to 1945, from 1957 to 1960, from 1962 to 1963. Periods when the hotel had been closed, he guessed. When it had been between suckers grabbing for the brass ring.

Ullman's explanations of the Overlook's checkered career still didn't ring quite true to him. It seemed that the Overlook's spectacular location alone should have guaranteed its continuing success. There had always been an American jetset, even before jets were invented, and it seemed to Jack that the Overlook should have been one of the bases they touched in their migrations. It even sounded right. The Waldorf in May, the Bar Harbor House in June and July, the Overlook in August and early September, before moving on to Bermuda, Havana, Rio, wherever. He found a pile of old desk registers and they bore him out. Nelson Rockefeller in 1950. Henry Ford & Fam. in 1927. Jean Harlow in 1930. Clark Gable and Carole Lombard. In 1956 the whole top floor had been taken for a week by 'Darryl F. Zanuck & Party.' The money must have rolled down the corridors and into the cash registers like a twentieth-century Comstock Lode. The management must have been spectacularly bad.

There was history here, all right, and not just in newspaper headlines. It was buried between the entries in these ledgers and account books and room-service chits where you couldn't quite see it. In 1922 Warren G. Harding had ordered a whole salmon at ten o'clock in the evening, and a case of Coors beer. But whom had he been eating and drinking with? Had it been a poker game? A strategy session? What?

Jack glanced at his watch and was surprised to see that forty-five minutes had somehow slipped by since he had come down here. His hands and arms were grimy, and he probably smelled bad. He decided to go up and take a shower before Wendy and Danny got back.

He walked slowly between the mountains of paper, his mind alive and ticking over possibilities in a speedy way that was exhilarating. He hadn't felt this way in years. It suddenly seemed that the book he had semijokingly promised himself might really happen. It might even be right here, buried in these untidy heaps of paper. It could be a work of fiction, or history, or both – a long book exploding out of this central place in a hundred directions.

He stood beneath the cobwebby light, took his handkerchief from his back pocket without thinking, and scrubbed at his lips with it. And that was when he saw the scrapbook.

A pile of five boxes stood on his left like some tottering Pisa. The one on top was stuffed with more invoices and ledgers. Balanced on top of those, keeping its angle of repose for who knew how many years, was a thick scrapbook with white leather covers, its pages bound with two hanks of gold string that had been tied along the binding in gaudy bows.

Curious, he went over and took it down. The top cover was thick with dust. He held it on a plane at lip level, blew the dust off in a cloud, and opened it. As he did so a card fluttered out and he grabbed it in mid-air before it could fall to the stone floor. It was rich and creamy, dominated by a raised engraving of the Overlook with every window alight. The lawn and playground were decorated with glowing Japanese lanterns. It looked almost as though you could step right into it, an Overlook Hotel that had existed thirty years ago.

Horace M. Derwent Requests
The Pleasure of Your Company
At a Masked Ball to Celebrate
The Grand Opening of

THE OVERLOOK HOTEL

Dinner Will Be Served At 8 p.m.
Unmasking And Dancing At Midnight
August 29, 1945 RSVP

Dinner at eight! Unmasking at midnight!

He could almost see them in the dining room, the richest men in America and their women. Tuxedos and glimmering starched shirts; evening gowns; the band playing; gleaming high-heeled pumps. The clink of glasses, the jocund pop of champagne corks. The war was over, or almost over. The future lay ahead, clean and shining. America was the colossus of the world and at last she knew it and accepted it.

And later, at midnight, Derwent himself crying: 'Unmask! Unmask!' The masks coming off and . . .

(*The Red Death held sway over all!*)

He frowned. What left field had that come out of? That was Poe, the Great American Hack. And surely the Overlook – this shining, glowing Overlook on the invitation he held in his hands – was the farthest cry from E. A. Poe imaginable.

He put the invitation back and turned to the next page. A paste-up from one of the Denver papers, and scratched beneath it the date: May 15, 1947.

POSH MOUNTAIN RESORT REOPENS WITH
STELLAR GUEST REGISTER

Derwent Says Overlook Will be 'Showplace of the World'

By David Felton, Features Editor

The Overlook Hotel has been opened and reopened in its thirty-eight-year history, but rarely with such style and dash as that promised by Horace Derwent, the mysterious California millionaire who is the latest owner of the hostelry.

Derwent, who makes no secret of having sunk more than one million dollars into his newest venture – and some say the figure is closer to three million – says that 'The new Overlook will be one of the world's showplaces, the kind of hotel you will remember overnighting in thirty years later.'

When Derwent, who is rumored to have substantial Las Vegas holdings, was asked if his purchase and refurbishing of the Overlook signaled the opening gun in a battle to legalize casino-style gambling in Colorado, the aircraft, movie, munitions, and shipping magnate denied it . . . with a smile. 'The Overlook would be cheapened by gambling,' he said, 'and don't think I'm knocking Vegas! They've got too many of my markers out there for me to do that! I have no interest in lobbying for legalized gambling in Colorado. It would be spitting into the wind.'

When the Overlook opens officially (there was a gigantic and hugely successful party there some time ago when the actual work was finished), the newly painted, papered, and decorated rooms will be occupied by a stellar guest list, ranging from Chic designer Corbat Stani to . . .

Smiling bemusedly, Jack turned the page. Now he was looking at a full-page ad from the New York Sunday *Times* travel section. On the page after that a story on Derwent himself, a balding man with eyes that pierced you even from an old newsprint photo. He was wearing rimless spectacles and a forties-style pencil-line mustache that did nothing at all to make him look like Errol Flynn. His face was that of an accountant. It was the eyes that made him look like someone or something else.

Jack skimmed the article rapidly. He knew most of the information from a *Newsweek* story on Derwent the year before. Born poor in St. Paul, never finished high school, joined the Navy instead. Rose rapidly, then left in a bitter wrangle over the patent on a new type of propeller that he had designed. In the tug of war between the Navy and an unknown young man named Horace Derwent, Uncle Sam came off the predictable winner. But Uncle Sam had never gotten another patent, and there had been a lot of them.

In the late twenties and early thirties, Derwent turned to aviation. He bought out a bankrupt cropdusting company, turned it into an airmail service, and prospered. More patents followed: a new monoplane wing design, a bomb carriage used on the Flying Fortresses that had rained fire on Hamburg and Dresden and Berlin, a machine gun that was cooled by alcohol, a prototype of the ejection seat later used in United States jets.

And along the line, the accountant who lived in the same skin as the inventor kept piling up the investments. A piddling string of munition factories in New York and New Jersey. Five textile mills in New England. Chemical factories in the bankrupt and groaning South. At the end of the Depression his wealth had been nothing but a handful of controlling interests, bought at abysmally low prices, salable only at lower prices still. At one point Derwent boasted that he could liquidate completely and realize the price of a three-year-old Chevrolet.

There had been rumors, Jack recalled, that some of the means employed by Derwent to keep his head above water were less than savory. Involvement with bootlegging. Prostitution in the Midwest. Smuggling in the coastal areas of the South where his fertilizer factories were. Finally an association with the nascent western gambling interests.

Probably Derwent's most famous investment was the purchase of the foundering Top Mark Studios, which had not had a hit since their child star, Little Margery Morris, had died of a heroin overdose in 1934. She was fourteen. Little Margery, who had specialized in sweet seven-year-olds who saved marriages and the lives of dogs unjustly accused of killing chickens, had been given the biggest Hollywood funeral in history by Top Mark – the official story was that Little Margery had contracted a 'wasting disease' while entertaining at a New York orphanage – and some cynics suggested the studio had laid out all that long green because it knew it was burying itself.

Derwent hired a keen businessman and raging sex maniac named Henry Finkel to run Top Mark, and in the two years before Pearl Harbor the studio ground out sixty movies, fifty-five of which glided right into the face of the Hayes Office and spit on its large blue nose. The other five were government training films. The feature films were huge successes. During one of them an unnamed costume designer had jury-rigged a strapless bra for the heroine to appear in during the Grand Ball scene, where she revealed everything except possibly the birthmark just below the cleft of her buttocks. Derwent received credit for this invention as well, and his reputation – or notoriety – grew.

The war had made him rich and he was still rich. Living in Chicago, seldom seen except for Derwent Enterprises board meetings (which he ran with an iron hand), it was rumored that he owned United Air Lines, Las Vegas (where he was known to have controlling interests in four hotel-casinos and some involvement in at least six others), Los Angeles, and the U.S.A. itself. Reputed to be a friend of royalty, presidents, and underworld kingpins, it was supposed by many that he was the richest man in the world.

But he had not been able to make a go of the Overlook, Jack thought. He put the scrapbook down for a moment and took the small notebook and mechanical pencil he always kept with him out of his breast pocket. He jotted 'Look into H. Derwent, Sidwndr lbry?' He put the notebook back and picked up the scrapbook again. His face was preoccupied, his eyes distant. He wiped his mouth constantly with his hand as he turned the pages.

He skimmed the material that followed, making a mental note to read it more closely later. Press releases were pasted into many of the pages. So-and-so was expected at the Overlook next week, thus-and-such would be entertaining in the lounge (in Derwent's time it had been the Red-Eye Lounge). Many of the entertainers were Vegas names, and many of the guests were Top Mark executives and stars.

Then, in a clipping marked February 1, 1952:

MILLIONAIRE EXEC TO SELL COLORADO INVESTMENTS
Deal Made with California Investors on Overlook, Other Investments, Derwent Reveals

By Rodney Conklin, Financial Editor

In a terse communique yesterday from the Chicago offices of the

> monolithic Derwent Enterprises, it was revealed that millionaire (perhaps billionaire) Horace Derwent has sold out of Colorado in a stunning financial power play that will be completed by October 1, 1954. Derwent's investments include natural gas, coal, hydro-electric power, and a land development company called Colorado Sunshine, Inc., which owns or holds options on better than 500,000 acres of Colorado land.
>
> The most famous Derwent holding in Colorado, the Overlook Hotel, has already been sold, Derwent revealed in a rare interview yesterday. The buyer was a California group of investors headed by Charles Grondin, a former director of the California Land Development Corporation. While Derwent refused to discuss price, informed sources . . .

He had sold out everything, lock, stock, and barrel. It wasn't just the Overlook. But somehow . . . somehow . . .

He wiped his lips with his hand and wished he had a drink. This would go better with a drink. He turned more pages.

The California group had opened the hotel for two seasons, and then sold it to a Colorado group called Mountainview Resorts. Mountainview went bankrupt in 1957 amid charges of corruption, nest-feathering, and cheating the stockholders. The president of the company shot himself two days after being subpoenaed to appear before a grand jury.

The hotel had been closed for the rest of the decade. There was a single story about it, a Sunday feature headlined FORMER GRAND HOTEL SINKING INTO DECAY. The accompanying photos wrenched at Jack's heart: the paint on the front porch peeling, the lawn a bald and scabrous mess, windows broken by storms and stones. This would be a part of the book, if he actually wrote it, too – the phoenix going down into the ashes to be reborn. He promised himself he would take care of the place, very good care. It seemed that before today he had never really understood the breadth of his responsibility to the Overlook. It was almost like having a responsibility to history.

In 1961 four writers, two of them Pulitzer Prize winners, had leased the Overlook and reopened it as a writers' school. That had lasted one year. One of the students had gotten drunk in his third-floor room, crashed out of the window somehow, and fell to his death on the cement terrace below. The paper hinted that it might have been suicide.

Any big hotels have got scandals, Watson had said, *just like every big hotel has got a ghost. Why? Hell, people come and go . . .*

Suddenly it seemed that he could almost feel the weight of the Overlook bearing down on him from above, one hundred and ten guest rooms, the storage rooms, kitchen, pantry, freezer, lounge, ballroom, dining room . . .

(*In the room the women come and go*)

(*. . . and the Red Death held sway over all.*)

He rubbed his lips and turned to the next page in the scrapbook. He was in the last third of it now, and for the first time he wondered consciously whose book this was, left atop the highest pile of records in the cellar.

A new headline, this one dated April 10, 1963.

LAS VEGAS GROUP BUYS FAMED COLORADO HOTEL
Scenic Overlook to Become Key Club

Robert T. Leffing, spokesman for a group of investors going under the name of High Country Investments, announced today in Las Vegas that High Country has negotiated a deal for the famous Overlook Hotel, a resort located high in the Rockies. Leffing declined to mention the names of specific investors, but said the hotel would be turned into an exclusive 'key club.' He said that the group he represents hopes to sell memberships to high-echelon executives in American and foreign companies.

High Country also owns hotels in Montana, Wyoming, and Utah.

The Overlook became world-known in the years 1946 to 1952 when it was owned by elusive mega-millionaire Horace Derwent, who . . .

The item on the next page was a mere squib, dated four months later. The Overlook had opened under its new management. Apparently the paper hadn't been able to find out or wasn't interested in who the key holders were, because no name was mentioned but High Country Investments – the most anonymous-sounding company name Jack had ever heard except for a chain of bike and appliance shops in western New England that went under the name of Business, Inc.

He turned the page and blinked down at the clipping pasted there.

MILLIONAIRE DERWENT BACK IN COLORADO VIA BACK DOOR?
High Country Exec Revealed to be Charles Grondin

By Rodney Conklin, Financial Editor

The Overlook Hotel, a scenic pleasure palace in the Colorado high country and once the private plaything of millionaire Horace Derwent, is at the center of a financial tangle which is only now beginning to come to light.

On April 10 of last year the hotel was purchased by a Las Vegas firm, High Country Investments, as a key club for wealthy executives of both foreign and domestic breeds. Now informed sources say that High Country is headed by Charles Grondin, 53, who was the head of California Land Development Corp. until 1959, when he resigned to take the position of executive veep in the Chicago home office of Derwent Enterprises.

This has led to speculation that High Country Investments may be controlled by Derwent, who may have acquired the Overlook for the second time, and under decidedly peculiar circumstances.

Grondin, who was indicted and acquitted on charges of tax evasion in 1960, could not be reached for comment, and Horace Derwent, who guards his own privacy jealously, had no comment when reached by telephone. State Representative Dick Bows of Golden has called for a complete investigation into . . .

That clipping was dated July 27, 1964. The next was a column from a

Sunday paper that September. The byline belonged to Josh Brannigar, a muck-raking investigator of the Jack Anderson breed. Jack vaguely recalled that Brannigar had died in 1968 or '69.

MAFIA FREE-ZONE IN COLORADO?

By Josh Brannigar

It now seems possible that the newest r&r spot of Organization overlords in the U.S. is located at an out-of-the-way hotel nestled in the center of the Rockies. The Overlook Hotel, a white elephant that has been run lucklessly by almost a dozen different groups and individuals since it first opened its doors in 1910, is now being operated as a security-jacketed 'key club,' ostensibly for unwinding businessmen. The question is, what business are the Overlook's key holders *really* in?

The members present during the week of August 16–23 may give us an idea. The list below was obtained by a former employee of High Country Investments, a company first believed to be a dummy company owned by Derwent Enterprises. It now seems more likely that Derwent's interest in High Country (if any) is outweighed by those of several Las Vegas gambling barons. And these same gaming honchos have been linked in the past to both suspected and convicted underworld kingpins.

Present at the Overlook during that sunny week in August were:

Charles Grondin, President of High Country Investments. When it became known in July of this year that he was running the High Country ship it was announced – considerably after the fact – that he had resigned his position in Derwent Enterprises previously. The silver-maned Grondin, who refused to talk to me for this column, has been tried once and acquitted on tax evasion charges (1960).

Charles 'Baby Charlie' Battaglia, a 60-year-old Vegas empressario (controlling interests in The Greenback and The Lucky Bones on the Strip). Battaglia is a close personal friend of Grondin. His arrest record stretches back to 1932, when he was tried and acquitted in the gang-land-style murder of Jack 'Dutchy' Morgan. Federal authorities suspect his involvement in the drug traffic, prostitution, and murder for hire, but 'Baby Charlie' has only been behind bars once, for income tax evasion in 1955–56.

Richard Scarne, the principal stockholder of Fun Time Automatic Machines. Fun Time makes slot machines for the Nevada crowd, pinball machines, and jukeboxes (Melody-Coin) for the rest of the country. He has done time for assault with a deadly weapon (1940), carrying a concealed weapon (1948), and conspiracy to commit tax fraud (1961).

Peter Zeiss, a Miami-based importer, now nearing 70. For the last five years Zeiss has been fighting deportation as an undesirable person. He has been convicted on charges of receiving and concealing stolen property (1958), and conspiracy to commit tax fraud (1954). Charming, distinguished, and courtly, Pete Zeiss is called 'Poppa' by his intimates and has been tried on charges of murder and accessory to murder. A large stockholder in Scarne's Fun Time company, he also has known interests in four Las Vegas casinos.

Vittorio Gienelli, also known as 'Vito the Chopper,' tried twice for gangland-style murders, one of them the ax-murder of Boston vice overlord Frank Scoffy. Gienelli has been indicted twenty-three times, tried fourteen times, and convicted only once, for shoplifting in 1940. It has been said that in recent years Gienelli has become a power in the organization's western operation, which is centered in Las Vegas.

Carl 'Jimmy-Ricks' Prashkin, a San Francisco investor, reputed to be the heir apparent of the power Gienelli now wields. Prashkin owns large blocks of stock in Derwent Enterprises, High Country Investments, Fun Time Automatic Machines, and three Vegas casinos. Prashkin is clean in America, but was indicted in Mexico on fraud charges that were dropped quickly three weeks after they were brought. It has been suggested that Prashkin may be in charge of laundering money skimmed from Vegas casino operations and funneling the big bucks back into the organization's legitimate western operations. And such operations may now include the Overlook Hotel in Colorado.

Other visitors during the current season include . . .

There was more but Jack only skimmed it, constantly wiping his lips with his hand. A banker with Las Vegas connections. Men from New York who were apparently doing more in the Garment District than making clothes. Men reputed to be involved with drugs, vice, robbery, murder.

God, what a story! And they had all been here, right above him, in those empty rooms. Screwing expensive whores on the third floor, maybe. Drinking magnums of champagne. Making deals that would turn over millions of dollars, maybe in the very suite of rooms where Presidents had stayed. There was a story, all right. One hell of a story. A little frantically, he took out his notebook and jotted down another memo to check all of these people out at the library in Denver when the caretaking job was over. Every hotel has its ghost? The Overlook had a whole coven of them. First suicide, then the Mafia, what next?

The next clipping was an angry denial of Brannigar's charges by Charles Grondin. Jack smirked at it.

The clipping on the next page was so large that it had been folded. Jack unfolded it and gasped harshly. The picture there seemed to leap out at him: the wallpaper had been changed since June of 1966, but he knew that window and the view perfectly well. It was the western exposure of the Presidential Suite. Murder came next. The sitting room wall by the door leading into the bedroom was splashed with blood and what could only be white flecks of brain matter. A blank-faced cop was standing over a corpse hidden by a blanket. Jack stared, fascinated, and then his eyes moved up to the headline.

GANGLAND-STYLE SHOOTING AT COLORADO HOTEL
Reputed Crime Overlord Shot at Mountain Key Club Two Others Dead

SIDEWINDER, COLO (UPI) – Forty miles from this sleepy Colorado town, a gangland-style execution has occurred in the heart of the Rocky

Mountains. The Overlook Hotel, purchased three years ago as an exclusive key club by a Las Vegas firm, was the site of a triple shotgun slaying. Two of the men were either the companions or bodyguards of Vittorio Gienelli, also known as 'The Chopper' for his reputed involvement in a Boston slaying twenty years ago.

Police were summoned by Robert Norman, manager of the Overlook, who said he heard shots and that some of the guests reported two men wearing stockings on their faces and carrying guns had fled down the fire escape and driven off in a late-model tan convertible.

State Trooper Benjamin Moorer discovered two dead men, later identified as Victor T. Boorman and Roger Macassi, both of Las Vegas, outside the door of the Presidential Suite where two American Presidents have stayed. Inside, Moorer found the body of Gienelli sprawled on the floor. Gienelli was apparently fleeing his attackers when he was cut down. Moorer said Gienelli had been shot with heavy-gauge shotguns at close range.

Charles Grondin, the representative of the company which now owns the Overlook, could not be reached for . . .

Below the clipping, in heavy strokes of a ball-point pen, someone had written: *They took his balls along with them.* Jack stared at that for a long time, feeling cold. Whose book was this?

He turned the page at last, swallowing a click in his throat. Another column from Josh Branngar, this one dated early 1967. He only read the headline: NOTORIOUS HOTEL SOLD FOLLOWING MURDER OF UNDERWORLD FIGURE.

The sheets following that clipping were blank.

(*They took his balls along with them.*)

He flipped back to the beginning, looking for a name or address. Even a room number. Because he felt quite sure that whoever had kept this little book of memories had stayed at the hotel. But there was nothing.

He was getting ready to go through all the clippings, more closely this time, when a voice called down the stairs: 'Jack? Hon?'

Wendy.

He started, almost guiltily, as if he had been drinking secretly and she would smell the fumes on him. Ridiculous. He scrubbed his lips with his hand and called back, 'Yeah, babe. Lookin for rats.'

She was coming down. He heard her on the stairs, then crossing the boiler room. Quickly, without thinking why he might be doing it, he stuffed the scrapbook under a pile of bills and invoices. He stood up as she came through the arch.

'What in the world have you been doing down here? It's almost three o'clock!'

He smiled. 'Is it that late? I got rooting around through all this stuff. Trying to find out where the bodies are buried, I guess.'

The words clanged back viciously in his mind.

She came closer, looking at him, and he unconsciously retreated a step, unable to help himself He knew what she was doing. She was trying to smell liquor on him. Probably she wasn't even aware of it herself, but he was, and it made him feel both guilty and angry.

'Your mouth is bleeding,' she said in a curiously flat tone.

'Huh?' He put his hand to his lips and winced at the thin stinging. His index finger came away bloody. His guilt increased.

'You've been rubbing your mouth again,' she said.

He looked down and shrugged. 'Yeah, I guess I have.'

'It's been hell for you, hasn't it?'

'No, not so bad.'

'Has it gotten any easier?'

He looked up at her and made his feet start moving. Once they were actually in motion it was easier. He crossed to his wife and slipped an arm around her waist. He brushed aside a sheaf of her blond hair and kissed her neck. 'Yes,' he said. 'Where's Danny?'

'Oh, he's around somewhere. It's started to cloud up outside. Hungry?'

He slipped a hand over her taut, jeans-clad bottom with counterfeit lechery. 'Like ze bear, madame.'

'Watch out, slugger. Don't start something you can't finish.'

'Fig-fig, madame?' he asked, still rubbing. 'Dirty peectures? Unnatural positions?' As they went through the arch, he threw one glance back at the box where the scrapbook

(*whose?*)

was hidden. With the light out it was only a shadow. He was relieved that he had gotten Wendy away. His lust became less acted, more natural, as they approached the stairs.

'Maybe,' she said. 'After we get you a sandwich – *yeek!*' She twisted away from him, giggling. 'That tickles!'

'It teekles nozzing like Jock Torrance would like to teekle you, madame.'

'Lay off, Jock. How about a ham and cheese . . . for the first course?'

They went up the stairs together, and Jack didn't look over his shoulder again. But he thought of Watson's words:

Every big hotel has got a ghost. Why? Hell, people come and go . . .

Then Wendy shut the basement door behind them, closing it into darkness.

Chapter Nineteen

Outside 217

Danny was remembering the words of someone else who had worked at the Overlook during the season:

Her saying she'd seen something in one of the rooms where . . . a bad thing happened. That was in Room 217 and I want you to promise me you won't go in there, Danny . . . steer right clear . . .

It was a perfectly ordinary door, no different from any other door on the first two floors of the hotel. It was dark gray, halfway down a corridor that ran at right angles to the main second-floor hallway. The numbers on the door looked no different from the house numbers on the Boulder apartment building they had lived in. A 2, a 1, and a 7. Big deal. Just below them was a tiny glass circle, a peephole. Danny had tried several of them. From the inside you got a wide, fish-eye view of the corridor. From outside you could screw up your eye seven ways to Sunday and still not see a thing. A dirty gyp.

(*Why are you here?*)

After the walk behind the Overlook, he and Mommy had come back and she had fixed him his favorite lunch, a cheese and bologna sandwich plus Campbell's Bean Soup. They ate in Dick's kitchen and talked. The radio was on, getting thin and crackly music from the Estes Park station. The kitchen was his favorite place in the hotel, and he guessed that Mommy and Daddy must feel the same way, because after trying their meals in the dining room for three days or so, they had begun eating in the kitchen by mutual consent, setting up chairs around Dick Hallorann's butcher block, which was almost as big as their dining room table back in Stovington, anyway. The dining room had been too depressing, even with the lights on and the music playing from the tape cassette system in the office. You were still just one of three people sitting at a table surrounded by dozens of other tables, all empty, all covered with those transparent plastic dustcloths. Mommy said it was like having dinner in the middle of a Horace Walpole novel, and Daddy had laughed and agreed. Danny had no idea who Horace Walpole was, but he did know that Mommy's cooking had begun to taste better as soon as they began to eat it in the kitchen. He kept discovering little flashes of Dick Hallorann's personality lying around, and they reassured him like a warm touch.

Mommy had eaten half a sandwich, no soup. She said Daddy must have gone out for a walk of his own since both the VW and the hotel truck were in the parking lot. She said she was tired and might lie down for an hour or so, if he thought he could amuse himself and not get into trouble. Danny told her around a mouthful of cheese and bologna that he thought he could.

'Why don't you go out into the playground?' she asked him. 'I thought you'd love that place, with a sandbox for your trucks and all.'

He swallowed and the food went down his throat in a lump that was dry and hard. 'Maybe I will,' he said, turning to the radio and fiddling with it.

'And all those neat hedge animals,' she said, taking his empty plate. 'Your father's got to get out and trim them pretty soon.'

'Yeah,' he said.

(*Just nasty things . . . once it had to do with those damn hedges clipped to look like animals . . .*)

'If you see your father before I do, tell him I'm lying down.'

'Sure, Mom.'

She put the dirty dishes in the sink and came back over to him. 'Are you happy here, Danny?'

He looked at her guilelessly, a milk mustache on his lip. 'Uh-huh.'

'No more bad dreams?'

'No.' Tony had come to him once, one night while he was lying in bed, calling his name faintly and from far away. Danny had squeezed his eyes tightly shut until Tony had gone.

'You sure?'

'Yes, Mom.'

She seemed satisfied. 'How's your hand?'

He flexed it for her. 'All better.'

She nodded. Jack had taken the nest under the Pyrex bowl, full of frozen wasps, out to the incinerator in back of the equipment shed and burned it. They had seen no more wasps since. He had written to a lawyer in Boulder, enclosing the snaps of Danny's hand, and the lawyer had called back two days ago – that had put Jack in a foul temper all afternoon. The lawyer doubted if the company that had manufactured the bug bomb could be sued successfully because there was only Jack to testify that he had followed directions printed on the package. Jack had asked the lawyer if they couldn't purchase some others and test them for the same defect. Yes, the lawyer said, but the results were highly doubtful even if all the test bombs malfunctioned. He told Jack of a case that involved an extension ladder company and a man who had broken his back. Wendy had commiserated with Jack, but privately she had just been glad that Danny had gotten off as cheaply as he had. It was best to leave lawsuits to people who understood them, and that did not include the Torrances. And they had seen no more wasps since.

'Go and play, doc. Have fun.'

But he hadn't had fun. He had wandered aimlessly around the hotel, poking into the maids' closets and the janitor's rooms, looking for something interesting, not finding it, a small boy padding along a dark blue carpet woven with twisting black lines. He had tried a room door from time to time, but of course they were all locked. The passkey was hanging down in the office, he knew where, but Daddy had told him he shouldn't touch that. And he didn't want to. Did he?

(*Why are you here?*)

There was nothing aimless about it after all. He had been drawn to Room 217 by a morbid kind of curiosity. He remembered a story Daddy had read to him once when he was drunk. That had been a long time ago, but the story was just as vivid now as when Daddy had read it to him. Mommy had scolded Daddy and asked what he was doing, reading a three-year-old baby something so horrible. The name of the story was *Bluebeard*. That was clear in his mind too, because he had thought at first Daddy was saying *Bluebird*, and there were no bluebirds in the story, or birds of any kind for that matter. Actually the story was about *Bluebeard*'s wife, a pretty lady that had corn-colored hair like Mommy. After *Bluebeard* married her, they lived in a big and ominous castle that was not unlike the Overlook. And every day *Bluebeard* went off to work and every day he would tell his pretty little wife not to look in a certain room, although the key to that room was hanging right on a hook, just like the passkey was hanging on the office wall downstairs. *Bluebeard*'s wife had gotten more and more curious about the locked room. She tried to peep through the keyhole the way Danny had tried to look through Room 217's peephole with similar unsatisfying results. There was even a picture of her getting down on her knees and trying to look *under* the door, but the crack wasn't wide enough. The door swung wide and . . .

The old fairy tale book had depicted her discovery in ghastly, loving detail. The image was burned on Danny's mind. The severed heads of *Bluebeard*'s seven previous wives were in the room, each one on its own pedestal, the eyes turned up to whites, the mouths unhinged and gaping in silent screams.

They were somehow balanced on necks ragged from the broadsword's decapitating swing, and there was blood running down the pedestals.

Terrified, she had turned to flee from the room and the castle, only to discover *Bluebeard* standing in the doorway, his terrible eyes blazing. 'I told you not to enter this room,' *Bluebeard* said, unsheathing his sword. 'Alas, in your curiosity you are like the other seven, and though I loved you best of all, your ending shall be as was theirs. Prepare to die, wretched woman!'

It seemed vaguely to Danny that the story had had a happy ending, but that had paled to insignificance beside the two dominant images: the taunting, maddening locked door with some great secret behind it, and the grisly secret itself, repeated more than half a dozen times. The locked door and behind it the heads, the severed heads.

His hand reached out and stroked the room's doorknob, almost furtively. He had no idea how long he had been here, standing hypnotized before the bland gray locked door.

(*And maybe three times I've thought I've seen things . . . nasty things . . .*)

But Mr Hallorann – Dick – had also said he didn't think those things could hurt you. They were like scary pictures in a book, that was all. And maybe he wouldn't see anything. On the other hand . . .

He plunged his left hand into his pocket and it came out holding the passkey. It had been there all along, of course.

He held it by the square metal tab on the end which had OFFICE printed on it in Magic Marker. He twirled the key on its chain, watching it go around and around. After several minutes of this he stopped and slipped the passkey into the lock. It slid in smoothly, with no hitch, as if it had wanted to be there all along.

(*I've thought I've seen things . . . nasty things . . . promise me you won't go in there.*)

(*I promise.*)

And a promise was, of course, very important. Still, his curiosity itched at him as maddeningly as poison ivy in a place you aren't supposed to scratch. But it was a dreadful kind of curiosity, the kind that makes you peek through your fingers during the scariest parts of a scary movie. What was beyond that door would be no movie.

(*I don't think those things can hurt you . . . like scary pictures in a book . . .*)

Suddenly he reached out with his left hand, not sure of what it was going to do until it had removed the passkey and stuffed it back into his pocket. He stared at the door a moment longer, blue-gray eyes wide, then turned quickly and walked back down the corridor toward the main hallway that ran at right angles to the corridor he was in.

Something made him pause there and he wasn't sure what for a moment. Then he remembered that directly around this corner, on the way back to the stairs, there was one of those old-fashioned fire extinguishers curled up against the wall. Curled there like a dozing snake.

They weren't chemical-type extinguishers at all, Daddy said, although there were several of those in the kitchen. These were the forerunner of the modern sprinkler systems. The long canvas hoses hooked directly into the Overlook's plumbing system, and by turning a single valve you could become a one-man fire department. Daddy said that the chemical extinguishers, which sprayed foam or CO_2, were much better. The chemicals smothered fires, took away the oxygen they needed to burn, while a high-pressure spray might just spread the flames around. Daddy said that Mr Ullman should replace the old-fashioned hoses right along with the old-fashioned boiler, but Mr Ullman would probably do neither because he was a CHEAP PRICK. Danny knew that this was one of the worst epithets his father could summon. It was applied to certain doctors, dentists, and appliance repairmen, and also to the head of his English Department at Stovington, who had disallowed some of Daddy's book orders because he said the books would put them over budget. 'Over budget, hell,' he had fumed to Wendy – Danny had been listening from his bedroom where he was supposed to be asleep. 'He's just saving the last five hundred bucks for himself, the CHEAP PRICK.'

Danny looked around the corner.

The extinguisher was there, a flat hose folded back a dozen times on itself, the red tank attached to the wall. Above it was an ax in a glass case like a museum exhibit, with white words printed on a red background: IN CASE OF EMERGENCY, BREAK GLASS. Danny could read the word EMERGENCY, which was also the name of one of his favorite TV shows, but was unsure of the rest. But he didn't like the way the word was used in connection with that long flat hose. EMERGENCY was fire, explosions, car crashes, hospitals, sometimes death. And he didn't like the way that hose hung so blandly on the wall. When he was alone, he always skittered past these extinguishers as fast as he could. No particular reason. It just felt better to go fast. It felt safer.

Now, heart thumping loudly in his chest, he came around the corner and looked down the hall past the extinguisher to the stairs. Mommy was down there, sleeping. And if Daddy was back from his walk, he would probably be sitting in the kitchen, eating a sandwich and reading a book. He would just walk right past that old extinguisher and go downstairs.

He started toward it, moving closer to the far wall until his right arm was brushing the expensive silk paper. Twenty steps away. Fifteen. A dozen.

When he was ten steps away, the brass nozzle suddenly rolled off the fat loop it had been lying

(sleeping?)

on and fell to the hall carpet with a dull thump. It lay there, the dark bore of its muzzle pointing at Danny. He stopped immediately, his shoulders twitching forward with the suddenness of his scare. His blood thumped thickly in his ears and temples. His mouth had gone dry and sour, his hands curled into fists. Yet the nozzle of the hose only lay there, its brass casing glowing mellowly, a loop of flat canvas leading back up to the red-painted frame bolted to the wall.

So it had fallen off, so what? It was only a fire extinguisher, nothing else. It was stupid to think that it looked like some poison snake from 'Wide World of Animals' that had heard him and woken up. Even if the stitched canvas did look a little bit like scales. He would just step over it and go down the hall to the stairs, walking a little bit fast, maybe, to make sure it didn't snap out after him and curl around his foot . . .

He wiped his lips with his left hand, in unconscious imitation of his father, and took a step forward. No movement from the hose. Another step. Nothing. There, see how stupid you are? You got all worked up thinking about that dumb room and that dumb *Bluebeard* story and that hose was probably ready to fall off for the last five years. That's all.

Danny stared at the hose on the floor and thought of wasps.

Eight steps away, the nozzle of the hose gleamed peacefully at him from the rug as if to say: *Don't worry. I'm just a hose, that's all. And even if that isn't all, what I do to you won't be much worse than a bee sting. Or a wasp sting. What would I want to do to a nice little boy like you . . . except bite . . . and bite . . . and bite?*

Danny took another step, and another. His breath was dry and harsh in his throat. Panic was close now. He began to wish the hose *would* move, then at last he would know, he would be sure. He took another step and now he was within striking distance. But it's not going to *strike* at you, he thought hysterically. How can it *strike* at you, *bite* at you, when it's just a hose?

Maybe it's full of wasps.

His internal temperature plummeted to ten below zero. He stared at the black bore in the center of the nozzle, nearly hypnotized. Maybe it *was* full of wasps, secret wasps, their brown bodies bloated with poison, so full of autumn poison that it dripped from their stingers in clear drops of fluid.

Suddenly he knew that he was nearly frozen with terror; if he did not make his feet go now, they would become locked to the carpet and he would stay here, staring at the black hole in the center of the brass nozzle like a bird staring at a snake, he would stay here until his daddy found him and then what would happen?

With a high moan, he made himself run. As he reached the hose, some trick of the light made the nozzle seem to move, to revolve as if to strike, and he leaped high in the air above it; in his panicky state it seemed that his legs pushed him nearly all the way to the ceiling, that he could feel the stiff back hairs that formed his cowlick brushing the hallway's plaster ceiling, although later he knew that couldn't have been so.

He came down on the other side of the hose and ran, and suddenly he heard it behind him, coming for him, the soft dry whicker of that brass snake's head as it slithered rapidly along the carpet after him like a rattlesnake moving swiftly through a dry field of grass. It was coming for him, and suddenly the stairs seemed very far away; they seemed to retreat a running step into the distance for each running step he took toward them.

Daddy! he tried to scream, but his closed throat would not allow a word to pass. He was on his own. Behind him the sound grew louder, the dry sliding sound of the snake, slipping swiftly over the carpet's dry hackles. At his heels now, perhaps rising up with the clear poison dribbling from its brass snout.

Danny reached the stairs and had to pinwheel his arms crazily for balance. For one moment it seemed sure that he would cartwheel over and go head-for-heels to the bottom.

He threw a glance back over his shoulder.

The hose had not moved. It lay as it had lain, one loop off the frame, the brass nozzle on the hall floor, the nozzle pointing disinterestedly away from him. You see, stupid? he berated himself. You made it all up, scaredy-cat. It was all your imagination, scaredy-cat, scaredy-cat.

He clung to the stairway railing, his legs trembling in reaction.

(*It never chased you*)

his mind told him, and seized on that thought, and played it back.

(*never chased you, never chased you, never did, never did*)

It was nothing to be afraid of. Why, he could go back and put that hose right into its frame, if he wanted to. He could, but he didn't think he would. Because what if it had chased him and had gone back when it saw that it couldn't . . . quite . . . catch him?

The hose lay on the carpet, almost seeming to ask him if he would like to come back and try again.

Panting, Danny ran downstairs.

Chapter Twenty

Talking to Mr Ullman

The Sidewinder Public library was a small, retiring building one block down from the town's business area. It was a modest, vine-covered building, and the wide concrete walk up to the door was lined with the corpses of last summer's flowers. On the lawn was a large bronze statue of a Civil War general Jack had never heard of, although he had been something of a Civil War buff in his teenage years.

The newspaper files were kept downstairs. They consisted of the Sidewinder *Gazette* that had gone bust in 1963, the Estes Park daily, and the Boulder *Camera*. No Denver papers at all.

Sighing, Jack settled for the *Camera*.

When the files reached 1965, the actual newspapers were replaced by spools of microfilm ('A federal grant,' the librarian told him brightly. 'We hope to do 1958 to '64 when the next check comes through, but they're so slow, aren't they? You will be careful, won't you? I just know you will. Call if you need me.'). The only reading machine had a lens that had somehow gotten warped, and by the time Wendy put her hand on his shoulder forty-five minutes after he had switched from the actual papers, he had a juicy thumper of a headache.

'Danny's in the park,' she said, 'but I don't want him outside too long. How much longer do you think you'll be?'

'Ten minutes,' he said. Actually he had traced down the last of the Overlook's fascinating history – the years between the gangland shooting and the takeover by Stuart Ullman & Co. But he felt the same reticence about telling Wendy.

'What are you up to, anyway?' she asked. She ruffled his hair as she said it, but her voice was only half-teasing.

'Looking up some old Overlook history,' he said.

'Any particular reason?'

'No,

(*and why the hell are you so interested anyway?*)

just curiosity.'

'Find anything interesting?'

'Not much,' he said, having to strive to keep his voice pleasant now. She was prying, just the way she had always pried and poked at him when they had been at Stovington and Danny was still a crib-infant. *Where are you going, Jack? When will you be back? How much money do you have with you? Are you going to take the car? Is Al going to be with you? Will one of you stay sober?* On and on. She had, pardon the expression, driven him to drink. Maybe that hadn't been the only reason, but by Christ let's tell the truth here and admit it was one of them. Nag and nag and nag until you wanted to clout her one just to shut her up and stop the

(*Where? When? How? Are you? Will you?*)

endless flow of questions. It could give you a real

(*headache? hangover?*)

headache. The reader. The damned reader with its distorted print. That was why he had such a cunt of a headache.

'Jack, are you all right? You look pale—'

He snapped his head away from her fingers. '*I am fine!*'

She recoiled from his hot eyes and tried on a smile that was a size too small. 'Well . . . if you are . . . I'll just go and wait in the park with Danny . . .' She was starting away now, her smile dissolving into a bewildered expression of hurt.

He called to her: 'Wendy?'

She looked back from the foot of the stairs. 'What Jack?'

He got up and went over to her. 'I'm sorry, babe. I guess I'm really not all right. That machine . . . the lens is distorted. I've got a really bad headache. Got any aspirin?'

'Sure.' She pawed in her purse and came up with a tin of Anacin. 'You keep them.'

He took the tin. 'No Excedrin?' He saw the small recoil on her face and understood. It had been a bitter sort of joke between them at first, before the drinking had gotten too bad for jokes. He had claimed that Excedrin was the only nonprescription drug ever invented that could stop a hangover dead in its tracks. Absolutely the only one. He had begun to think of his morning-after thumpers as Excedrin Headache Number Vat 69.

'No Excedrin,' she said. 'Sorry.'

'That's okay,' he said, 'these'll do just fine.' But of course they wouldn't, and she should have known it, too. At times she could be the stupidest bitch . . .

'Want some water?' she asked brightly.

(*No I just want you to GET THE FUCK OUT OF HERE!*)

'I'll get some at the drinking fountain when I go up. Thanks.'

'Okay.' She started up the stairs, good legs moving gracefully under a short tan wool skirt. 'We'll be in the park.'

'Right.' He slipped the tin of Anacin absently into his pocket, went back to the reader, and turned it off. When he was sure she was gone, he went upstairs himself. God, but it was a lousy headache. If you were going to have a vise-gripper like this one, you ought to at least be allowed the pleasure of a few drinks to balance it off.

He tried to put the thought from his mind, more ill tempered than ever.

He went to the main desk, fingering a matchbook cover with a telephone number on it.

'Ma'am, do you have a pay telephone?'

'No, sir, but you can use mine if it's local.'

'It's long-distance, sorry.'

'Well then, I guess the drugstore would be your best bet. They have a booth.'

'Thanks.'

He went out and down the walk, past the anonymous Civil War general. He began to walk toward the business block, hands stuffed in his pockets, head thudding like a leaden bell. The sky was also leaden; it was November 7, and with the new month the weather had become threatening. There had been a number of snow flurries. There had been snow in October too, but that had melted. The new flurries had stayed, a light frosting over everything – it sparkled in the sunlight like fine crystal. But there had been no sunlight today, and even as he reached the drugstore it began to spit snow again.

The phone booth was at the back of the building, and he was halfway down an aisle of patent medicines, jingling his change in his pocket, when his eyes fell on the white boxes with their green print. He took one of them to the cashier, paid, and went back to the telephone booth. He pulled the door closed, put his change and matchbook cover on the counter, and dialed O.

'Your call, please?'

'Fort Lauderdale, Florida, operator.' He gave her the number there and the number in the booth. When she told him it would be a dollar ninety for the first three minutes he dropped eight quarters into the slot, wincing each time the bell bonged in his ear.

Then, left in limbo with only the faraway clickings and gabblings of connection-making, he took the green bottle of Excedrin out of its box, pried up the white cap, and dropped the wad of cotton batting to the floor of the booth. Cradling the phone receiver between his ear and shoulder, he shook out three of the white tablets and lined them up on the counter beside his remaining change. He recapped the bottle and put it in his pocket.

At the other end, the phone was picked up on the first ring.

'Surf-Sand Resort, how may we help you?' the perky female voice asked.

'I'd like to speak with the manager, please.'

'Do you mean Mr Trent or—'

'I mean Mr Ullman.'

'I believe Mr Ullman is busy, but if you would like me to check—'

'I would. Tell him it's Jack Torrance calling from Colorado.'

'One moment, please.' She put him on hold.

Jack's dislike for that cheap, self-important little prick Ullman came flooding back. He took one of the Excedrins from the counter, regarded it for a moment, then put it into his mouth and began to chew it, slowly and with relish. The taste flooded back like memory, making his saliva squirt in mingled pleasure and unhappiness. A dry, bitter taste, but a compelling one. He swallowed with a grimace. Chewing aspirin had been a habit with him in his drinking days; he hadn't done it at all since then. But when your headache was bad enough, a hangover headache or one like this one, chewing them seemed to make them get to work quicker. He had read somewhere that chewing aspirin could become addictive. Where had he read that, anyway? Frowning he tried to think. And then Ullman came on the line.

'Torrance? What's the trouble?'

'No trouble,' he said. 'The boiler's okay and I haven't even gotten around to murdering my wife yet. I'm saving that until after the holidays, when things get dull.'

'Very funny. Why are you calling? I'm a busy—'

'Busy man, yes, I understand that. I'm calling about some things that you didn't tell me during your history of the Overlook's great and honorable past. Like how Horace Derwent sold it to a bunch of Las Vegas sharpies who dealt it through so many dummy corporations that not even the IRS knew who really owned it. About how they waited until the time was right and then turned it into a playground for Mafia bigwigs, and about how it had to be shut down in 1966 when one of them got a little bit dead. Along with his bodyguards, who were standing outside the door to the Presidential Suite. Great place, the Overlook's Presidential Suite. Wilson, Harding, Roosevelt, Nixon, and Vito the Chopper, right?'

There was a moment of surprised silence on the other end of the line, and then Ullman said quietly: 'I don't see how that can have any bearing on your job, Mr Torrance. It—'

'The best part happened after Gienelli was shot, though, don't you think? Two more quick shuffles, now you see it and now you don't, and then the Overlook is suddenly owned by a private citizen, a woman named Sylvia Hunter . . . who just happened to be Sylvia Hunter Derwent from 1942 to 1948.'

'Your three minutes are up,' the operator said. 'Signal when through.'

'My dear Mr Torrance, all of this is public knowledge . . . and ancient history.'

'It formed no part of my knowledge,' Jack said. 'I doubt if many other people know it, either. Not all of it. They remember the Gienelli shooting maybe, but I doubt if anybody has put together all the wondrous and strange shuffles the Overlook has been through since 1945. And it always seems like Derwent or a Derwent associate comes up with the door prize. What was Sylvia Hunter running up there in '67 and '68, Mr Ullman? It was a whorehouse, wasn't it?'

'*Torrance!*' His shock crackled across two thousand miles of telephone cable without losing a thing.

Smiling, Jack popped another Excedrin into his mouth and chewed it.

'She sold out after a rather well known U.S. senator died of a heart attack up there. There were rumors that he was found naked except for black nylon stockings and a garter belt and a pair of high-heeled pumps. Patent-leather pumps, as a matter of fact.'

'That's a vicious, damnable lie!' Ullman cried.

'Is it?' Jack asked. He was beginning to feel better. The headache was draining away. He took the last Excedrin and chewed it up, enjoying the bitter, powdery taste as the tablet shredded in his mouth.

'It was a very unfortunate occurence,' Ullman said. 'Now what is the point, Torrance? If you're planning to write some ugly smear article . . . if this is some ill-conceived, stupid blackmail idea . . .'

'Nothing of the sort,' Jack said. 'I called because I didn't think you played square with me. And because—'

'Didn't play *square*?' Ullman cried. 'My God, did you think I was going to share a large pile of dirty laundry with the hotel's *caretaker*? Who in heaven's name do you think you are? And how could those old stories possibly affect you anyway? Or do you think there are ghosts parading up and down the halls of the west wing wearing bedsheets and crying "Woe!"?'

'No, I don't think there are any ghosts. But you raked up a lot of my personal history before you gave me the job. You had me on the carpet, quizzing me about my ability to take care of your hotel like a boy in front of the teacher's desk for peeing in the coatroom. You embarrassed me.'

'I just do not believe your cheek, your bloody damned impertinence,' Ullman said. He sounded as if he might be choking. 'I'd like to sack you. And perhaps I will.'

'I think Al Shockley might object. Strenuously.'

'And I think you may have finally overestimated Mr Shockley's commitment to you, Mr Torrance.'

For a moment Jack's headache came back in all its thudding glory, and he closed his eyes against the pain. As if from a distance away he heard himself ask: 'Who owns the Overlook now? Is it still Derwent Enterprises? Or are you too smallfry to know?'

'I think that will do, Mr Torrance. You are an employee of the hotel, no different from a busboy or a kitchen pot scrubber. I have no intention of—'

'Okay, I'll write Al,' Jack said. 'He'll know; after all, he's on the Board of Directors. And I might just add a little P.S. to the effect that—'

'Derwent doesn't own it.'

'What? I couldn't quite make that out.'

'I said Derwent doesn't own it. The stockholders are all Easterners. Your friend Mr Shockley owns the largest block of stock himself, better than thirty-five per cent. You would know better than I if he has any ties to Derwent.'

'Who else?'

'I have no intention of divulging the names of the other stockholders to you, Mr Torrance. I intend to bring this whole matter to the attention of—'

'One other question.'

'I am under no obligation to you.'

'Most of the Overlook's history – savory and unsavory alike – I found in a scrapbook that was in the cellar. Big thing with white leather covers. Gold thread for binding. Do you have any idea whose scrapbook that might be?'

'None at all.'

'Is it possible it could have belonged to Grady? The caretaker who killed himself?'

'Mr Torrance,' Ullman said in tones of deepest frost, 'I am by no means sure that Mr Grady could read, let alone dig out the rotten apples you have been wasting my time with.'

'I'm thinking of writing a book about the Overlook Hotel. I thought if I actually got through it, the owner of the scrapbook would like to have an acknowledgment at the front.'

'I think writing a book about the Overlook would be very unwise,' Ullman said. 'Especially a book done from your . . . uh, point of view.'

'Your opinion doesn't surprise me.' His headache was all gone now. There had been that one flash of pain, and that was all. His mind felt sharp and accurate, all the way down to millimeters. It was the way he usually felt only when the writing was going extremely well or when he had a three-drink buzz on. That was another thing he had forgotten about Excedrin; he didn't know if it worked for others, but for him crunching three tablets was like an instant high.

Now he said: 'What you'd like is some sort of commissioned guidebook that you could hand out free to the guests when they checked in. Something with a lot of glossy photos of the mountains at sunrise and sunset and a lemon-meringue text to go with it. Also a section on the colorful people who have stayed there, of course excluding the really colorful ones like Gienelli and his friends.'

'If I felt I could fire you and be a hundred per cent certain of my own job instead of just ninety-five per cent,' Ullman said in clipped, strangled tones, 'I would fire you right this minute, over the telephone. But since I feel that five per cent of uncertainty, I intend to call Mr Shockley the moment you're off the line . . . which will be soon, or so I devoutly hope.'

Jack said, 'There isn't going to be anything in the book that isn't true, you know. There's no need to dress it up.'

(*Why are you baiting him? Do you want to be fired?*)

'I don't care if Chapter Five is about the Pope of Rome screwing the shade of the Virgin Mary,' Ullman said, his voice rising. 'I want you out of my hotel!'

'*It's not your hotel!*' Jack screamed, and slammed the receiver into its cradle.

He sat on the stool breathing hard, a little scared now,

(a little? hell, a lot)

wondering why in the name of God he had called Ullman in the first place.

(*You lost your temper again, Jack.*)

Yes. Yes, he had. No sense trying to deny it. And the hell of it was, he had no idea how much influence that cheap little prick had over Al, no more than he knew how much bullshit Al would take from him in the name of auld land syne. If Ullman was as good as he claimed to be, and if he gave Al a he-goes-or-I-go ultimatum, might not Al be forced to take it? He closed his eyes and tried to imagine telling Wendy. Guess what, babe? I lost another job. This time I had to go through two thousand miles of Bell Telephone cable to find someone to punch out, but I managed it.

He opened his eyes and wiped his mouth with his handkerchief. He wanted a drink. Hell, he *needed* one. There was a café just down the street, surely he had time for a quick beer on his way up to the park, just one to lay the dust . . .

He clenched his hands together helplessly.

The question recurred: Why had he called Ullman in the first place? The number of the Surf-Sand in Lauderdale had been written in a small notebook by the phone and the CB radio in the office – plumbers' numbers, carpenters, glaziers, electricians, others. Jack had copied it onto the matchbook cover shortly after getting out of bed, the idea of calling Ullman fullblown and gleeful in his mind. But to what purpose? Once, during the drinking phase,

Wendy had accused him of desiring his own destruction but not possessing the necessary moral fiber to support a full-blown deathwish. So he manufactured ways in which other people could do it, lopping a piece at a time off himself and their family. Could it be true? Was he afraid somewhere inside that the Overlook might be just what he needed to finish his play and generally collect up his shit and get it together? Was he blowing the whistle on himself? Please God no, don't let it be that way. Please.

He closed his eyes and an image immediately arose on the darkened screen of his inner lids: sticking his hand through that hole in the shingles to pull out the rotted flashing, the sudden needling sting, his own agonized, startled cry in the still and unheeding air: *Oh you goddamn fucking son of a bitch . . .*

Replaced with an image two years earlier, himself stumbling into the house at three in the morning, drunk, falling over a table and sprawling full-length on the floor, cursing, waking Wendy up on the couch. Wendy turning on the light, seeing his clothes ripped and smeared from some cloudy parking-lot scuffle that had occurred at a vaguely remembered honky-tonk just over the New Hampshire border hours before, crusted blood under his nose, now looking up at his wife, blinking stupidly in the light like a mole in the sunshine, and Wendy saying dully, *You son of a bitch, you woke Danny up. If you don't care about yourself, can't you care a little bit about us? Oh, why do I even bother talking to you?*

The telephone rang, making him jump. He snatched it off the cradle, illogically sure it must be either Ullman or Al Shockley. 'What?' he barked.

'Your overtime, sir. Three dollars and fifty cents.'

'I'll have to break some ones,' he said. 'Wait a minute.'

He put the phone on the shelf, deposited his last six quarters, then went out to the cashier to get more. He performed the transaction automatically, his mind running in a single closed circle like a squirrel on an exercise wheel.

Why had he called Ullman?

Because Ullman had embarrassed him? He had been embarrassed before, and by real masters – the Grand Master, of course, being himself. Simply to crow at the man, expose his hypocrisy? Jack didn't think he was that petty. His mind tried to seize on the scrapbook as a valid reason, but that wouldn't hold water either. The chances of Ullman knowing who the owner was were no more than two in a thousand. At the interview, he had treated the cellar as another country – a nasty underdeveloped one at that. If he had really wanted to know, he would have called Watson, whose winter number was also in the office notebook. Even Watson would not have been a sure thing, but surer than Ullman.

And telling him about the book idea, that had been another stupid thing. Incredibly stupid. Besides jeopardizing his job, he could be closing off wide channels of information once Ullman called around and told people to beware of New Englanders bearing questions about the Overlook Hotel. He could have done his researches quietly, mailing off polite letters, perhaps even arranging some interviews in the spring . . . and then laughed up his sleeve at Ullman's rage when the book came out and he was safely away – The Masked Author Strikes Again. Instead he had made that damned senseless call, lost his temper, antagonized Ullman, and brought out all of the hotel manager's Little Caesar tendencies. Why? If it wasn't an effort to get himself thrown out of the good job Al had snagged for him, then what was it?

He deposited the rest of the money in the slots and hung up the phone. It really was the senseless kind of thing he might have done if he had been drunk. But he had been sober; dead cold sober.

Walking out of the drugstore he crunched another Excedrin into his mouth, grimacing yet relishing the bitter taste.

On the walk outside he met Wendy and Danny.

'Hey we were just coming after you,' Wendy said. 'Snowing, don't you know.'

Jack blinked up. 'So it is.' It was snowing hard. Sidewinder's main street was already heavily powdered, the center line obscured. Danny had his head tilted up to the white sky, his mouth open and his tongue out to catch some of the fat flakes drifting down.

'Do you think this is it?' Wendy asked.

Jack shrugged. 'I don't know. I was hoping for another week or two of grace. We still might get it.'

Grace, that was it.

(*I'm sorry, Al. Grace, your mercy. For your mercy. One more chance. I am heartily sorry—*)

How many times, over how many years, had he – a grown man – asked for the mercy of another chance? He was suddenly so sick of himself, so revolted, that he could have groaned aloud.

'How's your headache?' She asked, studying him closely.

He put an arm around her and hugged her tight. 'Better. Come on, you two, let's go home while we still can.'

They walked back to where the hotel truck was slant-parked against the curb, Jack in the middle, his left arm around Wendy's shoulders, his right hand holding Danny's hand. He had called it home for the first time, for better or worse.

As he got behind the truck's wheel it occurred to him that while he was fascinated by the Overlook, he didn't much like it. He wasn't sure it was good for either his wife or his son or himself. Maybe that was why he had called Ullman.

To be fired while there was still time.

He backed the truck out of its parking space and headed them out of town and up into the mountains.

Chapter Twenty-one

Night Thoughts

It was ten o'clock. Their quarters were filled with counterfeit sleep.

Jack lay on his side facing the wall, eyes open, listening to Wendy's slow and regular breathing. The taste of dissolved aspirin was still on his tongue, making it feel rough and slightly numb. Al Shockley had called at quarter of six, quarter of eight back East. Wendy had been downstairs with Danny, sitting in front of the lobby fireplace and reading.

'Person to person,' the operator said, 'for Mr Jack Torrance.'

'Speaking.' He had switched the phone to his right hand, had dug his handkerchief out of his back pocket with his left, and had wiped his tender lips with it. Then he lit a cigarette.

Al's voice then, strong in his ear: 'Jacky-boy, what in the name of God are you up to?'

'Hi, Al.' He snuffed the cigarette and groped for the Excedrin bottle.

'What's going on, Jack? I got this *weird* phone call from Stuart Ullman this afternoon. And when Stu Ullman calls long-distance out of his own pocket, you know the shit has hit the fan.'

'Ullman has nothing to worry about, Al. Neither do you.'

'What exactly is the nothing we don't have to worry about? Stu made it sound like a cross between blackmail and a *National Enquirer* feature on the Overlook. Talk to me, boy.'

'I wanted to poke him a little,' Jack said. 'When I came up here to be interviewed, he had to drag out all my dirty laundry. Drinking problem. Lost your last job for racking over a student. Wonder if you're the right man for this. Et cetera. The thing that bugged me was that he was bringing all this up because he loved the goddamn hotel so much. The beautiful Overlook. The traditional Overlook. The bloody sacred Overlook. Well, I found a scrapbook in the basement. Somebody had put together all the less savory aspects of Ullman's cathedral, and it looked to me like a little black mass had been going on after hours.'

'I hope that's metaphorical, Jack.' Al's voice sounded frighteningly cold.

'It is. But I did find out—'

'I know the hotel's history.'

Jack ran a hand through his hair. 'So I called him up and poked him with it. I admit it wasn't very bright, and I sure wouldn't do it again. End of story.'

'Stu says you're planning to do a little dirty-laundry-airing yourself.'

'Stu is an asshole!' he barked into the phone. 'I told him I had an idea of writing about the Overlook, yes. I do. I think this place forms an index of the whole post-World War II American character. That sounds like an inflated claim, stated so baldly . . . I know it does . . . but it's all here, Al!

My God, it could be a *great* book. But it's far in the future, I can promise you that, I've got more on my plate right now than I can eat, and—'

'Jack, that's not good enough.'

He found himself gaping at the black receiver of the phone, unable to believe what he had surely heard. 'What? Al, did you say—?'

'I said what I said. How long is far in the future, Jack? For you it may be two years, maybe five. For me it's thirty or forty, because I expect to be associated with the Overlook for a long time. The thought of you doing some sort of a scum-job on my hotel and passing it off as a great piece of American writing, that makes me sick.'

Jack was speechless.

'I tried to help you, Jacky-boy. We went through the war together, and I thought I owed you some help. You remember the war?'

'I remember it,' he muttered, but the coals of resentment had begun to glow around his heart. First Ullman, then Wendy, now Al. What was this? National Let's Pick Jack Torrance Apart Week? He clamped his lips more tightly together, reached for his cigarettes, and knocked them off onto the floor. Had he ever liked this cheap prick talking to him from his mahogany-lined den in Vermont? Had he really?

'Before you hit that Hatfield kid,' Al was saying, 'I had talked the Board out of letting you go and even had them swung around to considering tenure. You blew that one for yourself. I got you this hotel thing, a nice quiet place for you to get yourself together, finish your play, and wait it out until Harry Effinger and I could convince the rest of those guys that they made a big mistake. Now it looks like you want to chew my arm off on your way to a bigger killing. Is that the way you say thanks to your friends, Jack?'

'No,' he whispered.

He didn't dare say more. His head was throbbing with the hot, acid-etched words that wanted to get out. He tried desperately to think of Danny and Wendy, depending on him, Danny and Wendy sitting peacefully downstairs in front of the fire and working on the first of the second-grade reading primers, thinking everything was A-OK. If he lost this job, what then? Off to California in that tired old VW with the disintegrating fuel pump like a family of dustbowl Okies? He told himself he would get down on his knees and beg Al before he let that happen, but still the words struggled to pour out, and the hand holding the hot wires of his rage felt greased.

'What?' Al said sharply.

'No,' he said. 'That is not the way I treat my friends. And you know it.'

'How do I know it? At the worst, you're planning to smear my hotel by digging up bodies that were decently buried years ago. At the best, you call up my temperamental but extremely competent hotel manager and work him into a frenzy as part of some . . . some stupid kid's game.'

'It was more than a game, Al. It's easier for you. You don't have to take some rich friend's charity. You don't need a friend in court because you *are* the court. The fact that you were one step from a brown-bag lush goes pretty much unmentioned, doesn't it?'

'I suppose it does,' Al said. His voice had dropped a notch and he sounded tired of the whole thing. 'But Jack, Jack . . . I can't help that. I can't change that.'

'I know,' Jack said emptily. 'Am I fired? I guess you better tell me if I am.'

'Not if you'll do two things for me.'

'All right.'

'Hadn't you better hear the conditions before you accept them?'

'No. Give me your deal and I'll take it. There's Wendy and Danny to think about. If you want my balls, I'll send them airmail.'

'Are you sure selfpity is a luxury you can afford, Jack?'

He had closed his eyes and slid an Excedrin between his dry lips. 'At this point I feel it's the only one I can afford. Fire away . . . no pun intended.'

Al was silent for a moment. Then he said: 'First, no more calls to Ullman. Not even if the place burns down. If that happens, call the maintenance man, that guy who swears all the time, you know who I mean . . .'

'Watson.'

'Yes.'

'Okay. Done.'

'Second, you promise me, Jack. Word of honor. No book about a famous Colorado mountain hotel with a history.'

For a moment his rage was so great that he literally could not speak. The blood beat loudly in his ears. It was like getting a call from some twentieth-century Medici prince . . . no portraits of my family with their warts showing, please, or back to the rabble you'll go. I subsidize no pictures but pretty pictures. When you paint the daughter of my good friend and business partner, please omit birthmark or back to the rabble you'll go. Of course we're friends . . . we are both civilized men aren't we? We've shared bed and board and bottle. We'll always be friends, and the dog collar I have on you will always be ignored by mutual consent, and I'll take good and benevolent care of you. All I ask in return is your soul. Small item. We can even ignore the fact that you've handed it over, the way we ignore the dog collar. Remember, my talented friend, there are Michelangelos begging everywhere in the streets of Rome . . .

'Jack? You there?'

He made a strangled noise that was intended to be the word yes.

Al's voice was firm and very sure of itself. 'I really don't think I'm asking so much, Jack. And there will be other books. You just can't expect me to subsidize you while you . . .'

'All right, agreed.'

'I don't want you to think I'm trying to control your artistic life, Jack. You know me better than that. It's just that—'

'Al?'

'What?'

'Is Derwent still involved with the Overlook? Somehow?'

'I don't see how that can possibly be any concern of yours, Jack.'

'No,' he said distantly. 'I suppose it isn't. Listen Al, I think I hear Wendy calling me for something. I'll get back to you.'

'Sure thing, Jacky-boy. We'll have a good talk. How are things? Dry?'

(YOU'VE GOT YOUR POUND OF FLESH BLOOD AND ALL NOW CAN'T YOU LEAVE ME ALONE?)

'As a bone.'

'Here too. I'm actually beginning to enjoy sobriety. If—'

'I'll get back, Al. Wendy—'

'Sure. Okay.'

And so he had hung up and that was when the cramps had come, hitting him like lightning bolts, making him curl up in front of the telephone like a penitent, hands over his belly, head throbbing like a monstrous bladder.

The moving wasp, having stung, moves on . . .

It had passed a little when Wendy came upstairs and asked him who had been on the phone.

'Al,' he said. 'He called to ask how things were going. I said they were fine.'

'Jack, you look terrible. Are you sick?'

'Headache's back. I'm going to bed early. No sense trying to write.'

'Can I get you some warm milk?'

He smiled wanly. 'That would be nice.'

And now he lay beside her, feeling her warm and sleeping thigh against his own. Thinking of the conversation with Al, how he had groveled, still made him hot and cold by turns. Someday there would be a reckoning. Someday there would be a book, not the soft and thoughtful thing he had first considered, but a gem-hard work of research, photo section and all, and he would pull apart the entire Overlook history, nasty, incestuous ownership deals and all. He would spread it all out for the reader like a dissected crayfish. And if Al Shockley had connections with the Derwent empire, then God help him.

Strung up like piano wire, he lay staring into the dark, knowing it might be hours yet before he could sleep.

Wendy Torrance lay on her back, eyes closed, listening to the sound of her husband's slumber – the long inhale, the brief hold, the slightly guttural exhale. Where did he go when he slept, she wondered. To some amusement park, a Great Barrington of dreams where all the rides were free and there was no wife-mother along to tell them they'd had enough hotdogs or that they'd better be going if they wanted to get home by dark? Or was it some fathoms-deep bar where the drinking never stopped and the batwings were always propped open and all the old companions were gathered around the electronic hockey game, glasses in hand, Al Shockley prominent among them with his tie loosened and the top button of his shirt undone? A place where both she and Danny were excluded and the boogie went on endlessly?

Wendy was worried about him, the old, helpless worry that she had hoped was behind her forever in Vermont, as if worry could somehow not cross state lines. She didn't like what the Overlook seemed to be doing to Jack and Danny.

The most frightening thing, vaporous and unmentioned, perhaps unmentionable, was that all of Jack's drinking symptoms had come back, one by one . . . all but the drink itself. The constant wiping of the lips with hand or handkerchief, as if to rid them of excess moisture. Long pauses at the typewriter, more balls of paper in the wastebasket. There had been a bottle of Excedrin on the telephone table tonight after Al had called him, but no water glass. He had been chewing them again. He got irritated over little things. He would unconsciously start snapping his fingers in a nervous rhythm when things got too quiet. Increased profanity. She had begun to worry about his temper, too. It would almost come as a relief if he would lose it, blow off steam, in much the same way that he went down to the basement first thing in the morning and last thing at night to dump the press on the boiler. It would almost be good to see him curse and kick a chair across the room or slam a door. But those things, always an integral part of his temperament, had almost wholly ceased. Yet she had the feeling that Jack was more and more often angry with her or Danny, but was refusing to let it out. The boiler had a pressure gauge: old, cracked, clotted with grease, but still workable. Jack had none. She had never been able to read him very well. Danny could, but Danny wasn't talking.

And the call from Al. At about the same time it had come, Danny had lost all interest in the story they had been reading. He left her to sit by the fire and crossed to the main desk where Jack had constructed a roadway for his matchbox cars and trucks. The Violent Violet Volkswagen was there and Danny had begun to push it rapidly back and forth. Pretending to read her own book but actually looking at Danny over the top of it, she had seen an odd amalgam of the ways she and Jack expressed anxiety. The wiping of the lips. Running both hands nervously through his hair, as she had done while waiting for Jack to come home from his round of the bars. She couldn't believe Al had called just to 'ask how things were going.' If you wanted to shoot the bull, you called Al. When Al called you, that was business.

Later, when she had come back downstairs, she had found Danny curled up by the fire again, reading the second-grade-primer adventures of Joe and Rachel at the circus with their daddy in complete, absorbed attention. The fidgety distraction had completely disappeared. Watching him, she had been struck again by the eerie certainty that Danny knew more and understood more than there was room for in Dr ('Just call me Bill') Edmonds's philosophy.

'Hey, time for bed, doc,' she'd said.

'Yeah, okay.' He marked his place in the book and stood up.

'Wash up and brush your teeth.'

'Okay.'

'Don't forget to use the floss.'

'I won't.'

They stood side by side for a moment, watching the wax and wane of the coals of the fire. Most of the lobby was chilly and drafty, but this circle around the fireplace was magically warm, and hard to leave.

'It was Uncle Al on the phone,' she said casually.

'Oh yeah?' Totally unsurprised.

'I wonder if Uncle Al was mad at Daddy,' she said, still casually.

'Yeah, he sure was,' Danny said, still watching the fire. 'He didn't want Daddy to write the book.'

'What book, Danny?'

'About the hotel.'

The question framed on her lips was one she and Jack had asked Danny a thousand times: *How do you know that*? She hadn't asked him. She didn't want to upset him before bed, or make him aware that they were casually discussing his knowledge of things he had no way of knowing at all. And he *did* know, she was convinced of that. Dr Edmond's patter about inductive reasoning and subconscious logic was just that: patter. Her sister . . . how had Danny known she was thinking about Aileen in the waiting room that day? And

(*I dreamed Daddy had an accident.*)

She shook her head, as if to clear it. 'Go wash up, doc.'

'Okay.' He ran up the stairs toward their quarters. Frowning, she had gone into the kitchen to warm Jack's milk in a saucepan.

And now, lying wakeful in her bed and listening to her husband's breathing and the wind outside (miraculously, they'd had only another flurry that afternoon; still no heavy snow), she let her mind turn fully to her lovely, troubling son, born with a caul over his face, a simple tissue of membrane that doctors saw perhaps once in every seven hundred births, a tissue that the old wives' tales said betokened the second sight.

She decided that it was time to talk to Danny about the Overlook . . . and high time she tried to get Danny to talk to her. Tomorrow. For sure. The two of them would be going down to the Sidewinder Public Library to see if they could get him some second-grade-level books on an extended loan through the winter, and she would talk to him. And frankly. With that thought she felt a little easier, and at last began to drift toward sleep.

Danny lay awake in his bedroom, eyes open, left arm encircling his aged and slightly worse-for-wear Pooh (Pooh had lost one shoe-button eye and was oozing stuffing from half a dozen sprung seams), listening to his parents sleep in their bedroom. He felt as if he were standing unwilling guard over them. The nights were the worst of all. He hated the nights and the constant howl of the wind around the west side of the hotel.

His glider floated overhead from a string. On his bureau the VW model, brought up from the roadway setup downstairs, glowed a dimly fluorescent purple. His books were in the bookcase, his coloring books on the desk. *A place for everything and everything in its place*, Mommy said. *Then you know where it is when you want it.* But now things had been misplaced. Things were missing. Worse still, things had been *added*, things you couldn't quite see, like in one of those pictures that said CAN YOU SEE THE INDIANS? And if you strained and squinted, you could see some of them – the thing you had taken for a cactus at first glance was really a brave with a knife clamped in his teeth, and there were others hiding in rocks, and you could even see one of their evil, merciless faces peering through the spokes of a covered wagon wheel. But you could never see all of them, and that was what made you uneasy. Because it was the ones you couldn't see that would sneak up behind you, a tomahawk in one hand and a scalping knife in the other . . .

He shifted uneasily in his bed, his eyes searching out the comforting glow of the night light. Things were worse here. He knew that much for sure. At first they hadn't been so bad, but little by little . . . his daddy thought about drinking a lot more. Sometimes he was angry at Mommy and didn't know why. He went around wiping his lips with his handkerchief and his eyes were far away and cloudy. Mommy was worried about him and Danny, too. He didn't have to shine into her to know that; it had been in the anxious way she had questioned him on the day the fire hose had seemed to turn into a snake. Mr Hallorann said he thought all mothers could shine a little bit, and she had known on that day that something had happened. But not what.

He had almost told her, but a couple of things had held him back. He knew that the doctor in Sidewinder had dismissed Tony and the things that Tony showed him as perfectly

(well almost)

normal. His mother might not believe him if he told her about the hose. Worse, she might believe him in the wrong way, might think he was LOSING HIS MARBLES. He understood a little about LOSING YOUR MARBLES, not as much as he did about GETTING A BABY, which his mommy had explained to him the year before at some length, but enough.

Once, at nursery school, his friend Scott had pointed out a boy named Robin Stenger, who was moping around the swings with a face almost long enough to step on. Robin's father taught arithmetic at Daddy's school, and Scott's daddy taught history there. Most of the kids at the nursery school were associated either with Stovington Prep or with the small IBM plant just outside of town. The prep kids chummed in one group, the IBM kids in another. There were cross-friendships, of course, but it was natural enough for the kids whose fathers knew each other to more or less stick together. When there was an adult scandal in one group, it almost always filtered down to the children in some wildly mutated form or other, but it rarely jumped to the other group.

He and Scotty were sitting in the play rocketship when Scotty jerked his thumb at Robin and said: 'You know that kid?'

'Yeah,' Danny said.

Scott leaned forward. 'His dad LOST HIS MARBLES last night. They took him away.'

'Yeah? Just for losing some marbles?'

Scotty looked disgusted. 'He went crazy. You know.' Scott crossed his eyes, flopped out his tongue, and twirled his index fingers in large elliptical orbits around his ears. 'They took him to THE BUGHOUSE.'

'Wow,' Danny said. 'When will they let him come back?'

'Never-never-never,' Scotty said darkly.

In the course of that day and the next, Danny heard that

a.) Mr Stenger had tried to kill everybody in his family, including Robin, with his World War II souvenir pistol;

b.) Mr Stenger ripped the house to pieces while he was STINKO;

c.) Mr Stenger had been discovered eating a bowl of dead bugs and grass like they were cereal and milk and crying while he did it;

d.) Mr Stenger had tried to strangle his wife with a stocking when the Red Sox lost a big ball game.

Finally, too troubled to keep it to himself, he had asked Daddy about Mr Stenger. His daddy had taken him on his lap and had explained that Mr Stenger had been under a great deal of strain, some of it about his family and some about his job and some of it about things that nobody but doctors could understand. He had been having crying fits, and three nights ago he had gotten crying and couldn't stop it and had broken a lot of things in the Stenger home. It wasn't LOSING YOUR MARBLES, Daddy said, it was HAVING A BREAK-DOWN, and Mr Stenger wasn't in a BUGHOUSE but in a SANNY-TARIUM. But despite Daddy's careful explanations, Danny was scared. There didn't seem to be any difference at all between LOSING YOUR MARBLES and HAVING A BREAK-DOWN, and whether you called it a BUGHOUSE or a SANNY-

TARIUM, there were still bars on the windows and they wouldn't let you out if you wanted to go. And his father, quite innocently, had confirmed another of Scotty's phrases unchanged, one that filled Danny with a vague and unformed dread. In the place where Mr Stenger now lived, there were THE MEN IN THE WHITE COATS. They came to get you in a truck with no windows, a truck that was gravestone gray. It rolled up to the curb in front of your house and THE MEN IN THE WHITE COATS got out and took you away from your family and made you live in a room with soft walls. And if you wanted to write home, you had to do it with Crayolas.

'When will they let him come back?' Danny asked his father.

'Just as soon as he's better, doc.'

'But when will that be?' Danny had persisted.

'Dan,' Jack said, 'NO ONE KNOWS.'

And that was the worst of all. It was another way of saying never-never-never. A month later, Robin's mother took him out of nursery school and they moved away from Stovington without Mr Stenger.

That had been over a year ago, after Daddy stopped taking the Bad Stuff but before he had lost his job. Danny still thought about it often. Sometimes when he fell down or bumped his head or had a bellyache, he would begin to cry and the memory would flash over him, accompanied by the fear that he would not be able to stop crying, that he would just go on and on, weeping and wailing, until his daddy went to the phone, dialed it, and said: 'Hello? This is Jack Torrance at 149 Mapleline Way. My son here can't stop crying. Please send THE MEN IN THE WHITE COATS to take him to the SANNY-TARIUM. That's right, he's LOST HIS MARBLES. Thank you.' And the gray truck with no windows would come rolling up to *his* door, they would load him in, still weeping hysterically, and take him away. When would he see his mommy and daddy again? NO ONE KNOWS.

It was this fear that had kept him silent. A year older, he was quite sure that his daddy and mommy wouldn't let him be taken away for thinking a fire hose was a snake, his *rational* mind was sure of that, but still, when he thought of telling them, that old memory rose up like a stone filling his mouth and blocking words. It wasn't like Tony; Tony had always seemed perfectly natural (until the bad dreams, of course), and his parents had also seemed to accept Tony as a more or less natural phenomenon. Things like Tony came from being BRIGHT, which they both assumed he was (the same way they assumed they were BRIGHT), but a fire hose that turned into a snake, or seeing blood and brains on the wall of the Presidential Sweet when no one else could, those things would not be natural. They had already taken him to see a regular doctor. Was it not reasonable to assume that THE MEN IN THE WHITE COATS might come next?'

Still he might have told them except he was sure, sooner or later, that they would want to take him away from the hotel. And he wanted desperately to get away from the Overlook. But he also knew that this was his daddy's last chance, that he was here at the Overlook to do more than take care of the place. He was here to work on his papers. To get over losing his job. To love Mommy/Wendy. And until very recently, it had seemed that all those things were happening. It was only lately that Daddy had begun to have trouble. Since he found those papers.

(*This inhuman place makes human monsters.*)

What did that mean? He had prayed to God, but God hadn't told him. And what would Daddy do if he stopped working here? He had tried to find out from Daddy's mind, and had become more and more convinced that Daddy didn't know. The strongest proof had come earlier this evening when Uncle Al had called his daddy up on the phone and said mean things and Daddy didn't dare say anything back because Uncle Al could fire him from this job just the way that Mr Crommert, the Stovington headmaster, and the Board of Directors had fired him from his schoolteaching job. And Daddy was scared to death of that, for him and Mommy as well as himself.

So he didn't dare say anything. He could only watch helplessly and hope that there really weren't any Indians at all, or if there were that they would be content to wait for bigger game and let their little three-wagon train pass unmolested.

But he couldn't believe it, no matter how hard he tried.

Things were worse at the Overlook now.

The snow was coming, and when it did, any poor options he had would be abrogated. And after the snow, what? What then, when they were shut in and at the mercy of whatever might have only been toying with them before?

(*Come out here and take your medicine!*)

What then? REDRUM.

Hc shivered in his bed and turned over again. He could read more now. Tomorrow maybe he would try to call Tony, he would try to make Tony show him exactly what REDRUM was and if there was any way he could prevent it. He would risk the nightmares. He had to *know*.

Danny was still awake long after his parents' false sleep had become the real thing. He rolled in his bed, twisting the sheets, grappling with a problem years too big for him, awake in the night like a single sentinel on picket. And sometime after midnight, he slept too and then only the wind was awake, prying at the hotel and hooting in its gables under the bright gimlet gaze of the stars.

Chapter Twenty-two

In the Truck

I see a bad moon a-rising.
I see trouble on the way.
I see earthquakes and lightnin'
I see bad times today.
Don't go 'round tonight,
It's bound to take your life,
There's a bad moon on the rise.*

* 'Bad Moon Rising,' by J. C. Fogerty, © 1969 Jondora Music, Berkeley, California. Used by permission. All rights reserved. International copyright secured.

Someone had added a very old Buick car radio under the hotel truck's dashboard, and now, tinny and choked with static, the distinctive sound of John Fogerty's Creedence Clearwater Revival band came out of the speaker. Wendy and Danny were on their way down to Sidewinder. The day was clear and bright. Danny was turning Jack's orange library card over and over in his hands and seemed cheerful enough, but Wendy thought he looked drawn and tired, as if he hadn't been sleeping enough and was going on nervous energy alone.

The song ended and the disc jockey came on. 'Yeah, that's Creedence. And speakin of bad moon, it looks like it may be risin over the KMTX listening area before long, hard as it is to believe with the beautiful, springlike weather we've enjoyed for the last couple-three days. The KMTX Fearless Forecaster says high pressure will give way by one o'clock this afternoon to a widespread low-pressure area which is just gonna grind to a stop in our KMTX area, up where the air is rare. Temperatures will fall rapidly, and precipitation should start around dusk. Elevations under seven thousand feet, including the metro-Denver area, can expect a mixture of sleet and snow, perhaps freezing on some roads, and nothin but snow up here, cuz. We're lookin at one to three inches below seven thousand and possible accumulations of six to ten inches in Central Colorado and on the Slope. The Highway Advisory Board says that if you're plannin to tour the mountains in your car this afternoon or tonight, you should remember that the chain law will be in effect. And don't go nowhere unless you have to. Remember,' the announcer added jocularly, 'that's how the Donners got into trouble. They just weren't as close to the nearest Seven-Eleven as they thought.'

A Clairol commercial came on, and Wendy reached down and snapped the radio off. 'You mind?'

'Huh-uh, that's okay.' He glanced out at the sky, which was bright blue. 'Guess Daddy picked just the right day to trim those hedge animals, didn't he?'

'I guess he did,' Wendy said.

'Sure doesn't look much like snow, though,' Danny added hopefully.

'Getting cold feet?' Wendy asked. She was still thinking about that crack the disc jockey had made about the Donner Party.

'Nah, I guess not.'

Well, she thought, this is the time. If you're going to bring it up, do it now or forever hold your peace.

'Danny,' she said, making her voice as casual as possible, 'would you be happier if we went away from the Overlook? If we didn't stay the winter?'

Danny looked down at his hands. 'I guess so,' he said. 'Yeah. But it's Daddy's job.'

'Sometimes,' she said carefully, 'I get the idea that Daddy might be happier away from the Overlook, too.' They passed a sign which read SIDEWINDER 18 MI. and then she took the truck cautiously around a hairpin and shifted up into second. She took no chances on these downgrades; they scared her silly.

'Do you really think so?' Danny asked. He looked at her with interest for a moment and then shook his head. 'No, I don't think so.'

'Why not"

'Because he's worried about us,' Danny said, choosing his words carefully. It was hard to explain, he understood so little of it himself. He found himself harking back to an incident he had told Mr Hallorann about, the big kid looking at department store TV sets and wanting to steal one. That had been distressing, but at least it had been clear what was going on, even to Danny, then little more than an infant. But grownups were always in a turmoil, every possible action muddied over by thoughts of the consequences, by self-doubt, by *selfimage*, by feelings of love and responsibility. Every possible choice seemed to have drawbacks, and sometimes he didn't understand why the drawbacks *were* drawbacks. It was very hard.

'He thinks . . .' Danny began again, and then looked at his mother quickly. She was watching the road, not looking at him, and he felt he could go on.

'He thinks maybe we'll be lonely. And then he thinks that he likes it here and it's a good place for us. He loves us and doesn't want us to be lonely . . . or sad . . . but he thinks even if we are, it might be okay in the LONGRUN. Do you know LONGRUN?'

She nodded. 'Yes, dear. I do.'

'He's worried that if we left he couldn't get another job. That we'd have to beg, or something.'

'Is that all?'

'No, but the rest is all mixed up. Because he's different now.'

'Yes,' she said, almost sighing. The grade eased a little and she shifted cautiously back to third gear.

'I'm not making this up, Mommy. Honest to God.'

'I know that,' she said, and smiled. 'Did Tony tell you?'

'No,' he said. 'I just know. That doctor didn't believe in Tony, did he?'

'Never mind that doctor,' she said. 'I believe in Tony. I don't know what he is or who he is, if he's a part of you that's special or if he comes from . . . somewhere outside, but I do believe in him, Danny. And if you . . . he . . . think we should go, we will. The two of us will go and be together with Daddy again in the spring.'

He looked at her with sharp hope. 'Where? A motel?'

'Hon, we couldn't afford a motel. It would have to be at my mother's.'

The hope in Danny's face died out. 'I know—' he said, and stopped.

'What?'

'Nothing,' he muttered.

She shifted back to second as the grade steepened again. 'No, doc, please don't say that. This talk is something we should have had weeks ago, I think. So please. What is it you know? I won't be mad. I can't be mad, because this is too important. Talk straight to me.'

'I know how you feel about her,' Danny said, and sighed.

'How do I feel?'

'Bad,' Danny said, and then rhyming, singsong, frightening her: 'Bad. Sad. Mad. It's like she wasn't your mommy at all. Like she wanted to eat you.' He looked at her, frightened. 'And I don't like it there. She's always thinking about how she would be better for me than you. And how she could get me away from you. Mommy, I don't want to go there. I'd rather be at the Overlook than there.'

Wendy was shaken. Was it that bad between her and her mother? God, what hell for the boy if it was and he could really read their thoughts for each other. She suddenly felt more naked than naked, as if she had been caught in an obscene act.

'All right,' she said. 'All right, Danny.'

'You're mad at me,' he said in a small, near-to-tears voice.

'No, I'm not. Really I'm not. I'm just sort of shook up.'

They were passing a SIDEWINDER 15 MI. sign, and Wendy relaxed a little. From here on in the road was better.

'I want to ask you one more question, Danny. I want you to answer it as truthfully as you can. Will you do that?'

'Yes, Mommy,' he said, almost whispering.

'Has your daddy been drinking again?'

'No,' he said, and smothered the two words that rose behind his lips after that simple negative: *Not yet.*

Wendy relaxed a little more. She put a hand on Danny's jeans-clad leg and squeezed it. 'Your daddy has tried very hard,' she said softly. 'Because he loves us. And we love him, don't we?'

He nodded gravely.

Speaking almost to herself she went on: 'He's not a perfect man, but he has tried . . . Danny, he's tried so hard! When he . . . stopped . . . he went through a kind of hell. He's still going through it. I think if it hadn't been for us, he would have just let go. I want to do what's right. And I don't know. Should we go? Stay? It's like a choice between the fat and the fire.'

'I know.'

'Would you do something for me doc?'

'What?'

'Try to make Tony come. Right now. Ask him if we're safe at the Overlook.'

'I already tried,' Danny said slowly. 'This morning.'

'What happend?' Wendy asked. 'What did he say?'

'He didn't come,' Danny said. 'Tony didn't come.' And he suddenly burst into tears.

'Danny,' she said, alarmed. 'Honey, don't do that. Please—' The truck swerved across the double yellow line and she pulled it back, scared.

'Don't take me to Gramma's,' Danny said through his tears. 'Please, Mommy, I don't want to go there, I want to stay with Daddy—'

'All right,' she said softly. 'All right, that's what we'll do.' She took a Kleenex out of the pocket of her Western-style shirt and handed it to him. 'We'll stay. And everything will be fine. Just fine.'

Chapter Twenty-three

In the Playground

Jack came out onto the porch, tugging the tab of his zipper up under his chin, blinking into the bright air. In his left hand he was holding a battery-powered hedge-clipper. He tugged a fresh handkerchief out of his back pocket with his right hand, wiped his lips with it, and tucked it away. Snow, they had said on the radio. It was hard to believe, even though he could see the clouds building up on the far horizon.

He started down the path to the topiary, switching the hedge-clipper over to the other hand. It wouldn't be a long job, he thought; a little touch-up would do it. The cold nights had surely stunted their growth. The rabbit's ears looked a little fuzzy, and two of the dog's legs had grown fuzzy green bonespurs, but the lions and the buffalo looked fine. Just a little haircut would do the trick, and then let the snow come.

The concrete path ended as abruptly as a diving board. He stepped off it and walked past the drained pool to the gravel path which wound through the hedge sculptures and into the playground itself. He walked over to the rabbit and pushed the button on the handle of the clippers. It hummed into quiet life.

'Hi, Br'er Rabbit,' Jack said. 'How are you today? A little off the top and get some of the extra off your ears? Fine. Say, did you hear the one about the traveling salesman and the old lady with a pet poodle?'

His voice sounded unnatural and stupid in his ears, and he stopped. It occurred to him that he didn't care much for these hedge animals. It had always seemed slightly perverted to him to clip and torture a plain old hedge into something that it wasn't. Along one of the highways in Vermont there had been a hedge billboard on a high slope overlooking the road, advertising some kind of ice cream. Making nature peddle ice cream, that was just wrong. It was grotesque.

(*You weren't hired to philosophize, Torrance.*)

Ah, that was true. So true. He clipped along the rabbit's ears, brushing a small litter of sticks and twigs off onto the grass. The hedge-clipper hummed in that low and rather disgustingly metallic way that all battery-powered appliances seem to have. The sun was brilliant but it held no warmth, and now it wasn't so hard to believe that snow was coming.

Working quickly, knowing that to stop and think when you were at this kind of task usually meant making a mistake, Jack touched up the rabbit's 'face' (up this close it didn't look like a face at all, but he knew that at a distance of twenty paces or so light and shadow would seem to suggest one; that, and the viewer's imagination) and then zipped the clippers along its belly.

That done, he shut the clippers off, walked down toward the playground, and then turned back abruptly to get it all at once, the entire rabbit. Yes, it looked all right. Well, he would do the dog next.

'But if it was my hotel,' he said, 'I'd cut the whole damn bunch of you down.' He would, too. Just cut them down and resod the lawn where they'd been and put in half a dozen small metal tables with gaily colored umbrellas. People could have cocktails on the Overlook's lawn in the summer sun. Sloe gin fizzes and margaritas and pink ladies and all those sweet tourist drinks. A rum and tonic, maybe. Jack took his handkerchief out of his back pocket and slowly rubbed his lips with it.

'Come on, come on,' he said softly. That was nothing to be thinking about.

He was going to start back, and then some impulse made him change his mind and he went down to the playground instead. It was funny how you never knew kids, he thought. He and Wendy had expected Danny would love the playground; it had everything a kid could want. But Jack didn't think the boy had been down half a dozen times, if that. He supposed if there had been another kid to play with, it would have been different.

The gate squeaked slightly as he let himself in, and then there was crushed gravel crunching under his feet. He went first to the playhouse, the perfect scale model of the Overlook itself. It came up to his lower thigh, just about Danny's height when he was standing up. Jack hunkered down and looked in the third-floor windows.

'The giant has come to eat you all up in your beds,' he said hollowly. 'Kiss your Triple A rating goodbye.' But that wasn't funny, either. You could open the house simply by pulling it apart – it opened on a hidden hinge. The inside was a disappointment. The walls were painted, but the place was mostly hollow. But of course it would have to be, he told himself, or how else could the kids get inside? What play furniture might go with the place in the summer was gone, probably packed away in the equipment shed. He closed it up and heard the small click as the latch closed.

He walked over to the slide, set the hedge-clipper down, and after a glance back at the driveway to make sure Wendy and Danny hadn't returned, he climbed to the top and sat down. This was the big kids' slide, but the fit was still uncomfortably tight for his grownup ass. How long had it been since he had been on a slide? Twenty years? It didn't seem possible it could be that long, it didn't *feel* that long, but it had to be that, or more. He could remember his old man taking him to the park in Berlin when he had been Danny's age, and he had done the whole bit – slide, swings, teeter-totters, everything. He and the old man would have a hotdog lunch and buy peanuts from the man with the cart afterward. They would sit on a bench to eat them and dusky clouds of pigeons would flock around their feet.

'Goddam scavenger birds,' his dad would say, 'don't you feed them, Jacky.' But they would both end up feeding them, and giggling at the way they ran after the nuts, the greedy way they ran after the nuts. Jack didn't think the old man had ever taken his brothers to the park. Jack had been his favorite, and even so Jack had taken his lumps when the old man was drunk, which was a lot of the time. But Jack had loved him for as long as he was able, long after the rest of the family could only hate and fear him.

He pushed off with his hands and went to the bottom, but the trip was unsatisfying. The slide, unused, had too much friction and no really pleasant speed could be built up. And his ass was just too big. His adult feet thumped into the slight dip where thousands of children's feet had landed before him. He stood up, brushed at the seat of his pants, and looked at the hedge-clipper. But instead of going back to it he went to the swings, which were also a disappointment. The chains had built up rust since the close of the season, and they squealed like things in pain. Jack promised himself he would oil them in the spring.

You better stop it, he advised himself. You're not a kid anymore. You don't need this place to prove it.

But he went on to the cement rings – they were too small for him and he passed them up – and then to the security fence which marked the edge of the grounds. He curled his fingers through the links and looked through, the sun crosshatching shadow-lines on his face like a man behind bars. He recognized the similarity himself and he shook the chain link, put a harried expression on his face, and whispered: 'Lemme outta here! Lemme outta here!' But for the third time, not funny. It was time to get back to work.

That was when he heard the sound behind him.

He turned around quickly, frowning, embarrassed, wondering if someone had seen him fooling around down here in kiddie country. His eyes ticked off the slides, the opposing angles of the seesaws, the swings in which only the wind sat. Beyond all that to the gate and the low fence that divided the playground from the lawn and the topiary – the lions gathered protectively around the path, the rabbit bent over as if to crop grass, the buffalo ready to charge, the crouching dog. Beyond them, the putting green and the hotel itself. From here he could even see the raised lip of the roque court on the Overlook's western side.

Everything was just as it had been. So why had the flesh of his face and hands begun to creep, and why had the hair along the back of his neck begun to stand up, as if the flesh back there had suddenly tightened?

He squinted up at the hotel again, but that was no answer. It simply stood there, its windows dark, a tiny thread of smoke curling from the chimney, coming from the banked fire in the lobby.

(Buster, you better get going or they're going to come back and wonder if you were doing anything all the while.)

Sure, get going. Because the snow was coming and he had to get the damn hedges trimmed. It was part of the agreement. Besides, they wouldn't dare—

(Who wouldn't? What wouldn't? Dare do what?)

He began to walk back toward the hedge-clipper at the foot of the big kids' slide, and the sound of his feet crunching on the crushed stone seemed abnormally loud. Now the flesh on his testicles had begun to creep too, and his buttocks felt hard and heavy, like stone.

(*Jesus, what is this?*)

He stopped by the hedge-clipper, but made no move to pick it up. Yes, there was something different. In the topiary. And it was so simple, so easy to see, that he just wasn't picking it up. Come on, he scolded himself, you just trimmed the fucking rabbit, so what's the

(that's it)

His breath stopped in his throat.

The rabbit was down on all fours, cropping grass. Its belly was against the ground. But not ten minutes ago it had been up on its hind legs, of course it had been, he had trimmed its ears . . . and its belly.

His eyes darted to the dog. When he had come down the path it had been sitting up, as if begging for a sweet. Now it was crouched, head tilted, the clipped wedge of mouth seeming to snarl silently. And the lions—

(oh no, baby, oh no, uh-uh, no way)

the lions were closer to the path. The two on his right had subtly changed positions, had drawn closer together. The tail of the one on the left now almost jutted out over the path. When he had come past them and through the gate, that lion had been on the right and he was quite sure its tail had been curled around it.

They were no longer protecting the path; they were blocking it.

Jack put his hand suddenly over his eyes and then took it away. The picture didn't change. A soft sigh, too quiet to be a groan, escaped him. In his drinking days he had always been afraid of something like this happening. But when you were a heavy drinker you called it the DTs – good old Ray Milland in *Lost Weekend*, seeing the bugs coming out of the walls.

What did you call it when you were cold sober?

The question was meant to be rhetorical, but his mind answered it

(you call it insanity)

nevertheless.

Staring at the hedge animals, he realized something *had* changed while he had his hand over his eyes. The dog had moved closer. No longer crouching, it seemed to be in a running posture, haunches flexed, one front leg forward, the other back. The hedge mouth yawned wider, the pruned sticks looked sharp and vicious. And now he fancied he could see faint eye indentations in the greenery as well. Looking at him.

Why do they have to be trimmed? he thought hysterically. *They're perfect.*

Another soft sound. He involuntarily backed up a step when he looked at the lions. One of the two on the right seemed to have drawn slightly ahead of the other. Its head was lowered. One paw had stolen almost all the way to the low fence. Dear God, what next?

(*next it leaps over and gobbles you up like something in an evil nursery fable*)

It was like that game they had played when they were kids, red light. One person was 'it,' and while he turned his back and counted to ten, the other players crept forward. When 'it' got to ten, he whirled around and if he caught anyone moving, they were out of the game. The others remained frozen in statue postures until 'it' turned his back and counted again. They got closer and closer, and at last, somewhere between five and ten, you would feel a hand on your back . . .

Gravel rattled on the path.

He jerked his head around to look at the dog and it was halfway down the pathway, just behind the lions now, its mouth wide and yawning. Before, it had only been a hedge clipped in the general shape of a dog, something that lost all definition when you got up close to it. But now Jack could see that it had been clipped to look like a German shepherd, and shepherds could be mean. You could train shepherds to kill.

A low rustling sound.

The lion on the left had advanced all the way to the fence now; its muzzle was touching the boards. It seemed to be grinning at him. Jack backed up another two steps. His head was thudding crazily and he could feel the dry rasp of his breath in his throat. Now the buffalo had moved, circling to the right, behind and around the rabbit. The head was lowered, the green hedge horns pointing at him. The thing was, you couldn't watch all of them. Not all at once.

He began to make a whining sound, unaware in his locked concentration that he was making any sound at all. His eyes darted from one hedge creature to the next, trying to *see* them move. The wind gusted, making a hungry rattling sound in the close-matted branches. What kind of sound would there be if they got him? But of course he knew. A snapping, rending, breaking sound. It would be—

(*no no NO NO I WILL NOT BELIEVE THIS NOT AT ALL!*)

He clapped his hands over his eyes, clutching at his hair, his forehead, his throbbing temples. And he stood like that for a long time, dread building until he could stand it no longer and he pulled his hands away with a cry.

By the putting green the dog was sitting up, as if begging for a scrap. The buffalo was gazing with disinterest back toward the roque court, as it had been when Jack had come down with the clippers. The rabbit stood on its hind legs, ears up to catch the faintest sound, freshly clipped belly exposed. The lions, rooted into place, stood beside the path.

He stood frozen for a long time, the harsh breath in his throat finally slowing. He reached for his cigarettes and shook four of them out onto the gravel. He stooped down and picked them up, groped for them, never taking his eyes from the topiary for fear the animals would begin to move again. He picked them up, stuffed three carelessly back into the pack, and lit the fourth. After two deep drags he dropped it and crushed it out. He went to the hedge-clipper and picked it up.

'I'm very tired,' he said, and now it seemed okay to talk out loud. It didn't seem crazy at all. 'I've been under a strain. The wasps . . . the play . . . Al calling me like that. But it's all right.'

He began to trudge back up to the hotel. Part of his mind tugged fretfully at him, tried to make him detour around the hedge animals, but he went directly up the gravel path, through them. A faint breeze rattled through them, that was all. He had imagined the whole thing. He had had a bad scare but it was over now.

In the Overlook's kitchen he paused to take two Excedrin and then went downstairs and looked at papers until he heard the dim sound of the hotel truck rattling into the driveway. He went up to meet them. He felt all right. He saw no need to mention his hallucination. He'd had a bad scare but it was over now.

Chapter Twenty-four

Snow

It was dusk.

They stood on the porch in the fading light, Jack in the middle, his left arm around Danny's shoulders and his right arm around Wendy's waist. Together they watched as the decision was taken out of their hands.

The sky had been completely clouded over by two-thirty and it had begun to snow an hour later, and this time you didn't need a weatherman to tell you it was serious snow, no flurry that was going to melt or blow away when the evening wind started to whoop. At first it had fallen in perfectly straight lines, building up a snowcover that coated everything evenly, but now, an hour after it had started, the wind had begun to blow from the northwest and the snow had begun to drift against the porch and the sides of the Overlook's driveway. Beyond the grounds the highway had disappeared under an even blanket of white. The hedge animals were also gone, but when Wendy and Danny had gotten home, she had commended him on the good job he had done. Do you think so? he had asked, and said no more. Now the hedges were buried under amorphous white cloaks.

Curiously, all of them were thinking different thoughts but feeling the same emotion: relief. The bridge had been crossed.

'Will it ever be spring?' Wendy murmured.

Jack squeezed her tighter. 'Before you know it. What do you say we go in and have some supper? It's cold out here.'

She smiled. All afternoon Jack had seemed distant and . . . well, odd. Now he sounded more like his normal self. 'Fine by me. How about you, Danny?'

'Sure.'

So they went in together, leaving the wind to build to the low-pitched scream that would go on all night – a sound they would get to know well. Flakes of snow swirled and danced across the porch. The Overlook faced it as it had for nearly three quarters of a century, its darkened windows now bearded with snow, indifferent to the fact that it was now cut off from the world. Or possibly it was pleased with the prospect. Inside its shell the three of them went about their early evening routine, like microbes trapped in the intestine of a monster.

Chapter Twenty-five

Inside 217

A week and a half later two feet of snow lay white and crisp and even on the grounds of the Overlook Hotel. The hedge menagerie was buried up to its haunches; the rabbit, frozen on its hind legs, seemed to be rising from a white pool. Some of the drifts were over five feet deep. The wind was constantly changing them, sculpting them into sinuous, dunelike shapes. Twice Jack had snowshoed clumsily around to the equipment shed for his shovel to clear the porch, the third time he shrugged, simply cleared a path through the towering drift lying against the door, and let Danny amuse himself by sledding to the right and left of the path. The truly heroic drifts lay against the Overlook's west side; some of them towered to a height of twenty feet, and beyong them the ground was scoured bare to the grass by the constant windflow. The first-floor windows were covered, and the view from the dining room which Jack had so admired on closing day was now no more exciting than a view of a blank movie screen. Their phone had been out for the last eight days, and the CB radio in Ullman's office was now their only communications link with the outside world.

It snowed every day now, sometimes only brief flurries that powdered the glittering snow crust, sometimes for real, the low whistle of the wind cranking up to a womanish shriek that made the old hotel rock and groan alarmingly even in its deep cradle of snow. Night temperatures had not gotten above 10°, and although the thermometer by the kitchen service entrance sometimes got as high as 25° in the early afternoons, the steady knife edge of the wind made it uncomfortable to go out without a ski mask. But they all did go out on the days when the sun shone, usually wearing two sets of clothing and mittens on over their gloves. Getting out was almost a compulsive thing; the hotel was circled with the double track of Danny's Flexible Flyer. The permutations were nearly endless: Danny riding while his parents pulled; Daddy riding and laughing while Wendy and Danny tried to pull (it was just possible for them to pull him on the icy crust, and flatly impossible when powder covered it); Danny and Mommy riding; Wendy riding by herself while her menfolk pulled and puffed white vapor like drayhorses, pretending she was heavier than she was. They laughed a great deal on these sled excursions around the house, but the whooping and impersonal voice of the wind, so huge and hollowly sincere, made their laughter seem tinny and forced.

They had seen caribou tracks in the snow and once the caribou themselves, a group of five standing motionlessly below the security fence. They had all taken turns with Jack's Zeiss-Ikon binoculars to see them better, and looking at them had given Wendy a weird, unreal feeling: they were standing leg-deep in the snow that covered the highway, and it came to her that between now and the spring thaw, the road belonged more to the caribou than it did to them. Now the things that men had made up here were neutralized. The caribou understood that, she believed. She had put the binoculars down and had said something about starting lunch and in the kitchen she had cried a little, trying to rid herself of the awful pent-up feeling that sometimes fell on her like a large, pressing hand over her heart. She thought of the caribou. She thought of the wasps Jack had put out on the service entrance platform, under the Pyrex bowl, to freeze.

There were plenty of snowshoes hung from nails in the equipment shed, and Jack found a pair to fit each of them, although Danny's pair was quite a bit outsized. Jack did well with them. Although he had not snowshoed since his boyhood in Berlin, New Hampshire, he retaught himself quickly. Wendy didn't care much for it – even fifteen minutes of tramping around on the outsized laced paddles made her legs and ankles ache outrageously – but Danny was intrigued and working hard to pick up the knack. He still fell often, but Jack was pleased with his progress. He said that by February Danny would be skipping circles around both of them.

This day was overcast, and by noon the sky had already begun to spit snow. The radio was promising another eight to twelve inches and chanting hosannas to Precipitation, that great god of Colorado skiers. Wendy, sitting in the bedroom and knitting a scarf, thought to herself that she knew exactly what the skiers could do with all that snow. She knew exactly where they could put it.

Jack was in the cellar. He had gone down to check the furnace and boiler – such checks had become a ritual with him since the snow had closed them in – and after satisfying himself that everything was going well he had wandered through the arch, screwed the lightbulb on, and had seated himself in an old and cobwebby camp chair he had found. He was leafing through the old records and papers, constantly wiping his mouth with his handkerchief as he did so. Confinement had leached his skin of its autumn tan, and as he sat hunched over the yellowed, crackling sheets, his reddish-blond hair tumbling untidily over his forehead, he looked slightly lunatic. He had found some odd things tucked in among the invoices, bills of lading, receipts. Disquieting things. A bloody strip of sheeting. A dismembered teddy bear that seemed to have been slashed to pieces. A crumpled sheet of violet ladies' stationery, a ghost of perfume still clinging to it beneath the musk of age, a note begun and left unfinished in faded blue ink: '*Dearest Tommy, I can't think so well up here as I'd hoped, about us I mean, of course, who else? Ha. Ha. Things keep getting in the way. I've had strange dreams about things going bump in the night, can you believe that and*' That was all. The note was dated June 27, 1934. He found a hand puppet that seemed to be either a witch or a warlock . . . something with long teeth and a pointy hat, at any rate. It had been improbably tucked between a bundle of natural-gas receipts and a bundle of receipts for Vichy water. And something that seemed to be a poem, scribbled on the back of a menu in dark pencil: '*Medoc/are you here?/I've been sleepwalking again, my dear./The plants are moving under the rug.*' No date on the menu, and no name on the poem, if it was a poem. Elusive, but fascinating. it seemed to him that these things were like pieces in a jigsaw, things that would eventually fit together if he could find the right linking pieces. And so he kept looking, jumping and wiping his lips every time the furnace roared into life behind him.

Danny was standing outside Room 217 again.

The passkey was in his pocket. He was staring at the door with a kind of drugged avidity, and his upper body seemed to twitch and jiggle beneath his flannel shirt. He was humming softly and tunelessly.

He hadn't wanted to come here, not after the fire hose. He was scared to come here. He was scared that he had taken the passkey again, disobeying his father.

He *had* wanted to come here. Curiosity

(killed the cat; satisfaction brought him back)

was like a constant fishhook in his brain, a kind of nagging siren song that would not be appeased. And hadn't Mr. Hallorann said, 'I don't think there's anything here that can hurt you'?

(You promised.)

(*Promises were made to be broken.*)

He jumped at that. It was as if that thought had come from outside, insectile, buzzing, softly cajoling.

(*Promises were made to be broken my dear redrum, to be broken. splintered. shattered. hammered apart. FORE!*)

His nervous humming broke into low, atonal song: 'Lou, Lou, skip to m'Lou, skip to m'Lou my daaarlin . . .'

Hadn't Mr Hallorann been right? Hadn't that been, in the end, the reason why he had kept silent and allowed the snow to close them in?

Just close your eyes and it will be gone.

What he had seen in the Presidential Sweet had gone away. And the snake had only been a fire hose that had fallen onto the rug. Yes, even the blood in the Presidential Sweet had been harmless, something old, something that had happened long before he was born or even thought of, something that was done with. Like a movie that only he could see. There was nothing, really nothing, in this hotel that could hurt him, and if he had to prove that to himself by going into this room, shouldn't he do so?

'Lou, Lou, skip to m'Lou . . .'

(*Curiosity killed the cat my dear redrum, redrum my dear, satisfaction brought him back safe and sound, from toes to crown; from head to ground he was safe and sound. He knew that those things*)

(*are like scary pictures, they can't hurt you, but oh my god*)

(*what big teeth you have grandma and is that a wolf in a BLUEBEARD suit or a BLUEBEARD in a wolf suit and i'm so*)

(*glad you asked because curiosity killed that cat and it was the HOPE of satisfaction that brought him*)

up the hall, treading softly over the blue and twisting jungle carpet. He had stopped by the fire extinguisher, had put the brass nozzle back in the frame, and then had poked it repeatedly with his finger, heart thumping, whispering: 'Come on and hurt me. Come on and hurt me, you cheap prick. Can't do it, can you? Huh? You're nothing but a cheap fire hose. Can't do nothin but lie there. Come on, come on!' He had felt insane with bravado. And nothing had happened. It was only a hose after all, only canvas and brass, you could hack it to pieces and it would never complain, never twist and jerk and bleed green slime all over the blue carpet, because it was only a hose, not a nose and not a rose, not glass buttons or satin bows, not a snake in a sleepy doze . . . and he had hurried on, had hurried on because he was

('late, I'm late,' said the white rabbit.)

the white rabbit. Yes. Now there was a white rabbit out by the playground, once it had been green but now it was white, as if something had shocked it repeatedly on the snowy, windy nights and turned it old . . .

Danny took the passkey from his pocket and slid it into the lock.

'Lou, Lou . . .'

(*the white rabbit had been on its way to a croquet party to the Red Queen's croquet party storks for mallets hedgehogs for balls*)

He touched the key, let his fingers wander over it. His head felt dry and sick. He turned the key and the tumblers thumped back smoothly.

(*OFF WITH HIS HEAD! OFF WITH HIS HEAD! OFF WITH HIS HEAD!*)

(*this game isn't croquet though the mallets are too short this game is*)

(*WHACK-BOOM! Straight through the wicket.*)

OFF WITH HIS HEEEEEAAAAAAD—)

Danny pushed the door open. It swung smoothly, without a creak. He was standing just outside a large combination bed-sitting room, and although the snow had not reached up this far – the highest drifts were still a foot below the second-floor windows – the room was dark because Daddy had closed all the shutters on the western exposure two weeks ago.

He stood in the doorway, fumbled to his right, and found the switch plate. Two bulbs in an overhead cut-glass fixture came on. Danny stepped further in and looked around. The rug was deep and soft, a quiet rose color. Soothing. A double bed with a white coverlet. A writing desk

(*Pray tell me: Why is a raven like a writing desk?*)

by the large shuttered window. During the season the Constant Writer

(*having a wonderful time, wish you were fear*)

would have a pretty view of the mountains to describe to the folks back home.

He stepped further in. Nothing here, nothing at all. Only an empty room, cold because Daddy was heating the east wing today. A bureau. A closet, its door open to reveal a clutch of hotel hangers, the kind you can't steal. A Gideon Bible on an endtable. To his left was the bathroom door, a full-length mirror on it reflecting his own white-faced image. That door was ajar and—

He watched his double nod slowly.

Yes, that's where it was, whatever it was. In there. In the bathroom. His double walked forward, as if to escape the glass. It put its hand out, pressed it against his own. Then it fell away at an angle as the bathroom door swung open. He looked in.

A long room, old-fashioned, like a Pullman car. Tiny white hexagonal tiles on the floor. At the far end, a toilet with the lid up. At the right, a washbasin and another mirror above it, the kind that hides a medicine cabinet. To the left, a huge white tub on claw feet, the shower curtain pulled closed. Danny stepped into the bathroom and walked toward the tub dreamily, as if propelled from outside himself, as if this whole thing were one of the dreams Tony had brought him, that he would perhaps see something nice when he pulled the shower curtain back, something Daddy had forgotten or Mommy had lost, something that would make them both happy—

So he pulled the shower curtain back.

The woman in the tub had been dead for a long time. She was bloated and purple, her gas-filled belly rising out of the cold, ice-rimmed water like some fleshy island. Her eyes were fixed on Danny's, glassy and huge, like marbles. She was grinning, her purple lips pulled back in a grimace. Her breasts lolled. Her pubic hair floated. Her hands were frozen on the knurled porcelain sides of the tub like crab claws.

Danny shrieked. But the sound never escaped his lips; turning inward and inward, it fell down in his darkness like a stone in a well. He took a single blundering step backward, hearing his heels clack on the white hexagonal tiles, and at the same moment his urine broke, spilling effortlessly out of him.

The woman was sitting up.

Still grinning, her huge marble eyes fixed on him, she was sitting up. Her dead palms made squittering noises on the porcelain. Her breasts swayed like ancient cracked punching bags. There was the minute sound of breaking ice shards. She was not breathing. She was a corpse, and dead long years.

Danny turned and ran. Bolting through the bathroom door, his eyes starting from their sockets, his hair on end like the hair on a hedgehog about to be turned into a sacrificial

(croquet? or roque?)

ball, his mouth open and soundless. He ran full-tilt into the outside door of 217, which was now closed. He began hammering on it, far beyond realizing that it was unlocked, and he had only to turn the knob to let himself out. His mouth pealed forth deafening screams that were beyond human auditory range. He could only hammer on the door and hear the dead woman coming for him, bloated belly, dry hair, outstretched hands – something that had lain slain in that tub for perhaps years, embalmed there in magic.

The door would not open, would not, would not, would not.

And then the voice of Dick Hallorann came to him, so sudden and unexpected, so calm, that his locked vocal cords opened and he began to cry weakly – not with fear but with blessed relief.

(*I don't think they can hurt you . . . they're like pictures in a book . . . close your eyes and they'll be gone.*)

His eyelids snapped down. His hands curled into balls. His shoulders hunched with the effort of his concentration:

(*Nothing there nothing there not there at all NOTHING THERE THERE IS NOTHING!*)

Time passed. And he was just beginning to relax, just beginning to realize that the door must be unlocked and he could go, when the years-damp, bloated, fish-smelling hands closed softly around his throat and he was turned implacably around to stare into that dead and purple face.

BOOK FOUR

SNOWBOUND

Chapter Twenty-six

Dreamland

Knitting made her sleepy. Today even Bartók would have made her sleepy, and it wasn't Bartók on the little phonograph, it was Bach. Her hands grew slower and slower, and at the time her son was making the acquaintance of Room 217's long-term resident, Wendy was asleep with her knitting on her lap. The yarn and needles rose in the slow time of her breathing. Her sleep was deep and she did not dream.

Jack Torrance had fallen asleep too, but his sleep was light and uneasy, populated by dreams that seemed too vivid to be mere dreams – they were certainly more vivid than any dreams he had ever had before.

His eyes had begun to get heavy as he leafed through packets of milk bills, a hundred to a packet, seemingly tens of thousands all together. Yet he gave each one a cursory glance, afraid that by not being thorough he might miss exactly the piece of Overlookiana he needed to make the mystic connection that he was sure must be here somewhere. He felt like a man with a power cord in one hand, groping around a dark and unfamiliar room for a socket. If he could find it he would be rewarded with a view of wonders.

He had come to grips with Al Shockley's phone call and his request; his strange experience in the playground had helped him to do that. That had been too damned close to some kind of breakdown, and he was convinced that it was his mind in revolt against Al's high-goddam-handed request that he chuck his book project. It had maybe been a signal that his own sense of self-respect could only be pushed so far before disintegrating entirely. He would write the book. If it meant the end of his association with Al Shockley, that would have to be. He would write the hotel's biography, write it straight from the shoulder, and the introduction would be his hallucination that the topiary animals had moved. The title would be uninspired but workable: *Strange Resort, The Story of the Overlook Hotel.* Straight from the shoulder, yes, but it would not be written vindictively, in any effort to get back at Al or Stuart Ullman or George Hatfield or his father (miserable, bullying drunk that he had been) or anyone else, for that matter. He would write it because the Overlook had enchanted him – could any other explanation be so simple or so true? He would write it for the reason he felt that all great literature, fiction and nonfiction, was written: truth comes out, in the end it always comes out. He would write it because he felt he had to.

Five hundred gals whole milk. One hundred gals skim milk. Pd. Billed to acc't. Three hundred pts orange juice. Pd.

He slipped down further in his chair, still holding a clutch of the receipts, but his eyes no longer looking at what was printed there. They had come unfocused. His lids were slow and heavy. His mind had slipped from the Overlook to his father, who had been a male nurse at the Berlin Community Hospital. Big man. A fat man who had towered to six feet two inches, he had been taller than Jack even when Jack got his full growth of six feet even – not that the old man had still been around then. 'Runt of the litter,' he would say say, and then cuff Jack lovingly and laugh. There had been two other brothers, both taller than their father, and Becky, who at five-ten had only been two inches shorter than Jack and taller than he for most of their childhood.

His relationship with his father had been like the unfurling of some flower of beautiful potential, which, when wholly opened, turned out to be blighted inside. Until he had been seven he had loved the tall, big-bellied man uncritically and strongly in spite of the spankings, the black-and-blues, the occasional black eye.

He could remember velvet summer nights, the house quiet, oldest brother Brett out with his girl, middle brother Mike studying something, Becky and their mother in the living room, watching something on the balky old TV; and he would sit in the hall dressed in a pajama singlet and nothing else, ostensibly playing with his trucks, actually waiting for the moment when the silence would be broken by the door swinging open with a large bang, the bellow of his father's welcome when he saw Jacky was waiting, his own happy squeal in answer as this big man came down the hall, his pink scalp glowing beneath his crewcut in the glow of the hall light. In that light he always looked like some soft and flapping oversized ghost in his hospital whites, the shirt always untucked (and sometimes bloody), the pants cuffs dropping down over the black shoes.

His father would sweep him into his arms and Jacky would be propelled deliriously upward, so fast it seemed he could feel air pressure settling against his skull like a cap make out of lead, up and up, both of them crying 'Elevator! Elevator!'; and there had been nights when his father in his drunkenness had not stopped the upward lift of his slabmuscled arms soon enough and Jacky had gone right over his father's flattopped head like a human projectile to crash-land on the hall floor behind his dad. But on other nights his father would only sweep him into a giggling ecstasy, through the zone of air where beer hung around his father's face like a mist of raindrops, to be twisted and turned and shaken like a laughing rag, and finally to be set down on his feet, hiccupping with reaction.

The receipts slipped from his relaxing hand and seesawed down through the air to land lazily on the floor; his eyelids, which had settled shut with his father's image tattooed on their backs like stereopticon images, opened a little bit and then slipped back down again. He twitched a little. Consciousness, like the receipts, like autumn aspen leaves, seesawed lazily downward.

That had been the first phase of his relationship with his father, and as it was drawing to its end he had become aware that Becky and his brothers, all of them older, hated the father and that their mother, a nondescript woman who rarely spoke above a mutter, only suffered him because her Catholic upbringing said that she must. In those days it had not seemed strange to Jack that the father won all his arguments with his children by use of his fists, and it had not seemed strange that his own love should go hand-in-hand with his fear: fear of the elevator game which might end in a splintering crash on any given night; fear that his father's bearish good humor on his day off might suddenly change to boarish bellowing and the smack of his '*good right hand*'; and sometimes, he remembered, he had even been afraid that his father's shadow might fall over him while he was at play. It was near the end of this phase that he began to notice that Brett never brought his dates home, or Mike and Becky their chums.

Love began to curdle at nine, when his father put his mother into the hospital with his cane. He had begun to carry the cane a year earlier, when a car accident had left him lame. After that he was never without it, long and black and thick and gold-headed. Now, dozing, Jack's body twitched in a remembered cringe at the sound it made in the air, a murderous swish, and its heavy crack against the wall . . . or against flesh. He had beaten their mother for no good reason at all, suddenly and without warning. They had been at the supper table. The cane had been standing by his chair. It was a Sunday night, the end of a three-day weekend for Daddy, a weekend which he had boozed away in his usual inimitable style. Roast chicken. Peas. Mashed potatoes. Daddy at the head of the table, his plate heaped high, snoozing or nearly snoozing. His mother passing plates. And suddenly Daddy had been wide awake, his eyes set deeply into their fat eye-sockets, glittering with a kind of stupid, evil petulance. They flickered from one member of the family to the next, and the vein in the center of his forehead was standing out prominently, always a bad sign. One of his large freckled hands had dropped to the gold knob of his cane, caressing it. He said something about coffee – to this day Jack was sure it had been 'coffee' that his father said. Momma had opened her mouth to answer and then the cane was whickering through the air, smashing against her face. Blood spurted from her nose. Becky screamed. Momma's spectacles dropped into her gravy. The cane had been drawn back, had come down again, this time on top of her head, splitting the scalp. Momma had dropped to the floor. He had been out of his chair and around to where she lay dazed on the carpet, brandishing the cane, moving with a fat man's grotesque speed and agility, little eyes flashing, jowls quivering as he spoke to her just as he had always spoken to his children during such outbursts. 'Now. Now by Christ. I guess you'll take your medicine now. Goddam puppy. Whelp. Come on and take your medicine.' The cane had gone up and down on her seven more times before Brett and Mike got hold of him, dragged him away, wrestled the cane out of his hand. Jack

(little Jacky now he was little Jacky now dozing and mumbling on a cobwebby camp chair while the furnace roared into hollow life behind him)

knew exactly how many blows it had been because each soft *whump* against his mother's body had been engraved on his memory like the irrational swipe of a chisel on stone. Seven *whumps*. No more, no less. He and Becky crying, unbelieving, looking at their mother's spectacles lying in her mashed potatoes, one cracked lens smeared with gravy. Brett shouting at Daddy from the back hall, telling him he'd kill him if he moved. And Daddy saying over and over: 'Damn little puppy. Damn little whelp. Give me my cane, you damn little pup. Give it to me.' Brett brandishing it hysterically, saying yes, yes, I'll give it to you, just you move a little bit and I'll give you all you want and two extra. I'll give you *plenty*. Momma getting slowly to her feet, dazed, her face already puffed and swelling like an old tire with too much air in it, bleeding in four or five different places, and she had said a terrible thing, perhaps the only thing Momma had ever said which Jacky could recall word for word: 'Who's got the newspaper? Your daddy wants the funnies. Is it raining yet?' And then she sank to her knees again, her hair hanging in her puffed and bleeding face. Mike calling the doctor, babbling into the phone. Could he come right away? It was their mother. No, he couldn't say what the trouble was, not over the phone, not over a party line he couldn't. Just *come*. The doctor came and took Momma away to the hospital where Daddy had worked all of his adult life. Daddy, sobered up some (or perhaps only with the stupid cunning of any hard-pressed animal), told the doctor she had fallen downstairs. There was blood on the tablecloth because he had tried to wipe her dear face with it. Had her glasses flown all the way through the living room and into the dining room to land in her mashed potatoes and gravy? the doctor asked with a kind of horrid, grinning sarcasm. Is that what happened, Mark? I have heard of folks who can get a radio station on their gold fillings and I have seen a man get shot between the eyes and live to tell about it, but that is a new one on me. Daddy had merely shook his head and said he didn't know; they must have fallen off her face when he brought her through the dining room. The four children had been stunned to silence by the calm stupendousness of the lie. Four days later Brett quit his job in the mill and joined the Army. Jack had always felt it was not just the sudden and irrational beating his father had administered at the dinner table but the fact that, in the hospital, their mother had corroborated their father's story while holding the hand of the parish priest. Revolted, Brett had left them to whatever might come. He had been killed in Dong Ho province in 1965, the year when Jack Torrance, undergraduate, had joined the active college agitation to end the war. He had waved his brother's bloody shirt at rallies that were increasingly well attended, but it was not Brett's face that hung before his eyes when he spoke – it was the face of his mother, a dazed, uncomprehending face, his mother saying: 'Who's got the newspaper?'

Mike escaped three years later when Jack was twelve – he went to UNH on a hefty Merit Scholarship. A year after that their father died of a sudden, massive stroke which occurred while he was prepping a patient for surgery. He had collapsed in his flapping and untucked hospital whites, dead possibly even before he hit the industrial black-and-red hospital tiles, and three days later the man who had dominated Jacky's life, the irrational white ghost-god, was under ground.

The stone read *Mark Anthony Torrance, Loving Father.* To that Jack would have added one line: *He Knew How to Play Elevator.*

There had been a great lot of insurance money. There are people who collect insurance as compulsively as others collect coins and stamps, and Mark Torrance had been that type. The insurance money came in at the same time the monthly policy payments and liquor bills stopped. For five years they had been rich. Nearly rich . . .

In his shallow, uneasy sleep his face rose before him as if in a glass, his face but not his face, the wide eyes and innocent bowed mouth of a boy sitting in the hall with his trucks, waiting for his daddy, waiting for the white ghost-god, waiting for the elevator to rise up with dizzying exhilarating speed through the salt-and-sawdust mist of exhaled taverns, waiting perhaps for it to go crashing down, spilling old clock-springs out of his ears while his daddy roared with laughter, and it

(transformed into Danny's face, so much like his own had been, his eyes had been light blue while Danny's were cloudy gray, but the lips still made a bow and the complexion was fair; Danny in his study, wearing training pants, all his papers soggy and the fine misty smell of beer rising . . . a dreadful batter all in ferment, rising on the wings of yeast, the breath of taverns . . . snap of bone . . . his own voice, mewling drunkenly *Danny, you okay doc? . . . Oh God oh God your poor sweet arm* . . . and that face transformed into)

(momma's dazed face rising up from below the table, punched and bleeding, and momma was saying)

('*—from your father. I repeat, an enormously important announcement from your father. Please stay tuned or tune immediately to the Happy Jack frequency. Repeat, tune immediately to the Happy Hour frequency. I repeat—*')

A slow dissolve. Disembodied voices echoing up to him as if along an endless, cloudy hallway.

(*Things keep getting in the way, dear Tommy . . .*)

(*Medoc, are you here? I've been sleepwalking again, my dear. It's the inhuman monsters that I fear . . .*)

(*'Excuse me, Mr Ullman, but isn't this the . . .'*)

. . . office, with its file cabinets, Ullman's big desk, a blank reservations book for next year already in place – never misses a trick, that Ullman – all the keys hanging neatly on their hooks

(except for one, which one, which key, passkey – passkey, passkey, who's got the passkey? if we went upstairs perhaps we'd see)

and the big two-way radio on its shelf.

He snapped it on. CB transmissions coming in short, crackly bursts. He switched the band and dialed across burst of music, news, a preacher haranguing a softly moaning congregation, a weather report. And another voice which he dialed back to. It was his father's voice.

'—kill him. You have to kill him, Jacky, and her, too. Because a real artist must suffer. Because each man kills the thing he loves. Because they'll always be conspiring against you, trying to hold you back and drag you down. Right this minute that boy of yours is in where he shouldn't be. Trespassing. That's what he's doing. He's a goddam little pup. Cane him for it, Jacky, cane him within an inch of his life. Have a drink, Jacky my boy, and we'll play the elevator game. Then I'll go with you while you give him his medicine. I know you can do it, of course you can. You must kill him. You have to kill him, Jacky, and her, too. Because a real artist must suffer. Because each man—'

His father's voice, going up higher and higher, becoming something maddening, not human at all, something squealing and petulant and maddening, the voice of the Ghost-God, the Pig-God, coming dead at him out of the radio and

'*No!*' he screamed back. 'You're *dead*, you're in your *grave*, you're not in me at all!' Because he had cut all the father out of him and it was not right that he should come back, creeping through this hotel two thousand miles from the New England town where his father had lived and died.

He raised the radio up and brought it down, and it smashed on the floor spilling old clocksprings and tubes like the result of some crazy elevator game gone awry, making his father's voice gone, leaving only his voice, Jack's voice, Jacky's voice, chanting in the cold reality of the office:

'*—dead, you're dead, you're dead!*'

And the startled sound of Wendy's feet hitting the floor over his head, and Wendy's startled, frightened voice: 'Jack? *Jack!*'

He stood, blinking down at the shattered radio. Now there was only the snowmobile in the equipment shed to link them to the outside world.

He put his hands over his eyes and clutched at his temples. He was getting a headache.

Chapter Twenty-seven

Catatonic

Wendy ran down the hall in her stocking feet and ran down the main stairs to the lobby two at a time. She didn't look up at the carpeted flight that led to the second floor, but if she had, she would have seen Danny standing at the top of them, still and silent, his unfocused eyes directed out into indifferent space, his thumb in his mouth, the collar and shoulders of his shirt damp. There were puffy bruises on his neck and just below his chin.

Jack's cries had ceased, but that did nothing to ease her fear. Ripped out of her sleep by his voice, raised in that old hectoring pitch she remembered so well, she still felt that she was dreaming – but another part knew she was awake, and that terrified her more. She half-expected to burst into the office and find him standing over Danny's sprawled-out body, drunk and confused.

She pushed through the door and Jack was standing there, rubbing at his temples with his fingers. His face was ghost-white. The two-way CB radio lay at his feet in a sprinkling of broken glass.

'Wendy?' he asked uncertainly. 'Wendy—?'

The bewilderment seemed to grow and for a moment she saw his true face, the one he ordinarily kept so well hidden, and it was a face of desperate unhappiness, the face of an animal caught in a snare beyond its ability to decipher and render harmless. Then the muscles began to work, began to writhe under the skin, the mouth began to tremble infirmly, the Adam's apple began to rise and fall.

Her own bewilderment and surprise were overlaid by shock: he was going to cry. She had seen him cry before, but never since he stopped drinking ... and never in those days unless he was very drunk and pathetically remorseful. He was a tight man, drum-tight, and his loss of control frightened her all over again.

He came toward her, the tears brimming over his lower lids now, his head shaking involuntarily as if in a fruitless effort to ward off this emotional storm, and his chest drew in a convulsive gasp that was expelled in a huge, racking sob. His feet, clad in Hush Puppies, stumbled over the wreck of the radio and he almost fell into her arms, making her stagger back with his weight. His breath blew into her face and there was no smell of liquor on it. Of course not; there was no liquor up here.

'What's wrong?' She held him as best she could. 'Jack, what is it?'

But he could do nothing at first but sob, clinging to her, almost crushing the wind from her, his head turning on her shoulder in that helpless, shaking, warding-off gesture. His sobs were heavy and fierce. He was shuddering all over, his muscles jerking beneath his plaid shirt and jeans.

'Jack? What? Tell me what's wrong!'

At last the sobs began to change themselves into words, most of them incoherent at first, but coming clearer as his tears began to spend themselves.

'... dream, I guess it was a dream, but it was so real, I ... it was my mother saying that Daddy was going to be on the radio and I ... he was ... he was telling me to ... I don't know, he was *yelling* at me ... and so I broke the radio ... to shut him up. To shut him up. He's dead. I don't even want to dream about him. He's dead. My God, Wendy, my God. I never had a nightmare like that. I never want to have another one. Christ! It was awful.'

'You just fell asleep in the office?'

'No ... not here. Downstairs.' He was straightening a little now, his weight coming off her, and the steady back-and-forth motion of his head first slowed and then stopped.

'I was looking through those old papers. Sitting on a chair I set up down there. Milk receipts. Dull stuff. And I guess I just drowsed off. That's when I started to dream. I must have sleepwalked up here.' He essayed a shaky little laugh against her neck. 'Another first.'

'Where is Danny, Jack?'

'I don't know. Isn't he with you?'

'He wasn't ... downstairs with you?'

He looked over his shoulder and his face tightened at what he saw on her face.

'Never going to let me forget that, are you, Wendy?'

'Jack—'

'When I'm on my deathbed you'll lean over and say, "It serves you right, remember the time you broke Danny's arm?" '

'Jack!'

'Jack what?' he asked hotly, and jumped to his feet. 'Are you denying that's what you're thinking? That I hurt him? That I hurt him once before and I could hurt him again?'

'I want to know where he is, that's all!'

'Go ahead, yell your fucking head off, that'll make everything okay, won't it?'

She turned and walked out the door.

He watched her go, frozen for a moment, a blotter covered with fragments of broken glass in one hand. Then he dropped it into the wastebasket, went after her, and caught her by the lobby desk. He put his hands on her shoulders and turned her around. Her face was carefully set.

'Wendy, I'm sorry. It was the dream. I'm upset. Forgive?'

'Of course,' she said, her face not changing expression. Her wooden shoulders slipped out of his hands. She walked to the middle of the lobby and called: '*Hey, doc! Where are you?*'

Silence came back. She walked toward the double lobby doors, opened one of them, and stepped out onto the path Jack had shoveled. It was more like a trench; the packed and drifted snow through which the path was cut came to her shoulders. She called again, her breath coming out in a white plume. When she came back in she had begun to look scared.

Controlling his irritation with her, he said reasonably: 'Are you *sure* he's not sleeping in his room?'

'I told you, he was playing somewhere when I was knitting. I could hear him downstairs.'

'Did you fall asleep?'

'What's that got to do with it? Yes. *Danny?*'

'Did you look in his room when you came downstairs just now?'

'I—' She stopped.

He nodded. 'I didn't really think so.'

He started up the stairs without waiting for her. She followed him, half-running, but he was taking the risers two at a time. She almost crashed into his back when he came to a dead stop on the first-floor landing. He was rooted there, looking up, his eyes wide.

'What—?' she began, and followed his gaze.

Danny still stood there, his eyes blank, sucking his thumb. The marks on his throat were cruelly visible in the light of the hall's electric flambeaux.

'*Danny!*' she shrieked.

It broke Jack's paralysis and they rushed up the stairs together to where he stood. Wendy fell on her knees beside him and swept the boy into her arms. Danny came pliantly enough, but he did not hug her back. It was like hugging a padded stick, and the sweet taste of horror flooded her mouth. He only sucked his thumb and stared with indifferent blankness out into the stairwell beyond both of them.

'Danny, what happened?' Jack asked. He put out his hand to touch the puffy side of Danny's neck. 'Who did this to y—'

'*Don't you touch him!*' Wendy hissed. She clutched Danny in her arms, lifted him, and had retreated halfway down the stairs before Jack could do more than stand up, confused.

'What? Wendy, what the hell are you t—'

'Don't you touch him! I'll kill you if you lay your hands on him again!'

'Wendy—'

'You bastard!'

She turned and ran down the rest of the stairs to the first floor. Danny's head jounced mildly up and down as she ran. His thumb was lodged securely in his mouth. His eyes were soaped windows. She turned right at the foot of the stairs, and Jack heard her feet retreat to the end of it. Their bedroom door slammed. The bolt was run home. The lock turned. Brief silence. Then the soft, muttered sounds of comforting.

He stood for an unknown length of time, literally paralyzed by all that had happened in such a short space of time. His dream was still with him, painting everything a slightly unreal shade. It was as if he had taken a very mild mescaline hit. Had he maybe hurt Danny as Wendy thought? Tried to strangle his son at his dead father's request? No. He would never hurt Danny.

(*He fell down the stairs, Doctor.*)

He would never hurt Danny *now.*

(*How could I know the bug bomb was defective?*)

Never in his life had he been willfully vicious when he was sober.

(*Except when you almost killed George Hatfield.*)

'No!' he cried into the darkness. He brought both fists crashing down on his legs, again and again and again.

Wendy sat in the overstuffed chair by the window with Danny on her lap, holding him, crooning the old meaningless words, the ones you never remember afterward no matter how a thing turns out. He had folded onto her lap with neither protest nor gladness, like a paper cutout of himself, and his eyes didn't even shift toward the door when Jack cried out 'No!' somewhere in the hallway.

The confusion had receded a little bit in her mind, but she now discovered something even worse behind it. Panic.

Jack had done this, she had no doubt of it. His denials meant nothing to her. She thought it was perfectly possible that Jack had tried to throttle Danny in his sleep just as he had smashed the CB radio in his sleep. He was having a breakdown of some kind. But what was she going to do about it? She couldn't stay locked in here forever. They would have to eat.

There was really only one question, and it was asked in a mental voice of utter coldness and pragmatism, the voice of her maternity, a cold and passionless voice once it was directed away from the closed circle of mother and child and out toward Jack. It was a voice that spoke of self-preservation only after son-preservation and its question was.

(*Exactly how dangerous is he?*)

He had denied doing it. He had been horrified at the bruises, at Danny's soft and implacable disconnection. If he had done it, a separate section of himself had been responsible. The fact that he had done it when he was asleep was – in a terrible, twisted way – encouraging. Wasn't it possible that he could be trusted to get them out of here? To get them down and away. And after that . . .

But she could see no further than she and Danny arriving safe at Dr Edmonds's office in Sidewinder. She had no particular need to see further. The present crisis was more than enough to keep her occupied.

She crooned to Danny, rocking him on her breasts. Her fingers, on his shoulder, had noticed that his T-shirt was damp, but they had not bothered reporting the information to her brain in more than a cursory way. If it had been reported, she might have remembered that Jack's hands, as he had hugged her in the office and sobbed against her neck, had been dry. It might have given her pause. But her mind was still on other things. The decision had to be made – to approach Jack or not?

Actually it was not much of a decision. There was nothing she could do alone, not even carry Danny down to the office and call for help on the CB radio. He had suffered a great shock. He ought to be taken out quickly before any permanent damage could be done. She refused to let herself believe that permanent damage might already have been done.

And still she agonized over it, looking for another alternative. She did not want to put Danny back within Jack's reach. She was aware now that she had made one bad decision when she had gone against her feelings (and Danny's) and allowed the snow to close them in . . . for Jack's sake. Another bad decision when she had shelved the idea of divorce. Now she was nearly paralyzed by the idea that she might be making another mistake, one she would regret every minute of every day of the rest of her life.

There was not a gun in the place. There were knives hanging from the magnetized runners in the kitchen, but Jack was between her and them.

In her striving to make the right decision, to find the alternative, the bitter irony of her thoughts did not occur: an hour ago she had been asleep, firmly convinced that things were all right and soon would be even better. Now she was considering the possibility of using a butcher knife on her husband if he tried to interfere with her and her son.

At last she stood up with Danny in her arms, her legs trembling. There was no other way. She would have to assume that Jack awake was Jack sane, and that he would help her get Danny down to Sidewinder and Dr Edmonds. And if Jack tried to do anything *but* help, God help *him*.

She went to the door and unlocked it. Shifting Danny up to her shoulder, she opened it and went out into the hall.

'Jack?' she called nervously, and got no answer.

With growing trepidation she walked down to the stairwell, but Jack was not there. And as she stood there on the landing, wondering what to do next, the singing came up from below, rich, angry, bitterly satiric:

'*Roll me over*
In the clo-ho-ver,
Roll me over, lay me down and do it again.'

She was frightened even more by the sound of him than she had been by his silence, but there was still no alternative. She started down the stairs.

Chapter Twenty-eight

'It Was Her!'

Jack had stood on the stairs, listening to the crooning, comforting sounds coming muffled through the locked door, and slowly his confusion had given way to anger. Things had never really changed. Not to Wendy. He could be off the juice for twenty years and still when he came home at night and she embraced him at the door, he would see/sense that little flare of her nostrils as she tried to divine scotch or gin fumes riding the outbound train of his exhalation. She was always going to assume the worst; if he and Danny got in a car accident with a drunken blindman who had had a stroke just before the collision, she would silently blame Danny's injuries on him and turn away.

Her face as she had snatched Danny away – it rose up before him and he suddenly wanted to wipe the anger that had been on it out with his fist.

She had no goddam right!

Yes, maybe at first. He had been a lush, he had done terrible things. Breaking Danny's arm had been a terrible thing. But if a man reforms, doesn't he deserve to have his reformation credited sooner or later? And if he doesn't get it, doesn't he deserve the game to go with the name? If a father constantly accuses his virginal daughter of screwing every boy in junior high, must she not at last grow weary (enough) of it to earn her scoldings? And if a wife secretly – and not so secretly – continues to believe that her teetotaling husband is a drunk . . .

He got up, walked slowly down to the first-floor landing, and stood there for a moment. He took his handkerchief from his back pocket, wiped his lips with it, and considered going down and pounding on the bedroom door, demanding to be let in so he could see his son. She had no right to be so goddam highhanded.

Well, sooner or later she'd have to come out, unless she planned a radical sort of diet for the two of them. A rather ugly grin touched his lips at the thought. Let her come to him. She would in time.

He went downstairs to the ground floor, stood aimlessly by the lobby desk for a moment, then turned right. He went into the dining room and stood just inside the door. The empty tables, their white linen cloths neatly cleaned and pressed beneath their clear plastic covers, glimmered up at him. All was deserted now but

(*Dinner Will Be Served at 8 p.m.*
Unmasking and Dancing At Midnight)

Jack walked among the tables, momentarily forgetting his wife and son upstairs, forgetting the dream, the smashed radio, the bruises. He trailed his fingers over the slick plastic dustcovers, trying to imagine how it must have been on that hot August night in 1945, the war won, the future stretching ahead so various and new, like a land of dreams. The bright and particolored Japanese lanterns hung the whole length of the circular drive, the golden-yellow light spilling from these high windows that were now drifted over with snow. Men and women in costume, here a glittering princess, there a high-booted cavalier, flashing jewelry and flashing wit everywhere, dancing, liquor flowing freely, first wine and then cocktails and then perhaps boiler-makers, the level of conversation going up and up and up until the jolly cry rang out from the bandmaster's podium, the cry of 'Unmask! Unmask!'

(*And the Red Death held sway . . .*)

He found himself standing on the other side of the dining room, just outside the stylized batwing doors of the Colorado Lounge where, on that night in 1945, all the booze would have been free.

(*Belly up to the bar, pardner, the drinks're on the house.*)

He stepped through the batwings and into the deep, folded shadows of the bar. And a strange thing occurred. He had been in here before, once to check the inventory sheet Ullman had left, and he knew the place had been stripped clean. The shelves were totally bare. But now, lit only murkily by the light which filtered through from the dining room (which was itself only dimly lit because of the snow blocking the windows), he thought he saw ranks and ranks of bottles twinkling mutedly behind the bar, and syphons, and even beer dripping from the spigots of all three highly polished taps. Yes, he could even *smell* beer, that damp and fermented and yeasty odor, no different from the smell that had hung finely misted around his father's face every night when he came home from work.

Eyes widening, he fumbled for the wall switch, and the low, intimate bar-lighting came on, circles of twenty-watt bulbs emplanted on the tops of the three wagon-wheel chandeliers overhead.

The shelves were all empty. They had not even as yet gathered a good coat of dust. The beer taps were dry, as were the chrome drains beneath them. To his left and right, the velvet-upholstered booths stood like men with high backs, each one designed to give a maximum of privacy to the couple inside. Straight ahead, across the red-carpeted floor, forty barstools stood around the horseshoe-shaped bar. Each stool was upholstered in leather and embossed with cattle brands – Circle H, Bar D Bar (that was fitting), Rocking W, Lazy B.

He approached it, giving his head a little shake of bewilderment as he did so. It was like that day on the playground when . . . but there was no sense in thinking about that. Still he could have sworn he had seen those bottles, vaguely, it was true, the way you see the darkened shapes of furniture in a room where the curtains have been drawn. Mild glints on glass. The only thing that remained was that smell of beer, and Jack knew that was a smell that faded into the woodwork of every bar in the world after a certain period of time, not to be eradicated by any cleaner invented. Yet the smell here seemed sharp . . . almost fresh.

He sat down on one of the stools and propped his elbows on the bar's leather-cushioned edge. At his left hand was a bowl for peanuts – now empty, of course. The first bar he'd been in for nineteen months and the damned thing was dry – just his luck. All the same, a bitterly powerful wave of nostalgia swept over him, and the physical craving for a drink seemed to work itself up from his belly to his throat to his mouth and nose, shriveling and wrinkling the tissues as it went, making them cry out for something wet and long and cold.

He glanced at the shelves again in wild, irrational hope but the shelves were just as empty as before. He grinned in pain and frustration. His fists, clenching slowly, made minute scratchings on the bar's leather-padded edge.

'Hi, Lloyd,' he said. 'A little slow tonight, isn't it?'

Lloyd said it was. Lloyd asked him what it would be.

'Now I'm really glad you asked me that,' Jack said, 'really glad. Because I happen to have two twenties and two tens in my wallet and I was afraid they'd be sitting there until sometime next April. There isn't a Seven-Eleven around here, would you believe it? And I thought they had Seven-Elevens on the fucking *moon*.'

Lloyd sympathized.

'So here's what,' Jack said. 'You set me up an even twenty martinis. An even twenty, just like that, kazang. One for every month I've been on the wagon and one to grow on. You can do that, can't you? You aren't too busy?'

Lloyd said he wasn't busy at all.

'Good man. You line those martians up right along the bar and I'm going to take them down, one by one. White man's burden, Lloyd my man.'

Lloyd turned to do the job. Jack reached into his pocket for his money clip and came out with an Excedrin bottle instead. His money clip was on the bedroom bureau, and of course his skinny-shanks wife had locked him out of the bedroom. Nice going, Wendy. You bleeding bitch.

'I seem to be momentarily light,' Jack said. 'How's my credit in this joint, anyhow?'

Lloyd said his credit was fine.

'That's super. I like you, Lloyd. You were always the best of them. Best damned barkeep between Barre and Portland, Maine, Portland, *Oregon*, for that matter.'

Lloyd thanked him for saying so.

Jack thumped the cap from his Excedrin bottle, shook two tablets out, and flipped them into his mouth. The familiar acid-compelling taste flooded in.

He had a sudden sensation that people were watching him, curiously and with some contempt. The booths behind him were full – there were graying, distinguished men and beautiful young girls, all of them in costume, watching this sad exercise in the dramatic arts with cold amusement.

Jack whirled on his stool.

The booths were all empty, stretching away from the lounge door to the left and right, the line on his left cornering to flank the bar's horseshoe curve down the short length of the room. Padded leather seats and backs. Gleaming dark Formica tables, an ashtray on each one, a book of matches in each ashtray, the words *Colorado Lounge* stamped on each in gold leaf above the batwing-door logo.

He turned back, swallowing the rest of the dissolving Excedrin with a grimace.

'Lloyd, you're a wonder,' he said. 'Set up already. Your speed is only exceeded by the soulful beauty of your Neopolitan eyes. *Salud.*'

Jack contemplated the twenty imaginary drinks, the martini glasses blushing droplets of condensation, each with a swizzle poked through a plump green olive. He could almost smell gin on the air.

'The wagon,' he said. 'Have you ever been acquainted with a gentleman who has hopped up on the wagon?'

Lloyd allowed as how he had met such men from time to time.

'Have you ever renewed acquaintances with such a man after he hopped back off?'

Lloyd could not, in all honesty, recall.

'You never did, then,' Jack said. He curled his hand around the first drink, carried his fist to his mouth, which was open, and turned his fist up. He swallowed and then tossed the imaginary glass over his shoulder. The people were back again, fresh from their costume ball, studying him, laughing behind their hands. He could feel them. If the backbar had featured a mirror instead of those damn stupid empty shelves, he could have seen them. Let them stare. Fuck them. Let anybody stare who wanted to stare.

'No, you never did,' he told Lloyd. 'Few men ever return from the fabled Wagon, but those who do come with a fearful tale to tell. When you jump on, it seems like the brightest, cleanest Wagon you ever saw, with ten-foot wheels to keep the bed of it high out of the gutter where all the drunks are laying around with their brown bags and their Thunderbird and their Granddad Flash's Popskull Bourbon. You're away from all the people who throw you nasty looks and tell you to clean up your act or go put it on in another town. From the gutter, that's the finest-lookin Wagon you ever saw, Lloyd my boy. All hung with bunting and a brass band in front and three majorettes to each side, twirling their batons and flashing their panties at you. Man, you got to get on that Wagon and away from the juicers that are straining canned heat and smelling their own puke to get high again and poking along the gutter for butts with half an inch left below the filter.'

He drained two more imaginary drinks and tossed the glasses back over his shoulder. He could almost hear them smashing on the floor. And goddam if he wasn't starting to feel high. It was the Excedrin.

'So you climb up,' he told Lloyd. 'and ain't you glad to be there. My God yes, that's affirmative. That Wagon is the biggest and best float in the whole parade, and everybody is lining the streets and clapping and cheering and waving, all for you. Except for the winos passed out in the gutter. Those guys used to be your friends, but that's all behind you now.'

He carried his empty fist to his mouth and sluiced down another – four down, sixteen to go. Making excellent progress. He swayed a little on the stool. Let em stare, if that was how they got off. Take a picture, folks, it'll last longer.

'Then you start to see things, Lloydy-my-boy. Things you missed from the gutter. Like how the floor of the Wagon is nothing but straight pine boards, so fresh they're still bleeding sap, and if you took your shoes off you'd be sure to get a splinter. Like how the only furniture in the Wagon is these long benches with high backs and no cushions to sit on, and in fact they are nothing but pews with a songbook every five feet or so. Like how all the people sitting in the pews on the Wagon are these flatchested el birdos in long dresses with a little lace around the collar and their hair pulled back into buns until it's so tight you can almost hear it screaming. And every face is flat and pale and shiny, and they're all singing "Shall we gather at the riiiiver, the beautiful, the beautiful, the *riiiiiver*," and up front there's this reekin bitch with blond hair, playing the organ and tellin em to sing louder, sing louder. And somebody slams a songbook into your hands and says, "Sing it out brother. If you expect to stay on this Wagon, you got to sing morning, noon, and night. Especially at night." And that's when you realize what the Wagon really is, Lloyd. It's a church with bars on the windows, a church for women and a prison for you.'

He stopped. Lloyd was gone. Worse still, he had never been there. The drinks had never been there. Only the people in the booths, the people from the costume party, and he could almost hear their muffled laughter as they held their hands to their mouths and pointed, their eyes sparkling with cruel pinpoints of light.

He whirled around again. 'Leave me—'

(alone?)

All the booths were empty. The sound of laughter had died like a stir of autumn leaves. Jack stared at the empty lounge for a tick of time, his eyes wide and dark. A pulse beat noticeably in the center of his forehead. In the very center of him a cold certainty was forming and the certainty was that he was losing his mind. He felt an urge to pick up the bar stool next to him, reverse it, and go through the place like an avenging whirlwind. Instead he whirled back around to the bar and began to bellow:

'Roll me over
In the clo-ho-ver,
Roll me over, lay me down and do it again.'

Danny's face rose before him, not Danny's normal face, lively and alert, the eyes sparkling and open, but the catatonic, zombielike face of a stranger, the eyes dull and opaque, the mouth pursed babyishly around his thumb. What was he doing, sitting here and talking to himself like a sulky teen-ager when his son was upstairs, someplace, acting like something that belonged in a padded room, acting the way Wally Hollis said Vic Stenger had been before the men in the white coats had to come and take him away?

(*But I never put a hand on him! Goddammit, I didn't!*)

'Jack?' The voice was timid, hesitant.

He was so startled he almost fell off the stool whirling it around. Wendy was standing just inside the batwing doors, Danny cradled in her arms like some waxen horror show dummy. The three of them made a tableau that Jack felt very strongly; it was just before the curtain of Act II in some oldtime temperance play, one so poorly mounted that the prop man had forgotten to stock the shelves of the Den of Iniquity.

'I never touched him,' Jack said thickly. 'I never have since the night I broke his arm. Not even to spank him.'

'Jack, that doesn't matter now. What matters is—'

'*This matters!*' he shouted. He brought one fist crashing down on the bar, hard enough to make the empty peanut dishes jump. '*It matters, goddammit, it matters!*'

'Jack, we have to get him off the mountain. He's—'

Danny began to stir in her arms. The slack, empty expression on his face had begun to break up like a thick matte of ice over some buried surface. His lips twisted, as if at some weird taste. His eyes widened. His hands came up as if to cover them and then dropped back.

Abruptly he stiffened in her arms. His back arched into a bow, making Wendy stagger. And he suddenly began to shriek, mad sounds that escaped his straining throat in bolt after crazy, echoing bolt. The sound seemed to fill the empty downstairs and come back at them like banshees. There might have been a hundred Dannys, all screaming at once.

'*Jack!*' she cried in terror. '*Oh God Jack what's wrong with him?*'

He came off the stool, numb from the waist down, more frightened than he had ever been in his life. What hole had his son poked through and into? What dark nest? And what had been in there to sting him?

'Danny!' he roared. '*Danny!*'

Danny saw him. He broke his mother's grip with a sudden, fierce strength that gave her no chance to hold him. She stumbled back against one of the booths and nearly fell into it.

'*Daddy!*' he screamed, running to Jack, his eyes huge and affrighted. '*Oh Daddy Daddy, it was her! Her! Her! Oh Daaaaahdeee—*'

He slammed into Jack's arms like a blunt arrow, making Jack rock on his feet. Danny clutched at him furiously, at first seeming to pummel him like a fighter, then clutching his belt and sobbing against his shirt. Jack could feel his son's face, hot and working, against his belly.

Daddy, it was her.

Jack looked slowly up into Wendy's face. His eyes were like small silver coins.

'Wendy?' Voice soft, nearly purring. 'Wendy, what did you do to him?'

Wendy stared back at him in stunned disbelief, her face pallid. She shook her head.

'Oh Jack, you must know—'

Outside it had begun to snow again.

Chapter Twenty-nine

Kitchen Talk

Jack carried Danny into the kitchen. The boy was still sobbing wildly, refusing to look up from Jack's chest. In the kitchen he gave Danny back to Wendy, who still seemed stunned and disbelieving.

'Jack, I don't know what he's talking about. Please, you must believe that.'

'I do believe it,' he said, although he had to admit to himself that it gave him a certain amount of pleasure to see the shoe switched to the other foot with such dazzling, unexpected speed. But his anger at Wendy had been only a passing gut twitch. In his heart he knew Wendy would pour a can of gasoline over herself and strike a match before harming Danny.

The large tea kettle was on the back burner, poking along on low heat. Jack dropped a teabag into his own large ceramic cup and poured hot water halfway.

'Got cooking sherry, don't you?' he asked Wendy.

'What? . . . oh, sure. Two or three bottles of it.'

'Which cupboard?'

She pointed, and Jack took one of the bottles down. He poured a hefty dollop into the teacup, put the sherry back, and filled the last quarter of the cup with milk. Then he added three tablespoons of sugar and stirred. He brought it to Danny, whose sobs had tapered off to snifflings and hitchings. But he was trembling all over, and his eyes were wide and starey.

'Want you to drink this, doc,' Jack said. 'It's going to taste frigging awful, but it'll make you feel better. Can you drink it for your daddy?'

Danny nodded that he could and took the cup. He drank a little, grimaced, and looked questioningly at Jack. Jack nodded, and Danny drank again. Wendy felt the familiar twist of jealousy somewhere in her middle, knowing the boy would not have drunk it for her.

On the heels of that came an uncomfortable, even startling thought: Had she *wanted* to think Jack was to blame? Was she that jealous? It was the way her mother would have thought, that was the really horrible thing. She could remember a Sunday when her Dad had taken her to the park and she had toppled from the second tier of the jungle gym, cutting both knees. When her father brought her home, her mother had shrieked at him: *What did you do? Why weren't you watching her? What kind of a father are you?*

(She had hounded him to his grave; by the time he divorced her it was too late.)

She had never even given Jack the benefit of the doubt. Not the smallest. Wendy felt her face burn yet knew with a kind of helpless finality that if the whole thing were to be played over again, she would do and think the same way. She carried part of her mother with her always, for good or bad.

'Jack—' she began, not sure if she meant to apologize or justify. Either, she knew, would be useless.

'Not now,' he said.

It took Danny fifteen minutes to drink half of the big cup's contents, and by that time he had calmed visibly. The shakes were almost gone.

Jack put his hands solemnly on his son's shoulders. 'Danny, do you think you can tell us exactly what happened to you? It's very important.'

Danny looked from Jack to Wendy, then back again. In the silent pause, their setting and situation made themselves known: the whoop of the wind outside, driving fresh snow down from the northwest; the creaking and groaning of the old hotel as it settled into another storm. The fact of their disconnect came to Wendy with unexpected force as it sometimes did, like a blow under the heart.

'I want . . . to tell you everything,' Danny said. 'I wish I had before.' He picked up the cup and held it, as if comforted by the warmth.

'Why didn't you, son?' Jack brushed Danny's sweaty, tumbled hair back gently from his brow.

'Because Uncle Al got you the job. And I couldn't figure out how it was good for you here and bad for you here at the same time. It was . . .' He looked at them for help. He did not have the necessary word.

'A dilemma?' Wendy asked gently. 'When neither choice seems any good?'

'Yes, that.' He nodded, relieved.

Wendy said: 'The day you trimmed the hedges, Danny and I had a talk in the truck. The day the first real snow came. Remember?'

Jack nodded. The day he had trimmed the hedges was very clear in his mind.

Wendy sighed. 'I guess we didn't talk enough. Did we, doc?'

Danny, the picture of woe, shook his head.

'Exactly what did you talk about?' Jack asked. 'I'm not sure how much I like my wife and son—'

'—discussing how much they love you?'

'Whatever it was, I don't understand it. I feel like I came into a movie just after the intermission.'

'We were discussing you,' Wendy said quietly. 'And maybe we didn't say it all in words, but we both knew. Me because I'm your wife and Danny because he . . . just understands things.'

Jack was silent.

'Danny said it just right. The place seemed good for you. You were away from all the pressures that made you so unhappy at Stovington. You were your own boss, working with your hands so you could save your brain – all of your brain – for your evenings writing. Then . . . I don't know just when . . . the place began to seem bad for you. Spending all that time down in the cellar, sifting through those old papers, all that old history. Talking in your sleep—'

'In my sleep?' Jack asked. His face wore a cautious, startled expression. 'I talk in my sleep?'

'Most of it is slurry. Once I got up to use the bathroom and you were saying, "To hell with it, bring in the slots at least, no one will know, no one will ever know." Another time you woke me right up, practically yelling, "Unmask, unmask, unmask." '

'Jesus Christ,' he said, and rubbed a hand over his face. He looked ill.

'All your old drinking habits, too. Chewing Excedrin. Wiping your mouth all the time. Cranky in the morning. And you haven't been able to finish the play yet, have you?'

'No. Not yet, but it's only a matter of time. I've been thinking about something else . . . a new project—'

'This hotel. The project Al Shockley called you about. The one he wanted you to drop.'

'How do you know about that?' Jack barked. 'Were you listening in? You—'

'No,' she said. 'I couldn't have listened in if I'd wanted to, and you'd know that if you were thinking straight. Danny and I were downstairs that night. The switchboard is shut down. Our phone upstairs was the only one in the hotel that was working, because it's patched directly into the outside line. You told me so yourself.'

'Then how could you know what Al told me?'

'Danny told me. Danny knew. The same way he sometimes knows when things are misplaced, or when people are thinking about divorce.'

'The doctor said—'

She shook her head impatiently. 'The doctor was full of shit and we both know it. We've known it all the time. Remember when Danny said he wanted to see the firetrucks? That was no hunch. *He was just a baby.* He *knows* things. And now I'm afraid . . .' She looked at the bruises on Danny's neck.

'Did you really know Uncle Al had called me, Danny?'

Danny nodded. 'He was really mad, Daddy. Because you called Mr Ullman and Mr Ullman called him. Uncle Al didn't want you to write anything about the hotel.'

'Jesus,' Jack said again. 'The bruises, Danny. Who tried to strangle you?'

Danny's face went dark. '*Her*,' he said, 'The woman in that room. In 217. The dead lady.' His lips began to tremble again, and he seized the teacup and drank.

Jack and Wendy exchanged a scared look over his bowed head.

'Do you know anything about this?' he asked her.

She shook her head. 'Not about this, no.'

'Danny?' He raised the boy's frightened face. 'Try son. We're right here.'

'I knew it was bad here,' Danny said in a low voice. 'Ever since we were in Boulder. Because Tony gave me dreams about it.'

'What dreams?'

'I can't remember everything. He showed me the Overlook at night, with a skull and crossbones on the front. And there was pounding. Something . . . I don't remember what . . . chasing after me. A monster. Tony showed me about redrum.'

'What's that, doc?' Wendy asked.

He shook his head. 'I don't know.'

'Rum, like yo-ho-ho and a bottle of rum?' Jack asked.

Danny shook his head again. 'I don't know. Then we got here, and Mr Hallorann talked to me in his car. Because he has the shine, too.'

'Shine?'

'It's . . .' Danny made a sweeping, all-encompassing gesture with his hands. 'It's being able to understand things. To know things. Sometimes you see things. Like me knowing Uncle Al called. And Mr Hallorann knowing you call me doc. Mr Hallorann, he was peeling potatoes in the Army when he knew his brother got killed in a train crash. And when he called home it was true.'

'Holy God,' Jack whispered. 'You're not making this up, are you, Dan?'

Danny shook his head violently. 'No, I swear to God.' Then, with a touch of pride he added: 'Mr Hallorann said I had the best shine of anyone he ever met. We could talk back and forth to each other without hardly opening our mouths.'

His parents looked at each other again, frankly stunned.

'Mr Hallorann got me alone because he was worried,' Danny went on. 'He said this was a bad place for people who shine. He said he'd seen things. I saw something, too. Right after I talked to him. When Mr Ullman was taking us around.'

'What was it?' Jack asked.

'In the Presidential Sweet. On the wall by the door going into the bedroom.

A whole lot of blood and some other stuff. Gushy stuff. I think . . . that the gushy stuff must have been brains.'

'Oh my God,' Jack said.

Wendy was now very pale, her lips nearly gray.

'This place,' Jack said. 'Some pretty bad types owned it awhile back. Organization people from Las Vegas.'

'Crooks?' Danny asked.

'Yeah, crooks.' He looked at Wendy. 'In 1966 a big-time hood named Vito Gienelli got killed up there, along with his two bodyguards. There was a picture in the newspaper. Danny just described the picture.'

'Mr Hallorann said he saw some other stuff,' Danny told them. 'Once about the playground. And once it was something bad in that room. 217. A maid saw it and lost her job because she talked about it. So Mr Hallorann went up and he saw it too. But he didn't talk about it because he didn't want to lose his job. Except he told me never to go in there. But I did. Because I believed him when he said the things you saw here couldn't hurt you.' This last was nearly whispered in a low, husky voice, and Danny touched the puffed circle of bruises on his neck.

'What about the playground?' Jack asked in a strange, casual voice.

'I don't know. The playground, he said. And the hedge animals.'

Jack jumped a little, and Wendy looked at him, curiously.

'Have you seen anything down there, Jack?'

'No,' he said. 'Nothing.'

Danny was looking at him.

'Nothing,' he said again, more calmly. And that was true. He had been the victim of an hallucination. And that was *all*.

'Danny, we have to hear about the woman,' Wendy said gently.

So Danny told them, but his words came in cyclic bursts, sometimes almost verging on incomprehensible garble in his hurry to spit it out and be free of it. He pushed tighter and tighter against his mother's breasts as he talked.

'I went in,' he said. 'I stole the passkey and went in. It was like I couldn't help myself. I had to know. And she . . . the lady . . . was in the tub. She was dead. All swelled up. She was nuh-nuh . . . didn't have no clothes on.' He looked miserably at his mother. 'And she started to get up and she wanted me. I know she did because I could feel it. She wasn't even thinking, not the way you and Daddy think. It was black . . . it was hurt-think . . . like . . . like the wasps that night in my room! Only wanting to hurt. Like the wasps.'

He swallowed and there was silence for a moment, all quiet while the image of the wasps sank into them.

'So I ran,' Danny said. 'I ran but the door was closed. I left it open but it was closed. I didn't think about just opening it again and running out. I was scared. So I just . . . I leaned against the door and closed my eyes and thought of how Mr Hallorann said the things here were just like pictures in a book and if I . . . kept saying to myself . . . *you're not there, go away, you're not there* . . . she would go away. But it didn't work.'

His voice began to rise hysterically.

'She grabbed me . . . turned me around . . . I could see her eyes . . . how her eyes were . . . and she started to choke me . . . I could smell her . . . *I could smell how dead she was . . .*'

'Stop now, shhh,' Wendy said, alarmed. 'Stop, Danny. It's all right. It—'

She was getting ready to go into her croon again. The Wendy Torrance All-purpose Croon. Pat. Pending.

'Let him finish,' Jack said curtly.

'There isn't any more,' Danny said. 'I passed out. Either because she was choking me or just because I was scared. When I came to, I was dreaming you and Mommy were fighting over me and you wanted to do the Bad Thing again, Daddy. Then I knew it wasn't a dream at all . . . and I was awake . . . and . . . I wet my pants. I wet my pants like a baby.' His head fell back against Wendy's sweater and he began to cry with horrible weakness, his hands lying limp and spent in his lap.

Jack got up. 'Take care of him.'

'What are you going to do?' Her face was full of dread.

'I'm going up to that room, what did you think I was going to do? Have coffee?'

'No! Don't, Jack, please *don't!*'

'Wendy if there's someone else in the hotel, we have to know.'

'*Don't you dare leave us alone!*' she shrieked at him. Spittle flew from her lips with the force of her cry.

Jack said: 'Wendy, that's a remarkable imitation of your mom.'

She burst into tears then, unable to cover her face because Danny was on her lap.

'I'm sorry,' Jack said. 'But I have to, you know. I'm the goddam caretaker. It's what I'm paid for.'

She only cried harder and he left her that way, going out of the kitchen, rubbing his mouth with his handkerchief as the door swung shut behind him.

'Don't worry, mommy,' Danny said. 'He'll be all right. He doesn't shine. Nothing here can hurt him.'

Through her tears she said, 'No, I don't believe that.'

Chapter Thirty

217 Revisited

He took the elevator up and it was strange, because none of them had used the elevator since they moved in. He threw the brass handle over and it wheezed vibratoriously up the shaft, the brass grate rattling madly. Wendy had a true claustrophobe's horror of the elevator, he knew. She envisioned the three of them trapped in it between floors while the winter storms raged outside, she could see them growing thinner and weaker, starving to death. Or perhaps dining on each other, the way those Rugby players had. He remembered a bumper sticker he had seen in Boulder, RUGBY PLAYERS EAT THEIR OWN DEAD. He could think of others. YOU ARE WHAT YOU EAT. Or menu items. Welcome to the Overlook Dining Room, Pride of the Rockies. Eat in

Splendor at the Roof of the World. Human Haunch Broiled Over Matches *La Spécialité de la Maison*. The contemptuous smile flicked over his features again. As the number 2 rose on the shaft wall, he threw the brass handle back to the home position and the elevator car creaked to a stop. He took his Excedrin from his pocket, shook three of them into his hand, and opened the elevator door. Nothing in the Overlook frightened him. He felt that he and it were *simpático*.

He walked up the hall flipping his Excedrin into his mouth and chewing them one by one. He rounded the corner into the short corridor off the main hall. The door to Room 217 was ajar, and the passkey hung from the lock on its white paddle.

He frowned, feeling a wave of irritation and even real anger. Whatever had come of it, the boy had been trespassing. He had been told, and told bluntly, that certain areas of the hotel were off limits: the equipment shed, the basement, and all of the guest rooms. He would talk to Danny about that just as soon as the boy was over his fright. He would talk to him reasonably but sternly. There were plenty of fathers who would have done more than just talk. They would have administered a good shaking, and perhaps that was what Danny needed. If the boy had gotten a scare, wasn't that at least his just deserts?

He walked down to the door, removed the passkey, dropped it into his pocket, and stepped inside. The overhead light was on. He glanced at the bed, saw it was not rumpled, and then walked directly across to the bathroom door. A curious certainty had grown in him. Although Watson had mentioned no names or room numbers, Jack felt sure sure that this was the room the lawyer's wife and her stud had shared, that this was the bathroom where she had been found dead, full of barbiturates and Colorado Lounge booze.

He pushed the mirror-backed bathroom door open and stepped through. The light in here was off. He turned it on and observed the long, Pullman-car room, furnished in the distinctive early nineteen-hundreds-remodeled-in-the-twenties style that seemed common to all Overlook bathrooms, except for the ones on the third floor – those were properly Byzantine, as befitted the royalty, politicians, movie stars, and capos who had stayed there over the years.

The shower curtain, a pallid pastel pink, was drawn protectively around the long claw-footed tub.

(nevertheless they *did* move)

And for the first time he felt his new sense of sureness (almost cockiness) that had come over him when Danny ran to him shouting *It was her! It was her!* deserting him. A chilled finger pressed gently against the base of his spine, cooling him off ten degrees. It was joined by others and they suddenly rippled all the way up his back to his medulla oblongata, playing his spine like a jungle instrument.

His anger at Danny evaporated, and as he stepped forward and pushed the shower curtain back his mouth was dry and he felt only sympathy for his son and terror for himself.

The tub was dry and empty.

Relief and irritation vented in a sudden '*Pah!*' sound that escaped his compressed lips like a very small explosive. The tub had been scrubbed clean at the end of the season; except for the rust stain under the twin faucets, it sparkled. There was a faint but definable smell of cleanser, the kind that can irritate your nose with the smell of its own righteousness for weeks, even months, after it has been used.

He bent down and ran his fingertips along the bottom of the tub. Dry as a bone. Not even a hint of moisture. The boy had been either hallucinating or outright lying. He felt angry again. That was when the bathmat on the floor caught his attention. He frowned down at it. What was a bathmat doing in here? It should be down in the linen cupboard at the end of the wing with the rest of the sheets and towels and pillow slips. All the linen was supposed to be there. Not even the beds were really made up in these guest rooms; the mattresses had been zipped into clear plastic and then covered with bedspreads. He supposed Danny might have gone down and gotten it – the passkey would open the linen cupboard – but why? He brushed the tips of his fingers back and forth across it. The bathmat was bone dry.

He went back to the bathroom door and stood in it. Everything was all right. The boy had been dreaming. There was not a thing out of place. It was a little puzzling about the bathmat, granted, but the logical explanation was that some chambermaid, hurrying like mad on the last day of the season, had just forgotten to pick it up. Other than that, everything was—

His nostrils flared a little. Disinfectant, that self-righteous smell, cleaner-than-thou. And—

Soap?

Surely not. But once the smell had been identified, it was too clear to dismiss. Soap. And not one of those postcard-size bars of Ivory they provide you with in hotels and motels, either. This scent was light and perfumed, a lady's soap. It had a pink sort of smell. Camay or Lowila, the brand that Wendy had always used in Stovington.

(*It's nothing. It's your imagination.*)

(*yes like the hedges nevertheless they did move*)

(*They did not move!*)

He crossed jerkily to the door which gave on the hall, feeling the irregular thump of a headache beginning at his temples. Too much had happened today, too much by far. He wouldn't spank the boy or shake him, just talk to him, but by God, he wasn't going to add Room 217 to his problems. Not on the basis of a dry bathmat and a faint smell of Lowila soap. He—

There was a sudden rattling, metallic sound behind him. It came just as his hand closed around the doorknob, and an observer might have thought the brushed steel of the knob carried an electric charge. He jerked convulsively, eyes widening, other facial features drawing in, grimacing.

Then he had control of himself, a little, anyway, and he let go of the doorknob and turned carefully around. His joints creaked. He began to walk back to the bathroom door, step by leaden step.

The shower curtain which he had pushed back to look into the tub, was now drawn. The metallic rattle, which had sounded to him like a stir of bones in a crypt, had been the curtain rings on the overhead bar. Jack stared at the curtain. His face felt as if it had been heavily waxed, all dead skin on the outside, live, hot rivulets of fear on the inside. The way he had felt on the playground.

There was something behind the pink plastic shower curtain. There was something in the tub.

He could see it, ill defined and obscure through the plastic, a nearly amorphous shape. It could have been anything. A trick of the light. The shadow of the shower attachment. A woman long dead and reclining in her bath, a bar of Lowila in one stiffening hand as she waited patiently for whatever lover might come.

Jack told himself to step forward boldly and rake the shower curtain back. To expose whatever might be there. Instead he turned with jerky, marionette strides, his heart whamming frightfully in his chest, and went back into the bed/sitting room.

The door to the hall was shut.

He stared at it for a long, immobile second. He could taste his terror now. It was in the back of his throat like a taste of gone-over cherries.

He walked to the door with that same jerky stride and forced his fingers to curl around the knob.

(*It won't open.*)

But it did.

He turned off the light with a fumbling gesture, stepped out into the hall, and pulled the door shut without looking back. From inside, he seemed to hear an odd wet thumping sound, far off, dim, as if something had just scrambled belatedly out of the tub, as if to greet a caller, as if it had realized the caller was leaving before the social amenities had been completed and so it was now rushing to the door, all purple and grinning, to invite the caller back inside. Perhaps forever.

Footsteps approaching the door or only the heartbeat in his ears?

He fumbled at the passkey. It seemed sludgy, unwilling to turn in the lock. He attacked the passkey. The tumblers suddenly fell and he stepped back against the corridor's far wall, a little groan of relief escaping him. He closed his eyes and all the old phrases began to parade through his mind, it seemed there must be hundreds of them.

(cracking up not playing with a full deck lostya marbles guy just went loony tunes he went up and over the high side went bananas lost his football crackers nuts half a seabag)

all meaning the same thing: *losing your mind.*

'No,' he whimpered, hardly aware that he had been reduced to this, whimpering with his eyes shut like a child. 'Oh no, God. Please, God, no.'

But below the tumble of his chaotic thoughts, below the triphammer beat of his heart, he could hear the soft and futile sound of the doorknob being turned to and fro as something locked in tried helplessly to get out, something that wanted to meet him, something that would like to be introduced to his family as the storm shrieked around them and white daylight became black night. If he opened his eyes and saw that doorknob moving he would go mad. So he kept them shut, and after an unknowable time, there was stillness.

Jack forced himself to open his eyes, half-convinced that when he did, she would be standing before him. But the hall was empty.

He felt watched just the same.

He looked at the peephole in the center of the door and wondered what would happen if he approached it, stared into it. What would he be eyeball to eyeball with?

His feet were moving

(*feets don't fail me now*)

before he realized it. He turned them away from the door and walked down to the main hall, his feet whispering on the blue-black jungle carpet. He stopped halfway to the stairs and looked at the fire extinguisher. He thought that the folds of canvas were arranged in a slightly different manner. And he was quite sure that the brass nozzle had been pointing toward the elevator when he came up the hall. Now it was pointing the other way.

'I didn't see that at all,' Jack Torrance said quite clearly. His face was white and haggard and his mouth kept trying to grin.

But he didn't take the elevator back down. It was too much like an open mouth. Too much by half. He took the stairs.

Chapter Thirty-one

The Verdict

He stepped into the kitchen and looked at them, bouncing the passkey a few inches up off his left hand, making the chain on the white metal tongue jingle, then catching it again. Danny was pallid and worn out. Wendy had been crying, he saw; her eyes were red and darkly circled. He felt a sudden burst of gladness at this. He wasn't suffering alone, that was sure.

They looked at him without speaking.

'Nothing there,' he said, astounded by the heartiness of his voice. 'Not a thing.'

He bounced the passkey up and down, up and down, smiling reassuringly at them, watching the relief spread over their faces, and thought he had never in his life wanted a drink so badly as he did right now.

Chapter Thirty-two

The Bedroom

Late that afternoon Jack got a cot from the first-floor storage room and put it in the corner of their bedroom. Wendy had expected that the boy would be half the night getting to sleep, but Danny was nodding before 'The Waltons' was half over, and fifteen minutes after they had tucked him in he was far down in sleep, moveless, one hand tucked under his cheek. Wendy sat watching him, holding her place in a fat paper-back copy of *Cashelmara* with one finger. Jack sat at his desk, looking at his play.

'Oh shit,' Jack said.

Wendy looked up from her contemplation of Danny. 'What?'

'Nothing.'

He looked down at the play with smoldering ill-temper. How could he have thought it was good? It was puerile. It had been done a thousand times. Worse, he had no idea how to finish it. Once it had seemed simple enough. Denker in a fit of rage, seizes the poker from beside the fireplace and beats saintly Gary to death. Then, standing spread-legged over the body, the bloody poker in one hand, he screams at the audience: 'It's here somewhere and I *will* find it!' Then, as the lights dim and the curtain is slowly drawn, the audience sees Gary's body face down on the forestage as Denker strides to the upstage bookcase and feverishly begins pulling books from the shelves, looking at them, throwing them aside. He had thought it was something old enough to be new, a play whose novelty alone might be enough to see it through a successful Broadway run: a tragedy in five acts.

But, in addition to his sudden diversion of interest to the Overlook's history, something else had happened. He had developed opposing feelings about his characters. This was something quite new. Ordinarily he liked all of his characters, the good and the bad. He was glad he did. It allowed him to try to see all of their sides and understand their motivations more clearly. His favorite story, sold to a small southern Maine magazine called Contraband for copies, had been a piece called 'The Monkey Is Here, Paul DeLong.' It had been about a child molester about to commit suicide in his furnished room. The child molester's name had been Paul DeLong, Monkey to his friends. Jack had liked Monkey very much. He sympathized with Monkey's bizarre needs, knowing that Monkey was not the only one to blame for the three rape-murders in his past. There had been bad parents, the father a beater as his own father had been, the mother a limp and silent dishrag as his mother had been. A homosexual experience in grammar school. Public humiliation. Worse experiences in high school and college. He had been arrested and sent to an institution after exposing himself to a pair of little girls getting off a school bus. Worst of all, he had been dismissed from the institution, let back out onto the streets, because the man in charge had decided he was all right. This man's name had been Grimmer. Grimmer had known that Monkey DeLong was exhibiting deviant symptoms, but he had written the good, hopeful report and had let him go anyway. Jack liked and sympathized with Grimmer, too. Grimmer had to run an understaffed and underfunded institution and try to keep the whole thing together with spit, baling wire, and nickle-and-dime appropriations from a state legislature who had to go back and face the voters. Grimmer knew that Monkey could interact with other people, that he did not soil his pants or try to stab his fellow inmates with the scissors. He did not think he was Napoleon. The staff psychiatrist in charge of Monkey's case thought there was a better-than-even chance that Monkey could make it on the street, and they both knew that the longer a man is in an institution the more he comes to need that closed environment, like a junkie with his smack. And meanwhile, people were knocking down the doors. Paranoids, schizoids, cycloids, semi-catatonics, men who claimed to have gone to heaven in flying saucers, women who had burned their children's sex organs off with Bic lighters, alcoholics, pyromaniacs, kleptomaniacs, manic-depressives, suicidals. Tough old world, baby. If you're not bolted together tightly, you're gonna shake, rattle, and roll before you turn thirty. Jack could sympathize with Grimmer's problem. He could sympathize with the parents of the murder victims. With the murdered children themselves, of course. And with Monkey DeLong. Let the reader lay blame. In those days he hadn't wanted to judge. The cloak of the moralist sat badly on his shoulders.

He had started *The Little School* in the same optimistic vein. But lately he had begun to choose up sides, and worse still, he had come to loathe his hero, Gary Benson. Originally conceived as a bright boy more cursed with money than blessed with it, a boy who wanted more than anything to compile a good record so he could go to a good university because he had earned admission and not because his father had pulled strings, he had become to Jack a kind of simpering Goody Two-shoes, a postulant before the altar of knowledge rather than a sincere acolyte, an outward paragon of Boy Scout virtues, inwardly cynical, filled not with real brilliance (as he had first been conceived) but only with sly animal cunning. All through the play he unfailingly addressed Denker as 'sir,' just as Jack had taught his own son to address those older and those in authority as 'sir.' He thought that Danny used the word quite sincerely, and Gary Benson as originally conceived had too, but as he had begun Act V, it had come more and more strongly to him that Gary was using the word satirically, outwardly straight-faced while the Gary Benson inside was mugging and leering at Denker. Denker, who had never had any of the things Gary had. Denker, who had had to work all his life just to become head of a single little school. Who was now faced with ruin over this handsome, innocent-seeming rich boy who had cheated on his Final Composition and had then cunningly covered his tracks. Jack had seen Denker the teacher as not much different from the strutting South American little Caesars in their banana kingdoms, standing dissidents up against the wall of the handiest squash or handball court, a super-zealot in a comparatively small puddle, a man whose every whim becomes a crusade. In the beginning he had wanted to use his play as a microcosm to say something about the abuse of power. Now he tended more and more to see Denker as a Mr Chips figure, and the tragedy was not the intellectual racking of Gary Benson but rather the destruction of a kindly old teacher and headmaster unable to see through the cynical wiles of this monster masquerading as a boy.

He hadn't been able to finish the play.

Now he sat looking down at it, scowling, wondering if there was any way he could salvage the situation. He didn't really think there was. He had begun with one play and it had somehow turned into another, presto-chango. Well, what the hell. Either way it had been done before. Either way it was a load of shit. And why was he driving himself crazy about it tonight anyway? After the day just gone by it was no wonder he couldn't think straight.

'—get him down?'

He looked up, trying to blink the cobwebs away. 'Huh?'

'I said, how are we going to get him down? We've got to get him out of here, Jack.'

For a moment his wits were so scattered that he wasn't even sure what she was talking about. Then he realized and uttered a short, barking laugh.

'You say that as if it were so easy.'

'I didn't mean—'

'No problem, Wendy. I'll just change clothes in that telephone booth down in the lobby and fly him to Denver on my back. Superman Jack Torrance, they called me in my salad days.'

Her face registered slow hurt.

'I understand the problem, Jack. The radio is broken. The snow . . . but you have to understand Danny's problem. My God, don't you? He was nearly catatonic, Jack! What if he hadn't come out of that?'

'But he did,' Jack said, a trifle shortly. He had been frightened at Danny's blank-eyed, slack-faced state too, of course he had. At first. But the more he thought about it, the more he wondered if it hadn't been a piece of play-acting put on to escape his punishment. He had, after all, been trespassing.

'All the same,' she said. She came to him and sat on the end of the bed by his desk. Her face was both surprised and worried. 'Jack the bruises on his neck! Something got at him! And I want him away from it!'

'Don't shout,' he said. 'My head aches, Wendy. I'm as worried about this as you are, so please . . . don't . . . shout.'

'All right,' she said, lowering her voice. 'I won't shout. But I don't understand you, Jack. Someone is in here with us. And not a very nice someone, either. We have to get down to Sidewinder, not just Danny but all of us. Quickly. And you . . . you're sitting there reading your *play!*'

"We have to get down, we have to get down," you keep saying that. You must think I really am Superman.'

'I think you're my husband,' she said softly, and looked down at her hands.

His temper flared. He slammed the playscript down, knocking the edges of the pile out of true again and crumpling the sheets on the bottom.

'It's time you got some of the home truths into you, Wendy. You don't seem to have internalized them, as the sociologists say. They're knocking around up in your head like a bunch of loose cueballs. You need to shoot them into the pockets. You need to understand that *we are snowed in*.'

Danny had suddenly become active in his bed. Still sleeping, he had begun to twist and turn. The way he always did when we fought, Wendy thought dismally. And we're doing it again.

'Don't wake him up, Jack. Please.'

He glanced over at Danny and some of the flush went out of his cheeks. 'Okay. I'm sorry. I'm sorry I sounded mad, Wendy. It's not really for you. But I broke the radio. If it's anybody's fault it's mine. That was our big link to the outside. Olly-olly-in-for-free. Please come get us, Mister Ranger. We can't stay out this late.'

'Don't,' she said, and put a hand on his shoulder. He leaned his head against it. She brushed his hair with the other hand. 'I guess you've got a right, after what I accused you of. Sometimes I am like my mother. I can be a bitch. But you have to understand that some things . . . are hard to get over. You have to understand that.'

'Do you mean his arm?' His lips had thinned.

'Yes,' Wendy said, and then she rushed on: 'But it's not just you. I worry when he goes out to play. I worry about him wanting a two-wheeler next year, even one with training wheels. I worry about his teeth and his eyesight and about this thing, what he calls his shine. I worry. Because he's little and he seems very fragile and because . . . because something in this hotel seems to want him. And it will go through us to get him if it has to. That's why we must get him out, Jack. I know that! I feel that! *We must get him out!*'

Her hand had tightened painfully on his shoulder in her agitation, but he didn't move away. One hand found the firm weight of her left breast and he began to stroke it through her shirt.

'Wendy,' he said, and stopped. She waited for him to rearrange whatever he had to say. His strong hand on her breast felt good, soothing. 'I could maybe snowshoe him down. He could walk part of the way himself, but I would mostly have to carry him. It would mean camping out one, two, maybe three nights. That would mean building a travois to carry supplies and bedrolls on. We have the AM/FM radio, so we could pick a day when the weather forecast called for a three-day spell of good weather. But if the forecast was wrong,' he finished, his voice soft and measured, 'I think we might die.'

Her face had paled. It looked shiny, almost ghostly. He continued to stroke her breast, rubbing the ball of his thumb gently over the nipple.

She made a soft sound – from his words or in reaction to his gentle pressure on her breast, he couldn't tell. He raised his hand slightly and undid the top button of her shirt. Wendy shifted her legs slightly. All at once her jeans seemed too tight, slightly irritating in a pleasant sort of way.

'It would mean leaving you alone because you can't snowshoe worth beans. It would be maybe three days of not knowing. Would you want that?' His hand dropped to the second button, slipped it, and the beginning of her cleavage was exposed.

'No,' she said in a voice that was slightly thick. She glanced over at Danny. He had stopped twisting and turning. His thumb had crept back into his mouth. So that was all right. But Jack was leaving something out of the picture. It was too bleak. There was something else . . . what?

'If we stay put,' Jack said, unbuttoning the third and fourth buttons with that same deliberate slowness, 'a ranger from the park or a game warden is going to poke in here just to find out how we're doing. At that point we simply tell him we want down. He'll see to it.' He slipped her naked breasts into the wide V of the open shirt, bent, and molded his lips around the stem of a nipple. It was hard and erect. He slipped his tongue slowly back and forth across it in a way he knew she liked. Wendy moaned a little and arched her back.

(*?Something I've forgotten?*)

'Honey?' she asked. On their own her hands sought the back of his head so that when he answered his voice was muffled against her flesh.

'How would the ranger take us out?'

He raised his head slightly to answer and then settled his mouth against the other nipple.

'If the helicopter was spoken for I guess it would have to be by snowmobile.'

(*!!!*)

'But we have one of those! Ullman said so!'

His mouth froze against her breast for a moment, and then he sat up. Her own face was slightly flushed, her eyes overbright. Jack's, on the other hand, was calm, as if he had been reading a rather dull book instead of engaging in foreplay with his wife.

'If there's a snowmobile there's no problem,' she said excitedly. 'We can all three go down together.'

'Wendy, I've never driven a snowmobile in my life.'

'It can't be that hard to learn. Back in Vermont you see ten-year-olds driving them in the fields . . . although what their parents can be thinking of I don't know. And you had a motorcycle when we met.' He had, a Honda 350cc. He had traded it in on a Saab shortly after he and Wendy took up residence together.

'I suppose I could,' he said slowly. 'But I wonder how well it's been maintained. Ullman and Watson . . . they run this place from May to October. They have summertime minds. I know it won't have gas in it. There may not be plugs or a battery, either. I don't want you to get your hopes up over your head, Wendy.'

She was totally excited now, leaning over him, her breasts tumbling out of her shirt. He had a sudden impulse to seize one and twist it until she shrieked. Maybe that would teach her to shut up.

'The gas is no problem,' she said. 'The VW and the hotel truck are both full. There's gas for the emergency generator downstairs, too. And there must be a gascan out in that shed so you could carry extra.'

'Yes,' he said. 'There is.' Actually there were three of them, two five-gallons and a two-gallon.

'I'll bet the sparkplugs and the battery are out there too. Nobody would store their snowmobile in one place and the plugs and battery someplace else, would they?'

'Doesn't seem likely, does it?' He got up and walked over to where Danny lay sleeping. A spill of hair had fallen across his forehead and Jack brushed it away gently. Danny didn't stir.

'And if you can get it running you'll take us out?' she asked from behind him. 'On the first day the radio says good weather?'

For a moment he didn't answer. He stood looking down at his son, and his mixed feelings dissolved in a wave of love. He was the way she had said, vulnerable, fragile. The marks on his neck were very prominent.

'Yes,' he said. 'I'll get it running we'll get out as quick as we can.'

'Thank God!'

He turned around. She had taken off her shirt and lay on the bed, her belly flat, her breasts aimed perkily at the ceiling. She was playing with them lazily, flicking at the nipples. 'Hurry up, gentlemen,' she said softly, 'time.'

After, with no light burning in the room but the night light that Danny had brought with him from his room, she lay in the crook of his arm, feeling deliciously at peace. She found it hard to believe they could be sharing the Overlook with a murderous stowaway.

'Jack?'

'Hmmmm?'

'What got at him?'

He didn't answer her directly. 'He does have something. Some talent the rest of us are missing. The most of us, beg pardon. And maybe the Overlook has something, too.'

'Ghosts?'

'I don't know. Not in the Algernon Blackwood sense, that's for sure. More like the residues of the feelings of the people who have stayed here. Good things and bad things. In that sense, I suppose that every big hotel has got its ghosts. Especially the old ones.'

'But a dead woman in the tub . . . Jack, he's not losing his mind, is he?'

He gave her a brief squeeze. 'We know he goes into . . . well, trances, for want of a better word . . . from time to time. We know that when he's in them he sometimes . . . sees? . . . things he doesn't understand. If precognitive trances are possible, they're probably functions of the subconscious mind. Freud said that the subconscious never speaks to us in literal language. Only in symbols. If you dream about being in a bakery where no one speaks English, you may be worried about your ability to support your family. Or maybe just that no one understands you. I've read that the falling dream is a standard outlet for feelings of insecurity. Games, little games. Conscious on one side of the net, subconscious on the other, serving some cockamamie image back and forth. Same with mental illness, with hunches, all of that. Why should precognition be any different? Maybe Danny really did see blood all over the walls of the Presidential Suite. To a kid his age, the image of blood and the concept of death are nearly interchangeable. To kids, the image is always more accessible than the concept, anyway. William Carlos Williams knew that, he was a pediatrician. When we grow up, concepts gradually get easier and we leave the images to the poets . . . and I'm just rambling on.'

'I like to hear you ramble.'

'She said it, folks. She said it. You all heard it.'

'The marks on his neck, Jack. Those are real.'

'Yes.'

There was nothing else for a long time. She had begun to think he must have gone to sleep and she was slipping into a drowse herself when he said:

'I can think of two explanations for those. And neither of them involves a fourth party in the hotel.'

'What?' She came up on one elbow.

'Stigmata, maybe,' he said.

'Stigmata? Isn't that when people bleed on Good Friday or something?'

'Yes. Sometimes people who believe deeply in Christ's divinity exhibit bleeding marks on their hands and feet during the Holy Week. It was more common in the Middle Ages than now. In those days such people were considered blessed by God. I don't think the Catholic Church proclaimed any of it as out-and-out miracles, which was pretty smart of them. Stigmata isn't much different from some of the things the yogis can do. It's better understood now, that's all. The people who understand the interaction between the mind and the body – study it, I mean, no one understands it – believe we have a lot more control over our involuntary functions than they used to think. You can slow your heartbeat if you think about it enough. Speed up your own metabolism. Make yourself sweat more. Or make yourself bleed.'

'You think Danny *thought* those bruises onto his neck? Jack, I just can't believe that.'

'I can believe it's possible, although it seems unlikely to me, too. What's more likely is that he did it to himself.'

'*To himself?*'

'He's gone into these "trances" and hurt himself in the past. Do you remember the time at the supper table? About two years ago, I think. We were super-pissed at each other. Nobody talking very much. Then, all at once, his eyes rolled up in his head and he went face-first into his dinner. Then onto the floor. Remember?'

'Yes,' she said. 'I sure do. I thought he was having a convulsion.'

'Another time we were in the park,' he said. 'Just Danny and I. Saturday afternoon. He was sitting on a swing, coasting back and forth. He collapsed onto the ground. It was like he'd been shot. I ran over and picked him up and all of a sudden he just came around. He sort of blinked at me and said, "I hurt my tummy. Tell Mommy to close the bedroom windows if it rains." And that night it rained like hell.'

'Yes, but—'

'And he's always coming in with cuts and scraped elbows. His shins look like a battlefield in distress. And when you ask him how he got this one or that one, he just says "Oh, I was playing," and that's the end of it.'

'Jack, all kids get bumped and bruised up. With little boys it's almost constant from the time they learn to walk until they're twelve or thirteen.'

'And I'm sure Danny gets his share,' Jack responded. 'He's an active kid. But I remember that day in the park and that night at the supper table. And I wonder if some of our kid's bumps and bruises come from just keeling over. That Dr Edmonds said Danny did it right in his office, for Christ's sake!'

'All right. But those bruises were *fingers*. I'd swear to it. He didn't get them falling down.'

'He goes into a trance,' Jack said. 'Maybe he sees something that happened in that room. An argument. Maybe a suicide. Violent emotions. It isn't like watching a movie; he's in a highly suggestible state. He's right in the damn thing. His subconscious is maybe visualizing whatever happened in a symbolic way . . . as a dead woman who's alive again, zombie, undead, ghoul, you pick your term.'

'You're giving me goose-bumps,' she said thickly.

'I'm giving myself a few. I'm no psychiatrist, but it seems to fit so well. The walking dead woman as a symbol for dead emotions, dead lives, that just won't give up and go away . . . but because she's a subconscious figure, she's also *him*. In the trance state, the conscious Danny is submerged. The subconscious figure is pulling the strings. So Danny put his hands around his own neck and—'

'Stop,' she said. 'I get the picture. I think that's more frightening than having a stranger creeping around the halls, Jack. You can move away from a stranger. You can't move away from yourself. You're talking about schizophrenia.'

'Of a very limited type,' he said, but a trifle uneasily. 'And of a very special nature. Because he does seem able to read thoughts, and he really does seem to have precognitive flashes from time to time. I can't think of that as mental illness no matter how hard I try. We all have schizo deposits in us anyway. I think as Danny gets older, he'll get this under control.'

'If you're right, then it's imperative that we get him out. Whatever he has, this hotel is making it worse.'

'I wouldn't say that,' he objected. 'If he'd done as he was told, he never would have gone up to that room in the first place. It never would have happened.'

'My God, Jack! Are you implying that being half-strangled was a. . . a fitting punishment for being off limits?'

'No . . . no. Of course not. But—'

'No buts,' she said, shaking her head violently. 'The truth is, we're guessing. We don't have any idea when he might turn a corner and run into one of those . . . air pockets, one-reel horror movies, whatever they are. We have to get him *away*.' She laughed a little in the darkness. 'Next thing we'll be seeing things.'

'Don't talk nonsense,' he said, and in the darkness of the room he saw the hedge lions bunching around the path, no longer flanking it but guarding it, hungry November lions. Cold sweat sprang out on his brow.

'You didn't really see anything, did you?' she was asking. 'I mean, when you went up to that room. You didn't see anything?'

The lions were gone. Now he saw a pink pastel shower curtain with a dark shape lounging behind it. The closed door. That muffled, hurried thump, and sounds after it that might have been running footsteps. The horrible, lurching beat of his own heart as he struggled with the passkey.

'Nothing,' he said, and that was true. He had been strung up, not sure of what was happening. He hadn't had a chance to sift through his thoughts for a reasonable explanation concerning the bruises on his son's neck. He had been pretty damn suggestible himself. Hallucinations could sometimes be catching.

'And you haven't changed your mind? About the snowmobile, I mean?'

His hands clamped into sudden tight fists

(*Stop nagging me!*)

by his sides. 'I said I would, didn't I? I will. Now go to sleep. It's been a long hard day.'

'And how,' she said. There was a rustle of bedclothes as she turned toward him and kissed his shoulder. 'I love you, Jack.'

'I love you too,' he said, but he was only mouthing the words. His hands were still clenched into fists. They felt like rocks on the ends of his arms. The pulse beat prominently in his forehead. She hadn't said a word about what was going to happen to them *after* they got down, when the party was over. Not one word. It had been Danny this and Danny that and Jack I'm so scared. Oh yes, she was scared of a lot of closet boogeymen and jumping shadows, plenty scared. But there was no lack of real ones, either. When they got down to Sidewinder they would arrive with sixty dollars and the clothes they stood up in. Not even a car. Even if Sidewinder had a pawnshop, which it didn't, they had nothing to hock but Wendy's ninety-dollar diamond engagement ring and the Sony AM/FM radio. A pawnbroker might give them twenty bucks. A *kind* pawnbroker. There would be no job, not even part-time or seasonal, except maybe shoveling out driveways for three dollars a shot. The picture of John Torrance, thirty years old, who had once published in *Esquire* and who had harbored dreams – not at all unreasonable dreams, he felt – of becoming a major American writer during the next decade, with a shovel from the Sidewinder Western Auto on his shoulder, ringing doorbells . . . that picture suddenly came to him much more clearly than the hedge lions and he clenched his fists tighter still, feeling the fingernails sink into his palms and draw blood in mystic quarter-moon shapes. John Torrance, standing in line to change his sixty dollars into food stamps, standing in line again at the Sidewinder Methodist Church to get donated commodities and dirty looks from the locals. John Torrance explaining to Al that they'd just had to leave, had to shut down the boiler, had to leave the Overlook and all it contained open to vandals or thieves on snow machines because you see, Al, *attendez-vous*, Al, there are ghosts up there and they have it in for my boy. Good-by Al. Thoughts of Chapter Four, Spring Comes for John Torrance. What then? Whatever then? They might be able to get to the West Coast in the VW, he supposed. A new fuel pump would do it. Fifty miles west of here and it was all downhill, you could damn near put the bug in neutral and coast to Utah. On to sunny California, land of oranges and opportunity. A man with his sterling record of alcoholism, student-beating and ghost-chasing would undoubtedly be able to write his own ticket. Anything you like. Custodial engineer – swamping out Greyhound buses. The automotive business – washing cars in a rubber suit. The culinary arts, perhaps, washing dishes in a diner. Or possible a more responsible position, such as pumping gas. A job like that even held the intellectual stimulation of making change and writing out credit slips. *I can give you twenty-five hours a week at the minimum wage.* That was heavy tunes in a year when Wonder bread went for sixty cents a loaf.

Blood had begun to trickle down from his palms. Like stigmata, oh yes. He squeezed tighter, savaging himself with pain. His wife was asleep beside him, why not? There were no problems. He had agreed to take her and Danny away from the big bad boogeyman and there were no problems. *So you see, Al, I thought the best thing to do would be to—*

(*kill her.*)

The thought rose up from nowhere, naked and unadorned. The urge to tumble her out of bed, naked, bewildered, just beginning to wake up; to pounce on her, seize her neck like the green limb of a young aspen and to throttle her, thumbs on windpipe, fingers pressing against the top of her spine, jerking her head up and ramming it back down against the floorboards, again and again, whamming, whacking, smashing, crashing. Jitter and jive, baby. Shake, rattle, and roll. He would make her take her medicine. Every drop. Every last bitter drop.

He was dimly aware of a muffled noise somewhere, just outside his hot and racing inner world. He looked across the room and Danny was thrashing again, twisting in his bed and rumpling the blankets. The boy was moaning deep in his throat, a small caged sound. What nightmare? A purple woman, long dead, shambling after him down twisting hotel corridors? Somehow he didn't think so. Something else chased Danny in his dreams, Something worse.

The bitter lock of his emotions was broken. He got out of bed and went across to the boy, feeling sick and ashamed of himself. It was Danny he had to think of, not Wendy, not himself. Only Danny. And no matter what shape he wrestled the facts into, he knew in his heart that Danny must be taken out. He straightened the boy's blankets and added the quilt from the foot of the bed. Danny had quieted again now. Jack touched the sleeping forehead

(what monsters capering just behind that ridge of bone?)

and found it warm, but not overly so. And he was sleeping peacefully again. Queer.

He got back into bed and tried to sleep. It eluded him.

It was so unfair that things should turn out this way – bad luck seemed to stalk them. They hadn't been able to shake it by coming up here after all. By the time they arrived in Sidewinder tomorrow afternoon, the golden opportunity would have evaporated – gone the way of the blue suede shoe, as an old roommate of his had been wont to say. Consider the difference if they didn't go down, if they could somehow stick it out. The play would get finished. One way or the other, he would tack an ending onto it. His own uncertainty about his characters might add an appealing touch of ambiguity to his original ending. Perhaps it would even make him some money, it wasn't impossible. Even lacking that, Al might well convince the Stovington Board to rehire him. He would be on pro of course, maybe for as long as three years, but if he could stay sober and keep writing, he might not have to stay at Stovington for three years. Of course he hadn't cared much for Stovington before, he had felt stifled, buried alive, but that had been an immature reaction. Furthermore, how much could a man enjoy teaching when he went through his first three classes with a skull-busting hangover every second or third day? It wouldn't be that way again. He would be able to handle his responsibilities much better. He was sure of it.

Somewhere in the midst of that thought, things began to break up and he drifted down into sleep. His last thought followed him down like a sounding bell:

It seemed that he might be able to find peace here. At last. If they would only let him.

When he woke up he was standing in the bathroom of 217.

(been walking in my sleep again – why? – no radios to break up here)

The bathroom light was on, the room behind him in darkness. The shower curtain was drawn around the long claw-footed tub. The bathmat beside it was wrinkled and wet.

He began to feel afraid, but the very dreamlike quality of his fear told him this was not real. Yet that could not contain the fear. So many things at the Overlook seemed like dreams.

He moved across the floor to the tub, not wanting to be helpless to turn his feet back.

He flung the curtain open.

Lying in the tub, naked, lolling almost weightless in the water, was George Hatfield, a knife stuck in his chest. The water around him was stained a bright pink. George's eyes were closed. His penis floated limply, like kelp.

'George—' he heard himself say.

At the word, George's eyes snapped open. They were silver, not human eyes at all. George's hands, fish-white, found the sides of the tub and he pulled himself up to a sitting position. The knife stuck straight out from his chest, equidistantly placed between nipples. The wound was lipless.

'You set the timer ahead,' silver-eyed George told him.

'No, George, I didn't. I—'

'I don't stutter.'

George was standing now, still fixing him with that inhuman silver glare, but his mouth had drawn back in a dead and grimacing smile. He threw one leg over the porcelained side of the tub. One white and wrinkled foot placed itself on the bathmat.

'First you tried to run me over on my bike and then you set the timer ahead and then you tried to stab me to death but *I still don't stutter.*' George was coming for him, his hands out, the fingers slightly curled. He smelled moldy and wet, like leaves that had been rained on.

'It was for your own good,' Jack said, backing up. 'I set it ahead for your own good. Furthermore, I happen to know you cheated on your Final Composition.'

'I don't cheat . . . and I don't stutter.'

George's hands touched his neck.

Jack turned and ran, ran with the floating, weightless slowness that is so common to dreams.

'You did! You did cheat!' he screamed in fear and anger as he crossed the darkened bed/sitting room. 'I'll prove it!'

George's hands were on his neck again. Jack's heart swelled with fear until he was sure it would burst. And then, at last, his hand curled around the doorknob and it turned under his hand and he yanked the door open. He plunged out, not into the second-floor hallway, but into the basement room beyond the arch. The cobwebby light was on. His campchair, stark and geometrical, stood beneath it. And all around it was a miniature mountain range of boxes and crates and banded bundles of records and invoices and God knew what. Relief surged through him.

'I'll find it!' he heard himself screaming. He seized a damp and moldering cardboard box; it split apart in his hands, spilling out a waterfall of yellow flimsies. 'It's here somewhere! *I will find it!*' He plunged his hands deep into the pile of papers and came up with a dry, papery wasps' nest in one hand and a timer in the other. The timer was ticking. Attached to its back was a length of electrical cord and attached to the other end of the cord was a bundle of dynamite. *'Here!'* he screamed. *'Here, take it!'*

His relief became absolute triumph. He had done more than escape George; he had conquered. With these talismanic objects in his hands, George would never touch him again. George would flee in terror.

He began to turn so he could confront George, and that was when George's hands settled around his neck, squeezing, stopping his breath, damming up his respiration entirely after one final dragging gasp.

'I don't stutter,' whispered George from behind him.

He dropped the wasps' nest and wasps boiled out of it in a furious brown and yellow wave. His lungs were on fire. His wavering sight fell on the timer and the sense of triumph returned, along with a cresting wave of righteous wrath. Instead of connecting the timer to dynamite, the cord ran to the gold knob of a stout black cane, like the one his father had carried after the accident with the milk truck.

He grasped it and the cord parted. The cane felt heavy and right in his hands. He swung it back over his shoulder. On the way up it glanced against the wire from which the light bulb depended and the light began to swing back and forth, making the room's hooded shadows rock monstrously against the floor and walls. On the way down the cane struck something much harder. George screamed. The grip on Jack's throat loosened.

He tore free of George's grip and whirled. George was on his knees, his head drooping, his hands laced together on top of it. Blood welled through his fingers.

'Please,' George whispered humbly. 'Give me a break Mr Torrance.'

'Now you'll take your medicine,' Jack grunted. 'Now by God, won't you. Young pup. Young worthless cur. Now by God, right now. Every drop. Every single damn drop!'

As the light swayed above him and the shadows danced and flapped, he began to swing the cane, bringing it down again and again, his arm rising and falling like a machine. George's bloody protecting fingers fell away from his head and Jack brought the cane down again and again, and on his neck and shoulders and back and arms. Except that the cane was no longer precisely a cane; it seemed to be a mallet with some kind of brightly striped handle. A mallet with a hard side and soft side. The business end was clotted with blood and hair. And the flat, whacking sound of the mallet against flesh had been replaced with a hollow booming sound, echoing and reverberating. His own voice had taken on this same quality, bellowing, disembodied. And yet, paradoxically, it sounded weaker, slurred, petulant . . . as if he were drunk.

The figure on its knees slowly raised its head, as if in supplication. There was not a face, precisely, but only a mask of blood through which eyes peered. He brought the mallet back for a final whistling downstroke and it was fully launched before he saw that the supplicating face below him was not George's but Danny's. It was the face of his son.

'Daddy—'

And then the mallet crashed home, striking Danny right between the eyes, closing them forever. And something somewhere seemed to be laughing—

(*! No !*)

He came out of it standing naked over Danny's bed, his hands empty, his body sheened with sweat. His final scream had only been in his mind. He voiced it again, this time in a whisper.

'No. No, Danny. Never.'

He went back to bed on legs that had turned to rubber. Wendy was sleeping deeply. The clock on the nightstand said it was quarter to five. He lay sleepless until seven, when Danny began to stir awake. Then he put his legs over the edge of the bed and began to dress. It was time to go downstairs and check the boiler.

Chapter Thirty-three

The Snowmobile

Sometime after midnight, while they all slept uneasily, the snow had stopped after dumping a fresh eight inches on the old crust. The clouds had broken, a fresh wind had swept them away, and now Jack stood in a dusty ingot of sunlight, which slanted through the dirty window set into the eastern side of the equipment shed.

The place was about as long as a freight car, and about as high. It smelled of grease and oil and gasoline and – faint, nostalgic smell – sweet grass. Four power lawnmowers were ranked like soldiers on review against the south wall, two of them the riding type that look like small tractors. To their left were posthole diggers, round-bladed shovels made for doing surgery on the putting green, a chain saw, the electric hedge-clippers, and a long thin steel pole with a red flag at the top. Caddy, fetch my ball in under ten seconds and there's a quarter in it for you. Yes, *sir*.

Against the eastern wall, where the morning sun slanted in most strongly, three Ping-Pong tables leaned one against the other like a drunken house of cards. Their nets had been removed and flopped down from the shelf above. In the corner was a stack of shuffleboard weights and a roque set – the wickets banded together with twists of wire, the brightly painted balls in an egg-carton sort of thing (strange hens you have up here, Watson . . . yes, and you should see the animals down on the front lawn, ha-ha), and the mallets, two sets of them, standing in their racks.

He walked over to them, stepping over an old eight-cell battery (which had once sat beneath the hood of the hotel truck, no doubt) and a battery charger and a pair of J. C. Penney jumper cables coiled between them. He slipped one of the short-handled mallets out of the front rack and held it up in front of his face, like a knight bound for battle saluting his king.

Fragments of his dream (it was all jumbled now, fading) recurred, something about George Hatfield and his father's cane, just enough to make him uneasy and, absurdly enough, a trifle guilty about holding a plain old garden-variety roque mallet. Not that roque was such a common garden-variety game anymore; its more modern cousin, croquet, was much more popular now . . . and a child's version of the game at that. Roque, however . . . that must have been quite a game. Jack had found a mildewed rule book down in the basement, from one of the years in the early twenties when a North American Roque Tournament had been held at the Overlook. Quite a game.

(*schizo*)

He frowned a little, then smiled. Yes, it was a schizo sort of game at that. The mallet expressed that perfectly. A soft end and a hard end. A game of finesse and aim, and a game of raw, bludgeoning power.

He swung the mallet through the air . . . *whhhoooop*. He smiled a little at the powerful, whistling sound it made. Then he replaced it in the rack and turned to his left. What he saw there made him frown again.

The snowmobile sat almost in the middle of the equipment shed, a fairly new one, and Jack didn't care for its looks at all. *Bombardier Skidoo* was written on the side of the engine cowling facing him in black letters which had been raked backward, presumably to connote speed. The protruding skis were also black. There was black piping to the right and left of the cowling, what they would call racing stripes on a sports car. But the actual paintjob was a bright, sneering yellow, and that was what he didn't like about it. Sitting there in its shaft of morning sun, yellow body and black piping, black skis and black upholstered open cockpit, it looked like a monstrous mechanized wasp. When it was running it would sound like that too. Whining and buzzing and ready to sting. But then, what else should it look like? It wasn't flying under false colors, at least. Because after it had done its job, they were going to be hurting plenty. All of them. By spring the Torrance family would be hurting so badly that what those wasps had done to Danny's hand would look like a mother's kisses.

He pulled his handkerchief from his back pocket, wiped his mouth with it, and walked over to the Skidoo. He stood looking down at it, the frown very deep now, and stuffed his handkerchief back into his pocket. Outside a sudden gust of wind slammed against the equipment shed, making it rock and creak. He looked out the window and saw the gust carrying a sheet of sparkling snow crystals toward the drifted-in rear of the hotel, whirling them high into the hard blue sky.

The wind dropped and he went back to looking at the machine. It was a disgusting thing, really. You almost expected to see a long, limber stinger protruding from the rear of it. He had always disliked the goddam snowmobiles. They shivered the cathedral silence of winter into a million rattling fragments. They startled the wildlife. They sent out huge and pollutive clouds of blue and billowing oilsmoke behind them – cough, cough, gag, gag, let me breathe. They were perhaps the final grotesque toy of the unwinding fossil fuel age, given to ten-year-olds for Christmas.

He remembered a newspaper article he had read in Stovington, a story datelined someplace in Maine. A kid on a snowmobile, barrel assing up a road he'd never traveled before at better than thirty miles an hour. Night. His headlight off. There had been a heavy chain strung between two posts with a NO TRESPASSING sign hung from the middle. They said that in all probability the kid never saw it. The moon might have gone behind a cloud. The chain had decapitated him. Reading the story Jack had been almost glad, and now, looking down at this machine, the feeling recurred.

(If it wasn't for Danny, I would take great pleasure in grabbing one of those mallets, opening the cowling, and just pounding until)

He let his pent-up breath escape him in a long slow sigh. Wendy was right. Come hell, high water, or the welfare line, Wendy was right. Pounding this machine to death would be the height of folly, no matter how pleasant an aspect that folly made. It would almost be tantamount to pounding his own son to death.

'Fucking Luddite,' he said aloud.

He went to the back of the machine and unscrewed the gascap. He found a dipstick on one of the shelves that ran at chest-height around the walls and slipped it in. The last eighth of an inch came out wet. Not very much, but enough to see if the damn thing would run. Later he could siphon more from the Volks and the hotel truck.

He screwed the cap back on and opened the cowling. No sparkplugs, no battery. He went to the shelf again and began to poke along it, pushing aside screwdrivers and adjustable wrenches, a one-lung carburetor that had been taken out of an old lawnmower, plastic boxes of screws and nails and bolts of varying sizes. The shelf was thick and dark with old grease, and the years' accumulation of dust had stuck to it like fur. He didn't like touching it.

He found a small, oil-stained box with the abbreviation *Skid.* laconically marked on it in pencil. He shook it and something rattled inside. Plugs. He held one of them up to the light, trying to estimate the gap without hunting around for the gapping tool. Fuck it, he thought resentfully, and dropped the plug back into the box. If the gap's wrong, that's just too damn bad. Tough fucking titty.

There was a stool behind the door. He dragged it over, sat down, and installed the four sparkplugs, then fitted the small rubber caps over each. That done, he let his fingers play briefly over the magneto. They laughed when I sat down at the piano.

Back to the shelves. This time he couldn't find what he wanted, a small battery. A three- or four-cell. There were socket wrenches, a case filled with drills and drillbits, bags of lawn fertilizer and Vigoro for the flower beds, but no snowmobile battery. It didn't bother him in the slightest. In fact, it made him feel glad. He was relieved. I did my best, Captain, but I could not get through. That's fine, son. I'm going to put you in for the Silver Star and the Purple Snowmobile. You're a credit to your regiment. Thank you, sir. I did try.

He began to whistle 'Red River Valley' uptempo as he poked along the last two or three feet of shelf. The notes came out in little puffs of white smoke. He had made a complete circuit of the shed and the thing wasn't there. Maybe somebody had lifted it. Maybe Watson had. He laughed aloud. The old office bootleg trick. A few paperclips, a couple of reams of paper, nobody will miss this tablecloth or this Golden Regal place setting . . . and what about this fine snowmobile battery? Yes, that might come in handy. Toss it in the sack. White-collar crime, Baby. Everybody has sticky fingers. Under-the-jacket discount, we used to call it when we were kids.

He walked back to the snowmobile and gave the side of it a good healthy kick as he went by. Well, that was the end of it. He would just have to tell Wendy sorry, baby, but—

There was a box sitting in the corner by the door. The stool had been right over it. Written on the top, in pencil, was the abbreviation *Skid.*

He looked at it, the smile drying up on his lips. Look, sir, it's the cavalry. Looks like your smoke signals must have worked after all.

It wasn't fair.

Goddammit, it just wasn't fair.

Something – luck, fate, providence – had been trying to save him. Some other luck, white luck. And at the last moment bad old Jack Torrance luck had stepped back in. The lousy run of cards wasn't over yet.

Resentment, a gray, sullen wave of it, pushed up his throat. His hands had clenched into fists again.

(*Not fair, goddammit, not fair!*)

Why couldn't he have looked someplace else? Anyplace! Why hadn't he had a crick in his neck or an itch in his nose or the need to blink? Just one of those little things. He never would have seen it.

Well, he hadn't. That was all. It was an hallucination, no different from what had happened yesterday outside that room on the second floor or the goddam hedge menagerie. A momentary strain, that was all. Fancy, I thought I saw a snowmobile battery in that corner. Nothing there now. Combat fatigue, I guess, sir. Sorry. Keep your pecker up, son. It happens to all of us sooner or later.

He yanked the door open almost hard enough to snap the hinges and pulled his snowshoes inside. They were clotted with snow and he slapped them down hard enough on the floor to raise a cloud of it. He put his left foot on the left shoe . . . and paused.

Danny was out there, by the milk platform. Trying to make a snowman, by the looks. Not much luck; the snow was too cold to stick together. Still, he was giving it the old college try, out there in the flashing morning, a speck of a bundled-up boy above the brilliant snow and below the brilliant sky. Wearing his hat turned around backward like Carlton Fiske.

(*What in the name of God were you thinking of?*)

The answer came back with no pause.

(*Me. I was thinking of me.*)

He suddenly remembered lying in bed the night before, lying there and suddenly he had been contemplating the murder of his wife.

In that instant, kneeling there, everything came clear to him. It was not just Danny the Overlook was working on. It was working on him, too. It wasn't Danny who was the weak link, it was him. He was the vulnerable one, the one who could be bent and twisted until something snapped.

(until i let go and sleep . . . and when i do that if i do that)

He looked up at the banks of windows and the sun threw back an almost blinding glare from their many-paned surfaces but he looked anyway. For the first time he noticed how much they seemed like eyes. They reflected away the sun and held their own darkness within. It was not Danny they were looking at. It was him.

In those few seconds he understood everything. There was a certain black-and-white picture he remembered seeing as a child, in catechism class. The nun had presented it to them on an easel and called it a miracle of God. The class had looked at it blankly, seeing nothing but a jumble of whites and blacks, senseless and patternless. Then one of the children in the third row had gasped, 'It's Jesus!' and that child had gone home with a brand-new Testament and also a calendar because he had been first. The others stared even harder, Jacky Torrance among them. One by one the other kids had given a similar gasp, one little girl transported in near-ecstasy, crying out shrilly: 'I *see* Him! I *see* Him!' She had also been rewarded with a Testament. At last everyone had seen the face of Jesus in the jumble of blacks and whites except Jacky. He strained harder and harder, scared now, part of him cynically thinking that everyone else was simply putting on to please Sister Beatrice, part of him secretly convinced that he wasn't seeing it because

God had decided he was the worst sinner in the class. 'Don't you see it, Jacky?' Sister Beatrice had asked him in her sad, sweet manner. I see your *tits*, he had thought in vicious desperation. He began to shake his head, then faked excitement and said: 'Yes, I do! Wow! It *is* Jesus!' And everyone in class had laughed and applauded him, making him feel triumphant, ashamed, and scared. Later, when everyone else had tumbled their way up from the church basement and out onto the street he had lingered behind, looking at the meaningless black-and-white jumble that Sister Beatrice had left on the easel. He hated it. They had all made it up the way he had, even Sister herself. It was a big fake. 'Shitfire-hellfire-shitfire,' he had whispered under his breath, and as he turned to go he had seen the face of Jesus from the corner of his eye, sad and wise. He turned back, his heart in his throat. Everything had suddenly clicked into place and he had stared at the picture with fearful wonder, unable to believe he had missed it. The eyes, the zigzag of shadow across the care-worn brow, the fine nose, the compassionate lips. Looking at Jack Torrance. What had only been a meaningless sprawl had suddenly been transformed into a stark black-and-white etching of the face of Christ-Our-Lord. Fearful wonder became terror. He had cussed in front of a picture of Jesus. He would be damned. He would be in hell with the sinners. The face of Christ had been in the picture all along. All along.

Now, kneeling in the sun and watching his son playing in the shadow of the hotel, he knew that it was all true. The hotel wanted Danny, maybe all of them but Danny for sure. The hedges had really walked. There was a dead woman in 217, a woman that was perhaps only a spirit and harmless under most circumstances, but a woman who was now an active danger. Like some malevolent clockwork toy she had been wound up and set in motion by Danny's own odd mind . . . and his own. Had it been Watson who had told him a man had dropped dead of a stroke one day on the roque court? Or had it been Ullman? It didn't matter. There had been an assassination on the third floor. How many old quarrels, suicides, strokes? How many murders? Was Grady lurking somewhere in the west wing with his ax, just waiting for Danny to start him up so he could come back out of the woodwork?

The puffed circle of bruises around Danny's neck.

The twinkling, half-seen bottles in the deserted lounge.

The radio.

The dreams.

The scrapbook he had found in the cellar.

(*Medoc, are you here? I've been sleepwalking again, my dear . . .*)

He got up suddenly, thrusting the snowshoes back out the door. He was shaking all over. He slammed the door and picked up the box with the battery in it. It slipped through his shaking fingers

(*oh christ what if i cracked it*)

and thumped over on its side. He pulled the flaps of the carton open and yanked the battery out, heedless of the acid that might be leaking through the battery's casing if it had cracked. But it hadn't. It was whole. A little sigh escaped his lips.

Cradling it, he took it over to the Skidoo and put it on its platform near the front of the engine. He found a small adjustable wrench on one of the shelves and attached the battery cables quickly and with no trouble. The battery was live; no need to use the charger on it. There had been a crackle of electricity and a small odor of ozone when he slipped the positive cable onto its terminal. The job done, he stood away, wiping his hands nervously on his faded denim jacket. There. It should work. No reason why not. No reason at all except that it was part of the Overlook and the Overlook really didn't want them out of here. Not at all. The Overlook was having one hell of a good time. There was a little boy to terrorize, a man and his woman to set one against the other, and if it played its cards right they could end up flitting through the Overlook's halls like insubstantial shades in a Shirley Jackson novel, whatever walked in Hill House walked alone, but you wouldn't be alone in the Overlook, oh no, there would be plenty of company here. But there was really no reason why the snowmobile shouldn't start. Except of course

(*Except he still didn't really want to go.*)

yes, except for that.

He stood looking at the Skidoo, his breath puffing out in frozen little plumes. He wanted it to be the way it had been. When he had come in here he'd had no doubts. Going down would be the wrong decision, he had known that then. Wendy was only scared of the boogeyman summoned up by a single hysterical little boy. Now suddenly, he could see her side. It was like his play, his damnable play. He no longer knew which side he was on, or how things should come out. Once you saw the face of a god in those jumbled blacks and whites, it was everybody out of the pool – you could never unsee it. Others might laugh and say it's nothing, just a lot of splotches with no meaning, give me a good old Craft-master paint-by-the-numbers any day, but *you* would always see the face of Christ-Our-Lord looking out at you. You had seen it in one gestalt leap, the conscious and unconscious melding in that one shocking moment of understanding. You would always see it. You were damned to always see it.

(*I've been sleepwalking again, my dear . . .*)

It had been all right until he had seen Danny playing in the snow. It was Danny's fault. Everything had been Danny's fault. He was the one with the shining, or whatever it was. It wasn't a shining. It was a curse. If he and Wendy had been here alone, they could have passed the winter quite nicely. No pain, no strain on the brain.

(*Don't want to leave.? Can't?*)

The Overlook didn't want them to go and he didn't want them to go either. Not even Danny. Maybe he was a part of it, now. Perhaps the Overlook, large and rambling Samuel Johnson that it was, had picked him to be its Boswell. You say the new caretaker writes? Very good, sign him on. Time we told our side. Let's get rid of the woman and his snot-nosed kid first, however. We don't want him to be distracted. We don't—

He was standing by the snowmobile's cockpit, his head starting to ache again. What did it come down to? Go or stay. Very simple. Keep it simple. Shall we go or shall we stay?

If we go, how long will it be before you find the local hole in Sidewinder? a voice inside him asked. The dark place with the lousy color TV that unshaven and unemployed men spend the day watching game shows on? Where the piss in the men's room smells two thousand years old and there's always a sodden Camel butt unraveling in the toilet bowl? Where the beer is thirty cents a glass and you cut it with salt and the jukebox is loaded with seventy country oldies?

How long? Oh Christ, he was so afraid it wouldn't be long at all.

'I can't win,' he said, very softly. That was it. It was like trying to play solitaire with one of the aces missing from the deck.

Abruptly he leaned over the Skidoo's motor compartment and yanked off the magneto. It came off with sickening ease. He looked at it for a moment, then went to the equipment shed's back door and opened it.

From here the view of the mountains was unobstructed, picture-postcard beautiful in the twinkling brightness of morning. An unbroken field of snow rose to the first pines about a mile distant. He flung the magneto as far out into the snow as he could. It went much further than it should have. There was a light puff of snow when it fell. The light breeze carried the snow granules away to fresh resting places. Disperse there, I say. There's nothing to see. It's all over. Disperse.

He felt at peace.

He stood in the doorway for a long time, breathing the good mountain air, and then he closed it firmly and went back out the other door to tell Wendy they would be staying. On the way, he stopped and had a snowball fight with Danny.

Chapter Thirty-four

The Hedges

It was November 29, three days after Thanksgiving. The last week had been a good one, the Thanksgiving dinner the best they'd ever had as a family, Wendy had cooked Dick Hallorann's turkey to a turn and they had all eaten to bursting without even coming close to demolishing the jolly bird. Jack had groaned that they would be eating turkey for the rest of the winter – creamed turkey, turkey sandwiches, turkey and noodles, turkey surprise.

No, Wendy told him with a little smile. Only until Christmas. Then we have the capon.

Jack and Danny groaned together.

The bruises on Danny's neck had faded, and their fears seemed to have faded with them. On Thanksgiving afternoon Wendy had been pulling Danny around on his sled while Jack worked on the play, which was now almost done.

'Are you still afraid, doc?' she had asked, not knowing how to put the question less baldly.

'Yes,' he answered simply. 'But now I stay in the safe places.'

'Your daddy says that sooner or later the forest rangers will wonder why we're not checking in on the CB radio. They'll come to see if anything is wrong. We might go down then. You and I. And let your daddy finish the winter. He has good reasons for wanting to. In a way, doc . . . I know this is hard for you to understand . . . our backs are against the wall.'

'Yes,' he had answered noncommittally.

On this sparkling afternoon the two of them were upstairs, and Danny knew that they had been making love. They were dozing now. They were happy, he knew. His mother was still a little bit afraid, but his father's attitude was strange. It was a feeling that he had done something that was very hard and had done it right. But Danny could not seem to see exactly what the something was. His father was guarding that carefully, even in his own mind. Was it possible, Danny wondered, to be glad you had done something and still be so ashamed of that something that you tried not to think of it? The question was a disturbing one. He didn't think such a thing was possible . . . in a normal mind. His hardest probings at his father had only brought him a dim picture of something like an octopus, whirling up into the hard blue sky. And on both occasions that he had concentrated hard enough to get this, Daddy had suddenly been staring at him in a sharp and frightening way, as if he knew what Danny was doing.

Now he was in the lobby, getting ready to go out. He went out a lot, taking his sled or wearing his snowshoes. He liked to get out of the hotel. When he was out in the sunshine, it seemed like a weight had slipped from his shoulders.

He pulled a chair over, stood on it, and got his parka and snow pants out of the ballroom closet, and then sat down on the chair to put them on. His boots were in the boot box and he pulled them on, his tongue creeping out into the corner of his mouth in concentration as he laced them and tied the rawhide into careful granny knots. He pulled on his mittens and his ski mask and was ready.

He tramped out through the kitchen to the back door, then paused. He was tired of playing out back, and at this time of day the hotel's shadow would be cast over his play area. He didn't even like being in the Overlook's shadow. He decided he would put on his snowshoes and go down to the playground instead. Dick Hallorann had told him to stay away from the topiary, but the thought of the hedge animals did not bother him much. They were buried under snowdrifts now, nothing showing but a vague hump that was the rabbit's head and the lions' tails. Sticking out of the snow the way they were, the tails looked more absurd than frightening.

Danny opened the back door and got his snowshoes from the milk platform. Five minutes later he was strapping them to his feet on the front porch. His daddy had told him that he (Danny) had the hang of using the snowshoes – the lazy, shuffling stride, the twist of ankle that shook the powdery snow from the lacings just before the boot came back down – and all that remained was for him to build up the necessary muscles in his thighes and calves and ankles. Danny found that his ankles got tired the fastest. Snowshoeing was almost as hard on your ankles as skating, because you had to keep clearing the lacings. Every five minutes or so he had to stop with his legs spread and the snowshoes flat on the snow to rest them.

But he didn't have to rest on his way down to the playground because it was all downhill. Less than ten minutes after he struggled up and over the monstrous snow-dune that had drifted in on the Overlook's front porch he was standing with his mittened hand on the playground slide. He wasn't even breathing hard.

The playground seemed much nicer in the deep snow than it ever had during the autumn. It looked like a fairyland sculpture. The swing chains had been frozen in strange positions, the seats of the big kids' swings resting flush against the snow. The jungle gym was an ice-cave guarded by dripping icicle teeth. Only the chimneys of the play-Overlook stuck up over the snow

(wish the other one was buried that way only not with us in it)

and the tops of the cement rings protruded in two places like Eskimo igloos. Danny tramped over there, squatted, and began to dig. Before long he had uncovered the dark mouth of one of them and he slipped into the cold tunnel. In his mind he was Patrick McGoohan, the Secret Agent Man (they had shown the reruns of that program twice on the Burlington TV channel and his daddy never missed them; he would skip a party to stay home and watch 'Secret Agent' or 'The Avengers' and Danny had always watched with him), on the run from KGB agents in the mountains of Switzerland. There had been avalanches in the area and the notorious KGB agent Slobbo had killed his girlfriend with a poison dart, but somewhere near was the Russian antigravity machine. Perhaps at the end of this very tunnel. He drew his automatic and went along the concrete tunnel, his eyes wide and alert, his breath pluming out.

The far end of the concrete ring was solidly blocked with snow. He tried digging through it and was amazed (and a little uneasy) to see how solid it was, almost like ice from the cold and the constant weight of more snow on top of it.

His make-believe game collapsed around him and he was suddenly aware that he felt closed in and extremely nervous in this tight ring of cement. He could hear his breathing; it sounded dank and quick and hollow. He was under the snow, and hardly any light filtered down the hole he had dug to get in here. Suddenly he wanted to be out in the sunlight more than anything, suddenly he remembered his daddy and mommy were sleeping and didn't know where he was, that if the hole he dug caved in he would be trapped, and the Overlook didn't like him.

Danny got turned around with some difficulty and crawled back along the length of the concrete ring, his snowshoes clacking woodenly together behind him, his palms crackling in last fall's dead aspen leaves beneath him. He had just reached the end and the cold spill of light coming down from above when the snow *did* give in, a minor fall, but enough to powder his face and clog the opening he had wriggled down through and leave him in darkness.

For a moment his brain froze in utter panic and he could not think. Then, as if from far off, he heard his daddy telling him that he must never play at the Stovington dump, because sometimes stupid people hauled old refrigerators off to the dump without removing the doors and if you got in one and the door happened to shut on you, there was no way to get out. You would die in the darkness.

(You wouldn't want a thing like that to happen to you, would you, doc?)

(No, Daddy.)

But it *had* happened, his frenzied mind told him, it *had* happened, he was in the dark, he was closed in, and it was as cold as a refrigerator. And—

(*something is in here with me.*)

His breath stopped in a gasp. An almost drowsy terror stole through his veins. Yes. Yes. There was something in here with him, some awful thing the Overlook had saved for just such a chance as this. Maybe a huge spider that had burrowed down under the dead leaves, or a rat . . . or maybe the corpse of some little kid that had died here on the playground. Had that ever happened? Yes, he thought maybe it had. He thought of the woman in the tub. The blood and brains on the wall of the Presidential Sweet. Of some little kid, its head split open from a fall from the monkey bars or a swing, crawling after him in the dark, grinning, looking for one final playmate in its endless playground. Forever. In a moment he would hear it coming.

At the far end of the concrete ring, Danny heard the stealthy crackle of dead leaves as something came for him on its hands and knees. At any moment he would feel its cold hand close over his ankle—

That thought broke his paralysis. He was digging at the loose fall of snow that choked the end of the concrete ring, throwing it back between his legs in powdery bursts like a dog digging for a bone. Blue light filtered down from above and Danny thrust himself up at it like a diver coming out of deep water. He scraped his back on the lip of the concrete ring. One of his snowshoes twisted behind the other. Snow spilled down inside his ski mask and into the collar of his parka. He dug at the snow, clawed at it. It seemed to be trying to hold him, to suck him back down, back into the concrete ring where that unseen, leaf-crackling *thing* was, and keep him there. Forever.

Then he was out, his face was turned up to the sun, and he was crawling through the snow, crawling away from the half-buried cement ring, gasping harshly, his face almost comically white with powdered snow – a living fright-mask. He hobbled over to the jungle gym and sat down to readjust his snowshoes and get his breath. As he set them to rights and tightened the straps again, he never took his eyes from the hole at the end of the concrete ring. He waited to see if something would come out. Nothing did, and after three or four minutes, Danny's breathing began to slow down. Whatever it was, it couldn't stand the sunlight. It was cooped up down there, maybe only able to come out when it was dark . . . or when both ends of its circular prison were plugged with snow.

(*but i'm safe now i'm safe i'll just go back because now i'm*)

Something thumped softly behind him.

He turned around, toward the hotel, and looked. But even before he looked

(*Can you see the Indians in this picture?*)

he knew what he would see, because he knew what that soft thumping sound had been. It was the sound of a large clump of snow falling, the way it sounded when it slid off the roof of the hotel and fell to the ground.

(*Can you see—?*)

Yes. He could. The snow had fallen off the hedge dog. When he came down it had only been a harmless lump of snow outside the playground. Now it stood revealed, an incongruous splash of green in all the eye-watering whiteness. It was sitting up, as if to beg a sweet or a scrap.

But this time he wouldn't go crazy, he wouldn't blow his cool. Because at least he wasn't trapped in some dark old hole. He was in the sunlight. And it was just a dog. It's pretty warm out today, he thought hopefully.

Maybe the sun just melted enough snow off that old dog so the rest fell off in a bunch. Maybe that's all it is.

(*Don't go near that place . . . steer right clear.*)

His snowshoe bindings were as tight as they were ever going to be. He stood up and stared back at the concrete ring, almost completely submerged in the snow, and what he saw at the end he had exited from froze his heart. There was a circular patch of darkness at the end of it, a fold of shadow that marked the hole he'd dug to get down inside. Now, in spite of the snow-dazzle, he thought he could see something there. Something moving. A hand. The waving hand of some desperately unhappy child, waving hand, pleading hand, drowning hand.

(*Save me O please save me If you can't save me at least come play with me . . . Forever. And Forever. And Forever.*)

'No,' Danny whispered huskily. The word fell dry and bare from his mouth, which was stripped of moisture. He could feel his mind wavering now, trying to go away the way it had when the woman in the room had . . . no, better not think of that.

He grasped at the strings of reality and held them tightly. He had to get out of here. Concentrate on that. Be cool. Be like the Secret Agent Man. Would Patrick McGoohan be crying and peeing in his pants like a little baby?

Would his daddy?

That calmed him somewhat.

From behind him, that soft *flump* sound of falling snow came again. He turned around and the head of one of the hedge lions was sticking out of the snow now, snarling at him. It was closer than it should have been, almost up to the gate of the playground.

Terror tried to rise up and he quelled it. He was the Secret Agent Man, and he *would* escape.

He began to walk out of the playground, taking the same roundabout course his father had taken on the day that the snow flew. He concentrated on operating the snowshoes. Slow, flat strides. Don't lift your foot too high or you'll lose your balance. Twist your ankle and spill the snow off the crisscrossed lacings. It seemed so *slow*. He reached the corner of the playground. The snow was drifted high here and he was able to step over the fence. He got halfway over and then almost fell flat when the snowshoe on his behind foot caught on one of the fence posts. He leaned on the outside edge of gravity, pinwheeling his arms, remembering how hard it was to get up once you fell down.

From his right, that soft sound again, falling clumps of snow. He looked over and saw the other two lions, clear of snow now down to their forepaws, side by side, about sixty paces away. The green indentations that were their eyes were fixed on him. The dog had turned its head.

(*It only happens when you're not looking.*)

'Oh! Hey—'

His snowshoes had crossed and he plunged forward into the snow, arms waving uselessly. More snow got inside his hood and down his neck and into the tops of his boots. He struggled out of the snow and tried to get the snowshoes under him, heart hammering crazily now

(*Secret Agent Man remember you're the Secret Agent*)

and overbalanced backward. For a moment he lay there looking at the sky, thinking it would be simpler to just give up.

Then he thought of the thing in the concrete tunnel and knew he could not. He gained his feet and stared over at the topiary. All three lions were bunched together now, not forty feet away. The dog had ranged off to their left, as if to block Danny's retreat. They were bare of snow except for powdery ruffs around their necks and muzzles. They were all staring at him.

His breath was racing now, and the panic was like a rat behind his forehead, twisting and gnawing. He fought the panic and he fought the snowshoes.

(*Daddy's voice: No, don't fight them, doc. Walk on them like they were your own feet. Walk* with *them.*)

(*Yes, Daddy.*)

He began to walk again, trying to regain the easy rhythm he had practiced with his daddy. Little by little it began to come, but with the rhythm came an awareness of just how tired he was, how much his fear had exhausted him. The tendons of his thighs and calves and ankles were hot and trembly. Ahead he could see the Overlook, mockingly distant, seeming to stare at him with its many windows, as if this were some sort of contest in which it was mildly interested.

Danny looked back over his shoulder and his hurried breathing caught for a moment and then hurried on even faster. The nearest lion was now only twenty feet behind, breasting through the snow like a dog paddling in a pond. The two others were to its right and left, pacing it. They were like an army platoon on patrol, the dog, still off to their left, the scout. The closest lion had its head down. The shoulders bunched powerfully above its neck. The tail was up, as if in the instant before he had turned to look it had been swishing back and forth, back and forth. He thought it looked like a great big housecat that was having a good time playing with a mouse before killing it.

(*—falling—*)

No, if he fell he was dead. They would never let him get up. They would pounce. He pinwheeled his arms madly and lunged ahead, his center of gravity dancing just beyond his nose. He caught it and hurried on, snapping glances back over his shoulder. The air whistled in and out of his dry throat like hot glass.

The world closed down to the dazzling snow, the green hedges, and the whispery sound of his snowshoes. And something else. A soft, muffled padding sound. He tried to hurry faster and couldn't. He was walking over the buried driveway now, a small boy with his face almost buried in the shadow of his parka hood. The afternoon was still and bright.

When he looked back again, the point lion was only five feet behind. It was grinning. Its mouth was open, its haunches tensed down like a clock-spring. Behind it and the others he could see the rabbit, its head now sticking out of the snow, bright green, as if it had turned its horrid blank face to watch the end of the stalk.

Now, on the Overlook's front lawn between the circular drive and the porch, he let the panic loose and began to run clumsily in the snowshoes, not daring to look back now, tilting further and further forward, his arms out ahead of him like a blind man feeling for obstacles. His hood fell back, revealing his complexion, paste white giving way to hectic red blotches on his cheeks, his eyes bulging with terror. The porch was very close now.

Behind him he heard the sudden hard crunch of snow as something leaped.

He fell on the porch steps, screaming without sound, and scrambled up them on his hands and knees, snowshoes clattering and askew behind him.

There was a slashing sound in the air and sudden pain in his leg. The ripping sound of cloth. Something else that might have – *must* have – been in his mind.

Bellowing, angry roar.

Smell of blood and evergreen.

He fell full-length on the porch, sobbing hoarsely, the rich, metallic taste of copper in his mouth. His heart was thundering in his chest. There was a small trickle of blood coming from his nose.

He had no idea how long he lay there before the lobby doors flew open and Jack ran out, wearing just his jeans and a pair of slippers. Wendy was behind him.

'*Danny!*' she screamed.

'Doc! Danny, for Christ's sake! What's wrong? What happened?'

Daddy was helping him up. Below the knee his snowpants were ripped open. Inside, his woollen ski sock had been ripped open and his calf had been shallowly scratched . . . as if he had tried to push his way through a closely grown evergreen hedge and the branches had clawed him.

He looked over his shoulder. Far down the lawn, past the putting green, were a number of vague, snow-cowled humps. The hedge animals. Between them and the playground. Between them and the road.

His legs gave way. Jack caught him. He began to cry.

Chapter Thirty-five

The Lobby

He had told them everything except what had happened to him when the snow had blocked the end of the concrete ring. He couldn't bring himself to repeat that. And he didn't know the right words to express the creeping, lassitudinous sense of terror he had felt when he heard the dead aspen leaves begin to crackle furtively down there in the cold darkness. But he told them about the soft sound of snow falling in clumps. About the lion with its head and its bunched shoulders working its way up and out of the snow to chase him. He even told them about how the rabbit had turned its head to watch near the end.

The three of them were in the lobby. Jack had built a roaring blaze in the fireplace. Danny was bundled up in a blanket on the small sofa where once, a million years ago, three nuns had sat laughing like girls while they waited for the line at the desk to thin out. He was sipping hot noodle soup from a mug. Wendy sat beside him, stroking his hair. Jack had sat on the floor, his face seeming to grow more and more still, more and more set as Danny told his story. Twice he pulled his handkerchief out of his back pocket and rubbed his sore-looking lips with it.

'Then they chased me,' he finished. Jack got up and went over to the window, his back to them. He looked at his mommy. 'They chased me all the way up to the porch.' He was struggling to keep his voice calm, because if he stayed calm maybe they would believe him. Mr Stenger hadn't stayed calm. He had started to cry and hadn't been able to stop so THE MEN IN THE WHITE COATS had come to take him away because if you couldn't stop crying it meant you had LOST YOUR MARBLES and when would you be back? NO ONE KNOWS. His parka and snowpants and the clotted snowshoes lay on the rug just inside the big double doors.

(I won't cry I won't let myself cry)

And he thought he could do that, but he couldn't stop shaking. He looked into the fire and waited for Daddy to say something. High yellow flames danced on the dark stone hearth. A pine-knot exploded with a bang and sparks rushed up the flue.

'Danny, come over here.' Jack turned around. His face still had that pinched, deathly look. Danny didn't like to look at it.

'Jack—'

'I just want the boy over here for a minute.'

Danny slipped off the sofa and came over beside his daddy.

'Good boy. Now what do you see?'

Danny had known what he would see even before he got to the window. Below the clutter of boot tracks, sled tracks, and snowshoe tracks that marked their usual exercise area, the snowfield that covered the Overlook's lawns sloped down to the topiary and the playground beyond. It was marred by two sets of tracks, one of them in a straight line from the porch to the playground, the other a long, looping line coming back up.

'Only my tracks, Daddy. But—'

'What about the hedges, Danny?'

Danny's lips began to tremble. He was going to cry. What if he couldn't stop?

(i won't cry I Won't Cry Won't Won't WON'T)

'All covered with snow,' he whispered. 'But, Daddy—'

'What? I couldn't hear you!'

'Jack, you're cross-examing him! Can't you see he's upset, he's—'

'Shut up! Well, Danny?'

'They scratched me, Daddy. My leg—'

'You must have cut your leg on the crust of the snow.'

Then Wendy was between them, her face pale and angry. 'What are you trying to make him do?' she asked him. 'Confess to murder? *What's wrong with you?*'

The strangeness in his eyes seemed to break then. 'I'm trying to help him find the difference between something real and something that was only an hallucination, that's all.' He squatted by Danny so they were on an eye-to-eye level, and then hugged him tight. 'Danny, it didn't really happen. Okay? It was like one of those trances you have sometimes. That's all.'

'Daddy?'

'What, Dan?'

'I didn't cut my leg on the crust. There isn't any crust. It's all powdery snow. It won't even stick together to make snowballs. Remember we tried to have a snowball fight and couldn't?'

He felt his father stiffen against him. 'The porch step, then.'

Danny pulled away. Suddenly he had it. It had flashed into his mind all at once, the way things sometimes did, the way it had about the woman wanting to be in that gray man's pants. He stared at his father with widening eyes.

'You know I'm telling the truth,' he whispered, shocked.

'Danny—' Jack's face, tightening.

'You know because you saw—'

The sound of Jack's open palm striking Danny's face was flat, not dramatic at all. The boy's head rocked back, the palmprint reddening on his cheek like a brand.

Wendy made a moaning noise.

For a moment they were still, the three of them, and then Jack grabbed for his son and said, 'Danny, I'm sorry, you okay, doc?'

'You hit him, you bastard!' Wendy cried. 'You dirty bastard!'

She grabbed his other arm and for a moment Danny was pulled between them.

'Oh please stop pulling me!' he screamed at them, and there was such agony in his voice that they both let go of him, and then the tears had to come and he collapsed, weeping, between the sofa and the window, his parents staring at him helplessly, the way children might stare at a toy broken in a furious tussle over to whom it belonged. In the fireplace another pine-knot exploded like a hand grenade, making them all jump.

Wendy gave him baby aspirin and Jack slipped him, unprotesting, between the sheets of his cot. He was asleep in no time with his thumb in his mouth.

'I don't like that,' she said. 'It's a regression.'

Jack didn't reply.

She looked at him softly, without anger, without a smile, either. 'You want me to apologize for calling you a bastard? All right, I apologize. I'm sorry. You still shouldn't have hit him.'

'I know,' he muttered. 'I know that. I don't know what the hell came over me.'

'You promised you'd never hit him again.'

He looked at her furiously, and then the fury collapsed. Suddenly, with pity and horror, she saw what Jack would look like as an old man. She had never seen him look that way before.

(?what way?)

Defeated, she answered herself. *He looks beaten*.

He said: 'I always thought I could keep my promises.'

She went to him and put her hands on his arm. 'All right, it's over. And when the ranger comes to check us, we'll tell him we all want to go down. All right?'

'All right,' Jack said, and at that moment, at least, he meant it. The same way he had always meant it on those mornings after, looking at his pale and haggard face in the bathroom mirror. *I'm going to stop, going to cut it off flat*. But morning gave way to afternoon, and in the afternoons he felt a little better. And afternoons gave way to night. As some great twentieth-century thinker had said, night must fall.

He found himself wishing that Wendy would ask him about the hedges, would ask him what Danny meant when he said *You know because you saw*— If she did, he would tell her everything. Everything. The hedges, the woman in the room, even about the fire hose that seemed to have switched positions. But where did confession stop? Could he tell her he'd thrown the magneto away, that they could all be down in Sidewinder right now if he hadn't done that?

What she said was, 'Do you want tea?'

'Yes. A cup of tea would be good.'

She went to the door and paused there, rubbing her forearms through her sweater. 'It's my fault as much as yours,' she said. 'What were we doing while he was going through that . . . dream, or whatever it was?'

'Wendy—'

'We were sleeping,' she said. 'Sleeping like a couple of teenage kids with their itch nicely scratched.'

'Stop it,' he said. 'It's over.'

'No,' Wendy answered, and gave him a strange, restless smile. 'It's not over.'

She went out to make tea, leaving him to keep watch over their son.

Chapter Thirty-six

The Elevator

Jack awoke from a thin and uneasy sleep where huge and ill-defined shapes chased him through endless snowfields to what he first thought was another dream: darkness, and in it, a sudden mechanical jumble of noises – clicks and clanks, hummings, rattling, snaps and whooshes.

Then Wendy sat up beside him and he knew it was no dream.

'What's that?' Her hand, cold marble, gripped his wrist. He restrained an urge to shake it off – how in the hell was he supposed to know what it was? The illuminated clock on his nightstand said it was five minutes to twelve.

The humming sound again. Loud and steady, varying the slightest bit. Followed by a clank as the humming ceased. A rattling bang. A thump. Then the humming resumed.

It was the elevator.

Danny was sitting up. 'Daddy? *Daddy?*' His voice was sleepy and scared.

'Right here, doc,' Jack said. 'Come on over and jump in. Your mom's awake, too.'

The bedclothes rustled as Danny got on the bed between them. 'It's the elevator,' he whispered.

'That's right,' Jack said. 'Just the elevator.'

'What do you mean, *just?*' Wendy demanded. There was an ice-skim of hysteria on her voice. 'It's the middle of the night. *Who's running it?*'

Hummmmmmm. Click/clank. Above them now. The rattle of the gate accordioning back, the bump of the doors opening and closing. Then the hum of the motor and the cables again.

Danny began to whimper.

Jack swung his feet out of bed and onto the floor. 'It's probably a short. I'll check.'

'Don't you dare go out of this room!'

'Don't be stupid,' he said, pulling on his robe. 'It's my job.'

She was out of bed herself a moment later, pulling Danny with her.

'We'll go, too.'

'Wendy—'

'What's wrong?' Danny asked somberly. 'What's wrong, Daddy?'

Instead of answering he turned away, his face angry and set. He belted his robe around him at the door, opened it, and stepped out into the dark hall.

Wendy hesitated for a moment, and it was actually Danny who began to move first. She caught up quickly, and they went out together.

Jack hadn't bothered with the lights. She fumbled for the switch that lit the four spaced overheads in the hallway that led to the main corridor. Up ahead, Jack was already turning the corner. This time Danny found the switchplate and flicked all three switches up. The hallway leading down to the stairs and the elevator shaft came alight.

Jack was standing at the elevator station, which was flanked by benches and cigarette urns. He was standing motionless in front of the closed elevator door. In his faded tartan bathrobe and brown leather slippers with the rundown heels, his hair all in sleep corkscrews and Alfalfa cowlicks, he looked to her like an absurd twentieth-century Hamlet, an indecisive figure so mesmerized by onrushing tragedy that he was helpless to divert its course or alter it in any way.

(*jesus stop thinking so crazy—*)

Danny's hand had tightened painfully on her own. He was looking up at her intently, his face strained and anxious. He had been catching the drift of her thoughts, she realized. Just how much or how little of them he was getting was impossible to say, but she flushed, feeling much the same as if he had caught her in a masturbatory act.

'Come on,' she said, and they went down the hall to Jack.

The hummings and clankings and thumpings were louder here, terrifying in a disconnected, benumbed way. Jack was staring at the closed door with feverish intensity. Through the diamond-shaped window in the center of the elevator door she thought she could make out the cables, thrumming slightly. The elevator clanked to a stop below them, at lobby level. They heard the doors thump open. And . . . (*party*)

Why had she thought party? The word had simply jumped into her head for no reason at all. The silence in the Overlook was complete and intense except for the weird noises coming up the elevator shaft.

(must have been quite a party)

(*???WHAT PARTY???*)

For just a moment her mind had filled with an image so real that it seemed to be a memory . . . not just any memory but one of those you treasure, one of those you keep for very special occasions and rarely mention aloud. Lights . . . hundreds, maybe thousands of them. Lights and colors, the pop of champagne corks, a forty-piece orchestra playing Glenn Miller's 'In the Mood.' But Glenn Miller had gone down in his bomber before she was born, how could she have a memory of Glenn Miller?

She looked down at Danny and saw his head had cocked to one side, as if he was hearing something she couldn't hear. His face was very pale.

Thump.

The door had slid shut down there. A humming whine as the elevator began to rise. She saw the engine housing on top of the car first through the diamond-shaped window, then the interior of the car, seen through the further diamond shapes made by the brass gate. Warm yellow light from the car's overhead. It was empty. The car was empty. It was empty but

(on the night of the party they must have crowded in by the dozens, crowded the car way beyond its safety limit but of course it had been new then and all of them wearing masks)

(*????WHAT MASKS????*)

The car stopped above them, on the third floor. She looked at Danny. His face was all eyes. His mouth was pressed into a frightened, bloodless slit. Above them, the brass gate rattled back. The elevator door thumped open, it thumped open because it was time, the time had come, it was time to say

(*Goodnight . . . goodnight . . . yes, it was lovely . . . no, i really can't stay for the unmasking . . . early to bed, early to rise . . . oh, was that Sheila? . . . the monk? . . . isn't that witty, Sheila coming as a monk? . . . yes, goodnight . . . good*)

Thump.

Gears clashed. The motor engaged. The car began to whine back down.

'Jack,' she whispered. 'What is it? What's wrong with it?'

'A short circuit,' he said. His face was like wood. 'I told you, it was a short circuit.'

'I keep hearing voices in my head!' she cried. 'What is it? What's wrong? I feel like I'm going crazy!'

'What voices?' He looked at her with deadly blandness.

She turned to Danny. 'Did you—?'

Danny nodded slowly. 'Yes. And music. Like from a long time ago. In my head.'

The elevator car stopped again. The hotel was silent, creaking, deserted. Outside, the wind whined around the eaves in the darkness.

'Maybe you are both crazy,' Jack said conversationally. 'I don't hear a goddamned thing except that elevator having a case of the electrical hiccups. If you two want to have duet hysterics, fine. But count me out.'

The elevator was coming down again.

Jack stepped to the right, where a glass-fronted box was mounted on the wall at chest height. He smashed his bare fist against it. Glass tinkled inward. Blood dripped from two of his knuckles. He reached in and took out a key with a long, smooth barrel.

'Jack, no. Don't.'

'I am going to do my job. Now leave me alone, Wendy!'

She tried to grab his arm. He pushed her backward. Her feet tangled in the hem of her robe and she fell to the carpet with an ungainly thump. Danny cried out shrilly and fell on his knees beside her. Jack turned back to the elevator and thrust the key into the socket.

The elevator cables disappeared and the bottom of the car came into view in the small window. A second later Jack turned the key hard. There was a grating, screeching sound as the elevator car came to an instant standstill. For a moment the declutched motor in the basement whined even louder, and then its circuit breaker cut in and the Overlook went unearthly still. The night wind outside seemed very loud by comparison. Jack looked stupidly at the gray metal elevator door. There were three splotches of blood below the keyhole from his lacerated knuckles.

He turned back to Wendy and Danny for a moment. She was sitting up, and Danny had his arm around her. They were both staring at him carefully, as if he was a stranger they had never seen before, possibly a dangerous one. He opened his mouth, not sure what was going to come out.

'It . . . Wendy, it's my job.'

She said clearly: 'Fuck your job.'

He turned back to the elevator, worked his fingers into the crack that ran down the right side of the door, and got it to open a little way. Then he was able to get his whole weight on it and threw the door open.

The car had stopped halfway, its floor at Jack's chest level. Warm light still spilled out of it, contrasting with the oily darkness of the shaft below.

He looked in for what seemed a long time.

'It's empty,' he said then. 'A short circuit, like I said.' He hooked his fingers into the slot behind the door and began to pull it closed . . . then her hand was on his shoulder, surprisingly strong, yanking him away.

'Wendy!' he shouted. But she had already caught the car's bottom edge and pulled herself up enough so she could look in. Then, with a convulsive heave of her shoulder and belly muscles, she tried to boost herself all the way up. For a moment the issue was in doubt. Her feet tottered over the blackness of the shaft and one pink slipper fell from her foot and slipped out of sight.

'*Mommy!*' Danny screamed.

Then she was up, her cheeks flushed, her forehead as pale and shining as a spirit lamp. 'What about this, Jack? Is this a short circuit?' She threw something and suddenly the hall was full of drifting confetti, red and white and blue and yellow. 'Is *this?*' A green party streamer, faded to a pale pastel color with age.

'And *this?*'

She tossed it out and it came to rest on the blue-black jungle carpet, a black silk cat's-eye mask, dusted with sequins at the temples.

'*Does that look like a short circuit to you, Jack?*' she screamed at him.

Jack stepped slowly away from it, shaking his head mechanically back and forth. The cat's-eye mask stared up blankly at the ceiling from the confetti-strewn hallway carpet.

Chapter Thirty-seven

The Ballroom

It was the first of December.

Danny was in the east-wing ballroom, standing on an over-stuffed, high-backed wing chair, looking at the clock under glass. It stood in the center of the ballroom's high, ornamental mantelpiece, flanked by two large ivory elephants. He almost expected the elephants would begin to move and try to gore him with their tusks as he stood there, but they were moveless. They were 'safe.' Since the night of the elevator he had come to divide all things at the Overlook into two categories. The elevator, the basement, the playground, Room 217, and the Presidential Suite (it was Suite, not Sweet; he had seen the correct spelling in an account book Daddy had been reading at supper last night and had memorized it carefully) – those places were 'unsafe.' Their quarters, the lobby, and the porch were 'safe.' Apparently the ballroom was, too.

(The elephants are, anyway.)

He was not sure about other places and so avoided them on general principle.

He looked at the clock inside the glass dome. It was under glass because all its wheels and cogs and springs were showing. A chrome or steel track ran around the outside of these works, and directly below the clockface there was a small axis bar with a pair of meshing cogs at either end. The hands of the clock stood at quarter past XI, and although he didn't know Roman numerals he could guess by the configuration of the hands at what time the clock had stopped. The clock stood on a velvet base. In front of it, slightly distorted by the curve of the dome, was a carefully carved silver key.

He supposed that the clock was one of the things he wasn't supposed to touch, like the decorative fire-tools in their brass-bound cabinet by the lobby fireplace or the tall china highboy at the back of the dining room.

A sense of injustice and a feeling of angry rebellion suddenly rose in him and

(*never mind what i'm not supposed to touch, just never mind. touched me, hasn't it? played with me, hasn't it?*)

It had. And it hadn't been particularly careful not to break him, either.

Danny put his hands out, grasped the glass dome, and lifted it aside. He let one finger play over the works for a moment, the pad of his index finger denting against the cogs, running smoothly over the wheels. He picked up the silver key. For an adult it would have been uncomfortably small, but it fitted his own fingers perfectly. He placed it in the keyhole at the center of the clockface. It went firmly home with a tiny click, more felt than heard. It wound to the right, of course; clockwise.

Danny turned the key until it would turn no more and then removed it.

The clock began to tick. Cogs turned. A large balance wheel rocked back and forth in semicircles. The hands were moving. If you kept your head perfectly motionless and your eyes wide open, you could see the minute hand inching along toward its meeting some forty-five minutes from now with the hour hand. At XII.

(*And the Red Death held sway over all.*)

He frowned, and then shook the thought away. It was a thought with no meaning or reference for him.

He reached his index finger out again and pushed the minute hand up to the hour, curious about what might happen. It obviously wasn't a cuckoo clock, but that steel rail had to have some purpose.

There was a small, ratcheting series of clicks, and then the clock began to tinkle Strauss's 'Blue Danube Waltz.' A punched roll of cloth no more than two inches in width began to unwind. A small series of brass strikers rose and fell. From behind the clockface two figures glided into view along the steel track, ballet dancers, on the left a girl in a fluffy skirt and white stockings, on the right a boy in a black leotard and ballet slippers. Their hands were held in arches over their heads. They came together in the middle, in front of VI.

Danny espied tiny grooves in their sides, just below their armpits. The axis bar slipped into these grooves and he heard another small click. The cogs at either end of the bar began to turn. 'The Blue Danube' tinkled. The dancers' arms came down around each other. The boy flipped the girl up over his head and then whirled over the bar. They were now lying prone, the boy's head buried beneath the girl's short ballet skirt, the girl's face pressed against the center of the boy's leotard. They writhed in a mechanical frenzy.

Danny's nose wrinkled. They were kissing peepees. That made him feel sick.

A moment later and things began to run backward. The boy whirled back over the axis bar. He flipped the girl into an upright position. They seemed to nod knowingly at each other as their hands arched back over their heads. They retreated the way they had come, disappearing just as 'The Blue Danube' finished. The clock began to strike a count of silver chimes.

(*Midnight! Stroke of midnight!*)

(*Hooray for masks!*)

Danny whirled on the chair, almost falling down. The ballroom was empty. Beyond the double cathedral window he could see fresh snow beginning to sift down. The huge ballroom rug (rolled up for dancing, of course), a rich tangle of red and gold embroidery, lay undisturbed on the floor. Spaced around it were small, intimate tables for two, the spidery chairs that went with each upended with legs pointing at the ceiling.

The whole place was empty.

But it wasn't really empty. Because here in the Overlook things just went on and on. Here in the Overlook all times were one. There was an endless night in August of 1945, with laughter and drinks and a chosen shining few going up and coming down in the elevator, drinking champange and popping party favors in each other's faces. It was a not-yet-light morning in June some twenty years later and the organization hitters endlessly pumped shotgun shells into the torn and bleeding bodies of three men who went through their agony endlessly. In a room on the second floor a woman lolled in her tub and waited for visitors.

In the Overlook all things had a sort of life. It was as if the whole place had been wound up with a silver key. The clock was running. The clock was running.

He was that key, Danny thought sadly. Tony had warned him and he had just let things go on.

(*I'm just five!*)

he cried to some half-felt presence in the room.

(*Doesn't it make any difference that I'm just five?*)

There was no answer.

He turned reluctantly back to the clock.

He had been putting it off, hoping that something would happen to help him avoid trying to call Tony again, that a ranger would come, or a helicopter, or the rescue team; they always came in time on his TV programs, the people were saved. On TV the rangers and the SWAT squad and the paramedics were a friendly white force counterbalancing the confused evil that he perceived in the world; when people got in trouble they were helped out of it, they were fixed up. They did not have to help themselves out of trouble.

(*Please?*)

There was no answer.

No answer, and if Tony came would it be the same nightmare? The booming, the hoarse and petulant voice, the blue-black rug like snakes? *Redrum?*

But what else?

(*Please oh please*)

No answer.

With a trembling sigh, he looked at the clockface. Cogs turned and meshed with other cogs. The balance wheel rocked hypnotically back and forth. And if you held your head perfectly still, you could see the minute hand creeping inexorably down from XII to V. If you held your head perfectly still you could see that—

The clockface was gone. In its place was a round black hole. It led down into forever. It began to swell. The clock was gone. The room behind it. Danny tottered and then fell into the darkness that had been hiding behind the clockface all along.

The small boy in the chair suddenly collapsed and lay in it at a crooked unnatural angle, his head thrown back, his eyes staring sightlessly at the high ballroom ceiling.

Down and down and down and down to—

—the hallway, crouched in the hallway, and he had made a wrong turn, trying to get back to the stairs he had made a wrong turn and now AND NOW—

—he saw he was in the short dead-end corridor that led only to the Presidential Suite and the booming sound was coming closer, the roque mallet whistling savagely through the air, the head of it embedding itself into the wall, cutting the silk paper, letting out small puffs of plaster dust.

(*Goddammit, come out here! Take your*)

But there was another figure in the hallway. Slouched nonchalantly against the wall just behind him. Like a ghost.

No, not a ghost, but all dressed in white. Dressed in whites.

(*I'll find you, you goddam little whoremastering RUNT!*)

Danny cringed back from the sound. Coming up the main third-floor hall now. Soon the owner of that voice would round the corner.

(*Come here! Come here, you little shit!*)

The figure dressed in white straightened up a little, removed a cigarette from the corner of his mouth, and plucked a shred of tobacco from his full lower lip. It was Hallorann, Danny saw. Dressed in his cook's whites instead of the blue suit he had been wearing on closing day.

'If there *is* trouble,' Hallorann said, 'you give a call. A big loud holler like the one that knocked me back a few minutes ago. I might hear you even way down in Florida. And if I do, I'll come on the run. I'll come on the run. I'll come on the—'

(*Come now, then! Come now, come NOW! Oh Dick I need you we all need*)

'—run. Sorry, but I got to run. Sorry, Danny ole kid ole doc, but I got to run. It's sure been fun, you son of a gun, but I got to hurry, I got to run.'

(*No!*)

But as he watched, Dick Hallorann turned, put his cigarette back into the corner of his mouth, and stepped nonchalantly through the wall.

Leaving him alone.

And that was when the shadow-figure turned the corner, huge in the hallway's gloom, only the reflected red of its eyes clear.

(*There you are! Now I've got you, you fuck! Now I'll teach you!*)

It lurched toward him in a horrible, shambling run, the roque mallet swinging up and up and up. Danny scrambled backward, screaming, and suddenly he was through the wall and falling, tumbling over and over, down the hole, down the rabbit hole and into a land full of sick wonders.

Tony was far below him, also falling.

(*I can't come anymore, Danny . . . he won't let me near you . . . none of them will let me near you . . . get Dick . . . get Dick . . .*)

'*Tony!*' he screamed.

But Tony was gone and suddenly he was in a dark room. But not entirely dark. Muted light spilling from somewhere. It was Mommy and Daddy's bedroom. He could see Daddy's desk. But the room was a dreadful shambles. He had been in this room before. Mommy's record player overturned on the floor. Her records scattered on the rug. The mattress half off the bed. Pictures ripped from the walls. His cot lying on its side like a dead dog, the Violent Violet Volkswagen crushed to purple shards of plastic.

The light was coming from the bathroom door, half-open. Just beyond it a hand dangled limply, blood dripping from the tips of the fingers. And in the medicine cabinet mirror, the word REDRUM flashing off and on.

Suddenly a huge clock in a glass bowl materialized in front of it. There were no hands or numbers on the clockface, only a date written in red: DECEMBER 2. And then, eyes widening in horror, he saw the word REDRUM reflecting dimly from the glass dome, now reflected twice. And he saw that it spelled MURDER.

Danny Torrance screamed in wretched terror. The date was gone from the clockface. The clockface itself was gone, replaced by a circular black hole that swelled and swelled like a dilating iris. It blotted out everything and he fell forward, beginning to fall, falling, he was—

—falling off the chair.

For a moment he lay on the ballroom floor, breathing hard.

REDRUM.
MURDER.
REDRUM.
MURDER.

(*The Red Death held sway over all!*)

(*Unmask! Unmask!*)

And behind each glittering lovely mask, the as-yet unseen face of the shape that chased him down these dark hallways, its red eyes widening, blank and homicidal.

Oh, he was afraid of what face might come to light when the time for unmasking came around at last.

(*DICK!*)

he screamed with all his might. His head seemed to shiver with the force of it.

(*!!! OH DICK OH PLEASE PLEASE PLEASE COME!!!*)

Above him the clock he had wound with the silver key continued to mark off the seconds and minutes and hours.

BOOK FIVE

MATTERS OF LIFE AND DEATH

Chapter Thirty-eight

Florida

Mrs Hallorann's third son, Dick, dressed in his cook's whites, a Lucky Strike parked in the corner of his mouth, backed his reclaimed Cadillac limo out of its space behind the One-A Wholesale Vegetable Mart and drove slowly around the building. Masterton, part owner now but still walking with the patented shuffle he had adopted back before World War II, was pushing a bin of lettuces into the high, dark building.

Hallorann pushed the button that lowered the passenger side window and hollered: 'Those avocadoes is too damn high, you cheapskate!'

Masterton looked back over his shoulder, grinned widely enough to expose all three gold teeth, and yelled back, 'And I know exactly where you can put em, my good buddy.'

'Remarks like that I keep track of, *bro.*'

Masterton gave him the finger. Hallorann returned the compliment.

'Get your cukes, did you?' Masterton asked.

'I did.'

'You come back early tomorrow, I gonna give you some of the nicest new potatoes you ever seen.'

'I send the boy,' Hallorann said. 'You comin up tonight?'

'You supplyin the juice, *bro?*'

'That's a big ten-four.'

'I be there. You keep that thing off the top end goin home, you hear me? Every cop between here an St. Pete knows your name.'

'You know all about it, huh?' Hallorann asked, grinning.

'I know more than you'll ever learn, my man.'

'Listen to this sassy nigger. Would you listen?'

'Go on, get outta here fore I start throwin these lettuces.'

'Go on an throw em. I'll take anything for free.'

Masterton made as if to throw one. Hallorann ducked, rolled up the window, and drove on. He was feeling fine. For the last half hour or so he had been smelling oranges, but he didn't find that queer. For the last half hour he had been in a fruit and vegetable market.

It was 4:30 p.m., EST, the first day of December, Old Man Winter settling his frostbitten rump firmly onto most of the country, but down here the men wore open-throated short-sleeve shirts and the women were in light summer dresses and shorts. On top of the First Bank of Florida building, a digital thermometer bordered with huge grapefruits was flashing 79° over and over. Thank God for Florida, Hallorann thought, mosquitoes and all.

In the back of the limo were two dozen avocados, a crate of cucumbers, ditto oranges, ditto grapefruit. Three shopping sacks filled with Bermuda onions, the sweetest vegetable a loving God ever created, some pretty good sweet peas, which would be served with the entree and come back uneaten nine times out of ten, and a single blue Hubbard squash that was strictly for personal consumption.

Hallorann stopped in the turn lane at the Vermont Street light, and when the green arrow showed he pulled out onto state highway 219, pushing up to forty and holding it there until the town began to trickle away into an exurban sprawl of gas stations, Burger Kings, and McDonalds. It was a small order today, he could have sent Baedecker after it, but Baedecker had been chafing for his chance to buy the meat, and besides, Hallorann never missed a chance to bang it back and forth with Frank Masterton if he could help it. Masterton might show up tonight to watch some TV and drink Hallorann's Bushmill's, or he might not. Either way was all right. But seeing him mattered. Every time it mattered now, because they weren't young anymore. In the last few days it seemed he was thinking of that very fact a great deal. No so young anymore, when you got up near sixty years old (or – tell the truth and save a lie – past it) you had to start thinking about stepping out. You could go anytime. And that had been on his mind this week, not in a heavy way but as a fact. Dying was a part of living. You had to keep tuning in to that if you expected to be a whole person. And if the fact of your own death was hard to understand, at least it wasn't impossible to accept.

Why this should have been on his mind he could not have said, but his other reason for getting this small order himself was so he could step upstairs to the small office over Frank's Bar and Grill. There was a lawyer up there now (the dentist who had been there last year had apparently gone broke), a young black fellow named McIver. Hallorann had stepped in and told this McIver that he wanted to make a will, and could McIver help him out? Well, McIver asked, how soon do you want the document? Yesterday, said Hallorann, and threw his head back and laughed. Have you got anything complicated in mind? was McIver's next question. Hallorann did not. He had his Cadillac, his bank account – some nine thousand dollars – a piddling checking account, and a closet of clothes. He wanted it all to go to his sister. And if your sister predeceases you? McIver asked. Never mind, Hallorann said. If that happens, I'll make a new will. The document had been completed and signed in less than three hours – fast work for a shyster – and now resided in Hallorann's breast pocket, folded into a stiff blue envelope with the word WILL on the outside in Old English letters.

He could not have said why he had chosen this warm sunny day when he felt so well to do something he had been putting off for years, but the impulse had come on him and he hadn't said no. He was used to following his hunches.

He was pretty well out of town now. He cranked the limo up to an illegal sixty and let it ride there in the left-hand lane, sucking up most of the Petersburg-bound traffic. He knew from experience that the limo would still ride as solid as iron at ninety, and even at a hundred and twenty it didn't seem to lighten up much. But his screamin days were long gone. The thought of putting the limo up to a hundred and twenty on a straight stretch only scared him. He was getting old.

(*Jesus, those oranges smell strong. Wonder if they gone over?*)

Bugs splattered against the window. He dialed the radio to a Miami soul station and got the soft, wailing voice of Al Green.

> '*What a beautiful time we had together,*
> *Now it's getting late and we must leave each other . . .*'

He unrolled the window, pitched his cigarette butt out, then rolled it further down to clear out the smell of the oranges. He tapped his fingers against the wheel and hummed along under his breath. Hooked over the rearview mirror, his St. Christopher's medal swung gently back and forth.

And suddenly the smell of oranges intensified and he knew it was coming, something was coming at him. He saw his own eyes in the rearview, widening, surprised. And then it came all at once, came in a huge blast that drove out everything else: the music, the road ahead, his own absent awareness of himself as a unique human creature. It was as if someone had put a psychic gun to his head and shot him with a .45 caliber scream.

(*!!!OH DICK OH PLEASE PLEASE PLEASE COME!!!*)

The limo had just drawn even with a Pinto station wagon driven by a man in workman's clothes. The workman saw the limo drifting into his lane and laid on the horn. When the Cadillac continued to drift he snapped a look at the driver and saw a big black man bolt upright behind the wheel, his eyes looking vaguely upward. Later the workman told his wife that he knew it was just one of those niggery hairdos they were all wearing these days, but at the time it had looked just as if every hair on that coon's head was standing on end. He thought the black man was having a heart attack.

The workman braked hard, dropping back into a luckily-empty space behind him. The rear end of the Cadillac pulled ahead of him, still cutting in, and the workman stared with bemused horror as the long, rocket-shaped rear taillights cut into his lane no more than a quarter of an inch in front of his bumper.

The workman cut to the left, still laying on his horn, and roared around the drunkenly weaving limousine. He invited the driver of the limo to perform an illegal sex act on himself. To engage in oral congress with various rodents and birds. He articulated his own proposal that all persons of Negro blood return to their native continent. He expressed his sincere belief in the position the limo-driver's soul would occupy in the afterlife. He finished by saying that he believed he had met the limo-driver's mother in a New Orleans house of prostitution.

Then he was ahead and out of danger and suddenly aware that he had wet his pants.

In Hallorann's mind the thought kept repeating

(*COME DICK PLEASE COME DICK PLEASE*)

but it began to fade off the way a radio station will as you approach the limits of its broadcasting area. He became fuzzily aware that his car was tooling along the soft shoulder at better than fifty miles an hour. He guided it back onto the road, feeling the rear end fishtail for a moment before regaining the composition surface.

There was an A/W Rootbeer stand just ahead. Hallorann signaled and turned in, his heart thudding painfully in his chest, his face a sickly gray color. He pulled into a parking slot, took his handkerchief out of his pocket, and mopped his forehead with it.

(*Lord God!*)

'May I help you?'

The voice startled him again, even though it wasn't the voice of God but that of a cute little carhop, standing by his open window with an order pad.

'Yeah, baby, a rootbeer float. Two scoops of vanilla, okay?'

'Yes, sir.' She walked away, hips rolling nicely beneath her red nylon uniform.

Hallorann leaned back against the leather seat and closed his eyes. There was nothing left to pick up. The last of it had faded out between pulling in here and giving the waitress his order. All that was left was a sick, thudding headache, as if his brain had been twisted and wrung out and hung up to dry. Like the headache he'd gotten from letting that boy Danny shine at him up there at Ullman's Folly.

But this had been much louder. Then the boy had only been playing a game with him. This had been pure panic, each word screamed aloud in his head.

He looked down at his arms. Hot sunshine lay on them but they had still goose-bumped. He had told the boy to call him if he needed help, he remembered that. And now the boy was calling.

He suddenly wondered how he could have left that boy up there at all, shining the way he did. There was bound to be trouble, maybe bad trouble.

He suddenly keyed the limo, put it in reverse, and pulled back onto the highway, peeling rubber. The waitress with the rolling hips stood in the A/W stand's archway, a tray with a rootbeer float on it in her hands.

'What is it with you, a fire?' she shouted, but Hallorann was gone.

The manager was a man named Queems, and when Hallorann came in Queems was conversing with his bookie. He wanted the four-horse at Rockaway. No, no parlay, no quinella, no exacta, no goddam futura. Just the little old four, six hundred dollars on the nose. And the Jets on Sunday. What did he mean, the Jets were playing the Bills? Didn't he know who the Jets were playing? Five hundred, seven-point spread. When Queems hung up, looking put-out, Hallorann understood how a man could make fifty grand a year running this little spa and still wear suits with shiny seats. He regarded Hallorann with an eye that was still bloodshot from too many glances into last night's bourbon bottle.

'Problems, Dick?'

'Yes, sir, Mr Queems, I guess so. I need three days off.'

There was a package of Kents in the breast pocket of Queems's sheer yellow shirt. He reached one out of the pocket without removing the pack, tweezing it out, and bit down morosely on the patented Micronite filter. He lit it with his desktop Cricket.

'So do I,' he said. 'But what's on your mind?'

'I need three days,' Hallorann repeated. 'It's my boy.'

Queems's eyes dropped to Hallorann's left hand, which was ringless.

'I been divorced since 1964,' Hallorann said patiently.

'Dick, you know what the weekend situation is. We're full. To the gunnels. Even the cheap seats. We're even filled up in the Florida Room on Sunday night. So take my watch, my wallet, my pension fund. Hell, you can even take my wife if you can stand the sharp edges. But please don't ask me for time off. What is he, sick?'

'Yes, sir,' Hallorann said, still trying to visualize himself twisting a cheap cloth hat and rolling his eyeballs. 'He shot.'

'Shot!' Queems said. He put his Kent down in an ashtray which bore the emblem of Ole Miss, of which he was a business admin graduate.

'Yes, sir,' Hallorann said somberly.

'Hunting accident?'

'No, sir,' Hallorann said, and let his voice drop to a lower, huskier note, 'Jana, she's been livin with this truck driver. A white man. He shot my boy. He's in a hospital in Denver, Colorado. Critical condition.'

'How in hell did you find out? I thought you were buying vegetables.'

'Yes, sir, I was.' He had stopped at the Western Union office just before coming here to reserve an Avis car at Stapleton Airport. Before leaving he had swiped a Western Union flimsy. Now he took the folded and crumpled blank form from his pocket and flashed it before Queems's bloodshot eyes. He put it back in his pocket and, allowing his voice to drop another notch, said: 'Jana sent it. It was waitin in my letterbox when I got back just now.'

'Jesus. Jesus Christ,' Queems said. There was a peculiar tight expression of concern on his face, one Hallorann was familiar with. It was as close to an expression of sympathy as a white man who thought of himself as 'good with the coloreds' could get when the object was a black man or his mythical black son.

'Yeah, okay, you get going,' Queems said. 'Baedecker can take over for three days, I guess. The potboy can help out.'

Hallorann nodded, letting his face get longer still, but the thought of the potboy helping out Baedecker made him grin inside. Even on a good day Hallorann doubted if the potboy could hit the urinal on the first squirt.

'I want to rebate back this week's pay,' Hallorann said. 'The whole thing. I know what a bind this puttin you in, Mr Queems, sir.'

Queems's expression got tighter still; it looked as if he might have a fishbone caught in his throat. 'We can talk about that later. You go on and pack. I'll talk to Baedecker. Want me to make you a plane reservation?'

'No, sir, I'll do it.'

'All right.' Queems stood up, leaned sincerely forward, and inhaled a raft of ascending smoke from his Kent. He coughed heartily, his thin white face turning red. Hallorann struggled hard to keep his somber expression. 'I hope everything turns out, Dick. Call when you get word.'

'I'll do that.'

They shook hands over the desk.

Hallorann made himself get down to the ground floor and across to the hired help's compound before bursting into rich, head-shaking laughter. He was still grinning and mopping his streaming eyes with his handkerchief when the smell of oranges came, thick and gagging, and the bolt followed it, striking him in the head, sending him back against the pink stucco wall in a drunken stagger.

(!!!PLEASE COME DICK PLEASE COME COME QUICK!!!)

He recovered a little at a time and at last felt capable of climbing the outside stairs to his apartment. He kept the latchkey under the rush-plaited doormat, and when he reached down to get it, something fell out of his inner pocket and fell to the second-floor decking with a flat thump. His mind was still so much on the voice that had shivered through his head that for a moment he could only look at the blue envelope blankly, not knowing what it was.

Then he turned it over and the word WILL stared up at him in the black spidery letters.

(*Oh my God is it like that?*)

He didn't know. But it could be. All week long the thought of his own ending had been on his mind like a . . . well, like a

(*Go on, say it*)

like a premonition.

Death? For a moment his whole life seemed to flash before him, not in a historical sense, no topography of the ups and downs that Mrs Hallorann's third son, Dick, had lived through, but his life as it was now. Martin Luther King had told them not long before the bullet took him down to his martyr's grave that he had been to the mountain. Dick could not claim that. No mountain, but he had reached a sunny plateau after years of struggle. He had good friends. He had all the references he would ever need to get a job anywhere. When he wanted fuck, why, he could find a friendly one with no questions asked and no big shitty struggle about what it all meant. He had come to terms with his blackness – happy terms. He was up past sixty and thank God, he was cruising.

Was he going to chance the end of that – the end of *him* – for three white people he didn't even know?

But that was a lie, wasn't it?

He knew the boy. They had shared each other the way good friends can't even after forty years of it. He knew the boy and the boy knew him, because they each had a kind of searchlight in their heads, something they hadn't asked for, something that had just been given.

(*Naw, you got a flashlight,* he *the one with the searchlight.*)

And sometimes that light, that shine, seemed like a pretty nice thing. You could pick the horses, or like the boy had said, you could tell your daddy where his trunk was when it turned up missing. But that was only dressing, the sauce on the salad, and down below there was as much bitter vetch in that salad as there was cool cucumber. You could taste pain and death and tears. And now the boy was stuck in that place, and he would go. For the boy. Because, speaking to the boy, they had only been different colors when they used their mouths. So he would go. He would do what he could, because if he didn't, the boy was going to die right inside his head.

But because he was human he could not help a bitter wish that the cup had never been passed his way.

(*She had started to get out and come after him.*)

He had been dumping a change of clothes into an overnight bag when the thought came to him, freezing him with the power of the memory as it always did when he thought of it. He tried to think of it as seldom as possible.

The maid, Delores Vickery her name was, had been hysterical. Had said some things to the other chambermaids, and worse still, to some of the guests. When the word got back to Ullman, as the silly quiff should have known it would do, he had fired her out of hand. She had come to Hallorann in tears, not about being fired, but about the things she had seen in that second-floor room. She had gone into 217 to change the towels, she said, and there had been that Mrs Massey, lying dead in the tub. That, of course, was impossible. Mrs Massey had been discreetly taken away the day before and was even then winging her way back to New York – in the shipping hold instead of the first class she'd been accustomed to.

Hallorann hadn't liked Delores much, but he had gone up to look that evening. The maid was an olive-complected girl of twenty-three who waited table near the end of the season when things slowed down. She had a small shining, Hallorann judged, really not more than a twinkle; a mousy-looking man and his escort, wearing a faded cloth coat, would come in for dinner and Delores would trade one of her tables for theirs. The mousy little man would leave a picture of Alexander Hamilton under his plate, bad enough for the girl who had made the trade, but worse, Delores would crow over it. She was lazy, a goof-off in an operation run by a man who allowed no goof-offs. She would sit in a linen closet, reading a confession magazine and smoking, but whenever Ullman went on one of his unscheduled prowls (and woe to the girl he caught resting her feet) he found her working industriously, her magazine hidden under the sheets on a high shelf, her ashtray tucked safely into her uniform pocket. Yeah, Hallorann thought, she'd been a goof-off and a sloven and the other girls had resented her, but Delores had had that little twinkle. It had always greased the skids for her. But what she had seen in 217 had scared her badly enough so she was more than glad to pick up the walking papers Ullman had issued her and go.

Why had she come to him? A shine knows a shine, Hallorann thought, grinning at the pun.

So he had gone up that night and had let himself into the room, which was to be reoccupied the next day. He had used the office passkey to get in, and if Ullman had caught him with that key, he would have joined Delores Vickery on the unemployment line.

The shower curtain around the tub had been drawn. He had pushed it back, but even before he did he'd had a premonition of what he was going to see. Mrs Massey, swollen and purple, lay soggily in the tub, which was half-full of water. He had stood looking down at her, a pulse beating thickly in his throat. There had been other things at the Overlook: a bad dream that recurred at irregular intervals – some sort of costume party and he was catering it in the Overlook's ballroom and at the shout to unmask, everybody exposed faces that were those of rotting insects – and there had been the hedge animals. Twice, maybe three times, he had (or thought he had) seen them move, ever so slightly. That dog would seem to change from his sitting-up posture to a slightly crouched one, and the lions seemed to move forward, as if menacing the little tykes on the playground. Last year in May Ullman had sent him up to the attic to look for the ornate set of firetools that now stood beside the lobby fireplace. While he had been up there the three lightbulbs strung overhead had gone out and he had lost his way back to the trapdoor. He had stumbled around for an unknown length of time, closer and closer to panic, barking his shins on boxes and bumping into things, with a stronger and stronger feeling that something was stalking him in the dark. Some great and frightening creature that had just oozed out of the woodwork when the lights went out. And when he had literally stumbled over the trapdoor's ringbolt he had hurried down as fast as he could, leaving the trap open, sooty and disheveled, with a feeling of disaster barely averted. Later Ullman had come down to the kitchen personally, to inform him he had left the attic trapdoor open and the lights burning up there. Did Hallorann think the guests wanted to go up there and play treasure hunt? Did he think electiricity was free?

And he suspected – no, was nearly positive – that several of the guests had seen or heard things, too. In the three years he had been there, the Presidential Suite had been booked nineteen times. Six of the guests who had put up there had left the hotel early, some of them looking markedly ill. Other guests had left other rooms with the same abruptness. One night in August of 1974, near dusk, a man who had won the Bronze and Silver Stars in Korea (that man now sat on the boards of three major corporations and was said to have personally pink-slipped a famous TV news anchorman) unaccountably went into a fit of screaming hysterics on the putting green. And there had been dozens of children during Hallorann's association with the Overlook who simply refused to go into the playground. One child had had a convulsion while playing in the concrete rings, but Hallorann didn't know if that could be attributed to the Overlook's deadly siren song or not – word had gone around among the help that the child, the only daughter of a handsome movie actor, was a medically controlled epileptic who had simply forgotten her medicine that day.

And so, staring down at the corpse of Mrs Massey, he had been frightened but not completely terrified. It was not completely unexpected. Terror came when she opened her eyes to disclose blank silver pupils and began to grin at him. Horror came when

(*she had started to get out and come after him.*)

He had fled, heart racing, and had not felt safe even with the door shut and locked behind him. In fact, he admitted to himself now as he zipped the flightbag shut, he had never felt safe anywhere in the Overlook again.

And now the boy – calling, screaming for help.

He looked at his watch. It was 5:30 p.m. He went to the apartment's door, remembered it would be heavy winter now in Colorado, especially up in the mountains, and went back to his closet. He pulled his long, sheepskin-lined overcoat out of its polyurethane dry-cleaning bag and put it over his arm. It was the only winter garment he owned. He turned off all the lights and looked around. Had he forgotten anything? Yes. One thing. He took the will out of his breast pocket and slipped it into the margin of the dressing table mirror. With luck he would be back to get it.

Sure, with luck.

He left the apartment, locked the door behind him, put the key under the rush mat, and ran down the outside steps to his converted Cadillac.

Halfway to Miami International, comfortably away from the switchboard where Queems or Queems's toadies were known to listen in, Hallorann stopped at a shopping center Laundromat and called United Air Lines. Flights to Denver?

There was one due out at 6:36 p.m. Could the gentleman make that?

Hallorann looked at his watch, which showed 6:02, and said he could. What about vacancies on the flight?

Just let me check.

A clunking sound in his ear followed by saccharine Montavani, which was supposed to make being on hold more pleasant. It didn't. Hallorann danced from one foot to the other, alternating glances between his watch and a young girl with a sleeping baby in a hammock on her back unloading a coin-op Maytag. She was afraid she was going to get home later than she planned and the roast would burn and her husband – Mark? Mike? Matt? – would be mad.

A minute passed. Two. He had just about made up his mind to drive ahead and take his chances when the canned-sounding voice of the flight reservations clerk came back on. There was an empty seat, a cancellation. It was in first class. Did that make any difference?

No. He wanted it.

Would that be cash or credit card?

Cash, baby, cash. I've got to fly.

And the name was—?

Hallorann, two *l*'s, two *n*'s. Catch you later.

He hung up and hurried toward the door. The girl's simple thought, worry for the roast, broadcast at him over and over until he thought he would go mad. Sometimes it was like that, for no reason at all you would catch a thought, completely isolated, completely pure and clear . . . and usually completely useless.

He almost made it.

He had the limo cranked up to eighty and the airport was actually in sight when one of Florida's Finest pulled him over.

Hallorann unrolled the electric window and opened his mouth at the cop, who was flipping up pages in his citation book.

'I *know*,' the cop said comfortingly. 'It's a funeral in Cleveland. Your father. It's a wedding in Seattle. Your sister. A fire in San Jose that wiped out your gramp's candy store. Some really fine Cambodian Red just waiting in a terminal locker in New York City. I love this piece of road just outside the airport. Even as a kid, story hour was my favorite part of school.'

'Listen, officer, my son is—'

'The only part of the story I can never figure out until the end,' the officer said, finding the right page in his citation book, 'is the driver's-license number of the offending motorist/storyteller and his registration information. So be a nice guy. Let me peek.'

Hallorann looked into the cop's calm blue eyes, debated telling his my-son-is-in-critical-condition story anyway, and decided that would make things worse. This Smokey was no Queems. He dug out his wallet.

'Wonderful,' the cop said. 'Would you take them out for me, please? I just have to see how it's all going to come out in the end.'

Silently, Hallorann took out his driver's license and his Florida registration and gave them to the traffic cop.

'That's very good. That's so good you win a present.

'What?' Hallorann asked hopefully.

'When I finish writing down these numbers, I'm going to let you blow up a little balloon for me.'

'Oh, *Jeeeesus!*' Hallorann moaned. 'Officer, my flight—'

'Shhhh,' the traffic cop said. 'Don't be naughty.'

Hallorann closed his eyes.

He got to the United desk at 6:49, hoping against hope that the flight had been delayed. He didn't even have to ask. The departure monitor over the incoming passengers desk told the story. Flight 901 for Denver, due out at 6:36 EST, had left at 6:40. Nine minutes before.

'Oh shit,' Dick Hallorann said.

And suddenly the smell of oranges, heavy and cloying, he had just time to reach the men's room before it came, deafening, terrified:

(!!!COME PLEASE COME DICK PLEASE PLEASE COME!!!)

Chapter Thirty-nine

On the Stairs

One of the things they had sold to swell their liquid assets a little before moving from Vermont to Colorado was Jack's collection of two hundred old rock 'n' roll and r & b albums; they had gone at the yard sale for a dollar apiece. One of these albums, Danny's personal favorite, had been an Eddie Cochran double-record set with four pages of bound-in liner notes by Lenny Kaye. Wendy had often been struck by Danny's fascination for this one particular album by a man-boy who had lived fast and died young . . . had died, in fact, when she herself had only been ten years old.

Now, at quarter past seven (mountain time), as Dick Hallorann was telling Queems about his ex-wife's white boyfriend, she came upon Danny sitting halfway up the stairs between the lobby and the first floor, tossing a red rubber ball from hand to hand and singing one of the songs from that album. His voice was low and tuneless.

'So I climb one-two flight three flight four,' Danny sang, 'five flight six flight seven flight more . . . when I get to the top, I'm too tired to rock . . .'

She came around him, sat down on one of the stair risers, and saw that his lower lip had swelled to twice its size and that there was dried blood on his chin. Her heart took a frightened leap in her chest, but she managed to speak neutrally.

'What happened, doc?' she asked, although she was sure she knew. Jack had hit him. Well, of course. That came next, didn't it? The wheels of progress; sooner or later they took you back to where you started from.

'I called Tony,' Danny said. 'In the ballroom. I guess I fell off the chair. It doesn't hurt anymore. Just feels . . . like my lip's too big.'

'Is that what really happened?' she asked, looking at him, troubled.

'Daddy didn't do it,' he answered. 'Not today.'

She gazed at him, feeling eerie. The ball traveled from one hand to the other. He had read her mind. Her son had read her mind.

'What . . . what did Tony tell you, Danny?'

'It doesn't matter.' His face was calm, his voice chillingly indifferent.

'*Danny—*' She gripped his shoulder, harder than she had intended. But he didn't wince, or even try to shake her off.

(*Oh we are wrecking this boy. It's not just Jack, it's me too, and maybe it's not even just us, Jack's father, my mother, are they here too? Sure, why not? The place is lousy with ghosts anyway, why not a couple more? Oh Lord in heaven he's like one of those suitcases they show on TV, run over, dropped from planes, going through factory crushers. Or a Timex watch. Takes a licking and keeps on ticking. Oh Danny I'm so sorry*)

'It doesn't matter,' he said again. The ball went from hand to hand. 'Tony can't come anymore. They won't let him. He's licked.'

'Who won't?'

'The people in the hotel,' he said. He looked at her then, and his eyes weren't indifferent at all. They were deep and scared. 'And the . . . the *things* in the hotel. There's all kinds of them. The hotel is *stuffed* with them.'

'You can see—'

'I don't want to see,' he said low, and then looked back at the rubber ball, arcing from hand to hand. 'But I can hear them sometimes, late at night. They're like the wind, all sighing together. In the attic. The basement. The rooms. All over. I thought it was my fault, because of the way I am. The key. The little silver key.'

'Danny, don't . . . don't upset yourself this way.'

'But it's *him* too,' Danny said. 'It's Daddy. And it's you. It wants all of us. It's tricking Daddy, it's fooling him, trying to make him think it wants him the most. It wants me the most, but it will take all of us.'

'If only that snowmobile—'

'They wouldn't let him,' Danny said in that same low voice. 'They made him throw part of it away into the snow. Far away. I dreamed it. And he knows that woman really is in 217.' He looked at her with his dark, frightened eyes. 'It doesn't matter whether you believe me or not.'

She slipped an arm around him.

'I believe you, Danny, tell me the truth. Is Jack . . . is he going to try to hurt us?'

'They'll try to make him,' Danny said. 'I've been calling for Mr Hallorann. He said if I ever needed him to just call. And I have been. But it's awful hard. It makes me tired. And the worst part is I don't know if he's hearing me or not. I don't think he can call back because it's too far for him. And I don't know if it's too far for me or not. Tomorrow—'

'What about tomorrow?'

He shook his head. 'Nothing.'

'Where is he now?' she asked. 'Your daddy?'

'He's in the basement. I don't think he'll be up tonight.'

She stood up suddenly. 'Wait right here for me. Five minutes.'

The kitchen was cold and deserted under the overhead fluorescent bars. She went to the rack where the carving knives hung from their magnetized strips. She took the longest and sharpest, wrapped it in a dish towel, and left the kitchen, turning off the lights as she went.

Danny sat on the stairs, his eyes following the course of his red rubber ball from hand to hand. He sang: 'She lives on the twentieth floor uptown, the elevator is broken down. So I walk one-two flight three flight four . . .'

(*—Lou, Lou, skip to m' Lou—*)

His singing broke off. He listened.

(*—Skip to m' Lou my darlin'—*)

The voice was in his head, so much a part of him, so frighteningly close that it might have been a part of his own thoughts. It was soft and infinitely sly. Mocking him. Seeming to say:

(*Oh yes, you'll like it here. Try it, you'll like it. Try it, you'll liiiiike it—*)

Now his ears were open and he could hear them again, the gathering, ghosts or spirits or maybe the hotel itself, a dreadful funhouse where all the sideshows ended in death, where all the specially painted boogies were really alive, where hedges walked, where a small silver key could start the obscenity. Soft and sighing, rustling like the endless winter wind that played under the eaves at night, the deadly lulling wind the summer tourists never heard. It was like the somnolent hum of summer wasps in a ground nest, sleepy, deadly, beginning to wake up. They were ten thousand feet high.

(*Why is a raven like a writing desk? The higher the fewer, of course! Have another cup of tea!*)

It was a living sound, but not voices, not breath. A man of a philosophical bent might have called it the sound of souls. Dick Hallorann's Nana, who had grown up on southern roads in the years before the turn of the century, would have called it ha'ants. A psychic investigator might have had a long name for it – psychic echo, psychokinesis, a telesmic sport. But to Danny it was only the sound of the hotel, the old monster, creaking steadily and ever more closely around them: halls that now stretched back through time as well as distance, hungry shadows, unquiet guests who did not rest easy.

In the darkened ballroom the clock under glass struck seven-thirty with a single musical note.

A hoarse voice, made brutal with drink, shouted: *'Unmask and let's fuck!'*

Wendy, halfway across the lobby, jerked to a standstill.

She looked at Danny on the stairs, still tossing the ball from hand to hand. 'Did you hear something?'

Danny only looked at her and continued to toss the ball from hand to hand.

There would be little sleep for them that night, although they slept together behind a locked door.

And in the dark, his eyes open, Danny thought:

(*He wants to be one of them and live forever. That's what he wants.*)

Wendy thought:

(*If I have to, I'll take him further up. If we're going to die I'd rather do it in the mountains.*)

She had left the butcher knife, still wrapped in the towel, under the bed. She kept her hand close to it. They dozed off and on. The hotel creaked around them. Outside snow had begun to spit down from a sky like lead.

Chapter Forty

In the Basement

(*!!! The boiler the goddam boiler !!!*)

The thought came into Jack Torrance's mind full-blown, edged in bright, warning red. On its heels, the voice of Watson:

(*If you forget it'll just creep an creep and like as not you an your fambly will end up on the fuckin moon . . . she's rated for two-fifty but she'd blow long before that now . . . I'd be scared to come down and stand next to her at a hundred and eighty.)*

He'd been down here all night, poring over the boxes of old records, possessed by a frantic feeling that time was getting short and he would have to hurry. Still the vital clues, the connections that would make everything clear, eluded him. His fingers were yellow and grimy with crumbling old paper. And he'd become so absorbed he hadn't checked the boiler once. He'd dumped it the previous evening around six o'clock, when he first came down. It was now . . .

He looked at his watch and jumped up, kicking over a stack of old invoices.

Christ, it was quarter of five in the morning.

Behind him, the furnace kicked on. The boiler was making a groaning, whistling sound.

He ran to it. His face, which had become thinner in the last month or so, was now heavily shadowed with beardstubble and he had a hollow concentration-camp look.

The boiler pressure gauge stood at two hundred and ten pounds per square inch. He fancied he could almost see the sides of the old patched and welded boiler heaving out with the lethal strain.

(*She creeps . . . I'd be scared to come down and stand next to her at a hundred and eighty . . .*)

Suddenly a cold and tempting inner voice spoke to him.

(*Let it go. Go get Wendy and Danny and get the fuck out of here. Let it blow sky-high.*)

He could visualize the explosion. A double thunderclap that would first rip the heart from this place, then the soul. The boiler would go with an orange-violet flash that would rain hot and burning shrapnel all over the cellar. In his mind he could see the redhot trinkets of metal careening from floor to walls to ceiling like strange billiard balls, whistling jagged death through the air. Some of them, surely, would whizz right through that stone arch, light on the old papers on the other side, and they would burn merry hell. Destroy the secrets, burn the clues, it's a mystery no living hand will ever solve. Then the gas explosion, a great rumbling crackle of flame, a giant pilot light that would turn the whole center of the hotel into a broiler. Stairs and hallways and ceilings and rooms aflame like the castle in the last reel of a Frankenstein movie. The flame spreading into the wings, hurrying up the black-and-blue-twined carpets like eager guests. The silk wallpaper charring and curling. There were no sprinklers, only those outmoded hoses and no one to use them. And there wasn't a fire engine in the world that could get here before late March. Burn, baby, burn. In twelve hours there would be nothing left but the bare bones.

The needle on the gauge had moved up to two-twelve. The boiler was creaking and groaning like an old woman trying to get out of bed. Hissing jets of steam had begun to play around the edges of old patches; beads of solder had begun to sizzle.

He didn't see, he didn't hear. Frozen with his hand on the valve that would dump off the pressure and damp the fire, Jack's eyes glittered from their sockets like sapphires.

(*It's my last chance.*)

The only thing not cashed in now was the life-insurance policy he had taken out jointly with Wendy in the summer between his first and second years at Stovington. Forty-thousand-dollar death benefit, double indemnity if he or she died in a train crash, a plane crash, or a fire. Seven-come-eleven, die the secret death and win a hundred dollars.

(*A fire . . . eighty thousand dollars.*)

They would have time to get out. Even if they were sleeping, they would have time to get out. He believed that. And he didn't think the hedges or anything else would try to hold them back if the Overlook was going up in flames.

(*Flames.*)

The needle inside the greasy, almost opaque dial had danced up to two hundred and fifteen pounds per square inch.

Another memory occurred to him, a childhood memory. There had been a wasps' nest in the lower branches of their apple tree behind the house. One of his older brothers – he couldn't remember which one now – had been stung while swinging in the old tire Daddy had hung from one of the tree's lower branches. It had been later summer, when wasps tend to be at their ugliest.

Their father, just home from work, dressed in his whites, the smell of beer hanging around his face in a fine mist, had gathered all three boys, Brett, Mike, and little Jacky, and told them he was going to get rid of the wasps.

'Now watch,' he had said, smiling and staggering a little (he hadn't been using the cane then, the collision with the milk truck was years in the future). 'Maybe you'll learn something. My father showed me this.'

He had raked a big pile of rain-dampened leaves under the branch where the wasps' nest rested, a deadlier fruit than the shrunken but tasty apples their tree usually produced in late September, which was then still half a month away. He lit the leaves. The day was clear and windless. The leaves smoldered but didn't really burn, and they made a smell – a fragrance – that had echoed back to him each fall when men in Saturday pants and light Windbreakers raked leaves together and burned them. A sweet smell with a bitter undertone, rich and evocative. The smoldering leaves produced great rafts of smoke that drifted up to obscure the nest.

Their father had let the leaves smolder all that afternoon, drinking beer on the porch and dropping the empty Black Label cans into his wife's plastic floorbucket while his two older sons flanked him and little Jacky sat on the steps at his feet, playing with his Bolo Bouncer and singing monotonously over and over: 'Your cheating heart . . . will make you weep . . . your cheating heart . . . is gonna tell on you.'

At quarter of six, just before supper, Daddy had gone out to the apple tree with his sons grouped carefully behind him. In one hand he had a garden hoe. He knocked the leaves apart, leaving little clots spread around to smolder and die. Then he reached the hoe handle up, weaving and blinking, and after two or three tries he knocked the nest to the ground.

The boys fled for the safety of the porch, but Daddy only stood over the nest, swaying and blinking down at it. Jacky crept back to see. A few wasps were crawling sluggishly over the paper terrain of their property, but they were not trying to fly. From the inside of the nest, the black and alien place, came a never-to-be-forgotten sound: a low, somnolent buzz, like the sound of high-tension wires.

'Why don't they try to sting you, Daddy?' he had asked.

'The smoke makes em drunk, Jacky. Go get my gascan.'

He ran to fetch it. Daddy doused the nest with amber gasoline.

'Now step away, Jacky, unless you want to lose your eyebrows.'

He had stepped away. From somewhere in the voluminous folds of his white overblouse, Daddy had produced a wooden kitchen match. He lit it with his thumbnail and flung it onto the nest. There had been a white-orange explosion, almost soundless in its ferocity. Daddy had stepped away, cackling wildly. The wasps' nest had gone up in no time.

'Fire,' Daddy had said, turning to Jacky with a smile. 'Fire will kill anything.'

After supper the boys had come out in the day's waning light to stand solemnly around the charred and blackened nest. From the hot interior had come the sound of wasp bodies popping like corn.

The pressure gauge stood at two-twenty. A low iron wailing sound was building up in the guts of the thing. Jets of steam stood out erect in a hundred places like porcupine quills.

(*Fire will kill anything.*)

Jack suddenly started. He had been dozing off . . . and he had almost dozed himself right into kingdom come. What in God's name had he been thinking of? Protecting the hotel was his job. He was the caretaker.

A sweat of terror sprang to his hands so quickly that at first he missed his grip on the large valve. Then he curled his fingers around its spokes. He whirled it one turn, two, three. There was a giant hiss of steam, dragon's breath. A warm tropical mist rose from beneath the boiler and veiled him. For a moment he could no longer see the dial but thought he must have waited too long; the groaning, clanking sound inside the boiler increased, followed by a series of heavy rattling sounds and the wrenching screech of metal.

When some of the steam blew away he saw that the pressure gauge had dropped back to two hundred and was still sinking. The jets of steam escaping around the soldered patches began to lose their force. The wrenching, grinding sounds began to diminish.

One-ninety . . . one-eighty . . . one seventy-five . . .

(*He was going downhill, going ninety miles an hour, when the whistle broke into a scream—*)

But he didn't think it would blow now. The press was down to one-sixty.

(*—they found him in the wreck with his hand on the throttle, he was scalded to death by the steam.*)

He stepped away from the boiler, breathing hard, trembling. He looked at his hands and saw that blisters were already rising on his palms. Hell with the blisters, he thought, and laughed shakily. He had almost died with his hand on the throttle, like Casey the engineer in 'The Wreck of the Old 97.' Worse still, he would have killed the Overlook. The final crashing failure. He had failed as a teacher, a writer, a husband, and a father. He had even failed as a drunk. But you couldn't do much better in the old failure category than to blow up the building you were supposed to be taking care of. And this was no ordinary building.

By no means.

Christ, but he needed a drink.

The press had dropped down to eighty psi. Cautiously, wincing a little at the pain in his hands, he closed the dump valve again. But from now on the boiler would have to be watched more closely than ever. It might have been seriously weakened. He wouldn't trust it at more than one hundred psi for the rest of the winter. And if they were a little chilly, they would just have to grin and bear it.

He had broken two of the blisters. His hands throbbed like rotten teeth.

A drink. A drink would fix him up, and there wasn't a thing in the goddamn house besides cooking sherry. At this point a drink would be medicinal. That was just it, by God. An anesthetic. He had done his duty and now he could use a little anesthetic – something stronger than Excedrin. But there was nothing.

He remembered bottles glittering in the shadows.

He had saved the hotel. The hotel would want to reward him. He felt sure of it. He took his handkerchief out of his back pocket and went to the stairs. He rubbed at his mouth. Just a little drink. Just one. To ease the pain.

He had served the Overlook, and now the Overlook would serve him. He was sure of it. His feet on the stair risers were quick and eager, the hurrying steps of a man who has come home from a long and bitter war. It was 5:20 a.m., MST.

Chapter Forty-one

Daylight

Danny awoke with a muffled gasp from a terrible dream. There had been an explosion. A fire. The Overlook was burning up. He and his mommy were watching it from the front lawn.

Mommy had said: 'Look, Danny, look at the hedges.'

He looked at them and they were all dead. Their leaves had turned a suffocant brown. The tightly packed branches showed through like the skeletons of half-dismembered corpses. And then his daddy had burst out of the Overlook's big double doors, and he was burning like a torch. His clothes were in flames, his skin had acquired a dark and sinister tan that was growing darker by the moment, his hair was a burning bush.

That was when he woke up, his throat tight with fear, his hands clutching at the sheet and blankets. Had he screamed? He looked over at his mother. Wendy lay on her side, the blankets up to her chin, a sheaf of straw-colored hair lying against her cheek. She looked like a child herself. No, he hadn't screamed.

Lying in bed, looking upward, the nightmare began to drain away. He had a curious feeling that some great tragedy

(fire? explosion?)

had been averted by inches. He let his mind drift out, searching for his daddy, and found him standing somewhere below. In the lobby. Danny pushed a little harder, trying to get inside his father. It was not good. Because Daddy was thinking about the Bad Thing. he was thinking how

(good just one or two would be i don't care sun's over the yardarm somewhere in the world remember how we used to say that al? gin and tonic bourbon with just a dash of bitters scotch and soda rum and coke tweedledum and tweedledee a drink for me and a drink for thee the martians have landed somewhere in the world princeton or houston or stokely on carmichael some fucking place after all tis the season and none of us are)

(GET OUT OF HIS MIND, YOU LITTLE SHIT!)

He recoiled in terror from that mental voice, his eyes widening, his hands tightening into claws on the counterpane. It hadn't been the voice of his father but a clever mimic. A voice he knew. Hoarse, brutal, yet underpointed with a vacuous sort of humor.

Was it so near, then?

He threw the covers back and swung his feet out onto the floor. He kicked his slippers out from under the bed and put them on. He went to the door and pulled it open and hurried up to the main corridor, his slippered feet whispering on the nap of the carpet runner. He turned the corner.

There was a man on all fours halfway down the corridor, between him and the stairs.

Danny froze.

The man looked up at him. His eyes were tiny and red. He was dressed in some sort of silvery, spangled costume. A dog costume, Danny realized. Protruding from the rump of his strange creation was a long and floppy tail with a puff on the end. A zipper ran up the back of the costume to the neck. To the left of him was a dog's or wolf's head, blank eyesockets above the muzzle, the mouth open in a meaningless snarl that showed the rug's black and blue pattern between fangs that appeared to be papier-mâché.

The man's mouth and chin and cheeks were smeared with blood.

He began to growl at Danny. He was grinning, but the growl was real. It was deep in his throat, a chilling primitive sound. Then he began to bark. His teeth were also stained red. He began to crawl toward Danny, dragging his boneless tail behind him. The costume dog's head lay unheeded on the carpet, glaring vacantly over Danny's shoulder.

'Let me by,' Danny said.

'I'm going to eat you, little boy,' the dogman answered, and suddenly a fusillade of barks came from his grinning mouth. They were human imitations, but the savagery in them was real. The man's hair was dark, greased with sweat from his confining costume. There was a mixture of scotch and champagne on his breath.

Danny flinched back but didn't run. 'Let me by.'

'Not by the hair of my chinny-chin-chin,' the dogman replied. His small red eyes were fixed attentively on Danny's face. He continued to grin. 'I'm going to eat you up, little boy. And I think I'll start with your plump little *cock*.'

He began to prance skittishly forward, making little leaps and snarling.

Danny's nerve broke. He fled back into the short hallway that led to their quarters, looking back over his shoulder. There was a series of mixed howls and barks and growls, broken by slurred mutterings and giggles.

Danny stood in the hallway, trembling.

'Get it up!' the drunken dogman cried out from around the corner. His voice was both violent and despairing. 'Get it up, Harry you bitch-bastard! I don't care how many casinos and airlines and movie companies you own! I know what you like in the privacy of your own h-home! Get it up! I'll *huff* . . . and I'll *puff* . . . until Harry Derwent's *all bloowwwwn down!*' He ended with a long, chilling howl that seemed to turn into a scream of rage and pain just before it dwindled off.

Danny turned apprehensively to the closed bedroom door at the end of the hallway and walked quietly down to it. He opened it and poked his head through. His mommy was sleeping in exactly the same position. No one was hearing this but him.

He closed the door softly and went back up to the intersection of their corridor and the main hall, hoping the dogman would be gone, the way the blood on the walls of the Presidential Suite had been gone. He peeked around the corner carefully.

The man in the dog costume was still there. He had put his head back on and was now prancing on all fours by the stairwell, chasing his tail. He occasionally leaped off the rug and came down making dog grunts in his throat.

'Woof! Woof! Bowwowwow! *Grrrrrr!*'

These sounds came hollowly out of the mask's stylized snarling mouth, and among them were sounds that might have been sobs or laughter.

Danny went back to the bedroom and sat down on his cot, covering his eyes with his hands. The hotel was running things now. Maybe at first the things that had happened had only been accidents. Maybe at first the things he had seen really *were* like scary pictures that couldn't hurt him. But now the hotel was controlling those things and they *could* hurt. The Overlook hadn't wanted him to go to his father. That might spoil all the fun. So it had put the dogman in his way, just as it had put the hedge animals between them and the road.

But his daddy could come here. And sooner or later his daddy would.

He began to cry, the tears rolling silently down his cheeks. It was too late. They were going to die, all three of them, and when the Overlook opened next late spring, they would be right here to greet the guests along with the rest of the spooks. The woman in the tub. The dogman. The horrible dark thing that had been in the cement tunnel. They would be—

(*Stop! Stop that now!*)

He knuckled the tears furiously from his eyes. He would try as hard as he could to keep that from happening. Not to himself, not to his daddy and mommy. He would try as hard as he could.

He closed his eyes and sent his mind out in a high, hard crystal bolt.

(*!!! DICK PLEASE COME QUICK WE'RE IN BAD TROUBLE DICK WE NEED*)

And suddenly, in the darkness behind his eyes the thing that chased him down the Overlook's dark halls in his dreams was *there*, right *there*, a huge creature dressed in white, its prehistoric club raised over its head:

'I'll make you stop it! You goddam puppy! I'll make you stop it because I am your FATHER!'

'*No!*' He jerked back to the reality of the bedroom, his eyes wide and staring, the screams tumbling helplessly from his mouth as his mother bolted awake, clutching the sheet to her breasts.

'*No Daddy no no no—*'

And they both heard the vicious, descending swing of the invisible club, cutting the air somewhere very close, then fading away to silence as he ran to his mother and hugged her, trembling like a rabbit in a snare.

The Overlook was not going to let him call Dick. That might spoil the fun, too.

They were alone.

Outside the snow came harder, curtaining them off from the world.

Chapter Forty-two

Mid-Air

Dick Hallorann's flight was called at 6:45 a.m., EST, and the boarding clerk held him by Gate 31, shifting his flight bag nervously from hand to hand, until the last call at 6:55. They were both looking for a man named Carlton Vecker, the only passenger on TWA's flight 196 from Miami to Denver who hadn't checked in.

'Okay,' the clerk said, and issued Hallorann a blue first-class boarding pass. 'You lucked out. You can board, sir.'

Hallorann hurried up the enclosed boarding ramp and let the mechanically grinning stewardess tear his pass off and give him the stub.

'We're serving breakfast on the flight,' the stew said. 'If you'd like—'

'Just coffee, babe,' he said, and went down the aisle to a seat in the smoking section. He kept expecting the no-show Vecker to pop through the door like a jack-in-the-box at the last second. The woman in the seat by the window was reading *You Can Be Your Own Best Friend* with a sour, unbelieving expression on her face. Hallorann buckled his seat belt and then wrapped his large black hands around the seat's armrests and promised the absent Carlton Vecker that it would take him and five strong TWA flight attendants to drag him out of his seat. He kept his eye on his watch. It dragged off the minutes to the 7:00 takeoff time with maddening slowness.

At 7:05 the stewardess informed them that there would be a slight delay while the ground crew rechecked one of the latches on the cargo door.

'Shit for brains,' Dick Hallorann muttered.

The sharp-faced woman turned her sour, unbelieving expression on him and then went back to her book.

He had spent the night at the airport, going from counter to counter – United, American, TWA, Continental, Braniff – haunting the ticket clerks. Sometime after midnight, drinking his eighth or ninth cup of coffee in the canteen, he had decided he was being an asshole to have taken this whole thing on his own shoulders. There were authorities. He had gone down to the nearest bank of telephones, and after talking to three different operators, he had gotten the emergency number of the Rocky Mountain National Park Authority.

The man who answered the telephone sounded utterly worn out. Hallorann had given a false name and said there was trouble at the Overlook Hotel, west of Sidewinder. Bad trouble.

He was put on hold.

The ranger (Hallorann assumed he was a ranger) came back on in about five minutes.

'They've got a CB,' the ranger said.

'Sure they've got a CB,' Hallorann said.

'We haven't had a Mayday call from them.'

'Man, that don't *matter*. They—'

'Exactly what kind of trouble are they in, Mr Hall?'

'Well, there's a family. The caretaker and his family. I think maybe he's gone a little nuts, you know. I think maybe he might hurt his wife and his little boy.'

'May I ask how you've come by this information, sir?'

Hallorann closed his eyes. 'What's your name, fellow?'

'Tom Staunton, sir.'

'Well, Tom, I *know*. Now I'll be just as straight with you as I can be. There's bad trouble up there. Maybe killin bad, do you dig what I'm sayin?'

'Mr Hall, I really have to know how you—'

'Look,' Hallorann had said. 'I'm telling you I *know*. A few years back there was a fellow up there name of Grady. He killed his wife and his two daughters and then pulled the string on himself. I'm telling you it's going to happen again if you guys don't haul your asses out there and stop it!'

'Mr Hall, you're not calling from Colorado.'

'No. But what difference—'

'If you're not in Colorado, you're not in CB range of the Overlook Hotel. If you're not in CB range you can't possibly have been in contact with the, uh . . .' Faint rattle of papers. 'The Torrance family. While I had you on hold I tried to telephone. It's out, which is nothing unusual. There are still twenty-five miles of aboveground telephone lines between the hotel and the Sidewinder switching station. My conclusion is that you must be some sort of crank.'

'Oh man, you stupid . . .' But his despair was too great to find a noun to go with the adjective. Suddenly, illumination. 'Call them!' he cried.

'Sir?'

'You got the CB, they got the CB. So call them! Call them and ask them what's up!'

There was a brief silence, and the humming of long-distance wires.

'You tried that too, didn't you?' Hallorann asked. 'That's why you had me on hold so long. You tried the phone and then you tried the CB and you didn't get *nothing* but you don't think nothing's wrong . . . what are you guys doing up there? Sitting on your asses and playing gin rummy?'

'No, we are not,' Staunton said angrily. Hallorann was relieved at the sound of anger in the voice. For the first time he felt he was speaking to a man and not to a recording. 'I'm the only man here, sir. Every other ranger in the park, *plus* game wardens, *plus* volunteers, are up in Hasty Notch, risking their lives because three stupid assholes with six months' experience decided to try the north face of King's Ram. They're stuck halfway up there and maybe they'll get down and maybe they won't. There are two choppers up there and the men who are flying them are risking their lives because it's night here and it's starting to snow. So if you're still having trouble putting it all together, I'll give you a hand with it. Number one, I don't have anybody to send to the Overlook. Number two, the Overlook isn't a priority here – what happens in the park is a priority. Number three, by day-break neither one of those choppers will be able to fly because it's going to snow like crazy, according to the National Weather Service. Do you understand the situation?'

'Yeah,' Hallorann had said softly. 'I understand.'

'Now my guess as to why I couldn't raise them on the CB is very simple. I don't know what time it is where you are, but out here it's nine-thirty. I think they may have turned it off and gone to bed. Now if you—'

'Good luck with your climbers, man,' Hallorann said. 'But I want you to know that they are not the only ones who are stuck up high because they didn't know what they were getting into.'

He had hung up the phone.

At 7:20 a.m. the TWA 747 backed lumberingly out of its stall, turned, and rolled out toward the runway. Hallorann let out a long, soudless exhale. Carlton Vecker, wherever you are, eat your heart out.

Flight 196 parted company with the ground at 7:28, and at 7:31, as it gained altitude, the thought-pistol went off in Dick Hallorann's head again. His shoulders hunched uselessly against the smell of oranges and then jerked spasmodically. His forehead wrinkled, his mouth drew down in a grimace of pain.

(*!!! DICK PLEASE COME QUICK WE'RE IN BAD TROUBLE DICK WE NEED*)

And that was all. It was suddenly gone. No fading out this time. The communication had been chopped off cleanly, as if with a knife. It scared him. His hands, still clutching the seat rests, had gone almost white. His mouth was dry. Something had happened to the boy. He was sure of it. If anyone had hurt that little child—

'Do you always react so violently to takeoffs?'

He looked around. It was the woman in the horn-rimmed glasses.

'It wasn't that,' Hallorann said. 'I've got a steel plate in my head. From Korea. Every now and then it gives me a twinge. Vibrates, don't you know. Scrambles the signal.'

'Is that so?'

'Yes, ma'am.'

'It is the line soldier who ultimately pays for any foreign intervention,' the sharp-faced woman said grimly.

'Is that so?'

'It is. This country must swear off its dirty little wars. The CIA has been at the root of every dirty little war America has fought in this century. The CIA and dollar diplomacy.'

She opened her book and began to read. The NO SMOKING sign went off.

Hallorann watched the receding land and wondered if the boy was all right. He had developed an affectionate feeling for that boy, although his folks hadn't seemed all that much.

He hoped to God they were watching out for Danny.

Chapter Forty-three

Drinks on the House

Jack stood in the dining room just outside the batwing doors leading into the Colorado Lounge, his head cocked, listening. He was smiling faintly.

Around him, he could hear the Overlook Hotel coming to life.

It was hard to say just how he knew, but he guessed it wasn't greatly different from the perceptions Danny had from time to time . . . like father, like son. Wasn't that how it was popularly expressed?

It wasn't a perception of sight or sound, although it was very near to those things, separated from those senses by the filmiest of perceptual curtains. It was as if another Overlook now lay scant inches beyond this one, separated from the real world (if there is such a thing as a 'real world,' Jack thought) but gradually coming into balance with it. He was reminded of the 3-D movies he'd seen as a kid. If you looked at the screen without the special glasses, you saw a double image – the sort of thing he was feeling now. But when you put the glasses on, it made sense.

All the hotel's eras were together now, all but this current one, the Torrance Era. And this would be together with the rest very soon now. That was good. That was very good.

He could almost hear the self-important *ding!ding!* of the silver-plated bell on the registration desk, summoning bellboys to the front as men in the fashionable flannels of the 1920s checked in and men in fashionable 1940s double-breated pinstripes checked out. There would be three nuns sitting in front of the fireplace as they waited for the check-out line to thin, and standing behind them, nattily dressed with diamond stickpins holding their blue-and-white-figured ties, Charles Grondin and Vito Gienelli discussed profit and loss, life and death. There were a dozen trucks in the loading bays out back, some laid one over the other like bad time exposures. In the east-wing ballroom, a dozen different business conventions were going on at the same time within temporal centimeters of each other. There was a costume ball going on. There were soirees, wedding receptions, birthday and anniversary parties. Men talking about Neville Chamberlain and the Archduke of Austria. Music. Laughter. Drunkenness. Hysteria. Little love, not here, but a steady undercurrent of sensuousness. And he could almost hear all of them together, drifting through the hotel and making a graceful cacophony. In the dining room where he stood, breakfast, lunch, and dinner for seventy years were all being served simultaneously just behind him. He could almost . . . no, strike the *almost*. He *could* hear them, faintly as yet, but clearly –

the way one can hear thunder miles off on a hot summer's day. He could hear all of them, the beautiful strangers. He was becoming aware of them as they must have been aware of him from the very start.

All the rooms of the Overlook were occupied this morning.

A full house.

And beyond the batwings, a low murmur of conversation drifted and swirled like lazy cigarette smoke. More sophisticated, more private. Low, throaty female laughter, the kind that seems to vibrate in a fairy ring around the viscera and the genitals. The sound of a cash register, its window softly lighted in the warm halfdark, ringing up the price of a gin rickey, a Manhattan, a depression bomber, a sloe gin fizz, a zombie. The jukebox, pouring out its drinkers' melodies, each one overlapping the other in time.

He pushed the batwings open and stepped through.

'Hello, boys,' Jack Torrance said softly. 'I've been away but now I'm back.'

'Good evening, Mr Torrance,' Lloyd said, genuinely pleased. 'It's good to see you.'

'It's good to be back, Lloyd,' he said gravely, and hooked his leg over a stool between a man in a sharp blue suit and a bleary-eyed woman in a black dress who was peering into the depths of a singapore sling.

'What will it be, Mr Torrance?'

'Martini,' he said with great pleasure. He looked at the backbar with its rows of dimly gleaming bottles, capped with their silver siphons. Jim Beam. Wild Turkey. Gilby's. Sharrod's Private Label. Toro. Seagram's. And home again.

'One large martian, if you please,' he said. 'They've landed somewhere in the world, Lloyd.' He took his wallet out and laid a twenty carefully on the bar.

As Lloyd made his drink, Jack looked over his shoulder. Every booth was occupied. Some of the occupants were dressed in costumes . . . a woman in gauzy harem pants and a rhinestone-sparkled brassiere, a man with a foxhead rising slyly out of his evening dress, a man in a silvery dog outfit who was tickling the nose of a woman in a sarong with the puff on the end of his long tail, to the general amusement of all.

'No charge to you, Mr Torrance,' Lloyd said, putting the drink down on Jack's twenty. 'Your money is no good here. Orders from the manager.'

'Manager?'

A faint unease came over him; nevertheless he picked up the martini glass and swirled it, watching the olive at the bottom bob slightly in the drink's chilly depths.

'Of course. The manager.' Lloyd's smile broadened, but his eyes were socketed in shadow and his skin was horribly white, like the skin of a corpse. 'Later he expects to see to your son's well-being himself. He is very interested in your son. Danny is a talented boy.'

The juniper fumes of the gin were pleasantly maddening, but they also seemed to be blurring his reason. Danny? What was all of this about Danny? And what was he doing in a bar with a drink in his hand?

He had TAKEN THE PLEDGE. He had GONE ON THE WAGON. He had SWORN OFF.

What could they want with his son? What could they want with Danny?

Wendy and Danny weren't in it. He tried to see into Lloyd's shadowed eyes, but it was too dark, too dark, it was like trying to read emotion into the empty orbs of a skull.

(*It's me they must want . . . isn't it? I am the one. Not Danny, not Wendy. I'm the one who loves it here. They wanted to leave. I'm the one who took care of the snowmobile . . . went through the old records . . . dumped the press on the boiler . . . lied . . . practically sold my soul . . . what can they want with him?*)

'Where is the manager?' He tried to ask it casually but his words seemed to come out between lips already numbed by the first drink, like words from a nightmare rather than those in a sweet dream.

Lloyd only smiled.

'What do you want with my son? Danny's not in this . . . is he?' He heard the naked plea in his own voice.

Lloyd's face seemed to be running, changing, becoming something pestilent. The white skin becoming a hepatitic yellow, cracking. Red sores erupting on the skin, bleeding foul-smelling liquid. Droplets of blood sprang out on Lloyd's forehead like sweat and somewhere a silver chime was striking the quarter-hour.

(*Unmask, unmask!*)

'Drink your drink, Mr Torrance,' Lloyd said softly. 'It isn't a matter that concerns you. Not at this point.'

He picked his drink up again, raised it to his lips, and hesitated. He heard the hard, horrible snap as Danny's arm broke. He saw the bicycle flying brokenly up over the hood of Al's car, starring the windshield. He saw a single wheel lying in the road, twisted spokes pointing into the sky like jags of piano wire.

He became aware that all conversation had stopped.

He looked back over his shoulder. They were all looking at him expectantly, silently. The man beside the woman in the sarong had removed his foxhead and Jack saw that it was Horace Derwent, his pallid blond hair spilling across his forehead. Everyone at the bar was watching, too. The woman beside him was looking at him closely, as if trying to focus. Her dress had slipped off one shoulder and looking down he could see a loosely puckered nipple capping one sagging breast. Looking back at her face he began to think that this might be the woman from 217, the one who had tried to strangle Danny. On his other hand, the man in the sharp blue suit had removed a small pearl-handled .32 from his jacket pocket and was idly spinning it on the bar, like a man with Russian roulette on his mind.

(*I want—*)

He realized the words were not passing through his frozen vocal cords and tried again.

'I want to see the manager. I . . . I don't think he understands. My son is not a part of this. He . . .'

'Mr Torrance,' Lloyd said, his voice coming with hideous gentleness from inside his plague-raddled face, 'you will meet the manager in due time. He has, in fact, decided to make you his agent in this matter. Now drink your drink.'

'Drink your drink,' they all echoed.

He picked it up with a badly trembling hand. It was raw gin. He looked into it, and looking was like drowning.

The woman beside him began to sing in a flat, dead voice: 'Roll . . . out . . . the barrel . . . and we'll have . . . a barrel . . . of fun . . .'

Lloyd picked it up. Then the man in the blue suit. The dog-man joined in, thumping one paw against the table

'*Now's the time to roll the barrel—*'

Derwent added his voice to the rest. A cigarette was cocked in one corner of his mouth at a jaunty angle. His right arm was around the shoulders of the woman in the sarong, and his right hand was gently and absently stroking her right breast. He was looking at the dog-man with amused contempt as he sang.

'*—because the gang's . . . all . . . here!*'

Jack brought the drink to his mouth and downed it in three long gulps, the gin highballing down his throat like a moving van in a tunnel, exploding in his stomach, rebounding up to his brain in one leap where it seized hold of him with a final convulsing fit of the shakes.

When that passed off, he felt fine.

'Do it again, please,' he said, and pushed the empty glass toward Lloyd.

'Yes, sir,' Lloyd said, taking the glass. Lloyd looked perfectly normal again. The olive-skinned man had put his .32 away. The woman on his right was staring into her singapore sling again. One breast was wholly exposed now, leaning on the bar's leather buffer. A vacuous crooning noise came from her slack mouth. The loom of conversation had begun again, weaving and weaving.

His new drink appeared in front of him.

'*Muchas gracias*, Lloyd,' he said, picking it up.

'Always a pleasure to serve you, Mr Torrance.' Lloyd smiled.

You were always the best of them, Lloyd.'

'Why, thank you, sir.'

He drank slowly this time, letting it trickle down his throat, tossing a few peanuts down the chute for good luck.

The drink was gone in no time, and he ordered another. Mr President, I have met the martians and am pleased to report they are friendly. While Lloyd fixed another, he began searching his pockets for a quarter to put in the jukebox. He thought of Danny again, but Danny's face was pleasantly fuzzed and nondescript now. He had hurt Danny once, but that had been before he had learned how to handle his liquor. Those days were behind him now. He would never hurt Danny again.

Not for the world.

Chapter Forty-four

Conversations at the Party

He was dancing with a beautiful woman.

He had no idea what time it was, how long he had spent in the Colorado Lounge or how long he had been here in the ballroom. Time had ceased to matter.

He had vague memories: listening to a man who had once been a successful radio comic and then a variety star in TV's infant days telling a very long and very hilarious joke about incest between Siamese twins; seeing the woman in the harem pants and the sequined bra do a slow and sinuous striptease to some bumping-and-grinding music from the jukebox (it seemed it had been David Rose's theme music from *The Stripper*); crossing the lobby as one of three, the other two men in evening dress that predated the twenties, all of them singing about the stiff patch on Rosie O'Grady's knickers. He seemed to remember looking out the big double doors and seeing Japanese lanterns strung in graceful, curving arcs that followed the sweep of the driveway – they gleamed in soft pastel colors like dusky jewels. The big glass globe on the porch ceiling was on, and night-insects bumped and flittered against it, and a part of him, perhaps the last tiny spark of sobriety, tried to tell him that it was 6 a.m. on a morning in December. But time had been canceled.

(*The arguments against insanity fall through with a soft shurring sound/layer on layer . . .*)

Who was that? Some poet he had read as an undergraduate? Some undergraduate poet who was now selling washers in Wausau or insurance in Indianapolis? Perhaps an original thought? Didn't matter.

(*The night is dark/the stars are high/a disembodied custard pie/is floating in the sky . . .*)

He giggled helplessly.

'What's funny, honey?'

And here he was again, in the ballroom. The chandelier was lit and couples were circling all around them, some in costume and some not, to the smooth sounds of some postwar band – but which war? Can you be certain?

No, of course not. He was certain of only one thing: he was dancing with a beautiful woman.

She was tall and auburn-haired, dressed in clinging white satin, and she was dancing close to him, her breasts pressed softly and sweetly against his chest. Her white hand was entwined in his. She was wearing a small and sparkly cat's-eye mask and her hair had been brushed over to one side in a soft and gleaming fall that seemed to pool in the valley between their touching shoulders. Her dress was full-skirted but he could feel her thighs against his legs from time to time and had become more and more sure that she was smooth-and-powdered naked under her dress,

(*the better to feel your erection with, my dear*)

and he was sporting a regular railspike. If it offended her she concealed it well; she snuggled even closer to him.

'Nothing funny, honey,' she said, and giggled again.

'I like you,' she whispered, and he thought that her scent was like lilies, secret and hidden in cracks furred with green moss – places where sunshine is short and shadows long.

'I like you, too.'

'We could go upstairs, if you want. I'm supposed to be with Harry, but he'll never notice. He's too busy teasing poor Roger.'

The number ended. There was a spatter of applause and then the band swung into 'Mood Indigo' with scarcely a pause.

Jack looked over her bare shoulder and saw Derwent standing by the refreshment table. The girl in the sarong was with him. There were bottles of champagne in ice buckets ranged along the white lawn covering the table, and Derwent held a foaming bottle in his hand. A knot of people had gathered, laughing. In front of Derwent and the girl in the sarong, Roger capered grotesquely on all fours, his tail dragging limply behind him. He was barking.

'Speak, boy, speak!' Harry Derwent cried.

'Rowf! Rowf!' Roger responded. Everyone clapped; a few of the men whistled.

'Now sit up. Sit up, doggy!'

Roger clambered up on his haunches. The muzzle of his mask was frozen in its eternal snarl. Inside the eyeholes, Roger's eyes rolled with frantic, sweaty hilarity. He held his arms out, dangling the paws.

'Rowf! Rowf!'

Derwent upended the bottle of champagne and it fell in a foamy Niagara onto the upturned mask. Roger made frantic slurping sounds, and everyone applauded again. Some of the women screamed with laughter.

'Isn't Harry a card?' his partner asked him, pressing close again. 'Everyone says so. He's AC/DC, you know. Poor Roger's only DC. He spent a weekend with Harry in Cuba once . . . oh, *months* ago. Now he follows Harry everywhere, wagging his little tail behind him.'

She giggled. The shy scent of lilies drifted up.

'But of course Harry never goes back for seconds . . . not on his DC side, anyway . . . and Roger is just *wild*. Harry told him if he came to the masked ball as a doggy, a *cute* little doggy, he might reconsider, and Roger is *such* a silly that he . . .'

The number ended. There was more applause. The band members were filing down for a break.

'Excuse me, sweetness,' she said. 'There's someone I just *must* . . . Darla! Darla, you *dear girl*, where have you *been?*'

She wove her way into the eating, drinking throng and he gazed after her stupidly, wondering how they had happened to be dancing together in the first place. He didn't remember. Incidents seemed to have occurred with no connections. First here, then there, then everywhere. His head was spinning. He smelled lilies and juniper berries. Up by the refreshment table Derwent was now holding a tiny triangular sandwich over Roger's head and urging him, to the general merriment of the onlookers, to do a somersault. The dogmask was turned upward. The silver sides of the dog costume bellowsed in and out. Roger suddenly leaped, tucking his head under, and tried to roll in mid-air. His leap was too low and too exhausted; he landed awkwardly on his back, rapping his head smartly on the tiles. A hollow groan drifted out of the dogmask.

Derwent led the applause. 'Try again, doggy! Try again!'

The onlookers took up the chant – *try again, try again* – and Jack staggered off the other way, feeling vaguely ill.

He almost fell over the drinks cart that was being wheeled along by a low-browed man in a white mess jacket. His foot rapped the lower chromed shelf of the cart; the bottles and siphons on top chattered together musically.

'Sorry,' Jack said thickly. He suddenly felt closed in and claustrophobic; he wanted to get out. He wanted the Overlook back the way it had been . . . free of these unwanted guests. His place was not honored, as the true opener of the way; he was only another of the ten thousand cheering extras, a doggy rolling over and sitting up on command.

'Quite all right,' the man in the white mess jacket said. The polite, clipped English coming from that thug's face was surreal. 'A drink?'

'Martini.'

From behind him, another comber of laughter broke; Roger was howling to the tune of 'Home on the Range.' Someone was picking out accompaniment on the Steinway baby grand.

'Here you are.'

The frosty cold glass was pressed into his hand. Jack drank gratefully, feeling the gin hit and crumble away the first inroads of sobriety.

'Is it all right, sir?'

'Fine.'

'Thank you, sir,' The cart began to roll again.

Jack suddenly reached out and touched the man's shoulder.

'Yes, sir?'

'Pardon me, but . . . what's your name?'

The other showed no surprise. 'Grady, sir. Delbert Grady.'

'But you . . . I mean that . . .'

The bartender was looking at him politely. Jack tried again, although his mouth was mushed by gin and unreality; each word felt as large as an ice cube.

'Weren't you once the caretaker here? When you . . . when . . .' But he couldn't finish. He couldn't say it.

'Why no, sir. I don't believe so.'

'But your wife . . . your daughters . . .'

'My wife is helping in the kitchen, sir. The girls are asleep, of course. It's much too late for them.'

'You were the caretaker. You—' *Oh say it!* 'You killed them.'

Grady's face remained blankly polite. 'I don't have any recollection of that at all, sir.' His glass was empty. Grady plucked it from Jack's unresisting fingers and set about making another drink for him. There was a small white plastic bucket on his cart that was filled with olives. For some reason they reminded Jack of tiny severed heads. Grady speared one deftly, dropped it into the glass, and handed it to him.

'But you—'

'*You're* the caretaker, sir,' Grady said mildly. 'You've *always* been the caretaker. I should know, sir. I've always been here. The same manager hired us both, at the same time. Is it all right, sir?'

Jack gulped at his drink. His head was swirling. 'Mr Ullman—'

'I know no one by that name, sir.'

'But he—'

'The manager,' Grady said. 'The *hotel*, sir. Surely you realize who hired you, sir.'

'No,' he said thickly. 'No, I—'

'I believe you must take it up further with your son, Mr Torrance, sir. He understands everything, although he hasn't enlightened you. Rather naughty of him, if I may be so bold, sir. In fact, he's crossed you at almost every turn, hasn't he? And him not yet six.'

'Yes,' Jack said. 'He has.' There was another wave of laughter from behind them.

'He needs to be corrected, if you don't mind me saying so. He needs a good talking-to, and perhaps a bit more. My own girls, sir, didn't care for the Overlook at first. One of them actually stole a pack of my matches and tried to burn it down. I corrected them. I corrected them most harshly. And when my wife tried to stop me from doing my duty, I corrected her.' He offered Jack a bland, meaningless smile. 'I find it a sad but true fact that women rarely understand a father's responsibility to his children. Husbands and fathers do have certain responsibilities, don't they, sir?'

'Yes,' Jack said.

'They didn't love the Overlook as I did,' Grady said, beginning to make him another drink. Silver bubbles rose in the upended gin bottle. 'Just as your son and wife don't love it . . . not at present, anyway. But they will come to love it. You must show them the error of their ways, Mr Torrance. Do you agree?'

'Yes. I do.'

He did see. He had been too easy with them. Husbands and fathers did have certain responsibilities. Father Knows Best. They did not understand. That in itself was no crime, but they were *willfully* not understanding. He was not ordinarily a harsh man. But he did believe in punishment. And if his son and his wife had willfully set themselves against his wishes, *against the things he knew were best for them*, then didn't he have a certain duty—?

'A thankless child is sharper than a serpent's tooth,' Grady said, handing him his drink. 'I do believe that the manager could bring your son into line. And your wife would shortly follow. Do you agree, sir?'

He was suddenly uncertain. 'I . . . but . . . if they could just leave . . . I mean, after all, it's me the manager wants, isn't it? It must be. Because—' Because why? He should know but suddenly he didn't. Oh, his poor brain was swimming.

'Bad dog!' Derwent was saying loudly, to a counterpoint of laughter. 'Bad dog to piddle on the floor.'

'Of course you know,' Grady said, leaning confidentially over the cart, 'your son is attempting to bring an outside party into it. Your son has a very great talent, one that the manager could use to even further improve the Overlook, to further . . . enrich it, shall we say? But your son is attempting to use that very talent against us. He is willful, Mr Torrance, sir. Willful.'

'Outside party?' Jack asked stupidly.

Grady nodded.

'Who?'

'A nigger,' Grady said. 'A nigger cook.'

'Hallorann?'

'I believe that is his name, sir, yes.'

Another burst of laughter from behind them was followed by Roger saying something in a whining, protesting voice.

'Yes! Yes! Yes!' Derwent began to chant. The others around him took it up, but before Jack could hear what they wanted Roger to do now, the band began to play again – the tune was 'Tuxedo Junction,' with a lot of mellow sax in it but not much soul.

(*Soul? Soul hasn't even been invented yet. Or has it?*)

(A nigger . . . a nigger cook.)

He opened his mouth to speak, not knowing what might come out. What did was:

'I was told you hadn't finished high school. But you don't talk like an uneducated man.'

'It's true that I left organized education very early, sir. But the manager takes care of his help. He finds that it pays. Education always pays, don't you agree, sir?'

'Yes,' Jack said dazedly.

'For instance, you show a great interest in learning more about the Overlook Hotel. Very wise of you, sir. Very noble. A certain scrapbook was left in the basement for you to find—'

'By whom?' Jack asked eagerly.

'By the manager, of course. Certain other materials could be put at your disposal, if you wished them . . .'

'I do. Very much.' He tried to control the eagerness in his voice and failed miserably.

'You're a true scholar,' Grady said. 'Pursue the topic to the end. Exhaust all sources.' He dipped his low-browed head, pulled out the lapel of his white mess jacket, and buffed his knuckles at a spot of dirt that was invisible to Jack.

'And the manager puts no strings on his largess,' Grady went on. 'Not at all. Look at me, a tenth-grade dropout. Think how much further you yourself could go in the Overlook's organizational structure. Perhaps . . . in time . . . to the very top.'

'Really?' Jack whispered.

'But that's really up to your son to decide, isn't it?' Grady asked, raising his eyebrows. The delicate gesture went oddly with the brows themselves, which were bushy and somehow savage.

'Up to Danny?' Jack frowned at Grady. 'No, of course not. I wouldn't allow my son to make decisions concerning my career. Not at all. What do you take me for?'

'A dedicated man,' Grady said warmly. 'Perhaps I put it badly, sir. Let us say that your future here is contingent upon how you decide to deal with your son's waywardness.'

'I make my own decisions,' Jack whispered.

'But you must deal with him.'

'I will.'

'Firmly.'

'I will.'

'A man who cannot control his own family holds very little interest for our manager. A man who cannot guide the courses of his own wife and son can hardly be expected to guide himself, let alone assume a position of responsibility in an operation of this magnitude. He—'

'*I said I'll handle him!*' Jack shouted suddenly, enraged.

'Tuxedo Junction' had just concluded and a new tune hadn't begun. His shout fell perfectly into the gap, and conversation suddenly ceased behind him. His skin suddenly felt hot all over. He became fixedly positive that everyone was staring at him. They had finished with Roger and would now commence with him. Roll over. Sit up. Play dead. If you play the game with us, we'll play the game with you. Position of responsibility. They wanted him to sacrifice his son.

(*—Now he follows Harry everywhere, wagging his little tail behind him—*)

(*Roll over. Play dead. Chastise your son.*)

'Right this way, sir,' Grady was saying. 'Something that might interest you.'

The conversation had begun again, lifting and dropping in its own rhythm, weaving in and out of the band music, now doing a swing version of Lennon and McCartney's 'Ticket to Ride.'

(*I've heard better over supermarket loudspeakers.*)

He giggled foolishly. He looked down at his left hand and saw there was another drink in it, half-full. He emptied it at a gulp.

Now he was standing in front of the mantelpiece, the heat from the crackling fire that had been laid in the hearth warming his legs.

(*a fire? . . . in August? . . . yes . . . and no . . . all times are one*)

There was a clock under a glass dome, flanked by two carved ivory elephants. Its hands stood at a minute to midnight. He gazed at it blearily. Had this been what Grady wanted him to see? He turned around to ask, but Grady had left him.

Halfway through 'Ticket to Ride,' the band wound up in a brassy flourish.

'The hour is at hand!' Horace Derwent proclaimed. 'Midnight! Unmask! Unmask!'

He tried to turn again, to see what famous faces were hidden beneath the glitter and paint and masks, but he was frozen now, unable to look away from the clock – its hands had come together and pointed straight up.

'*Unmask! Unmask!*' the chant went up.

The clock began to chime delicately. Along the steel runner below the clockface, from the left and right, two figures advanced. Jack watched, fascinated, the unmasking forgotten. Clockwork whirred. Cogs turned and meshed, brass warmly glowing. The balance wheel rocked back and forth precisely.

One of the figures was a man standing on tiptoe, with what looked like a tiny club clasped in his hands. The other was a small boy wearing a dunce cap. The clockwork figures glittered, fantastically precise. Across the front of the boy's dunce cap he could read the engraved word FOOLE.

The two figures slipped onto the opposing ends of a steel axis bar. Somewhere, tinkling on and on, were the strains of a Strauss waltz. An insane commercial jingle began to run through his mind to the tune: *Buy dog food, rowf-rowf, rowf-rowf, buy dog food* . . .

The steel mallet in the clockwork daddy's hands came down on the boy's head. The clockwork son crumpled forward. The mallet rose and fell, rose and fell. The boy's upstretched, protesting hands began to falter. The boy sagged from his crouch to a prone position. And still the hammer rose and fell to the light, tinkling air of the Strauss melody, and it seemed that he could see the man's face, working and knotting and constricting, could see the clockwork daddy's mouth opening and closing as he berated the unconscious, bludgeoned figure of the son.

A spot of red flew up against the inside of the glass dome.

Another followed. Two more splattered beside it.

Now the red liquid was spraying up like an obscene rain shower, striking the glass sides of the dome and running, obscuring what was going on inside, and flecked through the scarlet were tiny gray ribbons of tissue, fragments of bone and brain. And still he could see the hammer rising and falling as the clockwork continued to turn and the cogs continued to mesh the gears and teeth of this cunningly made machine.

'*Unmask! Unmask!*' Derwent was shrieking behind him, and somewhere a dog was howling in human tones.

(*But clockwork can't bleed clockwork can't bleed*)

The entire dome was splashed with blood, he could see clotted bits of hair but nothing else thank God he could see nothing else, and still he thought he would be sick because he could hear the hammerblows still falling, could hear them through the glass just as he could hear the phrases of 'The Blue Danube.' But the sounds were no longer the mechanical *tink-tink-tink* noises of a mechanical hammer striking a mechanical head, but the soft and squashy thudding sounds of a real hammer slicing down and whacking into a spongy, muddy ruin. A ruin that once had been—

'*UNMASK!*'

(*—the Red Death held sway over all!*)

With a miserable, rising scream, he turned away from the clock, his hands outstretched, his feet stumbling against one another like wooden blocks as he begged them to stop, to take him, Danny, Wendy, to take the whole world if they wanted it, but only to stop and leave him a little sanity, a little light.

The ballroom was empty.

The chairs with their spindly legs were upended on tables covered with plastic dust drops. The red rug with its golden tracings was back on the dance floor, protecting the polished hardwood surface. The bandstand was deserted except for a disassembled microphone stand and a dusty guitar leaning stringless against the wall. Cold morning light, winterlight, fell languidly through the high windows.

His head was still reeling, he still felt drunk, but when he turned back to the mantelpiece, his drink was gone. There were only the ivory elephants . . . and the clock.

He stumbled back across the cold, shadowy lobby and through the dining room. His foot hooked around a table leg and he fell full-length, upsetting the table with a clatter. He struck his nose hard on the floor and it began to bleed. He got up, snuffling back blood and wiping his nose with the back of his hand. He crossed to the Colorado Lounge and shoved through the batwing doors, making them fly back and bang into the walls.

The place was empty . . . but the bar was fully stocked. God be praised! Glass and the silver edging on labels glowed warmly in the dark.

Once, he remembered, a very long time ago, he had been angry that there was no backbar mirror. Now he was glad. Looking into it he would have seen just another drunk fresh off the wagon: bloody nose, untucked shirt, hair rumpled, cheeks stubbly.

(*This is what it's like to stick your whole hand into the nest.*)

Loneliness surged over him suddenly and completely. He cried out with sudden wretchedness and honestly wished he were dead. His wife and son were upstairs with the door locked against him. The others had all left. The party was over.

He lurched forward again, reaching the bar.

'Lloyd, where the fuck are you?' he screamed.

There was no answer. In this well-padded

(*cell*)

room, his words did not even echo back to give the illusion of company.

'*Grady!*'

No answer. Only the bottles, standing stiffly at attention.

(*Roll over. Play dead. Fetch. Play dead. Sit up. Play dead.*)

'Never mind, I'll do it myself, goddammit.'

Halfway over the bar he lost his balance and pitched forward, hitting his head a muffled blow on the floor. He got up on his hands and knees, his eyeballs moving disjointed from side to side, fuzzy muttering sounds coming from his mouth. Then he collapsed, his face turned to one side, breathing in harsh snores.

Outside, the wind whooped louder, driving the thickening snow before it. It was 8:30 a.m.

Chapter Forty-five

Stapleton Airport, Denver

At 8:31 a.m., MST, a woman on TWA's Flight 196 burst into tears and began to bugle her own opinion, which was perhaps not unshared among some of the other passengers (or even the crew, for that matter), that the plane was going to crash.

The sharp-faced woman next to Hallorann looked up from her book and offered a brief character analysis: 'Ninny,' and went back to her book. She had downed two screwdrivers during the flight, but they seemed not to have thawed her at all.

'It's going to crash!' the woman was crying out shrilly. 'Oh, I just know it is!'

A stewardess hurried to her seat and squatted beside her. Hallorann thought to himself that only stewardesses and very young housewives seemed able to squat with any degree of grace; it was a rare and wonderful talent. He thought about this while the stewardess talked softly and soothingly to the woman, quieting her bit by bit.

Hallorann didn't know about anyone else on 196, but he personally was almost scared enough to shit peachpits. Outside the window there was nothing to be seen but a buffeting curtain of white. The plane rocked sickeningly from side to side with gusts that seemed to come from everywhere. The engines were cranked up to provide partial compensation and as a result the floor was vibrating under their feet. There were several people moaning in Tourist behind them, one stew had gone back with a handful of fresh airsick bags, and a man three rows in front of Hallorann had whoopsed into his *National Observer* and had grinned apologetically at the stewardess who came to help him clean up. 'That's all right,' she comforted him, 'that's how I feel about the *Reader's Digest*.'

Hallorann had flown enough to be able to surmise what had happened. They had been flying against bad headwinds most of the way, the weather over Denver had worsened suddenly and unexpectedly, and now it was just a little late to divert for someplace where the weather was better. Feets don't fail me now.

(*Buddy-boy, this is some fucked-up cavalry charge.*)

The stewardess seemed to have succeeded in curbing the worst of the woman's hysterics. She was snuffling and honking into a lace handkerchief, but had ceased broadcasting her opinions about the flight's possible conclusion to the cabin at large. The stew gave her a final pat on the shoulder and stood up just as the 747 gave its worst lurch yet. The stewardess stumbled backward and landed in the lap of the man who had whoopsed into his paper, exposing a lovely length of nyloned thigh. The man blinked and then patted her kindly on the shoulder. She smiled back, but Hallorann thought the strain was showing. It had been one hell of a hard flight this morning.

There was a little ping as the NO SMOKING light reappeared.

'This is the captain speaking,' a soft, slightly southern voice informed them. 'We're ready to begin our descent to Stapleton International Airport. It's been a rough flight, for which I apologize. The landing may be a bit rough also, but we anticipate no real difficulty. Please observe the FASTEN SEAT BELTS and NO SMOKING signs, and we hope you enjoy your stay in the Denver metro area. And we also hope—'

Another hard bump rocked the plane and then dropped her with a sickening elevator plunge. Hallorann's stomach did a queasy hornpipe. Several people – not all women by any means – screamed.

'—that we'll see you again on another TWA flight real soon.'

'Not bloody likely,' someone behind Hallorann said.

'So silly,' the sharp-faced woman next to Hallorann remarked, putting a matchbook cover into her book and shutting it as the plane began to descend. 'When one has seen the horrors of a dirty little war . . . as you have . . . or sensed the degrading immorality of CIA dollar-diplomacy intervention . . . as I have . . . a rough landing *pales* into *insignificance*. Am I right, Mr Hallorann?'

'As rain, ma'am,' he said, and looked bleakly out into the wildly blowing snow.

'How is your steel plate reacting to all of this, if I might inquire?'

'Oh, my head's fine,' Hallorann said. 'It's just my stomach that's a mite queasy.'

'A shame.' She reopened her book.

As they descended through the impenetrable clouds of snow, Hallorann thought of a crash that had occurred at Boston's Logan Airport a few years ago. The conditions had been similar, only fog instead of snow had reduced visibility to zero. The plane had caught its undercarriage on a retaining wall near the end of the landing strip. What had been left of the eighty-nine people aboard hadn't looked much different from a Hamburger Helper casserole.

He wouldn't mind so much if it was just himself. He was pretty much alone in the world now, and attendance at his funeral would be mostly held down to the people he had worked with and that old renegade Masterton, who would at least drink to him. But the boy . . . the boy was depending on him. He was maybe all the help that child could expect, and he didn't like the way the boy's last call had been snapped off. He kept thinking of the way those hedge animals had seemed to move . . .

A thin white hand appeared over his.

The woman with the sharp face had taken off her glasses. Without them her features seemed much softer.

'It will be all right,' she said.

Hallorann made a smile and nodded.

As advertised the plane came down hard, reuniting with the earth forcefully enough to knock most of the magazines out of the rack at the front and to send plastic trays cascading out of the galley like oversized playing cards. No one screamed, but Hallorann heard several sets of teeth clicking violently together like gypsy castanets.

Then the turbine engines rose to a howl, braking the plane, and as they dropped in volume the pilot's soft southern voice, perhaps not completely steady, came over the intercom system. 'Ladies and gentlemen, we have landed at Stapleton Airport. Please remain in your seats until the plane has come to a complete stop at the terminal. Thank you.'

The woman beside Hallorann closed her book and uttered a long sigh. 'We live to fight another day, Mr Hallorann.'

'Ma'am, we aren't done with this one, yet.'

'True. Very true. Would you care to have a drink in the lounge with me?'

'I would, but I have an appointment to keep.'

'Pressing?'

'Very pressing,' Hallorann said gravely.

'Something that will improve the general situation in some small way, I hope.'

'I hope so too,' Hallorann said, and smiled. She smiled back at him, ten years dropping silently from her face as she did so.

Because he had only the flight bag he'd carried for luggage, Hallorann beat the crowd to the Hertz desk on the lower level. Outside the smoked glass windows he could see the snow still falling steadily. The gusting wind drove white clouds of it back and forth, and the people walking across to the parking area were struggling against it. One man lost his hat and Hallorann could commiserate with him as it whirled high, wide and handsome. The man stared after it and Hallorann thought:

(*Aw, just forget it, man. That homburg ain't comin down until it gets to Arizona.*)

On the heels of that thought:

(*If it's this bad in Denver, what's it going to be like west of Boulder?*)

Best not to think about that, maybe.

'Can I help you, sir?' a girl in a Hertz yellow asked him.

'If you got a car, you can help me,' he said with a big grin.

For a heavier-than-average charge he was able to get a heavier-than-average car, a silver and black Buick Electra. He was thinking of the winding mountain roads rather than style; he would have to stop somewhere along the way and get chains put on. He wouldn't get far without them.

'How bad is it?' he asked as she handed him the rental agreement to sign.

'They say it's the worst storm since 1969,' she answered brightly. 'Do you have far to drive, sir?'

'Farther than I'd like.'

'If you'd like sir, I can phone ahead to the Texaco station at the Route 270 junction. They'll put chains on for you.'

'That would be a great blessing, dear.'

She picked up the phone and made the call. 'They'll be expecting you.'

'Thank you much.'

Leaving the desk, he saw the sharp-faced woman standing on one of the queues that had formed in front of the luggage carousel. She was still reading her book. Hallorann winked at her as he went by. She looked up, smiled at him, and gave him a peace sign.

(*shine*)

He turned up his overcoat collar, smiling, and shifted his flight bag to the other hand. Only a little one, but it made him feel better. He was sorry he'd told her that fish story about having a steel plate in his head. He mentally wished her well and as he went out into the howling wind and snow, he thought she wished him the same in return.

The charge for putting on the chains at the service station was a modest one, but Hallorann slipped the man at work in the garage bay an extra ten to get moved up a little way on the waiting list. It was still quarter of ten before he was actually on the road, the windshield wipers clicking and the chains clinking with tuneless monotony on the Buick's big wheels.

The turnpike was a mess. Even with the chains he could go no faster than thirty. Cars had gone off the road at crazy angles, and on several of the grades traffic was barely struggling along, summer tires spinning helplessly in the drifting powder. It was the first big storm of the winter down here in the lowlands (if you could call a mile above sealevel 'low'), and it was a mother. Many of them were unprepared, common enough, but Hallorann still found himself cursing them as he inched around them, peering into his snow-clogged outside mirror to be sure nothing was

(*Dashing through the snow . . .*)

coming up in the left-hand lane to cream his black ass.

There was more bad luck waiting for him at the Route 36 entrance ramp. Route 36, the Denver-Boulder turnpike, also goes west to Estes Park, where it connects with Route 7. That road, also known as the Upland Highway, goes through Sidewinder, passes the Overlook Hotel, and finally winds down the Western Slope and into Utah.

The entrance ramp had been blocked by an overturned semi. Bright-burning flares had been scattered around it like birthday candles on some idiot child's cake.

He came to a stop and rolled his window down. A cop with a fur Cossack hat jammed down over his ears gestured with one gloved hand toward the flow of traffic moving north on I-25.

'You can't get up here!' he bawled to Hallorann over the wind. 'Go down two exits, get on 91, and connect with 36 at Broomfield!'

'I think I could get around him on the left!' Hallorann shouted back. 'That's twenty miles out of my way, what you're rappin!'

'I'll rap your friggin *head!*' the cop shouted back. 'This ramp's closed!'

Hallorann backed up, waited for a break in traffic, and continued on his way up Route 25. The signs informed him it was only a hundred miles to Cheyenne, Wyoming. If he didn't look out for his ramp, he'd wind up there.

He inched his speed up to thirty-five but dared no more; already snow was threatening to clog his wiper blades and the traffic patterns were decidedly crazy. Twenty-mile detour. He cursed, and the feeling that time was growing shorter for the boy welled up in him again, nearly suffocating with its urgency. And at the same time he felt a fatalistic certainty that he would not be coming back from this trip.

He turned on the radio, dialed past Christmas ads, and found a weather forecast.

'—six inches already, and another foot is expected in the Denver metro area by nightfall. Local and state police urge you not to take your car out of the garage unless it's absolutely necessary, and warn that most mountain passes have already been closed. So stay home and wax up your boards and keep tuned to—'

'Thanks, mother,' Hallorann said, and turned the radio off savagely.

Chapter Forty-six

Wendy

Around noon, after Danny had gone into the bathroom to use the toilet, Wendy took the towel-wrapped knife from under her pillow, put it in the pocket of her bathrobe, and went over to the bathroom door.

'Danny?'

'What?'

'I'm going down to make us some lunch. 'Kay?'

'Okay. Do you want me to come down?'

'No, I'll bring it up. How about a cheese omelet and some soup?'

'Sure.'

She hesitated outside the closed door a moment longer. 'Danny, are you sure it's okay?'

'Yeah,' he said. 'Just be careful.'

'Where's your father? Do you know?'

His voice came back, curiously flat: 'No. But it's okay.'

She stifled an urge to keep asking, to keep picking around the edges of the thing. The thing was there, they knew what it was, picking at it was only going to frighten Danny more . . . and herself.

Jack had lost his mind. They had sat together on Danny's cot as the storm began to pick up clout and meanness around eight o'clock this morning and had listened to him downstairs, bellowing and stumbling from one place to another. Most of it had seemed to come from the ballroom. Jack singing tuneless bits of song, Jack holding up one side of an argument, Jack screaming loudly at one point, freezing both of their faces as they stared into one another's eyes. Finally they had heard him stumbling back across the lobby, and Wendy thought she had heard a loud banging noise, as if he had fallen down or pushed a door violently open. Since eight-thirty or so – three and a half hours now – there had been only silence.

She went down the short hall, turned into the main first-floor corridor, and went to the stairs. She stood on the first-floor landing looking down into the lobby. It appeared deserted, but the gray and snowy day had left much of the long room in shadow. Danny could be wrong. Jack could be behind a chair or couch . . . maybe behind the registration desk . . . waiting for her to come down . . .

She wet her lips. 'Jack?'

No answer.

Her hand found the handle of the knife and she began to go down. She had seen the end of her marriage many times, in divorce, in Jack's death at the scene of a drunken car accident (a regular vision in the dark two o'clock of Stovington mornings), and occasionally in daydreams of being discovered by another man, a soap opera Galahad who would sweep Danny and her onto the saddle of his snow-white charger and take them away. But she had never envisioned herself prowling halls and staircases like a nervous felon, with a knife clasped in one hand to use against Jack.

A wave of despair struck through her at the thought and she had to stop halfway down the stairs and hold the railing, afraid her knees would buckle.

(*Admit it. It isn't just Jack, he's just the one solid thing in all of this you can hang the other things on, the things you can't believe and yet are being forced to believe, that thing about the hedges, the party favor in the elevator, the mask*)

She tried to stop the thought but it was too late.

(*and the voices.*)

Because from time to time it had not seemed that there was a solitary crazy man below them, shouting at and holding conversations with the phantoms in his own crumbling mind. From time to time, like a radio signal fading in and out she had heard – or thought she had – other voices, and music and laughter. At one moment she would hear Jack holding a conversation with someone named Grady (the name was vaguely familiar to her but she made no actual connection), making statements and asking questions into silence, yet speaking loudly, as if to make himself heard over a steady background racket. And then, eerily, other sounds would be there, seeming to slip into place – a dance band, people clapping, a man with an amused yet authoritative voice who seemed to be trying to persuade somebody to make a speech. For a period of thirty seconds to a minute she would hear this, long enough to grow faint with terror, and then it would be gone again and she would only hear Jack, talking in that commanding yet slightly slurred way she remembered as his drunk-speak voice. But there was nothing in the hotel to drink except cooking sherry. Wasn't that right? Yes, but if she could imagine that the hotel was full of voices and music, couldn't Jack imagine that he was drunk?

She didn't like that thought. Not at all.

Wendy reached the lobby and looked around. The velvet rope that had cordoned off the ballroom had been taken down; the steel post it had been clipped to had been knocked over, as if someone had carelessly bumped it going by. Mellow white light fell through the open door onto the lobby rug from the ballroom's high, narrow windows. Heart thumping, she went to the open ballroom doors and looked in. It was empty and silent, the only sound that curious subaural echo that seems to linger in all large rooms, from the largest cathedral to the smallest hometown bingo parlor.

She went back to the registration desk and stood undecided for a moment, listening to the wind howl outside. It was the worst storm so far, and it was still building up force. Somewhere on the west side a shutter latch had broken and the shutter banged back and forth with a steady flat cracking sound, like a shooting gallery with only one customer.

(*Jack, you really should take care of that. Before something gets in.*)

What would she do if he came at her right now, she wondered. If he should pop up from behind the dark, varnished registration desk with its pile of triplicate forms and its little silver-plated bell, like some murderous jack-in-the-box, pun intended, a grinning jack-in-the-box with a cleaver in one hand and no sense at all left behind his eyes. Would she stand frozen with terror, or was there enough of the primal mother in her to fight him for her son until one of them was dead? She didn't know. The very thought made her sick – made her feel that her whole life had been a long and easy dream to lull her helplessly into this waking nightmare. She was soft. When trouble came, she slept. Her past was unremarkable. She had never been tried in fire. Now the trial was upon her, not fire but ice, and she would not be allowed to sleep through this. Her son was waiting for her upstairs.

Clutching the haft of the knife tighter, she peered over the desk.

Nothing there.

Her relieved breath escaped her in a long, hitching sigh.

She put the gate up and went through, pausing to glance into the inner office before going in herself. She fumbled through the next door for the bank of kitchen light switches, coldly expecting a hand to close over hers at any second. Then the fluorescents were coming on with minuscule ticking and humming sounds and she could see Mr Hallorann's kitchen – her kitchen now, for better or worse – pale green tiles, gleaming Formica, spotless porcelain, glowing chrome edgings. She had promised him she would keep his kitchen clean, and she had. She felt as if it was one of Danny's safe places. Dick Hallorann's presence seemed to enfold and comfort her. Danny had called for Mr Hallorann, and upstairs, sitting next to Danny in fear as her husband ranted and raved below, that had seemed like the faintest of all hopes. But standing here, in Mr Hallorann's place, it seemed almost possible. Perhaps he was on his way now, intent on getting to them regardless of the storm. Perhaps it was so.

She went across to the pantry, shot the bolt back, and stepped inside. She got a can of tomato soup and closed the pantry door again, and bolted it. The door was tight against the floor. If you kept it bolted, you didn't have to worry about rat or mouse droppings in the rice or flour or sugar.

She opened the can and dropped the slightly jellied contents into a saucepan – *plop*. She went to the refrigerator and got milk and eggs for the omelet. Then to the walk-in freezer for cheese. All of these actions, so common and so much a part of her life before the Overlook had been a part of her life, helped to calm her.

She melted butter in the frying pan, diluted the soup with milk, and then poured the beaten eggs into the pan.

A sudden feeling that someone was standing behind her, reaching for her throat.

She wheeled around, clutching the knife. No one there.

(*!Get ahold of yourself, girl!*)

She grated a bowl of cheese from the block, added it to the omelet, flipped it, and turned the gas ring down to a bare blue flame. The soup was hot. She put the pot on a large tray with silverware, two bowls, two plates, the salt and pepper shakers. When the omelet had puffed slightly, Wendy slid it off onto one of the plates and covered it.

(*Now back the way you came. Turn off the kitchen lights. Go through the inner office. Through the desk gate, collect two hundred dollars.*)

She stopped on the lobby side of the registration desk and set the tray down beside the silver bell. Unreality would stretch only so far; this was like some surreal game of hide-and-seek.

She stood in the shadowy lobby, frowning in thought.

(*Don't push the facts away this time, girl. There are certain realities, as lunatic as this situation may seem. One of them is that you may be the only responsible person left in this grotesque pile. You have a five-going-on-six son to look out for. And your husband, whatever has happened to him and no matter how dangerous he may be . . . maybe he's part of your responsibility, too. And even if he isn't, consider this: Today is December second. You could be stuck up here another four months if a ranger doesn't happen by. Even if they do start to wonder why they haven't heard from us on the CB, no one is going to come today . . . or tomorrow . . . maybe not for weeks. Are you going to spend a month sneaking down to get meals with a knife in your pocket and jumping at every shadow? Do you really think you can avoid Jack for a month? Do you think you can keep Jack out of the upstairs quarters if he wants to get in? He has the passkey and one hard kick would snap the bolt.*)

Leaving the tray on the desk, she walked slowly down to the dining room and looked in. It was deserted. There was one table with chairs set up around it, the table they had tried eating at until the dining room's emptiness began to freak them out.

'Jack?' she called hesitantly.

At that moment the wind rose in a gust, driving snow against the shutters, but it seemed to her that there had been something. A muffled sort of groan.

'*Jack?*'

No returning sound this time, but her eyes fell on something beneath the batwing doors of the Colorado Lounge, something that gleamed faintly in the subdued light. Jack's cigarette lighter.

Plucking up her courage, she crossed to the batwings and pushed them open. The smell of gin was so strong that her breath snagged in her throat. It wasn't even right to call it a smell; it was a positive reek. But the shelves were empty. Where in God's name had he found it? A bottle hidden at the back of one of the cupboards? *Where?*

There was another groan, low and fuzzy, but perfectly audible this time. Wendy walked slowly to the bar.

'Jack?'

No answer.

She looked over the bar and there he was, sprawled out on the floor in a stupor. Drunk as a lord, by the smell. He must have tried to go right over the top and lost his balance. A wonder he hadn't broken his neck. An old proverb recurred to her: God looks after drunks and little children. Amen.

Yet she was not angry with him; looking down at him she thought he looked like a horribly overtired little boy who had tried to do too much and had fallen asleep in the middle of the living room floor. He had stopped drinking and it was not Jack who had made the decision to start again; there had been no liquor for him to start with . . . so where had it come from?

Resting at every five or six feet along the horseshoe-shaped bar there were wine bottles wrapped in straw, their mouths plugged with candles. Supposed to look bohemian, she supposed. She picked one up and shook it, half-expecting to hear the slosh of gin inside it

(*new wine in old bottles*)

but there was nothing. She set it back down.

Jack was stirring. She went around the bar, found the gate, and walked back on the inside to where Jack lay, pausing only to look at the gleaming chromium taps. They were dry, but when she passed close to them she could smell beer, wet and new, like a fine mist.

As she reached Jack he rolled over, opened his eyes, and looked up at her. For a moment his gaze was utterly blank, and then it cleared.

'Wendy?' he asked. 'That you?'

'Yes,' she said. 'Do you think you can make it upstairs? If you put your arms around me? Jack, where did you—'

His hand closed brutally around her ankle.

'Jack! What are you—'

'Gotcha!' he said, and began to grin. There was a stale odor of gin and olives about him that seemed to set off an old terror in her, a worse terror than any hotel could provide by itself. A distant part of her thought that the worst thing was that it had all come back to this, she and her drunken husband.

'Jack, I want to help.'

'Oh yeah. You and Danny only want to *help*.' The grip on her ankle was crushing now. Still holding onto her, Jack was getting shakily to his knees. 'You wanted to help us all right out of here. But now . . . I . . . *gotcha!*'

'Jack, you're hurting my ankle—'

'I'll hurt more than your ankle, you *bitch*.'

The word stunned her so completely that she made no effort to move when he let go of her ankle and stumbled from his knees to his feet, where he stood swaying in front of her.

'You never loved me,' he said. 'You want us to leave because you know that'll be the end of me. Did you ever think about my re . . . re . . . responsibilities? No, I guess to fuck you didn't. All you ever think about is ways to drag me down. You're just like my mother, you milksop *bitch!*'

'Stop it,' she said, crying. 'You don't know what you're saying. You're drunk. I don't know how, but you're drunk.'

'Oh, I know. I know now. You and him. That little pup upstairs. The two of you, planning together. Isn't that right?'

'No, no! We never planned anything! What are you—'

'*You liar!*' he screamed. 'Oh, I know how you do it! I guess I know that! When I say, "We're going to stay here and I'm going to do my job," you say, "Yes, dear," and he says, "Yes, Daddy," and then you lay your plans. You planned to use the snowmobile. You planned that. But I knew. I figured it out. *Did you think I wouldn't figure it out? Did you think I was stupid?*'

She stared at him, unable to speak now. He was going to kill her, and then he was going to kill Danny. Then maybe the hotel would be satisfied and allow him to kill himself. Just like that other caretaker. Just like

(*Grady*)

With almost swooning horror, she realized at last who it was that Jack had been conversing with in the ballroom.

'You turned my son against me. That was the worst.' His face sagged into lines of selfpity. 'My little boy. Now he hates me, too. You saw to that. That was your plan all along, wasn't it? You've always been jealous, haven't you? Just like your mother. You couldn't be satisfied unless you had all the cake, could you? *Could you?*'

She couldn't talk.

'Well, I'll fix you,' he said, and tried to put his hands around her throat.

She took a step backward, then another, and he stumbled against her. She remembered the knife in the pocket of her robe and groped for it, but now his left arm had swept around her, pinning her arm against her side. She could smell sharp gin and the sour odor of his sweat.

'Have to be punished,' he was grunting. 'Chastised. Chastised . . . harshly.'

His right hand found her throat.

As her breath stopped, pure panic took over. his left hand joined his right and now the knife was free to her own hand, but she forget about it. Both of her hands came up and began to yank helplessly at his larger, stronger ones.

'*Mommy!*' Danny shrieked from somewhere. '*Daddy, stop! You're hurting Mommy!*' He screamed piercingly, a high and crystal sound that she heard from far off.

Red flashes of light leaped in front of her eyes like ballet dancers. The room grew darker. She saw her son clamber up on the bar and throw himself at Jack's shoulder. Suddenly one of the hands that had been crushing her throat was gone as Jack cuffed Danny away with a snarl. The boy fell back against the empty shelves and dropped to the floor, dazed. The hand was on her throat again. The red flashes began to turn black.

Danny was crying weakly. Her chest was burning. Jack was shouting into her face: 'I'll fix you! Goddam you, I'll show you who is boss around here? I'll show you—'

But all sounds were fading down a long dark corridor. Her struggles began to weaken. One of her hands fell away from his and dropped slowly until the arm was stretched out at right angles to her body, the hand dangling limply from the wrist like the hand of a drowning woman.

It touched a bottle – one of the straw-wrapped wine bottles that served as decorative candleholders.

Sightlessly, with the last of her strength, she groped for the bottle's neck and found it, feeling the greasy beads of wax against her hand.

(*and O God if it slips*)

She brought it up and then down, praying for aim, knowing that if it only struck his shoulder or upper arm she was dead.

But the bottle came down squarely on Jack Torrance's head, the glass shattering violently inside the straw. The base of it was thick and heavy, and it made a sound against his skull like a medicine ball dropped on a hardwood floor. He rocked back on his heels, his eyes rolling up in their sockets. The pressure on her throat loosened, then gave way entirely. He put his hands out, as if to steady himself, and then crashed over on his back.

Wendy drew a long, sobbing breath. She almost fell herself, clutched the edge of the bar, and managed to hold herself up. Consciousness wavered in and out. She could hear Danny crying, but she had no idea where he was. It sounded like crying in an echo chamber. Dimly she saw dime-sized drops of blood falling to the dark surface of the bar – from her nose, she thought. She cleared her throat and spat on the floor. It sent a wave of agony up the column of her throat, but the agony subsided to a steady dull press of pain . . . just bearable.

Little by little, she managed to get control of herself.

She let go of the bar, turned around, and saw Jack lying full-length, the shattered bottle beside him. He looked like a felled giant. Danny was crouched below the lounge's cash register, both hands in his mouth, staring at his unconscious father.

Wendy went to him unsteadily and touched his shoulder. Danny cringed away from her.

'Danny, listen to me—'

'No, no,' he muttered in a husky old man's voice. 'Daddy hurt you ... you hurt Daddy ... Daddy hurt you ... I want to go to sleep. Danny wants to go to sleep.'

'Danny—'

'Sleep, sleep. Nighty-night.'

'*No!*'

Pain ripping up her throat again. She winced against it. But he opened his eyes. They looked at her warily from bluish, shadowed sockets.

She made herself speak calmly, her eyes never leaving his. Her voice was low and husky, almost a whisper. It hurt to talk. 'Listen to me, Danny. It wasn't your daddy trying to hurt me. And I didn't want to hurt him. The hotel has gotten into him, Danny. *The Overlook has gotten into your daddy.* Do you understand me?'

Some kind of knowledge came slowly back into Danny's eyes.

'The Bad Stuff,' he whispered. 'There was none of it here before, was there?'

'No. The hotel put it here. The ...' She broke off in a fit of coughing and spat out more blood. Her throat already felt puffed to twice its size. 'The hotel made him drink it. Did you hear those people he was talking to this morning?'

'Yes ... the hotel people ...'

'I heard them too. And that means the hotel is getting stronger. It wants to hurt all of us. But I think ... I hope ... that it can only do that through your daddy. He was the only one it could catch. Are you understanding me, Danny? It's desperately important that you understand.'

'The hotel caught Daddy.' He looked at Jack and groaned helplessly.

'I know you love your daddy. I do too. We have to remember that the hotel is trying to hurt him as much as it is us.' And she was convinced that was true. More, she thought that Danny might be the one the hotel really wanted, the reason it was going so far ... maybe the reason it was *able* to go so far. It might even be that in some unknown fashion it was Danny's shine that was powering it, the way a battery powers the electrical equipment in a car ... the way a battery gets a car to start. If they got out of here, the Overlook might subside to its old semi-sentient state, able to do no more than present penny-dreadful horror slides to the more psychically aware guests who entered it. Without Danny it was not much more than an amusement park haunted house, where a guest or two might hear rappings or the phantom sounds of a masquerade party, or see an occasional disturbing thing. But if it absorbed Danny ... Danny's shine or life-force or spirit ... whatever you wanted to call it ... into itself – what would it be then?

The thought made her cold all over.

'I wish Daddy was all better,' Danny said, and the tears began to flow again.

'Me too,' she said, and hugged Danny tightly. 'And honey, that's why you've got to help me put your daddy somewhere. Somewhere that the hotel can't make him hurt us and where he can't hurt himself. Then . . . if your friend Dick comes, or a park ranger, we can take him away. And I think he might be all right again. All of us might be all right. I think there's still a chance for that, if we're strong and brave, like you were when you jumped on his back. Do you understand?' She looked at him pleadingly and thought how strange it was; she had never seen him when he looked so much like Jack.

'Yes,' he said, and nodded, 'I think . . . if we can get away from here . . . everything will be like it was. Where could we put him?'

'The pantry. There's food in there, and a good strong bolt on the outside. It's warm. And we can eat up the things from the refrigerator and the freezer. There will be plenty for all three of us until help comes.'

'Do we do it now?'

'Yes, right now. Before he wakes up.'

Danny put the bargate up while she folded Jack's hands on his chest and listened to his breathing for a moment. It was slow but regular. From the smell of him she thought he must have drunk a great deal . . . and he was out of the habit. She thought it might be liquor as much as the crack on the head with the bottle that had put him out.

She picked up his legs and began to drag him along the floor. She had been married to him for nearly seven years, he had lain on top of her countless times – in the thousands – but she had never realized how heavy he was. Her breath whistled painfully in and out of her hurt throat. Nevertheless, she felt better than she had in days. She was alive. Having just brushed so close to death, that was precious. And Jack was alive, too. By blind luck rather than plan, they had perhaps found the only way that would bring them all safely out.

Panting harshly, she paused a moment, holding Jack's feet against her hips. The surroundings reminded her of the old seafaring captain's cry in *Treasure Island* after old blind Pew had passed him the Black spot: *We'll do em yet!*

And then she remembered, uncomfortably, that the old seadog had dropped dead mere seconds later.

'Are you all right, Mommy? Is he . . . is he too heavy?'

'I'll manage.' She began to drag him again. Danny was beside Jack. One of his hands had fallen off his chest, and Danny replaced it gently, with love.

'Are you sure, Mommy?'

'Yes. It's the best thing, Danny.'

'It's like putting him in jail.'

'Only for awhile.'

'Okay, then. Are you sure you can do it?'

'Yes.'

But it was a near thing, at that. Danny had been cradling his father's head when they went over the doorsills, but his hands slipped in Jack's greasy hair as they went into the kitchen. The back of his head struck the tiles, and Jack began to moan and stir.

'You got to use smoke,' Jack muttered quickly. 'Now run and get me that gascan.'

Wendy and Danny exchanged tight, fearful glances.

'Help me,' she said in a low voice.

For a moment Danny stood as if paralyzed by his father's face, and then he moved jerkily to her side and helped her hold the left leg. They dragged him across the kitchen floor in a nightmare kind of slow motion, the only sounds the faint, insectile buzz of the fluorescent lights and their own labored breathing.

When they reached the pantry, Wendy put Jack's feet down and turned to fumble with the bolt. Danny looked down at Jack, who was lying limp and relaxed again. The shirttail had pulled out of the back of his pants as they dragged him and Danny wondered if Daddy was too drunk to be cold. It seemed wrong to lock him in the pantry like a wild animal, but he had seen what he tried to do to Mommy. Even upstairs he had known Daddy was going to do that. He had heard them arguing in his head.

(If only we could all be out of here. Or if it was a dream I was having, back in Stovington. If only.)

The bolt was stuck.

Wendy pulled at it as hard as she could, but it wouldn't move. She couldn't retract the goddam bolt. It was stupid and unfair . . . she had opened it with no trouble at all when she had gone in to get the can of soup. Now it wouldn't move, and what was she going to do? They couldn't put him in the walk-in refrigerator; he would freeze or smother to death. But if they left him out and he woke up . . .

Jack stirred again on the floor.

'I'll take care of it,' he muttered. 'I understand.'

'He's waking up, Mommy!' Danny warned.

Sobbing now, she yanked at the bolt with both hands.

'Danny?' There was something softly menacing, if still blurry, in Jack's voice. 'That you, ole doc?'

'Just go to sleep, Daddy,' Danny said nervously. 'It's bedtime, you know.'

He looked up at his mother, still struggling with the bolt, and saw what was wrong immediately. She had forgotten to rotate the bolt before trying to withdraw it. The little catch was stuck in its notch.

'Here,' he said low, and brushed her trembling hands aside; his own were shaking almost as badly. He knocked the catch loose with the heel of his hand and the bold drew back easily.

'Quick,' he said. He looked down. Jack's eyes had fluttered open again and this time Daddy was looking directly at him, his gaze strangely flat and speculative.

'You copied it,' Daddy told him. 'I know you did, But it's here somewhere. And I'll find it. That I promise you. I'll find it . . .' His words slurred off again.

Wendy pushed the pantry door open with her knee, hardly noticing the pungent odor of dried fruit that wafted out. She picked up Jack's feet again and dragged him in. She was gasping harshly now, at the limit of her strength. As she yanked the chain pull that turned on the light, Jack's eyes fluttered open again.

'What are you doing? Wendy? What are you doing?'

She stepped over him.

He was quick; amazingly quick. One hand lashed out and she had to sidestep and nearly fall out the door to avoid his grasp. Still, he had caught a handful of her bathrobe and there was a heavy purring noise as it ripped. He was up on his hands and knees now, his hair hanging in his eyes, like some heavy animal. A large dog . . . or a lion.

'Damn you both. I know what you want. But you're not going to get it. This hotel . . . it's mine. It's me they want. Me! Me!'

'The door, Danny!' she screamed. '*Shut the door!*'

He pushed the heavy wooden door shut with a slam, just as Jack leaped. The door latched and Jack thudded uselessly against it.

Danny's small hands groped at the bolt. Wendy was too far away to help; the issue of whether he would be locked in or free was going to be decided in two seconds. Danny missed his grip, found it again, and shot the bolt across just as the latch began to jiggle madly up and down below it. Then it stayed up and there was a series of thuds as Jack slammed his shoulder against the door. The bolt, a quarter inch of steel in diameter, showed no signs of loosening. Wendy let her breath out slowly.

'Let me out of here!' Jack raged. 'Let me out! Danny, doggone it, this is your father and I want to get out! *Now do what I tell you!*'

Danny's hand moved automatically toward the bolt. Wendy caught it and pressed it between her breasts.

'You mind your daddy, Danny! You do what I say! You do it or I'll give you a hiding you'll never forget. *Open this door or I'll bash your fucking brains in!*'

Danny looked at her, pale as window glass.

They could hear his breath tearing in and out behind the half inch of solid oak.

'Wendy, you let me out! Let me out right now! You cheap nickle-plated cold-cunt bitch! You let me out! I mean it! Let me out of here and I'll let it go! If you don't, I'll mess you up! I mean it! I'll mess you up so bad your own mother would pass you on the street! *Now open this door!*'

Danny moaned. Wendy looked at him and saw he was going to faint in a moment.'

'Come on, doc,' she said, surprised at the calmness of her own voice. 'It's not your daddy talking, remember. It's the hotel.'

'*Come back here and let me out right NOW!*' Jack screamed. There was a scraping, breaking sound as he attacked the inside of the door with his fingernails.

'It's the hotel,' Danny said. 'It's the hotel. I remember.' But he looked back over his shoulder and his face was crumpled and terrified.

Chapter Forty-seven

Danny

It was three in the afternoon of a long, long day.

They were sitting on the big bed in their quarters. Danny was turning the purple VW model with the monster sticking out of the sun roof over and over in his hands, compulsively.

They had heard Daddy's batterings at the door all the way across the lobby, the batterings and his voice, hoarse and petulantly angry in a weakking sort of a way, vomiting promises of punishment, vomiting profanity, promising both of them that they would live to regret betraying him after he had slaved his guts out for them over the years.

Danny thought they would no longer be able to hear it upstairs, but the sounds of his rage carried perfectly up the dumb-waiter shaft. Mommy's face was pale, and there were horrible brownish bruises on her neck where Daddy had tried to . . .

He turned the model over and over in his hands, Daddy's prize for having learned his reading lessons.

(. . . where Daddy had tried to hug her too tight.)

Mommy put some of her music on the little record player, scratchy and full of horns and flutes. She smiled at him tiredly. He tried to smile back and failed. Even with the volume turned up loud he thought he could still hear Daddy screaming at them and battering the pantry door like an animal in a zoo cage. What if Daddy had to go to the bathroom? What would he do then?

Danny began to cry.

Wendy turned the volume down on the record player at once, held him, rocked him on her lap.

'Danny, love, it will be all right. It will. If Mr Hallorann didn't get your message, someone else will. As soon as the storm is over. No one could get up here until then anyway. Mr Hallorann or anyone else. But when the storm is over, everything will be fine again. We'll leave here. And do you know what we'll do next spring? The three of us?'

Danny shook his head against her breasts. He didn't know. It seemed there could never be spring again.

'We'll go fishing. We'll rent a boat and go fishing, just like we did last year on Chatterton Lake. You and me and your daddy. And maybe you'll catch a bass for our supper. And maybe we won't catch anything, but we're sure to have a good time.'

'I love you, Mommy,' he said, and hugged her.

'Oh, Danny, I love you, too.'

Outside, the wind whooped and screamed.

Around four-thirty, just as the daylight began to fail, the screams ceased.

They had both been dozing uneasily, Wendy still holding Danny in her arms, and she didn't wake. But Danny did. Somehow the silence was worse, more ominous than the screams and the blows against the strong pantry door. Was Daddy asleep again? Or dead? Or what?

(*Did he get out?*)

Fifteen minutes later the silence was broken by a hard, grating, metallic rattle. There was a heavy grinding, then a mechanical humming. Wendy came awake with a cry.

The elevator was running again.

They listened to it, wide-eyed, hugging each other. It went from floor to floor, the grate rattling back, the brass door slamming open. There was laughter, drunken shouts, occasional screams, and the sounds of breakage.

The Overlook was coming to life around them.

Chapter Forty-eight

Jack

He sat on the floor of the pantry with his legs out in front of him, a box of Triscuit crackers between them, looking at the door. He was eating the crackers one by one, not tasting them, only eating them because he had to eat something. When he got out of here, he was going to need his strength. All of it.

At this precise instant, he thought he had never felt quite so miserable in his entire life. His mind and body together made up a large-writ scripture of pain. His head ached terribly, the sick throb of a hangover. The attendant symptoms were there, too: his mouth tasted like a manure rake had taken a swing through it, his ears rung, his heart had an extra-heavy, thudding beat, like a tom-tom. In addition, both shoulders ached fiercely from throwing himself against the door and his throat felt raw and peeled from useless shouting. He had cut his right hand on the doorlatch.

And when he got out of here, he was going to kick some ass.

He munched the Triscuits one by one, refusing to give in to his wretched stomach, which wanted to vomit up everything. He thought of the Excedrins in his pocket and decided to wait until his stomach had quieted a bit. No sense swallowing a painkiller if you were going to throw it right back up. Have to use your brain. The celebrated Jack Torrance brain. Aren't you the fellow who once was going to live by his wits? Jack Torrance, best-selling author. Jack Torrance, acclaimed playwright and winner of the New York Critics Circle Award. John Torrance, man of letters, esteemed thinker, winner of the Pulitzer Prize at seventy for his trenchant book of memoirs, *My Life in the Twentieth Century*. All any of that shit boiled down to was living by your wits.

Living by your wits is always knowing where the wasps are.

He put another Triscuit into his mouth and crunched it up.

What it really came down to, he supposed, was their lack of trust in him. Their failure to believe that he knew what was best for them and how to get it. His wife had tried to usurp him, first by fair

(sort of)

means, then by foul. When her little hints and whining objections had been overturned by his own well-reasoned arguments, she had turned his boy against him, tried to kill him with a bottle, and then had locked him, of all places, in the goddamned fucking *pantry*.

Still, a small interior voice nagged him.

(*Yes but where did the liquor come from? Isn't that really the central point? You know what happens when you drink, you know it from bitter experience. When you drink, you lose your wits.*)

He hurled the box of Triscuits across the small room. They struck a shelf of canned goods and fell to the floor. He looked at the box, wiped his lips with his hand, and then looked at his watch. It was almost six-thirty. He had been in here for hours. His wife had locked him in here and he'd been here for fucking *hours*.

He could begin to sympathize with his father.

The thing he'd never asked himself, Jack realized now, was exactly what had driven his daddy to drink in the first place. And really . . . when you came right down to what his old students had been pleased to call the nitty-gritty . . . hadn't it been the woman he was married to? A milksop sponge of a woman, always dragging silently around the house with an expression of doomed martyrdom on her face? A ball and chain around Daddy's ankle? No, not ball and chain. She had never actively tried to make Daddy a prisoner, the way Wendy had done to him. For Jack's father it must have been more like the fate of McTeague the dentist at the end of Frank Norris's great novel: handcuffed to a dead man in the wasteland. Yes, that was better. Mentally and spiritually dead, his mother had been handcuffed to his father by matrimony. Still, Daddy had tried to do right as he dragged her rotting corpse through life. He had tried to bring the four children up to know right from wrong, to understand discipline, and above all, to respect their father.

Well, they had been ingrates, all of them, himself included. And now he was paying the price; his own son had turned out to be an ingrate, too. But there was hope. He would get out of here somehow. He would chastise them both, and harshly. He would set Danny an example, so that the day might come when Danny was grown, a day when Danny would know what to do better than he himself had known.

He remembered the Sunday dinner when his father had caned his mother at the table . . . how horrified he and the others had been. Now he could see how necessary that had been, how his father had only been feigning drunkenness, how his wits had been sharp and alive underneath all along, watching for the slightest sign of disrespect.

Jack crawled after the Triscuits and began to eat them again, sitting by the door she had so treacherously bolted. He wondered exactly what his father had seen, and how he had caught her out by his playacting. Had she been sneering at him behind her hand? Sticking her tongue out? Making obscene finger gestures? Or only looking at him insolently and arrogantly, convinced that he was too stupidly drunk to see? Whatever it had been, he had caught her at it, and he had chastised her sharply. And now, twenty years later, he could finally appreciate Daddy's wisdom.

Of course you could say Daddy had been foolish to marry such a woman, to have handcuffed himself to that corpse in the first place . . . and a disrespectful corpse at that. But when the young marry in haste they must repent in leisure, and perhaps Daddy's daddy had married the same type of woman, so that unconsciously Jack's daddy had also married one, as Jack himself had. Except that *his* wife, instead of being satisfied with the passive role of having wrecked one career and crippled another, had opted for the poisonously active task of trying to destroy his last and best chance: to become a member of the Overlook's staff, and possibly to rise . . . all the way to the position of manager, in time. She was trying to deny him Danny, and Danny was his ticket of admission. That was foolish, of course – why would they want the son when they could have the father? – but employers often had foolish ideas and that was the condition that had been made.

He wasn't going to be able to reason with her, he could see that now. He had tried to reason with her in the Colorado Lounge, and she had refused to listen, had hit him over the head with a bottle for his pains. But there would be another time, and soon. He would get out of here.

He suddenly held his breath and cocked his head. Somewhere a piano was playing boogie-woogie and people were laughing and clapping along. The sound was muffled through the heavy wooden door, but audible. The song was 'There'll Be a Hot Time in the Old Town Tonight.'

His hands curled helplessly into fists; he had to restrain himself from battering at the door with them. The party had begun again. The liquor would be flowing freely. Somewhere, dancing with someone else, would be the girl who had felt so maddeningly nude under her white silk gown.

'You'll pay for this!' he howled. 'Goddam you two, you'll pay! You'll take your goddam medicine for this, I promise you! You—'

'Here, here, now,' a mild voice said just outside the door. 'No need to shout, old fellow. I can hear you perfectly well.'

Jack lurched to his feet.

'Grady? Is that you?'

'Yes, sir. Indeed it is. You appear to have been locked in.'

'Let me out, Grady. Quickly.'

'I see you can hardly have taken care of the business we discussed, sir. The correction of your wife and son.'

'They're the ones who locked me in. Pull the bolt, for God's sake!'

'You let them lock you in?' Grady's voice registered well-bred surprise. 'Oh dear. A woman half your size and a little boy? Hardly sets you off as being of top managerial timber, does it?'

A pulse began to beat in the clockspring of veins at Jack's right temple. 'Let me out, Grady. I'll take care of them.'

'Will you indeed, sir? I wonder.' Well-bred surprise was replaced by well-bred regret. 'I'm pained to say that I doubt it. I – and others – have really come to believe that your heart is not in this, sir. That you haven't the . . . the belly for it.'

'I do!' Jack shouted. *'I do, I swear it!'*

'You would bring us your son?'

'Yes! Yes!'

'Your wife would object to that very strongly, Mr Torrance. And she appears to be . . . somewhat stronger than we had imagined. Somewhat more resourceful. She certainly seems to have gotten the better of *you*.'

Grady tittered.

'Perhaps, Mr Torrance, we should have been dealing with her all along.'

'I'll bring him, I swear it,' Jack said. His face was against the door now. He was sweating. 'She won't object. I swear she won't. She won't be able to.'

'You would have to kill her, I fear,' Grady said coldly.

'I'll do what I have to do. Just *let me out*.'

'You'll give your word on it, sir?' Grady persisted.

'My word, my promise, my sacred vow, whatever in hell you want. If you—'

There was a flat snap as the bolt was drawn back. The door shivered open a quarter of an inch. Jack's words and breath halted. For a moment he felt that death itself was outside that door.

The feeling passed.

He whispered: 'Thank you, Grady. I swear you won't regret it. I swear you won't.'

There was no answer. He became aware that all sounds had stopped except for the cold swooping of the wind outside.

He pushed the pantry door open; the hinges squealed faintly.

The kitchen was empty. Grady was gone. Everything was still and frozen beneath the cold white glare of the fluorescent bars. His eyes caught on the large chopping block where the three of them had eaten their meals.

Standing on top of it was a martini glass, a fifth of gin, and a plastic dish filled with olives.

Leaning against it was one of the roque mallets from the equipment shed.

He looked at it for a long time.

Then a voice, much deeper and much more powerful than Grady's, spoke from somewhere, everywhere . . . from inside him.

(*Keep your promise, Mr Torrance.*)

'I will,' he said. He heard the fawning servility in his own voice but was unable to control it. 'I will.'

He walked to the chopping block and put his hand on the handle of the mallet.

He hefted it.

Swung it.

It hissed viciously through the air.

Jack Torrance began to smile.

Chapter Forty-nine

Hallorann, Going Up the Country

It was quarter of two in the afternoon and according to the snow-clotted signs and the Hertz Buick's odometer, he was less than three miles from Estes Park when he finally went off the road.

In the hills, the snow was falling faster and more furiously than Hallorann had ever seen (which was, perhaps, not to say a great deal, since Hallorann had seen as little snow as he could manage in his lifetime), and the wind was blowing a capricious gale – now from the west, now backing around to the north, sending clouds of powdery snow across his field of vision, making him coldly aware again and again that if he missed a turn he might well plunge two hundred feet off the road, the Electra cartwheeling ass over teapot as it went down. Making it worse was his own amateur status as a winter driver. It scared him to have the yellow center line buried under swirling, drifting snow, and it scared him when the heavy gusts of wind came unimpeded through the notches in the hills and actually made the heavy Buick slew around. It scared him that the road information signs were mostly masked with snow and you could flip a coin as to whether the road was going to break right or left up ahead in the white drive-in movie screen he seemed to be driving through. He was scared, all right. He had driven in a cold sweat since climbing into the hills west of Boulder and Lyons, handling the accelerator and brake as if they were Ming vases. Between rock 'n' roll tunes on the radio, the disc jockey constantly adjured motorists to stay off the main highways and under no conditions to go into the mountains, because many roads were impassable and all of them were dangerous. Scores of minor accidents had been reported, and two serious ones: a party of skiers in a VW microbus and a family that had been bound for Albuquerque through the Sangre de Cristo Mountains. The combined score on both was four dead and five wounded. 'So stay off those roads and get into the good music here at KTLK,' the jock concluded cheerily, and then compounded Hallorann's misery by playing 'Seasons in the Sun.' 'We had joy, we had fun, we had—' Terry Jacks gibbered happily, and Hallorann snapped the radio off viciously, knowing he would have it back on in five minutes. No matter how bad it was, it was better than riding alone through this white madness.

(*Admit it. Dis heah black boy has got at least one long stripe of yaller . . . and it runs raht up his ebberlubbin back!*)

It wasn't even funny. He would have backed off before he even cleared Boulder if it hadn't been for his compulsion that the boy was in terrible trouble. Even now a small voice in the back of his skull – more the voice of reason than of cowardice, he thought – was telling him to hole up in an Estes Park motel for the night and wait for the plows to at least expose the center stripe again. That voice kept reminding him of the jet's shaky landing at Stapleton, of that sinking feeling that it was going to come in nose-first, delivering its passengers to the gates of hell rather than at Gate 39, Concourse B. But reason would not stand against the compulsion. It had to be today. The snowstorm was his own bad luck. He would have to cope with it. He was afraid that if he didn't, he might have something much worse to cope with in his dreams.

The wind gusted again, this time from the northeast, a little English on the ball if you please, and he was again cut off from the vague shapes of the hills and even from the embankments on either side of the road. He was driving through white null.

And then the high sodium lights of the snowplow loomed out of the soup, bearing down, and to his horror he saw that instead of being to one side, the Buick's nose was pointed directly between those headlamps. The plow was being none too choosy about keeping its own side of the road, and Hallorann had allowed the Buick to drift.

The grinding roar of the plow's diesel engine intruded over the bellow of the wind, and then the sound of its airhorn, hard, long, almost deafening.

Hallorann's testicles turned into two small wrinkled sacs filled with shaved ice. His guts seemed to have been transformed into a large mass of Silly Putty.

Color was materializing out of the white now, snow-clotted orange. He could see the high cab, even the gesticulating figure of the driver behind the single long wiper blade. He could see the V shape of the plow's wing blades, spewing more snow up onto the road's left-hand embankment like pallid, smoking exhaust.

WHAAAAAAAAA! the airhorn bellowed indignantly.

He squeezed the accelerator like the breast of a much-loved woman and the Buick scooted forward and toward the right. There was no embankment over here; the plows headed up instead of down had only to push the snow directly over the drop.

(*The drop, ah yes, the drop—*)

The wingblades on Hallorann's left, fully four feet higher than the Electra's roof, flirted by with no more than an inch or two to spare. Until the plow had actually cleared him, Hallorann had thought a crash inevitable. A prayer which was half an inarticulate apology to the boy flitted through his mind like a torn rag.

Then the plow was past, its revolving blue lights glinting and flashing in Hallorann's rearview mirror.

He jockeyed the Buick's steering wheel back to the left, but nothing doing. The scoot had turned into a skid, and the Buick was floating dreamily toward the lip of the drop, spuming snow from under its mudguards.

He flicked the wheel back the other way, in the skid's direction, and the car's front and rear began to swap places. Panicked now, he pumped the brake hard, and then felt a hard bump. In front of him the road was gone . . . he was looking into a bottomless chasm of swirling snow and vague greenish-gray pines far away and far below.

(*I'm going holy mother of Jesus I'm going off*)

And that was where the car stopped, canting forward at a thirty-degree angle, the left fender jammed against a guardrail, the rear wheels nearly off the ground. When Hallorann tried reverse, the wheels only spun helplessly. His heart was doing a Gene Krupa drumroll.

He got out – very carefully he got out – and went around to the Buick's back deck.

He was standing there, looking at the back wheels helplessly, when a cheerful voice behind him said: 'Hello there, fella. You must be shit right out of your mind.'

He turned around and saw the plow forty yards further down the road, obscured in the blowing snow except for the raftered dark brown streak of its exhaust and the revolving blue lights on top. The driver was standing just behind him, dressed in a long sheepskin coat and a slicker over it. A blue-and-white pinstriped engineer's cap was perched on his head, and Hallorann could hardly believe it was staying on in the teeth of the wind.

(*Glue. It sure-God must be glue.*)

'Hi,' he said. 'Can you pull me back onto the road?'

'Oh, I guess I could,' the plow driver said. 'What the hell you doing way up here, mister? Good way to kill your ass.'

'Urgent business.'

'Nothin is that urgent,' the plow driver said slowly and kindly, as if speaking to a mental defective. 'If you'd 'a hit that post a leetle mite harder, nobody woulda got you out till All Fools' Day. Don't come from these parts, do you?'

'No. And I wouldn't be here unless my business was as urgent as I say.'

'That so?' The driver shifted his stance companionably as if they were having a desultory chat on the back steps instead of standing in a blizzard halfway between hoot and holler, with Hallorann's car balanced three hundred feet above the tops of the trees below.

'Where you headed? Estes?'

'No, a place called the Overlook Hotel,' Hallorann said. 'It's a little way above Sidewinder—'

But the driver was shaking his head dolefully.

'I guess I know well enough where that is,' he said. 'Mister, you'll never get up to the old Overlook. Roads between Estes Park and Sidewinder is bloody damn hell. It's driftin in right behind us no matter how hard we push. I come through drifts a few miles back that was damn near six feet through the middle. And even if you could make Sidewinder, why, the road's closed from there all the way across to Buckland, Utah. Nope.' He shook his head. 'Never make it, mister. Never make it at all.'

'I have to try,' Hallorann said, calling on his last reserves of patience to keep his voice normal. 'There's a boy up there—'

'*Boy?* Naw. The Overlook closes down at the last end of September. No percentage keepin it open longer. Too many shit-storms like this.'

'He's the son of the caretaker. He's in trouble'

'How would you know that?'

His patience snapped.

'For Christ's sake are you going to stand there and flap y'jaw at me the rest of the day? *I know, I know!* Now are you going to pull me back on the road or not?'

'Kind of testy, aren't you?' the driver observed, not particularly perturbed. 'Sure, get back in there. I got a chain behind the seat.'

Hallorann got back behind the wheel, beginning to shake with delayed reaction now. His hands were numbed almost clear through. He had forgotten to bring gloves.

The plow backed up to the rear of the Buick, and he saw the driver get out with a long coil of chain. Hallorann opened the door and shouted: 'What can I do to help?'

'Stay out of the way, is all,' the driver shouted back. 'This ain't gonna take a blink.'

Which was true. A shudder ran through the Buick's frame as the chain pulled tight, and a second later it was back on the road, pointed more or less toward Estes Park. The plow driver walked up beside the window and knocked on the safety glass. Hallorann rolled down the window.

'Thanks,' he said. 'I'm sorry I shouted at you.'

'I been shouted at before,' the driver said with a grin. 'I guess you're sorta strung up. You take these.' A pair of bulky blue mittens dropped into Hallorann's lap. 'You'll need em when you go off the road again, I guess. Cold out. You wear em unless you want to spend the rest of your life pickin your nose with a crochetin hook. And you send em back. My wife knitted em and I'm partial to em. Name and address is sewed right into the linin. I'm Howard Cottrell, by the way. You just send em back when you don't need em anymore. And I don't want to have to go payin no postage due, mind.'

'All right,' Hallorann said. 'Thanks. One hell of a lot.'

'You be careful. I'd take you myself, but I'm busy as a cat in a mess of guitar strings.'

'That's okay. Thanks again.'

He started to roll up the window, but Cottrell stopped him.

'When you get to Sidewinder – *if* you get to Sidewinder – you go to Durkin's Conoco. It's right next to the li'brey. Can't miss it. You ask for Larry Durkin. Tell him Howie Cottrell sent you and you want to rent one of his snowmobiles. You mention my name and show those mittens, you'll get the cut rate.'

'Thanks again,' Hallorann said.

Cottrell nodded. 'It's funny. Ain't no way you could know someone's in trouble up there at the Overlook . . . the phone's out, sure as hell. But I believe you. Sometimes I get feelins.'

Hallorann nodded. 'Sometimes I do, too.'

'Yeah. I know you do. But you take care.'

'I will.'

Cottrell disappeared into the blowing dimness with a final wave, his engineer cap still mounted perkily on his head. Hallorann got going again, the chains flailing at the snowcover on the road, finally digging in enough to start the Buick moving. Behind him, Howard Cottrell gave a final good-luck blast on his plow's airhorn, although it was really unnecessary; Hallorann could feel him wishing him good luck.

That's two shines in one day, he thought, and that ought to be some kind of good omen. But he distrusted omens, good or bad. And meeting two people with the shine in one day (when he usually didn't run across more than four or five in the course of a year) might not mean anything. That feeling of finality, a feeling

(*like things are all wrapped up*)
he could not completely define was still very much with him. It was—

The Buick wanted to skid sideways around a tight curve and Hallorann jockeyed it carefully, hardly daring to breathe. He turned on the radio again and it was Aretha, and Aretha was just fine. He'd share his Hertz Buick with her any day.

Another gust of wind struck the car, making it rock and slip around. Hallorann cursed it and hunched more closely over the wheel. Aretha finished her song and then the jock was on again, telling him that driving today was a good way to get killed.

Hallorann snapped the radio off.

He did make it to Sidewinder, although he was four and a half hours on the road between Estes Park and there. By the time he got to the Upland Highway it was full dark, but the snowstorm showed no sign of abating. Twice he'd had to stop in front of drifts that were as high as his car's hood and wait for the plows to come along and knock holes in them. At one of the drifts the plow had come up on his side of the road and there had been another close call. The driver had merely swung around his car, not getting out to chew the fat, but he did deliver one of the two finger gestures that all Americans above the age of ten recognize, and it was not the peace sign.

It seemed that as he drew closer to the Overlook, his need to hurry became more and more compulsive. He found himself glancing at his wristwatch almost constantly. The hands seemed to be flying along.

Ten minutes after he had turned onto the Upland, he passed two signs. The whooping wind had cleared both of their snow pack so he was able to read them. SIDEWINDER 10, the first said. The second: ROAD CLOSED 12 MILES AHEAD DURING WINTER MONTHS.

'Larry Durkin,' Hallorann muttered to himself. His dark face was strained and tense in the muted green glow of the dashboard instruments. It was ten after six. 'The Conoco by the library. Larry—'

And that was when it struck him full-force, the smell of oranges and the thought-force, heavy and hateful, murderous:

(*GET OUT OF HERE YOU DIRTY NIGGER THIS IS NONE OF YOUR BUSINESS YOU NIGGER TURN AROUND TURN AROUND OR WE'LL KILL YOU HANG YOU UP FROM A TREE LIMB YOU FUCKING JUNGLE-BUNNY COON AND THEN BURN THE BODY THAT'S WHAT WE DO WITH NIGGERS SO TURN AROUND NOW*)

Hallorann screamed in the close confines of the car. The message did not come to him in words but in a series of rebuslike images that were slammed into his head with terrific force. He took his hands from the steering wheel to blot the pictures out.

Then the car smashed broadside into one of the embankments, rebounded, slewed halfway around, and came to a stop. The rear wheels spun uselessly.

Hallorann snapped the gearshift into park, and then covered his face with his hands. He did not precisely cry; what escaped him was an uneven huh-huh-huh sound. His chest heaved. He knew that if that blast had taken him on a stretch of road with a dropoff on one side or the other, he might well be dead now. Maybe that had been the idea. And it might hit him again, at any time. He would have to protect against it. He was surrounded by a red force of immense power that might have been memory. He was drowning in instinct.

He took his hands away from his face and opened his eyes cautiously. Nothing. If there was something trying to scare him again, it wasn't getting through. He was closed off.

Had that happened to the boy? Dear God, had that happened to the little boy?

And of all the images, the one that bothered him the most was that dull whacking sound, like a hammer splatting into thick cheese. What did that mean?

(*Jesus, not that little boy. Jesus, please.*)

He dropped the gearshift lever into low range and fed the engine gas a little at a time. The wheels spun, caught, spun, and caught again. The Buick began to move, its headlights cutting weakly through the swirling snow. He looked at his watch. Almost six-thirty now. And he was beginning to feel that was very late indeed.

Chapter Fifty

Redrum

Wendy Torrance stood indecisive in the middle of the bedroom, looking at her son, who had fallen fast asleep.

Half an hour ago the sounds had ceased. All of them, all at once. The elevator, the party, the sound of room doors opening and closing. Instead of easing her mind it made the tension that had been building in her even worse; it was like a malefic hush before the storm's final brutal push. But Danny had dozed off almost at once; first into a light, twitching doze, and in the last ten minutes or so a heavier sleep. Even looking directly at him she could barely see the slow rise and fall of his narrow chest.

She wondered when he had last gotten a full night's sleep, one without tormenting dreams or long periods of dark wakefulness, listening to revels that had only become audible – and visible – to her in the last couple of days, as the Overlook's grip on the three of them tightened.

(*Real psychic phenomena or group hypnosis?*)

She didn't know, and didn't think it mattered. What had been happening was just as deadly either way. She looked at Danny and thought

(*God grant he lie still*)

that if he was undisturbed, he might sleep the rest of the night through. Whatever talent he had, he was still a small boy and he needed his rest.

It was Jack she had begun to worry about.

She grimaced with sudden pain, took her hand away from her mouth, and saw she had torn off one of her fingernails. And her nails were one thing she'd always tried to keep nice. They weren't long enough to be called hooks, but still nicely shaped and

(*and what are you worrying about your fingernails for?*)

She laughed a little, but it was a shaky sound, without amusement.

First Jack had stopped howling and battering at the door. Then the party had begun again

(*or did it ever stop? did it sometimes just drift into a slightly different angle of time where they weren't meant to hear it?*)

counterpointed by the crashing, banging elevator. Then that had stopped. In that new silence, as Danny had been falling asleep, she had fancied she heard low, conspiratorial voices coming from the kitchen almost directly below them. At first she had dismissed it as the wind, which could mimic many different human vocal ranges, from a papery deathbed whisper around the doors and window frames to a full-out scream around the eaves . . . the sound of a woman fleeing a murderer in a cheap melodrama. Yet, sitting stiffly beside Danny, the idea that it was indeed voices became more and more convincing.

Jack and someone else, discussing his escape from the pantry.

Discussing the murder of his wife and son.

It would be nothing new inside these walls; murder had been done here before.

She had gone to the heating vent and had placed her ear against it, but at that exact moment the furnace had come on, and any sound was lost in the rush of warm air coming up from the basement. When the furnace had kicked off again, five minutes ago, the place was completely silent except for the wind, the gritty spatter of snow against the building, and the occasional groan of a board.

She looked down at her ripped fingernail. Small beads of blood were oozing up from beneath it.

(*Jack's gotten out.*)

(*Don't talk nonsense.*)

(*Yes, he's out. He's gotten a knife from the kitchen or maybe the meat cleaver. He's on his way up here right now, walking along the sides of the risers so the stairs won't creak.*)

(*! You're insane !*)

Her lips were trembling, and for a moment it seemed that she must have cried the words out loud. But the silence held.

She felt watched.

She whirled around and stared at the night-blackened window, and a hideous white face with circles of darkness for eyes was gibbering in at her, the face of a monstrous lunatic that had been hiding in these groaning walls all along—

It was only a pattern of frost on the outside of the glass.

She let her breath out in a long, susurrating whisper of fear, and it seemed to her that she heard, quite clearly this time, amused titters from somewhere.

(*You're jumping at shadows. It's bad enough without that. By tomorrow morning, you'll be ready for the rubber room.*)

There was only one way to allay those fears and she knew what it was.

She would have to go down and make sure Jack was still in the pantry.

Very simple. Go downstairs Have a peek. Come back up. Oh, by the way, stop and grab the tray on the registration counter. The omelet would be a washout, but the soup could be reheated on the hotplate by Jack's typewriter.

(*Oh yes and don't get killed if he's down there with a knife.*)

She walked to the dresser, trying to shake off the mantle of fear that lay on her. Scattered across the dresser's top was a pile of change, a stack of gasoline chits for the hotel truck, the two pipes Jack brought with him everywhere but rarely smoked . . . and his key ring.

She picked it up, held it in her hand for a moment, and then put it back down. The idea of locking the bedroom door behind her had occurred, but it just didn't appeal. Danny was asleep. Vague thoughts of fire passed through her mind, and something else nibbled more strongly, but she let it go.

Wendy crossed the room, stood indecisively by the door for a moment, then took the knife from the pocket of her robe and curled her right hand around the wooden haft.

She pulled the door open.

The short corridor leading to their quarters was bare. The electric wall flambeaux all shone brightly at their regular intervals, showing off the rug's blue background and sinuous, weaving pattern.

(*See? No boogies here.*)

(*No, of course not. They want you out. They want you to do something silly and womanish, and that is exactly what you are doing.*)

She hesitated again, miserably caught, not wanting to leave Danny and the safety of the apartment and at the same time needing badly to reassure herself that Jack *was* still . . . safely packed away.

(*Of course he is.*)

(*But the voices*)

(*There were no voices. It was your imagination. It was the wind.*)

'It wasn't the wind.'

The sound of her own voice made her jump. But the deadly certainty in it made her go forward. The knife swung by her side, catching angles of light and throwing them on the silk wallpaper. Her slippers whispered against the carpet's nap. Her nerves were singing like wires.

She reached the corner of the main corridor and peered around, her mind stiffened for whatever she might see there.

There was nothing to see.

After a moment's hesitation she rounded the corner and began down the main corridor. Each step toward the shadowy stairwell increased her dread and made her aware that she was leaving her sleeping son behind, alone and unprotected. The sound of her slippers against the carpet seemed louder and louder in her ears; twice she looked back over her shoulder to convince herself that someone wasn't creeping up behind her.

She reached the stairwell and put her hand on the cold newel post at the top of the railing. There were nineteen wide steps down to the lobby. She had counted them enough times to know. Nineteen carpeted stair risers, and nary a Jack crouching on any one of them. Of course not. Jack was locked in the pantry behind a hefty steel bolt and a thick wooden door.

But the lobby was dark and oh so full of shadows.

Her pulse thudded steadily and deeply in her throat.

Ahead and slightly to the left, the brass yaw of the elevator stood mockingly open, inviting her to step in and take the ride of her life.

(*No thank you*)

The inside of the car had been draped with pink and white crepe streamers. Confetti had burst from two tubular party favors. Lying in the rear left corner was an empty bottle of champagne.

She sensed movement above her and wheeled to look up the nineteen steps leading to the dark second-floor landing and saw nothing; yet there was a disturbing corner-of-the-eye sensation that things

(*things*)

had leaped back into the deeper darkness of the hallway up there just before her eyes could register them.

She looked down the stairs again.

Her right hand was sweating against the wooden handle of the knife; she switched it to her left, wiped her right palm against the pink terrycloth of her robe, and switched the knife back. Almost unaware that her mind had given her body the command to go forward, she began down the stairs, left foot then right, left foot then right, her free hand trailing lightly on the banister.

(*Where's the party? Don't let me scare you away, you bunch of moldy sheets! Not one scared woman with a knife! Let's have a little music around here! Let's have a little life!*)

Ten steps down, a dozen, a baker's dozen.

The light from the first-floor hall filtered a dull yellow down here, and she remembered that she would have to turn on the lobby lights either beside the entrance to the dining room or inside the manager's office.

Yet there was light coming from somewhere else, white and muted.

The fluorescents, of course. In the kitchen.

She paused on the thirteenth step, trying to remember if she had turned them off or left them on when she and Danny left. She simply couldn't remember.

Below her, in the lobby, highbacked chairs hulked in pools of shadow. The glass is in the lobby doors was pressed white with a uniform blanket of drifted snow. Brass studs in the sofa cushions gleamed faintly like cat's eyes. There were a hundred places to hide.

Her legs stilted with fear, she continued down.

Now seventeen, now eighteen, now nineteen.

(*Lobby level, madam. Step out carefully.*)

The ballroom doors were thrown wide, only blackness spilling out. From within came a steady ticking, like a bomb. She stiffened, then remembered the clock on the mantel, the clock under glass. Jack or Danny must have wound it . . . or maybe it had wound itself up, like everything else in the Overlook.

She turned toward the reception desk, meaning to go through the gate and the manager's office and into the kitchen. Gleaming dull silver, she could see the intended lunch tray.

Then the clock began to strike, little tinkling notes.

Wendy stiffened, her tongue rising to the roof of her mouth. Then she relaxed. It was striking eight, that was all. Eight o'clock

. . . *five, six, seven*

She counted the strokes. It suddenly seemed wrong to move again until the clock had stilled.

. . . eight . . . nine . . .

(?? Nine ??)

. . . ten . . . eleven . . .

Suddenly, belatedly, it came to her. She turned back clumsily for the stairs, knowing already she was too late. But how could she have known?

Twelve.

All the lights in the ballroom went on. There was a huge, shrieking flourish of brass. Wendy screamed aloud, the sound of her cry insignificant against the blare issuing from those brazen lungs.

'Unmask!' the cry echoed. *'Unmask! Unmask!'*

Then they faded, as if down a long corridor of time, leaving her alone again.

No, not alone.

She turned and he was coming for her.

It was Jack and yet not Jack. His eyes were lit with a vacant, murderous glow; his familiar mouth now wore a quivering, joyless grin.

He had the roque mallet in one hand.

'Thought you'd lock me in? Is that what you thought you'd do?'

The mallet whistled through the air. She stepped backward, tripped over a hassock, fell to the lobby rug.

'Jack—'

'You bitch,' he whispered. 'I know what you are.'

The mallet came down again with whistling, deadly velocity and buried itself in her soft stomach. She screamed, suddenly submerged in an ocean of pain. Dimly she saw the mallet rebound. It came to her with sudden numbing reality that he meant to beat her to death with the mallet he held in his hands.

She tried to cry out to him again, to beg him to stop for Danny's sake, but her breath had been knocked loose. She could only force out a weak whimper, hardly a sound at all.

'Now. Now, by Christ,' he said, grinning. He kicked the hassock out of his way. 'I guess you'll take your medicine now.'

The mallet whickered down. Wendy rolled to her left, her robe tangling above her knees. Jack's hold on the mallet was jarred loose when it hit the floor. He had to stoop and pick it up, and while he did she ran for the stairs, the breath at last sobbing back into her. Her stomach was a bruise of throbbing pain.

'Bitch,' he said through his grin, and began to come after her. 'You stinking bitch, I guess you'll get what's coming to you. I guess you will.'

She heard the mallet whistle through the air and then agony exploded on her right side as the mallet-head took her just below the line of her breasts, breaking two ribs. She fell forward on the steps and new agony ripped her as she struck on the wounded side. Yet instinct made her roll over, roll away, and the mallet whizzed past the side of her face, missing by a naked inch. It struck the deep pile of the stair carpeting with a muffled thud. That was when she saw the knife, which had been jarred out of her hand by her fall. It lay glittering on the fourth stair riser.

'Bitch,' he repeated. The mallet came down. She shoved herself upward and it landed just below her kneecap. Her lower leg was suddenly on fire. Blood began to trickle down her calf. And then the mallet was coming down again. She jerked her head away from it and it smashed into the stair riser in the hollow between her neck and shoulder, scraping away the flesh from her ear.

He brought the mallet down again and this time she rolled toward him, down the stairs, inside the arc of his swing. A shriek escaped her as her broken ribs thumped and grated. She struck his shins with her body while he was offbalance and he fell backward with a yell of anger and surprise, his feet jigging to keep their purchase on the stair riser. Then he thumped to the floor, the mallet flying from his hand. He sat up, staring at her for a moment with shocked eyes.

'I'll kill you for that,' he said.

He rolled over and stretched out for the handle of the mallet. Wendy forced herself to her feet. Her left leg sent bolt after bolt of pain all the way up to her hip. Her face was ashy pale but set. She leaped onto his back as his hand closed over the shaft of the roque mallet.

'Oh dear God!' she screamed to the Overlook's shadowy lobby, and buried the kitchen knife in his lower back up to the handle.

He stiffened beneath her and then shrieked. She thought she had never heard such an awful sound in her whole life; it was as if the very boards and windows and doors of the hotel had screamed. It seemed to go on and on while he remained board-stiff beneath her weight. They were like a parlor charade of horse and rider. Except that the back of his red-and-black-checked flannel shirt was growing darker, sodden, with spreading blood.

Then he collapsed forward on his face, bucking her off on her hurt side, making her groan.

She lay breathing harshly for a time, unable to move. She was an excruciating throb of pain from one end to the other. Every time she inhaled, something stabbed viciously at her, and her neck was wet with blood from her grazed ear.

There was only the sound of her struggle to breathe, the wind, and the ticking clock in the ballroom.

At last she forced herself to her feet and hobbled across to the stairway. When she got there she clung to the newel post, head down, waves of faintness washing over her. When it had passed a little, she began to climb, using her unhurt leg and pulling with her arms on the banister. Once she looked up, expecting to see Danny there, but the stairway was empty.

(*Thank God he slept through it thank God thank God*)

Six steps up she had to rest, her head down, her blond hair coiled on and over the banister. Air whistled painfully through her throat, as if it had grown barbs. Her right side was a swollen, hot mass.

(*Come on Wendy come on old girl get a locked door behind you and then look at the damage thirteen more to go not so bad. And you get to the upstairs corridor you can crawl. I give my permission.*)

She drew in as much breath as her broken ribs would allow and half-pulled, half-fell up another riser. And another.

She was on the ninth, almost halfway up, when Jack's voice came from behind and below her. He said thickly: 'You bitch. You killed me.'

Terror as black as midnight swept through her. She looked over her shoulder and saw Jack getting slowly to his feet.

His back was bowed over, and she could see the handle of the kitchen knife sticking out of it. His eyes seemed to have contracted, almost to have lost themselves in the pale, sagging folds of the skin around them. He was grasping the roque mallet loosely in his left hand. The end of it was bloody. A scrap of her pink terrycloth robe stuck almost in the center.

'I'll give you your medicine,' he whispered, and began to stagger toward the stairs.

Whimpering with fear, she began to pull herself upward again. Ten steps, a dozen, a baker's dozen. But still the first-floor hallway looked as far above her as an unattainable mountain peak. She was panting now, her side shrieking in protest. Her hair swung wildly back and forth in front of her face. Sweat stung her eyes. The ticking of the domed clock in the ballroom seemed to fill her ears, and counterpointing it, Jack's panting, agonized gasps as he began to mount the stairs.

Chapter Fifty-one

Hallorann Arrives

Larry Durkin was a tall and skinny man with a morose face overtopped with a luxuriant mane of red hair. Hallorann had caught him just as he was leaving the Conoco station, the morose face buried deeply inside an army-issue parka. He was reluctant to do any more business that stormy day no matter how far Hallorann had come, and even more reluctant to rent one of his two snowmobiles out to this wild-eyed black man who insisted on going up to the old Overlook. Among people who had spent most of their lives in the little town of Sidewinder, the hotel had a smelly reputation. Murder had been done up there. A bunch of hoods had run the place for a while, and cutthroat businessmen had run it for a while, too. And things had been done up at the old Overlook that never made the papers, because money has a way of talking. But the people in Sidewinder had a pretty good idea. Most of the hotel's chambermaids came from here, and chambermaids see a lot.

But when Hallorann mentioned Howard Cottrell's name and showed Durkin the tag inside one of the blue mittens, the gas station owner thawed.

'Sent you here, did he?' Durkin asked, unlocking one of the garage bays and leading Hallorann inside. 'Good to know the old rip's got some sense left. I thought he was plumb out of it.' He flicked a switch and a bank of very old and very dirty fluorescents buzzed wearily into life. 'Now what in the tarnal creation would you want up at that place, fella?'

Hallorann's nerve had begun to crack. The last few miles into Sidewinder had been very bad. Once a gust of wind that must have been tooling along at better than sixty miles an hour had floated the Buick all the way around in a 360° turn. And there were still miles to travel with God alone knew what at the other end of them. He was terrified for the boy. Now it was almost ten minutes to seven and he had this whole song and dance to go through again.

'Somebody is in trouble up there,' he said very carefully. 'The son of the caretaker.'

'Who? Torrance's boy? Now what kind of trouble could he be in?'

'I don't know,' Hallorann muttered. He felt sick with the time this was taking. He was speaking with a country man, and he knew that all country men feel a similar need to approach their business obliquely, to smell around its corners and sides before plunging into the middle of dealing. But there was no time, because now he was one scared nigger and if this went on much longer he just might decide to cut and run.

'Look,' he said. 'Please. I need to go up there and I have to have a snowmobile to get there. I'll pay your price, but for God's sake let me get on with my business!'

'All right,' Durkin said, unperturbed. 'If Howard sent you, that's good enough. You take this ArcticCat. I'll put five gallons of gas in the can. Tank's full. She'll get you up and back down, I guess.'

'Thank you,' Hallorann said, not quite steadily.

'I'll take twenty dollars. That includes the ethyl.'

Hallorann fumbled a twenty out of his wallet and handed it over. Durkin tucked it into one of his shirt pockets with hardly a look.

'Guess maybe we better trade jackets, too,' Durkin said, pulling off his parka. 'That overcoat of yours ain't gonna be worth nothin tonight. You trade me back when you return the snowsled.'

'Oh, hey, I couldn't—'

'Don't fuss with me,' Durkin interrupted, still mildly. 'I ain't sending you out to freeze. I only got to walk down two blocks and I'm at my own supper table. Give it over.'

Slightly dazed, Hallorann traded his overcoat for Durkin's fur-lined parka. Overhead the fluorescents buzzed faintly, reminding him of the lights in the Overlook's kitchen.

'Torrance's boy,' Durkin said, and shook his head. 'Good-lookin little tyke, ain't he? He n his dad was in here a lot before the snow really flew. Drivin the hotel truck, mostly. Looked to me like the two of em was just about as tight as they could get. That's one little boy that loves his daddy. Hope he's all right.'

'So do I.' Hallorann zipped the parka and tied the hood.

'Lemme help you push that out,' Durkin said. They rolled the snowmobile across the oil-stained concrete and toward the garage bay. 'You ever drove one of these before?'

'No.'

'Well, there's nothing to it. The instructions are pasted there on the dashboard, but all there really is, is stop and go. Your throttle's here, just like a motorcycle throttle. Brake on the other side. Lean with it on the turns. This baby will do seventy on hardpack, but on this powder you'll get no more than fifty and that's pushing it.'

Now they were in the service station's snow-filled front lot, and Durkin had raised his voice to make himself heard over the battering of the wind.

'Stay on the road!' he shouted at Hallorann's ear. 'Keep your eye on the guardrail posts and the signs and you'll be all right, I guess. If you get off the road, you're going to be dead. Understand?'

Hallorann nodded.

'Wait a minute!' Durkin told him, and ran back into the garage bay.

While he was gone, Hallorann turned the key in the ignition and pumped the throttle a little. The snowmobile coughed into brash, choppy life.

Durkin came back with a red and black ski mask.

'Put this on under your hood!' he shouted.

Hallorann dragged it on. It was a tight fit, but it cut the last of the numbing wind off from his cheeks and forehead and chin.

Durkin leaned close to make himself heard.

'I guess you must know about things the same way Howle does sometimes,' he said. 'It don't matter, except that place has got a bad reputation around here. I'll give you a rifle if you want it.'

'I don't think it would do any good,' Hallorann shouted back.

'You're the boss. But if you get that boy, you bring him to Sixteen Peach Lane. The wife'll have some soup on.'

'Okay. Thanks for everything.'

'You watch out!' Durkin yelled. 'Stay on the road!'

Hallorann nodded and twisted the throttle slowly. The snowmobile purred forward, the headlamp cutting a clean cone of light through the thickly falling snow. He saw Durkin's upraised hand in the rearview mirror, and raised his own in return. The he nudged the handlebars to the left and was traveling up Main Street, the snowmobile coursing smoothly through the white light thrown by the streetlamps. The speedometer stood at thirty miles an hour. It was ten past seven. At the Overlook, Wendy and Danny were sleeping and Jack Torrance was discussing matters of life and death with the previous caretaker.

Five blocks up Main, the streetlamps ended. For half a mile there were small houses, all buttoned tightly up against the storm, and then only wind-howling darkness. In the black again with no light but the thin spear of the snowmobile's headlamp, terror closed in on him again, a childlike fear, dismal and disheartening. He had never felt so alone. For several minutes, as the few lights of Sidewinder dwindled away and disappeared in the rearview, the urge to turn around and go back was almost insurmountable. He reflected that for all of Durkin's concern for Jack Torrance's boy, he had not offered to take the other snowmobile and come with him.

(*That place has got a bad reputation around here.*)

Clenching his teeth, he turned the throttle higher and watched the needle on the speedometer climb past forty and settle at forty-five. He seemed to be going horribly fast and yet he was afraid it wasn't fast enough. At this speed it would take him almost an hour to get to the Overlook. But at a higher speed he might not get there at all.

He kept his eyes glued to the passing guardrails and the dime-sized reflectors mounted on top of each one. Many of them were buried under drifts. Twice he saw curve signs dangerously late and felt the snowmobile riding up the drifts that masked the dropoff before turning back onto where the road was in the summertime. The odometer counted off the miles at a maddeningly slow clip – five, ten, finally fifteen. Even behind the knitted ski mask his face was beginning to stiffen up and his legs were growing numb.

(*Guess I'd give a hundred bucks for a pair of ski pants.*)

As each mile turned over, his terror grew – as if the place had a poison atmosphere that thickened as you neared it. Had it ever been like this before? He had never really liked the Overlook, and there had been others who shared his feeling, but it had never been like this.

He could feel the voice that had almost wrecked him outside of Sidewinder still trying to get in, to get past his defenses to the soft meat inside. If it had been strong twenty-five miles back, how much stronger would it be now? He couldn't keep it out entirely. Some of it was slipping through, flooding his brain with sinister subliminal images. More and more he got the image of a badly hurt woman in a bathroom, holding her hands up uselessly to ward off a blow, and he felt more and more that the woman must be—

(*Jesus, watch out!*)

The embankment was looming up ahead of him like a freight train. Woolgathering, he had missed a turn sign. He jerked the snowmobile's steering gear hard right and it swung around, tilting as it did so. From underneath came the harsh grating sound of the snowtread on rock. He thought the snowmobile was going to dump him, and it did totter on the knife-edge of balance before half-driving, half-skidding back down to the more or less level surface of the snow-buried road. Then the dropoff was ahead of him, the headlamp showing an abrupt end to the snowcover and darkness beyond that. He turned the snowmobile the other way, a pulse beating sickly in his throat.

(*Keep it on the road Dicky old chum.*)

He forced himself to turn the throttle up another notch. Now the speedometer needle was pegged just below fifty. The wind howled and roared. The headlamp probed the dark.

An unknown length of time later, he came around a drift-banked curve and saw a glimmering flash of light ahead. Just a glimpse, and then it was blotted out by a rising fold of land. The glimpse was so brief he was persuading himself it had been wishful thinking when another turn brought it in view again, slightly closer, for another few seconds. There was no question of its reality this time; he had seen it from just this angle too many times before. It was the Overlook. There were lights on the first floor and lobby levels, it looked like.

Some of his terror – the part that had to do with driving off the road or wrecking the snowmobile on an unseen curve – melted entirely away. The snowmobile swept surely into the first half of an S curve that he now remembered confidently foot for foot, and that was when the headlamp picked out the

(*oh dear jesus god what is it*)

in the road ahead of him. Limned in stark blacks and whites, Hallorann first thought it was some hideously huge timberwolf that had been driven down from the high country by the storm. Then, as he closed on it, he recognized it and horror closed his throat.

Not a wolf but a lion. A hedge lion.

Its features were a mask of black shadow and powdered snow, its haunches wound tight to spring. And it did spring, snow billowing around its pistoning rear legs in a silent burst of crystal glitter.

Hallorann screamed and twisted the handlebars hard right, ducking low at the same time. Scratching, ripping pain scrawled itself across his face, his neck, his shoulders. The ski mask was torn open down the back. He was hurled from the snowmobile. He hit the snow, plowed through it, rolled over.

He could feel it coming for him. In his nostrils there was a bitter smell of green leaves and holly. A huge hedge paw batted him in the small of the back and he flew ten feet through the air, splayed out like a rag doll. He saw the snowmobile, riderless, strike the embankment and rear up, its headlamp searching the sky. It fell over with a thump and stalled.

Then the hedge lion was on him. There was a crackling, rustling sound. Something raked across the front of the parka, shredding it. It might have been stiff twigs, but Hallorann knew it was claws.

'You're not there!' Hallorann screamed at the circling, snarling hedge lion. *'You're not there at all!'* He struggled to his feet and made it halfway to the snowmobile before the lion lunged, batting him across the head with a needle-tipped paw. Hallorann saw silent, exploding lights.

'Not there,' he said again, but it was a fading mutter. His knees unhinged and dropped him into the snow. He crawled for the snowmobile, the right side of his face a scarf of blood. The lion struck him again, rolling him onto his back like a turtle. It roared playfully.

Hallorann struggled to reach the snowmobile. What he needed was there. And then the lion was on him again, ripping and clawing.

Chapter Fifty-two

Wendy and Jack

Wendy risked another glance over her shoulder. Jack was on the sixth riser, clinging to the banister much as she was doing herself. He was still grinning, and dark blood oozed slowly through the grin and slipped down the line of his jaw. He bared his teeth at her.

'I'm going to bash your brains in. Bash them right to fuck in.' He struggled up another riser.

Panic spurred her, and the ache in her side diminished a little. She pulled herself up as fast as she could regardless of the pain, yanking convulsively at the banister. She reached the top and threw a glance behind her.

He seemed to be gaining strength rather than losing it. He was only four risers from the top, measuring the distance with the roque mallet in his left hand as he pulled himself up with his right.

'Right behind you,' he panted through his bloody grin, as if reading her mind. 'Right behind you now, bitch. With your medicine.'

She fled stumblingly down the main corridor, hands pressed to her side.

The door to one of the rooms jerked open and a man with a green ghoulmask on popped out. *'Great party, isn't it?'* He screamed into her face, and pulled the waxed string of a party-favor. There was an echoing bang and suddenly crepe streamers were drifting all around her. The man in the ghoulmask cackled and slammed back into his room. She fell forward onto the carpet, full-length. Her right side seemed to explode with pain, and she fought off the blackness of unconsciousness desperately. Dimly she could hear the elevator running again, and beneath her splayed fingers she could see that the carpet pattern appeared to move, swaying and twining sinuously.

The mallet slammed down behind her and she threw herself forward, sobbing. Over her shoulder she saw Jack stumble forward, overbalance, and bring the mallet down just before he crashed to the carpet, expelling a bright splash of blood onto the nap.

The mallet head struck her squarely between the shoulder blades and for a moment the agony was so great that she could only writhe, hands opening and clenching. Something inside her had snapped – she had heard it clearly, and for a few moments she was aware only in a muted, muffled way, as if she were merely observing these things through a cloudy wrapping of gauze.

Then full consciousness came back, terror and pain with it.

Jack was trying to get up so he could finish the job.

Wendy tried to stand and found it was impossible. Electric bolts seemed to course up and down her back at the effort. She began to crawl along in a sidestroke motion. Jack was crawling after her, using the roque mallet as a crutch or a cane.

She reached the corner and pulled herself around it, using her hands to yank at the angle of the wall. Her terror deepened – she would not have believed that possible, but it was. It was a hundred times worse not to be able to see him or know how close he was getting. She tore out fistfuls of the carpet napping pulling herself along, and she was halfway down this short hall before she noticed the bedroom door was standing wide open.

(*Danny! O Jesus*)

She forced herself to her knees and then clawed her way to her feet, fingers slipping over the silk wallpaper. Her nails pulled little strips of it loose. She ignored the pain and half-walked, half-shambled through the doorway as Jack came around the open door, leaning on the roque mallet.

She caught the edge of the dresser, held herself up against it, and grabbed the doorframe.

Jack shouted at her: 'Don't you shut that door! Goddam you, don't you *dare* shut it!'

She slammed it closed and shot the bolt. Her left hand pawed wildly at the junk on the dresser, knocking loose coins onto the floor where they rolled in every direction. Her hand seized the key ring just as the mallet whistled down against the door, making it tremble in its frame. She got the key into the lock on the second stab and twisted it to the right. At the sound of the tumblers falling, Jack screamed. The mallet came down against the door in a volley of booming blows that made her flinch and step back. How could he be doing that with a knife in his back? Where was he finding the strength? She wanted to shriek *Why aren't you dead?* at the locked door.

Instead she turned around. She and Danny would have to go into the attached bathroom and lock that door, too, in case Jack actually could break through the bedroom door. The thought of escaping down the dumb-waiter shaft crossed her mind in a wild burst, and then she rejected it. Danny was small enough to fit into it, but she would be unable to control the rope pull. He might go crashing all the way to the bottom.

The bathroom it would have to be. And if Jack broke through into there—

But she wouldn't allow herself to think of it.

'Danny, honey, you'll have to wake up n—'

But the bed was empty.

When he had begun to sleep more soundly, she had thrown the blankets and one of the quilts over him. Now they were thrown back.

'I'll get you!' Jack howled. 'I'll get both of you!' Every other word was punctuated with a blow from the roque hammer, yet Wendy ignored both. All of her attention was focused on that empty bed.

'Come out here! Unlock this goddam door!'

'Danny?' she whispered.

Of course . . . when Jack had attacked her. It had come through to him, as violent emotions always seemed to. Perhaps he'd even seen the whole thing in a nightmare. He was hiding.

She fell clumsily to her knees, enduring another bolt of pain from her swollen and bleeding leg, and looked under the bed. Nothing there but dustballs and Jack's bedroom slippers.

Jack screamed her name, and this time when he swung the mallet, a long splinter of wood jumped from the door and clattered off the hardwood planking. The next blow brought a sickening, splintering crack, the sound of dry kindling under a hatchet. The bloody mallet head, now splintered and gouged in its own right, bashed through the new hole in the door, was withdrawn, and came down again, sending wooden shrapnel flying across the room.

Wendy pulled herself to her feet again using the foot of the bed, and hobbled across the room to the closet. Her broken ribs stabbed at her, making her groan.

'Danny?'

She brushed the hung garments aside frantically; some of them slipped their hangers and ballooned gracelessly to the floor. He was not in the closet.

She hobbled toward the bathroom and as she reached the door she glanced back over her shoulder. The mallet crashed through again, widening the hole, and then a hand appeared, groping for the bolt. She saw with horror that she had left Jack's key ring dangling from the lock.

The hand yanked the bolt back, and as it did so it struck the bunched keys. They jingled merrily. The hand clutched them victoriously.

With a sob, she pushed her way into the bathroom and slammed the door just as the bedroom door burst open and Jack charged through, bellowing.

Wendy ran the bolt and twisted the spring lock, looking around desperately. The bathroom was empty. Danny wasn't here, either. And as she caught sight of her own blood-smeared, horrified face in the medicine cabinet mirror, she was glad. She had never believed that children should be witness to the little quarrels of their parents. And perhaps the thing that was now raving through the bedroom, overturning things and smashing them, would finally collapse before it could go after her son. Perhaps, she thought, it might be possible for her to inflict even more damage on it . . . kill it, perhaps.

Her eyes skated quickly over the bathroom's machine-produced porcelain surfaces, looking for anything that might serve as a weapon. There was a bar of soap, but even wrapped in a towel she didn't think it would be lethal enough. Everything else was bolted down. God, was there nothing she could do?

Beyond the door, the animal sounds of destruction went on and on, accompanied by thick shouts that they would 'take their medicine' and 'pay for that they'd done to him.' He would 'show them who's boss.' They were 'worthless puppies,' the both of them.

There was a thump as her record player was overturned, a hollow crash as the secondhand TV's picture tube was smashed, the tinkle of windowglass followed by a cold draft under the bathroom door. A dull thud as the mattresses were ripped from the twin beds where they had slept together, hip to hip. Boomings as Jack struck the walls indiscriminately with the mallet.

There was nothing of the real Jack in that howling, maundering, petulant voice, though. It alternately whined in tones of selfpity and rose in lurid screams; it reminded her chillingly of the screams that sometimes rose in the geriatrics ward of the hospital where she had worked summers as a high school kid. Senile dementia. Jack wasn't out there anymore. She was hearing the lunatic, raving voice of the Overlook itself.

The mallet smashed into the bathroom door, knocking out a huge chunk of the thin paneling. Half of a crazed and working face stared in at her. The mouth and cheeks and throat were lathered in blood, the single eye she could see was tiny and piggish and glittering.

'Nowhere left to run, you cunt,' it panted at her through its grin. The mallet descended again, knocking wood splinters into the tub and against the reflecting surface of the medicine cabinet—

(*!! The medicine cabinet !!*)

A desperate whining noise began to escape her as she whirled, pain temporarily forgotten, and threw the mirror door of the cabinet back. She began to paw through its contents. Behind her that hoarse voice bellowed: 'Here I come now! Here I come now, you pig!' It was demolishing the door in a machinelike frenzy.

Bottles and jars fell before her madly searching fingers—cough syrup, Vaseline, Clairol Herbal Essence shampoo, hydrogen peroxide, benzocaine – they fell into the sink and shattered.

Her hand closed over the dispenser of double-edged razor blades just as she heard the hand again, fumbling for the bolt and the spring lock.

She slipped one of the razor blades out, fumbling at it, her breath coming in harsh little gasps. She had cut the ball of her thumb. She whirled around and slashed at the hand, which had turned the lock and was now fumbling for the bolt.

Jack screamed. The hand was jerked back.

Panting, holding the razor blade between her thumb and index finger, she waited for him to try again. He did, and she slashed. He screamed again, trying to grab her hand, and she slashed at him again. The razor blade turned in her hand, cutting her again, and dropped to the tile floor by the toilet.

Wendy slipped another blade out of the dispenser and waited.

Movement in the other room—

(*?? going away ??*)

And a sound coming through the bedroom window. A motor. A high, insectile buzzing sound.

A roar of anger from Jack and then – yes, yes, she was sure of it – he was leaving the caretaker's apartment, plowing through the wreckage and out into the hall.

(*?? Someone coming a ranger Dick Hallorann ??*)

'Oh God,' she muttered brokenly through a mouth that seemed filled with broken sticks and old sawdust. 'Oh God, oh please.'

She had to leave now, had to go find her son so they could face the rest of this nightmare side by side. She reached out and fumbled at the bolt. Her arm seemed to stretch for miles. At last she got it to come free. She pushed the door open, staggered out, and was suddenly overcome by the horrible certainty that Jack had only pretended to leave, that he was lying in wait for her.

Wendy looked around. The room was empty, the living room too. Jumbled, broken stuff everywhere.

The closet? Empty.

The the soft shades of gray began to wash over her and she fell down on the mattress Jack had ripped from the bed, semiconscious.

Chapter Fifty-three

Hallorann Laid Low

Hallorann reached the overturned snowmobile just as, a mile and a half away, Wendy was pulling herself around the corner and into the short hallway leading to the caretaker's apartment.

It wasn't the snowmobile he wanted but the gascan held onto the back by a pair of elastic straps. His hands, still clad in Howard Cottrell's blue mittens, seized the top strap and pulled it free as the hedge lion roared behind him – a sound that seemed to be more in his head than outside of it. A hard, brambly slap to his left leg, making the knee sing with pain as it was driven in a way the joint had never been expected to bend. A groan escaped Hallorann's clenched teeth. It would come for the kill any time now, tired of playing with him.

He fumbled for the second strap. Sticky blood ran in his eyes.

(*Roar! Slap!*)

That one raked across his buttocks, almost tumbling him over and away from the snowmobile again. He held on – no exaggeration – for dear life.

Then he had freed the second strap. He clutched the gascan to him as the lion struck again, rolling him over on his back. He saw it again, only a shadow in the darkness and falling snow, as nightmarish as a moving gargoyle. Hallorann twisted at the can's cap as the moving shadow stalked him, kicking up snowpuffs. As it moved in again the cap spun free, releasing the pungent smell of the gasoline.

Hallorann gained his knees and as it came at him, low-slung and incredibly quick, he splashed it with the gas.

There was a hissing, spitting sound and it drew back.

'Gas!' Hallorann cried, his voice shrill and breaking. 'Gonna burn you, baby! Dig on it awhile!'

The lion came at him again, still spitting angrily. Hallorann splashed it again but this time the lion didn't give. It charged ahead. Hallorann sensed rather than saw its head angling at his face and he threw himself backward, partially avoiding it. Yet the lion still hit his upper rib cage a glancing blow, and a flare of pain struck there. Gas gurgled out of the can, which he still held, and doused his right hand and arm, cold as death.

Now he lay on his back in a snow angel, to the right of the snowmobile by about ten paces. The hissing lion was a bulking presence to his left, closing in again. Hallorann thought he could see its tail twitching.

He yanked Cottrell's mitten off his right hand, tasting sodden wool and gasoline. He ripped up the hem of the parka and jammed his hand into his pants pocket. Down in there, along with his keys and his change, was a very battered old Zippo lighter. He had bought it in Germany in 1954. Once the hinge had broken and he had returned it to the Zippo factory and they had repaired it without charge, just as advertised.

A nightmare flood of thoughts flooding through his mind in a split second.

(*Dear Zippo my lighter was swallowed by a crocodile dropped from an airplane lost in the Pacific trench saved me from a Kraut bullet in the Battle of the Bulge dear Zippo if this fucker doesn't go that lion is going to rip my head off*)

The lighter was out. He clicked the hood back. The lion, rushing at him, a growl like ripping cloth, his finger flicking the striker wheel, spark, *flame*,

(*my hand*)

his gasoline-soaked hand suddenly ablaze, the flames running up the sleeve of the parka, no pain yet, the lion shying from the torch suddenly blazing in front of it, a hideous flickering hedge sculpture with eyes and a mouth, shying away, too late.

Wincing at the pain, Hallorann drove his blazing arm into its stiff and scratchy side.

In an instant the whole creature was in flames, a prancing, writhing pyre on the snow. It bellowed in rage and pain, seeming to chase its flaming tail as it zigzagged away from Hallorann.

He thrust his own arm deep into the snow, killing the flames, unable to take his eyes from the hedge lion's death agonies for a moment. Then, gasping, he got to his feet. The arm of Durkin's parka was sooty but unburned, and that also described his hand. Thirty yards downhill from where he stood, the hedge lion had turned into a fireball. Sparks flew at the sky and were viciously snatched away by the wind. For a moment its ribs and skull were etched in orange flame and then it seemed to collapse, disintegrate, and fall into separate burning piles.

(*Never mind it. Get moving.*)

He picked up the gascan and struggled over to the snowmobile. His consciousness seemed to be flickering in and out, offering him cuttings and snippets of home movies but never the whole picture. In one of these he was aware of yanking the snowmobile back onto its tread and then sitting on it, out of breath and incapable of moving for a few moments. In another, he was reattaching the gascan, which was still half-full. His head was thumping horribly from the gasfumes (and in reaction to his battle with the hedge lion, he supposed), and he saw by the steaming hole in the snow beside him that he had vomited, but he was unable to remember when.

The snowmobile, the engine still warm, fired immediately. He twisted the throttle unevenly and started forward with a series of neck-snapping jerks that made his head ache even more fiercely. At first the snowmobile wove drunkenly from side to side, but by half-standing to get his face above the windscreen and into the sharp, needling blast of the wind, he drove some of the stupor out of himself. He opened the throttle wider.

(*Where are the rest of the hedge animals?*)

He didn't know, but at least he wouldn't be caught unaware again.

The Overlook loomed in front of him, the lighted first-floor windows throwing long yellow rectangles onto the snow. The gate at the foot of the drive was locked and he dismounted after a wary look around, praying he hadn't lost his keys when he pulled his lighter out of his pocket . . . no, they were there. He picked through them in the bright light thrown by the snowmobile headlamp. He found the right one and unsnapped the padlock, letting it drop into the snow. At first he didn't think he was going to be able to move the gate anyway; he pawed frantically at the snow surrounding it, disregarding the throbbing agony in his head and the fear that one of the other lions might be creeping up behind him. He managed to pull it a foot and a half away from the gatepost, squeezed into the gap, and pushed. He got it to move another two feet, enough room for the snowmobile, and threaded it through.

He became aware of movement ahead of him in the dark. The hedge animals, all of them, were clustered at the base of the Overlook's steps, guarding the way in, the way out. The lions prowled. The dog stood with its front paws on the first step.

Hallorann opened the throttle wide and the snowmobile leaped forward, puffing snow up behind it. In the caretaker's apartment, Jack Torrance's head jerked around at the high, wasplike buzz of the approaching engine, and suddenly began to move laboriously toward the hallway again. The bitch wasn't important now. The bitch could wait. Now it was this dirty nigger's turn. This dirty, interfering nigger with his nose in where it didn't belong. First him and then his son. He would show them. He would show them that . . . that he . . . that he was of *managerial timber!*

Outside, the snowmobile rocketed along faster and faster. The hotel seemed to surge toward it. Snow flew in Hallorann's face. The headlamp's oncoming glare spotlighted the hedge shepherd's face, its blank and socketless eyes.

Then it shrank away, leaving an opening. Hallorann yanked at the snowmobile's steering gear with all his remaining strength, and it kicked around in a sharp semicircle, throwing up clouds of snow, threatening to tip over. The rear end struck the foot of the porch steps and rebounded. Hallorann was off in a flash and running up the steps. He stumbled, fell, picked himself up. The dog was growling – again in his head – close behind him. Something ripped at the shoulder of the parka and then he was on the porch, standing in the narrow corridor Jack had shoveled through the snow, and safe. They were too big to fit in here.

He reached the big double doors which gave on the lobby and dug for his keys again. While he was getting them he tried the knob and it turned freely. He pushed his way in.

'Danny!' he cried hoarsely. *'Danny, where are you?'*

Silence came back.

His eyes traveled across the lobby to the foot of the wide stairs and a harsh gasp escaped him. The rug was splashed and matted with blood. There was a scrap of pink terrycloth robe. The trail of blood led up the stairs. The banister was also splashed with it.

'Oh Jesus,' he muttered, and raised his voice again. *'Danny! DANNY!'*

The hotel's silence seemed to mock him with echoes which were almost there, sly and oblique.

(*Danny? Who's Danny? Anybody here know a Danny? Danny, Danny, who's got the Danny? Anybody for a game of spin the Danny? Pin the tail on the Danny? Get of here, black boy. No one here knows Danny from Adam.*)

Jesus, had he come through everything just to be too late? Had it been done?

He ran up the stairs two at a time and stood at the top of the first floor. The blood led down toward the caretaker's apartment. Horror crept softly into his veins and into his brain as he began to walk toward the short hall. The hedge animals had been bad, but this was worse. In his heart he was already sure of what he was going to find when he got down there.

He was in no hurry to see it.

Jack had been hiding in the elevator when Hallorann came up the stairs. Now he crept up behind the figure in the snow-coated parka, a blood- and gore-streaked phantom with a smile upon its face. The roque mallet was lifted as high as the ugly, ripping pain in his back

(*?? did the bitch stick me can't remember ??*)

would allow.

'Black boy,' he whispered. 'I'll teach you to go sticking your nose in other people's business.'

Hallorann heard the whisper and began to turn, to duck, and the roque mallet whistled down. The blood of the parka matted the blow, but not enough. A rocket exploded in his head, leaving a contrail of stars . . . and then nothing.

He staggered against the silk wallpaper and Jack hit him again, the roque mallet slicing sideways this time, shattering Hallorann's cheekbone and most of the teeth on the left side of his jaw. He went down limply.

'Now,' Jack whispered. 'Now, by Christ.' Where was Danny? He had business with his trespassing son.

Three minutes later the elevator door banged open on the shadowed third floor. Jack Torrance was in it alone. The car had stopped only halfway into the doorway and he had to boost himself up onto the hall floor, wriggling painfully like a crippled thing. He dragged the splintered roque mallet after him. Outside the eaves, the wind howled and roared. Jack's eyes rolled wildly in their sockets. There was blood and confetti in his hair.

His son was up here, up here somewhere. He could feel it. Left to his own devices, he might do anything: scribble on the expensive silk wallpaper with his crayons, deface the furnishings, break the windows. He was a liar and a cheat and he would have to be chastised . . . harshly.

Jack Torrance struggled to his feet.

'Danny?' he called. 'Danny, come here a minute, will you? You've done something wrong and I want you to come and take your medicine like a man. Danny? *Danny!*'

Chapter Fifty-four

Tony

(*Danny* . . .)

(*Dannneee* . . .)

Darkness and hallways. He was wandering through darkness and hallways that were like those which lay within the body of the hotel but were somehow different. The silk-papered walls stretched up and up, and even when he craned his neck, Danny could not see the ceiling. It was lost in dimness. All the doors were locked, and they also rose up to dimness. Below the peepholes (in these giant doors they were the size of gunsights), tiny skulls and crossbones had been bolted to each door instead of room numbers.

And somewhere, Tony was calling him.

(Dannneee . . .)

There was a pounding noise, one he knew well, and hoarse shouts, faint with distance. He could not make out word for word, but he knew the text well enough by now. He had heard it before, in dreams and awake.

He paused, a little boy not yet three years out of diapers, and tried to decide where he was, where he might be. There was fear, but it was a fear he could live with. He had been afraid every day for two months now, to a degree that ranged from dull disquiet to outright, mind-bending terror. This he could live with. But he wanted to know why Tony had come, why he was making the sound of his name in this hall that was neither a part of real things nor of the dreamland where Tony sometimes showed him things. Why, where—

'Danny.'

Far down the giant hallway, almost as tiny as Danny himself, was a dark figure. Tony.

'Where am I?' he called softly to Tony.

'Sleeping,' Tony said. 'Sleeping in your mommy and daddy's bedroom. There was sadness in Tony's voice.

'Danny,' Tony said. 'Your mother is going to be badly hurt. Perhaps killed. Mr Hallorann, too.'

'No!'

He cried it out in a distant grief, a terror that seemed damped by these dreamy, dreary surroundings. Nonetheless, death images came to him: dead frog plastered to the turnpike like a grisly stamp; Daddy's broken watch lying on top of a box of junk to be thrown out; gravestones with a dead person under every one; dead jay by the telephone pole; the cold junk Mommy scraped off the plates and down the dark maw of the garbage disposal.

Yet he could not equate these simple symbols with the shifting complex reality of his mother; she satisfied his childish definition of eternity. She had been when he was not. She would continue to be when he was not again. He could accept the possibility of his own death, he had dealt with that since the encounter in Room 217.

But not hers.

Not Daddy's.

Not ever.

He began to struggle, and the darkness and the hallway began to waver. Tony's form became chimerical, indistinct.

'Don't!' Tony called. 'Don't, Danny, don't do that!'

'She's not going to be dead! *She's not!*'

'Then you have to help her. Danny . . . you're in a place deep down in your own mind. The place where I am. I'm a part of you, Danny.'

'You're *Tony*. You're not me. I want my mommy . . . I want my mommy . . .'

'I didn't bring you here, Danny. You brought yourself. Because you knew.'

'No—'

'You've always known,' Tony continued, and he began to walk closer. For the first time, Tony began to walk closer. 'You're deep down in yourself in a place where nothing comes through. We're alone here for a little while, Danny. This is an Overlook where no one can ever come. No clocks work here. None of the keys fit them and they can never be wound up. The doors have never been opened and no one has ever stayed in the rooms. But you can't stay long. Because it's coming.'

'It . . .' Danny whispered fearfully, and as he did so the irregular pounding noise seemed to grow closer, louder. His terror, cool and distant a moment ago, became a more immediate thing. Now the words could be made out. Hoarse, huckstering; they were uttered in a coarse imitation of his father's voice, but it wasn't Daddy. He knew that now. He knew

(*You brought yourself. Because you knew.*)

'Oh Tony, is it my daddy?' Danny screamed. *'Is it my daddy that's coming to get me?"*

Tony didn't answer. But Danny didn't need an answer. He knew. A long and nightmarish masquerade party went on here, and had gone on for years. Little by little a force had accrued, as secret and silent as interest in a bank account. Force, presence, shape, they were all only words and none of them mattered. It wore many masks, but it was all one. Now, somewhere, it was coming for him. It was hiding behind Daddy's face, it was imitating Daddy's voice, it was wearing Daddy's clothes.

But it was not his daddy.

It was not his daddy.

'I've got to help them!' he cried.

And now Tony stood directly in front of him, and looking at Tony was like looking into a magic mirror and seeing himself in ten years, the eyes widely spaced and very dark, the chin firm, the mouth handsomely molded. The hair was light blond like his mother's, and yet the stamp on his features was that of his father, as if Tony – as if the Daniel Anthony Torrance that would someday be – was a halfling caught between father and son, a ghost of both, a fusion.

'You have to try to help,' Tony said. 'But your father . . . he's with the hotel now, Danny. It's where he wants to be. It wants you too, because it's very greedy.'

Tony walked past him, into the shadows.

'Wait!' Danny cried. 'What can I—'

'He's close now,' Tony said, still walking away. 'You'll have to run . . . hide . . . keep away from him. Keep away.'

'Tony, I can't!'

'But you've already started,' Tony said. 'You will remember what your father forgot.'

He was gone.

And from somewhere near his father's voice came, coldly wheedling: 'Danny? You can come out, doc. Just a little spanking, that's all. Take it like a man and it will be all over. We don't need her, doc. Just you and me, right? When we get this little . . . spanking . . . behind us, it will be just you and me.'

Danny ran.

Behind him, the thing's temper broke through the shambling charade of normality.

'Come here, you little shit! Right now!'

Down a long hall, panting and gasping. Around a corner. Up a flight of stairs. And as he went, the walls that had been so high and remote began to come down; the rug which had only been a blur beneath his feet took on the familiar black and blue pattern, sinuously woven together; the doors became numbered again and behind them the parties that were all one went on and on, populated by generations of guests. The air seemed to be shimmering around him, the blows of the mallet against the walls echoing and re-echoing. He seemed to be bursting through some thin placental womb from sleep to

the rug outside the Presidential Suite on the third floor; lying near him in a bloody heap were the bodies of two men dressed in suits and narrow ties. They had been taken out by shotgun blasts and now they began to stir in front of him and get up.

He drew in breath to scream but didn't.

(*!! FALSE FACES !! NOT REAL !!*)

They faded before his gaze like old photographs and were gone.

But below him, the faint sound of the mallet against the walls went on and on, drifting up through the elevator shaft and the stairwell. The controlling force of the Overlook, in the shape of his father, blundering around on the first floor.

A door opened with a thin screeing sound behind him.

A decayed woman in a rotten silk gown pranced out, her yellowed and splitting fingers dressed with verdigris-caked rings. Heavy-bodied wasps crawled sluggishly over her face.

'Come in,' she whispered to him, grinning with black lips. 'Come in and we will daance the taaaango . . .'

'False face!' he hissed. 'Not real!' She drew back from him in alarm, and in the act of drawing back she faded and was gone.

'Where are you?' it screamed, but the voice was still only in his head. He could still hear the thing that was wearing Jack's face down on the first floor . . . and something else.

The high, whining sound of an approaching motor.

Danny's breath stopped in his throat with a little gasp. Was it just another face of the hotel, another illusion? Or was it Dick? He wanted – wanted desperately – to believe it *was* Dick, but he didn't dare take the chance.

He retreated down the main corridor, and then took one of the offshoots, his feet whispering on the nap of the carpet. Locked doors frowned down at him as they had done in the dreams, the visions, only now he was in the world of real things, where the game was played for keeps.

He turned to the right and came to a halt, his heart thudding heavily in his chest. Heat was blowing around his ankles. From the registers, of course. This must have been Daddy's day to heat the west wing and

(*You will remember what your father forgot.*)

What was it? He almost knew. Something that might save him and Mommy? But Tony said he would have to do it himself. What was it?

He sank down against the wall, trying desperately to think. It was so hard . . . the hotel kept trying to get into his head . . . the image of that dark and slumped form swinging the mallet from side to side, gouging the wallpaper . . . sending out puffs of plaster dust.

'Help me,' he muttered. 'Tony, help me.'

And suddenly he became aware that the hotel had grown deathly silent. The whining sound of the motor had stopped

(must not have been real)

and the sounds of the party had stopped and there was only the wind, howling and whooping endlessly.

The elevator whirred into sudden life.

It was coming up.

And Danny knew who – *what* – was in it.

He bolted to his feet, eyes staring wildly. Panic clutched around his heart. Why had Tony sent him to the third floor? He was trapped up here. All the doors were locked.

The attic!

There was an attic, he knew. He had come up here with daddy the day he had salted the rattraps around up there. He hadn't allowed Danny to come up with him because of the rats. He was afraid Danny might be bitten. But the trapdoor which led to the attic was set into the ceiling of the last short corridor in this wing. There was a pole leaning against the wall.

Daddy had pushed the trapdoor open with the pole, there had been a ratcheting whir of counterweights as the door went up and a ladder had swung down. If he could get up there and pull the ladder after him . . .

Somewhere in the maze of corridors behind him, the elevator came to a stop. There was a metallic, rattling crash as the gate was thrown back. And then a voice – not in his head now but terribly real – called out: 'Danny? Danny, come here a minute, will you? You've done something wrong and I want you to come and take your medicine like a man. Danny? *Danny!'*

Obedience was so strongly ingrained in him that he actually took two automatic steps toward the sound of that voice before stopping. His hands curled into fists at his sides.

(*Not real! False face! I know what you are! Take off your mask!*)

'Danny!' it roared. *'Come here, you pup! Come here and take it like a man!'* A loud, hollow boom as the mallet struck the wall. When the voice roared out his name again it had changed location. It had come closer.

In the world of real things, the hunt was beginning.

Danny ran. Feet silent on the heavy carpet, he ran past the closed doors, past the silk figured wallpaper, past the fire extinguisher bolted to the corner of the wall. He hesitated, and then plunged down the final corridor. Nothing at the end but a bolted door, and nowhere left to run.

But the pole was still there, still leaning against the wall where Daddy had left it.

Danny snatched it up. He craned his neck to stare up at the trapdoor. There was a hook on the end of the pole and you had to catch it on a ring set into the trapdoor. You had to—

There was a brand-new Yale padlock dangling from the trapdoor. The lock Jack Torrance had clipped around the hasp after laying his traps, just in case his son should take the notion into his head to go exploring up there someday.

Locked. Terror swept him.

Behind him it was coming, blundering and staggering past the Presidential Suite, the mallet whistling viciously through the air.

Danny backed up against the last closed door and waited for it.

Chapter Fifty-five

That Which Was Forgotten

Wendy came to a little at a time, the grayness draining away, pain replacing it: her back, her leg, her side . . . she didn't think she would be able to move. Even her fingers hurt, and at first she didn't know why.

(*The razor blade, that's why.*)

Her blond hair, now dank and matted, hung in her eyes. She brushed it away and her ribs stabbed inside, making her groan. Now she saw a field of blue and white mattress, spotted with blood. Her blood, or maybe Jack's.

Either way it was still fresh. She hadn't been out long. And that was important because—

(*?Why?*)

Because—

It was the insectile, buzzing sound of the motor that she remembered first. For a moment she fixed stupidly on the memory, and then in a single vertiginous and nauseating swoop, her mind seemed to pan back, showing her everything at once.

Hallorann. It must have been Hallorann. Why else would Jack have left so suddenly, without finishing it . . . without finishing *her?*

Because he was no longer at leisure. He had to find Danny quickly and . . . and do it before Hallorann could put a stop to it.

Or had it happened already?

She could hear the whine of the elevator rising up the shaft.

(*No God please no the blood the blood's still fresh don't let it have happened already*)

Somehow she was able to find her feet and stagger through the bedroom and across the ruins of the living room to the shattered front door. She pushed it open and made it out into the hall.

'Danny!' she cried, wincing at the pain in her chest. 'Mr Hallorann! Is anybody there? *Anybody?*'

The elevator had been running again and now it came to a stop. She heard the metallic crash of the gate being thrown back and then thought she heard a speaking voice. It might have been her imagination. The wind was too loud to really be able to tell.

Leaning against the wall, she made her way up to the corner of the short hallway. She was about to turn the corner when the scream froze her, floating down the stairwell and the elevator shaft:

'*Danny! Come here, you pup! Come here and take it like a man!*'

Jack. On the second or third floor. Looking for Danny.

She got around the corner, stumbled, almost fell. Her breath caught in her throat. Something

(someone?)

huddled against the wall about a quarter of the way down from the stairwell. She began to hurry faster, wincing every time her weight came down on her hurt leg. It was a man, she saw, and as she drew closer, she understood the meaning of that buzzing motor.

It was Mr Hallorann. He had come after all.

She eased to her knees beside him, offering up an incoherent prayer that he was not dead. His nose was bleeding, and a terrible gout of blood had spilled out of his mouth. The side of his face was a puffed purple bruise. But he was breathing, thank God for that. It was coming in long, harsh draws that shook his whole frame.

Looking at him more closely, Wendy's eyes widened. One arm of the parka he was wearing was blackened and singed. One side of it had been ripped open. There was blood in his hair and a shallow but ugly scratch down the back of his neck.

(*My God, what's happened to him?*)

'*Danny!*' the hoarse, petulant voice roared from above them. '*Get out here, goddammit!*'

There was no time to wonder about it now. She began to shake him, her face twisting at the flare of agony in her ribs. Her side felt hot and massive and swollen.

(*What if they're poking my lung whenever I move?*)

There was no help for that, either. If Jack found Danny, he would kill him, beat him to death with that mallet as he had tried to do to her.

So she shook Hallorann, and then began to slap the unbruised side of his face lightly.

'Wake up,' she said. 'Mr Hallorann, you've got to wake up. Please . . . please . . .'

From overhead, the restless booming sounds of the mallet as Jack Torrance looked for his son.

Danny stood with his back against the door, looking at the right angle where the hallways joined. The steady, irregular booming sound of the mallet against the walls grew louder. The thing that was after him screamed and howled and cursed. Dream and reality had joined together without a seam.

It came around the corner.

In a way, what Danny felt was relief. It was not his father. The mask of face and body had been ripped and shredded and made into a bad joke. It was not his daddy, not this Saturday Night Shock Show horror with its rolling eyes and hunched and hulking shoulders and blood-drenched shirt. It was not his daddy.

'Now, by God,' it breathed. It wiped its lips with a shaking hand. 'Now you'll find out who is the boss around here. You'll see. It's not you they want. It's me. *Me. Me!*'

It slashed out with the scarred hammer, its double head now shapeless and splintered with countless impacts. It struck the wall, cutting a circle in the silk paper. Plaster dust puffed out. It began to grin.

'Let's see you pull any of your fancy tricks now,' it muttered. 'I wasn't born yesterday, you know. Didn't just fall off the hay truck, by God. I'm going to do my fatherly duty by you, boy.'

Danny said: 'You're not my daddy.'

It stopped. For a moment it actually looked uncertain, as if not sure who or what it was. Then it began to walk again. The hammer whistled out, struck a door panel and made it boom hollowly.

'You're a liar,' it said. 'Who else would I be? I have the two birthmarks, I have the cupped navel, even the *pecker*, my boy. Ask your mother.'

'You're a mask,' Danny said. 'Just a false face. The only reason the hotel needs to use you is that you aren't as dead as the others. But when it's done with you, you won't be anything at all. You don't scare me.'

'I'll scare you!' it howled. The mallet whistled fiercely down, smashing into the rug between Danny's feet. Danny didn't flinch. 'You lied about me! You connived with her! You plotted against me! *And you cheated! You copied that final exam!*' The eyes glared out at him from beneath the furred brows. There was an expression of lunatic cunning in them. 'I'll find it, too. It's down in the basement somewhere. I'll find it. They promised me I could look all I want.' It raised the mallet again.

'Yes, they promise,' Danny said, 'but they lie.'

The mallet hesitated at the top of its swing.

Hallorann had begun to come around, but Wendy had stopped patting his cheeks. A moment ago the words *You cheated! You copied that final exam!* had floated down through the elevator shaft, dim, barely audible over the wind. From somewhere deep in the west wing. She was nearly convinced they were on the third floor and that Jack – whatever had taken possession of Jack – had found Danny. There was nothing she or Hallorann could do now.

'Oh doc,' she murmured. Tears blurred her eyes.

'Son of a bitch broke my jaw,' Hallorann muttered thickly, 'and my *head* . . .' He worked to sit up. His right eye was purpling rapidly and swelling shut. Still, he saw Wendy.

'Missus Torrance—'

'Shhhh,' she said.

'Where is the boy, Missus Torrance?'

'On the third floor,' she said, 'With his father.'

'They lie,' Danny said again. Something had gone through his mind, flashing like a meteor, too quick, too bright to catch and hold. Only the tail of the thought remained.

(*it's down in the basement somewhere*)

(*you will remember what your father forgot*)

'You . . . you shouldn't speak that way to your father,' it said hoarsely. The mallet trembled, came down. 'You'll only make things worse for yourself. Your . . . your punishment. Worse.' It staggered drunkenly and stared at him with maudlin selfpity that began to turn to hate. The mallet began to rise again.

'You're not my daddy,' Danny told it again. 'And if there's a little bit of my daddy left inside you, he knows they lie here. Everything is a lie and a cheat. Like the loaded dice my daddy got for my Christmas stocking last Christmas, like the presents they put in the store windows and my daddy says there's nothing in them, no presents, they're just empty boxes. Just for show, my daddy says. You're *it*, not my daddy. You're the hotel. And when you get what you want, you won't give my daddy anything because you're selfish. And my daddy knows that. You had to make him drink the Bad Stuff. That's the only way you could get him, you lying false face.'

'Liar! Liar!' The words came in a thin shriek. The mallet wavered wildy in the air.

'Go on and hit me. But you'll never get what you want from me.'

The face in front of him changed. It was hard to say how; there was no melting or merging of the features. The body trembled slightly, and then the bloody hands opened like broken claws. The mallet fell from them and thumped to the rug. That was all. But suddenly his daddy *was* there, looking at him in mortal agony, and a sorrow so great that Danny's heart flamed within his chest. The mouth drew down in a quivering bow.

'Doc,' Jack Torrance said. 'Run away. Quick. And remember how much I love you.'

'No,' Danny said.

'Oh Danny, for God's sake—'

'No,' Danny said. He took one of his father's bloody hands and kissed it. 'It's almost over.'

Hallorann got to his feet by propping his back against the wall and pushing himself up. He and Wendy stared at each other like nightmare survivors from a bombed hospital.

'We got to get up there,' he said. 'We have to help him.'

Her haunted eyes stared into his from her chalk-pale face, 'It's too late,' Wendy said. 'Now he can only help himself.'

A minute passed, then two. Three. And they heard it above them, screaming, not in anger or triumph now, but in mortal terror.

'Dear God,' Hallorann whispered. 'What's happening?'

'I don't know,' she said.

'Has it killed him?'

'I don't know.'

The elevator clashed into life and began to descend with the screaming, raving thing penned up inside.

Danny stood without moving. There was no place he could run where the Overlook was not. He recognized it suddenly, fully, painlessly. For the first time in his life he had an adult thought, an adult feeling, the essence of his experience in this bad place – a sorrowful distillation:

(*Mommy and Daddy can't help me and I'm alone.*)

'Go away,' he said to the bloody stranger in front of him. 'Go on. Get out of here.'

It bent over, exposing the knife handle in its back. Its hands closed around the mallet again, but instead of aiming at Danny, it reversed the handle, aiming the hard side of the roque mallet at its own face.

Understanding rushed through Danny.

Then the mallet began to rise and descend, destroying the last of Jack Torrance's image. The thing in the hall danced an eerie, shuffling polka, the beat counterpointed by the hideous sound of the mallet head striking again and again. Blood splattered across the wallpaper. Shards of bone leaped into the air like broken piano keys. It was impossible to say just how long it went on. But when it turned its attention back to Danny, his father was gone forever. What remained of the face became a strange, shifting composite, many faces mixed imperfectly into one. Danny saw the woman in 217; the dogman; the hungry boy-thing that had been in the concrete ring.

'Masks off, then,' it whispered. 'No more interruptions.'

The mallet rose for the final time. A ticking sound filled Danny's ears.

'Anything else to say?' it inquired. 'Are you sure you wouldn't like to run? A game of tag, perhaps? All we have is time, you know. An eternity of *time*. Or shall we end it? Might as well. After all, we're missing the party.'

It grinned with broken-toothed greed.

And it came to him. What his father had forgotten.

Sudden triumph filled his face; the thing saw it and hesitated puzzled.

'*The boiler!*' Danny screamed. '*It hasn't been dumped since this morning! It's going up! It's going to explode!*'

An expression of grotesque terror and dawning realization swept across the broken features of the thing in front of him. The mallet dropped from its fisted hands and bounced harmlessly on the black and blue rug.

'The boiler!' it cried. 'Oh no! That can't, be allowed! Certainly not! No! You goddamned little pup! Certainly not! Oh, oh, oh—'

'*It is!*' Danny cried back at it fiercely. He began to shuffle and shake his fists at the ruined thing before him. 'Any minute now! I know it! The boiler, Daddy forgot the boiler! *And you forgot it, too!*'

'No, oh no, it mustn't, it can't, you dirty little boy, I'll make you take your medicine, I'll make you take every drop, oh no, oh no—'.

It suddenly turned tail and began to shamble away. For a moment its shadow bobbed on the wall, waxing and waning. It trailed cries behind itself like wornout party streamers.

Moments later the elevator crashed into life.

Suddenly the shining was on him

(*mommy mr hallorann dick to my friends together alive they're alive got to get out it's going to blow going to blow sky-high*)

like a fierce and glaring sunrise and he ran. One foot kicked the bloody, misshapen roque mallet aside. He didn't notice.

Crying, he ran for the stairs.

They had to get out.

Chapter Fifty-six

The Explosion

Hallorann could never be sure of the progression of things after that. He remembered that the elevator had gone down and past them without stopping, and something had been inside. But he made no attempt to try to see in through the small diamond-shaped window, because what was in there did not sound human. A moment later there were running footsteps on the stairs. Wendy Torrance at first shrank back against him and then began to stumble down the main corridor to the stairs as fast as she could.

'Danny! Danny! Oh, thank God! Thank God!'

She swept him into a hug, groaning with joy as well as her pain.

(*Danny.*)

Danny looked at him from his mother's arms, and Hallorann saw how the boy had changed. His face was pale and pinched, his eyes dark and fathomless. He looked at if he had lost weight. Looking at the two of them together, Hallorann thought it was the mother who looked younger, in spite of the terrible beating she had taken.

(*Dick – we have to go – run – the place – it's going to*)

Picture of the Overlook, flames leaping out of its roof. Bricks raining down on the snow. Clang of firebells . . . not that any fire truck would be able to get up here much before the end of March. Most of all what came through in Danny's thought was a sense of urgent immediacy, a feeling that it was going to happen *at any time*.

'All right,' Hallorann said. He began to move toward the two of them and at first it was like swimming through deep water. His sense of balance was screwed, and the eye on the right side of his face didn't want to focus. His jaw was sending giant throbbing bursts of pain up to his temple and down his neck, and his cheek felt as large as a cabbage. But the boy's urgency had gotten him going, and it got a little easier.

'All right?' Wendy asked. She looked from Hallorann to her son and back to Hallorann. 'What do you mean, all right?'

'We have to go,' Hallorann said.

'I'm not dressed . . . my clothes . . .'

Danny darted out of her arms then and raced down the corridor. She looked after him, and as he vanished around the corner, back at Hallorann. 'What if he comes back?'

'Your husband?'

'He's not Jack,' she muttered. 'Jack's dead. This place killed him. *This damned place.*' She struck at the wall with her fist and cried out at the pain in her cut fingers. 'It's the boiler, isn't it?'

'Yes, ma'am. Danny says it's going to explode.'

'Good.' The word was uttered with dead finality. 'I don't know if I can get down those stairs again. My ribs . . . he broke my ribs. And something in my back. It hurts.'

'You'll make it,' Hallorann said. 'We'll all make it.' But suddenly he remembered the hedge animals, and wondered what they would do if they were guarding the way out.

Then Danny was coming back. He had Wendy's boots and coat and gloves, also his own coat and gloves.

'Danny,' she said. 'Your boots.'

'It's too late,' he said. His eyes stared at them with a desperate kind of madness. He looked at Dick and suddenly Hallorann's mind was fixed with an image of a clock under a glass dome, the clock in the ballroom that had been donated by a Swiss diplomat in 1949. The hands of the clock were standing at a minute to midnight.

'Oh my God,' Hallorann said. 'Oh my dear God.'

He clapped an arm around Wendy and picked her up. He clapped his other arm around Danny. He ran for the stairs.

Wendy shrieked in pain as he squeezed the bad ribs, as something in her back ground together, but Hallorann did not slow. He plunged down the stairs with them in his arms. One eye wide and desperate, the other puffed shut to a slit. He looked like a one-eyed pirate abducting hostages to be ransomed later.

Suddenly the shine was on him, and he understood what Danny had meant when he said it was too late. He could feel the explosion getting ready to rumble up from the basement and tear the guts out of this horrid place.

He ran faster, bolting headlong across the lobby toward the double doors.

It hurried across the basement and into the feeble yellow glow of the furnace room's only light. It was slobbering with fear. It had been so close, so close to having the boy and the boy's remarkable power. It could not lose now. It must not happen. It would dump the boiler and then chastise the boy harshly.

'Mustn't happen!' it cried. 'Oh no, mustn't happen!'

It stumbled across the floor to the boiler, which glowed a dull red halfway up its long tubular body. It was huffing and rattling and hissing off plumes of steam in a hundred directions, like a monster calliope. The pressure needle stood at the far end of the dial.

'*No, it won't be allowed!*' the manager/caretaker cried.

It laid its Jack Torrance hands on the valve, unmindful of the burning smell which arose or the searing of the flesh as the red-hot wheel sank in, as if into a mudrut.

The wheel gave, and with a triumphant scream, the thing spun it wide open. A giant roar of escaping steam bellowed out of the boiler, a dozen dragons hissing in concert. But before the steam obscured the pressure needle entirely, the needle had visibly begun to swing back.

'*I WIN!*' it cried. It capered obscenely in the hot, rising mist, waving its flaming hands over its head. '*NOT TOO LATE! I WIN! NOT TOO LATE! NOT TOO LATE! NOT—*'

Words turned into a shriek of triumph, and the shriek was swallowed in a shattering roar as the Overlook's boiler exploded.

Hallorann burst out through the double doors and carried the two of them through the trench in the big snowdrift on the porch. He saw the hedge animals clearly, more clearly than before, and even as he realized his worst fears were true, that they were between the porch and the snowmobile, the hotel exploded. It seemed to him that it happened all at once, although later he knew that couldn't have been the way it happened.

There was a flat explosion, a sound that seemed to exist on one low all-pervasive note

(*WHUMMMMMMMMMM—*)

and then there was a blast of warm air at their backs that seemed to push gently at them. They were thrown from the porch on its breath, the three of them, and a confused thought

(*this is what superman must feel like*)

slipped through Hallorann's mind as they flew through the air. He lost his hold on them and then he struck the snow in a soft billow. It was down his shirt and up his nose and he was dimly aware that it felt good on his hurt cheek.

Then he struggled to the top of it, for that moment not thinking about the hedge animals, or Wendy Torrance, or even the boy. He rolled over on his back so he could watch it die.

The Overlook's windows shattered. In the ballroom, the dome over the mantelpiece clock cracked, split in two pieces, and fell to the floor. The clock stopped ticking: cogs and gears and balance wheel all became motionless. There was a whispered, sighing noise, and a great billow of dust. In 217 the bathtub suddenly split in two, letting out a small flood of greenish, noxious-smelling water. In the Presidential Suite the wallpaper suddenly burst into flames. The batwing doors of the Colorado Lounge suddenly snapped their hinges and fell to the dining room floor. Beyond the basement arch, the great piles and stacks of old papers caught fire and went up with a blowtorch hiss. Boiling water rolled over the flames but did not quench them. Like burning autumn leaves below a wasps' nest, they whirled and blackened. The furnace exploded, shattering the basement's roofbeams, sending them crashing down like the bones of a dinosaur. The gasjet which had fed the furnace, unstoppered now, rose up in a bellowing pylon of flame through the riven floor of the lobby. The carpeting on the stair risers caught, racing up to the first-floor level as if to tell dreadful good news. A fusillade of explosions ripped the place. The chandelier in the dining room, a two-hundred-pound crystal bomb, fell with a splintering crash, knocking tables every which way. Flame belched out of the Overlook's five chimneys at the breaking clouds.

(*No! Mustn't! Mustn't! MUSTN'T!*)

It shrieked; it shrieked but now it was voiceless and it was only screaming panic and doom and damnation in its own ear, dissolving, losing thought and will, the webbing falling apart, searching, not finding, going out, going out to, fleeing, going out to emptiness, notness, crumbling.

The party was over.

Chapter Fifty-Seven

Exit

The roar shook the whole façade of the hotel. Glass belched out onto the snow and twinkled there like jagged diamonds. The hedge dog, which had been approaching Danny and his mother, recoiled away from it, its green and shadow-marbled ears flattening, its tail coming down between its legs as its haunches flattened abjectly. In his head, Hallorann heard it whine fearfully, and mixed with that sound was the fearful, confused yowling of the big cats. He struggled to his feet to go to the other two and help them, and as he did so he saw something more nightmarish than all the rest: the hedge rabbit, still coated with snow, was battering itself crazily at the chainlink fence at the far end of the playground, and the steel mesh was jingling with a kind of nightmare music, like a spectral zither. Even from here he could hear the sounds of the close-set twigs and branches which made up its body cracking and crunching like breaking bones.

'Dick! Dick!' Danny cried out. He was trying to support his mother, help her over to the snowmobile. The clothes he had carried out for the two of them were scattered between where they had fallen and where they now stood. Hallorann was suddenly aware that the woman was in her night-clothes, Danny jacketless, and it was no more than ten above zero.

(*my god she's in her bare feet*)

He struggled back through the snow, picking up her coat, her boots,

Danny's coat, odd gloves. Then he ran back to them, plunging hip-deep in the snow from time to time, having to flounder his way out.

Wendy was horribly pale, the side of her neck coated with blood, blood that was now freezing.

'I can't,' she muttered. She was no more than semiconscious. 'No, I . . . can't. Sorry.'

Danny looked up at Hallorann pleadingly.

'Gonna be okay,' Hallorann said, and gripped her again. 'Come on.'

The three of them made it to where the snowmobile had slewed around and stalled out. Hallorann sat the woman down on the passenger seat and put her coat on. He lifted her feet up – they were very cold but not frozen yet – and rubbed them briskly with Danny's jacket before putting on her boots. Wendy's face was alabaster pale, her eyes half-lidded and dazed, but she had begun to shiver. Hallorann thought that was a good sign.

Behind them, a series of three explosions rocked the hotel. Orange flashes lit the snow.

Danny put his mouth close to Hallorann's ear and screamed something.

'What?'

'I said do you need that?'

The boy was pointing at the red gascan that leaned at an angle in the snow.

'I guess we do.'

He picked it up and sloshed it. Still gas in there, he couldn't tell how much. He attached the can to the back of the snowmobile, fumbling the job several times before getting it right because his fingers were going numb. For the first time he became aware that he'd lost Howard Cottrell's mittens.

(*i get out of this i gonna have my sister knit you a dozen pair, howie*)

'Get on!' Hallorann shouted at the boy.

Danny shrank back. 'We'll freeze!'

'We have to go around to the equipment shed! There's stuff in there . . . blankets . . . stuff like that. Get on behind your mother!'

Danny got on, and Hallorann twisted his head so he could shout into Wendy's face.

'Missus Torrance! Hold onto me! You understand? *Hold on!*'

She put her arms around him and rested her cheek against his back. Hallorann started the snowmobile and turned the throttle delicately so they would start up without a jerk. The woman had the weakest sort of grip on him, and if she shifted backward, her weight would tumble both her and the boy off.

They began to move. He brought the snowmobile around in a circle and then they were traveling west parallel to the hotel. Hallorann cut in more to circle around behind it to the equipment shed.

They had a momentarily clear view into the Overlook's lobby. The gasflame coming up through the shattered floor was like a giant birthday candle, fierce yellow at its heart and blue around its flickering edges. In that moment it seemed only to be lighting, not destroying. They could see the registration desk with its silver bell, the credit card decals, the old-fashioned, scrolled cash register, the small figured throw rugs, the highbacked chairs, horsehair hassocks. Danny could see the small sofa by the fireplace where the three nuns had sat on the day they had come up – closing day. But this was the real closing day.

Then the drift on the porch blotted the view out. A moment later they were skirting the west side of the hotel. It was still light enough to see without the snowmobile's headlight. Both upper stories were flaming now, and pennants of flame shot out the windows. The gleaming white paint had begun to blacken and peel. The shutters which had covered the Presidential Suite's picture window – shutters Jack had carefully fastened as per instructions in mid-October – now hung in flaming brands, exposing the wide and shattered darkness behind them, like a toothless mouth yawing in a final, silent deathrattle.

Wendy had pressed her face against Hallorann's back to cut out the wind, and Danny had likewise pressed his face against his mother's back, and so it was only Hallorann who saw the final thing, and he never spoke of it. From the window of the Presidential Suite he thought he saw a huge dark shape issue, blotting out the snowfield behind it. For a moment it assumed the shape of a huge, obscene manta, and then the wind seemed to catch it, to tear it and shred it like old dark paper. It fragmented, was caught in a whirling eddy of smoke, and a moment later it was gone as if it had never been. But in those few seconds as it whirled blackly, dancing like negative motes of light, he remembered something from his childhood . . . fifty years ago, or more. He and his brother had come upon a huge nest of ground wasps just north of their farm. It has been tucked into a hollow between the earth and an old lightning-blasted tree. His brother had had a big old niggerchaser in the band of his hat, saved all the way from the Fourth of July. He had lighted it and tossed it at the nest. It had exploded with a loud bang, and an angry, rising hum – almost a low shriek – had risen from the blasted nest. They had run away as if demons had been at their heels. In a way, Hallorann supposed that demons had been. And looking back over his shoulder, as he was now, he had on that day seen a large dark cloud of hornets rising in the hot air, swirling together, breaking apart, looking for whatever enemy had done this to their home so that they – the single group intelligence – could sting it to death.

Then the thing in the sky was gone and it might only have been smoke or a great flapping swatch of wallpaper after all, and there was only the Overlook, a flaming pyre in the roaring throat of the night.

There was a key to the equipment shed's padlock on his key ring, but Hallorann saw there would be no need to use it.

The door was ajar, the padlock hanging open on its hasp.

'I can't go in there,' Danny whispered.

'That's okay. You stay with your mom. There used to be a pile of old horseblankets. Probably all moth-eaten by now, but better than freezin to death. Missus Torrance, you still with us?'

'I don't know,' the wan voice answered. 'I think so.'

'Good. I'll be just a second.'

'Come back as quick as you can,' Danny whispered. 'Please.'

Hallorann nodded. He had trained the headlamp on the door and now he floundered through the snow, casting a long shadow in front of himself. He pushed the equipment shed door open and stepped in. The horseblankets were still in the corner, by the roque set. He picked up four of them – they smelled musty and old and the moths certainly had been having a free lunch – and then he paused.

One of the roque mallets was gone.

(*Was that what he hit me with?*)

Well, it didn't matter what he'd been hit with, did it? Still, his fingers went to the side of his face and began to explore the huge lump there. Six hundred dollars' worth of dental work undone at a single blow. And after all

(*maybe he didn't hit me with one of those. Maybe one got lost. Or stolen. Or took for a souvenir. After all*)

it didn't really matter. No one was going to be playing roque here next summer. Or any summer in the foreseeable future.

No, it didn't really matter, except that looking at the racked mallets with the single missing member had a kind of fascination. He found himself thinking of the hard wooden *whack!* of the mallet head striking the round wooden ball. A nice summery sound. Watching it skitter across the

(*bone. blood.*)

gravel. It conjured up images of

(*bone. blood.*)

iced tea, porch swings, ladies in white straw hats, the hum of mosquitoes, and

(*bad little boys who don't play by the rules.*)

all that stuff. Sure. Nice game. Out of style now, but . . . nice.

'Dick?' The voice was thin, frantic, and, he thought, rather unpleasant. 'Are you all right, Dick? Come out now. *Please!*'

('*Come on out now nigguh de massa callin youall.*')

His hand closed tightly around one of the mallet handles, liking its feel.

(*Spare the rod, spoil the child.*)

His eyes went blank in the flickering, fire-shot darkness. Really, it would be doing them both a favor. She was messed up . . . in pain . . . and most of it

(*all of it*)

was that damn boy's fault. Sure. He had left his own daddy in there to burn. When you thought of it, it was damn close to murder. Patricide was what they called it. Pretty goddam low.

'Mr Hallorann?' Her voice was low, weak, querulous. He didn't much like the sound of it.

'*Dick!*' The boy was sobbing now, in terror.

Hallorann drew the mallet from the rack and turned toward the flood of white light from the snowmobile headlamp. His feet scratched unevenly over the boards of the equipment shed, like the feet of a clockwork toy that has been wound up and set in motion.

Suddenly he stopped, looked wonderingly at the mallet in his hands, and asked himself with rising horror what it was he had been thinking of doing. Murder? *Had he been thinking of murder?*

For a moment his entire mind seemed filled with an angry, weakly hectoring voice:

(*Do it! Do it, you weak-kneed no-balls nigger! Kill them! KILL THEM BOTH!*)

Then he flung the mallet behind him with a whispered, terrified cry. It clattered into the corner where the horseblankets had been, one of the two heads pointed toward him in an unspeakable invitation.

He fled.

Danny was sitting on the snowmobile seat and Wendy was holding him weakly. His face was shiny with tears, and he was shaking as if with ague. Between his clicking teeth he said: 'Where were you? We were *scared!*'

'It's a good place to be scared of,' Hallorann said slowly. 'Even if that place burns flat to the foundation, you'll never get me within a hundred miles of here again. Here, Missus Torrance, wrap these around you. I'll help. You too, Danny. Get yourself looking like an Arab.'

He swirled two of the blankets around Wendy, fashioning one of them into a hood to cover her head, and helped Danny tie his so they wouldn't fall off.

'Now hold on for dear life,' he said. 'We got a long way to go, but the worst is behind us now.'

He circled the equipment shed and then pointed the snowmobile back along their trail. The Overlook was a torch now, flaming at the sky. Great holes had been eaten into its sides, and there was a red hell inside, waxing and waning. Snowmelt ran down the charred gutters in steaming waterfalls.

They purred down the front lawn, their way well lit. The snowdunes glowed scarlet.

'Look!' Danny shouted as Hallorann slowed for the front gate. He was pointing toward the playground.

The hedge creatures were all in their original positions, but they were denuded, blackened, seared. Their dead branches were a stark interlacing network in the fireglow, their small leaves scattered around their feet like fallen petals.

'They're dead!' Danny screamed in hysterical triumph. '*Dead! They're dead!*'

'Shhh,' Wendy said. 'All right, honey, It's all right.'

'Hey, doc,' Hallorann said. 'Let's get to someplace warm. You ready?'

'Yes,' Danny whispered. 'I've been ready for so long—'

Hallorann edged through the gap between gate and post. A moment later they were on the road, pointed back toward Sidewinder. The sound of the snowmobile's engine dwindled until it was lost in the ceaseless roar of the wind. It rattled through the denuded branches of the hedge animals with a low, beating, desolate sound. The fire waxed and waned. Sometime after the sound of the snowmobile's engine had disappeared, the Overlook's roof caved in – first the west wing, then the east, and seconds later the central roof. A huge spiraling gout of sparks and flaming debris rushed up into the howling winter night.

A bundle of flaming shingles and a wad of hot flashing were wafted in through the open equipment shed door by the wind.

After a while the shed began to burn, too.

They were still twenty miles from Sidewinder when Hallorann stopped to pour the rest of the gas into the snowmobile's tank. He was getting very worried about Wendy Torrance, who seemed to be drifting away from them. It was still so far to go.

'*Dick!*' Danny cried. He was standing up on the seat, pointing. '*Dick, look! Look there!*'

The snow had stopped and a silver-dollar moon had peeked out through the raftering clouds. Far down the road but coming toward them, coming upward through a series of S-shaped switchbacks, was a pearly chain of lights. The wind dropped for a moment and Hallorann heard the faraway buzzing snarl of snowmobile engines.

Hallorann and Danny and Wendy reached them fifteen minutes later. They had brought extra clothes and brandy and Dr Edmonds.

And the long darkness was over.

Chapter Fifty-eight

Epilogue/Summer

After he had finished checking over the salads his understudy had made and peeked in on the home-baked beans they were using as appetizers this week, Hallorann untied his apron, hung it on a hook, and slipped out the back door. He had maybe forty-five minutes before he had to crank up for dinner in earnest.

The name of this place was the Red Arrow Lodge, and it was buried in the western Maine mountains, thirty miles from the town of Rangely. It was a good gig, Hallorann thought. The trade wasn't too heavy, it tipped well, and so far there hadn't been a single meal sent back. Not bad at all, considering the season was nearly half over.

He threaded his way between the outdoor bar and the swimming pool (although why anyone would want to use the pool with the lake so handy he would never know), crossed a greensward where a party of four was playing croquet and laughing, and crested a mild ridge. Pines took over here, and the wind soughed pleasantly in them, carrying the aroma of fir and sweet resin.

On the other side, a number of cabins with views of the lake were placed discreetly among the trees. The last one was the nicest, and Hallorann had reserved it for a party of two back in April when he had gotten this gig.

The woman was sitting on the porch in a rocking chair, a book in her hands. Hallorann was struck again by the change in her. Part of it was the stiff, almost formal way she sat, in spite of her informal surroundings – that was the back brace, of course. She'd had a shattered vertebra as well as three broken ribs and some internal injuries. The back was the slowest healing, and she was still in the brace . . . hence the formal posture. But the change was more than that. She looked older, and some of the laughter had gone out of her face. Now, as she sat reading her book, Hallorann saw a grave sort of beauty there that had been missing on the day he had first met her, some nine months ago. Then she had still been mostly girl. Now she was a woman, a human being who had been dragged around to the dark side of the moon and had come back able to put the pieces back together. But those pieces, Hallorann thought, they never fit just the same way again. Never in this world.

She heard his step and looked up, closing her book. 'Dick! Hi!' She started to rise, and a little grimace of pain crossed her face.

'Nope, don't get up,' he said. 'I don't stand on no ceremony unless it's white tie and tails.'

She smiled as he came up the steps and sat down next to her on the porch.

'How is it going?'

'Pretty fair,' he admitted. 'You try the shrimp creole tonight. You gonna like it.'

'That's a deal.'

'Where's Danny?'

'Right down there.' She pointed, and Hallorann saw a small figure sitting at the end of the dock. He was wearing jeans rolled up to the knee and a red-striped shirt. Further out on the calm water, a bobber floated. Every now and then Danny would reel it in, examine the sinker and hook below it, and then toss it out again.

'He's gettin brown,' Hallorann said.

'Yes. Very brown.' She looked at him fondly.

He took out a cigarette, tamped it, lit it. The smoke raftered away lazily in the sunny afternoon. 'What about those dreams he's been havin?'

'Better,' Wendy said. 'Only one this week. It used to be every night, sometimes two and three times. The explosions. The hedges. And most of all . . . you know.'

'Yeah. He's going to be okay, Wendy.'

She looked at him. 'Will he? I wonder.'

Hallorann nodded. 'You and him, you're coming back. Different, maybe, but okay. You ain't what you were, you two, but that isn't necessarily bad.'

They were silent for a while, Wendy moving the rocking chair back and forth a little, Hallorann with his feet up on the porch rail, smoking. A little breeze came up, pushing its secret way through the pines but barely ruffling Wendy's hair. She had cut it short.

'I've decided to take Al – Mr Shockley – up on his offer,' she said.

Hallorann nodded. 'It sounds like a good job. Something you could get interested in. When do you start?'

'Right after Labor Day. When Danny and I leave here, we'll be going right on to Maryland to look for a place. It was really the Chamber of Commerce brochure that convinced me, you know. It looks like a nice town to raise a kid in. And I'd like to be working again before we dig too deeply into the insurance money Jack left. There's still over forty thousand dollars. Enough to send Danny to college with enough left over to get him a start, if it's invested right.'

Hallorann nodded. 'Your mom?'

She looked at him and smiled wanly. 'I think Maryland is far enough.'

'You won't forget old friends, will you?'

'Danny wouldn't let me. Go on down and see him, he's been waiting all day.'

'Well, so have I.' He stood up and hitched his cook's whites at the hips. 'The two of you are going to be okay,' he repeated. 'Can't you feel it?'

She looked up at him and this time her smile was warmer. 'Yes,' she said. She took his hand and kissed it. 'Sometimes I think I can.'

'The shrimp creole,' he said, moving to the steps. 'Don't forget.'

'I won't.'

He walked down the sloping, graveled path that led to the dock and then out along the weather-beaten boards to the end, where Danny sat with his feet in the clear water. Beyond, the lake widened out, mirroring the pines along its verge. The terrain was mountainous around here, but the mountains were old, rounded and humbled by time. Hallorann liked them just fine.

'Catchin much?' Hallorann said, sitting down next to him. He took off one shoe, then the other. With a sigh, he let his hot feet down into the cool water.

'No. But I had a nibble a little while ago.'

'We'll take a boat out tomorrow morning. Got to get out in the middle if you want to catch an eatin fish, my boy. Out yonder is where the big ones lay.'

'How big?'

Hallorann shrugged. 'Oh . . . sharks, marlin, whales, that sort of thing.'

'There aren't any whales!'

'No *blue* whales, no. Of course not. These ones here run to no more than eighty feet. Pink whales.'

'How could they get here from the ocean?'

Hallorann put a hand on the boy's reddish-gold hair and rumpled it. 'They swim upstream, my boy. That's how.'

'Really?'

'Really.'

They were silent for a time, looking out over the stillness of the lake, Hallorann just thinking. When he looked back at Danny, he saw that his eyes had filled with tears.

Putting an arm around him, he said, 'What's this?'

'Nothing,' Danny whispered.

'You're missin your dad, aren't you?'

Danny nodded. 'You always know.' One of the tears spilled from the corner of his right eye and trickled slowly down his cheek.

'We can't have any secrets,' Hallorann agreed. 'That's just how it is.'

Looking at his pole, Danny said: 'Sometimes I wish it had been me. It was my fault. All my fault.'

Hallorann said, 'You don't like to talk about it around your mom, do you?'

'No. She wants to forget it ever happened. So do I, but—'

'But you can't.'

'No.'

'Do you need to cry?'

The boy tried to answer, but the words were swallowed in a sob. He leaned his head against Hallorann's shoulder and wept, the tears now flooding down his face. Hallorann held him and said nothing. The boy would have to shed his tears again and again, he knew, and it was Danny's luck that he was still young enough to be able to do that. The tears that heal are also the tears that scald and scourge.

When he had quieted a little, Hallorann said, 'You're gonna get over this. You don't think you are right now, but you will. You got the shi—'

'I wish I didn't!' Danny choked, his voice still thick with tears. 'I wish I didn't have it!'

'But you do,' Hallorann said quietly. 'For better or worse. You didn't get no say, little boy. But the worst is over. You can use it to talk to me when things get rough. And if they get too rough, you just call me and I'll come.'

'Even if I'm down in Maryland?'

'Even there.'

They were quiet, watching Danny's bobber drift around thirty feet out from the end of the dock. Then Danny said, almost too low to be heard, 'You'll be my friend?'

'As long as you want me.'

The boy held him tight and Hallorann hugged him.

'Danny? You listen to me. I'm going to talk to you about it this once and never again this same way. There's some things no six-year-old boy in the world should have to be told, but the way things should be and the way things are hardly ever get together. The world's a hard place, Danny. It don't care. It don't hate you and me, but it don't love us, either. Terrible things happen in the world, and they're things no one can explain. Good people die in bad, painful ways and leave the folks that love them all alone. Sometimes it seems like it's only the bad people who stay healthy and prosper. The world don't love you, but your momma does and so do I. You're a good boy. You grieve for your daddy, and when you feel you have to cry over what happened to him, you go into a closet or under your covers and cry until it's all out of you again. That's what a good son has to do. But see that you get on. That's your job in this hard world, to keep your love alive and see that you get on, no matter what. Pull your act together and just go on.'

'All right,' Danny whispered. 'I'll come see you again next summer if you want . . . if you don't mind. Next summer I'm going to be seven.'

'And I'll be sixty-two. And I'm gonna hug your brains out your ears. But let's finish one summer before we get on to the next.'

'Okay.' He looked at Hallorann. 'Dick?'

'Hmmm?'

'You won't die for a long time, will you?'

'I'm sure not studyin on it. Are you?'

'No, *sir*. I—'

'You got a bite, sonny.' He pointed. The red and white bobber had ducked under. It came up again glistening, and then went under again.

'*Hey!*' Danny gulped.

Wendy had come down and now joined them, standing in back of Danny. 'What is it?' she asked. 'Pickerel?'

'No, ma'am,' Hallorann said, 'I believe that's a pink whale.'

The tip of the fishing rod bent. Danny pulled it back and a long fish, rainbow-colored, flashed up in a sunny, winking parabola, and disappeared again.

Danny reeled frantically, gulping.

'Help me, Dick! I got him! I got him! Help me!'

Hallorann laughed. 'You're doin fine all by yourself, little man. I don't know if it's a pink whale or a trout, but it'll do. It'll do just fine.'

He put an arm around Danny's shoulders and the boy reeled the fish in, little by little. Wendy sat down on Danny's other side and the three of them sat on the end of the dock in the afternoon sun.

CARRIE

Carrie

This is for Tabby, who got me into it—
and then bailed me out of it.

BOOK ONE

BLOOD SPORT

News item from the Westover (Me.) weekly *Enterprise,* August 19, 1966:

RAIN OF STONES REPORTED

It was reliably reported by several persons that a rain of stones fell from a clear blue sky on Carlin Street in the town of Chamberlain on August 17th. The stones fell principally on the home of Mrs Margaret White, damaging the roof extensively and ruining two gutters and a downspout valued at approximately $25. Mrs White, a widow, lives with her three-year-old daughter, Carietta.

Mrs White could not be reached for comment.

Nobody was really surprised when it happened, not really, not at the subconscious level where savage things grow. On the surface, all the girls in the shower room were shocked, thrilled, ashamed, or simply glad that the White bitch had taken it in the mouth again. Some of them might also have claimed surprise, but of course their claim was untrue. Carrie had been going to school with some of them since the first grade, and this had been building since that time, building slowly and immutably, in accordance with all the laws that govern human nature, building with all the steadiness of a chain reaction approaching critical mass.

What none of them knew, of course, was that Carrie White was telekinetic.

Graffiti scratched on a desk of the Barker Street Grammar School in Chamberlain:

Carrie White eats shit.

The locker room was filled with shouts, echoes, and the subterranean sound of showers splashing on tile. The girls had been playing volleyball in Period One, and their morning sweat was light and eager.

Girls stretched and writhed under the hot water, squalling, flicking water, squirting white bars of soap from hand to hand. Carrie stood among them stolidly, a frog among swans. She was a chunky girl with pimples on her neck and back and buttocks, her wet hair completely without color. It rested against her face with dispirited sogginess and she simply stood, head slightly bent, letting the water splat against her flesh and roll off. She looked the part of the sacrificial goat, the constant butt, believer in left-handed monkey wrenches, perpetual foul-up, and she was. She wished forlornly and constantly that Ewen High had individual – and thus private – showers, like the high schools at Westover or Lewiston. They stared. They always *stared.*

Showers turning off one by one, girls stepping out, removing pastel bathing caps, toweling, spraying deodorant, checking the clock over the door. Bras were hooked, underpants stepped into. Steam hung in the air; the place might have been an Egyptian bathhouse except for the constant rumble of the Jacuzzi whirlpool in the corner. Calls and catcalls rebounded with all the snap and flicker of billiard balls after a hard break.

'—so Tommy said he *hated* it on me and I—'

'—I'm going with my sister and her husband. He picks his nose but so does she, so they're very—'

'—shower after school and—'

'—too cheap to spend a goddam penny so Cindi and I—'

Miss Desjardin, their slim, nonbreasted gym teacher, stepped in, craned her neck around briefly, and slapped her hands together once, smartly. 'What are you waiting for, Carrie? Doom? Bell in five minutes.' Her shorts were blinding white, her legs not too curved but striking in their unobtrusive muscularity. A silver whistle, won in college archery competition, hung around her neck.

The girls giggled and Carrie looked up, her eyes slow and dazed from the heat and the steady, pounding roar of the water. 'Ohuh?'

It was a strangely froggy sound, grotesquely apt, and the girls giggled again. Sue Snell had whipped a towel from her hair with the speed of a magician embarking on a wonderous feat and began to comb rapidly. Miss Desjardin made an irritated cranking gesture at Carrie and stepped out.

Carrie turned off the shower. It died in a drip and a gurgle.

It wasn't until she stepped out that they all saw the blood running down her leg.

From *The Shadow Exploded: Documented Facts and Specific Conclusions Derived from the Case of Carietta White,* by David R. Congress (Tulane University Press: 1981), p. 34:

It can hardly be disputed that failure to note specific instances of telekinesis during the White girl's earlier years must be attributed to the conclusion offered by White and Stearns in their paper *Telekinesis: A Wild Talent Revisited* – that the ability to move objects by effort of the will alone comes to the fore only in moments of extreme personal stress. The talent is well hidden indeed; how else could it have remained submerged for centuries with only the tip of the iceberg showing above a sea of quackery?

We have only skimpy hearsay evidence upon which to lay our foundation in this case, but even this is enough to indicate that a 'TK' potential of immense magnitude existed within Carrie White. The great tragedy is that we are now all Monday-morning quarterbacks . . .

'*Per*-iod!'

The catcall came first from Chris Hargensen. It struck the tiled walls, rebounded, and struck again. Sue Snell gasped laughter from her nose and felt an odd, vexing mixture of hate, revulsion, exasperation, and pity. She just look so *dumb*, standing there, not knowing what was going on. God, you'd think she never—

'*PER*-iod!'

It was becoming a chant, an incantation. Someone in the background (perhaps Hargensen again, Sue couldn't tell in the jungle of echoes) was yelling, *'Plug it up!'* with hoarse, uninhibited abandon.

'*PER*-iod, *PER*-iod, *PER*-iod!'

Carrie stood dumbly in the center of a forming circle, water rolling from her skin in beads. She stood like a patient ox, aware that the joke was on her (as always), dumbly embarrassed but unsurprised.

Sue felt welling disgust as the first dark drops of menstrual blood struck the tile in dime-sized drops. 'For God's sake, Carrie, you got your period!' she cried. 'Clean yourself up!'

'Ohuh?'

She looked around bovinely. Her hair stuck to her cheeks in a curving helmet shape. There was a cluster of acne on one shoulder. At sixteen, the elusive stamp of hurt was already marked clearly in her eyes.

'She thinks they're for lipstick!' Ruth Gogan suddenly shouted with cryptic glee, and then burst into a shriek of laughter. Sue remembered the comment later and fitted it into a general picture, but now it was only another senseless sound in the confusion. *Sixteen?* She was thinking. *She must know what's happening, she—*

More droplets of blood. Carrie still blinked around at her classmates in slow bewilderment.

Helen Shyres turned around and made mock throwing-up gestures.

'You're *bleeding!*' Sue yelled suddenly, furiously. 'You're *bleeding*, you big dumb pudding!'

Carrie looked down at herself.

She shrieked.

The sound was very loud in the humid locker room.

A tampon suddenly struck her in the chest and fell with a plop at her feet. A red flower stained the absorbent cotton and spread.

Then the laughter, disgusted, contemptuous, horrified, seemed to rise and bloom into something jagged and ugly, and the girls were bombarding her with tampons and sanitary napkins, some from purses, some from the broken dispenser on the wall. They flew like snow and the chant became: 'Plug it *up*, plug it *up*, plug it *up*, plug it—'

Sue was throwing them too, throwing and chanting with the rest, not really sure what she was doing – a charm had occurred to her mind and it glowed there like neon: *There's no harm in it really no harm in it really no harm—* It was still flashing and glowing, reassuringly, when Carrie suddenly began to howl and back away, flailing her arms and grunting and gobbling.

The girls stopped, realizing that fission and explosion had finally been reached. It was at this point, when looking back, that some of them would claim surprise. Yet there had been all these years, all these years of let's short-sheet Carrie's bed at Christian Youth Camp and I found this love letter from Carrie to Flash Bobby Pickett let's copy it and pass it around and hide her underpants somewhere and put this snake in her shoe and duck her *again*, duck her *again*; Carrie tagging along stubbornly on biking trips, known one year as pudd'n and the next year as truck-face, always smelling sweaty, not able to catch up; catching poison ivy from urinating in the bushes and everyone finding out (hey, scratch-ass, your bum itch?); Billy Preston putting peanut butter in her hair that time she fell asleep in study hall; the pinches, the legs outstretched in school aisles to trip her up, the books knocked from her desk, the obscene postcard tucked into her purse; Carrie on the church picnic and kneeling down clumsily to pray and the seam of her old madras skirt splitting along the zipper like the sound of a huge wind-breakage; Carrie always missing the ball, even in kickball, falling on her face in Modern Dance during their sophomore year and chipping a tooth, running into the net during volleyball; wearing stockings that were always run, running, or about to run, always showing sweat stains under the arms of her blouses; even the time Chris Hargensen called up after school from the Kelly Fruit Company downtown and asked her if she knew that *pig poop* was spelled C-A-R-R-I-E: Suddenly all this and the critical mass was reached. The ultimate shit-on, gross-out, put-down, long searched for, was found. Fission.

She backed away, howling in the new silence, fat forearms crossing her face, a tampon stuck in the middle of her pubic hair.

The girls watched her, their eyes shining solemnly.

Carrie backed into the side of one of the four large shower compartments and slowly collapsed into a sitting position. Slow, helpless groans jerked out of her. Her eyes rolled with wet whiteness, like the eyes of a hog in the slaughtering pen.

Sue said slowly, hesitantly: 'I think this must be the first time she ever—'

That was when the door pumped open with a flat and hurried bang and Miss Desjardin burst in to see what the matter was.

From *The Shadow Exploded* (p. 41):

Both medical and psychological writers on the subject are in agreement that Carrie White's exceptionally late and traumatic commencement of the menstrual cycle might well have provided the trigger for her latent talent.

It seems incredible that, as late as 1979, Carrie knew nothing of the mature woman's monthly cycle. It is nearly as incredible to believe that the girl's mother would permit her daughter to reach the age of nearly seventeen without consulting a gynecologist concerning the daughter's failure to menstruate.

Yet the facts are incontrovertible. When Carrie White realized she was bleeding from the vaginal opening, she had no idea of what was taking place. She was innocent of the entire concept of menstruation.

One of her surviving classmates, Ruth Gogan, tells of entering the girls' locker room at Ewen High School the year before the events we are concerned with and seeing Carrie using a tampon to blot her lipstick with. At that time Miss Gogan said: 'What the hell are you up to?' Miss White replied: 'Isn't this right?' Miss Gogan then replied: 'Sure. Sure it is.' Ruth Gogan let a number of her girl friends in on this (she later told this interviewer she thought it was 'sorta cute'), and if anyone tried in the future to inform Carrie of the true purpose of what she was using to make up with, she apparently dismissed the explanation as an attempt to pull her leg. This was a facet of her life that she had become exceedingly wary of. . . .

When the girls were gone to their Period Two classes and the bell had been silenced (several of them had slipped quietly out the back door before Miss Desjardin could begin to take names), Miss Desjardin employed the standard tactic for hysterics: She slapped Carrie smartly across the face. She hardly would have admitted the pleasure the act gave her, and she certainly would have denied that she regarded Carrie as a fat, whiny bag of lard. A first-year teacher, she still believed that she thought all children were good.

Carrie looked up at her dumbly, face still contorted and working. 'M-M-Miss D-D-Des-D—'

'Get up,' Miss Desjardin said dispassionately. 'Get up and tend to yourself.'

'I'm bleeding to death!' Carrie screamed, and one blind, searching hand came up and clutched Miss Desjardin's white shorts. It left a bloody handprint.

'I . . . you . . .' The gym teacher's face contorted into a pucker of disgust, and she suddenly hurled Carrie, stumbling, to her feet. *'Get over there!'*

Carrie stood swaying between the showers and the wall with its dime sanitary-napkin dispenser, slumped over, breasts pointing at the floor, her arms dangling limply. She looked like an ape. Her eyes were shiny and blank.

'Now,' Miss Desjardin said with hissing, deadly emphasis, 'you take one of those napkins out . . . no, never mind the coin slot, it's broken anyway . . . take one and . . . damn it, will you *do* it! You act as if you never had a period before.'

'Period?' Carrie said.

Her expression of complete unbelief was too genuine, too full of dumb and hopeless horror, to be ignored or denied. A terrible and black foreknowledge grew in Rita Desjardin's mind. It was incredible, could not be. She herself had begun menstruation shortly after her eleventh birthday and had gone to the head of the stairs to yell down excitedly: 'Hey, Mum, I'm on the rag!'

'Carrie?' she said now. She advanced toward the girl. 'Carrie?'

Carrie flinched away. At the same instant, a rack of softball bats in the corner fell over with a large, echoing bang. They rolled every which way, making Desjardin jump.

'Carrie, is this is your first period?'

But now that the thought had been admitted, she hardly had to ask. The blood was dark and flowing with terrible heaviness. Both of Carrie's legs were smeared and splattered with it, as though she had waded through a river of blood.

'It hurts,' Carrie groaned. 'My stomach . . .'

'That passes,' Miss Desjardin said. Pity and self-shame met in her and mixed uneasily. 'You have to . . . uh, stop the flow of blood. You—'

There was a bright flash overhead, followed by a flashgun-like pop as a lightbulb sizzled and went out. Miss Desjardin cried out with surprise, and it occurred to her

(the whole damn place is falling in)

that this kind of thing always seemed to happen around Carrie when she was upset, as if bad luck dogged her every step. The thought was gone almost as quickly as it had come. She took one of the sanitary napkins from the broken dispenser and unwrapped it.

'Look,' she said. 'Like this—'

From *The Shadow Exploded* (p. 54):

Carrie White's mother, Margaret White, gave birth to her daughter on September 21, 1963, under circumstances which can only be termed bizarre. In fact, an overview of the Carrie White case leaves the careful student with one feeling ascendent over all others: that Carrie was the only issue of a family as odd as any that has ever been brought to popular attention.

As noted earlier, Ralph White died in February of 1963 when a steel girder fell out of a carrying sling on a housing-project job in Portland. Mrs White continued to live alone in their suburban Chamberlain bungalow.

Due to the Whites' near fanatical fundamentalist religious beliefs, Mrs White had no friends to see her through her period of bereavement. And when her labor began seven months later, she was alone.

At approximately 1:30 p.m. on September 21, the neighbors on Carlin Street began to hear screams from the White bungalow. The police, however, were not summoned to the scene until after 6:00 p.m. We are left with two unappetizing alternatives to explain this time lag: Either Mrs White's neighbors on the street did not wish to become involved in a police investigation, or dislike for her had become so strong that they deliberately adopted a wait-and-see attitude. Mrs Georgia McLaughlin, the only one of three remaining residents who were on the street at that time and who would talk to me, said that she did not call the police because she thought the screams had something to do with 'holy rollin'.'

When the police did arrive at 6:22 p.m. the screams had become irregular. Mrs White was found in her bed upstairs, and the investigating officer, Thomas G. Mearton, at first thought she had been the victim of an assault. The bed was drenched with blood, and a butcher knife lay on the floor. It was only then that he saw the baby, still partially wrapped in the placental membrane, at Mrs White's breast. She had apparently cut the umbilical cord herself with the knife.

It staggers both imagination and belief to advance the hypothesis that Mrs Margaret White did not know she was pregnant, or even understand what the word entails, and recent scholars such as J. W. Bankson and George Fielding have made a more reasonable case for the hypothesis that the concept, linked irrevocably in her mind with the 'sin' of intercourse, had been blocked entirely from her mind. She may simply have refused to believe that such a thing could happen to her.

We have records of at least three letters to a friend in Kenosha, Wisconsin, that seem to prove conclusively that Mrs White believed, from her fifth month on, that she had 'a cancer of the womanly parts' and would soon join her husband in heaven. . . .

When Miss Desjardin led Carrie up to the office fifteen minutes later, the halls were mercifully empty. Classes droned onward behind closed doors.

Carrie's shrieks had finally ended, but she had continued to weep with steady regularity. Desjardin had finally placed the napkin herself, cleaned the girl up with wet paper towels, and gotten her back into her plain cotton underpants.

She tried twice to explain the commonplace reality of menstruation, but Carrie clapped her hands over her ears and continued to cry.

Mr Morton, the assistant principal, was out of his office in a flash when they entered. Billy deLois and Henry Trennant, two boys waiting for the lecture due them for cutting French I, goggled around from their chairs.

'Come in,' Mr Morton said briskly. 'Come right in.' He glared over Desjardin's shoulder at the boys, who were staring at the bloody handprint on her shorts. 'What are *you* looking at?'

'Blood,' Henry said, and smiled with a kind of vacuous surprise.

'Two detention periods,' Morton snapped. He glanced down at the bloody handprint and blinked.

He closed the door behind them and began pawing through the top drawer of his filing cabinet for a school accident form.

'Are you all right, uh—?'

'Carrie,' Desjardin supplied. 'Carrie White.' Mr Morton had finally located an accident form. There was a large coffee stain on it. 'You won't need that, Mr Morton.'

'I suppose it was the trampoline. We just . . . I won't?'

'No. But I think Carrie should be allowed to go home for the rest of the day. She's had a rather frightening experience.' Her eyes flashed a signal which he caught but could not interpret.

'Yes, okay, if you say so. Good. Fine.' Morton crumpled the form back into the filing cabinet, slammed it shut with his thumb in the drawer, and grunted. He whirled gracefully to the door, yanked it open, glared at Billy and Henry, and called: 'Miss Fish, could we have a dismissal slip here, please? Carrie Wright.'

'White,' said Miss Desjardin.

'White,' Morton agreed.

Billy deLois sniggered.

'Week's detention!' Morton barked. A blood blister was forming under his thumbnail. Hurt like hell. Carrie's steady, monotonous weeping went on and on.

Miss Fish brought the yellow dismissal slip and Morton scrawled his initials on it with his silver pocket pencil, wincing at the pressure on his wounded thumb.

'Do you need a ride, Cassie?' he asked. 'We can call a cab if you need one.'

She shook her head. He noticed with distaste that a large bubble of green mucus had formed at one nostril. Morton looked over her head and at Miss Desjardin.

'I'm sure she'll be all right,' she said. 'Carrie only has to go over to Carlin Street. The fresh air will do her good.'

Morton gave the girl the yellow slip. 'You can go now, Cassie,' he said magnanimously.

'That's not my name!' she screamed suddenly.

Morton recoiled, and Miss Desjardin jumped as if struck from behind. The heavy ceramic ashtray on Morton's desk (it was Rodin's *Thinker* with his head turned into a receptacle for cigarette butts) suddenly toppled to the rug, as if to take cover from the force of her scream. Butts and flakes of Morton's pipe tobacco scattered on the pale-green nylon rug.

'Now, listen,' Morton said, trying to muster sternness. 'I know you're upset, but that doesn't mean I'll stand for—'

'Please,' Miss Desjardin said quietly.

Morton blinked at her and then nodded curtly. He tried to project the image of a lovable John Wayne figure while performing the disciplinary functions that were his main job as Assistant Principal, but did not succeed very well. The administration (usually represented at Jay Cee suppers, P.T.A. functions, and American Legion award ceremonies by Principal Henry Grayle) usually termed him 'lovable Mort.' The student body was more apt to term him 'that crazy ass-jabber from the office.' But, as few students such as Billy deLois and Henry Trennant spoke at P.T.A. functions or town meetings, the administration's view tended to carry the day.

Now lovable Mort, still secretly nursing his jammed thumb, smiled at Carrie and said, 'Go along then if you like, Miss Wright. Or would you like to sit a spell and just collect yourself?'

'I'll go,' she muttered, and swiped at her hair. She got up, then looked around at Miss Desjardin. Her eyes were wide open and dark with knowledge. 'They laughed at me. Threw things. They've *always* laughed.'

Desjardin could only look at her helplessly.

Carrie left.

For a moment there was silence; Morton and Desjardin watched her go. Then, with an awkward throat-clearing sound, Mr Morton hunkered down carefully and began to sweep together the debris from the fallen ashtray.

'What was *that* all about?'

She sighed and looked at the drying maroon handprint on her shorts with distaste. 'She got her period. Her first period. In the shower.'

Morton cleared his throat again and his cheeks went pink. The sheet of paper he was sweeping with moved even faster. 'Isn't she a bit, uh—'

'Old for her first? Yes. That's what made it so traumatic for her. Although I can't understand why her mother . . .' The thought trailed off, forgotten for the moment. 'I don't think I handled it very well, Morty, but I didn't understand what was going on. She thought she was bleeding to death.'

He stared up sharply.

'I don't believe she knew there was such a thing as menstruation until half an hour ago.'

'Hand me that little brush there, Miss Desjardin. Yes, that's it.' She handed him a little brush with the legend *Chamberlain Hardware and Lumber Company NEVER Brushes You Off* written up the handle. He began to brush his pile of ashes onto the paper. 'There's still going to be some for the vacuum cleaner, I guess. This deep pile is miserable. I thought I set that ashtray back on the desk further. Funny how things fall over.' He bumped his head on the desk and sat up abruptly. 'It's hard for me to believe that a girl in this or any other high school could get through three years and still be alien to the fact of menstruation, Miss Desjardin.'

'It's even more difficult for me,' she said. 'But it's all I can think of to explain her reaction. And she's always been a group scapegoat.'

'Um.' He funneled the ashes and butts into the wastebasket and dusted his hands. 'I've placed her, I think. White. Margaret White's daughter. Must be. That makes it a little easier to believe.' He sat down behind his desk and smiled apologetically. 'There's so many of them. After five years or so, they all start to merge into one group face. You call boys by their brother's names, that type of thing. It's hard.'

'Of course it is.'

'Wait 'til you've been in the game twenty years, like me,' he said morosely, looking down at his blood blister. 'You get kids that look familiar and find out you had their daddy the year you started teaching. Margaret White was before my time, for which I am profoundly grateful. She told Mrs Bicente, God rest her, that the Lord was reserving a special burning seat in hell for her because she gave the kids an outline of Mr Darwin's beliefs on evolution. She was suspended twice while she was here – once for beating a classmate with her purse. Legend has it that Margaret saw the classmate smoking a cigarette. Peculiar religious views. Very peculiar.' His John Wayne expression suddenly snapped down. 'The other girls. Did they really laugh at her?'

'Worse. They were yelling and throwing sanitary napkins at her when I walked in. Throwing them like . . . like peanuts.'

'Oh. Oh, dear.' John Wayne disappeared. Mr Morton went scarlet. 'You have names?'

'Yes. Not all of them, although some of them may rat on the rest. Christine Hargensen appeared to be the ringleader . . . as usual.'

'Chris and her Mortimer Snerds,' Morton murmured.

'Yes. Tina Blake, Rachel Spies, Helen Shyres, Donna Thibodeau and her sister Mary Lila Grace, Jessica Upshaw. And Sue Snell.' She frowned. 'You wouldn't expect a trick like that from Sue. She's never seemed the type for this kind of a – a stunt.'

'Did you talk to the girls involved?'

Miss Desjardin chuckled unhappily. 'I got them the hell out of there. I was too flustered. And Carrie was having hysterics.'

'Um.' He steepled his fingers. 'Do you plan to talk to them?'

'Yes.' But she sounded reluctant.

'Do I detect a note of—'

'You probably do,' she said glumly. 'I'm living in a glass house, see. I understand how those girls felt. The whole thing just made me want to take the girl and *shake* her. Maybe there's some kind of instinct about menstruation that makes women want to snarl, I don't know. I keep seeing Sue Snell and the way she looked.'

'Um,' Mr Morton repeated wisely. He did not understand women and had no urge at all to discuss menstruation.

'I'll talk to them tomorrow,' she promised, rising. 'Rip them down one side and up the other.'

'Good. Make the punishment suit the crime. And if you feel you have to send any of them to, ah, to me, feel free—'

'I will,' she said kindly. 'By the way, a light blew out while I was trying to calm her down. It added the final touch.'

'I'll send a janitor right down,' he promised. 'And thanks for doing your best, Miss Desjardin. Will you have Miss Fish send in Billy and Henry?'

'Certainly.' She left.

He leaned back and let the whole business slide out of his mind. When Billy deLois and Henry Trennant, class-cutters *extraordinaire*, slunk in, he glowered at them happily and prepared to talk tough.

As he often told Hank Grayle, he ate class-cutters for lunch.

Grafitti scratched on a desk in Chamberlain Junior High School: *Roses are red, violets are blue, sugar is sweet, but Carrie White eats shit.*

She walked down Ewen Avenue and crossed over to Carlin at the stoplight on the corner. Her head was down and she was trying to think of nothing. Cramps came and went in great, gripping waves, making her slow down and speed up like a car with carburetor trouble. She stared at the sidewalk. Quartz glittering in the cement. Hopscotch grids scratched in ghostly, rain-faded chalk. Wads of gum stamped flat. Pieces of tinfoil and penny-candy wrappers. *They all hate and they never stop. They never get tired of it.* A penny lodged in a crack. She kicked it. *Imagine Chris Hargensen all bloody and screaming for mercy. With rats crawling all over her face. Good. Good. That would be good.* A dog turd with a foot-track in the middle of it. A roll of blackened caps that some kid had banged with a stone. Cigarette butts. *Crash in her head with a rock, with a boulder. Crash in all their heads. Good. Good.*

(savior jesus meek and mild)

That was good for Momma, all right for her. She didn't have to go among the wolves every day of every year, out into a carnival of laughers, joke-tellers, pointers, snickerers. And didn't Momma say there would be a Day of Judgement

(the name of that star shall be wormwood and they shall be scourged with scorpions)

and an angel with a sword?

If only it would be today and Jesus coming not with a lamb and a shepherd's crook, but with a boulder in each hand to crush the laughers and the snickerers, to root out the evil and destroy it screaming – a terrible Jesus of blood and righteousness.

And if only she could be His sword and His arm.

She had tried to fit. She had defied Momma in a hundred little ways had tried to erase the redplague circle that had been drawn around her from the first day she had left the controlled environment of the small house on Carlin Street and had walked up to the Barker Street Grammar School with her Bible under her arm. She could still remember that day, the stares, and the sudden, awful silence when she had gotten down on her knees before lunch in the school cafeteria – the laughter had begun on that day and had echoed up through the years.

The redplague circle was like blood itself – you could scrub and scrub and scrub and still it would be there, not erased, not clean. She had never gotten on her knees in a public place again, although she had not told Momma that. Still, the original memory remained, with her and with *them*. She had fought Momma tooth and nail over the Christian Youth Camp, and had earned the money to go herself by taking in sewing. Momma told her darkly that it was Sin, that it was Methodists and Baptists and Congregationalists and that it was Sin and Backsliding. She forbade Carrie to swim at the camp. Yet although she *had* swum and *had* laughed when they ducked her (until she couldn't get her breath any more and they kept doing it and she got panicky and began to scream) and had tried to take part in the camp's activities, a thousand practical jokes had been played on ol' prayin' Carrie and she had come home on the bus a week early, her eyes red and socketed from weeping, to be picked up by Momma at the station, and Momma had told her grimly that she should treasure the memory of her scourging as proof that Momma knew, that Momma was right, that the only hope of safety and salvation was inside the red circle. 'For strait is the gate,' Momma said grimly in the taxi, and at home she had sent Carrie to the closet for six hours.

Momma had, of course, forbade her to shower with the other girls; Carrie had hidden her shower things in her school locker and had showered anyway, taking part in a naked ritual that was shameful and embarrassing to her in hopes that the circle around her might fade a little, just a little—

(but today o today)

Tommy Erbter, age five, was biking up the other side of the street. He was a small, intense-looking boy on a twenty-inch Schwinn with bright-red training wheels. He was humming 'Scoobie Doo, where are you?' under his breath. He saw Carrie, brightened, and stuck out his tongue.

'Hey, ol' fart-face! Ol' prayin' Carrie!'

Carrie glared at him with sudden smoking rage. The bike wobbled on its training wheels and suddenly fell over. Tommy screamed. The bike was on top of him. Carrie smiled and walked on. The sound of Tommy's wails was sweet, jangling music in her ears.

If only she could make something like that happen whenever she liked.

(just did)

She stopped dead seven houses up from her own, staring blankly at nothing. Behind her, Tommy was climbing tearfully back onto his bike, nursing a scraped knee. He yelled something at her, but she ignored it. She had been yelled at by experts.

She had been thinking:

(*fall of that bike kid push you off that bike and split your rotten head*) and something had *happened*.

Her mind had . . . had . . . she groped for a word. Had *flexed*. That was not just right, but it was very close. There had been a curious mental bending, almost like an elbow curling a dumb-bell. That wasn't exactly right either, but it was all she could think of. An elbow with no strength. A weak baby muscle.

Flex.

She suddenly stared fiercely at Mrs Yorraty's big picture window. She thought:

(*stupid frumpy old bitch break that window*)

Nothing. Mrs Yorraty's picture window glittered serenely in the fresh nine o'clock glow of morning. Another cramp gripped Carrie's belly and she walked on.

But . . .

The light. And the ashtray; don't forget the ashtray.

She looked back

(*old bitch hates my momma*)

over her shoulder. Again it seemed that something flexed . . . but very weakly. The flow of her thoughts shuddered as if there had been a sudden bubbling from a wellspring deeper inside.

The picture window seemed to ripple. Nothing more. It could have been her eyes. *Could* have been.

Her head began to feel tired and fuzzy, and it throbbed with the beginning of a headache. Her eyes were hot, as if she had just sat down and read the Book of Revelations straight through.

She continued to walk down the street toward the small white house with the blue shutters. The familiar hate-love-dread feeling was churning inside her. Ivy had crawled up the west side of the bungalow (they always called it the bungalow because the White house sounded like a political joke and Momma said all politicians were crooks and sinners and would eventually give the country over to the Godless Reds who would put all the believers of Jesus - even the Catholics - up against the wall), and the ivy was picturesque, she *knew* it was, but sometimes she hated it. Sometimes, like now, the ivy looked like a grotesque giant hand ridged with great veins which had sprung up out of the ground to grip the building. She approached it with dragging feet.

Of course, there had been the stones.

She stopped again, blinking vapidly at the day. The stones. Momma never talked about that; Carrie didn't even know if her momma still remembered the day of the stones. It was surprising that she herself still remembered it. She had been a very little girl then. How old? Three? Four? There had been that girl in the white bathing suit, and then the stones came. And things had flown in the house. Here the memory was, suddenly bright and clear. As if it had been here all along, just below the surface, waiting for a kind of mental puberty.

Waiting, maybe, for today.

From *Carrie: The Black Dawn of T. K.* (*Esquire* magazine, September 12, 1980) by Jack Gaver:

Estelle Horan has lived in the neat San Diego suburb of Parrish for twelve years, and outwardly she is typical Ms California: She wears bright print shifts and smoked amber sunglasses; her hair is black-streaked blonde; she drives a neat maroon Volkswagen Formula Vee with a smile decal on the gas cap and a green-flag ecology sticker on the back window. Her husband is an executive at the Parrish branch of the Bank of America; her son and daughter are certified members of the Southern California Sun 'n Fun Crowd, burnished-brown beach creatures. There is a hibachi in the small, beautifully kept back yard, and the door chimes play a tinkly phrase from the refrain of 'Hey, Jude.'

But Ms Horan still carries the thin, difficult soil of New England somewhere inside her, and when she talks of Carrie White her face takes on an odd, pinched look that is more like Lovecraft out of Arkham than Kerouac out of Southern Cal.

'Of course she was strange,' Estelle Horan tells me, lighting a second Virginia Slim a moment after stubbing out her first. 'The whole family was strange. Ralph was a construction worker, and people on the street said he carried a Bible and a .38 revolver to work with him every day. The Bible was for his coffee break and lunch. The .38 was in case he met Antichrist on the job. I can remember the Bible myself. The revolver . . . who knows? He was a big olive-skinned man with his hair always shaved into a flattop crewcut. He always looked mean. And you didn't meet his eyes, not ever.

They were so intense they actually seemed to glow. When you saw him coming you crossed the street and you never stuck out your tongue at his back, not ever. That's how spooky *he* was,'

She pauses, puffing clouds of cigarette smoke toward the pseudo-redwood beams that cross the ceiling. Stella Horan lived on Carlin Street until she was twenty, commuting to day classes at Lewin Business College in Motton. But she remembers the incident of the stones very clearly.

'There are times,' she says, 'when I wonder if I might have caused it. Their back yard was next to ours, and Mrs White had put in a hedge but it hadn't grown out yet. She'd called my mother dozens of times about "the show" I was putting on in my back yard. Well, my bathing suit was perfectly decent – prudish by today's standards – nothing but a plain old one-piece Jantzen. Mrs White used to go on and on about what a scandal it was for "her baby." My mother . . . well, she tries to be polite, but her temper is *so* quick. I don't know what Margaret White said to finally push her over the edge – called me the Whore of Babylon, I suppose – but my mother told her our yard was our yard and I'd go out and dance the hootchie-kootchie buck naked if that was her pleasure and mine. She also told her that she was a dirty old woman with a can of worms for a mind. There was a lot more shouting, but that was the upshot of it.

'I wanted to stop sunbathing right then. I hate trouble. It upsets my stomach. But Mom – when she gets a case, she's a terror. She came home from Jordan Marsh with a little white bikini. Told me I might as well get all the sun I could. "After all," she said, "the privacy of our own back yard and all." '

Stella Horan smiles a little at the memory and crushes out her cigarette.

'I tried to argue with her, tell her I didn't want any more trouble, didn't want to be a pawn in their back-fence war. Didn't do a bit of good. Trying to stop my mom when she gets a bee in her hat is like trying to stop a Mack truck going downhill with no brakes. Actually, there was more to it. I was scared of the Whites. Real religious nuts are nothing to fool with. Sure, Ralph White was dead, but what if Margaret still had that .38 around?

'But there I was on Saturday afternoon, spread out on a blanket in the back yard, covered with suntan lotion and listening to Top Forty on the radio. Mom hated that stuff and usually she'd yell out at least twice for me to turn it down before she went nuts. But that day she turned it up twice herself. I started to feel like the Whore of Babylon myself.

'But nobody came out of the Whites' place. Not even the old lady to hang her wash. That's something else – she never hung any undies on the back line. Not even Carrie's, and she was only three back then. Always in the house.

'I started to relax. I guess I was thinking Margaret must have taken Carrie to the park to worship God in the raw or something. Anyway, after a little while I rolled on my back, put one arm over my eyes, and dozed off.

'When I woke up, Carrie was standing next to me and looking down at my body.'

She breaks off, frowning into space. Outside, the cars are whizzing by endlessly. I can hear the steady little whine my tape recorder makes. But it all seems a little too brittle, too glossy, just a cheap patina over a darker world – a real world where nightmares happen.

'She was such a *pretty* girl,' Stella Horan resumes, lighting another cigarette. 'I've seen some high school pictures of her, and that horrible fuzzy black-and-white photo on the cover of *Newsweek*. I look at them and all I can think is, Dear God, where did she go? What did that woman to do her? Then I feel sick and sorry. She was so pretty, with pink cheeks and bright brown eyes, and her hair the shade of blonde you know will darken and get mousy. Sweet is the only word that fits. Sweet and bright and innocent. Her mother's sickness hadn't touched her very deeply, not then.

'I kind of started up awake and tried to smile. It was hard to think what to do. I was logy from the sun and my mind felt sticky and slow. I said "Hi." She was wearing a little yellow dress, sort of cute but awfully long for a little girl in the summer. It came down to her shins.

'She didn't smile back. She just pointed and said, "What are those?"

'I looked down and saw that my top had slipped while I was asleep. So I fixed it and said, "Those are my breasts, Carrie."

'Then she said – very solemnly: "I wish I had some."

'I said: "You have to wait, Carrie. You won't start to get them for another . . . oh, eight or nine years."

' "No, I won't," she said. "Momma says good girls don't." She looked strange for a little girl, half sad and half self-righteous.

'I could hardly believe it, and the first thing that popped into my mind also popped right out of my mouth. I said: "Well, I'm a good girl. And doesn't your mother have breasts?"

'She lowered her head and said something so softly I couldn't hear it. When I asked her to repeat it, she looked at me defiantly and said that her momma had been bad when she made her and that was why she had them. She called them dirtypillows, as if it was all one word.

'I couldn't believe it. I was just dumbfounded. There was nothing at all I could think to say. We just stared at each other, and what I wanted to do was grab that sad little scrap of a girl and run away with her.

'And that was when Margaret White came out of her back door and saw us.

'For a minute she just goggled as if she couldn't believe it. Then she opened her mouth and whooped. That's the ugliest sound I've ever heard in my life. It was like the noise a bull alligator would make in a swamp. She just *whooped*. Rage. Complete, insane rage. Her face went just as red as the side of a fire truck and she curled her hands into fists and whooped at the sky. She was shaking all over. I thought she was having a stroke. Her face was all scrunched up, and it was a gargoyle's face.

'I thought Carrie was going to faint – or die on the spot. She sucked in all her breath and that little face went a cottage-cheesy color.

'Her mother yelled: "CAAAARRRIEEEEEE!"

'I jumped up and yelled back: "Don't you yell at her that way! You ought to be ashamed!" Something stupid like that. I don't remember. Carrie started to go back and then she stopped and then she started again, and just before she crossed over from our lawn to theirs she looked back at me and there was a look . . . oh, dreadful. I can't say it. Wanting and hating and fearing . . . and *misery*. As if life itself had fallen on her like stones, all at the age of three.

'My mother came out on the back stoop and her face just crumpled when she saw the child. And Margaret . . . oh, she was screaming things about sluts and strumpets and the sins of the fathers being visited even unto the seventh generation. My tongue felt like a little dried-up plant.

'For just a second Carrie stood swaying back and forth between the two yards, and then Margaret White looked upward and I swear sweet Jesus that woman *bayed* at the sky. And then she started to . . . to hurt herself, scourge herself. She was clawing at her neck and cheeks, making red marks and scratches. She tore her dress.

'Carrie screamed out "Momma!" and ran to her.

'Mrs White kind of . . . squatted, like a frog, and her arms swooped wide open. I thought she was going to crush her and I screamed. The woman was grinning. Grinning and drooling right down her chin. Oh, I was sick. Jesus, I was so sick.

'She gathered her up and they went in. I turned off my radio and I could hear her. Some of the words, but not all. You didn't have to hear all the words to know what was going on. Praying and sobbing and screeching. Crazy sounds. And Margaret telling the little girl to get herself into her closet and pray. The little girl crying and screaming that she was sorry, she forgot. Then nothing. And my mother and I just looked at each other. I never saw Mom look so bad, not even when Dad died. She said: "The child—" and that was all. We went inside.'

She gets up and goes to the window, a pretty woman in a yellow no-back sundress. 'It's almost like living it all over again, you know,' she says, not turning around. 'I'm all riled up inside again.' She laughs a little and cradles her elbows in her palms.

'Oh, she was so pretty. You'd never know from those pictures.'

Cars go by outside, back and forth, and I sit and wait for her to go on. She reminds me of a polevaulter eyeing the bar and wondering if it's set too high.

'My mother brewed us scotch tea, strong, with milk, the way she used to when I was tomboying around and someone would push me in the nettle patch or I'd fall off my bicycle. It was awful but we drank it anyway, sitting across from each other in the kitchen nook. She was in some old housedress with the hem falling down in back, and I was in my Whore of Babylon two-piece swimsuit. I wanted to cry but it was too real to cry about, not like the movies. Once when I was in New York I saw an old drunk leading a little girl in a blue dress by the hand. The girl had cried herself into a bloody nose. The drunk had goiter and his neck looked like an inner tube. There was a red bump in the middle of his forehead and a long white string on the blue serge jacket he was wearing. Everyone kept going and coming because, if you did, then pretty soon you wouldn't see them any more. That was real, too.

'I wanted to tell my mother that, and I was just opening my mouth to say it when the other thing happened . . . the thing you want to hear about, I guess. There was a big thump outside that made the glasses rattle in the china cabinet. It was a feeling as well as a sound, thick and solid, as if someone had just pushed an iron safe off the roof.'

She lights a new cigarette and begins to puff rapidly.

'I went to the window and looked out, but I couldn't see anything. Then, when I was getting ready to turn around, something else fell. The sun glittered on it. I thought it was a big glass globe for a second. Then it hit the edge of the Whites' roof and shattered, and it wasn't glass at all. It was a big chunk of ice. I was going to turn around and tell Mom, and that's when they started to fall all at once, in a shower.

'They were falling on the Whites' roof, on the back and front lawn, on the outside door to their cellar. That was a sheet-tin bulkhead, and when the first one hit it made a huge *bong* noise, like a church bell. My mother and I both screamed. We were clutching each other like a couple of girls in a thunderstorm.

'Then it stopped. There was no sound at all from their house. You could see the water from the melting ice trickling down their slate shingles in the sunshine. A great big hunk of ice was stuck in the angle of the roof and their little chimney. The light on it was so bright that my eyes hurt to look at it.

'My mother started to ask me if it was over, and then Margaret screamed. The sound came to us very clearly. In a way it was worse than before, because there was terror in this one. Then there were clanging, banging sounds, as if she was throwing every pot and pan in the house at the girl.

'The back door slammed open and slammed closed. No one came out. More screams. Mom said for me to call the police but I couldn't move. I was stuck to the spot. Mr Kirk and his wife Virginia came out on their lawn to look. The Smiths, too. Pretty soon everyone on the street that was home had come out, even old Mrs Warwick from up the block, and she was deaf in one ear.

'Things started to crash and tinkle and break. Bottles, glasses, I don't know what all. And then the side window broke open and the kitchen table fell halfway through. With God as my witness. It was a big mahogany thing and it took the screen with it and it must have weighed three hundred pounds. How could a woman – even a big woman – throw that?'

I ask her if she is implying something.

'I'm only *telling* you,' she insists, suddenly distraught. 'I'm not asking you to believe—'

She seems to catch her breath and then goes on flatly:

'There was nothing for maybe five minutes. Water was dripping out of the gutters over there. And there was ice all over the Whites' lawn. It was melting fast.'

She gives a short, chopping laugh and butts her cigarette.

'Why not? It *was* August.'

She wanders aimlessly back toward the sofa, then veers away. 'Then the stones. Right out of the blue, blue sky. Whistling and screaming like bombs. My mother cried out, "What, in the name of God!" and put her hands over her head. But I couldn't move. I watched it all and I couldn't move. It didn't matter anyway. They only fell on the Whites' property.

'One of them hit a downspout and knocked it onto the lawn. Others punched holes right through the roof and into the attic. The roof made a big cracking sound each time one hit, and puffs of dust would squirt up. The ones that hit the ground made everything vibrate. You could feel them hitting in your feet.

'Our china was tinkling and the fancy Welsh dresser was shaking and Mom's teacup fell on the floor and broke.

'They made big pits in the Whites' back lawn when they struck. Craters.

Mrs White hired a junkman from across town to cart them away, and Jerry Smith from up the street paid him a buck to let him chip a piece off one. He took it to B.U. and they looked at it and said it was ordinary granite.

'One of the last ones hit a little table they had in their back yard and smashed it to pieces.

'But nothing, nothing that wasn't on their property was hit.'

She stops and turns from the window to look at me, and her face is haggard from remembering all that. One hand plays forgetfully with her casually stylish shag haircut. 'Not much of it got into the local paper. By the time Billy Harris came around – he reported the Chamberlain news – she had already gotten the roof fixed, and when people told him the stones had gone right through it, I think he thought we were all pulling his leg.

'Nobody wants to believe it, not even now. You and all the people who'll read what you write will wish they could laugh it off and call me just another nut who's been out here in the sun too long. But it *happened*. There were lots of people on the block who *saw* it happen, and it was just as real as that drunk leading the little girl with the bloody nose. And now there's this other thing. No one can laugh that off, either. Too many people are dead.

'And it's not just on the Whites' property any more.'

She smiles, but there's not a drop of humor in it. She says: 'Ralph White was insured, and Margaret got a lot of money when he died . . . double indemnity. He left the house insured, too, but she never got a penny of that. The damage was caused by an act of God. Poetic justice, huh?'

She laughs a little, but there's no humor in that, either . . .

Found written repeatedly on one page of a Ewen Consolidated High School notebook owned by Carrie White:

Everybody's guessed/ that baby can't be blessed/ 'til she finally sees that she's like all the rest. . . . *

Carrie went into the house and closed the door behind her. Bright daylight disappeared and was replaced by brown shadows, coolness, and the oppressive smell of talcum powder. The only sound was the ticking of the Black Forest cuckoo clock in the living room. Momma had gotten the cuckoo clock with Green Stamps. Once, in the sixth grade, Carrie had set out to ask Momma if Green Stamps weren't sinful, but her nerve had failed her.

She walked up the hall and put her coat in the closet. A luminous picture above the coathooks limned a ghostly Jesus hovering grimly over a family seated at the kitchen table. Beneath was the caption (also luminous): *The Unseen Guest*.

She went into the living room and stood in the middle of the faded, starting-to-be-threadbare rug. She closed her eyes and watched the little dots flash by in the darkness. Her headache thumped queasily behind her temples.

Alone.

Momma worked on the speed ironer and folder down at the Blue Ribbon Laundry in Chamberlain Center. She had worked there since Carrie was five, when the compensation and insurance that had resulted from her father's accident had begun to run out. Her hours were from seven-thirty

* Lyrics from JUST LIKE A WOMAN by Bob Dylan. Copyright © 1966 Dwarf Music. Used by permission of Dwarf Music.

in the morning until four in the afternoon. The laundry was Godless. Momma had told her so many times. The foreman, Mr Elton Mott, was especially Godless. Momma said that Satan had reserved a special blue corner of Hell for Elt, as he was called at the Blue Ribbon.

Alone.

She opened her eyes. The living room contained two chairs with straight backs. There was a sewing table with a light where Carrie sometimes made dresses in the evening while Momma tatted doilies and talked about The Coming. The Black Forest cuckoo clock was on the far wall.

There were many religious pictures, but the one Carrie liked best was on the wall above her chair. It was Jesus leading lambs on a hill that was as green and smooth as the Riverside golf course. The others were not as tranquil: Jesus turning the moneychangers from the temple, Moses throwing the Tablets down upon the worshipers of the golden calf, Thomas the doubter putting his hand in Christ's wounded side (oh, the horrified fascination of that one and the nightmares it had given her as a girl!), Noah's ark floating above the agonized, drowning sinners, Lot and his family fleeing the great burning of Sodom and Gomorrah.

On a small deal table there were a lamp and a stack of tracts. The top pamphlet showed a sinner (his spiritual status was obvious from the agonized expression on his face) trying to crawl beneath a large boulder. The title blared: *Neither shall the rock hide him ON THAT DAY!*

But the room was actually dominated by a huge plaster crucifix on the far wall, fully four feet high. Momma had mail-ordered it special from St. Louis. The Jesus impaled upon it was frozen in a grotesque, muscle-straining rictus of pain, mouth drawn down in a groaning curve. His crown of thorns bled scarlet streams down temples and forehead. The eyes were turned up in a medieval expression of slanted agony. Both hands were also drenched with blood and the feet were nailed to a small plaster platform. This corpus had also given Carrie endless nightmares in which the mutilated Christ chased her through dream corridors, holding a mallet and nails, begging her to take up her cross and follow Him. Just lately these dreams had evolved into something less understandable but more sinister. The object did not seem to be murder but something even more awful.

Alone.

The pain in her legs and belly and privates had drained away a little. She no longer thought she was bleeding to death. The word was *menstruation*, and all at once it seemed logical and inevitable. It was her Time of the Month. She giggled a strange, affrighted giggle in the solemn stillness of the living room. It sounded like a quiz show. You too can win an all-expenses-paid trip to Bermuda on Time of the Month. Like the memory of the stones, the knowledge of menstruation seemed always to have been there, blocked but waiting.

She turned and walked heavily upstairs. The bathroom had a wooden floor and had been scrubbed nearly white (Cleanliness is next to Godliness) and a tub on claw feet. Rust stains dripped down the porcelain below the chrome spout, and there was no shower attachment. Momma said showers were sinful.

Carrie went in, opened the towel cabinet, and began to hunt purposefully but carefully, not leaving anything out of place. Momma's eyes were sharp.

The blue box was in the very back, behind the old towels they didn't use any more. There was a fuzzily silhouetted woman in a long, filmy gown on the side.

She took one of the napkins out and looked at it curiously. She had blotted the lipstick she snuck into her purse quite openly with these – once on a street corner. Now she remembered (or imagined she did) quizzical, shocked looks. Her face flamed. *They* had told her. The flush faded to a milky anger.

She went into her tiny bedroom. There were many more religious pictures here, but there were more lambs and fewer scenes of righteous wrath. A Ewen pennant was tacked over her dresser. On the dresser itself was a Bible and a plastic Jesus that glowed in the dark.

She undressed – first her blouse, then her hateful knee-length skirt, her slip, her girdle, her pettipants, her garter belt, her stockings. She looked at the pile of heavy clothes, their buttons and rubber, with an expression of fierce wretchedness. In the school library there was a stack of back issues of *Seventeen* and often she leafed through them, pasting an expression of idiotic casualness on her face. The models looked so easy and smooth in their short, kicky skirts, pantyhose, and frilly underwear with patterns on them. Of course *easy* was one of Momma's pet words (she knew what Momma would say o no question) to describe *them*. And it would make her dreadfully self-conscious, she knew that. Naked, evil, blackened with the sin of exhibitionism, the breeze blowing lewdly up the backs of her legs, inciting lust. And she knew that *they* would know how she felt. They always did. They would embarrass her somehow, push her savagely back down into clowndom. It was their way.

She could, she knew she could be

(what)

in another place. She was thick through the waist only because sometimes she felt so miserable, empty, bored, that the only way to fill that gaping, whistling hole was to eat and eat and eat – but she was not *that* thick through the middle. Her body chemistry would not allow her to go beyond a certain point. And she thought her legs were actually pretty, almost as pretty as Sue Snell's or Vicky Hanscom's. She could be

(what o what o what)

could stop the chocolates and her pimples would go down. They always did. She could fix her hair. Buy pantyhose and blue and green tights. Make little skirts and dresses from Butterick and Simplicity patterns. The price of a bus ticket, a train ticket. She could be, could be, could *be*—

Alive.

She unsnapped her heavy cotton bra and let it fall. Her breasts were milk-white, upright and smooth. The nipples were a light coffee color. She ran her hands over them and a little shiver went through her. Evil, bad, oh it was. Momma had told her there was Something. The Something was dangerous, ancient, unutterably evil. It could make you Feeble. *Watch*, Momma said. *It comes at night. It will make you think of the evil that goes on in parking lots and roadhouses.*

But, though this was only nine-twenty in the morning, Carrie thought that the Something had come to her. She ran her hands over her breasts

(dirtypillows)

again, and the skin was cool but the nipples were hot and hard, and when she tweaked one it made her feel weak and dissolving. Yes, this was the Something.

Her underpants were spotted with blood.

Suddenly she felt that she must burst into tears, scream, or rip the Something out of her body whole and beating, crush it, kill it.

The napkin Miss Desjardin had fixed was already wilting and she changed it carefully, knowing how bad she was, how bad *they* were, how she hated them and herself. Only Momma was good. Momma had battled the Black Man and had vanquished him. Carrie had seen it happen in a dream. Momma had driven him out of the front door with a broom, and the Black Man had fled up Carlin Street into the night, his cloven feet striking red sparks from the cement.

Her momma had torn the Something out of herself and was pure.

Carrie hated her.

She caught a glimpse of her own face in the tiny mirror she had hung on the back of the door, a mirror with a cheap green plastic rim, good only for combing hair by.

She hated her face, her dull, stupid, bovine face, the vapid eyes, the red, shiny pimples, the nests of blackheads. She hated her face most of all.

The reflection was suddenly split by a jagged, silvery crack. The mirror fell on the floor and shattered at her feet, leaving only the plastic ring to stare at her like a blinded eye.

From *Ogilvie's Dictionary of Psychic Phenomena*:

Telekinesis is the ability to move objects or to cause changes in objects by force of the mind. The phenomenon has most reliably been reported in times of crisis or in stress situations, when automobiles have been levitated from pinned bodies or debris from collapsed buildings, etc.

The phenomenon is often confused with the work of *poltergeists*, which are playful spirits. It should be noted that poltergeists are astral beings of questionable reality, while telekinesis is thought to be an empiric function of the mind, possibly electrochemical in nature. . . .

When they had finished making love, as she slowly put her clothes in order in the back seat of Tommy Ross's 1963 Ford, Sue Snell found her thoughts turning back to Carrie White.

It was Friday night and Tommy (who was looking pensively out the back window with his pants still down around his ankles; the effect was comic but oddly endearing) had taken her bowling. That, of course, was a mutually accepted excuse. Fornication had been on their minds from the word go.

She had been going out more or less steadily with Tommy ever since October (it was now May) and they had been lovers for only two weeks. Seven times, she amended. Tonight had been the seventh. There had been no fireworks yet, no bands playing 'Stars and Stripes Forever,' but it had gotten a little better.

The first time had hurt like hell. Her girl friends, Helen Shyres and Jeanne Gault, had both done It, and they both assured her that it only hurt for a minute – like getting a shot of penicillin – and then it was roses. But for Sue, the first time had been like being reamed out with a hoe handle.

Tommy had confessed to her since, with a grin, that he had gotten the rubber on wrong, too.

Tonight was only the second time she had begun to feel something like pleasure, and then it was over. Tommy had held out for as long as he could, but then it was just . . . over. It seemed like an awful lot of rubbing for a little warmth.

In the aftermath she felt low and melancholy, and her thoughts turned to Carrie in this light. A wave of remorse caught her with all emotional guards down, and when Tommy turned back from the view of Brickyard Hill, she was crying.

'Hey,' he said, alarmed. 'Oh, hey.' He held her clumsily.

' 'S all right,' she said, still weeping. 'It's not you. I did a not-so-good thing today. I was just thinking of it.'

'What?' He patted the back of her neck gently.

So she found herself launching into the story of that morning's incident, hardly believing it was herself she was listening to. Facing the thing frankly, she realized the main reason she had allowed Tommy to have her was because she was in

(love? infatuation? didn't matter results were the same)

with him, and now to put herself in this position – cohort in a nasty shower-room joke – was hardly the approved method to hook a fella. And Tommy was, of course, Popular. As someone who had been Popular herself all her life, it had almost seemed written that she would meet and fall in love with someone as Popular as she. They were almost certain to be voted King and Queen of the high school Spring Ball, and the senior class had already voted them class couple for the year-book. They had become a fixed star in the shifting firmament of the high school's relationships, the acknowledged Romeo and Juliet. And she knew with sudden hatefulness that there was one couple like them in every white suburban high school in America.

And having something she had always longed for – a sense of place, of security, of status – she found that it carried uneasiness with it like a darker sister. It was not the way she had conceived it. There were dark things lumbering around their warm circle of light. The idea that she had let him fuck her

(do you have to say it that way yes this time I do)

simply because he was Popular, for instance. The fact that they fit together walking, or that she could look at their reflection in a store window and think, *There goes a handsome couple*. She was quite sure

(or only hopeful)

that she wasn't that weak, not that liable to fall docilely into the complacent expectations of parents, friends, and even herself. But now there was this shower thing, where she had gone along and pitched in with high, savage glee. The word she was avoiding was expressed *To Conform*, in the infinitive, and it conjured up miserable images of hair rollers, long afternoons in front of the ironing board in front of the soap operas while hubby was off busting heavies in an anonymous Office; of joining the P.T.A. and then the country club when their income moved into five figures; of pills in circular yellow cases without number to insure against having to move out of the misses' sizes before it became absolutely necessary and against the intrusion of repulsive little strangers who shat in their pants and screamed for help at two in the morning; of fighting with desperate decorum to keep the niggers out of Kleen Korners, standing shoulder to shoulder with Terri Smith (Miss Potato Blossom of 1975) and Vicki Jones (Vice President of the Women's League), armed with signs and petitions and sweet, slightly desperate smiles.

Carrie, it was that goddamned Carrie, this was her fault. Perhaps before today she had heard distant, circling footfalls around their lighted place, but tonight, hearing her own sordid, crummy story, she saw the actual silhouettes of all these things, and yellow eyes that glowed like flashlights in the dark.

She had already bought her prom gown. It was blue. It was beautiful.

'You're right,' he said when she was done. 'Bad news. Doesn't sound a bit like you.' His face was grave and she felt a cool slice of terror. Then he smiled – he had a very jolly smile – and the darkness retreated a bit.

'I kicked a kid in the slats once when he was knocked out. Did I ever tell you about that?'

She shook her head.

'Yeah.' He rubbed his nose reminiscently and his cheek gave a small tic, the way it had when he made his confession about getting the rubber wrong the first time. 'The kid's name was Danny Patrick. He beat the living shit out of me once when we were in the sixth grade. I hated him, but I was scared, too. I was laying for him. You know how that is?'

She didn't, but nodded anyway.

'Anyway, he finally picked on the wrong kid a year or so later. Pete Taber. He was just a little guy, but he had lots of muscle. Danny got on him about something, and finally Peter just rose up righteous and beat the shit out of him. That was on the playground of the old Kennedy Junior High. Danny fell down and hit his head and went out cold. Everybody ran. We thought he might be dead. I ran away too, but first I gave him a good kick in the ribs. Felt really bad about it afterward. You going to apologize to her?'

It caught Sue flat-footed and all she could do was clinch weakly: 'Did you?'

'Huh? Hell no! I had better things to do than spend my time in traction. But there's a big difference, Susie.'

'There is?'

'It's not seventh grade any more. And I had some kind of reason, even if it was a piss-poor reason. What did that sad, silly bitch ever do to you?'

She didn't answer because she couldn't. She had never passed more than a hundred words with Carrie in her whole life, and three dozen or so had come today. Phys Ed was the only class they'd had in common since they had graduated from Chamberlain Junior High. Carrie was taking the commercial/business courses. Sue, of course, was in the college division.

She thought herself suddenly loathsome.

She found she could not bear that and so she twisted it at him. 'When did you start making all these big moral decisions? After you started fucking me?'

She saw the good humor fade from his face and was sorry.

'Guess I should have kept quiet,' he said, and pulled up his pants.

'It's not you, it's me.' She put a hand on his arm. 'I'm ashamed, see?'

'I know,' he said. 'But I shouldn't be giving advice. I'm not very good at it.'

'Tommy, do you ever hate being so . . . well, Popular?'

'Me?' The question wrote surprise on his face. 'Do you mean like football and class president and that stuff?'

'Yes.'

'No. It's not very important. High school isn't a very important place. When you're going you think it's a big deal, but when it's over nobody really thinks it was great unless they're beered up. That's how my brother and his buddies are, anyway.'

It did not soothe her; it made her fears worse. Little Susie mix 'n match from Ewen High School, Head Cupcake of the entire Cupcake Brigade. Prom gown kept forever in the closet, wrapped in protective plastic.

The night pressed dark against the slightly steamed car windows.

'I'll probably end up working at my dad's car lot,' he said. 'I'll spend my Friday and Saturday nights down at Uncle Billy's or out at The Cavalier drinking beer and talking about the Saturday afternoon I got that fat pitch from Saunders and we upset Dorchester. Get married to some nagging broad and always own last year's model, vote Democrat—'

'Don't,' she said, her mouth suddenly full of a dark, sweet horror. She pulled him to her. 'Love me. My head is so bad tonight. Love me. Love me.'

So he loved her and this time it was different, this time there finally seemed to be room and there was no tiresome rubbing but a delicious friction that went up and up: Twice he had to stop, panting, and held himself back, and then he went again

(he was a virgin before me and admitted it i would have believed a lie)

and went hard and her breath came in short, digging gasps and then she began to yell and hold at his back, helpless to stop, sweating, the bad taste washed away, every cell seeming to have its own climax, body filled with sunlight, musical notes in her mind, butterflies behind her skull in the cage of her mind.

Later, on the way home, he asked her formally if she would go to the Spring Ball with him. She said she would. He asked her if she had decided what to do about Carrie. She said she hadn't. He said that it made no difference, but she thought that it did. It had begun to seem that it meant all the difference.

From 'Telekinesis: Analysis and Aftermath' (*Science Yearbook* 1981), by Dean D.L. McGuffin:

There are, of course, still these scientists today – regretfully, the Duke University people are in their forefront – who reject the terrific underlying implications of the Carrie White affair. Like the Flatlands Society, the Rosicrucians, or the Corlies of Arizona, who are positive that the atomic bomb does not work, these unfortunates are flying in the face of logic with their heads in the sand – and beg your pardon for the mixed metaphor.

Of course one is able to understand the consternation, the raised voices, the angry letters and arguments at scientific convocations. The idea of telekinesis itself has been a bitter pill for the scientific community to swallow, with its horror-movie trappings of ouija boards and mediums and table rappings and floating coronets; but understanding will still not excuse scientific irresponsibility.

The outcome of the White affair raises grave and difficult questions. An earthquake has struck our ordered notions of the way the natural world is supposed to act and react. Can you blame even such a renowned physicist as Gerald Luponet for claiming the whole thing is a hoax and a fraud, even in the face of such overwhelming evidence as the White Commission presented? For if Carrie White is the truth, then what of Newton? . . .

They sat in the living room, Carrie and Momma, listening to Tennessee Ernie Ford singing 'Let the Lower Lights Be Burning' on a Webcor phonograph (which Momma called the victrola, or, if in a particularly good mood, the vic). Carrie sat at the sewing machine, pumping with her feet as she sewed the sleeves on a new dress. Momma sat beneath the plaster crucifix, tatting doilies and bumping her feet in time to the song, which was one of her favorites. Mr P. P. Bliss, who had written this hymn and others seemingly without number, was one of Momma's shining examples of God at work upon the face of the earth. He had been a sailor and a sinner (two terms that were synonymous in Momma's lexicon), a great blasphemer, a laugher in the face of the Almighty. Then a great storm had come up at sea the boat had threatened to capsize, and Mr P. P. Bliss had gotten down on his sin-sickly knees with a vision of Hell yawning beneath the ocean floor to receive him, and he had prayed to God. Mr P. P. Bliss promised God that if He saved him, he would dedicate the rest of his life to Him. The storm, of course, had cleared immediately.

Brightly beams our Father's mercy
From his lighthouse evermore,
But to us he gives the keeping
Of the lights along the shore . . .

All of Mr P. P. Bliss's hymns had a seagoing flavor to them.

The dress she was sewing was actually quite pretty, a dark wine color – the closest Momma would allow her to red – and the sleeves were puffed. She tried to keep her mind strictly on her sewing, but of course it wandered.

The overhead light was strong and harsh and yellow, the small dusty plush sofa was of course deserted (Carrie had never had a boy in To Sit), and on the far wall was a twin shadow: the crucified Jesus, and beneath Him, Momma.

The school had called Momma at the laundry and she had come home at noon. Carrie had watched her come up the walk, and her belly trembled.

Momma was a very big woman, and she always wore a hat. Lately her legs had begun to swell, and her feet always seemed on the point of overflowing her shoes. She wore a black cloth coat with a black fur collar. Her eyes were blue and magnified behind rimless bifocals. She always carried a large black satchel purse and in it was her change purse, her billfold (both black), a large King James Bible (also black) with her name stamped on the front in gold, and a stack of tracts secured with a rubber band. The tracts were usually orange, and smearily printed.

Carrie knew vaguely that Momma and Daddy Ralph had been Baptists once but had left the church when they became convinced that the Baptists were doing the work of the Antichrist. Since that time, all worship had taken place at home. Momma held worship on Sundays, Tuesdays, and Fridays. These were called Holy Days. Momma was the minister, Carrie the congregation. Services lasted from two to three hours.

Momma had opened the door and walked stolidly in. She and Carrie stared at each other down the short length of the front hall for a moment, like gunfighters before a shoot-out. It was one of those brief moments that seem

(fear could it really have been fear in momma's eyes)

much longer in retrospect.

Momma closed the door behind her. 'You're a woman,' she said softly.

Carrie felt her face twisting and crumpling and could not help it. 'Why didn't you *tell* me?' she cried. 'Oh Momma, I was so *scared*! And the girls all made fun and threw things and—'

Momma had been walking toward her, and now her hand flashed with sudden limber speed, a hard hand, laundry-callused and muscled. It struck her backhand across the jaw and Carrie fell down in the doorway between the hall and the living room, weeping loudly.

'And God made Eve from the rib of Adam,' Momma said. Her eyes were very large in the rimless glasses; they looked like poached eggs. She thumped Carrie with the side of her foot and Carric screamed. 'Get up, woman. Let's us get in and pray. Let's us pray to Jesus for our woman-weak, wicked, sinning souls.'

'*Momma—*'

The sobs were too strong to allow more. The latent hysterics had come out grinning and gibbering. She could not stand up. She could only crawl into the living room with her hair hanging in her face, braying huge, hoarse sobs. Every now and again Momma would swing her foot. So they progressed across the living room toward the place of the altar, which had once been a small bedroom.

'And Eve was weak and – say it, woman. Say it?'

'No, Momma, please help me—'

The foot swung. Carrie screamed.

'And Eve was weak and loosed the raven on the world,' Momma continued, '(and the raven was called Sin, and the first Sin was Intercourse. And the Lord visited Eve with a Curse, and the Curse was the Curse of Blood. And Adam and Eve were driven out of the Garden and into the World and Eve found that her belly had grown big with child.'

The foot swung and connected with Carrie's rump. Her nose scraped the wood floor. They were entering the place of the altar. There was a cross on a table covered with an embroidered silk cloth. On either side of the cross there were white candles. Behind this were several paint-by-the-numbers of Jesus and His apostles. And to the right was the worst place of all, the home of terror, the cave where all hope, all resistance to God's will – and Momma's – was extinguished. The closet door leered open. Inside, below a hideous blue bulb that was always lit, was Derrault's conception of Jonathan Edwards' famous sermon, *Sinners in the Hands of an Angry God.*

'And there was a second Curse, and this was the Curse of Childbearing, and Eve brought forth Cain in sweat and blood.'

Now Momma dragged her, half-standing and half-crawling, down to the altar, where they both fell on their knees. Momma gripped Carrie's wrist tightly.

'And following Cain, Eve gave birth to Abel, having not yet repented of the Sin of Intercourse. And so the Lord visited Eve with a third Curse, and this was the Curse of Murder. Cain rose up and slew Abel with a rock. And still Eve did not repent, nor all the daughters of Eve, and upon Eve did the Crafty Serpent found a kingdom of whoredoms and pestilences.'

'*Momma!*' she shrieked. 'Momma, please listen! *It wasn't my fault!*'

'Bow your head,' Momma said. 'Let's us pray.'

'*You should have told me!*'

Momma brought her hand down on the back of Carrie's neck and behind it was all the heavy muscle developed by eleven years of slinging heavy laundry bags and trucking piles of wet sheets. Carrie's eye-bulging face jerked forward and her forehead smacked the altar, leaving a mark and making the candles tremble.

'Let's us pray,' Momma said softly, implacably.

Weeping and snuffling, Carrie bowed her head. A runner of snot hung pendulously from her nose and she wiped it away

(if i had a nickel for every time she made me cry here)

with the back of her hand.

'O Lord,' Momma declaimed hugely, her head thrown back, 'help this sinning woman beside me here see the sin of her days and ways. Show her that if she had remained sinless the Curse of Blood never would have come on her. She may have committed the Sin of Lustful Thoughts. She may have been listening to rock 'n roll music on the radio. She may have been tempted by the Antichrist. Show her that this is Your kind, vengeful hand at work and—'

'No! Let me go!'

She tried to struggle to her feet and Momma's hand, as strong and pitiless as an iron manacle, forced her back to her knees.

' —and Your sign that she must walk the straight and narrow from here on out if she is to avoid the flaming agonies of the Eternal Pit. Amen.'

She turned her glittering, magnified eyes upon her daughter. 'Go to your closet now.'

'No!' She felt her breath go thick with terror.

'Go to your closet. Pray in secret. Ask forgiveness for your sin.'

'I didn't sin, Momma. *You* sinned. You didn't tell me and they laughed.'

Again she seemed to see a flash of fear in Momma's eyes, gone as quickly and soundlessly as summer lightning. Momma began to force Carrie toward the blue glare of the closet.

'Pray to God and your sins may be washed away.'

'Momma, you let me go.'

'Pray, woman.'

'I'll make the stones come again, Momma.'

Momma halted.

Even her breath seemed to stop in her throat for a moment. And then the hand tightened on her neck, tightened, until Carrie saw red, lurid dots in front of her eyes and felt her brain go fuzzy and far-off.

Momma's magnified eyes swam in front of her.

'You spawn of the devil,' she whispered. 'Why was I so cursed?'

Carrie's whirling mind strove to find something huge enough to express her agony, shame, terror, hate, fear. It seemed her whole life had narrowed to this miserable, beaten point of rebellion. Her eyes bulged crazily, her mouth, filled with spit, opened wide.

'*You SUCK!*' she screamed.

Momma hissed like a burned cat. 'Sin!' she cried. 'O, Sin!' She began to beat Carrie's back, her neck, her head. Carrie was driven, reeling, into the close blue glare of the closet.

'*You FUCK!*' Carrie screamed.

(there there o there it's out how else do you think she got you o god o good)

She was whirled into the closet headfirst and she struck the far wall and fell on the floor in a semidaze. The door slammed and the key turned.

She was alone with Momma's angry God.

The blue light glared on a picture of a huge and bearded Yahweh who was casting screaming multitudes of humans down through cloudy depths into an abyss of fire. Below them, black horrid figures struggled through the flames of perdition while the Black Man sat on a huge flame-colored throne with a trident in one hand. His body was that of a man, but he had a spiked tail and the head of a jackal.

She would not break this time.

But of course she did break. It took six hours but she broke, weeping and calling Momma to open the door and let her out. The need to urinate was terrible. The Black Man grinned at her with his jackal mouth, and his scarlet eyes knew all the secrets of woman-blood.

An hour after Carrie began to call, Momma let her out. Carrie scrabbled madly for the bathroom.

It was only now, three hours after that, sitting here with her head bowed over the sewing machine like a penitent, that she remembered the fear in Momma's eyes and she thought she knew the reason why.

There had been other times when Momma had kept her in the closet for as long as a day at a stretch – when she stole that forty-nine-cent finger ring from Shuber's Five and Ten, the time she had found that picture of Flash Bobby Pickett under Carrie's pillow – and Carrie had once fainted from the lack of food and the smell of her own waste. And she had never, never spoken back as she had done today. Today she had even said the Eff Word. Yet Momma had let her out almost as soon as she broke.

There. The dress was done. She removed her feet from the treadle and held it up to look at it. It was long. And ugly. She hated it.

She knew why Momma had let her out.

'Momma, may I go to bed?'

'Yes.' Momma did not look up from her doily.

She folded the dress over her arm. She looked down at the sewing machine. All at once the treadle depressed itself. The needle began to dip up and down, catching the light in steely flashes. The bobbin whirred and jerked. The sidewheel spun.

Momma's head jerked up, her eyes wide. The looped matrix at the edge of her doily, wonderfully intricate yet at the same time as precise and even, suddenly fell in disarray.

'Only clearing the thread,' Carrie said softly.

'Go to bed,' Momma said curtly, and the fear was back in her eyes.

'Yes,

(she was afraid i'd knock the closet door right off its hinges)

Momma.'

(and i think i could i think i could yes i think i could)

From *The Shadow Exploded* (p. 58):

Margaret White was born and raised in Motton, a small town which borders Chamberlain and sends its tuition students to Chamberlain's junior and senior high schools. Her parents were fairly well-to-do; they owned a prosperous night spot just outside the Motton town limits called The Jolly Roadhouse. Margaret's father, John Brigham, was killed in a barroom shooting incident in the summer of 1959.

Margaret Brigham, who was then almost thirty, began attending fundamentalist prayer meetings. Her mother had become involved with a new man (Harold Allison, whom she later married) and they both wanted Margaret out of the house – she believed her mother, Judith, and Harold Allison were living in sin and made her views known frequently. Judith Brigham expected her daughter to remain a spinster the rest of her life. In the more pungent phraseology of her soon-to-be stepfather, 'Margaret had a face like the ass end of a gasoline truck and a body to match.' He also referred to her as 'a little prayin' Jesus.'

Margaret refused to leave until 1960, when she met Ralph White at a revival meeting. In September of that year she left the Brigham residence in Motton and moved to a small flat in Chamberlain Center.

The courtship of Margaret Brigham and Ralph White terminated in marriage on March 23, 1962. On April 3, 1962, Margaret White was admitted briefly to Westover Doctors Hospital.

'Nope, she wouldn't tell us what was wrong,' Harold Allison said. 'The one time we went to see her she told us we were living in adultery even though we were hitched, and we were going to hell. She said God had put an invisible mark on our foreheads, but she could see it. Acted crazy as a bat in a henhouse, she did. Her mom tried to be nice, tried to find out what the matter with her was. She got hysterical and started to rave about an angel with a sword who would walk through the parking lots of roadhouses and cut down the wicked. We left.'

Judith Allison, however, had at least an idea of what might have been wrong with her daughter; she thought that Margaret had gone through a miscarriage. If so, the baby was conceived out of wedlock. Confirmation of this would shed an interesting light on the character of Carrie's mother.

In a long and rather hysterical letter to her mother dated August 19, 1962, Margaret said that she and Ralph were living sinlessly, without 'the Curse of Intercourse.' She urged Harold and Judith Allison to close their 'abode of wickedness' and do likewise. 'It is,' Margaret declares near the end of her letter, 'the oney [sic] way you & That Man can avoid the Rain of Blood yet to come. Ralph & I, like Mary & Joseph, will neither know or polute [sic] each other's flesh. If there is issue, let it be Divine.'

Of course, the calendar tells us that Carrie was conceived later that same year . . .

The girls dressed quietly for their Monday morning Period One gym class, with no horseplay or little screaming catcalls, and none of them were very surprised when Miss Desjardin slammed open the locker-room door and walked in. Her silver whistle dangled between her small breasts, and if her shorts were the ones she had been wearing on Friday, no trace of Carrie's bloody handprint remained.

The girls continued to dress sullenly, not looking at her.

'Aren't you the bunch to send out for graduation,' Miss Desjardin said softly. 'When is it? A month? And the Spring Ball even less than that. Most of you have your dates and gowns already, I bet. Sue, you'll be going with Tommy Ross. Helen, Roy Evarts. Chris, I imagine that you can take your pick. Who's the lucky guy?'

'Billy Nolan,' Chris Hargensen said sullenly.

'Well, isn't he the lucky one?' Desjardin remarked. 'What are you going to give him for a party favor, Chris, a bloody Kotex? Or how about some used toilet paper? I understand these things seem to be your sack these days.'

Chris went red. 'I'm leaving. I don't have to listen to that.'

Desjardin had not been able to get the image of Carrie out of her mind all weekend, Carrie screaming, blubbering, a wet napkin plastered squarely in the middle of her pubic hair – and her own sick, angry reaction.

And now, as Chris tried to storm out past her, she reached out and slammed her against a row of dented, olive-colored lockers beside the inner door. Chris's eyes widened with shocked disbelief. Then a kind of insane rage filled her face.

'You can't hit us!' she screamed. 'You'll get canned for this! See if you don't, you *bitch*!'

The other girls winced and sucked breath and stared at the floor. It was getting out of hand. Sue noticed out of the corner of her eye that Mary and Donna Thibodeau were holding hands.

'I don't really care, Hargensen,' Desjardin said. 'If you – or any of you girls – think I'm wearing my teacher hat right now, you're making a bad mistake. I just want you all to know that you did a shitty thing on Friday. A really shitty thing.'

Chris Hargensen was sneering at the floor. The rest of the girls were looking miserably at anything but their gym instructor. Sue found herself looking into the shower stall – the scene of the crime – and jerked her glance elsewhere. None of them had ever heard a teacher call anything shitty before.

'Did any of you stop to think that Carrie White has feelings? Do any of you *ever* stop to think? Sue? Fern? Helen? Jessica? Any of you? You think she's ugly. Well, you're all ugly. I saw it on Friday morning.'

Chris Hargensen was mumbling about her father being a lawyer.

'*Shut up*!' Desjardin yelled in her face. Chris recoiled so suddenly that her head struck the lockers behind her. She began to whine and rub her head.

'One more remark out of you,' Desjardin said softly, 'and I'll throw you across the room. Want to find out if I'm telling the truth?'

Chris, who had apparently decided she was dealing with a madwoman, said nothing.

Desjardin put her hands on her hips. 'The office has decided on punishment for you girls. Not *my* punishment, I'm sorry to say. My idea was three days' suspension and refusal of your prom tickets.'

Several girls looked at each other and muttered unhappily.

'That would have hit you where you live,' Desjardin continued. 'Unfortunately, Ewin is staffed completely by men in its administration wing. I don't believe they have any real conception of how utterly nasty what you did was. So. One week's detention.'

Spontaneous sighs of relief.

'But. It's to be *my* detention. In the gym. And I'm going to run you ragged.'

'I won't come,' Chris said. Her lips had thinned across her teeth.

'That's up to you, Chris. That's up to all of you. But punishment for skipping detention is going to be three days' suspension and refusal of your prom tickets. Get the picture?'

No one said anything.

'Right. Change up. And think about what I said.'

She left.

Utter silence for a long and stricken moment. Then Chris Hargensen said with loud, hysterical stridency:

'She can't get away with it!' She opened a door at random, pulled out a pair of sneakers and hurled them across the room. 'I'm going to get her! Goddammit! Goddammit! See if I don't't! If we all stick together we can—'

'Shut up, Chris,' Sue said, and was shocked to hear a dead, adult lifelessness in her voice. 'Just shut up.'

'This isn't over,' Chris Hargensen said, unzipping her skirt with a rough jab and reaching for her fashionably frayed green gym shorts. 'This isn't over by a long way.'

And she was right.

From *The Shadow Exploded* (pp. 60–61):

In the opinion of this researcher, a great many of the people who have researched the Carrie White matter – either for the scientific journals or for the popular press – have placed a mistaken emphasis on a relatively fruitless search for incidents of telekinesis in the girl's childhood. To strike a rough analogy, this is like spending years researching the early incidents of masturbation in a rapist's childhood.

The spectacular incident of the stones serves as a kind of red herring in this respect. Many researchers have adopted the erroneous belief that where there has been one incident, there must be others. To offer another analogy, this is like dispatching a crew of meteor watchers to Crater National Park because a huge asteroid struck there two million years ago.

To the best of my knowledge, there are no other *recorded* instances of TK in Carrie's childhood. If Carrie had not been an only child, we might have at least hearsay reports of dozens of other minor occurences.

In the case of Andrea Kolintz (see Appendix II for a fuller history), we are told that, following a spanking for crawling out on the roof, 'The medicine cabinet flew open, bottles fell to the floor or seemed to hurl themselves across the bathroom, doors flew open and slammed shut, and, at the climax of the manifestation, a 300-pound stereo cabinet tipped over and records flew all over the living room, dive-bombing the occupants and shattering against the walls.'

Significantly, this report is from one of Andrea's brothers, as quoted in the September 4, 1955, issue of *Life* magazine. *Life* is hardly the most scholarly or unimpeachable source, but there is a great deal of other documentation, and I think that the point of familiar witnesship is served.

In the case of Carrie White, the only witness to any possible prologue to the final climatic events was Margaret White, and she, of course is dead. . . .

Henry Grayle, principal of Ewen High School, had been expecting him all week, but Chris Hargensen's father didn't show up until Friday – the day after Chris had skipped her detention period with the formidable Miss Desjardin.

'Yes, Miss Fish?' He spoke formally into the intercom, although he could see the man in the outer office through his window, and certainly knew his face from pictures in the local paper.

'John Hargensen to see you, Mr. Grayle.'

'Send him in, please.' *Goddammit, Fish, do you have to sound so impressed*?

Grayle was an irrepressible paper-clip-bender, napkin-ripper, corner-folder. For John Hargensen, the town's leading legal light, he was bringing up the heavy ammunition – a whole box of heavy-duty clips in the middle of his desk blotter.

Hargensen was a tall, impressive man with a self-confident way of moving and the kind of sure, mobile features that said this was a man superior at the game of one-step-ahead social interaction.

He was wearing a brown Savile Row suit with subtle glints of green and gold running through the weave that put Grayle's local off-the-rack job to shame. His briefcase was thin, real leather, and bound with glittering stainless steel. The smile was faultless and full of many capped teeth – a smile to make the hearts of lady jurors melt like butter in a warm skillet. His grip was major league all the way – firm, warm, long.

'Mr Grayle. I've wanted to meet you for some time now.'

'I'm always glad to see interested parents,' Grayle said with a dry smile. 'That's why we have Parents Open House every October.'

'Of course.' Hargensen smiled. 'I imagine you're a busy man, and I have to be in court forty-five minutes from now. Shall we get down to specifics?'

'Surely.' Grayle dipped into his box of clips and began to mangle the first one. 'I suppose you are here concerning the disciplinary action against your daughter Christine. You should be informed that school policy on the matter has been set. As a man concerned with the workings of justice yourself, you should realize that bending the rules is hardly possible or—'

Hargensen waved his hand impatiently. 'Apparently you're laboring under a misconception, Mr Grayle. I am here because my daughter was manhandled by your gym teacher, Miss Rita Desjardin. And verbally abused, I'm afraid. I believe the term your Miss Desjardin used in connection with my daughter was "shitty." '

Grayle sighed inwardly. 'Miss Desjardin has been reprimanded.'

John Hargensen's smile cooled thirty degrees. 'I'm afraid a reprimand will not be sufficient. I believe this has been the young, ah, lady's first year in a teaching capacity?'

'Yes. We have found her to be eminently satisfactory.'

'Apparently your definition of eminently satisfactory includes throwing students up against lockers and the ability to curse like a sailor?'

Grayle fenced: 'As a lawyer, you must be aware that this state acknowledges the school's title to *in loco parentis* – along with full responsibility, we succeed to full parental rights during school hours. If you're not familiar, I'd advise you to check *Monondock Consolidated School District vs. Cranepool* or—'

'I'm familiar with the concept,' Hargensen said. 'I'm also aware that neither the Cranepool case that you administrators are so fond of quoting or the Frick case cover anything remotely concerned with physical or verbal abuse. There is, however, the case of *School District #4 vs. David.* Are you familiar with it?'

Grayle was. George Kramer, the assistant principal of the consolidated high school in S.D. 14 was a poker buddy. George wasn't playing much poker any more. He was working for an insurance company after taking it upon himself to cut a student's hair. The school district had ultimately paid seven thousand dollars in damages, or about a thousand bucks a snip.

Grayle started on another paper clip.

'Let's not quote cases at each other, Mr Grayle. We're busy men. I don't want a lot of unpleasantness. I don't want a mess. My daughter is at home, and she will stay there Monday and Tuesday. That will complete her three-day suspension. That's all right.' Another dismissive wave of the hand.

(catch fido good boy here's a nice bone)

'Here's what *I* want,' Hargensen continued. 'One, prom tickets for my daughter. A girl's senior prom is important to her, and Chris is very distressed. Two, no contract renewal of the Desjardin woman. That's for me. I believe that if I cared to take the School Department to court, I could walk out with both her dismissal and a hefty damage settlement in my pocket. But I don't want to be vindictive.'

'So court is the alternative if I don't agree to your demands?'

'I understand that a School Committee hearing would precede that, but only as a formality. But yes, court would be the final result. Nasty for you.'

Another paper clip.

'For physical and verbal abuse, is that correct?'

'Essentially.'

'Mr Hargensen, are you aware that your daughter and about ten of her peers threw sanitary napkins at a girl who was having her first menstrual period? A girl who was under the impression that she was bleeding to death?'

A faint frown creased Hargensen's features, as if someone had spoken in a distant room. 'I hardly think such an allegation is at issue. I am speaking of actions following—'

'Never mind,' Grayle said. 'Never mind what you were speaking of. This girl, Carietta White, was called "a dumb pudding" and was told to "plug it up" and was subjected to various obscene gestures. She has not been in school this week at all. Does that sound like physical and verbal abuse to you? It does to me.'

'I don't intend,' Hargensen said, 'to sit here and listen to a tissue of half-truths or your standard schoolmaster lecture, Mr Grayle. I know my daughter well enough to—'

'Here.' Grayle reached into the wire IN basket beside the blotter and tossed a sheaf of pink cards across the desk. 'I doubt very much if you know the daughter represented in these cards half so well as you think you do. If you did, you might realize that it was about time for a trip to the woodshed. It's time you snubbed her close before she does someone a major damage.'

'You aren't—'

'Ewen, four years,' Grayle overrode him. 'Graduation slated June seventy-nine; next month. Tested I.Q. of a hundred and forty. Eighty-three average. Nonetheless, I see she's been accepted at Oberlin. I'd guess someone – probably you, Mr Hargensen – has been yanking some pretty long strings. Seventy-four assigned detentions. *Twenty* of those have been for harassment of misfit pupils, I might add. Fifth wheels. I understand that Chris's clique calls them Mortimer Snerds. They find it all quite hilarious. She skipped out on fifty-one of those assigned detentions. At Chamberlain Junior High, one suspension for putting a firecracker in a girl's shoe . . . the note on the card says that little prank almost cost a little girl named Irma Swope two toes. The Swope girl has a harelip, I understand. I'm talking about your *daughter*, Mr Hargensen. Does that tell you anything?'

'Yes,' Hargensen said, rising. A thin flush had suffused his features. 'It tells me I'll see you in court. And when I'm done with you, you'll be lucky to get a job selling encyclopedias door to door.'

Grayle also rose, angrily, and the two men faced each other across the desk.

'Let it be court, then,' Grayle said.

He noted a faint flick of surprise on Hargensen's face, crossed his fingers, and went in for what he hoped would be a knockout – or at least a TKO that would save Desjardin's job and take this silk-ass son of a bitch down a notch.

'You apparently haven't realized all the implications of *in loco parentis* in this matter, Mr Hargensen. The same umbrella that covers your daughter also covers Carrie White. And the minute you file for damages on the grounds of physical and verbal abuse, we will cross-file against your daughter on those same grounds for Carrie White.'

Hargensen's mouth dropped open, then closed. 'You can't get away with a cheap gimmick like that, you—'

'Shyster lawyer? Is that the phrase you were looking for?' Grayle smiled grimly. 'I believe you know your way out, Mr Hargensen. The sanctions against your daughter stand. If you care to take the matter further, that is your right.'

Hargensen crossed the room stiffly, paused as if to add something, then left, barely restraining himself from the satisfaction of a hard doorslam.

Grayle blew out breath. It wasn't hard to see where Chris Hargensen came by her self-willed stubbornness.

A. P. Morton entered a minute later. 'How did it go?'

'Time'll tell, Morty,' Grayle said. Grimacing, he looked at the twisted pile of paper clips. 'He was good for seven clips, anyway. That's some kind of record.'

'Is he going to make it a civil matter?'

'Don't know. It rocked him when I said we'd cross-sue.'

'I bet it did.' Morton glanced at the phone on Grayle's desk. 'It's time we let the superintendent in on this bag of garbage, isn't it?'

'Yes.' Grayle said, picking up the phone. 'Thank God my unemployment insurance is paid up.'

'Me too,' Morton said loyally.

From *The Shadow Exploded* (Appendix III):

Carietta White passed in the following short verse as a poetry assignment in the seventh grade. Mr Edwin King, who had Carrie for grade seven English, says: 'I don't know why I saved it. She certainly doesn't stick out in my mind as a superior pupil, and this isn't a superior verse. She was very quiet and I can't remember her ever raising her hand even once in class. But something in this seemed to cry out.'

Jesus watches from the wall,
But his face is cold as stone,
And if he loves me
As she tells me
Why do I feel so all alone?

The border of the paper on which this little verse is written is decorated with a great many cruciform figures which almost seem to dance. . . .

Tommy was at baseball practice Monday afternoon, and Sue went down to the Kelly Fruit Company in The Center to wait for him.

Kelly's was the closest thing to a high school hangout the loosely sprawled community of Chamberlain could boast since Sheriff Doyle had closed the rec center following a large drug bust. It was run by a morose fat man named Hubert Kelly who dyed his hair black and complained constantly that his electronic pacemaker was on the verge of electrocuting him.

The place was a combination grocery, soda fountain, and gas station – there was a rusted Jenny gas pump out front that Hubie had never bothered to change when the company merged. He also sold beer, cheap wine, dirty books, and a wide selection of obscure cigarettes such as Murads, King Sano, and Marvel Straights.

The soda fountain was a slab of real marble, and there were four or five booths for kids unlucky enough or friendless enough to have no place to go and get drunk or stoned. An ancient pinball machine that always tilted on the third ball stuttered lights on and off in the back beside the rack of dirty books.

When Sue walked in she saw Chris Hargensen immediately. She was sitting in one of the back booths. Her current amour, Billy Nolan, was looking through the latest issue of *Popular Mechanics* at the magazine rack. Sue didn't know what a rich, Popular girl like Chris saw in Nolan, who was like some strange time traveler from the 1950s with his greased hair, zipper-bejeweled black leather jacket, and manifold-bubbling Chevrolet road machine.

'Sue!' Chris hailed. 'Come on over!'

Sue nodded and raised a hand, although dislike rose in her throat like a paper snake. Looking at Chris was like looking through a slanted doorway to a place where Carrie White crouched with hands over her head. Predictably, she found her own hypocrisy (inherent in the wave and the nod) incomprehensible and sickening. Why couldn't she just cut her dead?

'A dime root beer,' she told Hubie. Hubie had genuine draft root beer, and he served it in huge, frosted 1890s mugs. She had been looking forward to tipping a long one while she read a paper novel and waited for Tommy – in spite of the havoc the root beers raised with her complexion, she was hooked. But she wasn't surprised to find she'd lost her taste for this one.

'How's your heart, Hubie?' she asked.

'You kids,' Hubie said, scraping the head off Sue's beer with a table knife and filling the mug the rest of the way. 'You don't understand nothing. I plugged in my electric razor this morning and got a hundred and ten volts right through this pacemaker. You kids don't know what that's like, am I right?'

'I guess not.'

'No. Christ Jesus forbid you should ever have to find out. How long can my old ticker take it? You kids'll all find out when I buy the farm and those urban renewal poops turn this place into a parking lot. That's a dime.'

She pushed her dime across the marble.

'Fifty million volts right up the old tubes,' Hubie said darkly, and stared down at the small bulge in his breast pocket.

Sue went over and slid carefully into the vacant side of Chris's booth. She was looking exceptionally pretty, her black hair held by a shamrock-green band and a tight basque blouse that accentuated her firm, upthrust breasts.

'How are you, Chris?'

'Bitchin' good,' Chris said a little too blithely. 'You heard the latest? I'm out of the prom. I bet that cocksucker Grayle loses his job, though.'

She *had* heard the latest. Along with everyone at Ewen.

'Daddy's suing them,' Chris went on. Over her shoulder: '*Billeee*! Come over here and say hi to Sue.'

He dropped his magazine and sauntered over, thumbs hooked into his side-hitched garrison belt, fingers dangling limply toward the stuffed crotch of his pegged levis. Sue felt a wave of unreality surge over her and fought an urge to put her hands to her face and giggle madly.

'Hi, Suze,' Billy said. He slid in beside Chris and immediately began to massage her shoulder. His face was utterly blank. He might have been testing a cut of beef.

'I think we're going to crash the prom anyway,' Chris said. 'As a protest or something.'

'Is that right?' Sue was frankly startled.

'No,' Chris replied, dismissing it. 'I don't know.' Her face suddenly twisted into an expression of fury, as abrupt and surprising as a tornado funnel. 'That goddamned Carrie White! I wish she'd take her goddam holy joe routine and stuff it straight up her ass?'

'You'll get over it,' Sue said.

'If only the rest of you had walked out with me . . . Jesus, Sue, why didn't you? We could have had them by the balls. I never figured you for an establishment pawn.'

Sue felt her face grow hot. 'I don't know about anyone else, but I wasn't being anybody's pawn. I took the punishment because I thought I earned it. We did a suck-off thing. End of statement.'

'Bullshit. That fucking Carrie runs around saying everyone but her and her gilt-edged momma are going to hell and you can stick up for her? We should have taken those rags and stuffed them down her throat.'

'Sure. Yeah. See you around, Chris.' She pushed out of the booth.

This time it was Chris who colored; the blood slammed to her face in a sudden rush, as if a red cloud had passed over some inner sun.

'Aren't you getting to be the Joan of Arc around here! I seem to remember you were in there pitching with the rest of us.'

'Yes,' Sue said, trembling. 'But I stopped.'

'Oh, aren't you just *it*? Chris marveled. 'Oh, my *yes*. Take your root beer with you. I'm afraid I might touch it and turn to gold.'

She didn't take her root beer. She turned and half-walked, half-stumbled out. The upset inside her was very great, too great yet for either tears or anger. She was a get-along girl, and it was the first fight she had been in, physical or verbal, since grade-school pigtail pulling. And it was the first time in her life that she had actively espoused a Principle.

And of course Chris had hit her in just the right place, had hit her exactly where she was most vulnerable: She *was* being a hypocrite, there seemed no way to avoid that, and deeply, sheathed within her and hateful, was the knowledge that one of the reasons she had gone to Miss Desjardin's hour of calisthenics and sweating runs around the gym floor had nothing to do with nobility. She wasn't going to miss her last Spring Ball for anything. Not for *anything*.

Tommy was nowhere in sight.

She began to walk back toward the school, her stomach churning unhappily. Little Miss Sorority. Suzy Creemcheese. The Nice Girl who only does It with the boy she plans to marry – with the proper Sunday supplement coverage, of course. Two kids. Beat the living shit out of them if they show any signs of honesty: screwing, fighting, or refusing to grin each time some mythic honcho yelled frog.

Spring Ball. Blue gown. Corsage kept all the afternoon in the fridge. Tommy in a white dinner jacket, cummerbund, black pants, black shoes. Parents taking photos posed by the living-room sofa with Kodak Starflashes and Polaroid Big-Shots. Crepe masking the stark gymnasium girders. Two bands: one rock, one mellow. No fifth wheels need apply. Mortimer Snerd, please keep out. Aspiring country club members and future residents of Kleen Korners only.

The tears finally came and she began to run.

From *The Shadow Exploded* (p. 60):

The following excerpt is from a letter to Donna Kellogg from Christine Hargensen. The Kellogg girl moved from Chamberlain to Providence, Rhode Island, in the fall of 1978. She was apparently one of Chris Hargensen's few close friends and a confidante. The letter is postmarked May 17, 1979:

'So I'm out of the Prom and my yellow-guts father says he won't give them what they deserve. But they're not going to get away with it. I don't know exactly what I'm going to do yet, but I guarantee you everyone is going to get a big fucking surprise. . . .'

It was the seventeenth. May seventeenth. She crossed the day off the calendar in her room as soon as she slipped into her long white nightgown. She crossed off each day as it passed with a heavy black felt pen, and she supposed it expressed a very bad attitude toward life. She didn't really care. The only thing she really cared about was knowing that Momma was going to make her go back to school tomorrow and she would have to face all of Them.

She sat down in the small Boston rocker (bought and paid for with her own money) beside the window, closed her eyes, and swept Them and all the clutter of her conscious thoughts from her mind. It was like sweeping a floor. Lift the rug of your subconscious and sweep all the dirt under. Good-bye.

She opened her eyes. She looked at the hairbrush on her bureau.

Flex.

She was lifting the hairbrush. It was heavy. It was like lifting a barbell with very weak arms. Oh. Grunt.

The hairbrush slid to the edge of the bureau, slid out past the point where gravity should have toppled it, and then dangled, as if on an invisible string. Carrie's eyes had closed to slits. Veins pulsed in her temples. A doctor might have been interested in what her body was doing at that instant; it made no rational sense. Respiration had fallen to sixteen breaths per minute. Blood pressure up to 190/100. Heartbeat up to 140 – higher than astronauts under the heavy g-load of lift-off. Temperature down to 94.3°. Her body was burning energy that seemed to be coming from nowhere and seemed to be going nowhere. An electroencephalogram would have shown alpha waves that were no longer waves at all, but great, jagged spikes.

She let the hairbrush down carefully. Good. Last night she had dropped it. Lose all your points, go to jail.

She closed her eyes again and rocked. Physical functions began to revert to the norm; her respiration speeded until she was nearly panting. The rocker had a slight squeak. Wasn't annoying, though. Was soothing. Rock, rock. Clear your mind.

'Carrie?' Her mother's voice, slightly disturbed, floated up.

(she's getting interference like the radio when you turn on the blender good good)

'Have you said your prayers, Carrie?'

'I'm saying them,' she called back.

Yes. She was saying them, all right.

She looked at her small studio bed.

Flex.

Tremendous weight. Huge. Unbearable.

The bed trembled and then the end came up perhaps three inches.

It dropped with a crash. She waited, a small smile playing about her lips, for Momma to call upstairs angrily. She didn't. So Carrie got up, went to her bed, and slid between the cool sheets. Her head ached and she felt giddy, as she always did after these exercise sessions. Her heart was pounding in a fierce, scary way.

She reached over, turned off the light, and lay back. No pillow. Momma didn't allow her a pillow.

She thought of imps and familiars and witches

(am i a witch momma the devil's whore)

riding through the night, souring milk, overturning butter churns, blighting crops while They huddled inside their houses with hex signs scrawled on Their doors.

She closed her eyes, slept, and dreamed of huge, living stones crashing through the night, seeking out Momma, seeking out Them. They were trying to run, trying to hide. But the rock would not hide them; the dead tree gave no shelter.

From *My Name Is Susan Snell* by Susan Snell (New York: Simon & Schuster, 1986), pp. i–iv:

There's one thing no one has understood about what happened in Chamberlain on Prom Night. The press hasn't understood it, the scientists at Duke University haven't understood it, David Congress hasn't understood it – although his *The Shadow Exploded* is probably the only half-decent book written on the subject – and certainly the White Commission, which used me as a handy scapegoat, did not understand it.

This one thing is the most fundamental fact: We were kids.

Carrie was seventeen, Chris Hargensen was seventeen, I was seventeen, Tommy Ross was eighteen, Billy Nolan (who spent a year repeating the ninth grade, presumably before he learned how to shoot his cuffs during examinations) was nineteen. . . .

Older kids react in more socially acceptable ways than younger kids, but they still have a way of making bad decisions, of over-reacting, of underestimating.

In the first section which follows this introduction I must show these tendencies in myself as well as I am able. Yet the matter which I am going to discuss is at the root of my involvement in Prom Night, and if I am to clear my name, I must begin by recalling scenes which I find particularly painful. . . .

I have told this story before, most notoriously before the White Commission, which received it with incredulity. In the wake of two hundred deaths and the destruction of an entire town, it is so easy to forget one thing: We were kids. We were kids. We were kids trying to do our best. . . .

'You must be crazy.'

He blinked at her, not willing to believe that he had actually heard it. They were at his house, and the television was on but forgotten. His mother had gone over to visit Mrs Klein across the street. His father was in the cellar workroom making a birdhouse.

Sue looked uncomfortable but determined. 'It's the way I want it, Tommy.'

'Well, it's not the way I want it. I think it's the craziest goddam thing I ever heard. Like something you might do on a bet.'

Her face tightened. 'Oh? I thought you were the one making the big speeches the other night. But when it comes to putting your money where your big fat mouth is—'

'Wait, whoa.' He was unoffended, grinning. 'I didn't say no, did I? Not yet, anyway.'

'You—'

'Wait. Just wait. Let me talk. You want me to ask Carrie White to the Spring Ball. Okay, I got that. But there's a couple of things I don't understand.'

'Name them.' She leaned forward.

'First, what good would it do? And second, what makes you think she'd say yes if I asked her?'

'Not say yes! Why—' She floundered. 'You're . . . everybody likes you and—'

'We both know Carrie's got no reason to care much for people that everybody likes.'

'She'd go with you.'

'Why?'

Pressed, she looked defiant and proud at the same time. 'I've seen the way she looks at you. She's got a crush. Like half the girls at Ewen.'

He rolled his eyes.

'Well, I'm just telling you,' Sue said defensively. 'She won't be able to say no.'

'Suppose I believe you,' he said. 'What about the other thing?'

'You mean what good will it do? Why . . . it'll bring her out of her shell, of course. Make her . . .' She trailed off.

'A part of things? Come on, Suze. You don't believe that bullshit.'

'All right,' she said. 'Maybe I don't. But maybe I still think I've got something to make up for.'

'The shower room?'

'A lot more than that. Maybe if that was all I could let it go, but the means tricks have been going on ever since grammar school. I wasn't in on many of them, but I was on some. If I'd been in Carrie's groups, I bet I would have been in on even more. It seemed like . . . oh, a big laugh. Girls can be cat-mean about that sort of thing, and boys don't really understand. The boys would tease Carrie for a little while and then forget, but the girls . . . it went on and on and on and I can't even remember where it started any more. If I were Carrie, I couldn't even face showing myself to the world. I'd just find a big rock and hide under it.'

'You were kids,' he said. 'Kids don't know what they're doing. Kids don't even know their reactions really, actually, hurt other people. They have no, uh, empathy. Dig?'

She found herself struggling to express the thought this called up in her, for it suddenly seemed basic, bulking over the shower-room incident the way sky bulks over mountains.

'But hardly *anybody* ever finds out that their actions really, actually, hurt other people! People don't get better, they just get smarter. When you get smarter you don't stop pulling the wings off flies, you just think of better reasons for doing it. Lots of kids say they feel sorry for Carrie White – mostly girls, and *that's* a laugh – but I bet none of them understand what it's like to *be* Carrie White, every second of every day. And they don't really care.'

'Do you?'

'I don't know!' she cried. 'But someone ought to try and be sorry in a way that counts . . . in a way that means something.'

'All right. I'll ask her.'

'You will?' The statement came out in a flat, surprised way. She had not thought he actually would.

'Yes. But I think she'll say no. You've overestimated my box-office appeal. That popularity stuff is bullshit. You've got a bee in your bonnet about that.'

'Thank you,' she said, and it sounded odd, as if she had thanked an Inquisitor for torture.

'I love you,' he said.

She looked at him, startled. It was the first time he had said it.

From *My Name Is Susan Snell* (p. 6):

There are lots of people – mostly men – who aren't surprised that I asked Tommy to take Carrie to the Spring Ball. They are surprised that he did it, though, which shows you that the male mind expects very little in the way of altruism from its fellows.

Tommy took her because he loved me and because it was what I wanted. How, asks the skeptic from the balcony, did you know he loved you? Because he told me so, mister. And if you'd known him, that would have been good enough for you, too. . . .

He asked her on Thursday, after lunch, and found himself as nervous as a kid going to his first ice-cream party.

She sat four rows over from him in Period Five study hall, and when it was over he cut across to her through the mass of rushing bodies. At the teacher's desk, Mr Stephens, a tall man just beginning to run to fat, was folding papers abstractedly back into his ratty brown briefcase.

'Carrie?'

'Ohuh?'

She looked up from her books with a startled wince, as if expecting a blow. The day was overcast and the bank of flourescents embedded in the ceiling was not particularly kind to her pale complexion. But he saw for the first time (because it was the first time he had really looked) that she was far from repulsive. Her face was round rather than oval, and the eyes were so dark that they seemed to cast shadows beneath them, like bruises. Her hair was darkish blonde, slightly wiry, pulled back in a bun that was not becoming to her. The lips were full, almost lush, the teeth naturally white. Her body, for the most part, was indeterminate. A baggy sweater concealed her breasts except for token nubs. The skirt was colorful but awful all the same: It fell to a 1958 midshin hem in an odd and clumsy A-line. The calves were strong and rounded (the attempt to conceal these with heathery knee-socks was bizarre but unsuccessful) and handsome.

She was looking up with an expression that was slightly fearful, slightly something else. He was quite sure he knew what the something else was. Sue had been right, and being right, he had just time to wonder if this was doing a kindness or making things even worse.

'If you don't have a date for the Ball, would you want to go with me?'

Now she blinked, and as she did so, a strange thing happened. The time it took to happen could have been no more than the doorway to a second, but afterward he had no trouble recalling it, as one does with dreams or the sensation of *dêjà vu*. He felt a dizziness as if his mind was no longer controlling his body – the miserable, out-of-control feeling he associated with drinking too much and then coming to the vomiting point.

Then it was gone.

'What? What?'

She wasn't angry, at least. He had expected a brief gust of rage and then a sweeping retreat. But she wasn't angry; she seemed unable to cope with what he had said at all. They were alone in the study hall now, perfectly between the ebb of old students and the flow of new ones.

'The Spring Ball,' he said, a little shaken. 'It's next Friday and I know this is late notice but—'

'I don't like to be tricked,' she said softly, and lowered her head. She hesitated for just a second and then passed him by. She stopped and turned and he suddenly saw dignity in her, something so natural that he doubted if she was even aware of it. 'Do You People think you can just go on tricking me forever? I know who you go around with.'

'I don't go around with anyone I don't want to,' Tommy said patiently. 'I'm asking you because I want to ask you.' Ultimately, he knew this to be the truth. If Sue was making a gesture of atonement, she was doing it only at secondhand.

The Period Six students were coming in now, and some of them were looking over curiously. Dale Ullman said something to a boy Tommy didn't know and both of them snickered.

'Come on,' Tommy said. They walked out into the hall.

They were halfway to Wing Four – his class was the other way – walking together but perhaps only by accident, when she said, almost too quietly to hear: 'I'd love to. Love to.'

He was perceptive enough to know it was not an acceptance, and again doubt assailed him. Still, it was started. 'Do it, then. It will be all right. For both of us. We'll see to it.'

'No,' she said, and in her sudden pensiveness she could have been mistaken for beautiful. 'It will be a nightmare.'

'I don't have tickets,' he said, as if he hadn't heard. 'This is the last day they sell them.'

'Hey, Tommy, you're going the wrong way!' Brent Gillian yelled.

She stopped. 'You're going to be late.'

'Will you?'

'Your class,' she said, distraught. 'Your class. The bell is going to ring.'

'Will you?'

'Yes,' she said with angry helplessness. 'You knew I would.' She swiped at her eyes with the back of her hand.

'No,' he said. 'But now I do. I'll pick you up at seven-thirty.'

'Fine,' she whispered. 'Thank you.' She looked as if she might swoon.

And then, more uncertain than ever, he touched her hand.

From *The Shadow Exploded* (pp. 74 – 76):

Probably no other aspect of the Carrie White affair has been so misunderstood, second-guessed, and shrouded in mystery as the part played by Thomas Everett Ross, Carrie's ill-starred escort to the Ewen High School Spring Ball.

Morton Cratzchbarken, in an admittedly sensationalized address to The National Colloquim on Psychic Phenomena last year, said that the two most stunning events of the twentieth century have been the assassination of John F. Kennedy in 1963 and the destruction that came to Chamberlain, Maine, in May of 1979. Cratzchbarken points out that both events were driven home to the citizenry by mass media, and both events have almost shouted the frightening fact that, while something had ended, something else had been irrevocably set in motion, for good or ill. If the comparison can be made, then Thomas Ross played the part of a Lee Harvey Oswald – trigger man in a catastrophe. The question that still remains is: Did he do so wittingly or unwittingly?

Susan Snell, by her own admission, was to have been escorted by Ross to the annual event. She claims that she suggested Ross take Carrie to make up for her part in the shower-room incident. Those who oppose this story, most lately led by George Jerome of Harvard, claim that this is either a highly romantic distortion or an outright lie. Jerome argues with great force and eloquence that it is hardly typical of high-school-age adolescents to feel that they have to 'atone' for anything – particularly for an offense against a peer who has been ostracized from existing cliques.

'It would be uplifting if we could believe that adolescent human nature is capable of salvaging the pride and self-image of the low bird in the pecking order with such a gesture,' Jerome has said in a recent issue of *The Atlantic Monthly* 'but we know better. The low bird is not picked tenderly out of the dust by its fellows; rather, it is dispatched quickly and without mercy.'

Jerome, of course, is absolutely right – about birds, at any rate – and his eloquence is undoubtedly responsible in large part for the advancement of the 'practical joker' theory, which the White Commission approached but did not actually state. This theory hypothesizes that Ross and Christine Hargensen (see pp. 10–18) were at the center of a loose conspiracy to get Carrie White to the Spring Ball, and, once there, complete her humiliation. Some theorists (mostly crime writers) also claim that Sue Snell was an active part of this conspiracy. This casts the mysterious Mr Ross in the worst possible light, that of a practical joker deliberately maneuvering an unstable girl into a situation of extreme stress.

This author doesn't believe that likely in light of Mr Ross's character. This is a facet which has remained largely unexplored by his detractors, who have painted him as a rather dull clique-centered athlete; the phrase 'dumb jock' expresses this view of Tommy Ross perfectly.

It is true that Ross was an athlete of above-average ability. His best sport was baseball, and he was a member of the Ewen varsity squad from his Sophomore year. Dick O'Connell, general manager of the Boston Red Sox, has indicated that Ross would have been offered a fairly large bonus for signing a contract, had he lived.

But Ross was also a straight-A student (hardly fitting the 'dumb jock' image), and his parents have both said that he had decided pro baseball would have to wait until he had finished college, where he planned to study for an English degree. His interests included writing poetry, and a poem written six months prior to his death was published in an established 'little magazine' called *Everleaf*. This is available in Appendix V.

His surviving classmates also give him high marks, and this is significant. There were only twelve survivors of what has become known in the popular press as Prom Night. Those who were not in attendance were largely the unpopular members of the Junior and Senior classes. If these 'outs' remember Ross as a friendly, good-natured fellow (many referred to him as 'a hell of a good shit'), does not Professor Jerome's thesis suffer accordingly?

Ross's school records - which cannot, according to the state law, be photostated here - when taken with classmates' recollections and the comments of relatives, neighbors, and teachers, form a picture of an extraordinary young man. This is a fact that jells very badly with Professor Jerome's picture of a peer-worshiping, sly young tough. He apparently had a high enough tolerance to verbal abuse and enough independence from his peer group to ask Carrie in the first place. In fact, Thomas Ross appears to have been something of a rarity: a socially conscious young man.

No case will be made here for his sainthood. There is none to be made. But intensive research has satisfied me that neither was he a human chicken in a public-school barnyard, joining mindlessly in the ruin of a weaker hen . . .

She lay

(i am not afraid not afraid of her)

on her bed with an arm thrown over her eyes. It was Saturday night. If she was to make the dress she had in mind, she would have to start tomorrow at the

(i'm not afraid momma)

latest. She had already bought the material at John's in Westover. The heavy, crumpled velvet richness of it frightened her. The price had also frightened her, and she had been intimidated by the size of the place, the chic ladies wandering here and there in their light spring dresses, examining bolts of cloth. There was an echoing strangeness in the atmosphere and it was worlds from the Chamberlain Woolworth's, where she usually bought her material.

She was intimidated but not stopped. Because, if she wanted to, she could send them all screaming into the streets. Mannequins toppling over, light fixtures falling, bolts of cloth shooting through the air in unwinding streamers. Like Samson in the temple, she could rain destruction on their heads if she so desired.

(i am not afraid)

The package was now hidden on a dry shelf down in the cellar, and she was going to bring it up. Tonight.

She opened her eyes.

Flex.

The bureau rose into the air, trembled for a moment, and then rose until it nearly touched the ceiling. She lowered it. Lifted it. Lowered it. Now the bed, complete with her weight. Up. Down. Up. Down. Just like an elevator.

She was hardly tired at all. Well, a little. Not much. The ability, almost lost two weeks ago, was in full flower. It had progressed at a speed that was—

Well, almost terrifying.

And now, seemingly unbidden – like the knowledge of menstruation – a score of memories had come, as if some mental dam had been knocked down so that strange waters could gush forth. They were cloudy, distorted little-girl memories, but very real for all that. Making the pictures dance on the walls; turning on the water faucets from across the room; Momma asking her

(carrie shut the windows it's going to rain)

to do something and windows suddenly banging down all over the house; giving Miss Macaferty four flat tires all at once by unscrewing the valves in the tires of her Volkswagen; the stones—

(!!!!!!!no no no no no!!!!!!!)

—but now there was no denying the memory, no more than there could be a denying of the monthly flow, and that memory was not cloudy, no, not *that* one; it was harsh and brilliant, like jagged strokes of lightning: the little girl

(momma stop momma don't i can't breathe o my throat o momma i'm sorry i looked momma o my tongue blood in my mouth)

the poor little girl

(screaming: little slut o i know how it is with you i see what has to be done)

the poor little girl lying half in the closet and half out of it, seeing black stars dancing in front of everything, a sweet, faraway buzzing, swollen tongue lolling between her lips, throat circled with a bracelet of puffed, abraded flesh where Momma had throttled her and then Momma coming back, coming for her, Momma holding Daddy Ralph's long butcher knife

(cut it out i have to cut out the evil the nastiness sins of the flesh o i know about that the eyes cut out your eyes)

in her right hand, Momma's face twisted and working, drool on her chin, holding Daddy Ralph's Bible in her other hand

(you'll never look at that naked wickedness again)

and something flexed, not flex but *FLEX*, something huge and unformed and titanic, a well-spring of power that was not hers now and never would be again and then something on the roof and Momma screamed and dropped Daddy Ralph's Bible and that was *good*, and then more bumps and thumps and then the house began to throw its furnishings around and Momma dropped the knife and got on her knees and began to pray, holding up her hands and swaying on her knees while chairs whistled down the hall and the beds upstairs fell over and the dining room table tried to jam itself through a window and then Momma's eyes growing huge and crazed, bulging, her finger pointing at the little girl

(it's you it's you devilspawn witch imp of the devil it's *you* doing it)

and then the stones and Momma had fainted as their roof cracked and thumped as if with the footfalls of God and then—

Then she fainted herself. And after that there were no more memories. Momma did not speak of it. The butcher knife was back in its drawer. Momma dressed the huge black and blue bruises on her neck and Carrie thought she could remember asking Momma how she had gotten them and Momma tightening her lips and saying nothing. Little by little it was forgotten. The eye of memory opened only in dreams. The pictures no longer danced on the walls. The windows did not shut themselves. Carrie did not remember a time when things had been different. Not until now.

She lay on her bed, looking at the ceiling, sweating.

'Carrie! Supper!'

'Thank you,
(i am not afraid)
Momma.'

She got up and fixed her hair with a dark-blue headband. Then she went downstairs.

From *The Shadow Exploded* (p. 59):

How apparent was Carrie's 'wild talent' and what did Margaret White, with her extreme Christian ethic, think of it? We shall probably never know. But one is tempted to believe that Mrs White's reaction must have been extreme . . .

'You haven't touched your pie, Carrie.' Momma looked up from the tract she had been perusing while she drank her Constant Comment. 'It's homemade.'

'It makes me have pimples, Momma.'

'Your pimples are the Lord's way of chastising you. Now eat your pie.'

'Momma?'

'Yes?'

Carrie plunged. 'I've been invited to the Spring Ball next Friday by Tommy Ross—'

The tract was forgotten. Momma was staring at her with wide my-ears-are-deceiving-me eyes. Her nostrils flared like those of a horse that has heard the dry rattle of a snake.

Carrie tried to swallow an obstruction and only
(i am not afraid o yes i am)
got rid of part of it.

'—and he's a very nice boy. He's promised to stop in and meet you before and—'

'No.'

'—to have me in by eleven. I've—'

'No, no, *no!*'

'—accepted. Momma, please see that I have to start to . . . to try and get along with the world. I'm not like you. I'm funny – I mean, the kids think I'm funny. I don't want to be. I want to try and be a person before it's too late to—'

Mrs White threw her tea in Carrie's face.

It was only lukewarm, but it could not have shut off Carrie's words more suddenly if it had been scalding. She sat numbly, the amber fluid dripping from her chin and cheeks onto her white blouse, spreading. It was sticky and smelled like cinnamon.

Mrs White sat trembling, her face frozen except for her nostrils, which continued to flare. Abruptly she threw back her head and screamed at the ceiling.

'God! God! God!' Her jaw snapped brutally over each syllable.

Carrie sat without moving.

Mrs White got up and came around the table. Her hands were hooked into shaking claws. Her face bore a half-mad expression of compassion mixed with hate.

'The closet,' she said. 'Go to your closet and pray.'

'No, Momma.'

'Boys. Yes, boys come next. After the blood the boys come. Like sniffing dogs, grinning and slobbering, trying to find out where that smell is. *That . . . smell!*'

She swung her whole arm into the blow, and the sound of her palm against Carrie's face

(o god i am so afraid now)

was like that flat sound of a leather belt being snapped in air. Carrie remained seated, although her upper body swayed. The mark on her cheek was first white, then blood red.

'The mark,' Mrs White said. Her eyes were large but blank; she was breathing in rapid, snatching gulps of air. She seemed to be talking to herself as the claw hand descended onto Carrie's shoulder and pulled her out of her chair.

'I've seen it, all right. Oh yes. But. I. Never. Did. But for him. He. Took. Me . . . ' She paused, her eyes wandering vaguely toward the ceiling. Carrie was terrified. Momma seemed in the throes of some great revelation which might destroy her.

'Momma—'

'In cars. Oh, I know where they take you in their cars. City limits. Roadhouses. Whiskey. Smelling . . . *oh they smell it on you*!' Her voice rose to a scream. Tendons stood out on her neck, and her head twisted in a questing upward rotation.

'Momma, you better stop.'

This seemed to snap her back to some kind of hazy reality. Her lips twitched in a kind of elementary surprise and she halted, as if groping for old bearings in a new world.

'The closet,' she muttered. 'Go to your closet and pray.'

'No.'

Momma raised her hand to strike.

'*No!*'

The hand stopped in the dead air. Momma stared up at it, as if to confirm that it was still there, and whole.

The pie pan suddenly rose from the trivet on the table and hurled itself across the room to impact beside the living-room door in a splash of blueberry drool.

'*I'm going, Momma!*'

Momma's overturned teacup rose and flew past her head to shatter above the stove. Momma shrieked and dropped to her knees with her hands over her head.

'Devil's child,' she moaned. 'Devil's child, Satan spawn—'

'Momma, stand up.'

'Lust and licentiousness, the cravings of the flesh—'

'*Stand up!*'

Momma's voice failed her but she did stand up, with her hands still on her head, like a prisoner of war. Her lips moved. To Carrie she seemed to be reciting the Lord's Prayer.

'I don't want to fight with you, Momma,' Carrie said, and her voice almost broke from her and dissolved. She struggled to control it. 'I only want to be let to live my own life. I . . . I don't like yours.' She stopped, horrified in spite of herself. The ultimate blasphemy had been spoken, and it was a thousand times worse than the Eff Word.

'Witch,' Momma whispered. 'It says in the Lord's Book: "Thou shalt not suffer a witch to live." Your father did the Lord's work—'

'I don't want to talk about that,' Carrie said. It always disturbed her to hear Momma talk about her father. 'I just want you to understand that things are going to change around here, Momma.' Her eyes gleamed. '*They* better understand it, too.'

But Momma was whispering to herself again.

Unsatisfied, with a feeling of anticlimax in her throat and the dismal roiling of emotional upset in her belly, she went to the cellar to get her dress material.

It was better than the closet. There was that. Anything was better than the closet with its blue light and the overpowering stench of sweat and her own sin. Anything. Everything.

She stood with the wrapped package hugged against her breast and closed her eyes, shutting out the weak glow of the cellar's bare, cobweb-festooned bulb. Tommy Ross didn't love her; she knew that. This was some strange kind of atonement, and she could understand that and respond to it. She had lain cheek and jowl with the concept of penance since she had been old enough to reason.

He said it would be good – that they would see to it. Well, *she* would see to it. They better not start anything. They just better not. She did not know if her gift had come from the lord of light or of darkness, and now, finally finding that she did not care which, she was overcome with an almost indescribable relief, as if a huge weight, long carried, had slipped from her shoulders.

Upstairs, Momma continued to whisper. It was not the Lord's Prayer. It was the Prayer of Exorcism from Deuteronomy.

From *My Name Is Susan Snell* (p. 23):

They finally even made a movie about it. I saw it last April. When I came out, I was sick. Whenever anything important happens in America, they have to gold-plate it, like baby shoes. That way you can forget it. And forgetting Carrie White may be a bigger mistake than anyone realizes. . . .

Monday morning; Principal Grayle and his understudy, Pete Morton, were having coffee in Grayle's office.

'No word from Hargensen yet?' Morty asked. His lips curled into a John Wayne leer that was a little frightened around the edges.

'Not a peep. And Christine has stopped lipping off about how her father is going to send us down the road.' Grayle blew on his coffee with a long face.

'You don't exactly seem to be turning cartwheels.'

'I'm not. Did you know Carrie White is going to the prom?'

Morty blinked. 'With who? The Beak?' The Beak was Freddy Holt, another of Ewen's misfits. He weighed perhaps one hundred pounds soaking wet, and the casual observer might be tempted to believe that sixty of it was nose.

'No,' Grayle said. 'With Tommy Ross.'

Morty swallowed his coffee the wrong way and went into a coughing fit.

'That's the way I felt,' Grayle said.

'What about his girl friend? The little Snell girl?'

'I think she put him up to it,' Grayle said. 'She certainly seemed guilty enough about what happened to Carrie when I talked to her. Now she's on the Decoration Committee, happy as a clam, just as if not going to her Senior prom was nothing at all.'

'Oh,' Morty said wisely.

'And Hargensen – I think he must have talked to some people and discovered we really could sue him on behalf of Carrie White if we wanted to. I think he's cut his losses. It's the daughter that's worrying me.'

'Do you think there's going to be an incident Friday night?'

'I don't know. I do know Chris has got a lot of friends who are going to be there. And she's going around with that Billy Nolan mess; he's got a zooful of friends, too. The kind that make a career out of scaring pregnant ladies. Chris Hargensen has him tied around her finger, from what I've heard.'

'Are you afraid of anything specific?'

Grayle made a restless gesture. 'Specific? No. But I've been in the game long enough to know it's a bad situation. Do you remember the Stadler game in seventy-six?'

Morty nodded. It would take more than the passage of three years to obscure the memory of the Ewen-Stadler game. Bruce Trevor had been a marginal student but a fantastic basketball player. Coach Gaines didn't like him, but Trevor was going to put Ewen in the area tournament for the first time in ten years. He was cut from the team a week before Ewen's last must-win game against the Stadler Bobcats. A regular announced locker inspection had uncovered a kilo of marijuana behind Trevor's civics book. Ewen lost the game – and their shot at the tourney – 104–48. But no one remembered that; what they remembered was the riot that had interrupted the game in the fourth period. Led by Bruce Trevor, who righteously claimed he had been bum rapped, it resulted in four hospital admissions. One of them had been the Stadler coach, who had been hit over the head with a first-aid kit.

'I've got that kind of feeling,' Grayle said. 'A hunch. Someone's going to come with rotten apples or something.'

'Maybe you're psychic,' Morty said.

From *The Shadow Exploded* (pp. 92–93):

It is now generally agreed that the TK phenomenon is a genetic-recessive occurrence – but the opposite of a disease like hemophilia, which becomes overt only in males. In that disease, once called 'King's Evil,' the gene is recessive in the female and is carried harmlessly. Male offspring, however, are 'bleeders.' This disease is generated only if an afflicted male marries a woman carrying the recessive gene. If the offspring of such union is male, the result will be a hemophiliac son. If the offspring is female, the result will be a daughter who is a carrier. It should be emphasized that the hemophilia gene *may* be carried recessively in the male as a part of his genetic make-up. But if he marries a woman with the same outlaw gene, the result will be hemophilia if the offspring is male.

In the case of royal families, where intermarriage was common, the chance of the gene reproducing once it entered the family tree were high – thus the name King's Evil. Hemophilia also showed up in significant quantities in Appalachia during the earlier part of this century, and is commonly noticed in those cultures where incest and the marriage of first cousins is common.

With the TK phenomenon, the male appears to be the carrier; the TK gene *may* be recessive in the female, but dominates *only* in the female. It appears that Ralph White carried the gene. Margaret Brigham, by purest chance, also carried the outlaw gene sign, but we may be fairly confident that it was recessive, as no information has ever been found to indicate that she had telekinetic powers resembling her daughter's. Investigations are now being conducted into the life of Margaret Brigham's grandmother, Sadie Cochran – for, if the dominant/recessive pattern obtains with TK as it does with hemophilia, Mrs Cochran may have been TK dominant.

If the issue of the White marriage had been male, the result would have been another carrier. Chances that the mutation would have died with him would have been excellent, as neither side of the Ralph White–Margaret Brigham alliance had cousins of a comparable age for the theoretical male offspring to marry. And the chances of meeting and marrying another woman with the TK gene at random would be small. None of the teams working on the problem have yet isolated the gene.

Surely no one can doubt, in light of the Maine halocaust, that isolating this gene must become one of medicine's number-one priorities. The hemophiliac, or H gene, produces male issue with a lack of blood platelets. The telekinetic, or TK gene, produces female Typhoid Marys capable of destroying almost at will. . . .

Wednesday afternoon.

Susan and fourteen other students – The Spring Ball Decoration Committee, no less – were working on the huge mural that would hang behind the twin bandstands on Friday night. The theme was Springtime in Venice (who picked these hokey themes, Sue wondered. She had been a student at Ewen for four years, had attended two Balls, and she still didn't know. Why did the goddam thing *need* a theme, anyway? Why not just have a sock hop and be done with it?); George Chizmar, Ewen's most artistic student, had done a small chalk sketch of gondolas on a canal at sunset and a gondolier in a huge straw fedora leaning against the tiller as a gorgeous panoply of pinks and reds and oranges stained both sky and water. It *was* beautiful, no doubt about that. He had redrawn it in silhouette on a huge fourteen-by-twenty-foot canvas flat, numbering the various sections to go with various chalk hues. Now the Committee was patiently coloring it in, like children crawling over a huge page in a giant's coloring book. Still, Sue thought, looking at her hands and forearms, both heavily dusted with pink chalk, it was going to be the prettiest prom ever.

Next to her, Helen Shyres sat up on her haunches, stretched, and groaned as her back popped. She brushed a hank of hair from her forehead with the back of her hand, leaving a rose-colored smear.

'*How* in hell did you talk me into this?'

'You want it to be nice, don't you?' Sue mimicked Miss Geer, the spinster chairman (apt enough term for Miss Mustache) of the Decoration Committee.

'Yeah, but why not the Refreshment Committee or the Entertainment Committee? Less back, more mind. The mind, that's my area. Besides, you're not even—' She bit down on the words.

'Going?' Susan shrugged and picked up her chalk again. She had a monstrous writer's cramp. 'No, but I still want it to be nice.' She added shyly: 'Tommy's going.'

They worked in silence for a bit, and then Helen stopped again. No one was near them; the closest was Holly Marshall, on the other end of the mural, coloring the gondola's keel.

'Can I ask you about it, Sue?' Helen asked finally. 'God, everybody's talking.'

'Sure.' Sue stopped coloring and flexed her hand. 'Maybe I ought to tell someone, just so the story stays straight. I asked Tommy to take Carrie. I'm hoping it'll bring her out of herself a little . . . knock down some of the barriers. I think I owe her that much.'

'Where does that put the rest of us?' Helen asked without rancor.

Sue shrugged. 'You have to make up your own mind about what we did, Helen. I'm in no position to throw stones. But I don't want people to think I'm uh . . . '

'Playing martyr?'

'Something like that.'

'And Tommy went along with it?' This was the part that most fascinated her.

'Yes,' Sue said, and did not elaborate. After a pause: 'I suppose the other kids think I'm stuck up.'

Helen thought it over. 'Well . . . they're all talking about it. But most of them still think you're okay. Like you said, you make your own decisions. There is, however, a small dissenting faction.' She snickered dolefully.

'The Chris Hargensen people?'

'And the Billy Nolan people. God, he's scuzzy.'

'She doesn't like me much?' Sue said, making it a question.

'Susie, she hates your guts.'

Susan nodded, surprised to find the thought both distressed and excited her.

'I heard her father was going to sue the School Department and then he changed his mind,' she said.

Helen shrugged. 'She hasn't made any friends out of this,' she said. 'I don't know what got into us, any of us. It makes me feel like I don't even know my own mind.'

They worked on in silence. Across the room, Don Barrett was putting up an extension ladder preparatory to gilding the overhead steel beams with crepe paper.

'Look,' Helen said. 'There goes Chris now.'

Susan looked up just in time to see her walking into the cubby-hole office to the left of the gym entrance. She was wearing wine-colored velvet hot pants and a silky white blouse – no bra, from the way things were jiggling up front – a dirty old man's dream, Sue thought sourly, and then wondered what Chris could want in where the Prom Committee had set up shop. Of course Tina Blake was on the Committee and the two of them were thicker than thieves.

Stop it, she scolded herself. Do you want her in sackcloth and ashes?

Yes, she admitted. A part of her wanted just that.

'Helen?'

'Hmmmm?'

'Are they going to do something?'

Helen's face took on an unwilling masklike quality. 'I don't know.' The voice was light, over-innocent.

'Oh,' Sue said noncommittally.

(you know you know something: accept something goddammit if it's only yourself tell me)

They continued to color, and neither spoke. She knew it wasn't as all right as Helen had said. It couldn't be; she would never be quite the same golden girl in the eyes of her mates. She had done an ungovernable, dangerous thing – she had broken cover and shown her face.

The late afternoon sunlight, warm as oil and sweet as childhood, slanted through the high, bright gymnasium windows.

From *My Name Is Susan Snell* (p. 40):

I can understand some of what must have led up to the prom. Awful as it was, I can understand how someone like Billy Nolan could go along, for instance. Chris Hargensen led him by the nose – at least, most of the time. His friends were just as easily led by Billy himself. Kenny Garson, who dropped out of high school when he was eighteen, had a tested third-grade reading level. In the clinical sense, Steve Deighan was little more than an idiot. Some of the others had police records; one of them, Jackie Talbot, was first busted at the age of nine for stealing hubcaps. If you've got a social-worker mentality, you can even regard these people as unfortunate victims.

But what can you say for Chris Hargensen herself?

It seems to me that from first to last, her one and only object in view was the complete and total destruction of Carrie White. . . .

'I'm not supposed to,' Tina Blake said uneasily. She was a small, pretty girl with a billow of red hair. A pencil was pushed importantly in it. 'And if Norma comes back, she'll spill.'

'She's in the crapper,' Chris said. 'Come on.'

Tina, a little shocked, giggled in spite of herself. Still, she offered token resistance: 'Why do you want to see, anyway? You can't go.'

'Never mind,' Chris said. As always, she seemed to bubble with dark humor.

'Here,' Tina said, and pushed a sheet enclosed in limp plastic across the desk. 'I'm going out for a Coke. If that bitchy Norma Watson comes back and catches you, I never saw you.'

'Okay,' Chris murmured, already absorbed in the floor plan. She didn't hear the door close.

George Chizmar had also done the floor plan, so it was perfect. The dance floor was clearly marked. Twin bandstands. The stage where the King and Queen would be crowned

(i'd like to crown that fucking snell bitch carrie too)

at the end of the evening. Ranged along the three sides of the floor were the prom-goers' tables. Card tables, actually, but covered with a froth of crepe and ribbon, each holding party favors, prom programs, and ballots for King and Queen.

She ran a lacquered, spade-shaped fingernail down the tables to the right of the dance floor, then the left. There: *Tommy R. & Carrie W.* They were really going through with it. She could hardly believe it. Outrage made her tremble. Did they really think they would be allowed to get away with it? Her lips tautened grimly.

She looked over her shoulder. Norma Watson was still nowhere in sight.

Chris put the seating chart back and riffled quickly through the rest of the papers on the pitted and initial-scarred desk. Invoices, (mostly for crepe paper and ha'penny nails), a list of parents who had loaned card tables, petty-cash vouchers, a bill from Star Printers, who had run off the prom tickets, a sample King and Queen ballot—

Ballot! She snatched it up.

No one was supposed to see the actual King and Queen ballot until Friday, when the whole student body would hear the candidates announced over the school's intercom. The King and Queen would be voted in by those attending the prom, but blank nomination ballots had been circulated to home rooms almost a month earlier. The results were supposed to be top secret.

There was a gaining student move afoot to do away with the King and Queen business all together – some of the girls claimed it was sexist, the boys thought it was just plain stupid and a little embarrassing. Chances were good that this would be the last year the dance would be so formal or traditional.

But for Chris, this was the only year that counted. She stared at the ballot with greedy intensity.

George and Frieda. No way. Frieda Jason was a Jew.

Peter and Myra. No way here, either. Myra was one of the female clique dedicated to erasing the whole horse race. She wouldn't serve even if elected. Besides, she was about as goodlooking as the ass-end of old drayhorse Ethel.

Frank and Jessica. Quite possible. Frank Grier had made the All New England football team this year, but Jessica was another little sparrowfart with more pimples than brains.

Don and Helen. Forget it. Helen Shyres couldn't get elected dog catcher.

And the last pairing: *Tommy and Sue.* Only Sue, of course, had been crossed out, and Carrie's name had been written in. There was a pairing to conjure with! A kind of strange, shuffling laughter came over her, and she clapped a hand over her mouth to hold it in.

Tina scurried back in. 'Jesus, Chris, you still here? She's *coming!*'

'Don't sweat it, doll,' Chris said, and put the papers back on the desk. She was still grinning as she walked out, pausing to raise a mocking hand to Sue Snell, who was slaving her skinny butt off on that stupid mural.

In the outer hall, she fumbled a dime from her bag, dropped it into the pay phone, and called Billy Nolan.

From *The Shadow Exploded* (pp. 100–1):

One wonders just how much planning went into the ruination of Carrie White – was it a carefully made plan, rehearsed and gone over many times, or just something that happened in a bumbling sort of way?

. . . I favor the latter idea. I suspect that Christine Hargensen was the brains of the affair, but that she herself had only the most nebulous of ideas on how one might 'get' a girl like Carrie. I rather suspect it was she who suggested that William Nolan and his friends make the trip to Irwin Henty's farm in North Chamberlain. The thought of that trip's imagined result would have appealed to a warped sense of poetic justice, I am sure. . . .

The car screamed up the rutted Stack End Road in North Chamberlain at a sixty-five that was dangerous to life and limb on the washboard unpaved hardpan. A low-hanging branch, lush with May leaves, occasionally scraped the roof of the '61 Biscayne, which was fender-dented, rusted out, jacked in the back, and equipped with dual glasspack mufflers. One headlight was out; the other flickered in the midnight dark when the car struck a particularly rough bump.

Billy Nolan was at the pink fuzz-covered wheel. Jackie Talbot, Henry Blake, Steve Deighan, and the Garson brothers, Kenny and Lou, were also squeezed in. Three joints were going, passing through the inner dark like the lambent eyes of some rotating Cerberus.

'You sure Henty ain't around?' Henry asked. 'I got no urge to go back up, ole Sweet William. They feed you shit.'

Kenny Garson, who was wrecked to the fifth power, found this unutterably funny and emitted a slipstream of high-pitched giggles.

'He ain't around,' Billy said. Even those few words seemed to slip out grudgingly, against his will. 'Funeral.'

Chris had found this out accidentally. Old man Henty ran one of the few successful independent farms in the Chamberlain area. Unlike the crotchety old farmer with a heart of gold that is one of the staples of pastoral literature, old man Henty was as mean as cat dirt. He did not load his shotgun with rock salt at green-apple time, but with birdshot. He had also prosecuted several fellows for pilferage. One of them had been a friend of these boys, a luckless bastard named Freddy Overlock. Freddy had been caught red-handed in old man Henty's henhouse, and had received a double dose of number-six bird where the good Lord had split him. Good ole Fred had spent four raving, cursing hours on his belly in an Emergency Wing examining room while a jovial intern picked tiny pellets out of his butt and dropped them into a steel pan. To add insult to injury, he had been fined two hundred dollars for larceny and trespass. There was no love lost between Irwin Henty and the Chamberlain greaser squad.

'What about Red?' Steve asked.

'He's trying to get into some new waitress at The Cavalier,' Billy said, swinging the wheel and pulling the Biscayne through a juddering racing drift and onto the Henty Road. Red Trelawney was ole man Henty's hired hand. He was a heavy drinker and just as handy with the birdshot as his employer. 'He won't be back until they close up.'

'Hell of a risk for a joke' Jackie Talbot grumbled.

Billy stiffened. 'You want out?'

'No, uh-uh,' Jackie said hastily. Billy had produced an ounce of good grass to split among the five of them - and besides, it was nine miles back to town. 'It's a *good* joke, Billy.'

Kenny opened the glove compartment, took out an ornate scrolled roach clip (Chris's), and fixed the smoldering butt-end of a joint in it. This operation struck him as highly amusing, and he let out his high-pitched giggle again.

Now they were flashing past No Trespassing signs on either side of the road, barbed wire, newly turned fields. The smell of fresh earth was heavy and gravid and sweet on the warm May air.

Billy popped the headlights off as they breasted the next hill, dropped the gearshift into neutral and killed the ignition. They rolled, a silent hulk of metal, toward the Henty driveway.

Billy negotiated the turn with no trouble, and most of their speed bled away as they breasted another small rise and passed the dark and empty house. Now they could see the huge bulk of barn and beyond it, moonlight glittering dreamily on the cow pond and the apple orchard.

In the pigpen, two sows poked their flat snouts through the bars. In the barn, one cow lowed softly, perhaps in sleep.

Billy stopped the car with the emergency brake - not really necessary since the ignition was off, but it was a nice Commando touch - and they got out.

Lou Garson reached past Kenny and got something out of the glove compartment. Billy and Henry went around to the trunk and opened it.

'The bastard is going to shit where he stands when he comes back and gets a look,' Steve said with soft glee.

'For Freddy,' Henry said, taking the hammer out of the trunk.

Billy said nothing, but of course it was not for Freddy Overlock, who was an asshole. It was for Chris Hargensen, just as everything was for Chris, and had been since the day she swept down from her lofty college-course Olympus and made herself vulnerable to him. He would have done murder for her, and more.

Henry was swinging the nine-pound sledge experimentally in one hand. The heavy block of its business end made a portentous swishing noise in the night air, and the other boys gathered around as Billy opened the lid of the ice chest and took out the two galvanized steel pails. They were numbingly cold to the touch, lightly traced with frost.

'Okay,' he said.

The six of them walked quickly to the hogpen, their respiration shortening with excitement. The two sows were both as tame as tabbies, and the old boar lay asleep on his side at the far end. Henry swung the sledge once more through the air, but this time with no conviction. He handed it to Billy.

'I can't,' he said sickly. 'You.'

Billy took it and looked questioningly at Lou, who held the broad butcher knife he had taken from the glove compartment.

'Don't worry,' he said, and touched the ball of his thumb to the honed edge.

'The throat,' Billy reminded.

'I know.'

Kenny was crooning and grinning as he fed the remains of a crumpled bag of potato chips to the pigs. 'Doan worry, piggies, doan worry, big Bill's gonna bash your fuckin heads in and you woan have to worry about the bomb any more.' He scratched their bristly chins, and the pigs grunted and munched contentedly.

'Here it comes,' Billy remarked, and the sledge flashed down.

There was a sound that reminded him of the time he and Henry had dropped a pumpkin off Claridge Road overpass which crossed 495 west of town. One of the sows dropped dead with its tongue protruding, eyes still open, potato chip crumbs around its snout.

Kenny giggled. 'She didn't even have time to burp.'

'Do it quick, Lou,' Billy said.

Kenny's brother slid between the slats, lifted the pig's head toward the moon – the glazing eyes regarded the crescent with rapt blankness – and slashed.

The flow of blood was immediate and startling. Several of the boys were splattered and jumped back with little cries of disgust.

Billy leaned through and put one of the buckets under the main flow. The pail filled up rapidly, and he set it aside. The second was half full when the flow trickled and died.

'The other one,' he said.

'Jesus, Billy,' Jackie whines. 'Isn't that en—'

'Soo-*ee*, pig-pig-pig,' Kenny called, grinning and rattling the empty potato-chip bag. After a pause, the sow returned to the fence. The sledge flashed. The second bucket was filled and the remainder of the blood allowed to flow into the ground. A rank, coppery smell hung on the air. Billy found he was slimed in pig blood to the forearms.

Carrying the pails back to the trunk, his mind made a dim, symbolic connection. Pig blood. That was good. Chris was right. It was really good. It made everything solidify.

Pig blood for a pig.

He nestled the galvanized steel pails into the crushed ice, capped them, and slammed the lid of the chest. 'Let's go,' he said.

Billy got behind the wheel and released the emergency brake. The five boys got behind, put their shoulders into it, and the car turned in a tight, noiseless circle and trundled up past the barn to the crest of the hill across from Henty's house.

When the car began to roll on it's own, they trotted up beside the doors and climbed in, puffing and panting.

The car gained speed enough to slew a little as Billy whipped it out of the long driveway and onto the Henty Road. At the bottom of the hill he dropped the transmission into third and popped the clutch. The engine hitched and grunted into life.

Pig blood for a pig. Yes, that was good, all right. That was really good.

He smiled, and Lou Garson felt a start of surprise and fear. He was not sure he could recall ever having seen Billy Nolan smile before. There had not even been rumors.

'Whose funeral did ole man Henty go to?' Steve asked.

'His mother's,' Billy said.

'His *mother?*' Jackie Talbot said, stunned. 'Jesus Christ, she musta been older'n God.'

Kenny's high-pitched cackle drifted back on the redolent darkness that trembled at the edge of summer.

BOOK TWO

PROM NIGHT

She put the dress on for the first time on the morning of May 27, in her room. She had bought a special brassiere to go with it, which gave her breasts the proper uplift (not that they actually needed it) but left their top halves uncovered. Wearing it gave her a weird, dreamy feeling that was half shame and half defiant excitement.

The dress itself was nearly floor length. The skirt was loose, but the waist was snug, the material rich and unfamiliar against her skin, which was used to only cotton and wool.

The hang of it seemed to be right – or would be, with the new shoes. She slipped them on, adjusted the neckline, and went to the window. She could see only a maddening ghost image of herself, but everything seemed to be right. Maybe later she could—

The door swung open behind her with only a soft snick of the latch, and Carrie turned to look at her mother.

She was dressed for work, wearing her white sweater and holding her black pocketbook in one hand. In the other she was holding Daddy Ralph's Bible.

They looked at each other.

Hardly conscious of it, Carrie felt her back straighten until she stood straight in the patch of early spring sunshine that fell through the window.

'Red,' Momma murmured. 'I might have known it would be red.'

Carrie said nothing.

'I can see your dirtypillows. Everyone will. They'll be looking at your body. The Book says—'

'Those are my breasts, Momma. Every woman has them.'

'Take off that dress,' Momma said.

'No.'

'Take it off, Carrie. We'll go down and burn it in the incinerator together, and then pray for forgiveness. We'll do penance.' Her eyes began to sparkle with the strange, disconnected zeal that came over her at events which she considered to be tests of faith. 'I'll stay home from work and you'll stay home from school. We'll pray. We'll ask for a Sign. We'll get us down on our knees and ask for the Pentecostal Fire.'

'No, Momma.'

Her mother reached up and pinched her own face. It left a red mark. She looked to Carrie for reaction, saw none, hooked her right hand into claws and ripped it across her own cheek, bringing thin blood. She whined and rocked back on her heels. Her eyes glowed with exaltation.

'Stop hurting yourself, Momma. That's not going to make me stop either.'

Momma screamed. She made her right hand a fist and struck herself in the mouth, bringing blood. She dabbled her fingers in it, looked at it dreamily, and daubed a spot on the cover of the Bible.

'Washed in the Blood of the Lamb,' she whispered. 'Many times. Many times he and I—'

'Go away, Momma.'

She looked up at Carrie, her eyes glowing. There was a terrifying expression of righteous anger graven on her face.

'The Lord is not mocked,' she whispered. 'Be sure your sin will find you out. Burn it, Carrie! Cast that devil's red from you and burn it! Burn it! Burn it! *Burn it!*'

The door slammed open by itself.

'Go away, Momma.'

Momma smiled. Her bloody mouth made the smile grotesque, twisted. 'As Jezebel fell from the tower, let it be with you,' she said. 'And the dogs came and licked up the blood. It's in the Bible! It's—'

'Her feet began to slip along the floor and she looked down at them, bewildered. The wood might have turned to ice.

'Stop that!' she screamed.

She was in the hall now. She caught the doorjamb and held on for a moment; then her fingers were torn loose, seemingly by nothing.

'I love you, Momma,' Carrie said steadily. 'I'm sorry.'

She envisioned the door swinging shut, and the door did just that, as if moved by a light breeze. Carefully, so as not to hurt her, she disengaged the mental hands she had pushed her mother with.

A moment later, Margaret was pounding on the door. Carrie held it shut, her lips trembling.

'There's going to be a judgment!' Margaret White raved. 'I wash my hands of it! I tried!'

'Pilate said that,' Carrie said.

Her mother went away. A minute later Carrie saw her go down the walk and cross the street on her way to work.

'Momma,' she said softly, and put her forehead on the glass.

From *The Shadow Exploded* (p. 129):

Before turning to a more detailed analysis of Prom Night itself, it might be well to sum up what we know of Carrie White the person.

We know that Carrie was the victim of her mother's religious mania. We know that she possessed a latent telekinetic talent, commonly referred to as TK. We know that this so-called 'wild talent' is really a hereditary trait, produced by a gene that is usually recessive, if present at all. We suspect that the TK ability may be glandular in nature. We know that Carrie produced at least one demonstration of her ability as a small girl when she was put into an extreme situation of guilt and stress. We know that a second extreme situation of guilt and stress arose from a shower-room hazing incident. It has been theorized (especially by William G. Throneberry and Julia Givens, Berkeley) that resurgence of the TK ability at this point was caused by both psychological factors (i.e., the reaction of the other girls and Carrie herself to their first menstrual period) and physiological factors (i.e., the advent of puberty).

And finally, we know that on Prom Night, a third stress situation arose, causing the terrible events which we now must begin to discuss. We will begin with . . .

(i am not nervous not a bit nervous)

Tommy had called earlier with her corsage, and now she was pinning it to the shoulder of her gown herself. There was no momma, of course, to do it for her and make sure it was in the right place. Momma had locked herself in the chapel and had been in there for the last two hours, praying hysterically. Her voice rose and fell in frightening, incoherent cycles.

(i'm sorry momma but I can't be sorry)

When she had it fixed to her satisfaction, she dropped her hands and stood quietly for a moment with her eyes closed. There was no full-length mirror in the house,

(vanity vanity all is vanity)

but she thought she was all right. She *had* to be. She—

She opened her eyes again. The Black Forest cuckoo clock, bought with Green Stamps, said seven-ten.

(he'll be here in twenty minutes)

Would he?

Maybe it was all just an elaborate joke, the final crusher, the ultimate punch line. To leave her sitting here half the night in her crushed-velvet prom gown with its princess waistline, juliet sleeves and simple straight skirt – and her tea roses pinned to her left shoulder.

From the other room, on the rise now: '. . . in hallowed earth! We know thou bring'st the Eye That Watcheth, the hideous three-lobbed Eye, and the sound of black trumpets. We most heartily repent—'

Carrie did not think anyone could understand the brute courage it had taken to reconcile herself to this, to leave herself open to whatever fearsome possibilities the night might realize. Being stood up could hardly be the worst of them. In fact, in a kind of sneaking, wishful way she thought it might be for the best if—

(no stop that)

Of course it would be easier to stay here with Momma. Safer. She knew what They thought of Momma. Well, maybe Momma was a fanatic, a freak, but at least she was predictable. The house was predictable. She never came home to laughing, shrieking girls who threw things.

And if he didn't come, if she drew back and gave up? High school would be over in a month. Then what? A creeping, subterranean existence in this house, supported by Momma, watching game shows and soap operas all day on television at Mrs Garrison's house when she had Carrie In To Visit

(Mrs Garrison was eighty-six), walking down to the Center to get a malted after supper at the Kelly Fruit when it was deserted, getting fatter, losing hope, losing even the power to think?

No. Oh dear God, please no.

(please let it be a happy ending)

'—protect us from *he* with the split foot who waits in the alleys and in the parking lots of road-house, O Saviour—'

Seven twenty-five.

Restlessly, without thinking, she began to lift objects with her mind and put them back down, the way a nervous woman awaiting someone in a restaurant will fold and unfold her napkin. She could dangle half a dozen objects in air at one time, and not a sign of tiredness or headache. She kept waiting for the power to abate, but it remained at high water with no sign of waning. The other night on her way home from school, she had rolled a parked car

(oh please god let it not be a joke)

twenty feet down the main street curb with no strain at all. The courthouse idlers had stared at it as if their eyes would pop out, and of course she stared too, but she was smiling inside.

The cuckoo popped out of the clock and spoke once. Seven-thirty.

She had grown a little wary of the terrific strain using the power seemed to put on her heart and lungs and internal thermostat. She suspected it would be all too possible for her heart to literally burst with the strain. It was like being in another's body and forcing her to run and run and run. You would not pay the cost yourself; the other body would. She was beginning to realize that her power was perhaps not so different from the powers of Indian fakirs, who stroll across hot coals, run needles into their eyes, or blithely bury themselves for periods up to six weeks. Mind over matter in any form is a terrific drain on the body's resources.

Seven thirty-two.

(he's not coming)

(don't think about it a watched pot doesn't boil he'll come)

(no he won't he's out laughing at you with his friends and after a little bit they'll drive by in one of their fast noisy cars laughing and hooting and yelling)

Miserably, she began lifting the sewing machine up and down, swinging it in widening arcs through the air.

'—and protect us also from rebellious daughters imbued with the willfulness of the Wicked One—'

'Shut up!' Carrie screamed suddenly.

There was startled silence for a moment, and then the babbling chant began again.

Seven thirty-three.

Not coming.

(then i'll wreck the house)

The thought came to her naturally and cleanly. First the sewing machine, driven through the living-room wall. The couch through a window. Tables, chairs, books and tracts all flying. The plumbing ripped loose and still spurting, like arteries ripped free of flesh. The roof itself, if that were within her power, shingles exploding upward into the night like startled pigeons—

Lights splashed gaudily across the window.

Other cars had gone by, making her heart leap a little, but this one was going much more slowly.

(o)

She ran to the window, unable to restrain herself, and it was him, Tommy, just climbing out of his car, and even under the street light he was handsome and alive and almost . . . crackling. The odd word made her want to giggle.

Momma had stopped praying.

She grabbed her light silken wrap from where it had lain across the back of her chair and put it around her bare shoulders. She bit her lip, touched her hair, and would have sold her soul for a mirror. The buzzer in the hall made its harsh cry.

She made herself wait, controlling the twitch in her hands, for the second buzz. Then she went slowly, with silken swish.

She opened the door and he was there, nearly blinding in white dinner jacket and dark dress pants.

They looked at each other, and neither said a word.

She felt that her heart would break if he uttered so much as the wrong sound, and if he laughed she would die. She felt – actually, physically – her whole miserable life narrow to a point that might be an end or the beginning of a widening beam.

Finally, helpless, she said: 'Do you like me?'

He said: 'You're beautiful.'

She was.

From *The Shadow exploded* (p. 131):

While those going to the Ewen Spring Ball were gathering at the high school or just leaving pre-Prom buffets, Christine Hargensen and William Nolan had met in a room above a local town-limits tavern called The Cavalier. We know that they had been meeting there for some time; that is in the records of the White Commission. What we don't know is whether their plans were complete and irrevocable or if they went ahead almost on whim . . .

'Is it time yet?' she asked in the darkness.

He looked at his watch. 'No.'

Faintly, through the board floor, came the thump of the juke playing 'She's Got To Be a Saint,' by Ray Price. The Cavalier, Chris reflected, hadn't changed their records since the first time she'd been here with a forged ID two years ago. Of course then she'd been down in the taprooms, not in one of Sam Deveaux's 'specials.'

Billy's cigarette winked fitfully in the dark, like the eye of an uneasy demon. She watched it introspectively. She hadn't let him sleep with her until last Monday, when he had promised that he and his greaser friends would help her pull the string on Carrie White if she actually dared to go to the prom with Tommy Ross. But they had been here before, and had some pretty hot necking sessions – what she thought of as Scotch love and what he would call, in his unfailing ability to pinpoint the vulgar, the dry humps.

She had meant to make him wait until he had actually *done* something

(but of course he did he got the blood)

but it had all began to slip out of her hands, and it made her uneasy. If she had not given in willingly on Monday, he would have taken her by force.

Billy had not been her first lover, but he was the first she could not dance and dandle at her whim. Before him her boys had been clever marionettes with clear, pimple-free faces and parents with connections and country-club memberships. They drove their own VWs or Javelins or Dodge Chargers. They went to UMass or Boston College. They wore fraternity windbreakers in the fall and muscle-shirts with bright stripes in the summer. They smoked marijuana a great deal and talked about the funny things that happened to them when they were wrecked. They began by treating her with patronizing good fellowship (all high school girls, no matter how good-looking, were Bush League) and always ended up trotting after her with panting, doglike lust. If they trotted long enough and spent enough in the process, she usually let them go to bed with her. Quite often she lay passively beneath them, not helping or hindering, until it was over. Later, she achieved her own solitary climax while viewing the incident as a single closed loop of memory.

She had met Billy Nolan following a drug bust at a Portland apartment. Four students, including Chris's date for the evening, had been busted for possession. Chris and the other girls were charged with being present there. Her father took care of it with quiet efficiency, and asked her if she knew what would happen to her image and his practice if his daughter was taken up on a drug charge. She told him that she doubted if anything could hurt either one, and he took her car away.

Billy offered her a ride home from school one afternoon a week later and she accepted.

He was what the other kids called a white-soxer or a machine shop Chuck. Yet something about him excited her and now, lying drowsily in this illicit bed (but with an awakening sense of excitement and pleasurable fear), she thought it might have been his car – at least at the start.

It was a million miles from the machine-stamped, anonymous vehicles of her fraternity dates with their ventless windows, fold-up steering wheels, and vaguely unpleasant smell of plastic seat covers and windshield solvent.

Billy's car was old, dark, somehow sinister. The windshield was milky around the edges, as if a cataract was beginning to form. The seats were loose and unanchored. Beer bottles clicked and rolled in the back (her fraternity dates drank Budweiser; Billy and his friends drank Rheingold), and she had to place her feet around a huge, grease-clotted Craftsman toolkit without a lid. The tools inside were of many different makes, and she suspected that many of them were stolen. The car smelled of oil and gas. The sound of straight pipes came loudly and exhilaratingly through the thin floorboards. A row of dials slung under the dash registered amps, oil pressure, and tach (whatever that was). The back wheels were jacked and the hood seemed to point at the road.

And of course he drove fast.

On the third ride home one of the bald front tires blew at sixty miles an hour. The car went into a screaming slide and she shrieked aloud, suddenly positive of her own death. An image of her broken, bloody corpse, thrown against the base of a telephone pole like a pile of rags, flashed through her mind like a tabloid photograph. Billy cursed and whipped the fuzz-covered steering wheel from side to side.

They came to a stop on the left-hand shoulder, and when she got out of the car on knees that threatened to buckle at every step, she saw that they had left a looping trail of scorched rubber for seventy feet.

Billy was already opening the trunk, pulling out a jack and muttering to himself. Not a hair was out of place.

He passed her, a cigarette already dangling from the corner of his mouth. 'Bring that toolkit, babe.'

She was flabbergasted. Her mouth opened and closed twice, like a beached fish, before she could get the words out. 'I – I will not! You almost k – you – almost – you crazy *bastard!* Besides, it's *dirty!*'

He turned around and looked at her, his eyes flat. 'You bring it or I ain't taking you to the fuckin fights tomorrow night.'

'I hate the fights!' She had never been, but her anger and outrage required absolutes. Her faternity dates took her to rock concerts, which she hated. They always ended up next to someone who hadn't bathed in weeks.

He shrugged, went back to the front end, and began jacking.

She brought the toolkit, getting grease all over a brand-new sweater. He grunted without turning around. His tee shirt had pulled out of his jeans, and the flesh of his back was smooth, tanned, alive with muscles. It fascinated her, and she felt her tongue creep into the corner of her mouth. She helped him pull the tire off the wheel, getting her hands black. The car rocked alarmingly on the jack, and the spare was down to the canvas in two places.

When the job was finished and she got back in, there were heavy smears of grease across both the sweater and the expensive red skirt she was wearing.

'If you think—' she began as he got behind the wheel.

He slid across the seat and kissed her, his hands moving heavily on her, from waist to breasts. His breath was redolent of tobacco; there was the smell of Brylcreem and sweat. She broke it at last and stared down at herself, gasping for breath. The sweater was blotted with road grease and dirt now. Twenty-seven-fifty in Jordan Marsh and it was beyond anything but the garbage can. She was intensely, almost painfully excited.

'How are you going to explain that?' he asked, and kissed her again. His mouth felt as if he might be grinning.

'Feel me,' she said in his ear. 'Feel me all over. Get me dirty.'

He did. One nylon split like a gaping mouth. Her skirt, short to begin with, was pushed rudely up to her waist. He groped greedily, with no finesse at all. And something – perhaps that, perhaps the sudden brush with death – brought her to sudden, jolting orgasm. She had gone to the fights with him.

'Quarter of eight,' he said, and sat up in bed. He put on the lamp and began to dress. His body still fascinated her. She thought of last Monday night, and how it had been. He had—

(no)

Time enough to think of that later, maybe, when it would do something for her besides cause useless arousal. She swung her own legs over the edge of the bed and slid into gossamer panties.

'Maybe it's a bad idea,' she said, not sure if she was testing him or herself. 'Maybe we ought to just get back into bed and—'

'It's a good idea,' he said, and a shadow of humor crossed his face. 'Pig blood for a pig.'

'What?'

'Nothing. Come on. Get dressed.'

She did, and when they left by the back stairs she could feel a large excitement blooming, like a rapacious and night-flowering vine, in her belly.

From *My Name Is Susan Snell* (p. 45):

You know, I'm not as sorry about all of it as people seem to think I should be. Not that they say it right out; *they're* the ones who always say how dreadfully sorry they are. That's usually just before they ask for my autograph. But they expect you to be sorry. They expect you to get weepy, to wear a lot of black, to drink a little too much or take drugs. They say things like: 'Oh, it's such a shame. But you know what happened to her—' and blah, blah, blah.

But sorry is the Kool-Aid of human emotions. It's what you say when you spill a cup of coffee or throw a gutterball when you're bowling with the girls in the league. True sorrow is as rare as true love. I'm not sorry that Tommy is dead any more. He seems too much like a daydream I once had. You probably think that's cruel, but there's been a lot of water under the bridge since Prom Night. And I'm not sorry for my appearance before the White Commission. I told the truth – as much of it as I knew.

But I am sorry for Carrie.

They've forgotten her, you know. They've made her into some kind of a symbol and forgotten that she was a human being, as real as you reading this, with hopes and dreams and blah, blah, blah. Useless to tell you that, I suppose. Nothing can change her back now from something made out of newsprint into a person. But she was and she hurt. More than any of us probably know, she hurt.

And so I'm sorry and I hope it was good for her, that prom. Until the terror began, I hope it was good and fine and wonderful and magic. . . .

Tommy pulled into the parking lot beside the high school's new wing, let the motor idle for just a second, and then switched it off. Carrie sat on her side of the seat, holding her wrap around her bare shoulders. It suddenly seemed to her that she was living in a dream of hidden intentions and had just become aware of the fact. What could she be doing? She had left Momma alone.

'Nervous?' he asked, and she jumped.

'Yes.'

He laughed and got out. She was about to open her door when he opened it for her. 'Don't be nervous,' he said. 'You're like Galatea.'

'Who?'

'Galatea. We read about her in Mr Evers' class. She turned from a drudge into a beautiful women and nobody even knew her.'

She considered it. 'I want them to know me,' she said finally.

'I don't blame you. Come on.'

George Dawson and Frieda Jason were standing by the Coke machine. Frieda was in an orange tulle concoction, and looked a little like a tuba.

Donna Thibodeau was taking tickets at the door along with David Bracken. They were both National Honor Society members, part of Miss Geer's personal Gestapo, and they wore white slacks and red blazers – the school colors. Tina Blake and Norma Watson were handing out programs and seating people inside according to their chart. Both of them were dressed in black, and Carrie supposed they thought they were very chic, but to her they looked like cigarette girls in an old gangster movie.

All of them turned to look at Tommy and Carrie when they came in, and for a moment there was a stiff, awkward silence. Carrie felt a strong urge to wet her lips and controlled it. Then George Dawson said:

'Gawd, you look queer, Ross.'

Tommy smiled. 'When did you come out of the treetops, Bomba?

Dawson lurched forward with his fists up, and for a moment Carrie felt stark terror. In her keyed-up state, she came within an ace of picking George up and throwing him across the lobby. Then she realized it was an old game, often played, well-loved.

The two of them sparred in a growling circle. Then George, who had been tagged twice in the ribs, began to gobble and yell: 'Kill them Congs! Get them Gooks! Pongee sticks! Tiger cages!' and Tommy collapsed his guard, laughing.

'Don't let it bother you,' Frieda said, tilting her letter-opener nose and strolling over. 'If they kill each other, I'll dance with you.'

'They look too stupid to kill,' Carrie ventured. 'Like dinosaurs.' And when Frieda grinned, she felt something very old and rusty loosen inside her. A warmth came with it. Relief. Ease.

'Where'd you buy your dress?' Frieda asked. 'I love it.'

'I made it.'

'Made it?' Frieda's eyes opened in unaffected surprise. 'No shit!'

Carrie felt herself blushing furiously. 'Yes I did. I . . . I like to sew. I got the material at Johns' in Westover. The pattern is really quite easy.'

'Come on,' George said to all of them in general. 'Band's gonna start.' He rolled his eyes and went through a limber, satiric buck-and-wing 'Vibes, vibes, vibes. Us Gooks love them big Fender viyyybrations.'

When they went in, George was doing impressions of Flash Bobby Pickett and mugging, Carrie was telling Frieda about her dress, and Tommy was grinning, hands stuffed in his pockets. Spoiled the lines of his dinner jacket Sue would be telling him, but fuck it, it seemed to be working. So far it was working fine.

He and George and Frieda had less than two hours to live.

From *The Shadow Exploded* (p. 132):

The White Commission's stand on the trigger of the whole affair – two buckets of pig blood on a beam over the stage – seems to be overly weak and vacillating, even in the light of the scant concrete proof. If one chooses to believe the hearsay evidence of Nolan's immediate circle of friends (and to be brutally frank, they do not seem intelligent enough to lie convincingly), then Nolan took this part of the conspiracy entirely out of Christine Hargensen's hands and acted on his own initiative . . .

He didn't talk when he drove; he liked to drive. The operation gave him a feeling of power that nothing could rival, not even fucking.

The road unrolled before them in photographic blacks and whites, and the speedometer trembled just past seventy. He came from a broken home; his father had taken off after the failure of a badly managed gas-station venture when Billy was twelve, and his mother had four boy friends at last count. Brucie was in greatest favor right now. He was a Seagrams 7 man. She was turning into one ugly bag, too.

But the car: the car fed him power and glory from its own mystic lines of force. It made him someone to be reckoned with, someone with *mana*. It was not by accident that he had done most of his balling in the back seat. The car was his slave and his god. It gave, and it could take away. Billy had used it to take away many times. On long, sleepless nights when his mother and Brucie were fighting, Billy made popcorn and went out cruising for stray dogs. Some mornings he let the car roll, engine dead, into the garage he had constructed behind the house with its front bumper dripping.

She knew his habits well enough by now and did not bother making conversation that would simply be ignored anyway. She sat beside him with one leg curled under her, gnawing a knuckle. The lights of the cars streaking past them on 302 gleamed softly in her hair, streaking it silver.

He wondered how long she would last. Maybe not long after tonight. Somehow it had all led to this, even the early part, and when it was done the glue that had held them together would be thin and might dissolve, leaving them to wonder how it could have been in the first place. He thought she would start to look less like a goddess and more like the typical society bitch again, and that would make him want to belt her around a little. Or maybe a lot. Rub her nose in it.

They breasted the Brickyard Hill and there was the high school below them, the parking lot filled with plump, glistening daddies' cars. He felt the familiar gorge of disgust and hate rise in his throat. We'll give them something

(a night to remember)

all right. We can do that.

The classroom wings were dark and silent and deserted; the lobby was lit with a standard yellow glow, and the bank of glass that was the gymnasium's east side glowed with a soft, orangey light that was ethereal, almost ghostly. Again the bitter taste, and the urge to throw rocks.

'I see the lights, I see the party lights,' he murmured.

'Huh?' She turned to him, startled out of her own thoughts.

'Nothing.' He touched the nape of her neck. 'I think I'm gonna let you pull the string.'

Billy did it by himself, because he knew perfectly well that he could trust nobody else. That had been a hard lesson, much harder than the ones they taught you in school, but he had learned it well. The boys who had gone with him to Henty's place the night before had not even known what he wanted the blood for. They probably suspected Chris was involved, but they could not even be sure of that.

He drove to the school minutes after Thursday night had become Friday morning and cruised by twice to make sure it was deserted and neither of Chamberlain's two police cars was in the area.

He drove into the parking lot with his lights off and swung around in back of the building. Further back, the football field glimmered beneath a thin membrane of ground fog.

He opened the trunk and unlocked the ice chest. The blood had frozen solid, but that was all right. It would have the next twenty-two hours to thaw.

He put the buckets on the ground, then got a number of tools from his kit. He stuck them in his back pocket and grabbed a brown bag from the seat. Screws clinked inside.

He worked without hurry, with the easeful concentration of one who is unable to conceive of interruption. The gym where the dance was to be held was also the school auditorium, and the small row of windows looking toward where he had parked opened on the backstage storage area.

He selected a flat tool with a spatulate end and slid it through the small jointure between the upper and lower panes of one window. It was a good tool. He had made it himself in the Chamberlain metal shop. He wiggled it until the window's slip lock came free. He pushed the window up and slid in.

It was very dark. The predominant odor was of old paint from the Dramatics Club canvas flats. The gaunt shadows of Band Society music stands and instrument cases stood around like sentinels. Mr Downer's piano stood in one corner.

Billy took a small flashlight out of the bag and made his way to the stage and stepped through the red velvet curtains. The gym floor, with its painted basketball lines and highly varnished surface, glimmered at him like an amber lagoon. He shone his light on the apron in front of the curtain. There, in ghostly chalk lines, someone had drawn the floor silhouette of the King and Queen thrones which would be placed the following day. Then the entire apron would be strewn with paper flowers . . . why, Christ only knew.

He craned his neck and shone the beam of his light up into the shadows. Overhead, girders crisscrossed in shadowy lines. The girders over the dance floor had been sheathed in crepe paper, but the area directly over the apron hadn't been decorated. A short draw curtain obscured the girders up there, and they were invisible from the gym floor. The draw curtain also hid a bank of lights that would highlight the gondola mural.

Billy turned off the flashlight, walked to the left-hand edge of the apron, and mounted a steel-runged ladder bolted to the wall. The contents of his brown bag, which he had tucked into his shirt for safety, jingled with a strange, hollow jolliness in the deserted gymnasium.

At the top of the ladder was a small platform. Now, as he faced outward toward the apron, the stage flies were to his right, the gym itself on his left. In the flies the Dramatics Club props were stored, some of them dating back to the 1920s. A bust of Pallas, used in some ancient dramatic version of Poe's 'The Raven,' stared at Billy, with blind, floating eyes from atop a rusting bedspring. Straight ahead, a steel girder ran out over the apron. Lights to be used against the mural were bolted to the bottom of it.

He stepped out onto it and walked effortlessly, without fear, out over the drop. He was humming a popular tune under his breath. The beam was inch-thick with dust, and he left long, shuffling tracks. Halfway out he stopped, dropped to his knees, and peered down.

Yes. With the help of his light he could make out the chalk lines on the apron directly below. He made a soundless whistling.

(bombs away)

He X'd the precise spot on the dust, then beam-walked back to the platform. No one would be up here between now and the Ball; the lights that shone on the mural and on the apron where the King and Queen would be crowned

(they'll get crowned all right)

were controlled from a box backstage. Anyone looking up from directly below would be blinded by those same lights. His arrangements would be noticed only if someone went up into the flies for something. He didn't believe anyone would. It was an acceptable risk.

He opened the brown bag and took out a pair of Playtex rubber gloves, put them on, and then took out one of two small pullies he had purchased yesterday. He had gotten them at a hardware store in Lewiston, just to be safe. He popped a number of nails into his mouth like cigarettes and got the hammer. Still humming around his mouthful of nails, he fixed the pulley neatly in the corner a foot above the platform. Beside it he fixed a small eyehole screw.

He went back down the ladder, crossed backstage, and climbed another ladder not far from where he had come in. He was in the loft – sort of a catchall school attic. Here there were stacks of old yearbooks, moth-eaten athletic uniforms, and ancient textbooks that had been nibbled by mice.

Looking left, he could shine his light over the stage flies and spotlight the pulley he had just put up. Turning right, cool night air played on his face from a vent in the wall. Still humming, he took out the second pulley and nailed it up.

He went back down, crawled out the window he had forced, and got the two buckets of pig blood. He had been about his business for a half hour, but it showed no signs of thawing. He picked the buckets up and walked back to the window, silhouetted in the darkness like a farmer coming back from the first milking. He lifted them inside and went in after.

Beam-walking was easier with a bucket in each hand for balance. When he reached his dust-marked X, he put the buckets down, peered at the chalk marks on the apron once more, nodded, and walked back to the platform. He thought about wiping the buckets on his last trip out to them – Kenny's prints would be on them, Don's and Steve's as well – but it was better not to. Maybe they would have a little surprise on Saturday morning. The thought made his lips quirk.

The last item in the bag was a coil of jute twine. He walked back out to the buckets and tied the handles of both with running slipknots. He threaded the screw, then the pulley. He threw the uncoiling twine across to the loft, and then threaded that one. He probably would not have been amused to know that, in the gloom of the auditorium, covered and streaked with decades-old dust, gray kitties flying dreamily about his crow's-nest hair, he looked like a hunched, half-mad Rube Goldberg intent upon creating the better mousetrap.

He piled the slack twine on top of a stack of crates within reach of the vent. He climbed down for the last time and dusted off his hands. The thing was done.

He looked out the window, then wriggled through and thumped to the ground. He closed the window, reinserted his jimmy, and closed the lock as far as he could. Then he went back to his car.

Chris said chances were good that Tommy Ross and the White bitch would be the ones under the buckets; she had been doing a little quiet promoting among her friends. That would be good, if it happened. But, for Billy, any of the others would be all right too.

He was beginning to think that it would be all right if it was Chris herself.

He drove away.

From *My Name Is Susan Snell* (p. 48):

Carrie went to see Tommy the day before the prom. She was waiting outside one of his classes and he said she looked really wretched, as if she thought he'd yell at her to stop hanging around and stop bugging him.

She said she had to be in by eleven-thirty at the latest, or her momma would be worried. She said she wasn't going to spoil his time or anything, but it wouldn't be fair to worry her momma.

Tommy suggested they stop at the Kelly Fruit after and grab a root beer and a burger. All the other kids would be going to Westover or Lewiston, and they would have the place to themselves. Carrie's face lit up, he said. She told him that would be fine. Just fine.

This is the girl they keep calling a monster. I want you to keep that firmly in mind. The girl who could be satisfied with a hamburger and a dime root beer after her only school dance so her momma wouldn't be worried . . .

The first thing that struck Carrie when they walked in was Glamor. Not glamor but Glamor. Beautiful shadows rustled about in chiffon, lace, silk, satin. The air was redolent with the odor of flowers; the nose was constantly amazed by it. Girls in dresses with low backs, with scooped bodices showing actual cleavage, with Empire waists. Long skirts, pumps. Blinding white dinner jackets, cummerbunds, black shoes that had been spit-shined.

A few people were on the dance floor, not many yet, and in the soft revolving gloom they were wraiths without substance. She did not really want to see them as her classmates. She wanted them to be beautiful strangers.

Tommy's hand was firm on her elbow. 'The mural's nice,' he said.

'Yes,' she agreed faintly.

It had taken on a soft nether light under the orange spots, the boatman leaning with eternal indolence against his tiller while the sunset blazed around him and the buildings conspired together over urban waters. She knew with suddeness and ease that this moment would be with her always, within hand's reach of memory.

She doubted if they all sensed it – they had seen the world – but even George was silent for a minute as they looked, and the scene, the smell, even the sound of the band playing a faintly recognizable movie theme, was locked forever in her, and she was at peace. Her soul knew a moment's calm, as if it had been uncrumpled and smoothed under an iron.

'Viiiiiybes,' George yelled suddenly, and led Frieda out onto the floor. He began to do a sarcastic jitterbug to the old-timey big-band music, and someone catcalled over to him. George blabbered, leered, and went into a brief arms-crossed Cossack routine that nearly landed him on his butt.

Carrie smiled. 'George is funny,' she said.

'Sure he is. He's a good guy. There are lots of good people around. Want to sit down?'

'Yes,' she said gratefully.

He went back to the door and returned with Norma Watson, whose hair had been pulled into a huge, teased explosion for the affair.

'It's on the other SIDE,' she said, and her bright gerbel's eyes picked Carrie up and down, looking for an exposed strap, an eruption of pimples, any news to carry back to the door when her errand was done. 'That's a LOVELY dress, Carrie. Where did you EVER get it?'

Carrie told her while Norma led them around the dance floor to their table. She exuded odors of Avon soap, Woolworth's perfume, and Juicy Fruit gum.

There were two folding chairs at the table (looped and beribboned with the inevitable crepe paper), and the table itself was decked with crepe paper in the school colors. On top was a candle in a wine bottle, a dance program, a tiny gilded pencil, and two party favors - gondolas filled with Planters Mixed Nuts.

'I can't get OVER it,' Norma was saying. 'You look so DIFFERENT.' She cast an odd, furtive look at Carrie's face and it made her feel nervous. 'You're positively GLOWING. What's your SECRET?'

'I'm Don MacLean's secret lover,' Carrie said. Tommy sniggered and quickly smothered it. Norma's smile slipped a notch, and Carrie was amazed by her own wit - and audacity. That's what you looked like when the joke was on you. As though a bee had stung your rear end. Carrie found she liked Norma to look that way. It was distinctly unchristian.

'Well, I have to get back,' she said. 'Isn't it EXCITING, Tommy?' Her smile was sympathetic: *Wouldn't it be exciting if—?*

'Cold sweat is running down my thighs in rivers,' Tommy said gravely.

Norma left with an odd, puzzled smile. It had not gone the way things were supposed to go. Everyone knew how things were supposed to go with Carrie. Tommy sniggered again. 'Would you like to dance?' he asked.

She didn't know how, but wasn't ready to admit to *that* yet. 'Let's just sit down for a minute.'

While he held out her chair, she saw the candle and asked Tommy if he would light it. He did. Their eyes met over its flame. He reached out and took her hand. And the band played on.

From *The Shadow Exploded* (pp. 133-34)

Perhaps a complete study of Carrie's mother will be undertaken someday, when the subject of Carrie herself becomes more academic. I myself might attempt it, if only to gain access to the Brigham family tree. It might be extremely interesting to know what odd occurrences one might come across two or three generations back . . .

And there is, of course, the knowledge that Carrie went home on Prom

Night. Why? It is hard to tell just how sane Carrie's motives were by that time. She may have gone for absolution and forgiveness, or she may have gone for the express purpose of committing matricide. In any event, the physical evidence seems to indicate that Margaret White was waiting for her. . . .

The house was completely silent.

She was gone.

At night.

Gone.

Margaret White walked slowly from her bedroom into the living room. First had come the flow of blood and the filthy fantasies the Devil sent with it. Then this hellish Power the Devil had given to her. It came at the time of the blood and the time of hair on the body, of course. Oh, she knew the Devil's Power. Her own grandmother had it. She had been able to light the fireplace without ever stirring from her rocker by the window. It made her eyes glow with

(thou shalt not suffer a witch to live)

a kind of witch's light. And sometimes, at the supper table the sugar bowl would whirl madly like a dervish. Whenever it happened, Gram would cackle crazily and drool and make the sign of the Evil Eye all around her. Sometimes she panted like a dog on a hot day, and when she died of a heart attack at sixty-six, senile to the point of idiocy even at that early age, Carrie had not even been a year old. Margaret had gone into her bedroom not four weeks after Gram's funeral and there her girl-child had lain in her crib, laughing and gurgling, watching a bottle that was dangling in thin air over her head.

Margaret had almost killed her then. Ralph had stopped her.

She should not have let him stop her.

Now Margaret White stood in the middle of the living room. Christ on Calvary looked down at her with his wounded, suffering, reproachful eyes. The Black Forest cuckoo clock ticked. It was ten minutes after eight.

She had been able to feel, actually *feel*, the Devil's Power working in Carrie. It crawled all over you, lifting and pulling like evil, tickling little fingers. She had set out to do her duty again when Carrie was three, when she had caught her looking in sin at the Devil's slut in the next yard over. Then the stones had come, and she had weakened. And the power had risen again, after thirteen years. God was not mocked.

First the blood, then the power,

(you sign your name you sign it in blood)

now a boy and dancing and he would take her to a roadhouse after, take her into the parking lot, take her into the back seat, take her—

Blood, fresh blood. Blood was always at the root of it, and only blood could expiate it.

She was a big woman with massive upper arms that had dwarfed her elbows to dimples, but her head was surprisingly small on the end of her strong, corded neck. It had once been a beautiful face. It was still beautiful in a weird, zealous way. But the eyes had taken on a strange, wandering cast, and the lines had deepened cruelly around the denying but oddly weak mouth. Her hair, which had been almost all black a year ago, was now almost white.

The only way to kill sin, true black sin, was to drown it in the blood of

(she must be sacrificed)

a repentant heart. Surely God understood that, and had laid His finger upon her. Had not God Himself commanded Abraham to take his son Isaac up upon the mountain?

She shuffled out into the kitchen in her old and splayed slippers, and opened the kitchen utensil drawer. The knife they used for carving was long and sharp and arched in the middle from constant honing. She sat down on the high stool by the counter, found the sliver of whetstone in its small aluminum dish, and began to scrub it along the gleaming edge of the blade with the apathetic, fixated attention of the damned.

The Black Forest cuckoo clock ticked and ticked and finally the bird jumped out to call once and announce eight-thirty.

In her mouth she tasted olives.

THE SENIOR CLASS PRESENTS SPRING BALL '79

May 27, 1979

Music by The Billy Bosnan Band
Music by Josie and the Moonglows

ENTERTAINMENT

'Cabaret' – Baton Twirling by Sandra Stenchfield
'500 Miles'
'Lemon Tree'
'Mr Tambourine Man'
Folk Music by John Swithen and Maureen Cowan
'The Street Where You Live'
'Raindrops Keep Fallin' on My Head'
'Bridge Over Troubled Waters'
Ewen High School Chorus

CHAPERONES

Mr Stephens, Miss Geer, Mr and Mrs Lublin, Miss Desjardin
Coronation at 10:00 p.m.
Remember, it's YOUR prom; make it one to remember always!

When he asked her the third time, Carrie had to admit that she didn't know how to dance. She didn't add that, now the rock band had taken over for a half-hour set, she would feel out of place gyrating on the floor,

(and sinful)

yes, and sinful.

Tommy nodded, then smiled. He leaned forward and told her that he hated to dance. Would she like to go around and visit some of the other tables? Trepidation rose thickly in her throat, but she nodded. Yes, that would be nice. He was seeing to her. She must see to him (even if he really did not expect it); that was part of the deal. And she felt dusted over with the enchantment of the evening. She was suddenly hopeful that no one would stick out a foot or slyly paste a kick-me-hard sign on her back or suddenly squirt water in her face from a novelty carnation and retreat crackling while everyone laughed and pointed and catcalled.

And if here was enchantment, it was not divine but pagan

(momma untie your apron strings i'm getting big)

and she wanted it that way.

'Look,' he said as they got up.

Two or three stagehands were sliding the King and Queen thrones from the wings while Mr Lavoie, the head custodian, directed them with hand motions toward preset marks on the apron. She thought they looked quite Arthurian, those thrones, dressed all in blinding white, strewn with real flowers as well as huge crepe banners.

'They're beautiful,' she said.

'*You're* beautiful,' Tommy said, and she became quite sure that nothing bad could happen this night – perhaps they themselves might even be voted King and Queen of the Prom. She smiled at her own folly.

It was nine o'clock.

'Carrie?' a voice said hesitantly.

She had been so wrapped up in watching the band and the dance floor and the other tables that she hadn't seen anyone coming at all. Tommy had gone to get them punch.

She turned around and saw Miss Desjardin.

For a moment the two of them merely looked at each other, and the memory traveled between them, communicated

(she saw me she saw me naked and screaming and bloody)

without words or thought. It was in her eyes.

Then Carrie said shyly: 'You look very pretty, Miss Desjardin.'

She did. She was dressed in a glimmering silver sheath, a perfect complement to her blonde hair, which was up. A simple pendant hung around her neck. She looked very young, young enough to be attending rather than chaperoning.

'Thank you.' She hestitated, then put a gloved hand on Carrie's arm. 'You are beautiful,' she said, and each word carried a peculiar emphasis.

Carrie felt herself blushing again and dropped her eyes to the table. 'It's awfully nice of you to say so. I know I'm not . . . not really . . . but thank you anyway.'

'It's true,' Desjardin said. 'Carrie, anything that happened before . . . well, it's all forgotten. I wanted you to know that.'

'I can't forget it,' Carrie said. She looked up. The words that rose to her lips were: *I don't blame anyone any more*. She bit them off. It was a lie. She blamed them all and always would, and she wanted more than anything else to be honest. 'But it's over with. Now it's over with.'

Miss Desjardin smiled, and her eyes seemed to catch and hold the soft mix of lights in an almost liquid sparkling. She looked across toward the dance floor, and Carrie followed her gaze.

'I remember my own prom,' Desjardin said softly. 'I was two inches taller than the boy I went with when I was in my heels. He gave me a corsage that clashed with my gown. The tailpipe was broken on his car and the engine made . . . oh, an awful racket. But it was magic. I don't know why. But I've never had a date like it, ever again.' She looked at Carrie. 'Is it like that for you?'

It's very nice,' Carrie said.

'And is that all?'

'No. There's more. I couldn't tell it all. Not to anybody.'

Desjardin smiled and squeezed her arm. 'You'll never forget it,' she said. 'Never.'

'I think you're right.'

'Have a lovely time, Carrie.'

'Thank you.'

Tommy came up with two Dixie cups of punch as Desjardin left, walking around the dance floor toward the chaperones' table.

'What did she want?' he asked, putting the Dixie cups down carefully.

Carrie, looking after her, said: 'I think she wanted to say she was sorry.'

Sue Snell sat quietly in the living room of her home, hemming a dress and listening to the Jefferson Airplane *Long John Silver* album. It was old and badly scratched, but soothing.

Her mother and father had gone out for the evening. They knew what was going on, she was sure of that, but they had spared her the bumbling talks about how proud they were of Their Girl, or how glad they were that she was finally Growing Up. She was glad they had decided to leave her alone, because she was still uncomfortable about her own motives and afraid to examine them too deeply, lest she discover a jewel of selfishness glowing and winking at her from the black velvet of her subconscious.

She had done it; that was enough; she was satisfied.

(maybe he'll fall in love with her)

She looked up as if someone had spoken from the hallway, a startled smile curving her lips. That would be a fairy-tale ending, all right. The Prince bends over the Sleeping Beauty, touches his lips to hers.

Sue, I don't know how to tell you this but—

The smile faded.

Her period was late. Almost a week late. And she had always been as regular as an almanac.

The record changer clicked; another record dropped down. In the sudden, brief silence, she heard something within her turn over. Perhaps only her soul.

It was nine-fifteen.

Billy drove to the far end of the parking lot and pulled into a stall that faced the asphalt ramp leading to the highway. Chris started to get out and he jerked her back. His eyes glowed ferally in the dark.

'What?' she said with angry nervousness.

'They use a P.A. system to announce the King and Queen,' he said. 'Then one of the bands will play the school song. That means they're sitting there in those thrones, on target.'

'I know all that. Let go of me. You're hurting.'

He squeezed her wrist tighter still and felt small bones grind. It gave him a grim pleasure. Still, she didn't cry out. She was pretty good.

'You listen to me. I want you to know what you're getting into Pull the rope when the song is playing. Pull it hard. There will be a little slack between the pulleys, but not much. When you pull it and feel those buckets go, *run*. You don't stick around to hear the screams or anything else. This is out of the cute-little-joke league. This is criminal assault, you know? They don't fine you. They put you in jail and throw the key over their shoulder.'

It was an enormous speech for him.

Her eyes only glared at him, full of defiant anger.

'*Dig it*?'

'Yes.'

'All right. When the buckets go. I'm going to run. When I get to the car, I'm going to drive away. If you're there, you can come. If you're not, I'll leave you. If I leave you and you spill your guts, I'll kill you. Do you believe me?'

'Yes. Take your fucking hand off me.'

He did. An unwilling shadow-grin touched his face. 'Okay. It's going to be good.'

They got out of the car.

It was almost nine-thirty.

Vic Mooney, President of the Senior Class, was calling jovially into the mike: 'All right, ladies and gentlemen. Take your seats, please. It's time for the voting. We're going to vote for the King and Queen.'

'This contest insults women!' Myra Crewes called with uneasy good nature.

'It insults men, too!' George Dawson called back, and there was general laughter. Myra was silent. She had made her token protest.

'Take your seats, please!' Vic was smiling into the mike, smiling and blushing furiously, fingering a pimple on his chin. The huge Venetian boatman behind him looked dreamily over Vic's shoulder. 'Time to vote.'

Carrie and Tommy sat down. Tina Blake and Norma Watson were circulating mimeographed ballots, and when Norma dropped one at their table and breathed 'Good LUCK!' Carrie picked up the ballot and studied it. Her mouth popped open.

'Tommy, we're *on* here!'

'Yeah, I saw that,' he said. 'The school votes for single candidates and their dates get sort of shanghaied into it. Welcome aboard. Shall we decline?'

She bit her lip and looked at him. 'Do you want to decline?'

'Hell, no,' he said cheerfully. 'If you win, all you do is sit up there for the school song and one dance and wave a scepter and look like a goddam idiot. They take your picture for the yearbook so everyone can see you looked like a goddam idiot.'

'Who do we vote for?' She looked doubtfully from the ballot to the tiny pencil by her boatful of nuts. 'They're more your crowd than mine.' A little chuckle escaped her. 'In fact, I don't really have a crowd.'

He shrugged. 'Let's vote for ourselves. To the devil with false modesty.'

She laughed out loud, then clapped a hand over her mouth. The sound was almost entirely foreign to her. Before she could think, she circled their names, third from the top. The tiny pencil broke in her hand, and she gasped. A splinter had scratched the pad of one finger, and a small bead of blood welled.

'You hurt yourself?'

'No.' She smiled, but suddenly it was difficult to smile. The sight of the blood was distasteful to her. She blotted it away with her napkin. 'But I broke the pencil and it was a souvenir. Stupid me.'

'There's your boat,' he said, and pushed it toward her. 'Toot, toot.' Her throat closed, and she felt sure she would weep and then be ashamed. She did not, but her eyes glimmered like prisms and she lowered her head so he would not see.

The band was playing catchy fill-in music while the Honor Society ushers collected the folded-over ballots. They were taken to the chaperones' table by the door, where Vic and Mr Stephens and the Lublins counted them. Miss Geer surveyed it all with grim gimlet eyes.

Carrie felt an unwilling tension worm into her, tightening muscles in her stomach and back. She held Tommy's hand tightly. It was absurd, of course. No one was going to vote for them. The stallion, perhaps, but not when harnessed in tandem with a she-ox. It would be Frank and Jessica or maybe Don Farnham and Helen Shyres. Or – hell!

Two piles were growing larger than the others. Mr Stephens finished dividing the slips and all four of them took turns at counting the large piles, which looked about the same. They put their heads together, conferred, and counted once more. Mr Stephens nodded, thumbed the ballots once more like a man about to deal a hand of poker, and gave them back to Vic. He climbed back on stage and approached the mike. The Billy Bosnan Band played a flourish. Vic smiled nervously, harrumphed into the mike, and blinked at the sudden feedback whine. He nearly dropped the ballots to the floor, which was covered with heavy electrical cables, and somebody snickered.

'We've sort of hit a snag,' Vic said artlessly. 'Mr Lublin says this is the first time in the history of the Spring Ball—'

'How far does he go back?' someone behind Tommy grumbled. 'Eighteen hundred?'

'We've got a tie.'

This got a murmur from the crowd. 'Polka dots or striped?' George Dawson called, and there was some laughter. Vic gave a twitchy little smile and almost dropped the ballots again.

'Sixty-three votes for Frank Grier and Jessica MacLean, and sixty-three votes for Thomas Ross and Carrie White.'

This was followed by a moment of silence, and then sudden, swelling applause. Tommy looked across at his date. Her head was lowered, as if in shame, but he had a sudden feeling

(carrie carrie carrie)

not unlike the one he had had when he asked her to the prom. His mind felt as if something alien was moving in there, calling Carrie's name over and over again. As if—

'Attention!' Vic was calling. 'If I could have your attention, please.' The applause quieted. 'We're going to have a run-off ballot. When the people passing out the slips of paper get to you, please write the couple you favor on it.'

He left the mike, looking relieved.

The ballots were circulated; they had been hastily torn from leftover prom programs. The band played unnoticed and people talked excitedly.

'They weren't applauding for us' Carrie said, looking up. The thing he had felt (or thought he had felt) was gone. 'It couldn't have been for us.'

'Maybe it was for you.'

She looked at him, mute.

'What's taking it so long?' she hissed at him. 'I heard them clap. Maybe that was it. If you fucked up—' The length of jute cord hung between them limply, untouched since Billy had poked a screwdriver through the vent and lifted it out.

'Don't worry,' he said calmly. 'They'll play the school song. They always do.'

'But—'

'Shut up. You talk too fucking much.' The tip of his cigarette winked peacefully in the dark.

She shut. But

(oh when this is over you're going to get it buddy maybe you'll go to bed with lover's nuts tonight)

her mind ran furiously over his words, storing them. People did not speak to her in such a manner. Her father was a lawyer.

It was seven minutes of ten.

He was holding the broken pencil in his hand, ready to write, when she touched his wrist lightly, tentatively.

'Don't . . .'

'What?'

Don't vote for us,' she said finally.

He raised his eyebrows quizzically. 'Why not? In for a penny, in for a pound. That's what my mother always says.'

(mother)

A picture rose in her mind instantly, her mother droning endless prayers to a towering, faceless, columnar God who prowled roadhouse parking lots with a sword of fire in one hand. Terror rose in her blackly, and she had to fight with all her spirit to hold it back. She could not explain her dread, her sense of premonition. She could only smile helplessly and repeat: 'Don't. Please.'

The Honor Society ushers were coming back, collecting folded slips. He hesitated a moment longer, then suddenly scrawled *Tommy and Carrie* on the ragged slip of paper. 'For you,' he said 'Tonight you go first-class.'

She could not reply, for the premonition was on her: her mother's face.

The knife slipped from the whetstone, and in an instant it had sliced the cup of her palm below the thumb.

She looked at the cut. It bled slowly, thickly, from the open lips of the wound, running out of her hand and spotting the worn linoleum of the kitchen floor. Good, then. It was good. The blade had tasted flesh and let blood. She did not bandage it but tipped the flow over the cutting edge, letting the blood dull the blade's sharp glimmer. Then she began to sharpen again, heedless of the droplets which splattered her dress.

If thine right eye offend thee, pluck it out.

If it was a hard scripture, it was also sweet and good. A fitting scripture for those who lurked in the doorway shadows of one-night hotels and in the weeds behind bowling alleys.

Pluck it out.

(oh and the nasty music they play)

Pluck it

(the girls show their underwear how it sweats how it sweats blood)

out.

The Black Forest cuckoo clock began to strike ten *and*

(cut her guts out on the floor)

if thine right eye offend thee, pluck it out.

The dress was done and she could not watch the television or take out her books or call Nancy on the phone. There was nothing to do but sit on the sofa facing the blackness of the kitchen window and feel some nameless sort of fear growing in her like an infant coming to dreadful term.

With a sigh she began to massage her arms absently. They were cold and prickly. It was twelve after ten and there was no reason, really no reason, to feel that the world was coming to an end.

The stacks were higher this time, but they still looked exactly the same. Again, three counts were taken to make sure. Then Vic Mooney went to the mike again. He paused a moment, relishing the blue feel of tension in the air, and then announced simply:

'Tommy and Carrie win. By one vote.'

Dead silence for a moment. Then applause filled the hall again, some of it not without satiric overtones. Carrie drew in a startled, smothered gasp, and Tommy again felt (but for only a second) that weird vertigo in his mind

(carrie carrie carrie carrie)

that seemed to blank out all thought but the name and image of this strange girl he was with. For a fleeting second he was literally scared shit-less.

Something fell on the floor with a clink, and at the same instant the candle between them whiffed out.

Then Josie and the Moonglows were playing a rock version of 'Pomp and Circumstance,' the ushers appeared at their table (almost magically; all this had been rehearsed meticulously by Miss Geer who, according to rumor, ate slow and clumsy ushers for lunch), a scepter wrapped in aluminium foil was thrust into Tommys' hand, a robe with a lush dog-fur collar was thrown over Carrie's shoulders, and they were being led down the center aisle by a boy and a girl in white blazers. The band blared. The audience applauded. Miss Geer looked vindicated. Tommy Ross was grinning bemusedly.

They were ushered up the steps to the apron, led across to the thrones, and seated. Still the applause swelled. The sarcasm in it was lost now; it was honest and deep, a little frightening. Carrie was glad to sit down. It was all happening too fast. Her legs were trembling under her and suddenly, even with the comparatively high neck of her gown, her breasts

(dirtypillows)

felt dreadfully exposed. The sound of the applause in her ears made her feel woozy, almost punch-drunk. Part of her was actually convinced that all this was a dream from which she would wake with mixed feelings of loss and relief.

Vic boomed into the mike: 'The King and Queen of the 1979 Spring Ball – Tommy ROSS and Carrie WHITE!'

Still applause, swelling and booming and crackling. Tommy Ross, in the fading moments of his life now, took Carrie's hand and grinned at her, thinking that Suzie's intuition had been very right. Somehow she grinned back. Tommy

(she was right and i love her well i love this one too this carrie she is she is beautiful and it's right i love all of them the light the light in her eyes)

and Carrie

(can't see them the lights are too bright i can hear them but can't see them the shower remember the shower o momma it's too high i think i want to get down o are they laughing and ready to throw things to point and scream with laughter i can't see them i can't see them it's all too bright)

and the beam above them.

Both bands, in a sudden and serendipitous coalition of rock and brass, swung into the school song. The audience rose to its feet and began to sing, still applauding.

It was ten-o-seven.

Billy had just flexed his knees to make the joints pop. Chris Hargensen stood next to him with increasing signs of nervousness. Her hands played aimlessly along the seams of the jeans she had worn and she was biting the softness of her lower lip, chewing at it, making it a little ragged.

'You think they'll vote for *them*?' Billy said softly.

'They will,' she said. 'I set it up. It won't even be close. Why do they keep applauding? What's going on in there?'

'Don't ask me, babe. I—'

The school song suddenly roared out, full and strong on the soft May air, and Chris jumped as if stung. A soft gasp of surprise escaped her.

'*All rise high for Thomas Ewen Hiiiiyyygh* . . .

'Go on,' he said. 'They're there.' His eyes glowed softly in the dark. The odd half-grin had touched his features.

She licked her lips. They both stared at the length of jute cord.

We'll raise your banners to the skyyyyyy . . .

'Shut up,' she whispered. She was trembling, and he thought that her body had never looked so lush or exciting. When this was over he was going to have her until every other time she'd been had was like two pumps with a fag's little finger. He was going on her like a raw cob through butter.

'No guts, babe?'

He leaned forward. 'I won't pull it for you, babe. It can sit there till hell freezes.'

With pride we wear the red and whiiyyyyte . . .

A sudden smothered sound that might have been a half-scream came from her mouth, and she leaned forward and pulled violently on the cord with both hands. It came loose with slack for a moment, making her think that Billy had been having her on all this time, that the rope was attached to nothing but thin air. Then it snubbed tight, held for a second, and then came through her palms harshly, leaving a thin burn.

'I—' she began.

The music inside came to a jangling, discordant halt. For a moment ragged voices continued oblivious, and then they stopped. There was a beat of silence, and then someone screamed. Silence again.

They stared at each other in the dark, frozen by the actual act as thought never could have done. Her very breath turned to glass in her throat.

Then, inside, the laughter began.

It was ten twenty-five, and the feeling had been getting worse and worse. Sue stood in front of the gas range on one foot, waiting for the milk to began steaming so she could dump in the Nestlé's. Twice she had begun to go upstairs and put on a nightgown and twice she had stopped, drawn for no reason at all to the kitchen window that looked down Brickyard Hill and the spiral of Route 6 that led into town.

Now, as the whistle mounted atop the town hall on Main Street suddenly began to shriek into the night, rising and falling in cycles of panic, she did not even turn immediately to the window, but only turned the heat off under the milk so it would not burn.

The town hall whistle went off every day at twelve noon and that was all, except to call the volunteer fire department during grass fire season in August and September. It was strictly for major disasters, and its sound was dreamy and terrifying in the empty house.

She went to the window, but slowly. The shrieking of the whistle rose and fell, rose and fell. Somewhere, horns were beginning to blat, as if for a wedding. She could see her reflection in the darkened glass, lips parted, eyes wide, and then the condensation of her breath obscured it.

A memory, half-forgotten, came to her. As children in grammar school, they had practiced air-raid drills. When the teacher clapped her hands and said, 'The town whistle is blowing,' you were supposed to crawl under your desk and put your hands over your head and wait, either for the all-clear or for enemy missles to blow you to powder. Now, in her mind, as clearly as a leaf pressed in plastic,

(the town whistle is blowing)

she heard the words clang in her mind.

Far below, to the left, where the high school parking lot was – the ring of sodium arc lamps made it a sure landmark, although the school building itself was invisible in the dark – a spark glowed as if God had struck a flint-and-steel.

(that's where the oil tanks are)

The spark hesitated, then bloomed orange. Now you could see the school, and it was on fire.

She was already on her way to the closet to get her coat when the first dull, booming explosion shook the floor under her feet and made her mother's china rattle in the cupboards.

From *We Survived the Black Prom*, by Norma Watson (Published in the August, 1980, issue of *The Readers' Digest* as a 'Drama in Real Life' article):

... and it happened so quickly that no one really knew what was happening. We were all standing and applauding and singing the school song. Then – I was at the ushers' table just inside the main doors, looking at the stage – there was a sparkle as the big lights over the stage apron reflected on something metallic. I was standing with Tina Blake and Stella Horan, and I think they saw it, too.

All at once there was a huge red splash in the air. Some of it hit the mural and ran in long drips. I knew right away, even before it hit them, that it was blood. Stella Horan thought it was paint, but I had a premonition, just like the time my brother got hit by a hay truck.

They were drenched. Carrie got it the worst. She looked exactly like she had been dipped in a bucket of red paint. She just sat there. She never moved. The band that was closest to the stage, Josie and the Moonglows, got splattered. The lead guitarist had a white instrument, and it splattered all over it.

I said: 'My God, that's blood!'

When I said that, Tina screamed. It was very loud, and it rang out clearly in the auditorium.

People had stopped singing and everything was completely quiet. I couldn't move. I was rooted to the spot. I looked up and there were two buckets dangling high over the thrones, swinging and banging together. They were still dripping. All of a sudden they fell, with a lot of loose string paying out behind them. One of them hit Tommy Ross on the head. It made a very loud noise, like a gong.

That made someone laugh. I don't know who it was, but it wasn't the way a person laughs when they see something funny and gay. It was raw and hysterical and awful.

At that same instant, Carrie opened her eyes wide.

That was when they all started laughing. I did too, God help me. It was so . . . so weird.

When I was a little girl I had a Walt Disney storybook called *Song of the South*, and it had that Uncle Remus story about the tarbaby in it. There was a picture of the tarbaby sitting in the middle of the road, looking like one of those old-time Negro minstrels with the blackface and great big white eyes. When Carrie opened her eyes it was like that. They were the only part of her that wasn't completely red. And the light had gotten in them and made them glassy. God help me, but she looked for all the world like Eddie Cantor doing that pop-eyed act of his.

That was what made people laugh. We couldn't help it. It was one of those things where you laugh or go crazy. Carrie had been the butt of every joke for so long, and we all felt that we were part of something special that night. It was as if we were watching a person rejoin the human race, and I for one thanked the Lord for it. And *that* happened. That horror.

And so there was nothing else to do. It was either laugh or cry, and who could bring himself to cry over Carrie after all those years?

She just sat there, staring out at them, and the laughter kept swelling, getting louder and louder. People were holding their bellies and doubling up and pointing at her. Tommy was the only one who wasn't looking at her. He was sort of slumped over in his seat as if he'd gone to sleep. You couldn't tell he was hurt, though; he was splashed too bad.

And then her face . . . broke. I don't know how else to describe it. She put her hands up to her face and half-staggered to her feet. She almost got tangled in her own feet and fell over, and that made people laugh even more. Then she sort of . . . hopped off the stage. It was like watching a big red frog hopping off a lily pad. She almost fell again, but kept on her feet.

Miss Desjardin came running over to her, and she wasn't laughing any more. She was holding out her arms to her. But then she veered off and hit the wall beside the stage. It was the strangest thing. She didn't stumble or anything. It was is if someone had pushed her, but there was no one there.

Carrie ran through the crowd with her hands clutching her face, and somebody put his foot out. I don't know who it was, but she went sprawling on her face, leaving a long red streak on the floor. And she said, 'Oof!' I remember that. It made me laugh even harder, hearing Carrie say Oof like that. She started to crawl along the floor and then she got up and ran out. She ran right past me. You could smell the blood. It smelled like something sick and rotted.

She went down the stairs two at a time and then out the doors. And was gone.

The laughter just sort of faded off, a little at a time. Some people were still hitching and snorting. Lennie Brock had taken out a big white handkerchief and was wiping his eyes. Sally McManus looked all white, like she was going to throw up, but she was still giggling and she couldn't seem to stop. Billy Bosnan was just standing there with his little conductor's stick in his hand and shaking his head. Mr Lublin was sitting by Miss Desjardin and calling for a Kleenex. She had a bloody nose.

You have to understand that all this happened in no more than two minutes. Nobody could put it all together. We were stunned. Some of them were wandering around, talking a little, but not much. Helen Shyres burst into tears, and that made some of the others start up.

Then someone yelled: 'Call a doctor! Hey, call a doctor quick!'

It was Josie Vreck. He was up on the stage, kneeling by Tommy Ross, and his face was white as paper. He tried to pick him up, and the throne fell over and Tommy rolled onto the floor.

Nobody moved. They were all just staring. I felt like I was frozen in ice. My God, was all I could think. My God, my God, my God. And then this other thought crept in, and it was as if it wasn't my own at all. I was thinking about Carrie. And about God. It was all twisted up together, and it was awful.

Stella looked over at me and said: 'Carrie's back.'

And I said: 'Yes, that's right.'

The lobby doors all slammed shut. The sound was like hands clapping. Somebody in the back screamed, and that started the stampede. They ran for the doors in a rush. I just stood there, not believing it. And when I looked, just before the first of them got there and started to push, I saw Carrie looking in, her face all smeared, like an Indian with war paint on.

She was smiling.

They were pushing at the doors, hammering on them, but they wouldn't budge. As more of them crowded up against them, I could see the first ones to get there being battered against them, grunting and wheezing. They wouldn't open. And those doors are never locked. It's a state law.

Mr Stephens and Mr Lublin waded in, and began to pull them away, grabbing jackets, skirts, anything. They were all screaming and burrowing like cattle. Mr Stephens slapped a couple of girls and punched Vic Mooney in the eye. They were yelling for them to go out the back fire doors. Some did. Those were the ones who lived.

That's when it started to rain . . . at least, that's what I thought it was at first. There was water falling all over the place. I looked up and all the sprinklers were on, all over the gym. Water was hitting the basketball court and splashing. Josie Vreck was yelling for the guys in his band to turn off the electric amps and mikes quick, but they were all gone. He jumped down from the stage.

The panic at the doors stopped. People backed away, looking up at the ceiling. I heard somebody – Don Farnham, I think – say: 'This is gonna wreck the basketball court.'

A few other people started to go over and look at Tommy Ross. All at once I knew I wanted to get out of there. I took Tina Blake's hand and said, 'Let's run. Quick.'

To get to the fire doors, you had to go down a short corridor to the left of the stage. There were sprinklers there too, but they weren't on. And the doors were open – I could see a few people running out. But most of them were just standing around in little groups, blinking at each other. Some of them were looking at the smear of blood where Carrie fell down. The water was washing it away.

I took Tina's arm and started to pull her toward the exit sign. At that same instant there was a huge flash of light, a scream, and a horrible feedback whine. I looked around and saw Josie Vreck holding onto one of the mike stands. He couldn't let go. His eyes were bugging out and his hair was on end and it looked like he was dancing. His feet were sliding around in the water and smoke started to come out of his shirt.

He fell over on one of the amps – they were big ones, five or six feet high – and it fell into the water. The feedback went up to a scream that was head-splitting, and then there was another sizzling flash and it stopped. Josie's shirt was on fire.

'Run!' Tina yelled at me. 'Come on, Norma. *Please*!'

We ran out into the hallway, and something exploded backstage – the main power switches, I guess. For just a second I looked back. You could see right out onto the stage, where Tommy's body was, because the curtain was up. All the heavy light cables were in the air, flowing and jerking and writhing like snakes out of an Indian fakir's basket. Then one of them pulled in two. There was a violent flash when it hit the water, and then everybody was screaming at once.

Then we were out the door and running across the parking lot. I think I was screaming. I don't remember very well. I don't remember anything very well after they started screaming. After those high-voltage cables hit that water-covered floor . . .

For Tommy Ross, age eighteen, the end came swiftly and mercifully and almost without pain.

He was never even aware that something of importance was happening. There was a clanging, clashing noise that he associated momentarily with

(there go the milk buckets)

a childhood memory of his Uncle Galen's farm and then with
(somebody dropped something)
the band below him. He caught a glimpse of Josie Vreck looking over his head
(what have i got a halo or something)
and then the quarter-full bucket of blood struck him. The raised lip along the bottom of the rim struck him on top of the head and
(hey that hur)
he went swiftly down into unconsciousness. He was still sprawled on the stage when the fire originating in the electrical equipment of Josie and the Moonglows spread to the mural of the Venetian boatman, and then to the rat warren of old uniforms, books, and papers backstage and overhead.

He was dead when the oil tank exploded a half hour later.

From the New England AP ticker, 10:46 p.m.:

CHAMBERLAIN, MAINE (AP)

A FIRE IS RAGING OUT OF CONTROL AT EWEN (U-WIN) CONSOLIDATED HIGH SCHOOL AT THIS TIME. A SCHOOL DANCE WAS IN PROGRESS AT THE TIME OF THE OUTBREAK WHICH IS BELIEVED TO HAVE BEEN ELECTRICAL IN ORIGIN. WITNESSES SAY THAT THE SCHOOL'S SPRINKLER SYSTEM WENT ON WITHOUT WARNING, CAUSING A SHORT-CIRCUIT IN THE EQUIPMENT OF A ROCK BAND. SOME WITNESSES ALSO REPORT BREAKS IN MAIN POWER CABLES. IT IS BELIEVED THAT AS MANY AS ONE HUNDRED AND TEN PERSONS MAY BE TRAPPED IN THE BLAZING SCHOOL GYMNASIUM. FIRE FIGHTING EQUIPMENT FROM THE NEIGHBORING TOWNS OF WESTOVER, MOTTON, AND LEWISTON HAVE REPORTEDLY RECEIVED REQUESTS FOR ASSISTANCE AND ARE NOW OR SHORTLY WILL BE EN ROUTE. AS YET, NO CASUALTIES HAVE BEEN REPORTED. ENDS.

10:46 pm MAY 27 6904D AP

From the New England AP ticker, 11:22 p.m.

CHAMBERLAIN, MAINE (AP)

A TREMENDOUS EXPLOSION HAS ROCKED THOMAS EWIN (U-WIN) CONSOLIDATED HIGH SCHOOL IN THE SMALL MAINE TOWN OF CHAMBERLAIN. THREE CHAMBERLAIN FIRE TRUCKS, DISPATCHED EARLIER TO FIGHT A BLAZE AT THE GYMNASIUM WHERE A SCHOOL PROM WAS TAKING PLACE, HAVE ARRIVED TO NO AVAIL. ALL FIRE HYDRANTS IN THE AREA HAVE BEEN VANDALIZED, AND WATER PRESSURE FROM CITY MAINS IN THE AREA FROM SPRING STREET TO GRASS PLAZA IS REPORTED TO BE NIL. ONE FIRE OFFICIAL SAID: 'THE DAMN THINGS WERE STRIPPED OF THEIR NOZZLES. THEY MUST HAVE SPOUTED LIKE GUSHERS WHILE THOSE KIDS WERE BURNING.' THREE BODIES HAVE BEEN RECOVERED SO FAR. ONE HAS BEEN IDENTIFIED AS THOMAS B. MEARS, A CHAMBERLAIN FIREMAN. THE TWO OTHERS WERE APPARENT PROM-GOERS. THREE MORE CHAMBERLAIN FIREMEN HAVE BEEN TAKEN TO MOTTON RECEIVING HOSPITAL SUFFERING FROM MINOR BURNS AND SMOKE INHALATION. IT IS BELIEVED THAT THE EXPLOSION OCCURRED

WHEN THE FIRE REACHED THE SCHOOL'S FUEL-OIL TANKS, WHICH ARE SITUATED NEAR THE GYMNASIUM. THE FIRE ITSELF IS BELIEVED TO HAVE STARTED IN POORLY INSULATED ELECTRICAL EQUIPMENT FOLLOWING A SPRINKLER SYSTEM MALFUNCTION. ENDS.

11:22 pm MAY 27 70119E AP

Sue had only a driver's permit, but she took the keys to her mother's car from the pegboard beside the refrigerator and ran to the garage. The kitchen clock read exactly 11:00.

She flooded the car on her first try, and forced herself to wait before trying again. This time the motor coughed and caught, and she roared out of the garage heedlessly, dinging one fender. She turned around, and the rear wheels splurted gravel. Her mother's '77 Plymouth swerved onto the road, almost fishtailing onto the shoulder and making her feel sick to her stomach. It was only at this point that she realized she was moaning deep in her throat, like an animal in a trap.

She did not pause at the stop sign that marked the intersection of Route 6 and the Back Chamberlain Road. Fire sirens filled the night in the east, where Chamberlain bordered Westover, and from the south behind her – Motton.

She was almost at the base of the hill when the school exploded.

She jammed on the power brakes with both feet and was thrown into the steering wheel like a rag doll. The tires wailed on the pavement. Somehow she fumbled the door open and was out, shading her eyes against the glare.

A gout of flame had ripped skyward, trailing a nimbus of fluttering steel roof panels, wood, and paper. The smell was thick and oily. Main Street was lit as if by a flashgun. In that terrible hallway between seconds, she saw that the entire gymnasium wing of Ewen High was a gutted, flaming ruin.

Concussion struck a moment later, knocking her backward. Road litter blew past her in a sudden and tremendous rush, along with a blast of warm air that reminded her fleetingly of

(the smell of subways)

a trip she had taken to Boston the year before. The windows of Bill's Home Drugstore and the Kelly Fruit Company jingled and fell inward.

She had fallen on her side, and the fire lit the street with hellish noonday. What happened next happened in slow motion as her mind ran steadily onward

(dead are they all dead carrie why think carrie)

at its own clip. Cars were rushing toward the scene, and some people were running in robes, nightshirts, pajamas. She saw a man come out of the front door of Chamberlain's combined police station and courthouse. He was moving slowly. The cars were moving slowly. Even the people running were moving slowly.

She saw the man on the police-station steps cup his hand around his mouth and scream something; unclear over the shrieking town whistle, the fire sirens, the monster-mouth of the fire. Sounded like:

'*Heyret! Don't hey that ass!*'

The street was all wet down there. The light danced on the water. Down by Teddy's Amoco station.

'*—hey, that's—*'

And then the world exploded.

From the sworn testimony of Thomas K. Quillan, taken before The State Investigatory Board of Maine in connection with the events of May 27–28 in Chamberlain, Maine (abridged version which follows is from *Black Prom: The White Commission Report*, Signet Books: New York, 1980):

Q. Mr Quillan, are you a resident of Chamberlain?

A. Yes.

Q. What is your address?

A. I got a room over the pool hall. That's where I work. I mop the floors, vacuum the tables, work on the machines – pinball machines you know.

Q. Where were you on the night of May twenty-seventh at 10:30 p.m., Mr Quillan?

A. Well . . . actually, I was in a detention cell at the police station. I get paid on Thursdays, see. And I always go out and get bombed. I go out to The Cavalier, drink some Schlitz, play a little poker out back. But I get mean when I drink. Feels like the Roller Derby's going on in my head. Bummer, huh? Once I conked a guy over the head with a chair and—

Q. Was it your habit to go to the police station when you felt these fits of temper coming on?

A. Yeah. Big Otis, he's a friend of mine.

Q. Are you referring to Sheriff Otis Doyle of this county?

A. Yeah. He told me to pop in any time I started feeling mean. The night before the prom, a bunch of us guys were in the back room down at The Cavalier playing stud poker and I got to thinking Fast Marcel Dubay was cheating. I would have known better sober – a Frenchman's idea of pullin' a fast one is to look at his own cards – but that got me going. I'd had a couple of beers, you know, so I folded my hand and went on down to the station. Plessy was catching, and he locked me right up in Holding Cell Number 1. Plessy's a good boy. I knew his mom, but that was many years ago.

Q. Mr Quillan, do you suppose we could discuss the night of the twenty-seventh? 10:30 p.m.?

A. Ain't we?

Q. I devoutly hope so. Continue.

A. Well, Plessy locked me up around quarter of two on Friday morning, and I popped right off to sleep. Passed out, you might say. Woke up around four o'clock the next afternoon, took three Alka-Seltzers, and went back to sleep. I got a knack that way. I can sleep until my hangover's all gone. Big Otis says I should find out how I do it and take out a patent. He says I could save the world a lot of pain.

Q. I'm sure you could, Mr Quillan. Now when did you wake up again?'

A. Around ten o'clock on Friday night. I was pretty hungry, so I decided to go get some chow down at the diner.

Q. They left you all alone in an open cell?

A. Sure. I'm a fantastic guy when I'm sober. In fact, one time—

Q. Just tell the Committee what happened when you left the cell.

A. The fire whistle went off, that's what happened. Scared the bejesus out of me. I ain't heard that whistle at night since the Viet Nam war ended. So

I ran upstairs and sonofabitch, there's no one in the office. I say to myself, hot damn, Plessy's gonna get it for this. There's always supposed to be somebody catching, in case there's a call-in. So I went over to the window and looked out.

Q. Could the school be seen from the window?

A. Sure. It's on the other side of the street, a block and a half down. People were running around and yelling. And that's when I saw Carrie White.

Q. Had you ever seen Carrie White before?

A. Nope.

Q. Then how did you know it was she?

A. That's hard to explain.

Q. Could you see her clearly?

A. She was standing under a street light, by the fire hydrant on the corner of Main and Spring.

Q. Did something happen?

A. I guess to Christ. The whole top of the hydrant exploded off three different ways. Left, right, and straight up to heaven.

Q. What time did this . . . uh . . . malfunction occur?

A. Around twenty to eleven. Couldn't have been no later.

Q. What happened then?

A. She started downtown. Mister, she looked awful. She was wearing some kind of party dress, what was left of it, and she was all wet from that hydrant and covered with blood. She looked like she just crawled out of a car accident. But she was *grinning*. I never saw such a grin. It was like a death's head. And she kept looking at her hands and rubbing them on her dress, trying to get the blood off and thinking she'd never get it off and how she was going to pour blood on the whole town and make them pay. It was awful stuff.

Q. How would you have any idea what she was thinking?

A. I don't know. I can't explain.

Q. For the remainder of your testimony, I wish you would stick to what you *saw*, Mr Quillan.

A. Okay. There was a hydrant on the corner of Grass Plaza, and that one went, too. I could see that one better. The big lug nuts on the sides were unscrewing themselves. I *saw* that happening. It blew, just like the other one. And she was *happy*. She was saying to herself, that'll give 'em a shower, *that'll* . . . whoops, sorry. The fire trucks started to go by then, and I lost track of her. The new pumper pulled up to the school and they started on those hydrants and saw they wasn't going to get no water. Chief Burton was hollering at them, and that's when the school exploded. *Jesus*.

Q. Did you leave the police station?

A. Yeah. I wanted to find Plessy and tell him about that crazy broad and the fire hydrants. I glanced over at Teddy's Amoco, and I seen something that made my blood run cold. All six gas pumps was off their hooks. Teddy Duchamp's been dead since 1968, God love him, but his boy locked those pumps up every night just like Teddy himself used to do. Every one of them Yale padlocks was hanging busted by their hasps. The nozzles were laying on the tarmac, and the automatic feeds were set on every one. Gas was pouring out onto the sidewalk and into the street. Holy mother of God, when

I seen that, my balls drew right up. Then I saw this guy running along with a lighted cigarette.

Q. What did you do?

A. Hollered at him. Something like *Hey! Watch that cigarette! Hey don't, that's gas!* He never heard me. Fire sirens and the town whistle and cars rip-assing up and down the street, I don't wonder. I saw he was going to pitch it, so I started to duck back inside.

Q. What happened next?

A. Next? Why, next thing, the Devil came to Chamberlain . . .

When the buckets fell, she was at first only aware of a loud, metallic clang cutting through the music, and then she was deluged in warmth and wetness. She closed her eyes instinctively. There was a grunt from beside her, and in the part of her mind that had come so recently awake, she sensed brief pain.

(tommy)

The music came to a crashing, discordant halt, a few voices hanging on after it like broken strings, and in the sudden deadness of anticipation, filling the gap between event and realization, like doom, she heard someone say quite clearly:

'My God, that's blood.'

A moment later, as if to ram the truth of it home, to make it utterly and exactly clear, someone screamed.

Carrie sat with her eyes closed and felt the black bulge of terror rising in her mind. Momma had been right, after all. They had taken her again, gulled her again, made her the butt again. The horror of it should have been monotonous, but it was not; they had gotten her up here, up here in front of the whole school, and had repeated the shower-room scene . . . only the voice had said

(my god that's blood)

something too awful to be contemplated. If she opened her eyes and it was true, oh, what then? What then?

Someone began to laugh, a solitary, affrighted hyena sound, and she *did* open her eyes, opened them to see who it was and it *was* true, the final nightmare, she was red and dripping with it, they had drenched her in the very secretness of blood, in front of all of them and her thought

(oh . . . i . . . *COVERED* . . . with it)

was colored a ghastly purple with her revulsion and her shame. She could smell herself and it was the *stink* of blood, the awful wet, coppery smell. In a flickering kaleidoscope of images she saw the blood running thickly down her naked thighs, heard the constant beating of the shower on the tiles, felt the soft patter of tampons and napkins against her skin as voices exhorted her to *plug it UP*, tasted the plump, fulsome bitterness of horror. They had finally given her the shower they wanted.

A second voice joined the first, and she was followed by a third – girl's soprano giggle – a fourth, a fifth, six, a dozen, all of them, all laughing. Vic Mooney was laughing. She could see him. His face was utterly frozen shocked, but that laughter issued forth just the same.

She sat quite still, letting the noise wash over her like surf. They were still all beautiful and there was still enchantment and wonder, but she had crossed a line and now the fairy tale was green with corruption and evil. In this one she would bite a poison apple, be attacked by trolls, be eaten by tigers.

They were laughing at her again.

And suddenly it broke. The horrible realization of how badly she had been cheated came over her, and a horrible, soundless cry

(they're LOOKING at me)

tried to come out of her. She put her hands over her face to hide it and staggered out of the chair. Her only thought was to run, to get out of the light, to let the darkness have her and hide her.

But it was like trying to run through molasses. Her traitor mind had slowed time to a crawl; it was as if God had switched the whole scene from 78 rpm to 33⅓. Even the laughter seemed to have deepened and slowed to a sinister bass rumble.

Her feet tangled in each other, and she almost fell off the edge of the stage. She recovered herself, bent down, and hopped down to the floor. The grinding laughter swelled louder. It was like rocks rubbing together.

She wanted not to see, but she *did* see; the lights were too bright and she could see all their faces. Their mouths, their teeth, their eyes. She could see her own gore-streaked hands in front of her face.

Miss Desjardin was running toward her, and Miss Desjardin's face was filled with lying compassion. Carrie could see beneath the surface to where the real Miss Desjardin was giggling and chuckling with rancid old-maid ribaldry. Miss Desjardin's mouth opened and her voice issued forth, horrible and slow and deep:

'Let me help you, dear. Oh I am so sor—'

She struck out at her

(*flex*)

and Miss Desjardin went flying to rattle off the wall at the side of the stage and fall into a heap.

Carrie ran. She ran through the middle of them. Her hands were to her face but she could see through the prison of her fingers, could see them, how they were, beautiful, wrapped in light, swathed in the bright, angelic robes of Acceptance. The shined shoes, the clear faces, the careful beauty-parlor hairdos, the glittery gowns. They stepped back from her as if she was plague, but they kept laughing. Then a foot was stuck slyly out

(o yes that comes next o yes)

and she fell on her hands and knees and began to crawl, to crawl along the floor with her blood-clotted hair hanging in her face, crawling like St. Paul on the Damascus Road, whose eyes had been blinded by the light. Next someone would kick her ass.

But no one did and then she was scrabbling to her feet again. Things began to speed up. She was out through the door, out into the lobby, then flying down the stairs that she and Tommy had swept up so grandly two hours ago.

(tommy's dead full price paid full price for bringing a plague into the place of light)

She went down them in great, awkward leaps, with the sound of the laughter flapping around her like blackbirds.

Then, darkness.

She fled across the school's wide front lawn, losing both of her prom slippers and fleeing barefoot. The closely cut school lawn was like velvet, lightly dusted with dewfall, and the laughter was behind her. She began to calm slightly.

Then her feet *did* tangle and she fell at full length out by the flagpole. She lay quiescent, breathing raggedly, her hot face buried in the cool grass. The tears of shame began to flow, as hot and as heavy as that first flow of menstrual blood had been. They had beaten her, bested her, once and for all time. It was over.

She would pick herself up very soon now, and sneak home by the back streets, keeping to the shadows in case someone came looking for her, find Momma, admit she had been wrong –

(!!NO!!)

The steel in her – and there was a great deal of it – suddenly rose up and cried the word out strongly. The closet? The endless, wandering prayers? The tracts and the cross and only the mechanical bird in the Black Forest cuckoo clock to mark off the rest of the hours and days and years and decades of her life?

Suddenly, as if a videotape machine had been turned on in her mind, she saw Miss Desjardin running toward her, and saw her thrown out of her way like a rag doll as she used her mind on her, without even consciously thinking of it.

She rolled over on her back, eyes staring wildly at the stars from her painted face. She was forgetting

(!! THE POWER !!)

It was time to teach them a lesson. Time to show them a thing or two. She giggled hysterically. It was one of Momma's pet phrases.

(momma coming home putting her purse down eyeglasses flashing well i guess i showed that elt a thing or two at the shop today)

There was the sprinkler system. She could turn it on, turn it on easily. She giggled again and got up, began to walk barefoot back toward the lobby doors. Turn on the sprinkler system and close all the doors. Look in and let them *see* her looking in, watching and laughing while the shower ruined their dresses and their hairdos and took the shine off their shoes. Her only regret was that it couldn't be blood.

The lobby was empty. She paused halfway up the stairs and *FLEX*, the doors all slammed shut under the concentrated force she directed at them, the pneumatic door-closers snapping off. She heard some of them scream and it was music, sweet soul music.

For a moment nothing changed and then she could feel them pushing against the doors, wanting them to open. The pressure was negligible. They were trapped

(*trapped*)

and the word echoed intoxicatingly in her mind. They were under her thumb, in her power. *Power!* What a word that was!

She went the rest of the way up and looked in and George Dawson was smashed up against the glass, struggling, pushing, his face distorted with effort. There were others behind him, and they all looked like fish in an aquarium.

She glanced up and yes, there were the sprinkler pipes, with their tiny nozzles like metal daisies. The pipes went through small holes in the green cinderblock wall. There was a great many inside, she remembered. Fire laws, or something.

Fire laws. In a flash her mind recalled

(black thick cords like snakes)

the power cords strung all over the stage. They were out of the audience's sight, hidden by the footlights, but she had had to step carefully over them to get to the throne. Tommy had been holding her arm.

(fire and water)

She reached up with her mind, felt the pipes, traced them. Cold, full of water. She tasted iron in her mouth, cold wet metal, the taste of water drunk from the nozzle of a garden hose.

Flex.

For a moment nothing happened. Then they began to back away from the doors, looking around. She walked to the small oblong of glass in the middle door and looked inside.

It was raining in the gym.

Carrie began to smile.

She hadn't gotten all of them, only some. But she found that by looking up at the sprinkler system with her eyes, she could trace its course more easily with her mind. She began to turn on more of the nozzles, and more. Yet it wasn't enough. They weren't crying yet, so it wasn't enough.

(hurt them then hurt them)

There was a boy up on stage by Tommy, gesturing wildly and shouting something. As she watched, he climbed down and ran toward the rock band's equipment. He caught hold of one of the microphone stands and was transfixed. Carrie watched, amazed, as his body went through a nearly motionless dance of electricity. His feet shuffled in the water, his hair stood up in spikes, and his mouth jerked open, like the mouth of a fish. He looked funny. She began to laugh.

(by christ then let them all look funny)

And in a sudden, blind thrust, she yanked at all the power she could feel.

Some of the lights puffed out. There was a dazzling flash somewhere as a live power cord hit a puddle of water. There were dull thumps in her mind as circuit breakers went into hopeless operation. The boy who had been holding the mike stand fell over on one of his amps and there was an explosion of purple sparks and then the crepe bunting that faced the stage was burning.

Just below the thrones, a live 220-volt electricity cable was crackling on the floor and beside it Rhonda Simard was doing a crazed puppet dance in her green tulle formal. Its full skirt suddenly blazed into flame and she fell forward, still jerking.

It might have been at that moment that Carrie went over the edge. She leaned against the doors, her heart pumping wildly, yet her body as cold as ice cubes. Her face was livid, but dull red fever spots stood on each cheek. Her head throbbed thickly, and conscious thought was lost.

She reeled away from the doors, still holding them shut, doing it without thought or plan. Inside the fire was brightening and she realized dimly that the mural must have caught on fire.

She collapsed on the top step and put her head down on her knees, trying to slow her breathing. They were trying to get out the doors again, but she held them shut easily – that alone was no strain. Some obscure sense told her that a few were getting out the fire doors, but let them. She would get them later. She would get all of them. Every last one.

She went down the stairs slowly and out the front doors, still holding the gymnasium doors closed. It was easy. All you had to do was see them in your mind.

The town whistle went off suddenly, making her scream and put her hands in front of her face

(the whistle it's just the fire whistle)

for a moment. Her mind's eye lost sight of the gymnasium doors and some of them almost got out. No, no. Naughty. She slammed them shut again, catching somebody's fingers – it felt like Dale Norbert – in the jamb and severing one of them.

She began to reel across the lawn again, a scarecrow figure with bulging eyes, toward Main Street. On her right was downtown – the department store, the Kelly Fruit, the beauty parlor and barbershop, gas stations, police station, fire station—

(they'll put out my fire)

But they wouldn't. She began to giggle and it was an insane sound: triumphant, lost, victorious, terrified. She came to the first hydrant and tried to twist the huge painted lug nut on the side.

(ohuh)

It was heavy. It was very heavy. Metal twisted tight to balk her. Didn't matter.

She twisted harder and felt it give. Then the other side. Then the top. Then she twisted all three at once, standing back, and they unscrewed in a flash. Water exploded outward and upward, one of the lug nuts flying five feet in front of her at suicidal speed. It hit the street, caromed high into the air, and was gone. Water gushed with white pressure in a cruciform pattern.

Smiling, staggering, her heart beating at over two hundred per minute, she began to walk down toward Grass Plaza. She was unaware that she was scrubbing her bloodied hands against her dress like Lady Macbeth, or that she was weeping even as she laughed, or that one hidden part of her mind was keening over her final and utter ruin.

Because she was going to take them with her, and there was going to be a great burning, until the land was full of its stink.

She opened the hydrant at Grass Plaza, and then began to walk down to Teddy's Amoco. It happened to the first gas station she came to, but it was not the last.

From the sworn testimony of Sheriff Otis Doyle, taken before The State Investigatory Board of Maine (from *The White Commission Report*), p. 29–31:

Q. Sheriff, where were you on the night of May twenty-seventh?

A. I was on Route 179, known as Old Bentown Road, investigating an automobile accident. This was actually over the Chamberlain town line and into Durham, but I was assisting Mel Crager, who is the Durham constable.

Q. When were you first informed that trouble had broken out at Ewen High School?

A. I received a radio transmission from Officer Jacob Plessy at 10:21.

Q. What was the nature of the radio call?

A. Officer Plessy said there was trouble at the school, but he didn't know if it was serious or not. There was a lot of shouting going on, he said, and someone had pulled a couple of fire alarms. He said he was going over to try and determine the nature of the trouble.

Q. Did he say the school was on fire?

A. No, sir.

Q. Did you ask him to report back to you?

A. I did.

Q. Did Officer Plessy report back?

A. No. He was killed in the subsequent explosion of Teddy's Amoco gas station on the corner of Main and Summer.

Q. When did you next have a radio communication concerning Chamberlain?

A. At 10:42. I was at that time returning to Chamberlain with a suspect in the back of my car – a drunk driver. As I have said, the case was actually in Mel Crager's town, but Durham has no jail. When I got him to Chamberlain, we didn't have much of one, either.

Q. What communication did you receive at 10:42?

A. I got a call from the State Police that had been relayed from the Motton Fire Department. The State Police dispatcher said there was a fire and an apparent riot at Ewen High School, and a probable explosion. No one was sure of anything at that time. Remember, it all happened in a space of forty minutes.

Q. We understand that, Sheriff. What happened then?

A. I drove back to Chamberlain with siren and flasher. I was trying to raise Jake Plessy and not having any luck. That's when Tom Quillan came on and started to babble about the whole town going up in flames and no water.

Q. Do you know what time that was?

A. Yes, sir. I was keeping a record by then. It was 10:58.

Q. Quillan claims the Amoco station exploded at 11:00.

A. I'd take the average, sir. Call it 10:59.

Q. At what time did you arrive in Chamberlain?

A. At 11:10 p.m.

Q. What was your immediate impression upon arriving Sheriff Doyle?

A. I was stunned. I couldn't believe what I was seeing.

Q. What exactly *were* you seeing?

A. The entire upper half of the town's business section was burning. The Amoco station was gone. Woolworth's was nothing but a blazing frame. The fire had spread to three wooden store fronts next to that – Duffy's Bar and Grille, the Kelly Fruit Company, and the billiard parlor. The heat was ferocious. Sparks were flying onto the roofs of the Maitland Real Estate Agency and Doug Brann's Western Auto Store. Fire trucks were coming in, but they could do very little. Every fire hydrant on that side of the street was stripped. The only trucks doing any business at all were two old volunteer fire department pumpers from Westover, and about all they could do was wet the roofs of the surrounding buildings. And of course the high school.

It was just . . . gone. Of course it's fairly isolated – nothing close enough to it to burn – but my God, all those kids inside . . . all those kids . . .

Q. Did you meet Susan Snell upon entering town?

A. Yes, sir. She flagged me down.

Q. What time was this?

A. Just as I entered town . . . 11:12, no later.

Q. What did she say?

A. She was distraught. She'd been in a minor car accident – skidding – and she was barely making sense. She asked me if Tommy was dead. I asked her who Tommy was, but she didn't answer. She asked me if we had caught Carrie yet.

Q. The Commission is extremely interested in this part of your testimony, Sheriff Doyle.

A. Yes, sir, I know that.

Q. How did you respond to her question?

A. Well, there's only one Carrie in town as far as I know, and that's Margaret White's daughter. I asked her if Carrie had something to do with the fires. Miss Snell told me Carrie had done it. Those were her words. 'Carrie did it. Carrie did it.' She said it twice.

Q. Did she say anything else?

A. Yes, sir. She said: 'They've hurt Carrie for the last time.'

Q. Sheriff, are you sure she didn't say: *'We've* hurt Carrie for the last time'?

A. I am quite sure.

Q. Are you positive? One hundred per cent?

A. Sir, the town was burning around our heads. I—

Q. Had she been drinking?

A. I beg pardon?

Q. Had she been drinking? You said she had been involved in a car smash.

A. I believe I said a minor skidding accident.

Q. And you can't be sure she didn't say *we* instead of *they*?

A. I guess she might have, but—

Q. What did Miss Snell do then?

A. She burst into tears. I slapped her.

Q. Why did you do that?

A. She seemed hysterical.

Q. Did she quiet eventually?

A. Yes, sir. She quieted down and got control of herself pretty well, in light of the fact that her boy friend was probably dead.

Q. Did you interrogate her?

A. Well, not the way you'd interrogate a criminal, if that's what you mean. I asked her if she knew anything about what had happened. She repeated what she had already said, but in a calmer way. I asked her where she had been when the trouble began, and she told me that she had been at home.

Q. Did you interrogate her further?

A. No, sir.

Q. Did she say anything else to you?

A. Yes, sir. She asked me – begged me – to find Carrie White.

Q. What was your reaction to that?

A. I told her to go home.

Q. Thank you, Sheriff Doyle.

Vic Mooney lurched out of the shadows near the Bankers Trust drive-in office with a grin on his face. It was a huge and awful grin, a Cheshire cat grin, floating dreamily in the fireshot darkness like a trace memory of lunacy. His hair, carefully slicked down for his emcee duties was now sticking up in a crow's nest. Tiny drops of blood were branded across his forehead from some unremembered fall in his mad flight from the Spring Ball. One eye was swelled purple and screwed shut. He walked into Sheriff Doyle's squad car, bounced back like a pool ball, and grinned in at the drunk driver dozing in the back. Then he turned to Doyle who had just finished with Sue Snell. The fire cast wavering shadows of light across everything, turning the world into the maroon tones of dried blood.

As Doyle turned, Vic Mooney clutched him. He clutched Doyle as an amorous swain might clutch his lady in a hug dance. He clutched Doyle with both arms and squeezed him, all the while goggling upward into Doyle's face with his great crazed grin.

'Vic—' Doyle began.

'She pulled all the plugs,' Vic said lightly, grinning. 'Pulled all the plugs and turned on the water and buzz, buzz, buzz.'

'Vic—'

'We can't let 'em. Oh no. NoNoNo. We can't. Carrie pulled all the plugs. Rhonda Simard burnt up. *Oh Jeeeeeeeeeesuuuuuuuuusss—*'

Doyle slapped him twice, callused palm cracking flatly on the boy's face. The scream died with shocking suddenness, but the grin remained, like an echo of evil. It was loose and terrible.

'What happened?' Doyle said roughly. 'What happened at the school?'

'Carrie,' Vic muttered. 'Carrie happened at the school. She . . .' He trailed off and grinned at the ground.

Doyle gave him three brisk shakes. Vic's teeth clicked together like castanets.

'What about Carrie?'

'Queen of the Prom,' Vic muttered. 'They dumped blood on her and Tommy.'

'What—'

It was 11:15. Tony's Citgo on Summer Street suddenly exploded with a great, coughing roar. The street went daylight that made them both stagger back against the police car and shield their eyes. A huge, oily cloud of fire climbed over the elms in Courthouse Park, lighting the duck pond and the Little League diamond in scarlet. Amid the hungry crackling roar that followed, Doyle could hear glass and wood and hunks of gas-station cinder-block rattling back to earth. A secondary explosion followed, making them wince again. He still couldn't get it straight

(my town this is happening in my town)

that this was happening in Chamberlain, in *Chamberlain*, for God's sake, where he drank iced tea on his mother's sun porch and refereed PAL basketball and made one last cruise out Route 6 past The Cavalier before turning up at 2:30 every morning. His town was burning up.

Tom Quillan came out of the police station and ran down the sidewalk to Doyle's cruiser. His hair was standing up every which way, he was dressed in dirty green work fatigues and an undershirt and he had his loafers on the wrong feet, but Doyle thought he had never been so glad to see anyone in his life. Tom Quillan was as much Chamberlain as anything, and he was here – intact.

'Holy God,' he panted. 'Did you see *that?*'

'What's been happening?' Doyle asked curtly.

'I been monitorin' the radio,' Quillan said. 'Motton and Westover wanted to know if they should send ambulances and I said hell yes, send everything. Hearses too. Did I do right?'

'Yes.' Doyle ran his hands through his hair. 'Have you seen Harry Block?' Block was the town's Commissioner of Public Utilities, and that included water.

'Nope. But Chief Deighan says they got water in the old Rennett Block across town. They're laying hose now. I collared some kids, and they're settin' up a hospital in the police station. They're good boys, but they're gonna get blood on your floor, Otis.'

Otis Doyle felt unreality surge over him. Surely this conversation couldn't be happening in Chamberlain. *Couldn't.*

'That's all right, Tommy. You did right. You go back there and start calling every doctor in the phone book. I'm going over to Summer Street.'

'Okay, Otis. If you see that crazy broad, be careful.'

'Who?' Doyle was not a barking man, but now he did.

Tom Quillan flinched back. 'Carrie. Carrie White.'

'Who? How do you know?'

Quillan blinked slowly. 'I dunno. It just sort of . . . came to me.'

From the national AP ticker, 11:46 p.m.:

CHAMBERLAIN, MAINE (AP)

A DISASTER OF MAJOR PROPORTIONS HAS STRUCK THE TOWN OF CHAMBERLAIN, MAINE, TONIGHT. A FIRE, BELIEVED TO HAVE BEGUN AT EWIN (U-WIN) HIGH SCHOOL DURING A SCHOOL DANCE, HAS SPREAD TO THE DOWNTOWN AREA, RESULTING IN MULTIPLE EXPLOSIONS THAT HAVE LEVELED MUCH OF THE DOWNTOWN AREA. A RESIDENTIAL AREA TO THE WEST OF THE DOWNTOWN AREA IS ALSO REPORTED TO BE BURNING. HOWEVER, MOST CONCERN AT THIS TIME IS OVER THE HIGH SCHOOL WHERE A JUNIOR-SENIOR PROM WAS BEING HELD. IT IS BELIEVED THAT MANY OF THE PROM-GOERS WERE TRAPPED INSIDE. A WESTOVER FIRE OFFICIAL SUMMONED TO THE SCENE SAID THE KNOWN TOTAL OF DEAD STOOD AT SIXTY-SEVEN, MOST OF THEM HIGH SCHOOL STUDENTS. ASKED HOW HIGH THE TOTAL MIGHT GO HE SAID: 'WE DON'T KNOW. WE'RE AFRAID TO GUESS. THIS IS GOING TO BE WORSE THAN THE COCONUT GROVE.' AT LAST REPORT THREE FIRES WERE RAGING OUT OF CONTROL IN THE TOWN. REPORTS OF POSSIBLE ARSON ARE UNCONFIRMED. ENDS.

11:46 p.m. MAY 27 8943F AP

There were no more AP reports from Chamberlain. At 12:06 a.m., a Jackson Avenue gas main was opened. At 12:17, an ambulance attendant from Motton tossed out a cigarette butt as the rescue vehicle sped toward Summer Street.

The explosion destroyed nearly half a block at a stroke, including the offices of the Chamberlain *Clarion*. By 12:18 a.m., Chamberlain was cut off from the country that slept in reason beyond.

At 12:10, still seven minutes before the gas-main explosion, the telephone exchange experienced a softer explosion: a complete jam of every town phone line still in operation. The three harried girls on duty stayed at their posts but were utterly unable to cope. They worked with expressions of wooden horror on their faces, trying to place unplaceable calls.

And so Chamberlain drifted into the streets.

They came like an invasion from the graveyard that lay in the elbow crook formed by the intersection of the Bellsqueeze Road and Route 6; they came in white nightgowns and in robes, as if in winding shrouds. They came in pajamas and curlers (Mrs Dawson, she of the now-deceased son who had been a very funny fellow, came in a mudpack as if dressed for a minstrel show); they came to see what happened to their town, to see if it was indeed lying burned and bleeding. Many of them also came to die.

Carlin Street was thronged with them, a riptide of them, moving downtown through the hectic light in the sky, when Carrie came out of the Carlin Street Congregational Church, where she had been praying.

She had gone in only five minutes before, after opening the gas main (it had been easy; as soon as she pictured it lying there under the street it had been easy), but it seemed like hours. She had prayed long and deeply, sometimes aloud, sometimes silently. Her heart thudded and labored. The veins on her face and neck bulged. Her mind was filled with the huge knowledge of POWERS, and of an ABYSS. She prayed in front of the altar, kneeling in her wet and torn and bloody gown, her feet bare and dirty and bleeding from a broken bottle she had stepped on. Her breath sobbed in and out of her throat, and the church was filled with groanings and swayings and sunderings as psychic energy sprang from her. Pews fell, hymnals flew, and a silver Communion set cruised silently across the valuted darkness of the nave to crash into the far wall. She prayed and there was no answer. No one was there – or if there was, He/It was cowering from her. God had turned His face away, and why not? This horror was as much His doing as hers. And so she left the church, left it to go home and find her momma and make destruction complete.

She paused on the lower step, looking at the flocks of people streaming toward the center of town. Animals. Let them burn, then. Let the streets be filled with the smell of their sacrifice. Let this place be called racca, ichabod, wormwood.

Flex.

And power transformers atop lightpoles bloomed into nacreous purple light, spitting catherine-wheel sparks. High-tension wires fell into the streets in pick-up-sticks tangles and some of them ran, and that was bad for them because now the whole street was littered with wires and the stink began, the burning began. People began to scream and back away and some touched the cables and went into jerky electrical dances. Some had already slumped into the street their robes and pajamas smoldering.

Carrie turned back and looked fixedly at the church she had just left. The heavy door suddenly swung shut, as if in a hurricane wind.

Carrie turned toward home.

From the sworn testimony of Mrs Cora Simard, taken before The State Investigatory Board (from *The White Commission Report*), pp. 217–18:

Q. Mrs Simard, the Board understands that you lost your daughter on Prom Night, and we sympathize with you deeply. We will make this as brief as possible.

A. Thank you. I want to help if I can, of course.

Q. Were you on Carlin Street at approximately 12:12, when Carietta White came out of the First Congregational Church on that street?

A. Yes.

Q. Why were you there?

A. My husband had to be in Boston over the weekend on business and Rhonda was at the Spring Ball. I was home alone watching TV and waiting up for her. I was watching the Friday Night Movie when the town hall whistle went off, but I didn't connect that with the dance. But then the explosion . . . I didn't know what to do. I tried to call the police but got a busy signal after the first three numbers. I . . . I . . . Then . . .

Q. Take your time, Mrs Simard. All the time you need.

A. I was getting frantic. There was a second explosion – Teddy's Amoco station, I know now – and I decided to go downtown and see what was happening. There was a glow in the sky, an awful glow. That was when Mrs Shyres pounded on the door.

Q. Mrs Georgette Shyres?

A. Yes, they live around the corner. 217 Willow. That's just off Carlin Street. She was pounding and calling: 'Cora are you in there? Are you in there?' I went to the door. She was in her bathrobe and slippers. Her feet looked cold. She said they had called Westover to see if they knew anything and they told her the school was on fire. I said: 'Oh dear God, Rhonda's at the dance.'

Q. Is this when you decided to go downtown with Mrs Shyres?

A. We didn't decide anything. We just went. I put on a pair of slippers – Rhonda's, I think. They had little white puffballs on them. I should have worn my shoes, but I wasn't thinking. I guess I'm not thinking now. What do you want to hear about my shoes for?

Q. You tell it in your own way, Mrs Simard.

A. T-Thank you. I gave Mrs Shyres some old jacket that was around, and we went.

Q. Were there many people walking down Carlin Street?

A. I don't know. I was too upset. Maybe thirty. Maybe more.

Q. What happened?

A. Georgette and I were walking toward Main Street, holding hands just like two little girls walking across a meadow after dark. Georgette's teeth were clicking. I remember that. I wanted to ask her to stop clicking her teeth, but I thought it would be impolite. A block and a half from the Congo Church, I saw the door open and I thought: Someone has gone in to ask God's help. But a second later I knew that wasn't true.

Q. How did you know? It would be logical to assume just what you first assumed, wouldn't it?

A. I just knew.

Q. Did you know the person who came out of the church?

A. Yes. It was Carrie White.

Q. Had you ever seen Carrie White before?

A. No. She was not one of my daughter's friends.

Q. Had you ever seen a picture of Carrie White?

A. No.

Q. And in any case, it was dark and you were a block and a half from the church.

A. Yes, sir.

Q. Mrs Simard, how did you know it was Carrie White?

A. I just knew.

Q. This *knowing*, Mrs Simard: was it like a light going on in your head?

A. No, sir.

Q. What *was* it like?

A. I can't tell you. It faded away the way a dream does. An hour after you get up you can only remember you had a dream. But I knew.

Q. Was there an emotional feeling that went with this knowledge?

A. Yes. Horror.

Q. What did you do then?

A. I turned to Georgette and said: 'There she is.' Georgette said: 'Yes, that's her.' She started to say something else, and then the whole street was lit up by a bright glow and there were crackling noises and then the power lines started to fall into the street, some of them spitting live sparks. One of them hit a man in front of us and he b-burst into flames. Another man started to run and he stepped on one of them and his body just . . . arched backward, as if his back had turned into elastic. And then *he* fell down. Other people were screaming and running, just running blindly, and more and more cables fell. They were strung all over the place like snakes. And she was glad about it. *Glad!* I could *feel* her being glad. I knew I had to keep my head. The people who were running were getting electrocuted. Georgette said: 'Quick, Cora. Oh God, I don't want to get burned alive.' I said: 'Stop that. We have to use our heads, Georgette, or we'll never use them again.' Something foolish like that. But she wouldn't listen. She let go of my hand and started to run for the sidewalk. I screamed at her to stop – there was one of those heavy main cables broken off right in front of us – but she didn't listen. And she . . . she . . . oh, I could smell her when she started to burn. Smoke just seemed to *burst* out of her clothes and I thought: that's what it must be like when someone gets electrocuted. The smell was sweet, like pork. Have any of you ever smelled that? Sometimes I smell it in my dreams. I stood dead still, watching Georgette Shyres turn black. There was a big explosion over in the West End – the gas main, I suppose – but I never even noticed it. I looked around and I was all alone. Everyone else had either run away or was burning. I saw maybe six bodies. They were like piles of old rags. One of the cables had fallen onto the porch of a house to the left, and it was catching on fire. I could hear the old-fashioned shake shingles popping like corn. It seemed like I stood there a long time, telling myself to keep my head. It seemed like hours. I began to be afraid that I would faint and fall on one of the cables, or that I would panic and start to run. Like . . . like Georgette. So I started to walk. One step at a time. The street got even brighter, because of the burning house. I stepped over two live wires and went around a body that wasn't much more than a puddle. I – I – I had to look to see where I was going. There was a wedding ring on the body's hand, but it was all black. All *black*. Jesus, I was thinking. Oh dear Lord. I stepped over another cable and then there were three, all at once. I just stood there looking at them. I thought if I got over those I'd be all right but . . . I didn't dare. Do you know what I kept thinking of? That game you play when you're kids. Giant Step. A voice in my mind was saying, Cora, take one giant step over the live wires in the street. And I was thinking *May I? May I?* One of them was still spitting a few sparks, but the other two looked dead. But you can't tell. The third rail looks dead too. So I stood there, waiting for someone to come and nobody did. The house was still burning and the flames had spread to the lawn and the trees and the hedge beside it. But no fire trucks came. Of course they didn't. The whole west side was burning up by that time. And I felt so *faint*. And at last I knew it was take the giant step or faint and so I took it, as big a giant step as I could, and the heel of my slipper came down not an inch from the last wire. Then I got over and went around the end of one more wire and then I started to run. And that's all I remember. When morning came I was lying on a blanket in the police station with a lot of other people. Some of them – a few – were kids in their prom get-ups and I started to ask them if they had seen Rhonda. And they said . . . they s-s-said . . .

(A short recess)

Q. You are personally sure that Carrie White did this?
A. Yes.
Q. Thank you, Mrs Simard.
A. I'd like to ask a question, if you please.
Q. Of course.
A. What happens if there are others like her? What happens to the world?

From *The Shadow Exploded* (p. 151):

By 12:45 on the morning of May 28, the situation in Chamberlain was critical. The school had burned itself out on a fairly isolated piece of ground, but the entire downtown area was ablaze. Almost all the city water in that area had been tapped, but enough was available (at low pressure) from Deighan Street water mains to save the business buildings below the intersection of Main and Oak streets.

The explosion of Tony's Citgo on upper Summer Street had resulted in a ferocious fire that was not to be controlled until nearly ten o'clock that morning. There was water on Summer Street; there simply were no firemen or fire-fighting equipment to utilize it. Equipment was then on its way from Lewiston, Auburn, Lisbon, and Brunswick, but nothing arrived until one o'clock.

On Carlin Street, an electrical fire, caused by downed power lines, had begun. It was to eventually gut the entire north side of the street, including the bungalow where Margaret White gave birth to her daughter.

On the West End of town, just below what is commonly called Brickyard Hill, the worst disaster had taken place: the explosion of a gas main and a resulting fire that raged out of control through most of the next day.

And if we look at these flash points on a municipal map (see page facing), we can pick out Carrie's route – a wandering, looping path of destruction through the town, but one with an almost certain destination: home. . . .

Something toppled over in the living room, and Margaret White straightened up, cocking her head to one side. The butcher knife glittered dully in the light of the flames. The electric power had gone off sometime before, and the only light in the house came from the fire up the street.

One of the pictures fell from the wall with a thump. A moment later the Black Forest cuckoo clock fell. The mechanical bird gave a small, strangled squawk and was still.

From the town the sirens whooped endlessly, but she could still hear the footsteps when they turned up the walk.

The door blew open. Steps in the hall.

She heard the plaster plaques in the living room (CHRIST, THE UNSEEN GUEST; WHAT WOULD JESUS DO; THE HOUR DRAWETH NIGH: IF TONIGHT BECAME JUDGMENT, WOULD YOU BE READY) explode one after the other, like plaster birds in a shooting gallery.

(o i've been there and seen the harlots shimmy on wooden stages)

She sat up on her stool like a very bright scholar who has gone to the head of the class. But her eyes were deranged.

The living-room windows blew outward.

The kitchen door slammed and Carrie walked in.

Her body seemed to have become twisted, shrunken, cronelike. The prom dress was in tatters and flaps, and the pig blood had began to clot and streak. There was a smudge of grease on her forehead, and both knees were scraped and raw-looking.

'Momma,' she whispered. Her eyes were preternaturally bright, hawklike, but her mouth was trembling. If someone had been there to watch, he would have been struck by the resemblance between them.

Margaret White sat on her kitchen stool, the carving knife hidden among the folds of her dress in her lap.

'I should have killed myself when he put it in me,' she said clearly. 'After the first time, before we were married, he promised. Never again. He said we just . . . slipped. I believed him. I fell down and I lost the baby and that was God's judgment. I felt that the sin had been expiated. By blood. But sin never dies. *Sin . . . never . . . dies.*' Her eyes glittered.

'Momma, I—'

'At first it was all right. We lived sinlessly. We slept in the same bed, belly to belly sometimes, and o, I could feel the presence of the Serpent, but we. never. did. until.' She began to grin, and it was a hard, terrible grin. 'And that night I could see him looking at me That Way. We got down on our knees to pray for strength and he . . . touched me. In that place. That woman place. And I sent him out of the house. He was gone for hours, and I prayed for him. I could see him in my mind's eye, walking the midnight streets, wrestling with the devil as Jacob wrestled with the Angel of the Lord. And when he came back, my heart was filled with thanksgiving.'

She paused, grinning her dry, spitless grin into the shifting shadows of the room.

'Momma, I don't want to hear it?'

Plates began to explode in the cupboards like claypigeons.

'It wasn't until he came in that I smelled the whiskey on his breath. And he took me. *Took me!* With the stink of filthy roadhouse whiskey still on him he took me . . . *and I liked it!'* She screamed out the last words at the ceiling. *'I liked it o all that dirty fucking and his hands on me ALL OVER ME!'*

'MOMMA!'

(*!! MOMMA !!*)

She broke off as if slapped and blinked at her daughter. 'I almost killed myself,' she said in a more normal tone of voice. 'And Ralph wept and talked about atonement and I didn't and then he was dead and then I thought God had visited me with cancer; that He was turning my female parts into something as black and rotten as my sinning soul. But that would have been too easy. The Lord works in mysterious ways His wonders to perform. I see that now. When the pains began I went and got a knife – this knife—' she held it up '—and waited for you to come so I could make my sacrifice. But I was weak and backsliding. I took this knife in hand again when you were three, and I backslid again. So now the devil has come home.'

She held the knife up, and her eyes fastened hypnotically on the glittering hook of its blade.

Carrie took a slow, blundering step forward.

'I came to kill you, Momma. And you were waiting here to kill me. Momma, I . . . it's not right, Momma. It's not . . .'

'Let's pray,' Momma said softly. Her eyes fixed on Carrie's and there was a crazed, awful compassion in them. The firelight was brighter now, dancing on the walls like dervishes. 'For the last time, let us pray.'

'Oh Momma help me!' Carrie cried out.

She fell forward on her knees, head down, hands raised in supplication.

Momma leaned forward, and the knife came down in a shining arc.

Carrie, perhaps seeing out of the tail of her eye, jerked back, and instead of penetrating her back, the knife went into her shoulder to the hilt. Momma's feet tangled in the legs of her chair, and she collapsed in a sitting sprawl.

They stared at each other in silent tableau.

Blood began to ooze from around the handle of the knife and to splash onto the floor.

Then Carrie said softly: 'I'm going to give you a present, Momma.'

Margaret tried to get up, staggered, and fell back on her hands and knees. 'What are you doing?' she croaked hoarsely.

'I'm picturing your heart, Momma,' Carrie said. 'It's easier when you see things in your mind. Your heart is a big red muscle. Mine goes faster when I use my power. But yours is going a little slower now. A little slower.'

Margaret tried to get up again, failed, and forked the sign of the evil eye at her daughter.

'A little slower, Momma. Do you know what the present is, Momma? What you always wanted. Darkness. And whatever God lives there.'

Margaret White whispered: 'Our Father, Who art in heaven—'

'Slower, Momma, Slower.'

'—hallowed be Thy name—'

'I can see the blood draining back into you. Slower.'

'—Thy kingdom come—'

'Your feet and hands like marble, like alabaster. White.'

'—Thy will be done—'

'*My* will, Momma. Slower.'

'—on earth—'

'Slower.'

'—as . . . as . . . as it . . .'

She collapsed forward, hands twitching.

'—as it is in heaven.'

Carrie whispered: 'Full stop.'

She looked down at herself, and put her hands weakly around the haft of the knife.

(no o no that hurts that's too much hurt)

She tried to get up, failed, then pulled herself up by Momma's stool. Dizziness and nausea washed over her. She could taste blood, bright and slick, in the back of her throat. Smoke, acrid and choking, was drifting in through the windows now. The flames had reached next door; even now sparks would be lighting softly on the roof that rocks had punched brutally through a thousand years before.

Carrie went out the back door, staggered across the lawn, and rested

(where's my momma)

against a tree. There was something she was supposed to do. Something about

(roadhouses parking lots)

the Angel with the Sword. The Fiery Sword.

Never mind. It would come to her.

She crossed by back yards to Willow Street and then crawled up the embankment to Route 6.

It was 1:15 a.m.

It was 11:20 p.m. when Christine Hargensen and Billy Nolan got back to The Cavalier. They went up the back stairs, down the hall, and before she could do more than turn on the lights, he was yanking at her blouse.

'For God's sake let me unbutton it—'

'To hell with that.'

He ripped it suddenly down the back. The cloth tore with a sudden hard sound. One button popped free and winked on the bare wood floor. Honky-tonkin' music came faintly up to them, and the building vibrated subtly with the clumsy-enthusiastic dancing of farmers and truckers and millworkers and waitresses and hairdressers, of the greasers and their townie girl friends from Westover and Lewiston.

'Hey—'

'Be quiet.'

He slapped her, rocking her head back. Her eyes took on a flat and deadly shine.

'This is the end, Billy.' She backed away from him, breasts swelling into her bra, flat stomach pumping, legs long and tapering in her jeans; but she backed toward the bed. 'It's over.'

'Sure,' he said. He lunged for her and she punched him, a surprisingly hard punch that landed on his cheek.

He straightened and twitched his head a little.'You gave me a shiner, you bitch.'

'I'll give you more.'

'You're goddam right you will.'

They stared at each other, panting, glaring. Then he began to unbutton his shirt, a little grin beginning on his face.

'We got it on, Charlie. We really got it on.' He called her Charlie whenever he was pleased with her. It seemed to be, she thought with a cold blink of humor, a generic term for a good cunt.

She felt a little smile come to her own face, relaxed a little, and that was when he whipped his shirt across her face and came in low, butting her in the stomach like a goat, tipping her onto the bed. The springs screamed. She pounded her fists helplessly on his back.

'Get off me! Get off me! Get off me! You fucking greaseball, *get off me!*'

He was grinning at her, and with one quick, hard yank her zipper was broken her hips free.

'Call your daddy?' he was grunting. 'That what you gonna do? Huh? Huh? That it, ole Chuckie? Call big ole legal beagle daddy? Huh? I woulda done it to you, you know that? I woulda dumped it all over your fuckin squash. You know it? Huh? Know it? Pig blood for pigs, right? Right on your motherfuckin squash. You—'

She had suddenly ceased to resist. He paused, staring down at her, and she had an odd smile on her face. 'You wanted it this way all along, didn't you? You miserable little scumbag. That's right, isn't it? You creepy little one-nut low-cock dink-less wonder.'

His grin was slow, crazed. 'It doesn't matter.'

'No,' she said. 'It doesn't.' Her smile suddenly vanished, the cords on her neck stood out as she hawked back - and spit in his face.

They descended into a red, thrashing unconsciousness.

Downstairs the music thumped and wheezed ('*I'm poppin little white pills an my eyes are open wide/Six days on the road, and I'm gonna make it home tonight*'), c/w, full throttle, very loud, very bad, five-man band wearing sequined cowboy shirts and new pegged jeans with bright rivets, occasionally wiping mixed sweat and Vitalis from their brows, lead guitar, rhythm, steel, dobro guitar, drums: no one heard the town whistle, or the first explosion, or the second; and when the gas main blew and the music stopped and someone drove into the parking lot and began to yell the news, Chris and Billy were asleep.

Chris woke suddenly and the clock on the night table said five minutes of one. Someone was pounding on the door.

'Billy!' the voice was yelling. 'Get up! Hey! Hey!'

Billy stirred, rolled over, and knocked the cheap alarm clock onto the floor. 'What the Christ?' he said thickly, and sat up. His back stung. The bitch had covered it with long scratches. He'd barely noticed it at the time, but now he decided he was going to send her home bowlegged. Just to show her who was b—

Silence struck him. Silence. The Cavalier did not close until two; as a matter of fact, he could still see the neon twinkling and flicking through the dusty garret window. Except for the steady pounding

(something happened)

the place was a graveyard.

'Billy, you in there? Hey!'

'Who is it?' Chris whispered. Her eyes were glittering and watchful in the intermittent neon.

'Jackie Talbot,' he said absently, then raised his voice. 'What?'

'Lemme in, Billy. I got to talk to you!'

Billy got up and padded to the door, naked. He unlocked the old-fashioned hook-and-eye and opened it.

Jackie Talbot burst in. His eyes were wild and his face was smeared with soot. He had been drinking it up with Steve and Henry when the news came at ten minutes of twelve. They had gone back to town in Henry's elderly Dodge convertible and had seen the Jackson Avenue gas main explode from the vantage point of Brickyard Hill. When Jackie had borrowed the Dodge and started to drive back at 12:30, the town was a panicky shambles.

'Chamberlain's burning up,' he said to Billy. 'Whole fuckin town. The school's gone. The Center's gone. West End blew up – gas. And Carlin Street's on fire. And they're saying Carrie White did it!'

'Oh God,' Chris said. She started to get out of bed and grope for her clothes. 'What did—'

'Shut up,' Billy said mildly, 'or I'll kick your ass.' He looked at Jackie again and nodded for him to go on.

'They seen her. Lots of people seen her. Billy, they say she's all covered with blood. She was at that fuckin prom tonight . . . Steve and Henry didn't get it but . . . Billy, did you . . . that pig blood . . . was it—'

'Yeah,' Billy said.

'Oh, no.' Jackie stumbled back against the doorframe. His face was sickly yellow in the light of the one hall lightbulb. 'Oh Jesus, Billy, the whole town—'

'Carrie trashed the whole town? Carrie *White?* You're full of shit.' He said it calmly, almost serenely. Behind him, Chris was dressing rapidly.

'Go look out the window,' Jackie said.

Billy went over and looked out. The entire eastern horizon had gone crimson, and the sky was alight with it. Even as he looked, three fire trucks screamed by. He could make out the names on them in the glow of the street light that marked The Cavalier's parking lot.

'Son of a whore,' he said. 'Those trucks are from Brunswick.'

'Brunswick?' Chris said. 'That's forty miles away. That can't be . . .'

Billy turned back to Jackie Talbot. 'All right. What happened?'

Jackie shook his head. 'Nobody knows, not yet. It started at the high school. Carrie and Tommy Ross got the King and Queen, and then somebody dumped a couple of buckets of blood on them and she ran out. Then the school caught on fire, and they say nobody got out. Then Teddy's Amoco blew up, then that Mobil station on Summer Street—'

'Citgo,' Billy corrected. 'It's a Citgo.'

'*Who the fuck cares?*' Jackie screamed. 'It was her, every place something happened it was *her!* And those buckets . . . none of us wore gloves . . .'

'I'll take care of it,' Billy said.

'You don't get it, Billy. Carrie is—'

'Get out.'

'Billy—'

'Get out or I'll break your arm and feed it to you.'

Jackie backed out of the door warily.

'Go home. Don't talk to nobody. I'm going to take care of everything.'

'All right,' Jackie said. 'Okay. Billy, I just thought—'

Billy slammed the door.

Chris was on him in a second. 'Billy what are we going to do that bitch Carrie oh my Lord what are we going to—'

Billy slapped her, getting his whole arm into it, and knocked her onto the floor. Chris sat sprawled in stunned silence for a moment, and then held her face and began to sob.

Billy put on his pants, his tee shirt, his boots. Then he went to the chipped porcelain washstand in the corner, clicked on the light, wet his head, and began to comb his hair, bending down to see his reflection in the spotted, ancient mirror. Behind him, wavy and distorted, Chris Hargensen sat on the floor, wiping blood from her split lip.

'I'll tell you what we're going to do,' he said. 'We're going into town and watch the fires. Then we're coming home. You're going to tell your dear old daddy that we were out to The Cavalier drinking beers when it happened. I'm gonna tell my dear old mummy the same thing. Dig?'

'Billy, your fingerprints,' she said. Her voice was muffled, but respectful.

'*Their* fingerprints,' he said. 'I wore gloves.'

'Would they tell?' she asked. 'If the police took them in and questioned them—'

'Sure,' he said. 'They'd tell.' The loops an swirls were almost right. They glistened in the light of the dull, fly-specked globe like eddies in deep water. His face was calm, reposeful. The comb he used was a battered old Ace, clotted with grease. His father had given it to him on his eleventh birthday, and not one tooth was broken in it. Not one.

'Maybe they'll never find the buckets,' he said. 'If they do, maybe the fingerprints will be burnt off. I don't know. But if Doyle takes any of 'em in, I'm heading for California. You do what you want.'

'Would you take me with you?' she asked. She looked at him from the floor, her lip puffed to negroid size, her eyes pleading.

He smiled. 'Maybe.' But he wouldn't. Not any more. 'Come on. We're going to town.'

They went downstairs and through the empty dance hall, where chairs were still pushed back and beers were standing flat on the tables.

As they went out through the fire door Billy said: 'This place sucks, anyway.'

They got into his car, and he started it up. When he popped on the headlights, Chris began to scream, hands in fists up to her cheeks.

Billy felt it at the same time: Something in his mind,

(carrie carrie carrie carrie)

a presence.

Carrie was standing in front of them perhaps seventy feet away.

The high beams picked her out in ghastly horror-movie blacks and whites, dripping and clotted with blood. Now much of it was her own. The hilt of the butcher knife still protruded from her shoulder, and her gown was covered with dirt and grass stain. She had crawled much of the distance from Carlin Street, half fainting, to destroy this roadhouse – perhaps the very one where the doom of her creation had begun.

She stood swaying, her arms thrown out like the arms of a stage hypnotist, and she began to totter toward them.

It happened in the blink of a second. Chris had not had time to expend her first scream Billy's reflexes were very good and his reaction was instantaneous. He shifted into low, popped the clutch, and floored it.

The Chevrolet's tires screamed against the asphalt, and the car sprang forward like some old and terrible man-eater. The figure swelled in the windshield and as it did the presence became louder

(CARRIE CARRIE CARRIE)

and louder

(*CARRIE CARRIE CARRIE)*

like a radio being turned up to full volume. Time seemed to close around them in a frame and for a moment they were frozen even in motion: Billy

(*CARRIE* just like the dogs *CARRIE* just like the goddam dogs *CARRIE* brucie i wish it could *CARRIE* be *CARRIE* you)

and Chris

(*CARRIE* jesus not to kill her *CARRIE* didn't mean to kill *CARRIE* billy i don't *CARRIE* went to *CARRIE* see it *CA*)

and Carrie herself.

(see the wheel car wheel gas pedal wheel i see the *WHEEL* o god my heart my heart my heart)

And Billy suddenly felt his car turn traitor, come alive, slither in his hands. The Chevvy dug around in a smoking half-circle, straight pipes racketing, and suddenly the clapboard side of The Cavalier was swelling, swelling, swelling and

(this is)

they slammed into it at forty, still accelerating, and wood sprayed up in a neon-tinted detonation. Billy was thrown forward and the steering column speared him. Chris was thrown into the dashboard.

The gas tank split open, and fuel began to puddle around the rear of the car. Part of one straight pipe fell into it, and the gas bloomed into flame.

Carrie lay on her side, eyes closed, panting thickly. Her chest was on fire. She began to drag herself across the parking lot, going nowhere.

(momma i'm sorry it all went wrong o momma o please o please i hurt so bad momma what do i do)

And suddenly it didn't seem to matter any more, nothing would matter if she could turn over, turn over and see the stars, turn over and look once and die.

And that was how Sue found her at two o'clock.

When Sheriff Doyle left her, Sue walked down the street and sat on the steps of the Chamberlain U-Wash-It. She stared at the burning sky without seeing it. Tommy was dead. She knew it was true and accepted it with an ease that was dreadful.

And Carrie had done it.

She had no idea how she knew it, but the conviction was as pure and right as arithmetic.

Time passed. It didn't matter. Macbeth hath murdered sleep and Carrie hath murdered time. Pretty good. A *bon mot*. Sue smiled dolefully. Can this be the end of our heroine, Miss Sweet Little Sixteen? No worries about the country club and Kleen Korners now. Not ever. Gone. Burned out. Someone ran past, blabbering that Carlin Street was on fire. Good for Carlin Street. Tommy was gone. And Carrie had gone home to murder her mother.

(???????????)

She sat bolt upright, staring into the darkness.

(???????????)

She didn't know how she knew. It bore no relationship to anything she had ever read about telepathy. There were no pictures in her head, no great white flashes of revelation, only prosaic knowledge; the way you know summer follows spring, that cancer can kill you, that Carrie's mother was dead already, that—

(*!!!!!*)

Her heart rose thickly in her chest. Dead? She examined her knowledge of the incident, trying to disregard the insistent weirdness of knowing from nothing.

Yes, Margaret White was dead. Something to do with her heart. But she had stabbed Carrie. Carrie was badly hurt. She was—

There was nothing more.

She got up and ran back to her mother's car. Ten minutes later she parked on the corner of Branch and Carlin Street, which was on fire. No trucks were available to fight the blaze yet, but saw-horses had been put across both ends of the street, and greasily smoking road pots lit a sign which said:

DANGER! LIVE WIRES!

She cut through two back yards and forced her way through a budding hedge that scraped at her with short, stiff bristles. She came out one yard from the Whites' house and crossed over.

The house was in flames, the roof blazing. It was impossible to even think about getting close enough to look in. But in the strong firelight she saw something better: the splashed trail of Carrie's blood. She followed it with her head down, past the larger spots where Carrie had rested, through another hedge, across a Willow Street back yard, and then through an undeveloped tangle of scrub pine and oak. Beyond that, a short, unpaved spur – little more than a footpath – wound up the rise of land to the right, angling away from Route 6.

She stopped suddenly as doubt struck her with vicious and corrosive force. Suppose she could find her? What then? Heart failure? Set on fire? Controlled and forced to walk in front of an oncoming car or fire engine? Her peculiar knowledge told her Carrie would be capable of all these things.

(find a policeman)

She giggled a little at that one and sat down in the grass, which was silked with dew. She had already found a policeman. And even supposing Otis Doyle had believed her, what then? A mental picture came to her of a hundred desperate manhunters surrounding Carrie, demanding her to hand over her weapons and give up. Carrie obediently raises her hands and plucks her head from her shoulders. Hands it to Sheriff Doyle, who solemnly puts it in a wicker basket marked People's Exhibit A.

(and tommy's dead)

Well, well. She began to cry. She put her hands over her face and sobbed into them. A soft breeze snuffled through the juniper bushes on top of the hill. More fire engines screamed by on Route 6 like huge red hounds in the night.

(the town's burning down o well)

She had no idea how long she sat there, crying in a grainy half-doze. She was not even aware that she was following Carrie's progress toward The Cavalier, no more than she was aware of the process of respiration unless she thought about it. Carrie was hurt very badly, was going on brute determination alone at this point. It was three miles out to The Cavalier, even cross country, as Carrie was going. Sue

(watched? thought? doesn't matter)

as Carrie fell in a bro͝ok and dragged herself out, icy and shivering. It was really amazing that she kept going. But of course it was for Momma. Momma wanted her to be the Angel's fiery Sword, to destroy—

(she's going to destroy that too)

She got up and began to run clumsily, not bothering to follow the trail of blood. She didn't need to follow it any more.

From *The Shadow Exploded* (pp. 164–65):

Whatever any of us may think of the Carrie White affair, it is over. It's time to turn to the future. As Dean McGuffin points out, in his excellent *Science Yearbook* article, if we refuse to do this, we will almost certainly have to pay the piper - and the price is apt to be a high one.

A thorny moral question is raised here. Progress is already being made toward complete isolation of the TK gene. It is more or less assumed in the scientific community (see, for instance, Bourke and Hannegan's 'A View Toward Isolation of the TK Gene with Specific Recommendations for Control Parameters' in *Microbiology Annual*, Berkeley: 1982) that when a testing procedure is established all school-age children will undergo the test as routinely as they now undergo the TB skin-patch. Yet TK is not a germ; it is as much a part of the afflicted person as the color of his eyes.

If overt TK ability occurs as a part of puberty, and if this hypothetical TK test is performed on children entering the first grade, we shall certainly be forewarned. But in this case, is forewarned forearmed? If the TB test shows positive, a child can be treated or isolated. If the TK test shows positive, we have no treatment except a bullet in the head. And how is it possible to isolate a person who will eventually have the power to knock down all walls?

And even if isolation could be made successful, would the American people allow a small, pretty girl-child to be ripped away from her parents at the first sign of puberty to be locked in a bank vault for the rest of her life? I doubt it. Especially when the White Commission has worked so hard to convince the public that the nightmare in Chamberlain was a complete fluke.

Indeed, we seem to have returned to Square One . . .

From the sworn testimony of Susan Snell, taken before The State Investigatory Board of Maine (from *The White Commission Report*), pp. 306–472:

Q. Now, Miss Snell, the Board would like to go through your testimony concerning your alleged meeting with Carrie White in The Cavalier parking lot—

A. Why do you keep asking the same questions over and over? I've told you twice already.

Q. We want to make sure the record is correct in every—

A. You want to catch me in a lie, isn't that what you really mean? You don't think I'm telling the truth, do you?

Q. You say you came upon Carrie at—

A. Will you answer me?

Q. at approximately 2:00 on the morning of May 28th. Is that correct?

A. I'm not going to answer any more questions until you answer the one I just asked.

Q. Miss Snell, this body is empowered to cite you for contempt if you refuse to answer on any other ground than Constitutional ones.

A. I don't care what you're empowered to do. I've lost someone I love. Go and throw me in jail. I don't care. I – I – Oh, go to hell. All of you, go to hell. You're trying to . . . to . . . I don't know, crucify me or something. Just lay off me!

(*A short recess*)

Q. Miss Snell, are you willing to continue your testimony at this time?

A. Yes. But I won't be badgered, Mr Chairman.

Q. Of course not, young lady. No one wants to badger you. Now you claim to have come upon Carrie in the parking lot of this tavern at about 2:00. Is that correct?

A. Yes.

Q. You knew the time.

A. I was wearing the watch you see on my wrist right now.

Q. To be sure. Isn't The Cavalier better than six miles from where you left your mother's car?

A. It is by the road. It's closer to three as the crow flies.

Q. You walked this distance?

A. Yes.

Q. Now you testified earlier that you 'knew' you were getting close to Carrie. Can you explain this?

A. No.

Q. Could you smell her?

A. What?

Q. Did you follow your nose?

(*Laughter in the galleries*)

A. Are you playing games with me?

Q. Answer the question, please.

A. No, I didn't follow my nose.

Q. Could you see her?

A. No.

Q. Hear her?

A. No.

Q. Then how could you possibly know she was there?

A. How did Tom Quillan know? Or Cora Simard? Or poor Vic Mooney? How did any of them know?

Q. Answer the question, Miss. This is hardly the place or the time for impertinence.

A. But they did say they 'just knew,' didn't they? I read Mrs Simard's testimony in the paper! And what about the fire hydrants that opened themselves? And the gas pumps that broke their own locks and turned themselves on? The power lines that climbed down off their poles! And—

Q. Miss Snell, please—

A. Those things are in the record of this Commission's proceedings!

Q. That is not an issue here.

A. Then what *is*? Are you looking for the truth or just a scapegoat?

Q. You deny you had prior knowledge of Carrie White's whereabouts?

A. Of course I do. It's an absurd idea.

Q. Oh? And why is it absurd?

A. Well, if you're suggesting some kind of conspiracy, it's absurd because Carrie was dying when I found her. It could not have been an easy way to die.

Q. If you had no prior knowledge of her whereabouts, how could you go directly to her location?

A. Oh, you stupid man! Have you listened to anything that's been said here? Everybody knew it was Carrie! Anyone could have found her if they had put their minds to it.

Q. But not just anyone found her. You did. Can you tell us why people did not show up from all over, like iron filings drawn to a magnet?

A. She was weakening rapidly. I think that perhaps the . . . the zone of her influence was shrinking.

Q. I think you will agree that that is a relatively uninformed supposition.

A. Of course it is. On the subject of Carrie White, we're all relatively uninformed.

Q. Have it your way, Miss Snell. Now if we could turn to . . .

At first, when she climbed up the embankment between Henry Drain's meadow and the parking lot of The Cavalier, she thought Carrie was dead. Her figure was halfway across the parking lot, and she looked oddly shrunken and crumpled. Sue was reminded of dead animals she had seen on 95 – woodchucks, groundhogs, skunks – that had been crushed by speeding trucks and station wagons.

But the presence was still in her mind, vibrating stubbornly, repeating the call letters of Carrie White's personality over and over. An essence of Carrie, a *gestalt*. Muted now, not strident, not announcing itself with a clarion, but waxing and waning in steady oscillations.

Unconscious.

Sue climbed over the guard rail that bordered the parking lot, feeling the heat of the fire against her face. The Cavalier was a wooden frame building, and it was burning briskly. The charred remains of a car were limned in flame to the right of the back door. Carrie had done that, then. She did not go to look and see if anyone had been in it. It didn't matter, not now.

She walked over to where Carrie lay on her side, unable to hear her own footsteps under the hungry crackle of the fire. She looked down at the curled-up figure with a bemused and bitter pity. The knife hilt protruded cruelly from her and she was lying in a small pool of blood – some of it was trickling from her mouth. She looked as if she had been trying to turn herself over when unconsciousness had taken her. Able to start fires, pull down electric cables, able to kill almost by thought alone; lying here unable to turn herself over.

Sue knelt, took her by one arm and the unhurt shoulder, and gently turned her onto her back.

Carrie moaned thickly, and her eyes fluttered. The perception of her in Sue's mind sharpened, as if a mental picture was coming into focus.

(who's there)

And Sue, without thought, spoke in the same fashion:

(me sue snell)

Only there was no need to think of her name. The thought of herself as herself was neither words nor pictures. The realization suddenly brought everything up close, made it real, and compassion for Carrie broke through the dullness of her shock.

And Carrie, with faraway, dumb reproach:

(you tricked me you all tricked me)

(carrie i don't even know what happened is tommy)

(you tricked me that happened trick trick trick o dirty trick)

The mixure of image and emotion was staggering, indescribable. Blood, Sadness. Fear. The latest dirty trick in a long series of dirty tricks: they flashed by in a dizzying shuffle that made Sue's mind reel helplessly, hopelessly. They shared the awful totality of perfect knowledge.

(carrie don't don't don't hurts me)

Now the girls throwing sanitary napkins, chanting, laughing, Sue's face mirrored in her own mind: ugly, caricatured, all mouth, cruelly beautiful.

(see the dirty tricks see my whole life one long dirty trick)

(look carrie look inside me)

And Carrie looked.

The sensation was terrifying. Her mind and nervous system had become a library. Someone in desperate need ran through her, fingers trailing lightly over shelves of books, lifting some out, scanning them, putting them back, letting some fall, leaving the pages to flutter wildly

(glimpses that's me as a kid hate him daddy o mommy wide lips o teeth bobby pushed me o my knee car want to ride in the car we're going to see aunt cecily mommy come quick i made pee)

in the wind of memory; and still on and on, finally reaching a shelf marked TOMMY, subheaded PROM. Books thrown open, flashes of experience, marginal notations in all the hieroglyphs of emotion, more complex than the Rosetta Stone.

Looking. Finding more than Sue herself had suspected – love for Tommy, jealousy, selfishness, a need to subjugate him to her will on the matter of taking Carrie, disgust for Carrie herself, hate for Miss Desjardin, hate for herself.

(she could take better care of herself she does look just like a GODDAM TOAD)

But no ill will for Carrie personally, no plan to get her in front of everyone and undo her.

The feverish feeling of being raped in her most secret corridors began to fade. She felt Carrie pulling back, weak and exhausted.

(why didn't you just leave me alone)

(carrie i)

(momma would be alive i killed my momma i want her o it hurts my chest hurts my shoulder o o o i want my momma)

(carrie i)

And there was no way to finish that thought, nothing there to complete it with. Sue was suddenly overwhelmed with terror, the worse because she could put no name to it: The bleeding freak on this oil-stained asphalt suddenly seemed meaningless and awful in its pain and dying.

(o momma i'm scared momma MOMMA)

Sue tried to pull away, to disengage her mind, to allow Carrie at least the privacy of her dying, and was unable to. She felt that she was dying herself and did not want to see this preview of her own eventual end.

(carrie let me GO)

(Momma Momma Momma *oooooooooooooo OOOOOOOOOO*)

The mental scream reached a flaring, unbelievable crescendo and then suddenly faded. For a moment Sue felt as if she were watching a candle flame disappear down a long, black tunnel at a tremendous speed.

(she's dying o my god i'm feeling her die)

And then the light was gone, and the last conscious thought had been

(momma i'm sorry where)

and it broke up and Sue was tuned in only on the blank, idiot frequency of the physical nerve endings that would take hours to die.

She stumbled away from it, holding her arms out in front of her like a blind woman, toward the edge of the parking lot. She tripped over the knee-high guard rail and tumbled down the embankment. She got to her feet and stumbled into the field, which was filling with mystic white pockets of ground mist. Crickets chirruped mindlessly and a whippoorwill

(whippoorwill somebody's dying)

called in the great stillness of morning.

She began to run, breathing deep in her chest, running from Tommy, from the fires and explosions, from Carrie, but mostly from the final horror – that last lighted thought carried swiftly down into the black tunnel of eternity, followed by the blank, idiot hum of prosaic electricity.

The after-image began to fade reluctantly, leaving a blessed, cool darkness in her mind that knew nothing. She slowed, halted, and became aware that something had begun to happen. She stood in the middle of the great and misty field, waiting for realization.

Her rapid breathing slowed, slowed, caught suddenly as if on a thorn—

And suddenly vented itself in one howling, cheated scream.

As she felt the slow course of dark menstrual blood down her thighs.

ANDOVER MERCY HOSPITAL

REPORT OF DECEASE

Name White Carietta N. by
(Last) (First) (Middle)

Address 47 Carlin Street

Chamberlain, Maine 02249

Emergency Room None Ambulance #16

Treatment administered None D.O.A. X
Yes No

Time of Death May 28, 1979 - 2:00AM (approx.)

Cause of Death Hemorrhage, shock, coronary occlusion

and/or coronary thrombosis (possible)

Person identifying deceased Susan D. Snell

19 Back Chamberlain Road

Chamberlain, Maine 02249

Next of Kin None

Body to be released to Commonwealth of Maine

Doctor in attendance

Pathologist

BOOK THREE

WRECKAGE

From the national AP ticker, Friday, June 5, 1979:

CHAMBERLAIN, MAINE (AP)

STATE OFFICIALS SAY THAT THE DEATH TOLL IN CHAMBERLAIN STANDS AT 409, WITH 49 STILL LISTED AS MISSING. INVESTIGATION CONCERNING CARIETTA WHITE AND THE SO-CALLED 'TK' PHENOMENA CONTINUES AMID PERSISTENT RUMORS THAT AN AUTOPSY ON THE WHITE GIRL HAS UNCOVERED CERTAIN UNUSUAL FORMATIONS IN THE CEREBRUM AND CEREBELLUM OF THE BRAIN. THIS STATE'S GOVERNOR HAS APPOINTED A BLUE-RIBBON COMMITTEE TO STUDY THE ENTIRE TRAGEDY.

ENDS. FINAL JUNE 5 0303N AP

From *The Lewiston Daily Sun*, Sunday, September 7 (p. 3):

The Legacy of TK:
Scorched Earth and Scorched Hearts

CHAMBERLAIN – Prom Night is history now. Pundits have been saying for centuries that time heals all wounds, but the hurt of this small western Maine town may be mortal. The residential streets are still there on the town's East Side, guarded by graceful oaks that have stood for two hundred years. The trim saltboxes and ranch styles on Morin Street and Brickyard Hill are still neat and undamaged. But this New England pastoral lies on the rim of a blackened and shattered hub, and many of the neat houses have FOR SALES signs on their front lawns. Those still occupied are marked by black wreaths on front doors. Bright-yellow Allied vans and orange U-Hauls of varying sizes are a common sight on Chamberlain's streets these days.

The town's major industry, Chamberlain Mills and Weaving, still stands, untouched by the fire that raged over much of the town on those two days in May. But it has only been running one shift since June 4th, and according to mill president William A. Chamblis, further lay-offs are a strong possibility. 'We have the orders,' Chamblis said. 'but you can't run a mill without people to punch the time clock. We don't have them. I've gotten notice from thirty-four men since August 15th. The only thing we can see to do now is close up the dye house and job our work out. We'd hate to let the men go, but this thing is getting down to a matter of financial survival.'

Roger Fearon has lived in Chamberlain for twenty-two years, and has been with the mill for eighteen of those years. He has risen during that time from a third-floor bagger making seventy-three cents an hour to dye-house foreman; yet he seems strangely unmoved by the possibility of losing his job. 'I'd lose a damned good wage,' Fearon said. 'It's not something you take lightly. The wife and I have talked it over. We could sell the house – it's worth $20,000 easy – and although we probably won't realize half of that, we'll probably go ahead and put it up. Doesn't matter. We don't really want to live in Chamberlain any more. Call it what you want, but Chamberlain has gone bad for us.'

Fearon is not alone. Henry Kelly, proprietor of a tobacco shop and soda fountain called the Kelly Fruit until Prom Night leveled it, has no plans to rebuild. 'The kids are gone,' he shrugs. 'If I opened up again, there'd be too many ghosts in too many corners. I'm going to take the insurance money and retire to St. Petersburg.'

A week after the tornado of '54 had cut its path of death and destruction through Worcester, the air was filled with the sound of hammers, the smell of new timber, and a feeling of optimism and human resilence. There is none of that in Chamberlain this fall. The main road has been cleared of rubble and that is about the extent of it. The faces that you meet are full of dull hopelessness. Men drink beer without talking in Frank's Bar on the corner of Sullivan Street, and women exchange tales of grief and loss in back yards. Chamberlain has been declared a disaster area, and money is available to help put the town back on its feet and begin rebuilding the business district.

But the main business of Chamberlain in the last four months has been funerals.

Four hundred and forty are now known dead, eighteen more still unaccounted for. And sixty-seven of the dead were Ewen High School Seniors on the verge of graduation. It is this, perhaps, more than anything else, that has taken the guts out of Chamberlain.

They were buried on June 1 and 2 in three mass ceremonies. A memorial service was held on June 3 in the town square. It was the most moving ceremony that this reporter has ever witnessed. Attendance was in the thousands, and the entire assemblage was still as the school band, stripped from fifty-six to a bare forty, played the school song and taps.

There was a somber graduation ceremony the following week at neighboring Motton Academy, but there were only fifty-two Seniors left to graduate. The valedictorian, Henry Stampel, broke into tears halfway through his speech and could not continue. There were no Graduation Night parties following the ceremony; the Seniors merely took their diplomas and went home.

And still, as the summer progressed, the hearses continued to roll as more bodies were discovered. To some residents it seemed that each day the scab was ripped off again, so that the wound could bleed afresh.

If you are one of the many curiosity-seekers who have been through Chamberlain in the last week, you have seen a town that may be suffering from terminal cancer of the spirit. A few people, looking lost, wander through the aisles of the A&P. The Congregational Church on Carlin Street is gone, swept away by fire, but the brick Catholic Church still stands on Elm Street, and the trim Methodist Church on outer Main Street, although singed by fire, is unhurt. Yet attendance had been poor. The old men still sit on the benches in Courthouse Square, but there is little interest in the checkerboards or even in conversation.

The over-all impression is one of a town that is waiting to die. It is not enough, these days, to say that Chamberlain will never by the same. It may be closer to the truth to say that Chamberlain will simply never again be.

Excerpt from a letter dated June ninth from Principal Henry Grayle to Peter Philpott, Superintendent of Schools:

. . . and so I feel I can no longer continue in my present position, feeling, as I do, that such a tragedy might have been averted if I had only had more foresight. I would like you to accept my resignation effective as of July 1, if this is agreeable to you and your staff . . .

Exerpt from a letter dated June eleventh from Rita Desjardin, instructor of Physical Education, to Principal Henry Grayle:

. . . am returning my contract to you at this time. I feel that I would kill myself before ever teaching again. Late at night I keep thinking: If I had only reached out to that girl, if only, if only . . .

Found painted on the lawn of the house lot where the White bungalow had been located:

CARRIE WHITE IS BURNING FOR HER SINS
JESUS NEVER FAILS

From 'Telekinesis: Analysis and Aftermath' (*Science Yearbook*, 1981), by Dean D. L. McGuffin:

In conclusion, I would like to point out the grave risk authorities are taking by burying the Carrie White affair under the bureaucratic mat – and I am speaking specifically of the so-called White Commission. The desire among politicians to regard TK as a once-in-a-lifetime phenomenon seems very strong, and while this may be understandable it is not acceptable. The possibility of a recurrence, genetically speaking, is 99 percent. It's time we planned now for what may be . . .

From *Slang Terms Explained: A Parents' Guide*, by John R. Coombs (New York: The Lighthouse Press, 1985), p. 73:

to rip off a Carrie: To cause either violence or destruction; mayhem, confusion; (2) to commit arson (from Carrie White, 1963 – 1979)

From *The Shadow Exploded* (p. 201):

Elsewhere in this book mention is made of a page in one of Carrie White's school notebooks where a line from a famous rock poet of the '60s, Bob Dylan, was written repeatedly, as if in desperation.

It might not be amiss to close this book with a few lines from another Bob Dylan song, lines that might serve as Carrie's epitaph: *I wish I could write you a melody so plain/ That would save you, dear lady, from going insane/ That would ease you and cool you and cease the pain/ Of your useless and pointless knowledge. . .**

* Lyrics from TOMBSTONE BLUES by Bob Dylan.

From *My Name Is Susan Snell* (p. 98):

This little book is done now. I hope it sells well so I can go someplace where nobody knows me. I want to think things over, decide what I'm going to do between now and the time when my light is carried down that long tunnel into blackness. . .

From the conclusion of The State Investigatory Board of Maine in connection with the events of May 27–28 in Chamberlain, Maine:

. . . and so we must conclude that, while an autopsy performed on the subject indicates some cellular changes which *may* indicate the presence of *some* paranormal power, we find no reason to believe that a recurrence is likely or even possible . . .

Excerpt from a letter dated May 3, 1988, from Amelia Jenks, Royal Knob, Tennessee, to Sandra Jenks, Macon, Georgia:

. . . and your little neece is growin like a weed, awfull big for only 2. She has blue eyes like her daddy and my blond hair but that will porubly go dark. Still she is awfull pretty & I think sometimes when she is asleep how she looks like our momma.

The other day while she was playin in the dirt beside the house I sneeked around and saw the funnyest thing. Annie was playin with her brothers marbles only they were mooving around all by themselfs. Annie was giggeling and laffing but I was a little skared. Some of them marbles was going right up & down. It remined me of gramma, do you remember when the law came up that time after Pete and there guns flew out of there hands and grammie just laffed and laffed. And she use to be able to make her rocker go even when she wasen in it. It gave me a reel bad turn to think on it. I shure hope she don't get heartspels like grammie did, remember?

Well I must go & do a wash so give my best to Rich and take care to send us some pitchers when you can. Still our Annie is awfull pretty & her eyes are as brite as buttons. I bet she'll be a world-beeter someday.

All my love,

Melia

MISERY

This is for Stephanie and Jim Leonard,
who know why.

Boy, *do* they.

ACKNOWLEDGEMENTS

'King of the Road' by Roger Miller. © 1964 Tree Publishing Co., Inc. International copyright secured. All rights reserved. Used by permission of the publisher.

'The Collector' by John Fowles. © 1963 by John Fowles. Reproduced by permission of Jonathan Cape Ltd.

'Those Lazy, Hazy, Crazy Days of Summer' by Hans Carste and Charles Tobias. © 1963 ATV Music. Lyrics reproduced by permission of the publisher.

'Girls Just Want to Have Fun'. Words and music by Robert Hazard. © Heroic Music. British Publishers: Warner Bros. Music Ltd. Reproduced by kind permission.

'Santa Claus is comin' to Town' by Haven Gillespie and J. Fred Coots. © 1934, renewed 1962 Leo Feist Inc. Rights assigned to SBK Catalogue Partnership. All rights reserved. International copyright secured. Used by permission.

'Fifty Ways to Leave Your Lover' by Paul Simon. Copyright © 1975 by Paul Simon. Used by permission.

'Chug-a-Lug' by Roger Miller. © 1964 Tree Publishing Co., Inc. International copyright secured. All rights reserved. Used by permission of the publisher.

'Disco Inferno' by Leroy Green and Ron 'Have Mercy' Kersey. Copyright © 1977 by Six Strings Music and Golden Fleece Music; assigned to Six Strings Music, 1978. All rights reserved.

goddess

Africa

I'd like to gratefully acknowledge the help of three medical people who helped me with the factual material in this book. They are:

Russ Dorr, PA
Florence Dorr, RN
Janet Ordway, MD and Doctor of Psychiatry

As always, they helped with the things you don't notice. If you see a glaring error, it's mine.

There is, of course, no such drug as Novril, but there are several codeine-based drugs similar to it, and, unfortunately, hospital pharmacies and medical practice dispensaries are sometimes lax in keeping such drugs under tight lock and close inventory.

The places and characters in this book are fictional.

S.K.

PART ONE

ANNIE

'When you look into the abyss,
the abyss also looks into you'
FRIEDRICH NIETZSCHE

1

umber whunnnn
yerrrnnn umber whunnnn
fayunnnn
These sounds: even in the haze.

2

But sometimes the sounds – like the pain – faded, and then there was only the haze. He remembered darkness: solid darkness had come before the haze. Did that mean he was making progress? Let there be light (even of the hazy variety), and the light was good, and so on and so on? Had those sounds existed in the darkness? He didn't know the answers to any of these questions. Did it make sense to ask them? He didn't know the answer to that one, either.

The pain was somewhere below the sounds. The pain was east of the sun and south of his ears. That was all he *did* know.

For some length of time that seemed very long (and so was, since the pain and the stormy haze were the only two things which existed) those sounds were the only outer reality. He had no idea who he was or where he was and cared to know neither. He wished he was dead, but through the pain-soaked haze that filled his mind like a summer storm-cloud, he did not know he wished it.

As time passed, he became aware that there were periods of nonpain, and that these had a cyclic quality. And for the first time since emerging from the total blackness which had prologued the haze, he had a thought which existed apart from whatever his current situation was. This thought was of a broken-off piling which had jutted from the sand at Revere Beach. His mother and father had taken him to Revere Beach often when he was a kid, and he had always insisted that they spread their blanket where he could keep an eye on that piling, which looked to him like the single jutting fang of a buried monster. He liked to sit and watch the water come up until it covered the piling. Then, hours later, after the sandwiches and potato salad had been eaten, after the last few drops of Kool-Aid had been coaxed from his father's big Thermos, just before his mother said it was time to pack up and start home, the top of the rotted piling would begin to show again – just a peek and flash between the incoming waves at first, then more and more. By the time their trash was stashed in the big drum with KEEP YOUR BEACH CLEAN stencilled on the side, Paulie's beach-toys picked up

(*that's my name Paulie I'm Paulie and tonight ma'll put Johnson's Baby Oil on my sunburn* he thought inside the thunderhead where he now lived)

and the blanket folded again, the piling had almost wholly reappeared, its blackish, slime-smoothed sides surrounded by sudsy scuds of foam. It was the tide, his father had tried to explain, but he had always known it was the piling. The tide came and went; the piling stayed. It was just that sometimes you couldn't see it. Without the piling, there was *no* tide.

This memory circled and circled, maddening, like a sluggish fly. He groped for whatever it might mean, but for a long time the sounds interrupted.

fayunnnn

red everrrythinggg

umberrrr whunnnnn

Sometimes the sounds stopped. Sometimes he stopped.

His first really clear memory of this *now*, the *now* outside the storm-haze, was of stopping, of being suddenly aware he just couldn't pull another breath, and that was all right, that was good, that was in fact just peachy-keen; he could take a certain level of pain but enough was enough and he was glad to be getting out of the game.

Then there was a mouth clamped over his, a mouth which was unmistakably a woman's mouth in spite of its hard spitless lips, and the wind from this woman's mouth blew into his own mouth and down his throat, puffing his lungs, and when the lips were pulled back he smelled his warder for the first time, smelled her on the outrush of the breath she had forced into him the way a man might force a part of himself into an unwilling woman, a dreadful mixed stench of vanilla cookies and chocolate ice-cream and chicken gravy and peanut-butter fudge.

He heard a voice screaming, 'Breathe, goddammit! *Breathe*, Paul!'

The lips clamped down again. The breath blew down his throat again. Blew down it like the dank suck of wind which follows a fast subway train, pulling sheets of newspaper and candy-wrappers after it, and the lips were withdrawn, and he thought *For Christ's sake don't let any of it out through your nose* but he couldn't help it and oh that *stink*, that *stink* that *fucking* STINK.

'Breathe, goddam you!' the unseen voice shrieked, and he thought *I will, anything, please just don't do that anymore, don't infect me anymore,* and he *tried*, but before he could really get started her lips were clamped over his again, lips as dry and dead as strips of salted leather, and she raped him full of her air again.

When she took her lips away this time he did not *let* her breath out but *pushed* it and whooped in a gigantic breath of his own. Shoved it out. Waited for his unseen chest to go up again on its own, as it had been doing his whole life without any help from him. When it didn't, he gave another giant whooping gasp, and then he was breathing again on his own, and doing it as fast as he could to flush the smell and taste of her out of him.

Normal air had never tasted so fine.

He began to fade back into the haze again, but before the dimming world was gone entirely, he heard the woman's voice mutter: 'Whew! That was a close one!'

Not close enough, he thought, and fell asleep.

He dreamed of the piling, so real he felt he could almost reach out and slide his palm over its green-black fissured curve.

When he came back to his former state of semiconsciousness, he was able to make the connection between the piling and his current situation – it seemed to float into his hand. The pain wasn't tidal. That was the lesson of the dream which was really a memory. The pain only *appeared* to come and go. The pain was like the piling, sometimes covered and sometimes visible, but always there. When the pain wasn't harrying him through the deep stone grayness of his cloud, he was dumbly grateful, but he was no longer fooled – it was still there, waiting to return. And there was not just *one* piling but *two*; the pain was the pilings, and part of him knew for a long time before most of his mind had knowledge of knowing that the shattered pilings were his own shattered legs.

But it was still a long time before he was finally able to break the dried scum of saliva that had glued his lips together and croak out 'Where am I?' to the woman who sat by his bed with a book in her hands. The name of the man who had written the book was Paul Sheldon. He recognized it as his own with no surprise.

'Sidewinder, Colorado,' she said when he was finally able to ask the question. 'My name is Annie Wilkes. And I am –'

'I know,' he said. 'You're my number-one fan.'

'Yes,' she said, smiling. 'That's just what I am.'

3

Darkness. Then the pain and the haze. Then the awareness that, although the pain was constant, it was sometimes buried by an uneasy compromise which he supposed was relief. The first real memory: stopping, and being raped back into life by the woman's stinking breath.

Next real memory: her fingers pushing something into his mouth at regular intervals, something like Contac capsules, only since there was no water they only sat in his mouth and when they melted there was an incredibly bitter taste that was a little like the taste of aspirin. It would have been good to spit that bitter taste out, but he knew better than to do it. Because it was that bitter taste which brought the high tide in over the piling.

(PILINGS it's PILINGS there are TWO okay there are two fine now just hush just you know hush shhhhhh)

and made it seem gone for awhile.

These things all came at widely spaced intervals, but then, as the pain itself began not to recede but to erode (as that Revere Beach piling must itself have eroded, he thought, because nothing is forever – although the child he had been would have scoffed at such heresy), outside things began to impinge more rapidly until the objective world, with all its freight of memory, experience, and prejudice, had pretty much re-established itself. He was Paul Sheldon, who wrote novels of two kinds, good ones and best-sellers. He had been married and divorced twice. He smoked too much (or had before all this, whatever 'all this' was). Something very bad had happened to him but he was still alive. That dark-gray cloud began to dissipate faster and faster. It would be yet awhile before his number-one fan brought him the old clacking Royal with the grinning gapped mouth and the Ducky Daddles voice, but Paul understood long before then that he was in a hell of a jam.

4

That prescient part of his mind saw her before he knew he was seeing her, and must surely have understood her before he knew he was understanding her – why else did he associate such dour, ominous images with her? Whenever she came into the room he thought of the graven images worshiped by superstitious African tribes in the novels of H. Rider Haggard, and stones, and doom.

The image of Annie Wilkes as an African idol out of *She* or *King Solomon's Mines* was both ludicrous and queerly apt. She was a big woman who, other than the large but unwelcoming swell of her bosom under the gray cardigan sweater she always wore, seemed to have no feminine curves at all – there was no defined roundness of hip or buttock or even calf below the endless succession of wool skirts she wore in the house (she retired to her unseen bedroom to put on jeans before doing her outside chores). Her body was big but not generous. There was a feeling about her of clots and roadblocks rather than welcoming orifices or even open spaces, areas of hiatus.

Most of all she gave him a disturbing sense of *solidity*, as if she might not have any blood vessels or even internal organs; as if she might be only solid Annie Wilkes from side to side and top to bottom. He felt more and more convinced that her eyes, which appeared to move, were actually just painted on, and they moved no more than the eyes of portraits which appear to follow you to wherever you move in the room where they hang. It seemed to him that if he made the first two fingers of his hand into a V and attempted to poke them up her nostrils, they might go less than an eighth of an inch before encountering a solid (if slightly yielding) obstruction; that even her gray cardigan and frumpy house skirts and faded outside-work jeans were part of that solid fibrous unchanneled body. So his feeling that she was like an idol in a perfervid novel was not really surprising at all. Like an idol, she gave only one thing: a feeling of unease deepening steadily toward terror. Like an idol, she took everything else.

No, wait, that wasn't quite fair. She *did* give something else. She gave him the pills that brought the tide in over the pilings.

The pills were the tide; Annie Wilkes was the lunar presence which pulled them into his mouth like jetsam on a wave. She brought him two every six hours, first announcing her presence only as a pair of fingers poking into his mouth (and soon enough he learned to suck eagerly at those poking fingers in spite of the bitter taste), later appearing in her cardigan sweater and one of her half-dozen skirts, usually with a paperback copy of one of his novels tucked under her arm. At night she appeared to him in a fuzzy pink robe, her face shiny with some sort of cream (he could have named the main ingredient easily enough even though he had never seen the bottle from which she tipped it; the sheepy smell of the lanolin was strong and proclamatory), shaking him out of his frowzy, dream-thick sleep with the pills nestled in her hand and the poxy moon nestled in the window over one of her solid shoulders.

After awhile – after his alarm had become too great to be ignored – he was able to find out what she was feeding him. It was a pain-killer with a heavy codeine base called Novril. The reason she had to bring him the bedpan so infrequently was not only because he was on a diet consisting entirely of liquids and gelatines (earlier, when he was in the cloud, she had fed him intravenously), but also because Novril had a tendency to cause constipation in patients taking it. Another side-effect, a rather more serious one, was respiratory depression in sensitive patients. Paul was not particularly sensitive, even though he had been a heavy smoker for nearly eighteen years, but his breathing had *stopped* nonetheless on at least one occasion (there might have been others, in the haze, that he did not remember). That was the time she gave him mouth-to-mouth. It might have just been one of those things which happened, but he later came to suspect she had nearly killed him with an accidental overdose. She didn't know as much about what she was doing as she believed she did. That was only one of the things about Annie that scared him.

He discovered three things almost simultaneously, about ten days after having emerged from the dark cloud. The first was that Annie Wilkes had a great deal of Novril (she had, in fact, a great many drugs of all kinds). The second was that he was hooked on Novril. The third was that Annie Wilkes was dangerously crazy.

5

The darkness had prologued the pain and the storm-cloud; he began to remember what had prologued the darkness as she told him what had happened to him. This was shortly after he had asked the traditional when-the-sleeper-wakes question and she had told him he was in the little town of Sidewinder, Colorado. In addition she told him that she had read each of his eight novels at least twice, and had read her *very* favorites, the *Misery* novels, four, five, maybe six times. She only wished he would write them faster. She said she had hardly been able to believe that her patient was *really that Paul Sheldon* even after checking the ID in his wallet.

'Where is my wallet, by the way?' he asked.

'I've kept it safe for you,' she said. Her smile suddenly collapsed into a narrow watchfulness he didn't like much – it was like discovering a deep *crevasse* almost obscured by summer flowers in the midst of a smiling, jocund meadow. 'Did you think I'd steal something out of it?'

'No, of course not. It's just that -' *It's just that the rest of my life is in it,* he thought. *My life outside this room. Outside the pain. Outside the way time seems to stretch out like the long pink string of bubble-gum a kid pulls out of his mouth when he's bored. Because that's how it is in the last hour or so before the pills come.*

'Just *what,* Mister Man?' she persisted, and he saw with alarm that the narrow look was growing blacker and blacker. The *crevasse* was spreading, as if an earthquake was going on behind her brow. He could hear the steady, keen whine of the wind outside, and he had a sudden image of her picking him up and throwing him over her solid shoulder, where he would lie like a burlap sack slung over a stone wall, and taking him outside, and heaving him into a snowdrift. He would freeze to death, but before he did, his legs would throb and scream.

'It's just that my father always told me to keep my eye on my wallet,' he said, astonished by how easily this lie came out. His father had made a career out of not noticing Paul any more than he absolutely had to, and had, so far as Paul could remember, offered him only a single piece of advice in his entire life. On Paul's fourteenth birthday his father had given him a Red Devil condom in a foil envelope. 'Put that in your wallet,' Roger Sheldon said, 'and if you ever get excited while you're making out at the drive-in, take a second between excited enough to want to and too excited to care and slip that on. Too many bastards in the world already, and I don't want to see you going in the Army at sixteen.'

Now Paul went on: 'I guess he told me to keep my eye on my wallet so many times that it's stuck inside for good. If I offended you, I'm truly sorry.'

She relaxed. Smiled. The *crevasse* closed. Summer flowers nodded cheerfully once again. He thought of pushing his hand through that smile and encountering nothing but flexible darkness. 'No offense taken. It's in a safe place. Wait – I've got something for you.'

She left and returned with a steaming bowl of soup. There were vegetables floating in it. He was not able to eat much, but he ate more than he thought at first he could. She seemed pleased. It was while he ate the soup that she told him what had happened, and he remembered it all as she told him, and he supposed it was good to know how you happened to end up with your legs shattered, but the manner by which he was coming to this knowledge was disquieting – it was as if he was a character in a story or a play, a character whose history is not recounted like history but created like fiction.

She had gone into Sidewinder in the four-wheel drive to get feed for the livestock and a few groceries . . . also to check out the paperbacks at Wilson's Drug Center – that had been the Wednesday that was almost two weeks ago now, and the new paperbacks always came in on Tuesday.

'I was actually *thinking* of you,' she said, spooning soup into his mouth and then professionally wiping away a dribble from the corner with a napkin. 'That's what makes it such a remarkable coincidence, don't you see? I was hoping *Misery's Child* would finally be out in paperback, but no such luck.'

A storm had been on the way, she said, but until noon that day the weather forecasters had been confidently claiming it would veer south, toward New Mexico and the Sangre de Cristos.

'Yes,' he said, remembering as he said it: 'They said it would turn. That's why I went in the first place.' He tried to shift his legs. The result was an awful bolt of pain, and he groaned.

'Don't do that,' she said. 'If you get those legs of yours talking, Paul, they won't shut up . . . and I can't give you any more pills for two hours. I'm giving you too much as it is.'

Why aren't I in the hospital? This was clearly the question that wanted asking, but he wasn't sure it was a question either of them wanted asked. Not yet, anyway.

'When I got to the feed store, Tony Roberts told me I better step on it if I was going to get back here before the storm hit, and I said –'

'How far are we from this town?' he asked.

'A ways,' she said vaguely, looking off toward the window. There was a queer interval of silence, and Paul was frightened by what he saw on her face, because what he saw was nothing; the black nothing of a *crevasse* folded into an alpine meadow; a blackness where no flowers grew and into which the drop might be long. It was the face of a woman who has come momentarily untethered from all of the vital positions and landmarks of her life, a woman who has forgotten not only the memory she was in the process of recounting but memory itself. He had once toured a mental asylum – this was years ago, when he had been researching *Misery*, the first of the four books which had been his main source of income over the last eight years – and he had seen this look . . . or, more precisely, this unlook. The word which defined it was catatonia, but what frightened him had no such precise word – it was, rather, a vague comparison: in that moment he thought that her thoughts had become much as he had imagined her physical self: solid, fibrous, unchannelled, with no places of hiatus.

Then, slowly, her face cleared. Thoughts seemed to flow back into it. Then he realized *flowing* was just a tiny bit wrong. She wasn't filling up, like a pond or a tidal pool; she was waming up. *Yes . . . she is warming up, like some small electrical gadget. A toaster, or maybe a heating pad.*

'I said to Tony, "That storm is going south."' She spoke slowly at first, almost groggily, but then her words began to catch up to normal cadence and to fill with normal conversational brightness. But now he was alerted. *Everything* she said was a little strange, a little offbeat. Listening to Annie was like listening to a song played in the wrong key.

'But he said, "It changed its mind."

"'Oh poop!" I said. "I better get on my horse and ride."

"'I'd stay in town if you can, Miz Wilkes," he said. "Now they're saying on the radio that it's going to be a proper jeezer and nobody is prepared."

'But of course I had to get back – there's no one to feed the animals but me. The nearest people are the Roydmans, and they are miles from here. Besides, the Roydmans don't like me.'

She cast an eye shrewdly on him as she said this last, and when he didn't reply she tapped the spoon against the rim of the bowl in peremptory fashion.

'Done?'

'Yes, I'm full, thanks. It was very good. Do you have a lot of livestock?'

Because, he was already thinking, *if you do, that means you've got to have some help. A hired man, at least.* 'Help' was the operant word. Already that seemed like the operant word, and he had seen she wore no wedding ring.

'Not very much,' she said. 'Half a dozen laying hens. Two cows. And Misery.'

He blinked.

She laughed. 'You won't think I'm very nice, naming a sow after the brave and beautiful woman you made up. But that's her name, and I meant no disrespect.' After a moment's thought she added: 'She's very friendly.' The woman wrinkled up her nose and for a moment *became* a sow, even down to the few bristly whiskers that grew on her chin. She made a pig-sound: *'Whoink! Whoink! Whuh-Whuh-WHOINK!'*

Paul looked at her wide-eyed.

She did not notice; she had gone away again, her gaze dim and musing. Her eyes held no reflection but the lamp on the bed-table, twice reflected, dwelling faintly in each.

At last she gave a faint start and said: 'I got about five miles and then the snow started. It came fast – once it starts up here, it always does. I came creeping along, with my lights on, and then I saw your car off the road, overturned.' She looked at him disapprovingly. 'You didn't have your lights on.'

'It took me by surprise,' he said, remembering only at that moment how he had been taken by surprise. He did not yet remember that he had also been quite drunk.

'I stopped,' she said. 'If it had been on an upgrade, I might not have. Not very Christian, I know, but there were three inches on the road already, and even with a four-wheel drive you can't be sure of getting going again once you lose your forward motion. It's easier just to say to yourself, "Oh, they probably got out, caught a ride," et cetera, et cetera. But it was on top of the third big hill past the Roydmans', and it's flat there for awhile. So I pulled over, and as soon as I got out I heard groaning. That was you, Paul.'

She gave him a strange maternal grin.

For the first time, clearly, the thought surfaced in Paul Sheldon's mind: *I am in trouble here. This woman is not right.*

6

She sat beside him where he lay in what might have been a spare bedroom for the next twenty minutes or so and talked. As his body used the soup, the pain in his legs reawakened. He willed himself to concentrate on what she was saying, but was not entirely able to succeed. His mind had bifurcated. On one side he was listening to her tell how she had dragged him from the wreckage of his '74 Camaro – that was the side where the pain throbbed and ached like a couple of old splintered pilings beginning to wink and flash between the heaves of the withdrawing tide. On the other he could see himself at the Boulderado Hotel, finishing his new novel, which did not – thank God for small favors – feature Misery Chastain.

There were all sorts of reasons for him not to write about Misery, but one loomed above the rest, ironclad and unshakable. Misery – thank God for *large* favors – was finally dead. She had died five pages from the end of *Misery's Child*. Not a dry eye in the house when that had happened, including Paul's own – only the dew falling from his ocularies had been the result of hysterical laughter.

Finishing the new book, a contemporary novel about a car-thief, he had remembered typing the final sentence of *Misery's Child*: 'So Ian and Geoffrey left the Little Dunthorpe churchyard together, supporting themselves in their sorrow, determined to find their lives again.' While writing this line he had been giggling so madly it had been hard to strike the correct keys – he had to go back several times. Thank God for good old IBM Correct Tape. He had written THE END below and then had gone capering about the room – this same room in the Boulderado Hotel – and screaming *Free at last! Free at last! Great God Almighty, I'm free at last! The silly bitch finally bought the farm!*

The new novel was called *Fast Cars*, and he hadn't laughed when it was done. He just sat there in front of the typewriter for a moment, thinking *You may have just won next year's American Book Award, my friend.* And then he had picked up –

'– a little bruise on your right temple, but that didn't look like anything. It was your legs . . . . I could see right away, even with the light starting to fade, that your legs weren't –'

– the telephone and called room service for a bottle of Dom Pérignon. He remembered waiting for it to come, walking back and forth in the room where he had finished all of his books since 1974; he remembered tipping the waiter with a fifty-dollar bill and asking him if he had heard a weather forecast; he remembered the pleased, flustered, grinning waiter telling him that the storm currently heading their way was supposed to slide off to the south, toward New Mexico; he remembered the chill feel of the bottle, the discreet sound of the cork as he eased it free; he remembered the dry, acerbic-acidic taste of the first glass and opening his travel bag and looking at his plane ticket back to New York; he remembered suddenly, on the spur of the moment, deciding –

'– that I better get you home right away! It was a struggle getting you to the truck, but I'm a big woman – as you may have noticed – and I had a pile of blankets in the back. I got you in and wrapped you up, and even then, with the light fading and all, I thought you looked *familiar!* I thought maybe –'

– he would get the old Camaro out of the parking garage and just drive west instead of getting on the plane. What the hell was there in New York, anyway? The townhouse, empty, bleak, unwelcoming, possibly burgled.

Screw it! he thought, drinking more champagne. *Go west, young man, go west*! The idea had been crazy enough to make sense. Take nothing but a change of clothes and his –

'– bag I found. I put that in, too, but there wasn't anything else I could see and I was scared you might die on me or something so I fired up Old Bessie and I got your –'

– manuscript of *Fast Cars* and hit the road to Vegas or Reno or maybe even the City of the Angels. He remembered the idea had also seemed a bit silly at first – a trip the kid of twenty-four he had been when he had sold his first novel might have taken, but not one for a man two years past his fortieth birthday. A few more glasses of champagne and the idea no longer seemed silly at all. It seemed, in fact, almost noble. A kind of Grand Odyssey to Somewhere, a way to reacquaint himself with reality after the fictional terrain of the novel. So he had gone –

'– out like a light! I was sure you were going to die . . . . I mean, I was *sure!* So I slipped your wallet out of your back pocket, and I looked at your driver's license and I saw the name, Paul Sheldon, and I thought, "Oh, that must be a coincidence," but the picture on the license *also* looked like you, and then I got so scared I had to sit down at the kitchen table. I thought at first that I was going to faint. After awhile I started thinking maybe the *picture* was just a coincidence, too – those driver's-license photos really don't look like anybody – but then I found your Writers' Guild card, and one from PEN, and I knew you were –'

– in trouble when the snow started coming down, but long before that he had stopped in the Boulderado bar and tipped George twenty bucks to provide him with a second bottle of Dom, and he had drunk it rolling up I-70 into the Rockies under a sky the color of gunmetal, and somewhere east of the Eisenhower Tunnel he had diverted from the turnpike because the roads were bare and dry, the storm was sliding off to the south, what the hay, and also the goddam tunnel made him nervous. He had been playing an old Bo Diddley tape on the cassette machine under the dash and never turned on the radio until the Camaro started to seriously slip and slide and he began to realize that this wasn't just a passing upcountry flurry but the real thing. The storm was maybe not sliding off to the south after all; the storm was maybe coming right at him and he was maybe in a bucket of trouble

(*the way you are in trouble now*)

but he had been just drunk enough to think he could drive his way out of it. So instead of stopping in Cana and inquiring about shelter, he had driven on. He could remember the afternoon turning into a dull-gray chromium lens. He could remember the champagne beginning to wear off. He could remember leaning forward to get his cigarettes off the dashboard and that was when the last skid began and he tried to ride it out but it kept getting worse; he could remember a heavy dull thump and then the world's up and down had swapped places. He had –

'– *screamed!* And when I heard you screaming, I knew that you would live. Dying men rarely scream. They haven't the energy. I know. I decided I would *make* you live. So I got some of my pain medication and made you take it. Then you went to sleep. When you woke up and started to scream again, I gave you some more. You ran a fever for awhile, but I knocked that out, too. I gave you Keflex. You had one or two close calls, but that's all over now. I promise.' She got up. 'And now it's time you rested, Paul. You've got to get your strength back.'

'My legs hurt.'

'Yes, I'm sure they do. In an hour you can have some medication.'

'Now. Please.' It shamed him to beg, but he could not help it. The tide had gone out and the splintered pilings stood bare, jaggedly real, things which could neither be avoided nor dealt with.

'In an hour.' Firmly. She moved toward the door with the spoon and the soup-bowl in one hand.

'Wait!'

She turned back, looking at him with an expression both stern and loving. He did not like the expression. Didn't like it at *all.*

'Two weeks since you pulled me out?'

She looked vague again, and annoyed. He would come to know that her grasp of time was not good. 'Something like that.'

'I was unconscious.'

'Almost all the time.'

'What did I eat?'

She considered him.

'IV,' she said briefly.

'IV?' he said, and she mistook his stunned surprise for ignorance.

'I fed you intravenously,' she said. 'Through tubes. That's what those marks on your arms are.' She looked at him with eyes that were suddenly flat and considering. 'You owe me your life, Paul. I hope you'll remember that. I hope you'll keep that in mind.'

Then she left.

7

The hour passed. Somehow and finally, the hour passed.

He lay in bed, sweating and shivering at the same time. From the other room came first the sounds of Hawkeye and Hot Lips and then the disc jockeys on WKRP, that wild and crazy Cincinnati radio station. An announcer's voice came on, extolled Ginsu knives, gave an 800 number, and informed those Colorado watchers who had simply been panting for a good set of Ginsu knives that Operators Were Standing By.

Paul Sheldon was also Standing By.

She reappeared promptly when the clock in the other room struck eight, with two capsules and a glass of water.

He hoisted himself eagerly on his elbows as she sat on the bed.

'I *finally* got your new book two days ago,' she told him. Ice tinkled in the glass. It was a maddening sound. '*Misery's Child.* I love it . . . It's as good as all the rest. Better! The best!'

'Thank you,' he managed. He could feel the sweat standing out on his forehead. 'Please . . . my legs . . . very painful . . .'

'I *knew* she would marry Ian,' she said, smiling dreamily, 'and I believe Geoffrey and Ian will become friends again, eventually. *Do* they?' But immediately she said: 'No, don't tell! I want to find out for myself. I'm making it last. It always seems so long before there is another one.'

The pain throbbed in his legs and made a deep steel circlet around his crotch. He had touched himself down there, and he thought his pelvis was intact, but it felt twisted and weird. Below his knees it felt as if *nothing* was intact. He didn't want to look. He could see the twisted, lumpy shapes outlined in the bedclothes, and that was enough.

'Please? Miss Wilkes? The pain –'

'Call me Annie. All my friends do.'

She gave him the glass. It was cool and beaded with moisture. She kept the capsules. The capsules in her hand were the tide. She was the moon, and she had brought the tide which would cover the pilings. She brought them toward his mouth, which he immediately dropped open . . . and then she withdrew them.

'I took the liberty of looking in your little bag. You don't mind, do you?'

'No. No, of course not. The medicine –'

The beads of sweat on his forehead felt alternately hot and cold. Was he going to scream? He thought perhaps he was.

'I see there is a manuscript in there,' she said. She held the capsules in her right hand, which she now slowly tilted. They fell into her left hand. His eyes followed them. 'It's called *Fast Cars.* Not a *Misery* novel, I know that.' She looked at him with faint disapproval – but, as before, it was mixed with love. It was a *maternal* look. 'No cars in the nineteenth century, fast or otherwise!' She tittered at this small joke. 'I also took the liberty of glancing through it . . . You don't mind, do you?'

'Please,' he moaned. 'No, but please –'

Her left hand tilted. The capsules rolled, hesitated, and then fell back into her right hand with a minute clicking sound.

'And if I read it? You wouldn't mind if I read it?'

'No –' His bones were shattered, his legs filled with festering shards of broken glass. 'No . . .' He made something he hoped was a smile. 'No, of course not.'

'Because I would never presume to do such a thing without your permission,' she said earnestly. 'I respect you too much. In fact, Paul, I love you.' She crimsoned suddenly and alarmingly. One of the capsules dropped from her hand to the coverlet. Paul snatched at it, but she was quicker. He moaned, but she did not notice; after grabbing the capsule she went vague again, looking toward the window. 'Your *mind,*' she said. 'Your *creativity.* That is all I meant.'

In desperation, because it was the only thing he could think of, he said: 'I know. You're my number-one fan.'

She did not just warm up this time; she *lit* up. 'That's it!' she cried. 'That's it *exactly!* And you wouldn't mind if I read it in that spirit, would you? That spirit of . . . of fan-love? Even though I don't like your other books as well as the *Misery* stories?'

'No,' he said, and closed his eyes. *No, turn the pages of the manuscript into paper hats if you want, just . . . please . . . I'm dying in here . . .*

'You're *good,*' she said gently. 'I *knew* you would be. Just reading your books, I knew you would be. A man who could think of Misery Chastain, first think of her and then *breathe life* into her, could be nothing else.'

Her fingers were in his mouth suddenly, shockingly intimate, dirtily welcome. He sucked the capsules from between them and swallowed even before he could fumble the spilling glass of water to his mouth.

'Just like a baby,' she said, but he couldn't see her because his eyes were still closed and now he felt the sting of tears. 'But *good.* There is so much I want to ask you . . . so much I want to know.'

The springs creaked as she got up.

'We are going to be very happy here,' she said, and although a bolt of horror ripped into his heart, Paul still did not open his eyes.

8

He drifted. The tide came in and he drifted. The TV played in the other room for awhile and then didn't. Sometimes the clock chimed and he tried to count the chimes but he kept getting lost between.

IV. Through tubes. That's what those marks on your arms are.

He got up on one elbow and pawed for the lamp and finally got it turned on. He looked at his arms and in the folds of his elbows he saw fading, overlaped shades of purple and ocher, a hole filled with black blood at the center of each bruise.

He lay back, looking at the ceiling, listening to the wind. He was near the top of the Great Divide in the heart of winter, he was with a woman who was not right in her head, a woman who had fed him with IV drips when he was unconscious, a woman who had an apparently never-ending supply of dope, a woman who had told no one he was here.

These things were important, but he began to realize that something else was more important: the tide was going out again. He began to wait for the sound of her alarm clock upstairs. It would not go off for some long while yet, but it was time for him to start waiting for it to be time.

She was crazy but he needed her.

Oh I am in so much trouble he thought, and stared blindly up at the ceiling as the droplets of sweat began to gather on his forehead again.

9

The next morning she brought him more soup and told him she had read forty pages of what she called his 'manuscript-book'. She told him she didn't think it was as good as his others.

'It's hard to follow. It keeps jumping back and forth in time.'

'Technique,' he said. He was somewhere between hurting and not hurting, and so was able to think a little better about what she was saying. 'Technique, that's all it is. The subject . . . the subject dictates the form.' In some vague way he supposed that such tricks of the trade might interest, even fascinate her. God knew they had fascinated the attendees of the writers' workshops to whom he had sometimes lectured when he was younger. 'The boy's mind, you see, is confused and so –'

'Yes! He's *very* confused, and that makes him less interesting. Not *un*interesting – I'm sure you couldn't create an *un*interesting character – but *less* interesting. And the profanity! Every other word is that effword! It has –' She ruminated, feeding him the soup automatically, wiping his mouth when he dribbled almost without looking, the way an experienced typist rarely looks at the keys; so he came to understand, effortlessly, that she had been a nurse. Not a doctor, oh no; doctors would not know when the dribbles would come, or be able to forecast the course of each with such a nice exactitude.

If the forecaster in charge of that storm had been half as good at his job as Annie Wilkes is at hers, I would not be in this fucking jam, he thought bitterly.

'It has no *nobility!*' she cried suddenly, jumping and almost spilling beef-barley soup on his white, upturned face.

'Yes,' he said patiently. 'I understand what you mean, Annie. It's true that Tony Bonasaro has no nobility. He's a slum kid trying to get out of a bad environment, you see, and those words . . . everybody uses those words in –'

'They do *not!*' she said, giving him a forbidding look. 'What do you think I do when I go to the feed store in town? What do you think I *say*? "Now Tony, give me a bag of that effing pigfeed and a bag of that bitchly cow-corn and some of that Christing ear-mite medicine"? And what do you think he says to me? "You're effing right, Annie, coming right the eff up"?'

She looked at him, her face now like a sky which might spawn tornadoes at any instant. He lay back, frightened. The soup-bowl was tilting in her hands. One, then two drops fell on the coverlet.

'And then do I go down the street to the bank and say to Mrs Bollinger, "Here's one big bastard of a check and you better give me fifty effing dollars just as effing quick as you can"? Do you think that when they put me up there on the stand in Den –'

A stream of muddy-colored beef soup fell on the coverlet. She looked at it, then at him, and her face twisted. 'There! Look what you made me do!'

'I'm sorry.'

'*Sure! You! Are!*' she screamed, and threw the bowl into the corner, where it shattered. Soup splashed up the wall. He gasped.

She turned off then. She just sat there for what might have been thirty seconds. During that time Paul Sheldon's heart did not seem to beat at all.

She roused a little at a time, and suddenly she tittered.

'I have such a *temper*,' she said.

'I'm sorry,' he said out of a dry throat.

'You *should* be.' Her face went slack again and she looked moodily at the wall. He thought she was going to blank out again, but instead she fetched a sigh and lifted her bulk from the bed.

'You don't have any need to use such words in the *Misery* books, because they didn't use such words at all back then. They weren't even invented. Animal times demand animal words, I suppose, but that was a *better* time. You ought to stick to your *Misery* stories, Paul. I say that sincerely. As your number-one fan.'

She went to the door and looked back at him. 'I'll put that manuscript-book back in your bag and finish *Misery's Child.* I may go back to the other one later, when I'm done.'

'Don't do that if it makes you mad,' he said. He tried to smile. 'I'd rather not have you mad. I sort of depend on you, you know.'

She did not return his smile. 'Yes,' she said. 'You do. You do, don't you,

Paul?'

She left.

10

The tide went out. The pilings were back. He began to wait for the clock to chime. Two chimes. The chimes came. He lay propped up on the pillows, watching the door. She came in. She was wearing an apron over her cardigan and one of her skirts. In one hand she held a floor-bucket.

'I suppose you want your cockadoodie medication,' she said.

'Yes, please.' He tried to smile at her ingratiatingly and felt that shame again – he felt grotesque to himself, a stranger.

'I have it,' she said, 'but first I have to clean up the mess in the corner. The mess *you* made. You'll have to wait until I do that.'

He lay in the bed with his legs making shapes like broken branches under the coverlet and cold sweat running down his face in little slow creeks, he lay and watched as she crossed to the corner and set the bucket down and then picked up the pieces of the bowl and took them out and came back and knelt by the bucket and fished in it and brought out a soapy rag and wrung it out and began to wash the dried soup from the wall. He lay and watched and at last he began to shiver and the shivering made the pain worse but he could not help it. Once she turned around and saw him shivering and soaking the bedclothes in sweat, and she favored him with such a sly knowing smile that he could easily have killed her.

'It's dried on,' she said, turning her face back into the corner. 'I'm afraid this is going to take awhile, Paul.'

She scrubbed. The stain slowly disappeared from the plaster but she went on dipping the cloth, wringing it out, scrubbing, and then repeating the whole process. He could not see her face, but the idea – the *certainty* – that she had gone blank and might go on scrubbing the wall for hours tormented him.

At last – just before the clock chimed once, marking two-thirty – she got up and dropped the rag into the water. She took the bucket from the room without a word. He lay in bed, listening to the creaking boards which marked her heavy, stolid passage, listening as she poured the water out of her bucket – and, incredibly, the sound of the faucet as she drew more. He began to cry soundlessly. The tide had never gone out so far; he could see nothing but drying mudflats and those splintered pilings which cast their eternal damaged shadows.

She came back and stood for just a moment inside the doorway, observing his wet face with that same mixture of sternness and maternal love. Then her eyes drifted to the corner, where no sign of the splashed soup remained.

'Now I must rinse,' she said, 'or else the soap will leave a dull spot. I must do it all; I must make everything right. Living alone as I do is no excuse whatever for scamping the job. My mother had a motto, Paul, and I live by it. "Once nasty, never neat," she used to say.'

'Please,' he groaned. 'Please, the pain, I'm dying.'

'No. You're not dying.'

'I'll scream,' he said, beginning to cry harder. It hurt to cry. It hurt his legs and it hurt his heart. 'I won't be able to help it.'

'Then scream,' she said. 'But remember that you made that mess. Not me. It's nobody's fault but your own.'

Somehow he was able to keep from screaming. He watched as she dipped and wrung and rinsed, dipped and wrung and rinsed. At last, just as the clock in what he assumed was the parlor began to strike three, she rose and picked up the bucket.

She's going to go out now. She's going to go out and I'll hear her pouring the rinse-water down the sink and maybe she won't come back for hours because maybe she's not done punishing me yet.

But instead of leaving, she walked over to the bed and fished in her apron pocket. She brought out not two capsules but three.

'Here,' she said tenderly.

He gobbled them into his mouth, and when he looked up he saw her lifting the yellow plastic floor-bucket toward him. It filled his field of vision like a falling moon. Grayish water slopped over the rim onto the coverlet.

'Wash them down with this,' she said. Her voice was still tender.

He stared at her, and his face was all eyes.

'Do it,' she said. 'I know you can dry-swallow them, but please believe me when I say I can make them come right back up again. After all, it's only rinse-water. It won't hurt you.'

She leaned over him like a monolith, the bucket slightly tipped. He could see the rag twisting slowly in its dark depths like a drowned thing; he could see a thin scrum of soap on top. Part of him groaned but none of him hesitated. He drank quickly, washing the pills down, and the taste in his mouth was as it had been on the occasions when his mother made him brush his teeth with soap.

His belly hitched and he made a thick sound.

'I wouldn't throw them up, Paul. No more until nine tonight.'

She looked at him for a moment with a flat empty gaze, and then her face lit up and she smiled.

'You won't make me mad again, will you?'

'No,' he whispered. Anger the moon which brought the tide? What an idea! What a *bad* idea!

'I love you,' she said, and kissed him on the cheek. She left, not looking back, carrying the floor-bucket the way a sturdy countrywoman might carry a milk-pail, slightly away from her body with no thought at all, so that none would spill.

He lay back, tasting grit and plaster in his mouth and throat. Tasting soap.

I won't throw up . . . won't throw up . . . won't throw up.

At last the urgency of this thought began to fade and he realized he was going to sleep. He had held everything down long enough for the medication to begin its work. He had won.

This time.

11

He dreamed he was being eaten by a bird. It was not a good dream. There was a bang and he thought, *Yes, good, all right! Shoot it! Shoot the goddamned thing!*

Then he was awake, knowing it was only Annie Wilkes, pulling the back door shut. She had gone out to do the chores. He heard the dim crunch of her footsteps in the snow. She went past his window, wearing a parka with the hood up. Her breath plumed out, then broke apart on her moving face. She didn't look in at him, intent on her chores in the barn, he supposed. Feeding the animals, cleaning the stalls, maybe casting a few runes – he wouldn't put it past her. The sky was darkening purple – sunset. Five-thirty, maybe six o'clock.

The tide was still in and he could have gone back to sleep – *wanted* to go back to sleep – but he had to think about this bizarre situation while he was still capable of something like rational thought.

The worst thing, he was discovering, was that he didn't want to think of it even while he could, even when he knew he could not bring the situation to an end without thinking about it. His mind kept trying to push it away, like a child pushing away his meal even though he has been told he cannot leave the table until he has eaten it.

He didn't want to think about it because just *living* it was hard enough. He didn't want to think about it because whenever he did unpleasant images intervened – the way she went blank, the way she made him think of idols and stones, and now the way the yellow plastic floor-bucket had sped toward his face like a crashing moon. Thinking of *those* things would not change his situation, was in fact worse than not thinking at all, but once he turned his mind to Annie Wilkes and his position here in her house, they were the thoughts that came, crowding out all others. His heart would start to beat too fast, mostly in fear, but partly in shame, too. He saw himself putting his lips to the rim of the yellow floor-bucket, saw the rinse-water with its film of soap and the rag floating in it, saw these things but drank anyway, never hesitating a bit. He would never tell anyone about that, assuming he ever got out of this, and he supposed he might try to lie about it to himself, but he would never be able to do it.

Yet, miserable or not (and he was), he still wanted to live.

Think about it, goddammit! Jesus Christ, are you already so cowed you can't even try?

No – but *almost* that cowed.

Then an odd, angry thought occurred to him: *She doesn't like the new book because she's too stupid to understand what it's up to.*

The thought wasn't just odd; under the circumstances, how she felt about *Fast Cars* was totally immaterial. But thinking about the things she had said was at least a new avenue, and feeling angry at her was better than feeling scared *of* her, and so he went down it with some eagerness.

Too stupid? No. Too set. Not just unwilling to change, but antagonistic to the very idea *of change.*

Yes. And while she might be crazy, was she so different in her evaluation of his work from the hundreds of thousands of other people across the country – ninety percent of them women – who could barely wait for each new five-hundred-page episode in the turbulent life of the foundling who had risen to marry a peer of the realm? No, not at all. They wanted Misery, Misery, Misery. Each time he had taken a year or two off to write one of the other novels – what he thought of as his 'serious' work with what was at first certainty and then hope and finally a species of grim desperation – he had received a flood of protesting letters from these women, many of whom signed themselves 'your number-one fan'. The tone of these letters varied from bewilderment (that always hurt the most, somehow), to reproach, to outright anger, but the message was always the same: *It wasn't what I expected, it wasn't what I* wanted. *Please go back to Misery. I want to know what Misery is doing.* He could write a modern *Under the Volcano, Tess of the D'Urbervilles, The Sound and the Fury;* it wouldn't matter. They would still want Misery, Misery, Misery.

It's hard to follow . . . he's not interesting . . . and the profanity!

The anger sparked again. Anger at her obdurate density, anger that she could actually kidnap him – keep him prisoner here, force him into a choice between drinking dirty rinse-water from a floor-bucket or suffering the pain of his shattered legs – and then, on top of all that, find the nerve to *criticize* the best thing he had ever written.

'Bugger you and the effword you rode in on,' he said, and he suddenly felt better again, felt *himself* again, even though he knew this rebellion was petty and pitiful and meaningless – she was in the barn where she couldn't hear him, and the tide was safely in over the splintered pilings. Still . . .

He remembered her coming in here, withholding the capsules, coercing permission to read the manuscript of *Fast Cars.* He felt a flush of shame and humiliation warming his face, but now they were mixed with real anger: it had bloomed from a spark into a tiny sunken flame. He had never shown anyone a manuscript before he had proof-read it and then retyped it. *Never.* Not even Bryce, his agent. *Never.* Why, he didn't even –

For a moment his thoughts broke off cleanly. He could hear the dim sound of a cow mooing.

Why, he didn't even make a copy until the second draft was done.

The manuscript copy of *Fast Cars* which was now in Annie Wilkes's possession was, in fact, the only existing copy in the whole world. He had even burned his notes.

Two years of hard work, she didn't like it, and she was crazy.

Misery was what *she* liked; Misery was *who* she liked, not some foul-talking little spic car-thief from Spanish Harlem.

He remembered thinking: *Turn the pages of the manuscript into paper hats if you want, just . . . please . . .*

The anger and humiliation surged again, awakening the first dull answering throb in his legs. Yes. The work, the pride in your work, the worth of the work itself . . . all those things faded away to the magic-lantern shades they really were when the pain got bad enough. That she would do that to him – that she *could,* when he had spent most of his adult life thinking the word *writer* was the most important definition of himself – made her seem utterly monstrous, something he *must* escape. She really was an idol, and if she didn't kill him, she might kill what was *in* him.

Now he heard the eager squeal of the pig – she had thought he would mind, but he thought Misery was a wonderful name for a pig. He remembered how she had imitated it, the way her upper lip had wrinkled toward her nose, how her cheeks had seemed to flatten, how she had actually *looked* like a pig for a moment: *Whoink! WHOINKK!*

From the barn, her voice: '*Sooo-ey*, pig-pig-pig!'

He lay back, put his arm over his eyes, and tried to hold onto the anger, because the anger made him feel brave. A brave man could think. A coward couldn't.

Here was a woman who had been a nurse – he was sure of that. Was she still a nurse? No, because she did not go to work. Why did she no longer practice her trade? That seemed obvious. Not all her gear was stowed right; lots of it was rolling around in the holds. If it was obvious to him even through the haze of pain he had been living in, it would surely have been obvious to her colleagues.

And he had a little extra information on which to judge just how much of her gear wasn't stowed right, didn't he? She had dragged him from the wreck of his car and instead of calling the police or an ambulance she had installed him in her guest-room, put IV drips in his arms and a shitload of dope in his body. Enough so he had gone into what she called respiratory depression at least once. She had told no one he was here, and if she hadn't by now, that meant she didn't mean to.

Would she have behaved in this same fashion if it had been Joe Blow from Kokomo she had hauled out of the wreck? No. No, he didn't think so. She had kept *him* because he was Paul Sheldon, and *she* –

'She's my number-one fan,' Paul muttered, and put an arm over his eyes.

An awful memory bloomed there in the dark: his mother had taken him to the Boston Zoo, and he had been looking at a great big bird. It had the most beautiful feathers – red and purple and royal blue – that he had ever seen . . . and the saddest eyes. He had asked his mother where the bird came from and when she said *Africa* he had understood it was doomed to die in the cage where it lived, far away from wherever God had meant it to be, and he cried and his mother bought him an ice-cream cone and for awhile he had stopped crying and then he remembered and started again and so she had taken him home, telling him as they rode the trolley back to Lynn that he was a bawl-baby and a sissy.

Its feathers. Its *eyes.*

The throbbing in his legs began to cycle up.

No. No, no.

He pressed the crook of his elbow more tightly against his eyes. From the barn he could hear spaced thudding noises. Impossible to tell what they were, of course, but in his imagination

(your MIND your CREATIVITY that is all I meant)

he could see her pushing bales of hay out of the loft with the heel of her boot, could see them tumbling to the barn floor.

Africa. That bird came from Africa. From –

Then, cutting cleanly through this like a sharp knife, came her agitated, almost-screaming voice: *Do you think that when they put me up there on the stand in Den –*

Up on the stand. When they put me up on the stand in Denver.

Do you swear to tell the truth, the whole truth, and nothing but the truth, so help you God?

('I don't know where he gets it.')

I do.

('He's ALWAYS writing things like this down.')

State your name.

('Nobody on MY side of the family had an imagination like his.')

Annie Wilkes.

('So vivid!')

My name is Annie Wilkes.

He willed her to say more; she would not.

'Come on,' he muttered, his arm over his eyes – this was the way he thought best, the way he *imagined* best. His mother liked to tell Mrs Mulvaney on the other side of the fence what a marvelous imagination he had, so vivid, and what wonderful little stories he was always writing down (except, of course, when she was calling him a sissy and a bawl-baby). 'Come on, come on, come on.'

He could see the courtroom in Denver, could see Annie Wilkes on the stand, not wearing jeans now but a rusty purple-black dress and an awful hat. He could see that the courtroom was crowded with spectators, that the judge was bald and wearing glasses. The judge had a white moustache. There was a birthmark beneath the white moustache. The white moustache covered most of it but not quite all.

Annie Wilkes.

('He read at just three! Can you imagine!')

That spirit of . . . of fan-love . . .

('He's always writing things down, making things up.') Now I must rinse.

('Africa. That bird came from')

'Come *on*,' he whispered, but could get no further. The bailiff asked her to state her name, and over and over again she said it was Annie Wilkes, but she said no more; she sat there with her fibrous solid ominous body displacing air and said her name over and over again but no more than that.

Still trying to imagine why the ex-nurse who had taken him prisoner might have once been put on the stand in Denver, Paul drifted off to sleep.

12

He was in a hospital ward. Great relief swept through him – so great he felt like crying. Something had happened when he was asleep, someone had come, or perhaps Annie had had a change of heart or mind. It didn't matter. He had gone to sleep in the monster-woman's house and had awakened in the hospital.

But surely they would not have put him in a long ward like this? It was as big as an airplane hangar! Identical rows of men (with identical bottles of nutrient hung from identical IV trays beside their beds) filled the place.

He sat up and saw that the men themselves were also identical – they were all *him.* Then, distantly, he heard the clock chime, and understood that it was chiming from beyond the wall of sleep. This was a dream. Sadness replaced the relief.

The door at the far end of the huge ward opened and in came Annie Wilkes – only she was dressed in a long aproned dress and there was a mobcap on her head; she was dressed as Misery Chastain in *Misery's Love.* Over one arm she held a wicker basket. There was a towel over the contents. She folded the towel back as he watched. She reached in and took out a handful of something and flung it into the face of the first sleeping Paul Sheldon. It was sand, he saw – this was Annie Wilkes pretending to be Misery Chastain pretending to be the sandman. Sand*woman.*

Then he saw that the first Paul Sheldon's face had turned a ghastly white as soon as the sand struck it and fear jerked him out of the dream and into the bedroom, where Annie Wilkes was standing over him. She was holding the fat paperback of *Misery's Child* in one hand. Her bookmark suggested she was about three-quarters of the way through.

'You were moaning,' she said.

'I had a bad dream.'

'What was it about?'

The first thing which was not the truth that popped into his head was what he replied:

'Africa.'

13

She came in late the following morning, her face the color of ashes. He had been dozing, but he came awake at once, jerking up on his elbows.

'Miss Wilkes? Annie? Are you all r—'

'No.'

Christ, she's had a heart attack, he thought, and there was a moment's alarm which was immediately replaced by joy. *Let* her have one! A *big* one! A fucking chest-buster! He would be more than happy to crawl to the telephone, no matter how much it might hurt. He would crawl to the telephone over broken glass, if that was what it took.

And it *was* a heart attack . . . but not the right kind.

She came toward him, not quite staggering but *rolling,* the way a sailor will when he's just gotten off his ship at the end of a long voyage.

'What –' He tried to shrink away from her, but there was no place to go. There was only the headboard, and behind that, the wall.

'*No!*' She reached the side of the bed, bumped it, wavered, and for a moment seemed on the verge of falling on top of him. Then she just stood there, looking down at him out of her paper-white face, the cords on her neck standing out, one vein pulsing in the center of her forehead. Her hand, snapped open, hooked shut into solid rocklike fists, then snapped open again.

'You . . . you . . . you *dirty bird!*'

'What – I don't –' But suddenly he did, and his entire midsection first seemed to turn hollow and then to entirely disappear. He remembered where her bookmark had been last night, three-quarters of the way through. She had finished it. She knew all there was to know. She knew that Misery hadn't been the barren one, after all; it had been *Ian.* Had she sat there in her as-yet-unseen-by-him parlor with her mouth open and her eyes wide as Misery finally realized the truth and made her decision and sneaked off to Geoffrey? Had her eyes filled with tears when she realized that Misery and Geoffrey, far from having a clandestine affair behind the back of the man they both loved, were giving him the greatest gift they could – a child he would believe to be his own? And had her heart risen up when Misery told Ian she was pregnant and Ian had crushed her to him, tears flowing from his eyes, muttering 'My dear, oh, my dear!' over and over again? He was sure, in those few seconds, that all of those things had happened. But instead of weeping with exalted grief as she should have done when Misery expired giving birth to the boy whom Ian and Geoffrey would presumably raise together, she was mad as hell.

'She can't be dead!' Annie Wilkes shrieked at him. Her hands snapped open and hooked closed in a faster and faster rhythm. *'Misery Chastain CANNOT BE DEAD!'*

'Annie – Annie, please –'

There was a glass water-pitcher on the table. She seized it up and brandished it at him. Cold water splashed his face. An ice-cube landed beside his left ear and slid down the pillow into the hollow of his shoulder. In his mind

('So vivid!')

he saw her bringing the pitcher down into his face, he saw himself dying of a fractured skull and a massive cerebral hemorrhage in a freezing flood of ice-water while goose-pimples formed on his arms.

She wanted to do it; there was no question of that.

At the very last moment she pivoted away from him and flung the water-pitcher at the door instead, where it shattered as the soup-bowl had the other day.

She looked back at him and brushed her hair away from her face – two hard little spots of red had now bloomed in the white – with the backs of her hands.

'Dirty bird!' she panted. 'Oh you dirty birdie, how *could* you!'

He spoke rapidly, urgently, eyes flashing, riveted on her face – he was positive in that moment that his life might depend on what he was able to say in the next twenty seconds.

'Annie, in 1871 women *frequently* died in childbirth. Misery gave her life for her husband and her best friend and her child. The spirit of Misery will always –'

'I don't want her *spirit!*' she screamed, hooking her fingers into claws and shaking them at him, as if she would tear his eyes out. 'I want *her!* You *killed* her! You *murdered* her!' Her hands snapped shut into fists again and she drove them down like pistons, one on either side of his head. They punched deep into the pillow and he bounced like a ragdoll. His legs flared and he cried out.

'I didn't kill her!' he screamed.

She froze, staring at him with that narrow black expression – that look of *crevasse.*

'Of *course* not,' she said, bitterly sarcastic. 'And if you didn't, Paul Sheldon, who did?'

'No one,' he said more quietly. 'She just died.'

Ultimately he knew this to be the truth. If Misery Chastain had been a real person, he knew he might very well have been called upon 'to aid the police in their inquiries', as the euphemism went. After all, he had a motive – he had hated her. Ever since the third book, he had hated her. For April Fools' Day four years ago he'd had a small booklet privately printed and had sent it to a dozen close acquaintances. It had been called *Misery's Hobby.* In it Misery spent a cheerful country weekend boffing Growler, Ian's Irish Setter.

He might have murdered her . . . but he hadn't. In the end, in spite of his having grown to despise her, Misery's death had been something of a surprise to him. He had remained true enough to himself for art to imitate life – however feebly – to the very end of Misery's hackneyed adventures. She had died a mostly unexpected death. His cheerful capering had in no way changed the fact.

'You lie,' Annie whispered. 'I thought you were good, but you are *not* good. You are just a lying old dirty birdie.'

'She slipped away, that's all. Sometimes that happens. It was like life, when someone just –'

She overturned the table by the bed. The one shallow drawer spilled out. His wristwatch and pocket-change spilled out with it. He hadn't even known they were in there. He cringed back from her.

'You must think I was born *yesterday,*' she said. Her lips drew back from her teeth. 'In my job I saw dozens of people die – hundreds, now that I think about it. Sometimes they go screaming and sometimes they go in their sleep – they just slip away, the way you said, sure.

'But characters in stories DO NOT just slip away! God takes us when He thinks it's time and a writer is God to the people in a story, he made them up just like God made us up and no one can get hold of God to make Him explain, all right, okay, but as far as Misery goes I'll tell you one thing you dirty bird, I'll tell you that God just happens to have a couple of broken legs and God just happens to be in MY house eating MY food and . . . and . . .'

She went blank then. She straightened up with her hands hanging limply by her sides, looking at the wall where an old photograph of the Arc de Triomphe was hung. She stood there and Paul lay in his bed with round marks in the pillow beside his ears and looked at her. He could hear the water which had been in the pitcher dripping on the floor, and it came to him that he could commit murder. This was a question which had occurred to him from time to time, strictly academic, of course, only now it wasn't and he had the answer. If she hadn't thrown the pitcher, he would have shattered it on the floor himself and tried to shove one of the broken pieces of glass into her throat while she stood there, as inert as an umbrella-stand.

He looked down into the spillage from the drawer, but there was only the change, a pen, a comb, and his watch. No wallet. More important, no Swiss Army knife.

She came back a little at a time, and the anger, at least, was gone. She looked down at him sadly.

'I think I better go now. I don't think I better be around you for awhile. I don't think it's . . . wise.'

'Go? Where?'

'It doesn't matter. A place I know. If I stay here, I'll do something unwise. I need to think. Goodbye, Paul.'

She strode across the room.

'Will you be back to give me my medication?' he asked, alarmed.

She grasped the doorknob and pulled the door shut without answering. For the first time he heard the rattle of a key.

He heard her footsteps going off down the hall; he winced as she cried out angrily – words he couldn't understand – and something else fell and shattered. A door slammed. An engine cranked over and then started up. The low, crunching squeal of tires turning on packed snow. Now the motor-sound began to go away. It dwindled to a snore and then to a drone and was finally gone.

He was alone.

Alone in Annie Wilkes's house, locked in this room. Locked in this bed. The distance between here and Denver was like . . . well, like the distance between the Boston Zoo and Africa.

He lay in bed looking at the ceiling, his throat dry and his heart beating fast.

After awhile the parlor clock chimed noon and the tide began to go out.

14

Fifty-one hours.

He knew just how long because of the pen, the Flair Fine-Liner he had been carrying in his pocket at the time of the crash. He had been able to reach down and snag it. Every time the clock chimed he made a mark on his arm – four vertical marks and then a diagonal slash to seal the quintet. When she came back there were ten groups of five and one extra. The little groups, neat at first, grew increasingly jagged as his hands began to tremble. He didn't believe he had missed a single hour. He had dozed, but never really slept. The chiming of the clock woke him each time the hour came around.

After awhile he began to feel hunger and thirst – even through the pain. It became something like a horse race. At first King of Pain was far in the lead and I Got the Hungries was some twelve furlongs back. Pretty Thirsty was nearly lost in the dust. Then, around sun-up on the day after she had left, I Got the Hungries actually gave King of Pain a brief run for his money.

He had spent much of the night alternately dozing and waking in a cold sweat, sure he was dying. After awhile he began to *hope* he was dying. Anything to be out of it. He'd never had any idea how bad hurting could get. The pilings grew and grew. He could see the barnacles which encrusted them, could see pale drowned things lying limply in the clefts of the wood. They were the lucky things. For them the hurting was over. Around three he had lapsed into a bout of useless screaming.

By noon of the second day – Hour Twenty-Four – he realized that, as bad as the pain in his legs and pelvis was, something else was also making him hurt. It was withdrawal. Call this horse Junkie's Revenge, if you wanted. He needed the capsules in more ways than one.

He thought of trying to get out of bed, but the thought of the thump and the drop and the accompanying escalation of pain constantly deterred him. He could imagine all too well

('So vivid!')

how it would feel. He might have tried anyway, but she had locked the door. What could he do besides crawl across to it, snail-like, and lie there?

In desperation he pushed back the blankets with his hands for the first time, hoping against hope that it wasn't as bad as the shapes the blankets made seemed to suggest it was. It wasn't *as* bad; it was worse. He stared with horror at what he had become below the knees. In his mind he heard the voice of Ronald Reagan in *King's Row,* shrieking '*Where's the rest of me*?'

The rest of him was here, and he might get out of this; the prospects for doing so seemed ever more remote, but he supposed it was technically possible . . . but he might well never walk again – and surely not until each of his legs had been rebroken, perhaps in several places, and pinned with steel, and mercilessly overhauled, and subjected to half a hundred shriekingly painful indignities.

She had splinted them – of course he had known that, felt the rigid ungiving shapes, but until now he had not known what she had done it with. The lower parts of both legs were circled with slim steel rods that looked like the hacksawed remains of aluminum crutches. The rods had been strenuously taped, so that from the knees down he looked a bit like Im-Ho-Tep when he had been discovered in his tomb. The legs themselves meandered strangely up to his knees, turning outward here, jagging inward there. His left knee – a throbbing focus of pain – no longer seemed to exist at all. There was a calf, and a thigh, and then a sickening bunch in the middle that looked like a salt-dome. His upper legs were badly swollen and seemed to have bowed slightly outward. His thighs, crotch, even his penis, were all still mottled with fading bruises.

He had thought his lower legs might be shattered. That was not so, as it turned out. They had been *pulverized.*

Moaning, crying, he pulled the blankets back up. No rolling out of bed. Better to lie here, die here, better to accept this level of pain, terrific as it was, until all pain was gone.

Around four o'clock of the second day, Pretty Thirsty made its move. He had been aware of dryness in his mouth and throat for a long time, but now it began to seem more urgent. His tongue felt thick, too large. Swallowing hurt. He began to think of the pitcher of water she had dashed away.

He dozed, woke, dozed.

Day passed away. Night fell.

He had to urinate. He laid the top sheet over his penis, hoping to create a crude filter, and urinated through it into his cupped and shaking hands. He tried to think of it as recycling and drank what he had managed to hold and then licked his wet palms. Here was something else he reckoned he would not tell people about, if he lived long enough to tell them anything.

He began to believe she was dead. She was deeply unstable, and unstable people frequently took their own lives. He saw her

('So vivid')

pulling over to the side of the road in Old Bessie, taking a .44 from under the seat, putting it in her mouth, and shooting herself. *'With Misery dead I don't want to live. Goodbye, cruel world!'* Annie cried through a rain of tears, and pulled the trigger.

He cackled, then moaned, then screamed. The wind screamed with him . . . but took no other notice.

Or an accident? Was that possible? Oh, yes, sir! He saw her driving grimly, going too fast, and then

('He doesn't get it from MY side of the family!')

going blank and driving right off the side of the road. Down and down and down. Hitting once and bursting into a fireball, dying without even knowing it.

If she was dead he would die in here, a rat in a dry trap.

He kept thinking unconsciousness would come and relieve him, but unconsciousness declined; instead Hour Thirty came, and Hour Forty; now King of Pain and Pretty Thirsty merged into one single horse (I Got the Hungries had been left in the dust long since) and he began to feel like nothing more than a slice of living tissue on a microscope slide or a worm on a hook – something, anyway, twisting endlessly and waiting only to die.

15

When she came in he thought at first that she must be a dream, but then reality – or mere brute survival – took over and he began to moan and beg and plead, all of it broken, all of it coming from a deepening well of unreality. The one thing he saw clearly was that she was wearing a dark-blue dress and a sprigged hat – it was exactly the sort of outfit he had imagined her wearing on the stand in Denver.

Her color was high and her eyes sparkled with life and vivacity. She was as close to pretty as Annie Wilkes ever could be, and when he tried to remember that scene later the only clear images he could fix upon were her flushed cheeks and the sprigged hat. From some final stronghold of sanity and evaluative clarity the rational Paul Sheldon had thought: *She looks like a widow who just got fucked after a ten-year dry spell.*

In her hand she held a glass of water – a tall glass of water.

'Take this,' she said, and put a hand still cool from the out-of-doors on the back of his neck so he could sit up enough to drink without choking. He took three fast mouthfuls, the pores on the arid plain of his tongue widening and clamoring at the shock of the water, some of it spilling down his chin and onto the tee-shirt he wore, and then she drew it away from him.

He mewled for it, holding his shaking hands out.

'No,' she said. 'No, Paul. A little at a time, or you'll vomit.'

After a bit she gave it back to him and allowed two more swallows.

'The stuff,' he said, coughing. He sucked at his lips and ran his tongue over them and then sucked his tongue. He could vaguely remember drinking his own piss, how hot it had been, how salty. 'The capsules – pain – please, Annie, please, for God's sake please help me *the pain is so bad* –'

'I know it is, but you must listen to me,' she said, looking at him with that stern yet maternal expression. 'I had to get away and think. I have thought deeply, and I hope I've thought well. I was not entirely sure; my thoughts are often muddy, I know that. I accept that. It's why I couldn't remember where I was all those times they kept asking me about. So I prayed. There *is* a God, you know, and He answers prayers. He always does. So I prayed. I said, "Dear God, Paul Sheldon may be dead when I get back." But God said, "He will not be. I have spared him, so you may shew him the way he must go."'

She said *shew* as *shoe*, but Paul was barely hearing her anyway; his eyes were fixed on the glass of water. She gave him another three swallows. He slurped like a horse, burped, then cried out as shudder-cramps coursed through him.

During all of this she looked at him benignly.

'I will give you your medication and relieve your pain,' she said, 'but first you have a job to do. I'll be right back.'

She got up and headed for the door.

'No!' he screamed.

She took no notice at all. He lay in bed, cocooned in pain, trying not to moan and moaning anyway.

16

At first he thought he had lapsed into delirium. What he was seeing was too bizarre to be sane. When Annie returned, she was pushing a charcoal grill in front of her.

'Annie, I'm in terrible pain.' Tears coursed down his cheeks.

'I know, my dear.' She kissed his cheek, the touch of her lips as gentle as the fall of a feather. 'Soon.'

She left and he looked stupidly at the charcoal grill, something meant for an outdoor summer patio which now stood in his room, calling up relentless images of idols and sacrifices.

And sacrifice was what she had in mind, of course – when she came back she was carrying the manuscript of *Fast Cars*, the only existing result of his two years' work, in one hand. In the other she had a box of Diamond Blue Tip wooden matches.

17

'No,' he said, crying and shaking. One thought worked at him, burned in him like acid: for less than a hundred bucks he could have had the manuscript photocopied in Boulder. People – Bryce, both of his ex-wives, hell, even his mother – had always told him he was crazy not to make at least one copy of his work and put it aside; after all, the Boulderado could catch on fire, or the New York townhouse; there might be a tornado or a flood or some other natural disaster. He had constantly refused, for no rational reason: it was just that making copies seemed a jinx thing to do.

Well, here was the jinx and the natural disaster all rolled up in one; here was Hurricane Annie. In her innocence it had apparently never even crossed her mind that there might be another copy of *Fast Cars* someplace, and if he had just *listened*, if he had just invested the lousy hundred dollars –

'Yes,' she replied, holding out the matches to him. The manuscript, clean white Hammermill Bond with the title page topmost, lay on her lap. Her face was still clear and calm.

'No,' he said, turning his burning face away from her.

'Yes. It's filthy. That aside, it's also no good.'

'You wouldn't know good if it walked up and bit your nose off!' he yelled, not caring.

She laughed gently. Her temper had apparently gone on vacation. But, Paul thought, knowing Annie Wilkes, it could arrive back unexpectedly at any moment, bags in hand: *Couldn't stand to stay away! How ya doin?*

'First of all,' she said, 'good would *not* bite my nose off. *Evil* might, but not good. Second of all, I *do* know good when I see it – *you* are good, Paul. All you need is a little help. Now, take the matches.'

He shook his head stiffly back and forth. 'No.'

'Yes.'

'No!'

'Yes.'

'No goddammit!'

'Use all the profanity you want. I've heard it all before.'

'I won't do it.' He closed his eyes.

When he opened them she was holding out a cardboard square with the word NOVRIL printed across the top in bright blue letters. SAMPLE, the red letters just below the trade name read: NOT TO BE DISPENSED WITHOUT PHYSICIAN'S PRESCRIPTION. Below the warning were four capsules in blister-packs. He grabbed. She pulled the cardboard out of his reach.

'When you burn it,' she said. 'Then I'll give you the capsules – all four of these, I think – and the pain will go away. You will begin to feel serene again, and when you've got hold of yourself, I will change your bedding – I see you've wet it, and it must be uncomfortable – and I'll also change *you.* By then you will be hungry and I can give you some soup. Perhaps some unbuttered toast. But until you burn it, Paul, I can do nothing. I'm sorry.'

His tongue wanted to say *Yes! Yes, okay!* and so he bit it. He rolled away from her again – away from the enticing, maddening cardboard square, the white capsules in their lozenge-shaped transparent blisters. 'You're the devil,' he said.

Again he expected rage and got the indulgent laugh, with its undertones of knowing sadness.

'Oh yes! *Yes*! That's what a child thinks when mommy comes into the kitchen and sees him playing with the cleaning fluid from under the sink. He doesn't say it *that* way, of course, because he doesn't have your education. He just says, "Mommy, you're mean!"'

Her hand brushed his hair away from his hot brow. The fingers trailed down his cheek, across the side of his neck, and then squeezed his shoulder briefly, with compassion, before drawing away.

'The mother feels badly when her child says she's mean or if he cries for what's been taken away, as you are crying now. But she knows she's right, and so she does her duty. As I am doing mine.'

Three quick dull thumps as Annie dropped her knuckles on the manuscript – 190,000 words and five lives that a well and pain-free Paul Sheldon had cared deeply about, 190,000 words and five lives that he was finding more dispensable as each moment passed.

The pills. The pills. He had to have the goddam pills.

The lives were shadows. The pills were not. *They* were real.

'Paul?'

'No!' he sobbed.

The faint rattle of the capsules in their blisters – silence then the woody shuffle of the matches in their box.

'Paul?'

'No!'

'I'm waiting, Paul.'

Oh why in Christ's name are you doing this asshole Horatio-at-the-bridge act and who in Christ's name are you trying to impress? Do you think this is a movie or a TV show and you are getting graded by some audience on your bravery? You can do what she wants or you can hold out. If you hold out you'll die and then she'll burn the manuscript anyway. So what are you going to do, lie here and suffer for a book that would sell half as many copies as the least successful Misery book you ever wrote, and which Peter Prescott would shit upon in his finest genteel disparaging manner when he reviewed it for that great literary oracle, Newsweek*? Come on, come on, wise up! Even Galileo recanted when he saw they really meant to go through with it!*

'Paul? I'm waiting. I can wait all day. Although I rather suspect that you may go into a coma before too long; I believe you are in a near-comatose state now, and I have had a lot of . . .'

Her voice droned away.

Yes! Give me the matches! Give me a blowtorch! Give me a Baby Huey and a load of napalm! I'll drop a tactical nuke on it if that's what you want, you fucking beldame!

So spoke the opportunist, the survivor. Yet another part, failing now, near-comatose itself, went wailing off into the darkness: *A hundred and ninety thousand words! Five lives! Two years' work!* And what was the real bottom line – The *truth! What you knew about THE FUCKING TRUTH!*

There was the creak of bedsprings as she stood up.

'Well! You are a very stubborn little boy, I must say, and I can't sit by your bed all night, as much as I might like to! After all, I've been driving for nearly an hour, hurrying to get back here. I'll drop by in a bit and see if you've changed y –'

'*You* burn it, then!' he yelled at her.

She turned and looked at him. 'No,' she said, 'I cannot do that, as much as I would like to and spare you the agony you feel.'

'Why not?'

'Because,' she said primly, 'you must do it of your own free will.'

He began to laugh then, and her face darkened for the first time since she had come back, and she left the room with the manuscript under her arm.

18

When she came back an hour later he took the matches.

She laid the title page on the grill. He tried to light one of the Blue Tips and couldn't because it kept missing the rough strip or falling out of his hand.

So Annie took the box and lit the match and put the lit match in his hand and he touched it to the corner of the paper and then let the match fall into the pot and watched, fascinated, as the flame tasted, then gulped. She had a barbecue fork with her this time, and when the page began to curl up, she poked it through the gaps in the grill.

'This is going to take forever,' he said. 'I can't –'

'No, we'll make quick work of it,' she said. 'But you must burn a few of the single pages, Paul – as a symbol of your understanding.'

She now laid the first page of *Fast Cars* on the grill, words he remembered writing some twenty-four months ago, in the New York townhouse: *"'I don't have no wheels," Tony Bonasaro said, walking up to the girl coming down the steps, "and I am a slow learner, but I am a fast driver."'*

Oh it brought that day back like the right Golden Oldie on the radio. He remembered walking around the apartment from room to room, big with book, more than big, *gravid*, and here were the labor pains. He remembered finding one of Joan's bras under a sofa cushion earlier in the day, and she had been gone a full three months, showed you what kind of a job the cleaning service did; he remembered hearing New York traffic, and, faintly, the monotonous tolling of a church bell calling the faithful to mass.

He remembered sitting down.

As always, the blessed relief of starting, a feeling that was like falling into a hole filled with bright light.

As always, the glum knowledge that he would not write as well as he wanted to write.

As always, the terror of not being able to finish, of accelerating into a blank wall.

As always, the marvelous joyful nervy feeling of *journey* begun.

He looked at Annie Wilkes and said, clearly but not loud: 'Annie, please don't make me do this.'

She held the matches immovably before him and said:

'You can do as you choose.'

So he burned his book.

19

She made him burn the first page, the last page, and nine pairs of pages from various points in the manuscript – because nine, she said, was a number of power, and nine doubled was lucky. He saw that she had used a magic marker to black out the profanities, at least as far as she had read.

'Now,' she said, when the ninth pair was burned. 'You've been a good boy and a real sport and I know this hurts you almost as badly as your legs do and I won't draw it out any longer.'

She removed the grill and set the rest of the manuscript into the pot, crunching down the crispy black curls of the pages he had already burned. The room stank of matches and burned paper. *Smells like the devil's cloakroom,* he thought deliriously, and if there had been anything in the wrinkled walnut-shell that had once been his stomach, he supposed he would have vomited it up.

She lit another match and put it in his hand. Somehow he was able to lean over and drop the match into the pot. It didn't matter anymore. It didn't matter.

She was nudging him.

Wearily, he opened his eyes.

'It went out.' She scratched another match and put it in his hand.

So he somehow managed to lean over again, awakening rusty bandsaws in his legs as he did so, and touched the match to the corner of the pile of manuscript. This time the flame spread instead of shrinking and dying around the stick.

He leaned back, eyes shut, listening to the crackling sound, feeling the dull, baking heat.

'Goodness!' she cried, alarmed.

He opened his eyes and saw that charred bits of paper were wafting up from the barbecue on the heated air. Annie lumbered from the room. He heard water from the tub taps thud into the floorpail. He idly watched a dark piece of manuscript float across the room and land on one of the gauzy curtains. There was a brief spark – he had time to wonder if perhaps the room was going to catch on fire – that winked once and then went out, leaving a tiny hole like a cigarette burn. Ash sifted down on the bed. Some landed on his arms. He didn't really care, one way or the other. Annie came back, eyes trying to dart everywhere at once, trying to trace the course of each carbonized page as it rose and seesawed. Flames flipped and flickered over the edge of the pot.

'Goodness!' she said again, holding the bucket of water and looking around, trying to decide where to throw it or if it needed to be thrown at all. Her lips were trembling and wet with spit. As Paul watched, her tongue darted out and slicked them afresh. 'Goodness! Goodness!' It seemed to be all she could say.

Even caught in the squeezing vise of his pain, Paul felt an instant of intense pleasure – this was what Annie Wilkes looked like when she was frightened. It was a look he could come to love.

Another page wafted up, this one still running with little tendrils of low blue fire, and that decided her. With another 'Goodness!' she carefully poured the bucket of water into the barbecue pot. There was a monstrous hissing and a plume of steam. The smell was wet and awful, charred and yet somehow creamy.

When she left he managed to get up on his elbow one final time. He looked into the barbecue pot and saw something that looked like a charred lump of log floating in a brackish pond.

After awhile, Annie Wilkes came back.

Incredibly, she was humming.

She sat him up and pushed capsules into his mouth.

He swallowed them and lay back, thinking: *I'm going to kill her.*

20

'Eat,' she said from far away, and he felt stinging pain. He opened his eyes and saw her sitting beside him – for the first time he was actually on a level with her, facing her. He realized with bleary, distant surprise that for the first time in untold eons he was sitting, too . . . actually sitting up.

Who gives a shit? he thought, and let his eyes slip shut again. The tide was in. The pilings were covered. The tide had finally come in and the next time it went out it might go out forever and so he was going to ride the waves while there were waves left to ride, he could think about sitting up later . . .

'Eat!' she said again, and this was followed by a recurrence of pain. It buzzed against the left side of his head, making him whine and try to pull away.

'Eat, Paul! You've got to come out of it enough to eat or . . .'

Zzzzzing! His earlobe. She was pinching it.

''Kay,' he muttered. ''Kay! Don't yank it off, for God's sake.'

He forced his eyes open. Each lid felt as if it had a cement block dangling from it. Immediately the spoon was in his mouth, dumping hot soup down his throat. He swallowed to keep from drowning.

Suddenly, out of nowhere – *the most amazing comeback this announcer has ever seen, ladies and gentlemen!* – I Got the Hungries came bursting into view. It was as if that first spoonful of soup had awakened his gut from a hypnotic trance. He took the rest as fast as she could spoon it into his mouth, seeming to grow more rather than less hungry as he slurped and swallowed.

He had a vague memory of her wheeling out the sinister, smoking barbecue and then wheeling in something which, in his drugged and fading state, he had thought might be a shopping cart. The idea had caused him to feel neither surprise nor wonder; he *was* visiting with Annie Wilkes, after all. Barbecues, shopping carts; maybe tomorrow a parking meter or a nuclear warhead. When you lived in the funhouse, the laff riot just never stopped.

He had drifted off, but now he realized that the shopping cart had been a folded-up wheelchair. He was sitting in it, his splinted legs stuck stiffly out in front of him, his pelvic area feeling uncomfortably swollen and not very happy with the new position.

She put me in it while I was conked out, he thought. *Lifted me. Dead weight. Christ she must be strong.*

'Finished!' she said. 'I'm pleased to see how well you took that soup, Paul. I believe you are going to mend. We will not say "Good as new" – alas, no – but if we don't have any more of these . . . these *contretemps* . . . I believe you'll mend just fine. Now I'm going to change your nasty old bed, and when that's done I'm going to change nasty old *you*, and then, if you're not having too much pain and still feel hungry, I am going to let you have some toast.'

'Thank you, Annie,' he said humbly, and thought: *Your throat. If I can, I'll give you a chance to lick your lips and say 'Goodness!' But only once, Annie.*

Only once.

21

Four hours later he was back in bed and he would have burned all his books for even a single Novril. Sitting hadn't bothered him a bit while he was doing it – not with enough shit in his bloodstream to have put half the Prussian Army to sleep – but now it felt as if a swarm of bees had been loosed in the lower half of his body.

He screamed very loudly – the food must have done *something* for him, because he could not remember being able to scream so loudly since he had emerged from the dark cloud.

He sensed her standing just outside the bedroom door in the hallway for a long time before she actually came in, immobile, turned off, unplugged, gazing blankly at no more than the doorknob or perhaps the pattern of lines on her own hands.

'Here.' She gave him his medication – two capsules this time.

He swallowed them, holding her wrist to steady the glass. 'I bought you two presents in town,' she said, getting up.

'Did you?' he croaked.

She pointed at the wheelchair which brooded in the corner with its steel leg-rests stuck stiffly out.

'I'll show you the other one tomorrow. Now get some sleep, Paul.'

22

But for a long time no sleep came. He floated on the dope and thought about the situation he was in. It seemed a little easier now. It was easier to think about than the book which he had created and then uncreated.

Things . . . isolated things like pieces of cloth which may be pieced together to make a quilt.

They were miles from the neighbors who, Annie said, didn't like her. What was the name? Boynton. No, *Roydman*. That was it. Roydman. And how far from town? Not too far, surely. He was in a circle whose diameter might be as small as fifteen miles, or as large as forty-five. Annie Wilkes's house was in that circle, and the Roydmans', and downtown Sidewinder, however pitifully small that might be . . .

And my car. My Camaro's somewhere in that circle, too. Did the police find it?

He thought not. He was a well-known person; if a car had been found with tags registered in his name, a little elementary checking would have shown he had been in Boulder and had then dropped out of sight. The discovery of his wrecked and empty car would have prompted a search, stories on the news . . .

She never watches the news on TV, never listens to the radio at all – unless she's got one with an earplug, or phones.

It was all a little like the dog in the Sherlock Holmes story – the one that didn't bark. His car hadn't been found because the cops hadn't come. If it *had* been found, they would have checked everyone in his hypothetical circle, wouldn't they?

And just how many people could there be in such a circle, here close to the top of the Western Slope? The Roydmans, Annie Wilkes, maybe ten or twelve others?

And just because it hadn't been found so far didn't mean it *wouldn't* be found.

His vivid imagination (which he had not gotten from anyone on his mother's side of the family) now took over. The cop was tall, handsome in a cold way, his sideburns perhaps a bit longer than regulation. He was wearing dark sunglasses in which the person being questioned would see his own face in duplicate. His voice had a flat Midwestern twang.

We've found an overturned car halfway down Humbuggy Mountain which belongs to a famous writer named Paul Sheldon. There's some blood on the seats and the dashboard, but no sign of him. Must have crawled out, may even have wandered away in a daze –

That was a laugh, considering the state of his legs, but of course they would not know what injuries he might have sustained. They would only assume that, if he was not here, he must have been strong enough to get at least a little way. The course of their deductions was not apt to lead to such an unlikely possibility as kidnapping, at least not at first, and probably never.

Do you remember seeing anyone on the road the day of the storm? Tall man, forty-two years old, sandy hair? Probably wearing blue jeans and a checked flannel shirt and a parka? Might have looked sort of bunged up? Hell, might not even have known who he was?

Annie would give the cop coffee in the kitchen; Annie would be mindful that all the doors between there and the spare bedroom should be closed. In case he should groan.

Why, no, officer – I didn't see a soul. In fact, I came back from town just as quick as I could chase when Tony Roberts told me that bad old storm wasn't turning south after all.

The cop, setting down the coffee cup and getting up: *Well, if you should see anyone fitting the description, ma'am, I hope you'll get in touch with us just as fast as you can. He's quite a famous person. Been in* People *magazine. Some other ones, too.*

I certainly will, officer!

And away he would go.

Maybe something like that had *already* happened and he just didn't know about it. Maybe his imaginary cop's actual counterpart or counterparts had visited Annie while he was doped out. God knew he spent enough time doped out. More thought convinced him it was unlikely. He *wasn't* Joe Blow from Kokomo, just some transient blowing through. He had been in *People* (first best-seller) and *Us* (first divorce); there had been a question about him one Sunday in Walter Scott's *Personality Parade.* There would have been re-checks, maybe by phone, probably by the cops themselves. When a celebrity – even a quasi-celebrity like a writer – disappeared, the heat came on.

You're only guessing, man.

Maybe guessing, maybe deducing. Either way it was better than just lying here and doing nothing.

What about guardrails?

He tried to remember and couldn't. He could only remember reaching for his cigarettes, then the amazing way the ground and the sky had switched places, then darkness. But again, deduction (or educated guesswork, if you wanted to be snotty) made it easier to believe there had been none. Smashed guardrails and snapped guywires would have alerted roadcrews.

So what exactly *had* happened?

He had lost control at a place where there wasn't much of a drop, that was what – just enough grade to allow the car to flip over in space. If the drop had been steeper, there would have been guardrails. If the drop had been steeper, Annie Wilkes would have found it difficult or impossible to get to him, let alone drag him back to the road by herself.

So where was his car? Buried in the snow, of course.

Paul put his arm over his eyes and saw a town plow coming up the road where he has crashed only two hours earlier. The plow is a dim orange blob in the driving snow near the end of this day. The man driving is bundled to the eyes; on his head he wears an old-fashioned trainman's cap of blue-and-white pillowtick. To his right, at the bottom of a shallow slope which will, not far from here, deepen into a more typical upcountry gorge, lies Paul Sheldon's Camaro, with the faded blue HART FOR PRESIDENT sticker on the rear bumper just about the brightest thing down there. The guy driving the plow doesn't see the car; bumper sticker is too faded to catch his eye. The wing-plows block most of his side-vision, and besides, it's almost dark and he's beat. He just wants to finish this last run so he can turn the plow over to his relief and get a hot cup of joe.

He sweeps past, the plow spuming cloudy snow into the gully. The Camaro, already drifted to the windows, is now buried to the roof-line. Later, in the deepest part of a stormy twilight when even the things directly in front of you look unreal, the second-shift man drives by, headed in the opposite direction, and entombs it.

Paul opened his eyes and looked at the plaster ceiling.

There was a fine series of hairline cracks up there that seemed to make a trio of interlocked W's. He had become very familiar with them over the endless run of days he had lain here since coming out of the cloud, and now he traced them again, idly thinking of w words such as *wicked* and *wretched* and *witchlike* and *wriggling.*

Yes.

Could have been that way. Could have been.

Had she thought of what might happen when his car was found?

She *might* have. She was nuts, but being nuts didn't make her stupid.

Yet it had never crossed her mind that he might have a duplicate of *Fast Cars.*

Yeah. And she was right. The bitch was right. I didn't.

Images of the blackened pages floating up, the flames, the sounds, the smell of the uncreation – he gritted his teeth against the images and tried to shut his mind away from them; *vivid* was not always *good.*

*No, you didn't, but nine out of ten writers would have – at least they would if they were getting paid as much as you have been for even the non-*Misery *books. She never even* thought *of it.*

She's not a writer.

Neither is she stupid, as I think we have both agreed. I think that she is filled with herself – she does not just have a large ego but one which is positively grandiose. Burning it seemed to her the proper thing to do, and the idea that her concept of the proper thing to do might be short-circuited by something so piddling as a bank Xerox machine and a couple of rolls of quarters . . . that *blip just never crossed her screen, my friend*

His other deductions might be like houses built on quicksand, but this view of Annie Wilkes seemed to him as solid as the Rock of Gibraltar. Because of his researches for *Misery*, he had rather more than a layman's understanding of neurosis and psychosis, and he knew that although a borderline psychotic might have alternating periods of deep depression and almost aggressive cheerfulness and hilarity, the puffed and infected ego underlay all, positive that all eyes were upon him or her, positive that he or she was starring in a great drama; the outcome was a thing for which untold millions waited with held breath.

Such an ego simply forbade certain lines of thought. These lines were predictable because they all stretched in the same direction: from the unstable person to objects, situations, or other persons outside of the subject's field of control (or, fantasy: to the neurotic there might be some difference but to the psychotic they were one and the same).

Annie Wilkes had wanted *Fast Cars* destroyed, and so, to her, there had been only the one copy.

Maybe I could have saved the damn thing by telling her there were more. She would have seen destroying the manuscript was futile. She –

His breathing, which had been slowing toward sleep, suddenly caught in his throat and his eyes widened.

Yes, she would have seen it was futile. She would have been forced to acknowledge one of those lines leading to a place beyond her control. The ego would be hurt, squealing –

I have such a temper!

If she had been clearly faced with the fact that she *couldn't* destroy his 'dirty book', might she not have decided to destroy the *creator* of the dirty book instead? After all, there was no copy of Paul Sheldon.

His heart was beating fast. In the other room the clock began to bong, and overhead he heard her thumping footfalls cross his ceiling. The faint sound of her urinating. The toilet flushing. The heavy pad of her feet as she went back to bed.

The creak of the springs.

You won't make me mad again, will you?

His mind suddenly tried to break into a gallop, an overbred trotter trying to break stride. What, if anything, did all this dime-store psychoanalysis mean in terms of his car? About when it was found? What did it mean to *him?*

'Wait a minute,' he whispered in the dark. 'Wait a minute, wait a minute, just hold the phone. Slow down.'

He put his arm across his eyes again and again conjured up the state trooper with the dark sunglasses and the overlong sideburns. *We've found an overturned car halfway down Humbuggy Mountain,* the state trooper was saying, and blah-de-blah-de-blah.

Only *this* time Annie doesn't invite him to stay for coffee. This time she isn't going to feel safe until he's out of her house and far down the road. Even in the kitchen, even with two closed doors between them and the guest-room, even with the guest doped to the ears, the trooper might hear a groan.

If his car was found, Annie Wilkes would know she was in trouble, wouldn't she?

'Yes,' Paul whispered. His legs were beginning to hurt again, but in the dawning horror of this recognition he barely noticed.

She would be in trouble not because she had taken him to her house, especially if it was closer than Sidewinder (and so Paul believed it to be); for that they would probably give her a medal and a lifetime membership in the Misery Chastain Fan Club (to Paul's endless chagrin there actually was such a thing). The problem *was,* she had taken him to her house and installed him in the guest-room and told no one. No phone-call to the local ambulance service: 'This is Annie up on the Humbuggy Mountain Road and I've got a fellow here, looks a bit like King Kong used him for a trampoline.' The problem *was,* she had filled him full of dope to which she was certainly not supposed to have access – not if he was even half as hooked as he thought he *was.* The problem was, she had followed the dope with a weird sort of treatment, sticking needles in his arms, splinting his legs with sawed-off pieces of aluminum crutches. The problem *was,* Annie Wilkes had been on the stand up there in Denver . . . *and not as a supporting witness, either,* Paul thought. *I'd bet the house and lot on that.*

So she watches the cop go down the road in his spandy-clean cruiser (spandy-clean except for the caked chunks of snow and salt nestled in the wheel-wells and under the bumpers, that is), and she feels safe again . . . but not *too* safe, because now she is like an animal with its wind up. Way, *way* up.

The cops will look and look and look, because he is not just good old Joe Blow from Kokomo; he is Paul Sheldon, the literary Zeus from whose brow sprang Misery Chastain, darling of the dump-bins and sweetheart of the supermarkets. Maybe when they don't find him they'll stop looking, or at least look someplace else, but maybe one of the Roydmans saw her going by that night and saw something funny in the back of Old Bessie, something wrapped in a quilt, something vaguely manlike. Even if they hadn't seen a thing, she wouldn't put it past the Roydmans to make up a story to get her in trouble; they didn't like her.

The cops might come back, and next time her house-guest might not be so quiet.

He remembered her eyes darting around aimlessly when the fire in the barbecue pot was on the verge of getting out of control. He could see her tongue slicking her lips. He could see her walking back and forth, hands clenching and unclenching, peeking every now and then into the guest-room where he lay lost in his cloud. Every now and then she would utter

'Goodness!' to the empty rooms.

She had stolen a rare bird with beautiful feathers – a rare bird which came from Africa.

And what would they do if they found out?

Why, put her up on the stand again, of course. Put her up on the stand again in Denver. And this time she might not walk free.

He took his arm away from his eyes. He looked at the interlocking W's swaying drunkenly across the ceiling. He didn't need his elbow over his eyes to see the rest. She might hang on to him for a day or a week. It might take a follow-up phone-call or visit to make her decide to get rid of her *rara avis.* But in the end she would do it, just as wild dogs begin to bury their illicit kills after they have been hunted awhile.

She would give him five pills instead of two, or perhaps smother him with a pillow; perhaps she would simply shoot him. Surely there was a rifle around somewhere – almost everyone living in the high country had one – and that would take care of the problem.

No – not the gun.

Too messy.

Might leave evidence.

None of that had happened yet because no one had found the car. They might be looking for him in New York or in L.A., but no one was looking for him in Sidewinder, Colorado.

But in the spring.

The W's straggled across the ceiling. *Washed. Wiped. Wasted.*

The throbbing in his legs was more insistent; the next time the clock bonged she would come, but he was almost afraid she would read his thoughts on his face, like the bare premise of a story too gruesome to write. His eyes drifted left. There was a calendar on the wall. It showed a boy riding a sled down a hill. It was February according to the calendar, but if his calculations were right it was already early March. Annie Wilkes had just forgotten to turn the page.

How long before the melting snows revealed his Camaro with its New York plates and its registration in the glove compartment proclaiming the owner to be Paul Sheldon?

How long before that trooper called on her, or until she read it in the paper? How long until the spring melt?

Six weeks? Five?

That could be the length of my life, Paul thought, and began shuddering. By then his legs were fully awake, and it was not until she had come in and given him another dose of medicine that he was able to fall asleep.

23

The next evening she brought him the Royal. It was an office model from an era when such things as electric typewriters, color TVs, and touch-tone telephones were only science fiction. It was as black and as proper as a pair of high-button shoes. Glass panels were set into the sides, revealing the machine's levers, springs, ratchets, and rods. A steel return lever, dull with disuse, jutted to one side like a hitchhiker's thumb. The roller was dusty, its hard rubber scarred and pitted. The letters ROYAL ran across the front of the machine in a semicircle. Grunting, she set it down on the foot of the bed between his legs after holding it up for his inspection for a moment.

He stared at it.

Was it grinning?

Christ, it looked like it was.

Anyway, it already looked like trouble. The ribbon was a faded two-tone, red over black. He had forgotten there were such ribbons. The sight of this one called up no pleasant nostalgia.

'Well?' She was smiling eagerly. 'What do you think?'

'It's nice!' he said at once. 'A real antique.'

Her smile clouded. 'I didn't buy it for an antique. I bought it for second-hand. *Good* second-hand.'

He responded with immediate glibness. 'Hey! There ain't no such *thing* as an antique typewriter – not when you come right down to it. A good typewriter lasts damn near forever. These old office babies are *tanks!*'

If he could have reached it he would have patted it. If he could have reached it he would have *kissed* it.

Her smile returned. His heartbeat slowed a little.

'I got it at Used News. Isn't that a silly name for a store? But Nancy Dartmonger, the lady who runs it, is a silly woman.' Annie darkened a little, but he saw at once that she was not darkening at *him* – the survival instinct, he was discovering, might *be* only instinct in itself, but it created some really amazing shortcuts to empathy. He found himself becoming more attuned to her moods, her cycles; he listened to her tick as if she were a wounded clock.

'As well as silly, she's *bad*. Dartmonger! Her name ought to be *Whoremonger*. Divorced twice and now she's living with a *bartender*. That's why when you said it was an antique –'

'It looks fine,' he said.

She paused a long moment and then said, as if confessing: 'It has a missing n.'

'Does it?'

'Yes – see?'

She tilted the typewriter up so he could peer at the banked semicircle of keys and see the missing striker like a missing molar in a mouthful of teeth worn but otherwise complete.

'I see.'

She set it back down. The bed rocked a little. Paul guessed the typewriter might weigh as much as fifty pounds. It had come from a time when there were no alloys, no plastics . . . also no six-figure book advances, no movie tie-in editions, no *USA Today*, no *Entertainment Tonight*, no celebrities doing ads for credit cards or vodka.

The Royal grinned at him, promising trouble.

'She wanted forty-five dollars but gave me five off. Because of the missing n.' She offered him a crafty smile. No fool she, it said.

He smiled back. The tide was in. That made both smiling and lying easy. '*Gave* it to you? You mean you didn't dicker?'

Annie preened a little. 'I told her n was an important letter,' she allowed.

'Well good for you! *Damn!'* Here was a new discovery. Sycophancy was easy once you got the hang of it.

Her smile grew sly, inviting him to share a delicious secret.

'I told her n was one of the letters in my favorite writer's name.'

'It's *two* of the letters in my favorite *nurse's* name.'

Her smile became a glow. Incredibly, a blush rose in her solid cheeks. *That's what it would look like,* he thought, *if you built a furnace inside the mouth of one of those idols in the H. Rider Haggard stories. That is what it would look like at night.*

'You *fooler!'* she simpered.

'I'm not!' he said. 'Not at all.'

'Well!' She looked off for a moment, not blank but just pleased, a little flustered, taking a moment to gather her thoughts. Paul could have taken some pleasure in the way this was going if not for the weight of the typewriter, as solid as the woman and also damaged; it sat there grinning with its missing tooth, promising trouble.

'The wheelchair was much more expensive,' she said.

'Ostomy supplies have gone right out of *sight* since I –' She broke off, frowned, cleared her throat. Then she looked back at him, smiling. 'But it's *time* you began sitting up, and I don't begrudge the cost one tiny bit. And of course you can't type lying down, can you?'

'No . . .'

'I've got a board . . . I cut it to size . . . and paper . . . wait!'

She dashed from the room like a girl, leaving Paul and the typewriter to regard each other. His grin disappeared the moment her back was turned. The Royal's never varied.

He supposed later that he had pretty well known what all this was about, just as he supposed he had known what the typewriter would sound like, how it would clack through its grin like that old comic-strip character Ducky Daddles.

She came back with a package of Corrasable Bond in shrink-wrap and a board about three feet wide by four feet long.

'Look!' She put the board on the arms of the wheelchair that stood by his bed like some solemn skeletal visitor.

Already he could see the ghost of himself behind that board, pent in like a prisoner.

She put the typewriter on the board, facing the ghost, and put the package of Corrasable Bond – the paper he hated most in all the world because of the way the type blurred when the pages were shuffled together – beside it. She had now created a kind of cripple's study.

'What do you think?'

'It looks good,' he said, uttering the biggest lie of his life with perfect ease, and then asked the question to which he already knew the answer. 'What will I write there, do you think?'

'Oh, but Paul!' she said, turning to him, her eyes dancing animatedly in her flushed face. 'I don't *think,* I *know!* You're going to use this typewriter to write a new novel! Your best novel ! *Misery's Return!'*

24

Misery's Return. He felt nothing at all. He supposed a man who had just cut his hand off in a power saw might feel this same species of nothing as he stood regarding his spouting wrist with dull surprise.

'Yes!' Her face shone like a searchlight. Her powerful hands were clasped between her breasts. 'It will be a book just for me, Paul! My payment for nursing you back to health! The one and only copy of the newest *Misery* book! I'll have something no one else in the world has, no matter how much they might want it! *Think* of it!'

'Annie, Misery is dead.' But already, incredibly, he was thinking, *I could bring her back.* The thought filled him with tired revulsion but no real surprise. After all, a man who could drink from a floor-bucket should be capable of a little directed writing.

'No she's not,' Annie replied dreamily. 'Even when I was . . . when I was so mad at you, I knew she wasn't really dead. I knew you couldn't really kill her. Because you're *good.*'

'Am I?' he said, and looked at the typewriter. It grinned at him. *We're going to find out just how good you are, old buddy,* it whispered.

'Yes!'

'Annie, I don't know if I can sit in that wheelchair. Last time –'

'Last time it hurt, you bet it did. And it will hurt next time, too. Maybe even a little more. But there will come a day – and it won't be long, either, although it may seem longer to you than it really is – when it hurts a little less. And a little less. And a little less.'

'Annie, will you tell me one thing?'

'Of course, dear!'

'If I write this story for you –'

'*Novel!* A nice big one like all the others – maybe even bigger!'

He closed his eyes for a moment, then opened them.

'Okay – if I write this *novel* for you, will you let me go when it's done?'

For a moment unease slipped cloudily across her face, and then she was looking at him carefully, studiously. 'You speak as though I were keeping you *prisoner,* Paul.'

He said nothing, only looked at her.

'I think that by the time you finish, you should be up to the . . . up to the strain of meeting people again,' she said. 'Is that what you want to hear?'

'That's what I wanted to hear, yes.'

'Well, honestly! I knew writers were supposed to have big egos, but I guess I didn't understand that meant ingratitude, too!'

He went on looking at her and after a moment she looked away, impatient and a little flustered.

At last he said: 'I'll need all the *Misery* books, if you've got them, because I don't have my concordance.'

'Of course I have them!' she said. Then: 'What's a concordance?'

'It's a loose-leaf binder where I have all my *Misery* stuff,' he said.

'Characters and places, mostly, but cross-indexed three or four different ways. Time-lines. Historical stuff . . .'

He saw she was barely listening. This was the second time she'd shown not the slightest interest in a trick of the trade that would have held a class of would-be writers spellbound. The reason, he thought, was simplicity itself. Annie Wilkes was the perfect audience, a woman who loved stories without having the slightest interest in the mechanics of making them. She was the embodiment of that Victorian archetype, Constant Reader. She did not want to hear about his concordance and indices because to her Misery and the characters surrounding her were perfectly real. Indices meant nothing to her. If he had spoken of a village census in Little Dunthorpe, she might have shown some interest.

'I'll make sure you get the books. They're a little dog-eared, but that's a sign a book has been well read and well loved, isn't it?'

'Yes,' he said. No need to lie this time. 'Yes it is.'

'I'm going to study up on book-binding,' she said dreamily. 'I'm going to bind *Misery's Return* myself. Except for my mother's Bible, it will be the only *real* book I own.'

'That's good,' he said, just to say something. He was feeling a little sick to his stomach.

'I'll go out now so you can put on your thinking cap,' she said. 'This is exciting! Don't you think so?'

'Yes, Annie. I sure do.'

'I'll be in with some breast of chicken and mashed potatoes and peas for you in half an hour. Even a little Jell-O because you've been such a good boy. And I'll make sure you get your pain medication right on time. You can even have an extra pill in the night if you need it. I want to make sure you get your sleep, because you have to go back to work tomorrow. You'll mend faster when you're working, I'll bet!'

She went to the door, paused there for a moment, and then, grotesquely, blew him a kiss.

The door closed behind her. He did not want to look at the typewriter and for awhile resisted, but at last his eyes rolled helplessly toward it. It sat on the bureau, grinning. Looking at it was a little like looking at an instrument of torture – boot, rack, strappado – which is standing inactive, but only for the moment.

I think that by the time you finish, you should be . . . up to the strain of meeting people again.

Ah, Annie, you were lying to both of us. I knew it, and you did, too. I saw it in your eyes.

The limited vista now opening before him was extremely unpleasant: six weeks of life which he would spend suffering with his broken bones and renewing his acquaintance with Misery Chastain, née Carmichael, followed by a hasty interment in the back yard. Or perhaps she would feed his remains to Misery the pig – *that* would have a certain justice, black and gruesome though it might be.

Then don't do it. Make her mad. She's like a walking bottle of nitroglycerine as it is. Bounce her around a little. Make her explode. Better than lying here suffering.

He tried looking up at the interlocked W's, but all too soon he was looking at the typewriter again. It stood atop the bureau, mute and thick and full of words he did not want to write, grinning with its one missing tooth.

I don't think you believe that, old buddy. I think you want to stay alive even if it does hurt. If it means bringing Misery back for an encore, you'll do it. You'll try, anyway – but first you are going to have to deal with me . . . and I don't think I like your face.

'Makes us even,' Paul croaked.

This time he tried looking out the window, where fresh snow was falling. Soon enough, however, he was looking at the typewriter again with avid repulsed fascination, not even aware of just when his gaze had shifted.

25

Getting into the chair didn't hurt as much as he had feared, and that was good, because previous experience had shown him that he would hurt *plenty* afterward.

She set the tray of food down on the bureau, then rolled the wheelchair over to the bed. She helped him to sit up – there was a dull, thudding flare of pain in his pelvic area but it subsided – and then she leaned over, the side of her neck pressing against his shoulder like the neck of a horse. For an instant he could feel the thump of her pulse, and his face twisted in revulsion. Then her right arm was firmly around his back, her left under his buttocks.

'Try not to move from the knees down while I do this,' she said, and then simply slid him into the chair. She did it with the ease of a woman sliding a book into an empty slot in her bookcase. Yes, she was strong. Even in good shape the outcome of a fight between him and Annie would have been in doubt. As he was now it would be like Wally Cox taking on Boom Boom Mancini.

She put the board in front of him. 'See how well it fits?' she said, and went to the bureau to get the food.

'Annie?'

'Yes.'

'I wonder if you could turn that typewriter around. So it faces the wall.'

She frowned. 'Why in the world would you want me to do that?'

Because I don't want it grinning at me all night.

'Old superstition of mine,' he said. 'I always turn my typewriter to the wall before I start writing.' He paused and added: 'Every night while I *am* writing, as a matter of fact.'

'It's like step on a crack, break your mother's back,' she said. 'I never step on a crack if I can help it.' She turned it around so it grinned at nothing but blank wall. 'Better?'

'Much.'

'You are such a *silly*,' she said, and came over and began to feed him.

26

He dreamed of Annie Wilkes in the court of some fabulous Arabian caliph, conjuring imps and genies from bottles and then flying around the court on a magic carpet. When the carpet banked past him (her hair streamed out behind her; her eyes were as bright and flinty as the eyes of a sea-captain navigating among icebergs), he saw it was woven all in green and white; it made a Colorado license plate.

Once upon a time, Annie was calling. *Once upon a time it came to pass. This happened in the days when my grandfather's grandfather was a boy. This is the story of how a poor boy. I heard this from a man who. Once upon a time. Once upon a time.*

27

When he woke up Annie was shaking him and bright morning sun was slanting in the window – the snow had ended.

'Wake up, sleepyhead!' Annie was almost trilling. 'I've got yogurt and a nice boiled egg for you, and then it will be time for you to begin.'

He looked at her eager face and felt a strange new emotion – hope. He had dreamed that Annie Wilkes was Scheherazade, her solid body clad in diaphanous robes, her big feet stuffed into pink sequined slippers with curly toes as she rode on her magic carpet and chanted the incantatory phrases which open the doors of the best stories. But of course it wasn't *Annie* that was Scheherazade. *He* was. And if what he wrote was good enough, if she could not bear to kill him until she discovered how it all came out no matter how much or how loudly her animal instincts yelled for her to do it, that she *must* do it . . .

Might he not have a chance?

He looked past her and saw she had turned the typewriter around before waking him; it grinned resplendently at him with its missing tooth, telling him it was all right to hope and noble to strive, but in the end it was doom alone which would count.

28

She rolled him over to the window so the sun fell on him for the first time in weeks, and it seemed to him he could feel his pasty-white skin, dotted here and there with minor bedsores, murmur its pleasure and thanks. The windowpanes were edged on the inside with a tracery of frost, and when he held out his hand he could feel a bubble of cold like a dome around the window. The feel of it was both refreshing and somehow nostalgic, like a note from an old friend.

For the first time in weeks – it felt like years – he was able to look at a geography different from that of his room with its unchanging verities – blue wallpaper, picture of the Arc de Triomphe, the long, long month of February symbolized by the boy sliding downhill on his sled (he thought that his mind would turn to that boy's face and stocking cap each time January became February, even if he lived to see that change of months another fifty times). He looked into this new world as eagerly as he had watched his first movie – Bambi– as a child.

The horizon was near; it always was in the Rockies, where longer views of the world were inevitably cut off by uptilted plates of bedrock. The sky was a perfect early-morning blue, innocent of clouds. A carpet of green forest climbed the flank of the nearest mountain. There were perhaps seventy acres of open ground between the house and the edge of the forest – the snow-cover over it was a perfect and blazing white. It was impossible to tell if the land beneath was tilled earth or open meadow. The view of this open square was interrupted by only one building: a neat red barn. When she spoke of her livestock or when he saw her trudging grimly past his window, breaking her breath with the impervious prow of her face, he had imagined a ramshackle outbuilding like an illustration from a child's book of ghost stories – rooftree bowed and sagging from years of snow-weight, windows blank and dusty, some broken and blocked with pieces of cardboard, long double doors perhaps off their tracks and swaying outward. This neat and tidy structure with its dark-red paint and neat cream-colored trim looked like the five-car garage of a well-to-do country squire masquerading as a barn. In front of it stood a Jeep Cherokee, maybe five years old but obviously well cared for. To one side stood a Fisher plow in a home-made wooden cradle. To attach the plow to the Jeep, she would only need to drive the Jeep carefully up to the cradle so that the hooks on the frame matched the catches on the plow, and throw the locking lever on the dashboard. The perfect vehicle for a woman who lived alone and had no neighbor she could call upon for help (except for those dirty-birdie Roydmans, of course, and Annie probably wouldn't take a plate of pork chops from them if she was dying of starvation). The driveway was neatly plowed, a testament to the fact that she did indeed use the blade, but he could not see the road – the house cut off the view.

'I see you're admiring my barn, Paul.'

He looked around, startled. The quick and uncalculated movement awoke his pain from its doze. It snarled dully in what remained of his shins and in the bunched salt-dome that had replaced his left knee. It turned over, needling him from where it lay imprisoned in its cave of bones, and then fell lightly asleep again.

She had food on a tray. Soft food, invalid food . . . but his stomach growled at the sight of it. As she crossed to him he saw that she was wearing white shoes with crepe soles.

'Yes,' he said. 'It's very handsome.'

She put the board on the arms of the wheelchair and then put the tray on the board. She pulled a chair over beside him and sat down, watching him as he began to eat.

'Fiddle-de-foof! Handsome is as handsome does, my mother always said. I keep it nice because if I didn't, the neighbors would yap. They are always looking for a way to get at me, or start a rumor about me. So I keep everything nice. Keeping up appearances is very, very important. As far as the barn goes, it really isn't much work, as long as you don't let things pile up. Keeping the snow from breaking in the roof is the oogiest part.'

The oogiest part, he thought. *Save that one for the Annie Wilkes lexicon in your memoirs – if you ever get a chance to write your memoirs, that is. Along with dirty birdie and fiddle-de-foof and all the others which I'm sure will come up in time.*

'Two years ago I had Billy Haversham put heat-tapes in the roof. You throw a switch and they get hot and melt the ice. I won't need them much longer *this* winter, though – see how it's melting on its own?'

He had a forkful of egg halfway to his mouth. It stopped in midair as he looked out at the barn. There was a row of icicles along the eave. The tips of these icicles were dripping – dripping fast. Each drop sparkled as it fell onto a narrow canal of ice which lay at the base of the barn's side.

'It's up to forty-five degrees and it's not even nine o'clock!' Annie was going on gaily as Paul imagined the rear bumper of his Camaro surfacing through the rotted snow for the sun to twinkle on. 'Of course it won't last – we've got a hard snap or three ahead of us yet, and probably another big storm as well – but spring is coming, Paul, and my mother always used to say that the hope of spring is like the hope of heaven.'

He put his fork back down on the plate with the egg still on it.

'Don't want that last bite? All done?'

'All done,' he agreed, and in his mind he saw the Roydmans driving up from Sidewinder, saw a bright arrow of light strike Mrs Roydman's face, making her wince and put a shielding hand up – *What's down there, Ham? . . . Don't tell me I'm crazy, there's something down there! Reflection damn near burned m'eye out! Back up, I want to take another look.*

'Then I'll just take the tray,' she said, 'and you can get started.' She favored him with a glance that was very warm. 'I just can't tell you how excited I am, Paul.'

She went out, leaving him to sit in the wheelchair and look at the water running from the icicles which clung to the edge of the barn.

29

'I'd like some different paper, if you could get it,' he said when she came back to put the typewriter and paper on the board.

'Different from this?' she asked, tapping the cellophane – wrapped package of Corrasable Bond. 'But this is the most expensive of all! I asked when I went into the Paper Patch!'

'Didn't your mother ever tell you that the most expensive is not always the best?'

Annie's brow darkened. Her initial defensiveness had been replaced by indignation. Paul guessed her fury would follow.

'No, she did not. What she told me, Mister Smart Guy, is that when you *buy* cheap, you *get* cheap.'

The climate inside her, he had come to discover, was like springtime in the Midwest. She was a woman full of tornadoes waiting to happen, and if he had been a farmer observing a sky which looked the way Annie's face looked right now, he would have at once gone to collect his family and herd them into the storm cellar. Her brow was too white. Her nostrils flared regularly, like the nostrils of an animal scenting fire. Her hands had begun to spring limberly open and then snatch closed again, catching air and squashing it.

His need for her and his vulnerability to her screamed at him to back off, to placate her while there was still time – if indeed there still was – as a tribe in one of those Rider Haggard stories would have placated their goddess when she was angry, by making sacrifice to her effigy.

But there was another part of him, more calculating and less cowed, which reminded him that he could not play the part of Scheherazade if he grew frightened and placatory whenever she stormed. If he did, she would storm all the more. *If you didn't have something she badly wants,* this part of him reasoned, *she would have taken you to the hospital right away or killed you later on to protect herself from the Roydmans – because for Annie the world is full of Roydmans, for Annie they're lurking behind every bush. And if you don't bell this bitch right now, Paulie my boy, you may never be able to.*

She was beginning to breathe more rapidly, almost to hyperventilate; the rhythm of her clenching hands was likewise speeding up, and he knew that in a moment she would be beyond him.

Gathering up the little courage he had left, trying desperately to summon exactly the right note of sharp and yet almost casual irritability, he said: 'And you might as well stop that. Getting mad won't change a thing.'

She froze as if he had slapped her and looked at him, wounded.

'Annie,' he said patiently, 'this is no big deal.'

'It's a trick,' she said. 'You don't want to write my book and so you're making up tricks not to start. I knew you would. Oh boy. But it's not going to work. It –'

'That's silly,' he said. 'Did I say I wasn't going to start?'

'No . . . no, but –'

'That's right. Because I *am.* And if you come here and take a look at something, I'll show you what the problem is. Bring that Webster Pot with you, please.'

'The what?'

'Little jar of pens and pencils,' he said. 'On newspapers, they sometimes call them Webster Pots. After Daniel Webster.' This was a lie he had made up on the spur of the moment, but it had the desired effect– she looked more confused than ever, lost in a specialists' world of which she had not the slightest knowledge. The confusion had diffused (and thus defused) her rage even more; he saw she now didn't even know if she had any *right* to be angry.

She brought over the jar of pens and pencils and slammed them down on the board and he thought: *Goddam! I won!* No – that wasn't right. Misery had won.

But that isn't right, either. It was Scheherazade. Scheherazade won.

'What?' she said grumpily.

'Watch.'

He opened the package of Corrasable and took out a sheet. He took a freshly sharpened pencil and drew a line on the paper. Then he took a ballpoint pen and drew another line parallel to the first. Then he slid his thumb across the slightly waffled surface of the paper. Both lines blurred smudgily in the direction his thumb was traveling, the pencil-line slightly more than the one he had drawn with the pen.

'See?'

'So what?'

'Ribbon-ink will blur, too,' he said. 'It doesn't blur as much as that pencil-line, but it's worse than the ballpoint-ink line.'

'Were you going to sit and rub every page with your thumb?'

'Just the shift of the pages against each other will accomplish plenty of blurring over a period of weeks or even days,' he said, 'and when a manuscript is in work, it gets shifted around a lot. You're always hunting back through to find a name or a date. My God, Annie, one of the first things you find out in this business is that editors hate reading manuscripts typed on Corrasable Bond almost as much as they hate hand-written manuscripts.'

'Don't call it that. I hate it when you call it that.'

He looked at her, honestly puzzled. 'Call what *what?*'

'When you pervert the talent God gave you by calling it a business. I *hate* that.'

'I'm sorry.'

'You ought to be,' she said stonily. 'You might as well call yourself a whore.'

No, Annie, he thought, suddenly filled with fury. *I'm no whore.* Fast Cars *was about not being a whore. That's what killing that goddamned bitch Misery was about, now that I think about it. I was driving to the West Coast to celebrate my liberation from a state of whoredom. What you did was to pull me out of the wreck when I crashed my car and stick me back in the crib again. Two dollar straight up, four dollar I take you around the world. And every now and then I see a flicker in your eyes that tells me a part of you way back inside knows it too. A jury might let you off by reason of insanity, but not me, Annie. Not this kid.*

'A good point,' he said. 'Now, going back to the subject of the paper –'

'I'll get you your cockadoodie paper,' she said sullenly. 'Just tell me what to get and I'll get it.'

'As long as you understand I'm on your side –'

'Don't make me laugh. No one has been on my side since my mother died twenty years ago.'

'Believe what you want, then,' he said. 'If you're so insecure you can't believe I'm grateful to you for saving my life, that's your problem.'

He was watching her shrewdly, and again saw a flicker of uncertainty, of wanting to believe, in her eyes. Good. Very good. He looked at her with all the sincerity he could muster, and again in his mind he imagined shoving a chunk of glass into her throat, once and forever letting out the blood that serviced her crazy brain.

'At least you should be able to believe that I am on the book's side. You spoke of binding it. I assume that you meant binding the manuscript? The typed pages?'

'Of course that's what I meant.'

Yes, you bet. Because if you took the manuscript to a printer, it might raise questions. You may be naive about the world of books and publishing, but not that naive. Paul Sheldon is missing, and your printer might remember receiving a book-length manuscript concerning itself with Paul Sheldon's most famous character right around the time the man himself disappeared, mightn't he? And he'd certainly remember the instructions – instructions so queer any printer would remember them. One printed copy of a novel-length manuscript.

Just one.

'What did she look like, officer? Well, she was a big woman. Looked sort of like a stone idol in a H. Rider Haggard story. Just a minute, I've got her name and

address here in the files. Just let me look up the carbons of the invoices . . .'

'Nothing wrong with the idea, either,' he said. 'A bound manuscript can be damned handsome. Looks like a good folio edition. But a book should last a long time, Annie, and if I write this one on Corrasable, you're going to have nothing but a bunch of blank papers in ten years or so. Unless, of course, you just put it on the shelf.'

But she wouldn't want that, would she? Christ, no. She'd want to take it down every day, maybe every few hours. Take it down and gloat over it.

An odd stony look had come onto her face. He did not like this mulishness, this almost ostentatious look of obduracy. It made him nervous. He could calculate her rage, but there was something in this new expression which was as opaque as it was childish.

'You don't have to talk anymore,' she said. 'I already told you I'll get you your paper. What kind?'

'In this business-supply store you go to –'

'The Paper Patch.'

'Yes, the Paper Patch. You tell them you'd like two reams – a ream is a package of five hundred sheets –'

'I know that. I'm not stupid, Paul.'

'I know you're not,' he said, becoming more nervous still. The pain had begun to mutter up and down his legs again, and it was speaking even more loudly from the area of his pelvis – he had been sitting up for nearly an hour, and the dislocation down there was complaining about it.

Keep cool, for God's sake – don't lose everything you've gained!

But have I gained anything? Or is it only wishful thinking?

'Ask for two reams of white long-grain mimeo. Hammermill Bond is a good brand; so is Triad Modern. Two reams of mimeo will cost less than this one package of Corrasable, and it should be enough to do the whole job, write and rewrite.'

'I'll go right now,' she said, getting up suddenly.

He looked at her, alarmed, understanding that she meant to leave him without his medication again, and sitting up this time, as well. Sitting already hurt; the pain would be monstrous by the time she got back, even if she hurried.

'You don't have to do that,' he said, speaking fast. 'The Corrasable is good enough to start with – after all, I'll have to rewrite anyway –'

'Only a silly person would try to start a good work with a bad tool.' She took the package of Corrasable Bond, then snatched the sheet with the two smudged lines and crumpled it into a ball. She tossed both into the wastebasket and turned back to him. That stony, obdurate look covered her face like a mask. Her eyes glittered like tarnished dimes.

'I'm going to town now,' she said. 'I know you want to get started as soon as you can, since you're *on my side* –' she spoke these last words with intense, smoking sarcasm (and, Paul believed, more self-hate than she would ever know) '– and so I'm not even going to take time to put you back in your bed.'

She smiled, a pulling of the lips that was grotesquely puppet-like, and slipped to his side in her silent white nurse's shoes. Her fingers touched his hair. He flinched. He tried not to but couldn't help it. Her dead-alive smile widened.

'Although I suspect we may have to put off the actual start of *Misery's Return* for a day . . . or two . . . perhaps even three. Yes, it may be as long as three days before you are able to sit up again. Because of the pain. Too bad. I had champagne chilling in the fridge. I'll have to put it back in the shed.'

'Annie, really, I can start if you'll just –'

'No, Paul.' She moved to the door and then turned, looking at him with that stony face. Only her eyes, those tarnished dimes, were fully alive under the shelf of her brow. 'There is one thought I would like to leave you with. You may think you can fool me, or trick me; I know I look slow and stupid. But I am not stupid, Paul, and I am not slow.'

Suddenly her face broke apart. The stony obduracy shattered and what shone through was the countenance of an insanely angry child. For a moment Paul thought the extremity of his terror might kill him. Had he thought he had gained the upper hand? Had he? Could one possibly play Scheherazade when one's captor was insane?

She rushed across the room at him, thick legs pumping, knees flexing, elbows chopping back and forth in the stale sickroom air like pistons. Her hair bounced and joggled around her face as it came loose from the bobby-pins that held it up. Now her passage was not silent; it was like the tread of Goliath striding into the Valley of Bones. The picture of the Arc de Triomphe clacked affrightedly on the wall.

'Geeeee-yahhh!' she screamed, and brought her fist down on the bunched salt-dome that had been Paul Sheldon's left knee.

He threw his head back and howled, veins standing out in his neck and on his forehead. Pain burst out from his knee and shrouded him, whitely radiant, in the center of a nova.

She tore the typewriter off the board and slammed it down on the mantel, lifting its weight of dead metal as he might have lifted an empty cardboard box.

'So you just sit there,' she said, lips pulled back in that grinning rictus, 'and you think about who is in charge here, and all the things I can do to hurt you if you behave badly or try to trick me. You sit there and you scream if you want to, because no one can hear you. No one stops here because they all know Annie Wilkes is crazy, they all know what she did, even if they did find me innocent.'

She walked back to the door and turned again, and he screamed again when she did, in anticipation of another bull-like charge, and that made her grin more widely.

'I'll tell you something else,' she said softly. 'They think I got away with it, and they are right. Think about that, Paul, while I'm in town getting your cockadoodie paper.'

She left, slamming the bedroom door hard enough to shake the house. Then there was the click of the lock.

He leaned back in the chair, shaking all over, trying not to shake because it hurt, not able to help it. Tears streamed down his cheeks. Again and again he saw her flying across the room, again and again he saw her bringing her fist down on the remains of his knee with all the force of an angry drunk hammering on an oak bar, again and again he was swallowed in that terrible blue-white nova of pain.

'Please, God, please,' he moaned as the Cherokee started outside with a bang and a roar. 'Please, God, please – let me out of this or kill me . . . let me out of this or kill me.'

The roar of the engine faded off down the road and God did neither and he was left with his tears and the pain, which was now fully awake and raving through his body.

30

He thought later that the world, in its unfailing perversity, would probably construe those things which he did next as acts of heroism. And he would probably let them – but in fact what he did was nothing more than a final staggering grab for self-preservation.

Dimly he seemed to hear some madly enthusiastic sportscaster – Howard Cosell or Warner Wolf or perhaps that all-time crazy Johnny Most – describing the scene, as if his effort to get at her drug supply before the pain killed him was some strange sporting event – a trial substitution for *Monday Night Football*, perhaps. What would you call a sport like that, anyway? *Run for the Dope?*

'I just *can*not believe the guts this Sheldon kid is displaying today!' the sportscaster in Paul Sheldon's head was enthusing. 'I don't believe anyone in Annie Wilkes Stadium – or in the home viewing audience, for that matter – thought he had the *sly*-test chance of getting that wheelchair moving after the blow he took, but I believe . . . yes, it is! It's moving! Let's look at the replay!'

Sweat ran down his forehead and stung his eyes. He licked a mixture of salt and tears off his lips. The shuddering would not stop. The pain was like the end of the world. He thought: *There comes a point when the very discussion of pain becomes redundant. No one knows there is pain the size of this in the world. No one. It is like being possessed by demons.*

It was only the thought of the pills, the Novril that she kept somewhere in the house, which got him moving. The locked bedroom door . . . the possibility the dope might not be in the downstairs bathroom as he had surmised but hidden somewhere . . . the chance she might come back and catch him . . . these things mattered not at all, these things were only shadows behind the pain. He would deal with each problem as it came up or he would die. That was all.

Moving caused the band of fire below his waist and in his legs to sink in deeper, cinching his legs like belts studded with hot, inward-pointing spikes. But the chair *did* move. Very slowly the chair began to move.

He had managed about four feet before realizing he was going to do nothing more useful than roll the wheelchair past the door and into the far corner unless he could turn it.

He grasped the right wheel, shuddering,

(think of the pills, think of the relief of the pills)

and bore down on it as hard as he could. Rubber squeaked minutely on the wooden floor, the cries of mice. He bore down, once strong and now flabby muscles quivering like jelly, lips peeling back from his gritted teeth, and the wheelchair slowly pivoted.

He grasped both wheels and got the chair moving again. This time he rolled five feet before stopping to straighten himself out. Once he'd done it, he grayed out.

He swam back to reality five minutes later, hearing the dim, goading voice of that sportscaster in his head: 'He's trying to get going again! I just cannot be-*leeve* the guts of this Sheldon kid!'

The front of his mind only knew about the pain; it was the back that directed his eyes. He saw it near the door and rolled over to it. He reached down, but the tips of his fingers stopped a clear three inches short of the floor, where one of the two or three bobby-pins that had fallen from her hair as she charged him lay. He bit his lip, unaware of the sweat running down his face and neck and darkening his pajama shirt.

'I don't think he can get that pin, folks – it's been a fan-*tas*-tic effort, but I'm afraid this is where it all ends.'

Well, maybe not.

He let himself slouch to the right in the wheelchair, at first trying to ignore the pain in his right side – pain that felt like an increasing bubble of pressure, something similar to a tooth impaction – and then giving way and screaming. As she said, there was no one to hear him anyway.

The tips of his fingers still hung an inch from the floor, brushing back and forth just above the bobby-pin, and his right hip really felt as if it might simply explode outward in a squirt of some vile white bone-jelly.

Oh God please please help me –

He slumped farther in spite of the pain. His fingers brushed the pin but succeeded only in pushing it a quarter of an inch away. Paul slid down in the chair, still slumped to the right, and screamed again at the pain in his lower legs. His eyes were bulging, his mouth was open, his tongue straight down between his teeth like the pull on a window-shade. Little drops of spittle ran from its tip and spatted on the floor.

He pinched the bobby-pin between his fingers . . . tweezed it . . . almost lost it . . . and then it was locked in his fist.

Straightening up brought a fresh slough of pain, and when the act was accomplished he could do no more than sit and pant for awhile, his head tilted as far as the uncompromising back of the wheelchair would allow, the bobby-pin lying on the board across the chair's arms. For awhile he was quite sure he was going to puke, but that passed.

What are you doing? part of his mind scolded wearily after awhile. *Are you waiting for the pain to go away? It won't. She's always quoting her mother, but your own mother had a few sayings, too, didn't she?*

Yes. She had.

Sitting there, head thrown back, face shiny with sweat, hair plastered to his forehead, Paul spoke one of them aloud now, almost as an incantation: 'There may be fairies, there may be elves, but God helps those who help themselves.'

Yeah. So stop waiting, Paulie – the only elf that's going to show up here is that all-time heavyweight, Annie Wilkes.

He got moving again, rolling the wheelchair slowly across to the door. She had locked it, but he believed he might be able to unlock it. Tony Bonasaro, who was now only so many blackened flakes of ash, had been a car-thief. As part of his preparation for writing *Fast Cars,* Paul had studied the mechanics of car-thievery with a tough old ex-cop named Tom Twyford. Tom had shown him how to hot-wire an ignition, how to use the thin and limber strip of metal car-thieves called Slim Jims to yank the lock on a car door, how to short out a car burglar alarm.

Or, Tom had said on a spring day in New York some two and a half years ago, *let's say you don't want to steal a car at all. You got a car, but you're a little low on gas. You got a hose, but the car you pick for the free donation has got a locking gas-cap. Is this a problem? Not if you know what you're doing, because most gas-cap locks are strictly Mickey Mouse. All you really need is a bobby-pin.*

It took Paul five endless minutes of backing and filling to get the wheelchair exactly where he wanted it, with the left wheel almost touching the door.

The keyhole was the old-fashioned sort, reminding Paul of John Tenniel's *Alice in Wonderland* drawings, set in the middle of a tarnished keyplate. He slid down a bit in the wheelchair – giving out a single barking groan – and looked through it. He could see a short hallway leading down to what was clearly the parlor: a dark-red rug on the floor, an old-fashioned divan upholstered in similar material, a lamp with tassels hanging from its shade.

To his left, halfway down the hallway, was a door which stood ajar. Paul's pulsebeat quickened. That was almost surely the downstairs bathroom – he had heard her running enough water in there (including the time she had filled the floor-bucket from which he had enthusiastically drunk), and wasn't it also the place she always came from before giving him his medicine?

He thought it was.

He grasped the bobby-pin. It spilled out of his fingers onto the board and then skittered toward the edge.

'No!' he cried hoarsely, and clapped a hand over it just before it could fall. He clasped it in one fist and then grayed out again.

Although he had no way of telling for sure, he thought he was out longer this second time. The pain – except for the excruciating agony of his left knee – seemed to have abated a tiny bit. The bobby-pin was on the board across the arms of the wheelchair. This time he flexed the fingers of his right hand several times before picking it up.

Now, he thought, unbending it and holding it in his right hand. You will *not shake. Hold that thought. YOU WILL NOT SHAKE.*

He reached across his body with the pin and slipped it into the keyhole, listening as the sportscaster in his mind

(so vivid!)

described the action.

Sweat ran steadily down his face like oil. He listened . . . but even more, he *felt.*

The tumbler in a cheap lock is nothing but a rocker, Tom Twyford had said, seesawing his hand to demonstrate. You *want to turn a rocking chair over? Easiest thing in the world, right? Just grab the rockers and flip the mother right over . . . nothing to it. And that's all you got to do with a lock like this. Slide the tumbler up and then open the gas-cap quick, before it can snap back.*

He had the tumbler twice, but both times the bobby-pin slipped off and the tumbler snapped back before he could do more than begin to move it.

The bobby-pin was starting to bend. He thought that it would break after another two or three tries.

'Please God,' he said, sliding it in again. 'Please God, what do you say? Just a little break for the kid, that's all I'm asking.'

('Folks, Sheldon has performed heroically today, but this has got to be his last shot. The crowd has fallen silent . . .')

He closed his eyes, the sportscaster's voice fading as he listened avidly to the minute rattle of the pin in the lock. Now! Here was resistance! The tumbler! He could see it lying in there like the curved foot of a rocking chair, pressing the tongue of the lock, holding it in place, holding *him* in place.

It's strictly Mickey Mouse, Paul. Just stay cool.

When you hurt this badly, it was hard to stay cool.

He grasped the doorknob with his left hand, reaching under his right arm to do it, and began to apply gentle pressure to the bobby-pin. A little more . . . a little more . . .

In his mind he could see the rocker beginning to move in its dusty little alcove; he could see the lock's tongue begin to retract. No need for it to go all the way, good God, no – no need to overturn the rocking chair, to use Tom Twyford's metaphor. Just the instant it cleared the doorframe – a push –

The pin was simultaneously starting to bend and slip. He felt it happening, and in desperation he pushed upward as hard as he could, turned the knob, and shoved at the door. There was a *snap* as the pin broke in two, the part in the lock falling in, and he had a dull moment to consider his failure before he saw that the door was slowly swinging open with the tongue of the lock sticking out of the plate like a steel finger.

'Jesus,' he whispered. 'Jesus, thank you.'

Let's go to the videotape! Warner Wolf screamed exultantly in his mind as the thousands in Annie Wilkes Stadium – not to mention the untold millions watching at home – broke into thunderous cheers.

'Not now, Warner,' he croaked, and began the long, draining job of backing and filling the wheelchair so he could get a straight shot at the door.

31

He had a bad – no, not just bad; terrible, horrible – moment when it seemed the wheelchair was not going to fit. It was no more than two inches too wide, but that was two inches too much. *She brought it in collapsed, that's why you thought it was a shopping cart at first,* his mind informed him drearily.

In the end he was able to squeeze through – barely – by positioning himself squarely in the doorway and then leaning forward enough to grab the jambs of the door in his hands. The axle-caps of the wheels squalled against the wood, but he was able to get through.

After he did, he grayed out again.

32

Her voice called him out of his daze. He opened his eyes and saw she was pointing a shotgun at him. Her eyes glittered furiously. Spit shone on her teeth.

'If you want your freedom so badly, Paul,' Annie said, 'I'll be happy to grant it to you.'

She pulled back both hammers.

33

He jerked, expecting the shotgun blast. But she wasn't there, of course; his mind had already recognized the dream.

Not a dream – a warning. She could come back anytime. Anytime at all.

The quality of the light fanning through the half-open bathroom door had changed, grown brighter. It looked like noonlight. He wished the clock would chime and tell him just how close to right he was, but the clock was obstinately silent.

She stayed away fifty hours before.

So she did. And she might stay away eighty this time. Or you might hear that Cherokee pulling in five seconds from now. In case you didn't know it, friend, the Weather Bureau can post tornado warnings, but when it comes to telling exactly when and where they'll touch down, they don't know fuck-all.

'True enough,' he said, and rolled the wheelchair down to the bathroom. Looking in, he saw an austere room floored with hexagonal white tiles. A bathtub with rusty fans spreading below the faucets stood on clawed feet. Beside it was a linen closet. Across from the tub was a sink. Over the sink was a medicine cabinet.

The floor-bucket was in the tub – he could see its plastic top.

The hall was wide enough for him to swing the chair around and face the door, but now his arms were trembling with exhaustion. He had been a puny kid and so he had tried to take reasonably good care of himself as an adult, but his muscles were now the muscles of an invalid and the puny kid was back, as if all that time spent doing laps and jogging and working out on the Nautilus machine had only been a dream.

At least this doorway was wider – not much, but enough to make his passage less hair-raising. Paul bumped over the lintel, and then the chair's hard rubber wheels rolled smoothly over the tiles. He smelled something sour that he automatically associated with hospitals – Lysol, maybe. There was no toilet in here, but he had already suspected that – the only flushing sounds came from upstairs, and now that he thought of it, one of those upstairs flushes always followed his use of the bedpan. Here there was only the tub, the basin, and the linen closet with its door standing open.

He gazed briefly at the neat piles of blue towels and washcloths – he was familiar with both from the spongebaths she had given him – and then turned his attention to the medicine cabinet over the washstand.

It was out of reach.

No matter how much he strained, it was a good nine inches above the tips of his fingers. He could see this but reached anyway, unable to believe Fate or God or Whoever could be so cruel. He looked like an outfielder reaching desperately for a home-run ball he had absolutely no chance of catching.

Paul made a wounded, baffled noise, lowered his hand, and then leaned back, panting. The gray cloud lowered. He willed it away and looked around for something he could use to open the medicine cabinet's door and saw an O-Cedar mop leaning stiffly in the corner on a long blue pole.

You going to use that? Really? Well, I guess you could. Pry open the medicine cabinet door and then just knock a bunch of stuff out into the basin. But the bottles will break and even if there are no bottles, fat chance, everyone has at least a bottle of Listerine or Scope or something in their medicine cabinet, you have no way of putting back what you knock down. So when she comes back and sees the mess, what then?

'I'll tell her it was Misery,' he croaked. 'I'll tell her she dropped by looking for a tonic to bring her back from the dead.'

Then he burst into tears . . . but even through the tears his eyes were conning the room, looking for something, anything, inspiration, a break, just a fucking br –

He was looking into the linen closet again, and his rapid breath suddenly stopped. His eyes widened.

His first cursory glance had taken in the shelves with their stacks of folded sheets and pillow-cases and washcloths and towels. Now he looked at the *floor* and on the floor were a number of square cardboard cartons. Some were labeled UPJOHN. Some were labeled LILY. Some were labeled CAM PHARMACEUTICALS.

He turned the wheelchair roughly, hurting himself, not caring.

Please God don't let it be her cache of extra shampoo or her tampons or pictures of her dear old sainted mother or –

He fumbled for one of the boxes, dragged it out, and opened the flaps. No shampoo, no Avon samples. Far from it. There was a wild jumble of drugs in the carton, most of them in small boxes marked SAMPLES. At the bottom a few pills and capsules, different colors, rolled around loose. Some, like Motrim and Lopressor, the hypertension drug his father had taken during the last three years of his life, he knew. Others he had never heard of.

'Novril,' he muttered, raking wildly through the box while sweat ran down his face and his legs pounded and throbbed. 'Novril, where's the fucking *Novril?*'

No Novril. He pushed the flaps of the carton closed and shoved it back into the linen closet, making only a token effort to replace it in the same place it had been. Should be all right, the place looked like a goddam junk-heap –

Leaning far to his left, he was able to snag a second carton. He opened it and was hardly able to credit what he was seeing.

Darvon. Darvocet. Darvon Compound. Morphose and Morphose Complex. Librium. Valium. And Novril. Dozens and dozens and dozens of sample boxes. Lovely boxes. Dear boxes. O lovely dear sainted boxes. He clawed one open and saw the capsules she gave him every six hours, enclosed in their little blisters.

NOT TO BE DISPENSED WITHOUT PHYSICIAN'S PRESCRIPTION, the box said.

'Oh dear Jesus, the doctor is in!' Paul sobbed. He tore the cellophane apart with his teeth and chewed up three of the capsules, barely aware of the bruisingly bitter taste. He halted, stared at the five that were left encased in their mutilated cellophane sheet, and gobbled a fourth.

He looked around quickly, chin down on his breastbone, eyes crafty and frightened. Although he knew it was too soon to be feeling any relief, he did feel it – *having* the pills, it seemed, was even more important than *taking* the pills. It was as if he had been given control of the moon and the tides – or had just reached up and taken it. It was a huge thought, awesome . . . and yet also frightening, with undertones of guilt and blasphemy.

If she comes back now –

'All right – okay. I get the message.'

He looked into the carton, trying to calculate how many of the sample boxes he might be able to take without her realizing a little mouse named Paul Sheldon had been nibbling away at the supply.

He giggled at this, a shrill, relieved sound, and he realized the medication wasn't just working on his legs. He had gotten his fix, if you wanted to be perfectly vulgar about it.

Get moving, idiot. You have no time to enjoy being stoned.

He took five of the boxes – a total of thirty capsules. He had to restrain himself from taking more. He stirred the remaining boxes and bottles around, hoping the result would look no more or less helter-skelter than it had when he first peered into the box. He refolded the flaps and slipped the box back into the linen closet.

A car was coming.

He straightened up, eyes wide. His hands dropped to the arms of the wheelchair and gripped them with panicky tightness. If it was Annie, he was screwed and that was the end of it. He would never be able to maneuver this balky, oversized thing back to the bedroom in time. Maybe he could whack her once with the O-Cedar mop or something before she wrung his neck like a chicken.

He sat in the wheelchair with the sample boxes of Novril in his lap and his broken legs stuck stiffly out in front of him and waited for the car to pass or turn in.

The sound swelled endlessly . . . then began to diminish.

Okay. Do you need a more graphic warning, Paul-baby?

As a matter of fact, he did not. He took a final glance at the cartons. They looked to him about as they had when he had first seen them – although he had been looking at them through a haze of pain and could not be completely sure – but he knew that the piles of boxes might not be as random as they had looked, oh, not at all. She had the heightened awareness of the deep neurotic, and might have had the position of each box carefully memorized. She might take one casual glance in here and immediately realize in some arcane way what had happened. This knowledge did not bring fear but a sense of resignation – he had needed the medication, and he had somehow managed to escape his room and get it. If there were consequences, punishment, he could face them with at least the understanding that he could have done nothing but what he had done. And of all she had done to him, this resignation was surely a symptom of the worst – she had turned him into a pain-racked animal with no moral options at all.

He slowly backed the wheelchair across the bathroom, glancing behind himself occasionally to make sure he wasn't wandering off-course. Before, such a movement would have made him scream with pain, but now the pain was disappearing under a beautiful glassiness.

He rolled into the hall and then stopped as a terrible thought struck him: if the bathroom floor had been slightly damp, or even a bit dirty –

He stared at it, and for a moment the idea that he must have left tracks on those clean white tiles was so persuasive that he actually *saw* them. He shook his head and looked again. No tracks. But the door was open farther than it had been. He rolled forward, swung the wheelchair slightly to the right so he could lean over and grab the knob, and pulled the door half-closed. He eyed it, then pulled it a bit closer to the jamb. There. That looked right.

He was reaching for the wheels, meaning to pivot the chair so he could roll back to his room, when he realized he was pointed more or less toward the living room, and the living room was where most people kept their telephone and –

Light bursting in his mind like a flare over a foggy meadow.

'Hello, Sidewinder Police Station, Officer Humbuggy speaking.'

'Listen to me, Officer Humbuggy. Listen very carefully and don't interrupt, because I don't know how much time I have. My name is Paul Sheldon. I'm calling you from Annie Wilkes's house. I've been her prisoner here for at least two weeks, maybe as long as a month. I –'

'Annie Wilkes!'

'Get out here right away. Send an ambulance. And for Christ's sake get here before she gets back . . .'

'Before she gets back,' Paul moaned. 'Oh yeah. Far out.'

What makes you think she even has a phone? Who have you ever heard her call? Who would she call? Her good friends the Roydmans?

Just because she doesn't have anyone to chatter with all day doesn't mean she is incapable of understanding that accidents can happen; she could fall downstairs and break an arm or a leg, the barn might catch on fire –

How many times have you heard this supposed telephone ring?

So now there's a requirement? Your phone has to ring at least once a day or Mountain Bell comes and takes it out? Besides, I haven't even been conscious most of the time.

You're pushing your luck. You're pushing your luck and you know it.

Yes. He knew it, but the thought of that telephone, the imagined sensation of the cool black plastic under his fingers, the click of the rotary dial or the single booping sound as he touch-toned o – these were seductions too great to resist.

He worked the wheelchair around until it was directly facing the parlor, and then he rolled down to it.

The place smelled musty, unaired, obscurely tired. Although the curtains guarding the bow windows were only half-drawn, affording a lovely view of the mountains, the room seemed too dark – because its colors were too dark, he thought. Dark red predominated, as if someone had spilled a great deal of venous blood in here.

Over the mantel was a tinted photograph portrait of a forbidding woman with tiny eyes buried in a fleshy face. The rosebud mouth was pursed. The photograph, enclosed in a rococo frame of gold gilt, was the size of the President's photograph in the lobby of a big-city post office. Paul did not need a notarized statement telegram to tell him that this was Annie's sainted mother.

He rolled farther into the room. The left side of the wheelchair struck a small occasional table covered with ceramic gewgaws. They chattered together and one of them – a ceramic penguin sitting on a ceramic ice-block – fell off the side.

Without thinking, he reached out and grabbed it. The gesture was almost casual . . . and then reaction set in. He held the penguin tightly in his curled fist, trying to will the shakes away. *You caught it, no sweat, besides, there's a rug on the floor, probably wouldn't have broken anyway –*

But if it HAD! his mind screamed back. *If it HAD! Please, you have to go back to your room before you leave something . . . a track . . .*

No. Not yet. Not yet, no matter how frightened he was. Because this had cost him too much. If there was a payoff, he was going to have it.

He looked around the room, which was stuffed with heavy graceless furniture. It should have been dominated by the bow windows and the gorgeous view of the Rockies beyond them but was instead dominated by the picture of that fleshy woman imprisoned in the ghastly glaring frame with its twists and curlicues and frozen gilded swags.

On a table at the far end of the couch, where she would sit to watch TV, was a plain dialer telephone.

Gently, hardly daring to breathe, he put the ceramic penguin (NOW MY TALE IS TOLD! the legend on the block of ice read) back on the knick-knack table and rolled across the room toward the phone.

There was an occasional table in front of the sofa; he gave it a wide berth. On it was a spray of dried flowers in an ugly green vase, and the whole thing looked topheavy, ready to tip over if he so much as brushed it.

No cars coming outside – only the sound of the wind.

He grasped the handset of the phone in one hand and slowly picked it up.

A queer predestinate sense of failure filled his mind even before he got the handset to his ear and heard the nothing. He replaced the receiver slowly, a line from an old Roger Miller song occurring to him and seeming to make a certain senseless sense: *No phone, no pool, no pets . . . I ain't got no cigarettes . . .*

He traced the phone cord with his eye, saw the small square module on the baseboard, saw that the jack was plugged into it. Everything looked in perfect working order.

Like the barn, with its heat-tapes.

Keeping up appearances is very, very important.

He closed his eyes and saw Annie removing the jack and squeezing Elmer's Glue into the hole in the module. Saw her replacing the jack in the dead-white glue, where it would harden and freeze forever. The phone company would have no idea that anything was wrong unless someone attempted to call her and reported the line out of service, but no one called Annie, did they? She would receive regular monthly bills on her dead line and she would pay them promptly, but the phone was only stage dressing, part of her never ending battle to *keep up appearances,* like the neat barn with its fresh red paint and cream trim and heat-tapes to melt the winter ice. Had she castrated the phone in case of just such an expedition as this? Had she foreseen the possibility that he might get out of the room? He doubted it. The phone – the *working* phone – would have gotten on her nerves long before he came. She would have lain awake at night, looking up at the ceiling of her bedroom, listening to the high-country whine of the wind, imagining the people who must be thinking of her with either dislike or outright malevolence – all the world's Roydmans – people who might, any of them, at any time, take a notion to call her on the telephone and scream: *You did it, Annie! They took you all the way to Denver, and we know you did it! They don't take you all the way to Denver if you're innocent!* She would have asked for and gotten an unlisted number, of course – anyone tried for and acquitted of some major crime (and if it had been Denver, it had been major) would have done that – but even an unlisted number would not comfort a deep neurotic like Annie Wilkes for long. *They* were all in league against her, *they* could get the number if *they* wanted, probably the lawyers who had been against her would be glad to pass it out to anyone who asked for it, and people *would* ask, oh yes – for she would see the world as a dark place full of moving human masses like seas, a malevolent universe surrounding a single small stage upon which a single savagely bright pinspot illuminated . . . only her. So best to eradicate the phone, silence it, as she would silence *him* if she knew he had gotten even this far.

Panic burst shrilly up in his mind, telling him that he *had* to get out of here and back into his room, hide the pills somewhere, return to his place by the window so that when she returned she would see *no difference, no difference at all,* and this time he agreed with the voice. He agreed wholeheartedly. He backed carefully away from the phone, and when he gained the room's one reasonably clear area, he began the laborious job of turning the wheelchair around, careful not to bump the occasional table as he did so.

He had nearly finished the turn when he heard an approaching car and knew, simply *knew* it was her, returning from town.

34

He nearly fainted, in the grip of the greatest terror he had ever known, a terror that was filled with deep and unmanning guilt. He suddenly remembered the only incident in his life that came remotely close to this one in its desperate emotional quality. He had been twelve. It was summer vacation, his father working, his mother gone to spend the day in Boston with Mrs Kaspbrak from across the street. He had seen a pack of her cigarettes and had lit one of them. He smoked it enthusiastically, feeling both sick and fine, feeling the way he imagined robbers must feel when they stick up banks. Halfway through the cigarette, the room filled with smoke, he had heard her opening the front door. *'Paulie? It's me – I've forgotten my purse!'* He had begun to wave madly at the smoke, knowing it would do no good, knowing he was caught, knowing he would be spanked.

It would be more than a spanking this time.

He remembered the dream he'd had during one of his gray-outs: Annie cocking the shotgun's twin triggers and saying *If you want your freedom so badly, Paul, I'll be happy to grant it to you.*

The sound of the engine began to drop as the approaching car slowed down. It *was* her.

Paul settled hands he could barely feel on the wheels and rolled the chair toward the hallway, sparing one glance at the ceramic penguin on its block of ice. Was it in the same place it had been? He couldn't tell. He would have to hope.

He rolled down the hall toward the bedroom door, gaining speed. He hoped to shoot right through, but his aim was a little off. Only a little . . . but the fit was so tight that a little was enough. The wheelchair thumped against the right side of the doorway and bounced back a little.

Did you chip the paint? his mind screamed at him. *Oh Jesus Christ, did you chip the paint, did you leave a track?*

No chip. There was a small dent but no chip. Thank God. He backed and filled frantically, trying to navigate the fineness of the doorway's tight fit.

The car motor swelled, nearing, still slowing. Now he could hear the crunch of its snow tires.

Easy . . . easy does it . . .

He rolled forward and then the hubs of the wheels stuck solid against the sides of the bedroom door. He pushed harder, knowing it wasn't going to do any good, he was stuck in the doorway like a cork in a wine-bottle, unable to go either way –

He gave one final heave, the muscles in his arms quivering like overtuned violin strings, and the wheelchair passed through with that same low squealing noise.

The Cherokee turned into the driveway.

She'll have packages, his mind gibbered, the typewriter paper, maybe a few other things as well, and she'll be careful coming up the walk because of the ice, you're in here now, the worst is over, there's time, still time . . .

He rolled farther into the room, then turned in a clumsy semicircle. As he rolled the wheelchair parallel to the open bedroom door, he heard the Cherokee's engine shut off.

He leaned over, grasped the doorknob, and tried to pull the door shut. The tongue of the lock, still stuck out like a stiff steel finger, bumped the jamb. He pushed it with the ball of his thumb. It began to move . . . then stopped. Stopped dead, refusing to let the door close.

He stared at it stupidly for a moment, thinking of that old Navy maxim: *Whatever CAN go wrong WILL go wrong.*

Please God, no more, wasn't it enough she killed the phone?

He let go of the tongue. It sprang all the way out again. He pushed it in again and encountered the same obstruction. Inside the guts of the lock he heard an odd rattling and understood. It was the part of the bobby-pin which had broken off. It had fallen in some way that was keeping the lock's tongue from retracting completely.

He heard the Cherokee's door open. He even heard her grunt as she got out. He heard the rattle of paper bags as she gathered up her parcels.

'Come *on,'* he whispered, and began to chivvy the tongue gently back and forth. It went in perhaps a sixteenth of an inch each time and then stopped. He could hear the goddam bobby-pin rattling inside there. 'Come on . . . come on . . . come on . . .'

He was crying again and unaware of it, sweat and tears mingling freely on his cheeks; he was vaguely aware that he was still in great pain despite all the dope he had swallowed – that he was going to pay a high price for this little piece of work.

Not so high as the one she'll make you pay if you can't get this goddam door closed again, Paulie.

He heard her crunching, cautious footsteps as she made her way up the path. The rattle of bags . . . and now the rattle of her housekeys as she took them from her purse.

'Come on . . . come on . . . come on . . .'

This time when he pushed the tongue there was a flat click from inside the lock and the jut of metal slid a quarter of an inch into the door. Not enough to clear the jamb . . . but almost.

'Please . . . come on . . .'

He began to chivvy the tongue faster, diddling it, listening as she opened the kitchen door. Then, like a hideous flashback to that day when his mother had caught him smoking, Annie called cheerily: 'Paul? It's me! I've got your paper!'

Caught! I'm caught! Please God, no God, don't let her – hurt me God –

His thumb pressed convulsively tight against the tongue of the lock, and there was a muffled snap as the bobby-pin broke. The tongue slid all the way into the door. In the kitchen he heard a zipper-rasp as she opened her parka.

He closed the bedroom door. The click of the latch

(did she hear that? must have must have heard that!)

sounded as loud as a track-starter's gun.

He backed the wheelchair up toward the window. He was still backing and filling as her footsteps began to come down the hallway.

'I've got your paper, Paul! Are you awake?'

Never . . . never in time . . . She'll hear . . .

He gave the guide-lever a final wrench and rolled the wheelchair into place beside the window just as her key rattled in the lock.

It won't work . . . the bobby-pin . . . and she'll be suspicious . . .

But the piece of alien metal must have fallen all the way to the bottom of the lock, because her key worked perfectly. He sat in his chair, eyes half-closed, hoping madly that he had gotten the chair back where it had been (or at least close enough to it so she wouldn't notice), hoping that she would take his sweat-drenched face and quivering body simply as reactions to missing his medication, hoping most of all that he hadn't left a track –

It was as the door swung open that he looked down and saw that by looking for individual tracks with such agonized concentration, he had ignored a whole buffalo run: the boxes of Novril were still in his lap.

35

She had two packages of paper, and she held one up in each hand, smiling. 'Just what you asked for, isn't it? Triad Modern. Two reams here, and I have two more in the kitchen, just in case. So you see –'

She broke off, frowning, looking at him.

'You're *dripping* with sweat . . . and your color is very hectic.' She paused. 'What have you been doing?'

And although that set the panicky little voice of his lesser self to squealing again that he was caught and might as well give it up, might as well confess and hope for her mercy, he managed to meet her suspicious gaze with an ironic weariness.

'I think you know what I've been doing,' he said. 'I've been suffering.'

From the pocket of her skirt she took a Kleenex and wiped his brow. The Kleenex came away wet. She smiled at him with that terrible bogus maternity.

'Has it been very bad?'

'Yes. Yes, it has. Now can I –'

'I *told* you about making me mad. Live and learn, isn't that what they say? Well, if you live, I guess you'll learn.'

'Can I have my pills now?'

'In a minute,' she said. Her eyes never left his sweaty face, its waxy pallor and red rashlike blotches. 'First I want to make sure there's nothing *else* you want. Nothing else stupid old Annie Wilkes forgot because she doesn't know how a Mister Smart Guy goes about writing a book. I want to make sure you don't want me to go back to town and get you a tape recorder, or maybe a special pair of writing slippers, or something like that. Because if you want me to, I'll go. Your wish is my command. I won't even wait to give you your pills. I'll hop right into Old Bessie again and go. So what do you say, Mister Smart Guy? You all set?'

'I'm all set,' he said. 'Annie, please –'

'And you won't make me mad anymore?'

'No. I won't make you mad anymore.'

'Because when I get mad I'm not really myself.' Her eyes dropped. She was looking down to where his hands were cupped tightly together over the sample boxes of Novril. She looked for a very long time.

'Paul?' she asked softly. 'Paul, why are you holding your hands like that?'

He began to cry. It was guilt he cried from, and he hated that most of all: in addition to everything else that this monstrous woman had done to him, she had made him feel guilty as well. So he cried from guilt . . . but also from simple childish weariness.

He looked up at her, tears flowing down his cheeks, and played the absolute last card in his hand.

'I want my pills,' he said, 'and I want the urinal. I held it all the time you were gone, Annie, but I can't hold it much longer, and I don't want to wet myself again.'

She smiled softly, radiantly, and pushed his tumbled hair off his brow. 'You poor dear. Annie has put you through a lot, hasn't she? Too much! Mean old Annie! I'll get it right away.'

36

He wouldn't have dared put the pills under the rug even if he thought he had time to do so before she came back – the packages were small, but the bulges would still be all too obvious. As he heard her go into the downstairs bathroom, he took them, reached painfully around his body, and stuffed them into the back of his underpants. Sharp cardboard corners poked into the cleft of his buttocks.

She came back with the urinal, an old-fashioned tin device that looked absurdly like a blow-dryer, in one hand. She had two Novril capsules and a glass of water in the other.

Two more of those on top of the ones you took half an hour ago may drop you into a coma and then kill you, he thought, and a second voice answered at once: *Fine with me.*

He took the pills and swallowed them with water.

She held out the urinal. 'Do you need help?'

'I can do it,' he said.

She turned considerately away while he fumbled his penis into the cold tube and urinated. He happened to be looking at her when the hollow splashing sounds commenced, and he saw that she was smiling.

'All done?' she asked a few moments later.

'Yes.' He actually had needed to urinate quite badly – in all the excitement he hadn't had time to think of such things.

She took the urinal away from him and set it carefully on the floor. 'Now let's get you back in bed,' she said. 'You must be exhausted . . . and your legs must be singing grand opera.'

He nodded, although the truth was that he could not feel *anything* – this medication on top of what he'd already given himself was rolling him toward unconsciousness at an alarming rate, and he was beginning to see the room through gauzy layers of gray. He held onto one thought – she was going to lift him into bed, and when she did that she would have to be blind as well as numb not to notice that the back of his underwear happened to be stuffed with little boxes.

She got him over to the side of the bed.

'Just a minute longer, Paul, and you can take a snooze.'

'Annie, could you wait five minutes?' he managed.

She looked at him, gaze narrowing slightly.

'I thought you were in a lot of pain, buster.'

'I am,' he said. 'It hurts . . . too much. My knee, mostly. Where you . . . uh, where you lost your temper. I'm not ready to be picked up. Could I have five minutes to . . . to . . .'

He knew what he wanted to say but it was drifting away from him. Drifting away and into the gray. He looked at her helplessly, knowing he was going to be caught after all.

'To let the medication work?' she asked, and he nodded gratefully.

'Of course. I'll just put a few things away and come right back.'

As soon as she was out of the room he was reaching behind him, bringing out the boxes and stuffing them under the mattress one by one. The layers of gauze kept thickening, moving steadily from gray toward black.

Get them as far under as you can, he thought blindly. Make sure you do that so if she changes the bed she won't pull them out with the ground sheet. Get them as far under as you . . . you . . .

He shoved the last under the mattress, then leaned back and looked up at the ceiling, where the W's danced drunkenly across the plaster.

Africa, he thought.

Now I must rinse, he thought.

Oh, I am in so much trouble here, he thought.

Tracks, he thought. *Did I leave tracks? Did I –*

Paul Sheldon fell unconscious. When he woke up, fourteen hours had gone by and outside it was snowing again.

PART TWO

MISERY

'Writing does not *cause* misery,
it is born of misery.
MONTAIGNE

I

MISERY'S RETURN

By Paul Sheldon

For Annie Wilkes

CHAPTER 1

Although Ian Carmichael would not have moved from Little Dunthorpe for all the jewels in the Queen's treasury, he had to admit to himself that when it rained in Cornwall, it rained harder than anywhere else in England.

There was an old strip of towelling hung from a hook

in the entryway, and after hanging up his dripping coat and removing his boots, he used it to towel his dark-blonde hair dry.

Distantly, from the parlor, he could hear the rippling strains of Chopin, and he paused with the strip of towel still in his left hand, listening.

The moisture running down his cheeks now was not rainwater but tears.

He remembered Geoffrey saying You must not cry in front of her, old man--that is the one thing you must never do!

Geoffrey was right, of course--dear old Geoffrey was rarely wrong--but sometimes when he was alone, the nearness of Misery's escape from the Grim Reaper came forcibly home to him, and it was nearly impossible to hold the tears back. He loved her so much; without her he would die. Without Misery, there would simply be no life left for him, or in him.

Her labor had been long and hard, but no longer and no harder than that of many other young ladies she had seen, the midwife declared. It was only after midnight, an hour after Geoffrey had ridden into the gathering storm to try and fetch the doctor, that the midwife had grown alarmed. That was when the bleeding had started.

"Dear old Geoffrey!" He spoke it aloud this time as

he stepped into the huge and stuporously warm West Country kitchen.

"Did ye speak, young sair?" Mrs. Ramage, the Carmichaels' crotchety but lovable old housekeeper, asked him as she came in from the pantry. As usual, her mobcap was askew and she smelled of the snuff she still firmly believed, after all these years, to be a secret vice.

"Not on purpose, Mrs. Ramage," Ian said.

"By the sound o' ye coat a-drippin' out there in the entry, ye nairly drowned between the sheds and the hoose!"

"Aye, so I nearly did," Ian said, and thought: If Geoffrey had returned with the doctor even ten minutes later, I believe she would have died. This was a thought he tried consciously to discourage--it was both useless and gruesome--but the thought of life without Misery was so terrible that it sometimes crept up on him and surprised him.

Now, breaking into these gloomy meditations, there came the healthy bawl of a child--his son, awake and more than ready for his afternoon meal. Faintly he could hear the sound of Annie Wilkes, Thomas's capable nurse, as she began to soothe him and change his napkin.

"The wee bairn's in good voice today," Mrs. Ramage observed. Ian had one moment to think again, with surpassing wonder, that he was the father of a son, and then his wife spoke from the doorway:

"Hello, darling."

He looked up, looked at his Misery, his darling. She stood lightly poised in the doorway, her chestnut hair with its mysterious deep-red glints like dying embers flowing over her shoulders in gorgeous profusion. Her complexion was still too pallid, but in her cheeks Ian could see the first signs of returning color. Her eyes were dark and deep, and the glow of the kitchen lamps sparkled in each, like small and precious diamonds lying upon darkest jewellers' felt.

"My darling!" he cried, and ran to her, as he had that day in Liverpool, when it seemed certain that the pirates had taken her away as Mad Jack Wickersham had sworn they would.

Mrs. Ramage suddenly remembered something she had left undone in the parlor and left them together--she went, however, with a smile on her face. Mrs. Ramage, too, had her moments when she could not help wondering what life might have been like if Geoffrey and the doctor had arrived an hour later on that dark and stormy night two months ago, or if the experimental blood transfusion in which her young master had so bravely poured his own life's blood into Misery's depleted veins had not worked.

"Och, girrul," she told herself as she hurried down

the hall. "Some things dinna bear thinkin' a'." Good advice--advice Ian had given himself. But both had discovered that good advice was sometimes easier to give than receive.

In the kitchen, Ian hugged Misery tightly to him, feeling his soul live and die and then live again in the sweet smell of her warm skin.

He touched the swell of her breast and felt the strong and steady beat of her heart.

"If you had died, I should have died with you," he whispered.

She put her arms about his neck, bringing the firmness of her breast more fully into his hand. "Hush, my darling," Misery whispered, "and don't be silly. I'm here...right here. Now kiss me! If I die, I fear it will be with desire for you."

He pressed his mouth against hers and plunged his hands deeply into the glory of her chestnut hair, and for a few moments there was nothing at all, except for the two of them.

2

Annie laid the three pages of typescript on the night-table beside him and he waited to see what she would say about them. He was curious but not really nervous – he had been surprised, really, at how easy it had been to slip back into Misery's world. Her world was corny and melodramatic, but that did not change the fact that returning there had been nowhere near as distasteful as he had expected – it had been, in fact, rather comforting, like putting on a pair of old slippers. So his mouth dropped open and he was frankly and honestly flabbergasted when she said:

'It's not right.'

'You – you don't like it?' He could hardly believe it. How could she have liked the other *Misery* novels and not like this? It was so *Misery*-esque it was nearly a caricature, what with motherly old Mrs Ramage dipping snuff in the pantry, Ian and Misery pawing each other like a couple of horny kids just home from the Friday-night high-school dance, and –

Now *she* was the one who looked bewildered.

'Like it? Of course I like it. It's *beautiful.* When Ian swept her into his arms, I cried. I couldn't help it.' Her eyes actually were a bit red. 'And you naming baby Thomas's nurse after me . . . that was very sweet.'

He thought: *Smart, too – at least, I hope so. And by the way, toots, the baby's name started out to be Sean, in case you're interested; I changed it because I decided that was just too fucking many n's to fill in.*

'Then I'm afraid I don't understand –'

'No, you don't. I didn't say anything about not *liking* it, I said it wasn't *right.* It's a cheat. You'll have to change it.'

Had he once thought of her as the perfect audience? Oh boy. *Have to give you credit, Paul – when you make a mistake, you go whole hog.* Constant Reader had just become Merciless Editor.

Without his even being aware that it was happening, Paul's face rearranged itself into the expression of sincere concentration he always wore while listening to editors. He thought of this as his Can I Help You, Lady? expression. That was because most editors were like women who drive into service stations and tell the mechanic to fix whatever it is that's making that knocking sound under the hood or going wonk-wonk inside the dashboard, and please have it done an hour ago. A look of sincere concentration was good because it flattered them, and when editors were flattered, they would sometimes give in on some of their mad ideas.

'How is it a cheat?' he asked.

'Well, Geoffrey rode for the doctor,' she said. *'That's* all right. That happened in Chapter 38 of *Misery's Child.* But the doctor never came, as you well know, because Geoffrey's horse tripped on the top rail of that rotten Mr Cranthorpe's toll-gate when Geoffrey tried to jump it – I hope *that* dirty bird gets his comeuppance in *Misery's Return,* Paul, I really do – and Geoffrey broke his shoulder and some of his ribs and lay there most of the night in the rain until the sheep-herder's boy came along and found him. So the doctor never came. You see?'

'Yes.' He found himself suddenly unable to take his eyes from her face.

He had thought she was putting on an editor's hat – maybe even trying on a collaborator's chapeau, preparing to tell him what to write and how to write it. But that was not so. Mr Cranthorpe, for instance. She *hoped* Mr Cranthorpe would get his comeuppance, but she did not demand it. She saw the story's creative course as something outside of her hands, in spite of her obvious control of *him*. But some things simply could not be done. Creativity or the lack of it had no bearing on these things; to do them was as foolish as issuing a proclamation revoking the law of gravity or trying to play table-tennis with a brick. She really was Constant Reader, but Constant Reader did not mean Constant Sap.

She would not allow him to kill Misery . . . but neither would she allow him to cheat Misery back to life.

But Christ, I DID kill her, he thought wearily. *What am I going to do?*

'When I was a girl,' she said, 'they used to have chapter-plays at the movies. An episode a week. The Masked Avenger, and Flash Gordon, even one about Frank Buck, the man who went to Africa to catch wild animals and who could subdue lions and tigers just by staring at them. Do you remember the chapter-plays?'

'I remember them, but you can't be that old, Annie – you must have seen them on TV, or had an older brother or sister who told you about them.'

At the corners of her mouth dimples appeared briefly in the solidity of flesh and then disappeared. 'Go on with you, you fooler! I *did* have an older brother, though, and we used to go to the movies every Saturday afternoon. This was in Bakersfield, California, where I grew up. And while I always used to enjoy the newsreel and the color cartoons and the feature, what I really looked forward to was the next installment of the chapter-play. I'd find myself thinking about it at odd moments all week long. If a class was boring, or if I had to babysit Mrs Krenmitz's four brats downstairs. I used to hate those little brats.'

Annie lapsed into a moody silence, staring into the corner. She had become unplugged. It was the first time this had happened in some days, and he wondered uneasily if it meant she was slipping into the lower part of her cycle. If so, he had better batten down his hatches.

At last she came out of it, as always with an expression of faint surprise, as if she had not really expected the world to still be here.

'Rocket Man was my favorite. There he would be at the end of Chapter 6, Death in the Sky, unconscious while his plane went into a power dive. Or at the end of Chapter 9, Fiery Doom, he'd be tied to a chair in a burning warehouse. Sometimes it was a car with no brakes, sometimes poison gas, sometimes electricity.'

Annie spoke of these things with an affection which was bizarre in its unmistakable genuineness.

'Cliff-hangers, they called them,' he ventured.

She frowned at him. 'I know that, Mister Smart Guy. Gosh, sometimes I think you must believe I'm awful stupid!'

'I don't, Annie, really.'

She waved a hand at him impatiently, and he understood it would be better – today, at least – not to interrupt her. 'It was fun to try and think how he would get out of it. Sometimes I could, sometimes I couldn't. I didn't really care, as long as they played fair. The people who made the story.'

She looked at him sharply to make sure he was taking the point. Paul thought he could hardly have missed it.

'Like when he was unconscious in the airplane. He woke up, and there was a parachute under his seat. He put it on and jumped out of the plane and that was fair enough.'

Thousands of English-comp teachers would disagree with you, my dear, Paul thought. *What you're talking about is called a* deus ex machina, *the God from the machine, first used in Greek amphitheaters. When the playwright got his hero into an impossible jam, this chair decked with flowers came down from overhead. The hero sat down in it and was drawn up and out of harm's way. Even the stupidest swain could grasp the symbolism – the hero had been saved by God. But the* deus ex machina – *sometimes known in the technical jargon as 'the old parachute-under-the-airplane-seat trick', finally went out of vogue around the year 1700. Except, of course, for such arcana as the Rocket Man serials and the Nancy Drew books. I guess you missed the news, Annie.*

For one gruesome, never-to-be-forgotten moment, Paul thought he was going to have a laughing fit. Given her mood this morning, that would almost surely have resulted in some unpleasant and painful punishment. He raised a hand quickly to his mouth, pasting it over the smile trying to be born there, and manufactured a coughing fit.

She thumped him on the back hard enough to hurt.

'Better?'

'Yes, thanks.'

'Can I go on now, Paul, or were you planning to have a sneezing fit? Should I get the bucket? Do you feel as if you might have to vomit a few times?'

'No, Annie. Please go on. What you're saying is fascinating.'

She looked a little mollified – not much, but a little. 'When he found that parachute under the seat, it was fair. Maybe not all that *realistic,* but fair.'

He thought about this, startled – her occasional sharp insights never failed to startle him – and decided it was true.

Fair and *realistic* might be synonyms in the best of all possible worlds, but if so, this was not that world.

'But you take another episode,' she said, 'and this is *exactly* what's wrong with what you wrote yesterday, Paul, so listen to me.'

'I'm all ears.'

She looked at him sharply to see if he was joking. His face, however, was pale and serious – very much the face of a conscientious student. The urge to laugh had dissipated when he realized that Annie might know everything about the *deus ex machina* except the name.

'All right,' she said. 'This was a no-brakes chapter. The bad guys put Rocket Man – only it was Rocket Man in his secret identity – into a car that didn't have any brakes, and then they welded all the doors shut, and then they started the car rolling down this twisty-turny mountain road. I was on the edge of my seat that day, I can tell you.'

She was sitting on the edge of his bed – Paul was sitting across the room in the wheelchair. It had been five days since his expedition into the bathroom and the parlor, and he had recuperated from that experience faster than he would ever have believed. Just not being caught, it seemed, was a marvelous restorative.

She looked vaguely at the calendar, where the smiling boy rode his sled through an endless February.

'So there was poor old Rocket Man, stuck in that car without his rocket pack or even his special helmet with the one-way eyes, trying to steer and stop the car and open the side door, all at the same time. He was busier than a one-armed paperhanger, I can tell you!'

Yes, Paul could suddenly see it – and in an instinctive way he understood exactly how such a scene, absurdly melodramatic as it might be, could be milked for suspense. The scenery, all of it canted at an alarming downhill angle, rushing by. Cut to the brake-pedal, which sinks bonelessly to the mat when the man's foot (he saw the foot clearly, clad in a 1940s-style airtip shoe) stomps on it. Cut to his shoulder, hitting the door. Cut to the outside reverse, showing us an irregular bead of solder where the door has been sealed shut. Stupid, sure – not a bit literary – but you could do things with it. You could speed up pulses with it. No Chivas Regal here; this was the fictional equivalent of backwoods popskull.

'So then you saw that the road just ended at this cliff,' she said, 'and everyone in the theater knew that if Rocket Man didn't get out of that old Hudson before it got to the cliff, he was a gone goose. Oh boy! And here came the car, with Rocket Man still trying to put on the brakes or bash the door open, and then . . . over it went! It flew out into space, and then it went down. It hit the side of the cliff about halfway down and burst into flames, and then it went into the ocean, and then this ending message came up on the screen that said NEXT WEEK CHAPTER II, THE DRAGON FLIES.'

She sat on the edge of his bed, hands tightly clasped together, her large bosom rising and falling rapidly.

'Well!' she said, not looking at him, only at the wall, 'after that I hardly *saw* the movie. I didn't just think about Rocket Man once in awhile that next week; I thought about him *all* the time. How could he have gotten out of it? I couldn't even guess.

'Next Saturday, I was standing in front of the theater at noon, although the box office didn't open until one-fifteen and the movie didn't start until two. But, Paul . . . what happened . . . well, you'll never guess!'

Paul said nothing, but he could guess. He understood how she could like what he had written and still know it was not right – know it and say it not with an editor's sometimes untrustworthy literary sophistication but with Constant Reader's flat and uncontradictable certainty. He understood, and was amazed to find he was ashamed of himself. She was right. He *had* written a cheat.

'The new episode always started with the ending of the *last* one. They showed him going down the hill, they showed the cliff, they showed him banging on the car door, trying to open it. Then, just before the car got to the edge, the door banged open and out he flew onto the road! The car went over the cliff, and all the kids in the theater were cheering because Rocket Man got out, but I wasn't cheering, Paul. I was mad! I started yelling, "That isn't what happened last week! That isn't what happened last week!"'

Annie jumped up and began to walk rapidly back and forth in the room, her head down, her hair falling in a frizzy cowl about her face, smacking one fist steadily into her other palm, eyes blazing.

'My brother tried to make me stop and when I wouldn't, he tried to put his hand over my mouth to shut me up and I bit it and went on yelling "That isn't what happened last week! Are you all too stupid to remember? Did you all get amnesia?" And my brother said "You're crazy, Annie," but I knew I wasn't. And the manager came and said if I didn't shut up I'd have to leave and I said "You bet I'm going to leave because that was a dirty *cheat,* that wasn't what happened last week!"'

She looked at him and Paul saw clear murder in her eyes.

'He didn't get out of the cockadoodie car! It went over the edge and he was still inside it! Do you understand that?'

'Yes,' Paul said.

'DO YOU UNDERSTAND THAT?'

She suddenly leaped at him with that limber ferocity, and although he felt certain she meant to hurt him as she had before, possibly because she couldn't get at the dirty birdie of a scriptwriter who had cheated Rocket Man out of the Hudson before it went over the cliff, he did not move at all – he could see the seeds of her current instability in the window of past she had just opened for him, but he was also awed by it – the injustice she felt was, in spite of its childishness, completely, inarguably real.

She didn't hit him; she seized the front of the robe he was wearing and dragged him forward until their faces were nearly touching.

'DO YOU?'

'Yes, Annie, yes.'

She stared at him, that furious black gaze, and must have seen the truth in his face, because after a moment she slung him contemptuously back in the chair.

He grimaced against the thick, grinding pain, and after a while it began to subside.

'Then you know what is wrong,' she said.

'I suppose I do.' *Although I'll be goddamned if I know how I'm going to fix it.*

And that other voice returned at once: *I don't know if you'll be damned by God or saved by him, Paulie, but one thing I do know: if you don't find a way to bring Misery back to life – a way she can believe – she's going to kill you.*

'Then do it,' she said curtly, and left the room.

3

Paul looked at the typewriter. The typewriter was there. N's! He had never realized how many n's there were in an average line of type.

I thought you were supposed to be good, the typewriter said – his mind had invested it with a sneering and yet callow voice: the voice of a teen-age gunslinger in a Hollywood western, a kid intent on making a fast reputation here in Deadwood. *You're not so good. Hell, you can't even please one crazy overweight ex-nurse. Maybe you broke your writing bone in that crash, too . . . only that bone isn't healing.*

He leaned back as far as the wheelchair would allow and closed his eyes.

Her rejection of what he had written would be easier to bear if he could blame it on the pain, but the truth was that the pain had finally begun to subside a little.

The stolen pills were safely tucked away between the mattress and the box spring. He had taken none of them – knowing he had them put aside, a form of Annie-insurance, was enough. She would find them if she took it into her head to turn the mattress, he supposed, but that was a chance he was prepared to take.

There had been no trouble between them since the blow up over the typewriter paper. His medication came regularly, and he took it. He wondered if she knew he was hooked on the stuff.

Hey, come on now, Paul, that's a bit of a dramatization, isn't it?

No, it wasn't. Three nights ago, when he was sure she was upstairs, he had sneaked one of the sample boxes out and had read everything on the label, although he supposed he had read everything he needed when he saw what Novril's principal ingredient was. Maybe you spelled *relief* R-O-L-A-I-D-S, but you spelled Novril C-O-D-E-I-N-E.

The fact is, you're healing up, Paul. Below the knees your legs look like a four-year-old's stick-drawing, but you are healing up. You could get by on aspirin or Empirin now. It's not you *that needs the Novril; you're feeding it to the monkey.*

He would have to cut down, have to duck some of the caps. Until he could do that, she would have him on a chain as well as in a wheelchair – a chain of Novril capsules.

Okay. I'll duck one of the two capsules she gives me every other time she brings them. I'll put it under my tongue when I swallow the other one, then stick it under my mattress with the other pills when she takes the drinking glass out. Only not today. I don't feel ready to start today. I'll start tomorrow.

Now in his mind he heard the voice of the Red Queen lecturing Alice: *Down here we got our act clean yesterday, and we plan to start getting our act clean tomorrow, but we never clean up our act today.*

Ho-ho, Paulie, you're a real riot, the typewriter said in the tough gunsel's voice he had made up for it.

'Us dirty birdies are never all that funny, but we never stop trying – you have to give us that,' he muttered.

Well, you better start thinking about all the dope you are taking, Paul. You better start thinking about it very seriously.

He decided suddenly, on the spur of the moment, that he would start dodging some of the medication as soon as he got a first chapter that Annie liked on paper – a chapter which Annie decided wasn't a cheat.

Part of him – the part that listened to even the best, fairest editorial suggestions with ill-grace – protested that the woman was crazy, that there was no way to tell what she might or might not accept; that anything he tried would be only a crapshoot.

But another part – a far more sensible part – disagreed. He would know the real stuff when he found it. The real stuff would make the crap he had given Annie to read last night, the crap it had taken him three days and false starts without number to write, look like a dog turd sitting next to a silver dollar. Hadn't he known it was all wrong? It wasn't like him to labor so painfully, nor to half-fill a wastebasket with random jottings or half-pages which ended with lines like 'Misery turned to him, eyes shining, lips murmuring the magic words Oh you numb shithead THIS ISN'T WORKING AT ALL!!! He had chalked it off to the pain and to being in a situation where he was not just writing for his supper but for his life. Those ideas had been nothing but plausible lies. The fact was, things had gone badly because he was cheating and he had known it himself.

Well, she saw through you, shit-for-brains, the typewriter said in its nasty, insolent voice. *Didn't she? So what are you going to do now?*

He didn't know, but he supposed he would have to do something, and in a hurry. He hadn't cared for her mood this morning. He supposed he should count himself lucky that she hadn't re-broken his legs with a baseball bat or given him a battery-acid manicure or something similar to indicate her displeasure with the way he had begun her book – such critical responses were always possible, given Annie's unique view of the world. If he got out of this alive, he thought he might drop Christopher Hale a note. Hale reviewed books for the *New York Times.* The note would say: 'Whenever my editor called me up and told me you were planning to review one of my books in the daily *Times,* my knees used to knock together – you gave me some good ones, Chris old buddy, but you also torpedoed me more than once, as you well know. Anyway, I just wanted to tell you to go ahead and do your worst – I've discovered a whole new critical mode, my friend. We might call it the Colorado Barbecue and Floor-Bucket school of thought. It makes the stuff you guys do look about as scary as a ride on the Central Park carousel.'

This is all very amusing, Paul, writing critics little billets-doux *in one's head is always good for a giggle, but you really ought to find yourself a pot and get it boiling, don't you think?*

Yes. Yes indeed.

The typewriter sat there, smirking at him.

'I hate you,' Paul said morosely, and looked out the window.

4

The snow-storm to which Paul had awakened the day after his expedition to the bathroom had gone on for two days – there had been at least eighteen inches of new fall, and heavy drifting. By the time the sun finally peered through the clouds again, Annie's Cherokee was nothing but a vague hump in the driveway.

Now, however, the sun was out again and the sky was brilliant once more. That sun had heat as well as brilliance – he could feel it on his face and hands as he sat here. The icicles along the barn were dripping again. He thought briefly of his car in the snow, and then picked up a piece of paper and rolled it into the Royal. He typed the words MISERY'S RETURN in the upper left-hand corner, the number I in the upper right. He banged the carriage-return lever four or five times, centered the carriage, and typed Chapter I. He hit the keys harder than necessary, so she would be sure to hear he was typing *something,* at least.

Now there was all this white space below CHAPTER I, looking like a snowbank into which he could fall and die, smothered in frost.

Africa.

As long as they played fair.

That bird came from Africa.

There was a parachute under his seat.

Africa.

Now I must rinse.

He was drifting off and knew he shouldn't – if she came in here and caught him cooping instead of writing she would be mad – but he let himself drift anyway. He was not just dozing; he was, in an odd way, thinking. Looking. *Searching.*

Searching for what, Paulie?

But that was obvious. The plane was in a power-dive. He was searching for the parachute under the seat. Okay? Fair enough?

Fair enough. When he found the parachute under the seat, it was fair. Maybe not all that realistic, but fair.

For a couple of summers his mother had sent him to day-camp at the Malden Community Center. And they had played this game . . . they sat in a circle, and the game was like Annie's chapter-plays, and he almost always won . . . What was that game called?

He could see fifteen or twenty little boys and girls sitting in a circle in one shady corner of a playground, all of them wearing Malden Community Center tee-shirts, all listening intently as the counselor explained how the game was played. *Can You?, the name of that game was Can You?, and it really was just like the Republic cliff-hangers, the game you played then was Can You?, Paulie, and that's the name of the game now, isn't it?*

Yes, he supposed it was.

In Can You? the counselor would start a story about this guy named Careless Corrigan. Careless was lost in the trackless jungles of South America. Suddenly he looks around and sees there are lions behind him . . . lions on either side of him . . . and by God lions ahead of him. Careless Corrigan is surrounded by lions . . . and they are starting to move in. It's only five in the afternoon, but that is no problem for these kitties; as far as South American lions are concerned, that dinner-at-eight shit is for goofballs.

The counselor had had a stopwatch, and Paul Sheldon's dozing mind saw it with brilliant clarity, although he had last held its honest silver weight in his hand more than thirty years ago. He could see the fine copperplate of the numbers, the smaller needle at the bottom which recorded tenths of seconds, he could see the brand name printed in tiny letters: ANNEX.

The counselor would look around the circle and pick one of the day-campers. 'Daniel,' he would say. 'Can you?' The moment *Can you?* was out of his mouth, the counselor would click the stopwatch into motion.

Daniel then had exactly ten seconds to go on with the story. If he did not begin to speak during those ten seconds, he had to leave the circle. But if he got Careless away from the lions, the counselor would look at the circle again and ask the game's other question, one that recalled his current situation clearly to mind again. This question was *Did he?*

The rules for this part of the game were Annie's exactly. Realism was not necessary; fairness was. Daniel could say, for instance: 'Luckily, Careless had his Winchester with him and plenty of ammo. So he shot three of the lions and the rest ran away.' In a case like that, Daniel *did.* He got the stopwatch and went on with the story, ending his segment with Careless up to his hips in a pool of quicksand or something, and then he would ask someone else if he or she could, and bang down the button on the stopwatch.

But ten seconds wasn't long, and it was easy to get jammed up . . . easy to cheat. The next kid might well say something like 'Just then this great big bird – an Andean vulture, I think – flew down. Careless grabbed its neck and made it pull him out of that quicksand.'

When the counselor asked *Did she?*, you raised your hand if you thought she had, left it down if you thought she had blown it. In the case of the Andean vulture, the kid would almost surely have been invited to leave the circle.

Can you, Paul?

Yeah. That's how I survive. That's how come I'm able to maintain homes in both New York and L.A. and more rolling iron than there is in some used-car lots. Because I can, and it's not something to apologize for, goddammit. There are lots of guys out there who write a better prose line than I do and who have a better understanding of what people are really like and what humanity is supposed to mean – hell, I know that. But when the counselor asks Did he? *about those guys, sometimes only a few people raise their hands. But they raise their hands for me . . . or for* Misery *. . . and in the end I guess they're both the same.* Can *I? Yeah. You bet I can. There's a million things in this world I can't do. Couldn't hit a curve ball, even back in high school. Can't fix a leaky faucet. Can't roller-skate or make an F-chord on the guitar that sounds like anything but shit. I have tried twice to be married and couldn't do it either time. But if you want me to take you away, to scare you or involve you or make you cry or grin, yeah. I can. I can bring it to you and keep bringing it until you holler uncle. I am able. I CAN.*

The typewriter's insolent gunslinger-voice whispered into this deepening dream.

What we got here, friends, is a lot of two things – big talk and white space.

Can You?

Yes. Yes!

Did *he?*

No. He cheated. In Misery's Child *the doctor never came. Maybe the rest of you forgot what happened last week, but the stone idol never forgets. Paul has to leave the circle. Pardon me, please. Now I must rinse. Now I must*

5

'– rinse,' he muttered, and slid over to the right. This dragged his left leg slightly askew, and the bolt of pain in his crushed knee was enough to wake him up. Less than five minutes had gone by. He could hear Annie washing dishes in the kitchen. Usually she sang as she did her chores. Today she was not singing; there was only the rattle of plates and the occasional hiss of rinse-water. Another bad sign. *Here's a special weather bulletin for residents of Sheldon County – a tornado watch is in effect until 5.00 P.M. tonight. I repeat, a tornado watch –*

But it was time to stop playing games and get down to business. She wanted Misery back from the dead, but it had to be fair. Not necessarily realistic, just fair. If he could do it this morning, he could just maybe he could derail the depression he sensed coming on before it could get a real start.

Paul looked out the window, his chin on his palm. He was fully awake now, thinking fast and hard, but not really aware of the process. The top two or three layers of his conscious mind, which dealt with such things as when he had last shampooed, or whether or not Annie would be on time with his next dope allotment, seemed to have departed the scene entirely. That part of his head had quietly gone out to get a pastrami on rye, or something. There was sensory input, but he was not doing anything with it – not seeing what he was seeing, not hearing what he was hearing.

Another part of him was furiously trying out ideas, rejecting them, trying to combine them, rejecting the combinations. He sensed this going on but had no direct contact with it and wanted none. It was dirty down there in the sweatshops.

He understood what he was doing now as TRYING TO HAVE AN IDEA. TRYING TO HAVE AN IDEA wasn't the same thing as GETTING AN IDEA. GETTING AN IDEA was a more humble way of saying *I am inspired,* or *Eureka! My muse has spoken!*

The idea for *Fast Cars* had come to him one day in New York City. He had gone out with no more in mind than buying a VCR for the townhouse on 83rd Street. He had passed a parking lot and had seen an attendant trying to jimmy his way into a car. That was all. He had no idea if what he had seen was licit or illicit, and by the time he had walked another two or three blocks, he no longer cared. The attendant had become Tony Bonasaro. He knew everything about Tony but his name, which he later plucked from a telephone book. Half the story existed, full-blown, in his mind, and the rest was rapidly falling into place. He felt jivey, happy, almost drunk. The muse had arrived, every bit as welcome as an unexpected check in the mail. He had set out to get a video recorder and had gotten something much better instead. He had GOTTEN AN IDEA.

This other process – TRYING TO HAVE AN IDEA – was nowhere near as exalted or exalting, but it was every bit as mysterious . . . and every bit as necessary. Because when you were writing a novel you almost always got roadblocked somewhere, and there was no sense in trying to go on until you'd HAD AN IDEA.

His usual procedure when it was necessary to HAVE AN IDEA was to put on his coat and go for a walk. If he didn't need to HAVE AN IDEA, he took a book when he went for a walk. He recognized walking as good exercise, but it was boring. If you didn't have someone to talk to while you walked, a book was a necessity. But if you needed to HAVE AN IDEA, boredom could be to a roadblocked novel what chemotherapy was to a cancer patient.

Halfway through *Fast Cars,* Tony had killed Lieutenant Gray when the lieutenant tried to slap the cuffs on him in a Times Square movie theater. Paul wanted Tony to get away with the murder – for awhile, anyway – because there could be no third act with Tony sitting in the cooler. Yet Tony could not simply leave Gray sitting in the movie theater with the haft of a knife sticking out of his left armpit, because there were at least three people who knew Gray had gone to meet Tony.

Body disposal was the problem, and Paul didn't know how to solve it. It was a roadblock. It was the game. It was *Careless just killed this guy in a Times Square movie theater and now he's got to get the body back to his car without anyone saying 'Hey mister, is that guy as dead as he looks or did he just pitch a fit or something?' If he gets Gray's corpse back to the car, he can drive it to Queens and dump it in this abandoned building project he knows about. Paulie? Can You?*

There was no ten-second deadline, of course – he'd had no contract for the book, had written it on spec, and hence there was no delivery date to think about. Yet there was always a deadline, a time after which you had to leave the circle, and most writers knew it. If a book remained roadblocked long enough, it began to decay, to fall apart; all the little tricks and illusions started to show.

He had gone for a walk, thinking of nothing on top of his mind, the way he was thinking of nothing on top right now. He had walked three miles before someone sent up a flare from the sweatshops down below: Suppose he starts a fire in the theater?

That looked like it might work. There was no sense of giddiness, no true feeling of inspiration; he felt like a carpenter looking at a piece of lumber that might do the job.

He could set a fire in the stuffing of the seat next to him, how's that? Goddam seats in those theaters are always torn up. And there'd be smoke. Lots of it. He could hold off leaving as long as possible, then drag Gray out with him. He can pass Gray off as a smoke-inhalation victim. What do you think?

He had thought it was okay. Not great, and there were plenty of details still to be worked out, but it looked okay. He'd HAD AN IDEA. The work could proceed.

He'd never needed to HAVE AN IDEA to *start* a book, but he understood instinctively that it could be done.

He sat quietly in the chair, chin on hand, looking out at the barn. If he'd been able to walk, he would have been out there in the field. He sat quietly, almost dozing, waiting for something to happen, really aware of nothing at all except that things were happening down below, that whole edifices of make-believe were being erected, judged, found wanting, and torn down again in the wink of an eye. Ten minutes passed. Fifteen. Now she was running the vacuum cleaner in the parlor (but still not singing). He heard it but did nothing with the hearing of it; it was unconnected sound which ran into his head and then out again like water running through a flume.

Finally the guys down below shot up a flare, as they always eventually did. Poor buggers down there *never* stopped busting their balls, and he didn't envy them one little bit.

Paul sat quietly, beginning to HAVE AN IDEA. His conscious mind returned – THE DOCTOR IS *IN* – and picked the idea up like a letter pushed through the mail-slot in a door. He began to examine it. He almost rejected it (was that a faint groan from down there in the sweatshops?), reconsidered, decided half of it could be saved.

A second flare, this one brighter than the first.

Paul began to drum his fingers restlessly on the windowsill.

Around eleven o'clock he began to type. This went very slowly at first – individual clacks followed by spaces of silence, some as long as fifteen seconds. It was the aural equivalent of an island archipelago seen from the air – a chain of low humps broken by broad swaths of blue.

Little by little the spaces of silence began to shorten, and now there were occasional bursts of typing – it would have sounded fine on Paul's electric typewriter, but the clacking sound of the Royal was thick, actively unpleasant.

But after a while Paul did not notice the Ducky Daddles voice of the typewriter. He was warming up by the bottom of the first page. By the bottom of the second he was in high gear.

After awhile Annie turned off the vacuum cleaner and stood in the doorway, watching him. Paul had no idea she was there – had no idea, in fact, that *he* was. He had finally escaped. He was in Little Dunthorpe's churchyard, breathing damp night air, smelling moss and earth and mist; he heard the clock in the tower of the Presbyterian church strike two and dumped it into the story without missing a beat. When it was very good, he could see through the paper. He could see through it now.

Annie watched him for a long time, her heavy face unsmiling, moveless, but somehow satisfied. After awhile she went away. Her tread was heavy, but Paul didn't hear that, either.

He worked until three o'clock that afternoon, and at eight that night he asked her to help him back into the wheelchair again. He wrote another three hours, although by ten o'clock the pain had begun to be quite bad. Annie came in at eleven. He asked for another fifteen minutes.

'No, Paul, it's enough. You're white as salt.'

She got him into bed and he was asleep in three minutes. He slept the whole night through for the first time since coming out of the gray cloud, and his sleep was for the first time utterly without dreams.

He had been dreaming awake.

6

MISERY'S RETURN

By Paul Sheldon

For Annie Wilkes

CHAPTER 1

For a moment Geoffrey Alliburton was not sure who the old man at the door was, and this was not entirely because the bell had awakened him from a deepening doze. The irritating thing about village life, he thought, was that there weren't enough people for there to be any perfect strangers; instead there were just enough to keep one from knowing immediately who many of the villagers were. Sometimes all one really had to go on was a family resemblance --and such resemblances, of course, never precluded the unlikely but hardly impossible coincidence of bastardy. One could usually handle such moments--no matter how much one might feel one was entering one's dotage while trying to maintain an ordinary conversation with a person whose name one should be able to recall but could not; things only reached the more cosmic realms of embarrassment when <u>two</u> such familiar faces arrived at the same time, and one felt called upon to make introductions.

"I hope I'll not be disturbin' ye, sair," this visitor said. He was twisting a cheap cloth cap restlessly in his hands, and in the light cast by the lamp Geoffrey held up, his face looked lined and yellow and terribly worried--frightened, even. "It's just that I didn't want to go to Dr. Bookings, nor did I want to disturb His Lordship. Not, at least, until I'd spoken to you, if ye take my meaning, sair."

Geoffrey didn't, but quite suddenly he did know one thing--who this late-coming visitor was. The mention of Dr. Bookings, the C of E Minister, had done it. Three days ago Dr. Bookings had performed Misery's few last rites in the churchyard which lay behind the rectory, and this fellow had been there--but lurking considerately in the background, where he was less apt to be noticed.

His name was Colter. He was one of the church sextons. To be brutally frank, the man was a gravedigger.

"Colter," he said. "What can I do for you?"

Colter spoke hesitantly. "It's the noises, sair. The noises in the churchyard. Her Ladyship rests not easy, sair, so she doesn't, and I'm afeard. I--"

Geoffrey felt as if someone had punched him in the midsection. He pulled in a gasp of air and hot pain needled his side, where his ribs had been tightly taped by Dr. Shinebone. Shinebone's gloomy assessment had been that Geoffrey would almost certainly take pneumonia after lying in that ditch all night in the chilly rain, but three days had passed and there had been no onset of fever and coughing. He had known there would not be; God did not let off the guilty so easily. He believed that God would let him live to perpetuate his poor lost darling's memory for a long, long time.

"Are ye all right, sair?" Colter asked. "I heard ye were turrible bunged up t'other night." He paused. "The night herself died."

"I'm fine," Geoffrey said slowly. "Colter, these sounds you say you hear...you know they are just imaginings, don't you?"

Colter looked shocked.

"Imaginings?" he asked. "Sair! Next ye'll be tellin me ye have no belief in Jesus and the life everlastin'! Why, didn't Duncan Fromsley see old man Patterson not two days after his funeral, glowin' just as white as marsh-fire (which was just what it probably was, Geoffrey thought, marsh-fire plus whatever came out of old Fromsley's last bottle)? And ain't half the bleedin' town seen that old Papist monk that walks the battlements of Ridgeheath Manor? They even sent down a coupler ladies from the bleedin'

London Psychic Serciety to look inter that 'un!"

Geoffrey knew the ladies Colter meant; a couple of hysterical beldames probably suffering from the alternate calms and monsoons of midlife, both as dotty as a child's Draw-It-Name-It puzzle.

"Ghosts are just as real as you or me, sair," Colter was saying earnestly. "I don't mind the <u>idea</u> of them--but these noises are fearsome spooky, so they are, and I hardly even like to go near the churchyard--and I have to dig a grave for the little Roydman babe tomorrow, so I do."

Geoffrey said an inward prayer for patience. The urge to bellow at this poor sexton was almost insurmountable. He had been dozing peacefully enough in front of his own fire with a book in his lap when Colter came, waking him up...and he was coming more and more awake all the time, and at every second the dull sorrow settled more deeply over him, the awareness that his darling was gone. She was three days in her grave, soon to be a week...a month...a year...ten years. The sorrow, he thought, was like a rock on the shoreline of the ocean. When one was sleeping it was as if the tide was in, and there was some relief. Sleep was like a tide which covered the rock of grief. When one woke, however, the tide began to go out and soon the rock was visible again, a barnacle-encrusted thing of inarguable reality, a thing which would be there forever, or until God chose to wash it away.

And this fool dared to come here and prate of ghosts!

But the man's face looked so wretched that Geoffrey was able to control himself.

"Miss Misery--Her Ladyship--was much loved," Geoffrey said quietly.

"Aye, sair, so she was," Colter agreed fervently. He switched custody of his cloth cap to his left hand solely, and with his right produced a giant red handkerchief from his pocket. He honked mightily into it, his eyes watering.

"All of us sorrow at her passing." Geoffrey's hands went to his shirt and rubbed the heavy muslin wrappings beneath it restlessly.

"Aye, so we do, sair, so we do." Colter's words were muffled in the handkerchief, but Geoffrey could see his eyes; the man was really, honestly weeping. The last of his own selfish anger dissolved in pity. "She were a good lady, sair! Aye, she were a <u>great</u> lady, and it's a turrible thing the way His Lordship's took on about it--"

"Aye, she was fine," Geoffrey said gently, and found to his dismay that his own tears were now close, like a cloudburst which threatens on a late summer's afternoon.

"And sometimes, Colter, when someone especially fine passes away--someone especially dear to us all--we find it hard to let that someone go. So we may imagine that they have <u>not</u> gone. Do you follow me?"

"Aye, sair!" Colter said eagerly. "But these sounds... sair, if ye heard them!"

Patiently, Geoffrey said: "What sort of sounds do you mean?"

He thought Colter would then speak of sounds which might be no more than the wind in the trees, sounds amplified by his own imagination, of course--or perhaps a badger bumbling its way down to Little Dunthorpe Stream, which lay behind the churchyard. And so he was hardly prepared when Colter whispered in an affrighted voice: "Scratchin' sounds, sair! It sounds as if she were still alive down there and tryin' to work her way back up to the land o' the livin', so it does!"

CHAPTER 2

Fifteen minutes later, alone again, Geoffrey approached the dining-room sideboard. He was reeling from side to side like a man negotiating the foredeck of a ship in a gale. He <u>felt</u> like a man in a gale. He might have believed that the fever Dr. Shinebone had almost gleefully predicted had come on him at last, and with a vengeance, but it wasn't fever which had simultaneously brought wild red roses to his cheeks and turned his forehead to the color of candlewax, not fever which made his hands shake so badly that he almost dropped the decanter of brandy as he brought it out of the sideboard.

If there was a chance--the slightest chance--that the monstrous idea Colter had planted in his mind was true, then he had no business pausing here at all. But he felt that without a drink he might fall swooning to the floor.

Geoffrey Alliburton did something then he had never done before in his whole life; something he never did again. He lifted the decanter directly to his mouth, and drank from the neck.

Then he stepped back, and whispered: "We shall see about this. We shall see about this, by heaven. And if I go on this insane errand only to discover nothing at the end of it but an old gravedigger's imagination after all, I will have goodman Colter's earlobes on my watch chain, no matter how much he loved Misery."

CHAPTER 3

He took the pony-trap, driving under an eerie, not-quite-dark sky where a three-quarters moon ducked restlessly in and out between racing reefs of cloud. He had paused to throw on the first thing in the downstairs hall closet which came to hand--this turned out to be a dark-maroon smoking jacket. The tails blew out behind him as he whipped Mary on. The elderly mare did not like the speed upon which he was insisting; Geoffrey did not like the deepening pain in his shoulder and side...but the pain of neither could be helped.

<u>Scratchin' sounds, sair! It sounds as if she were still alive down there and tryin' to work her way back up to the land o' the livin'!</u>

This by itself would not have put him in a state of near-terror--but he remembered coming to Calthorpe Manor the day after Misery's death. He and Ian had looked at each other, and Ian had tried to smile, although his eyes were gemlike with unshed tears.

"It would somehow be easier," Ian had said, "if she looked...looked more <u>dead</u>. I know how that sounds--"

"Bosh," Geoffrey had said, trying to smile. "The undertaker doubtless exercised all his wit and--"

"Undertaker!" Ian nearly screamed, and for the first time Geoffrey had truly understood that his friend was tottering on the brink of madness. "Undertaker! <u>Ghoul</u>! I've had no undertaker and I will <u>have</u> no undertaker to come in and rouge my darling and paint her like a doll!"

"Ian! My dear fellow! Really, you mustn't--" Geoffrey had made as if to clap Ian on the shoulder and somehow that had turned into an embrace. The two men wept in each other's arms like tired children, while in some other room Misery's child, a boy now almost a day old and still unnamed, awoke and began to cry. Mrs. Ramage, whose own kindly heart was broken, began to sing it a cradle song in a voice cracked and full of tears.

At the time, deeply afraid for Ian's sanity, he had been less concerned with what Ian had said than how he had said it--only now, as he whipped Mary ever faster toward Little Dunthorpe in spite of his own deepening pain, did the words come back, haunting in light of Colter's tale: <u>If she looked more dead. If she looked more dead, old chap.</u>

Nor was that all. Late that afternoon, as the first of the village people had begun wending their way up Calthorpe Hill to pay their respects to the grieving lord, Shinebone had returned. He had looked tired, not very well himself; nor was this surprising in a man who claimed to have shaken hands with Wellington--the Iron Duke himself--when he (Shinebone, not Wellington) had been a boy. Geoffrey thought the Wellington story was probably an exaggeration, but Old Shinny, as he and Ian had called him as boys, had seen Geoffrey through all his childhood illnesses, and Shinny had seemed a very old man to him, even then. Always granting the eye of childhood, which tends to see anyone over the age of twenty-five as elderly, he thought Shinny must be all of seventy-five now.

He was old...he'd had a hectic, terrible last twenty-four hours...and might not an old, tired man have made a mistake?

A terrible, unspeakable mistake?

It was this thought more than any other which had sent him out on this cold and windy night, under a moon which stuttered uncertainly between the clouds.

Could he have made such a mistake? Part of him, a craven, cowardly part which would rather risk losing Misery forever tha look upon the inevitable results of such a mistake, denied it. But when Shinny came in...

Geoffrey had been sitting by Ian, who was remembering in a broken, scarcely coherent way how he and Ian had rescued Misery from the palace dungeons of the mad French viscount Leroux, how they had escaped in a wagonload of hay, and how Misery distracted one of the viscount's guards at a critical moment by slipping one gorgeously unclad leg out of the hay and waving it delicately. Geoffrey had been chiming in his own memories of the adventure, wholly in the grip of his grief by then, and he cursed that grief now, because to him (and to Ian as well, he supposed), Shinny had barely been there.

Hadn't Shinny seemed strangely distant, strangely preoccupied? Was it only weariness, or had it been something else...some suspicion...?

No, surely not, his mind protested uneasily. The pony-trap was flying up Calthorpe Hill. The manor house itself was dark, but--ah, good!--there was still a single light on in Mrs. Ramage's cottage.

"Hup, Mary!" he cried, and cracked the whip, wincing. "Not much further, girl, and you can rest a bit!"

Surely, surely not what you're thinking!!

But Shinny's examination of Geoffrey's broken ribs and sprained shoulder had seemed purely perfunctory, and he had spoken barely a word to Ian, in spite of the man's deep grief and frequent incoherent cries. No--after a visit which now seemed no longer than the most minimal sort of social convention would demand, Shinny had asked quietly: "Is she--?"

"Yes, in the parlor," Ian had managed. "My poor darling lies in the parlor. Kiss her for me, Shinny, a d tell her I'll be with her soon!"

Ian then had burst into tears again, and after muttering some half-heard word of condolence, Shinny had passed into the parlor. It now seemed to Geoffrey that the old sawbones had been in there a rather long time...or perhaps that was only faulty recollection. But when he came out he had looked almost cheerful, and there was nothing faulty about this recollection, Geoffrey felt sure--that expression was too out of place in that room of grief and tears, a room where Mrs. Ramage had already hung the black funerary curtains.

Geoffrey had followed the old doctor out and spoke hesitantly to him in the kitchen. He hoped, he said, that the doctor would prescribe a sleeping powder for Ian, who really did seem quite ill.

Shinny had seemed completely distracted, however. "It's not a bit like Miss Evelyn-Hyde," he said. "I have satisfied myself of <u>that</u>."

And he had returned to his calèche without so much as a response to Geoffrey's question. Geoffrey went back inside, already forgetting the doctor's odd remark, already chalking Shinny's equally odd behavior off to age, weariness, and his own sort of grief. His thoughts had turned to Ian again, and he determined that, with no sleeping powder forthcoming, he would simply have to pour whiskey down Ian's throat until the poor fellow passed out.

Forgetting...dismissing.

Until now.

<u>It's not a bit like Miss Evelyn-Hyde. I have satisfied myself of that.</u>

Of <u>what?</u>

Geoffrey did not know, but he intended to find out, no matter what the cost to his sanity might be--and he recognized that the cost might be high.

CHAPTER 4

Mrs. Ramage was still up when Geoffrey began to hammer on the cottage door, although it was already two hours past her normal bedtime. Since Misery had passed away, Mrs. Ramage found herself putting her bedtime further and further back. If she could not put an end to her restless tossing and turning, she could at least postpone the moment at which she began it.

Although she was the most levelheaded and practical of women, the sudden outburst of knocking startled a little scream from her, and she scalded herself with the hot milk she had been pouring from pot to cup. Lately she seemed always on edge, always on the verge of a scream. It was not grief, this feeling, although she was nearly overwhelmed with grief--this was a strange, thundery feeling that she couldn't ever remember having before. It sometimes seemed to her that thoughts better left unrecognized were circling around her, just beyond the grasp of her weary, bitterly sad mind.

"Who knocks at ten?" she cried at the door. "Whoever it is, I thank ye not for the burn I've given m'self!"

"It's Geoffrey, Mrs. Ramage! Geoffrey Alliburton! Open the door, for God's sake!"

Mrs. Ramage's mouth dropped open and she was halfway to the door before she remembered she was in her nightgown and cap. She had never heard Geoffrey sound so, and would not have believed it if someone had told her of it. If there was a man in all England with a heart stouter than that of her beloved My Lord, then it was Geoffrey--yet his voice trembled like the voice of a woman on the verge of hysterics.

"A minute, Mr. Geoffrey! I'm half-unclad!"

"Devil take it!" Geoffrey cried. "I don't care if you're starkers, Mrs. Ramage! Open this door! Open it in the name of Jesus!"

She stood only a second, then went to the door, unbarred it, and threw it open. Geoffrey's look did more than stun her, and again she heard the dim thunder of black thoughts somewhere back in her head.

Geoffrey stood on the threshold of the housekeeper's cottage in an odd slanting posture, as if his spine had been warped out of shape by long years carrying a peddler's sack. His right hand was pressed between his left arm and left side.

His hair was in a tangle. His dark-brown eyes burned out of his white face. His dress was remarkable for one as careful --dandified, some would have said--about his clothing as Geoffrey Alliburton usually was. He wore an old smoking jacket with the belt askew, an open-throated white shirt, and a pair of rough serge pants that would have looked more at home upon the legs of a itinerant gardener than upon those of the richest man in Little Dunthorpe. On his feet were a pair of threadbare slippers.

Mrs. Ramage, hardly dressed for a court ball herself in her long white nightgown and muskrat's-nightcap with the untied curling ribbons hanging around her face like the fringe on a lampshade, stared at him with mounting concern. He had re-injured the ribs he had broken riding after the doctor three nights ago, that was obvious, but it wasn't just pain that made his eyes blaze from his whitened face like that. It was terror, barely held in check.

"Mr. Geoffrey! What--"

"No questions!" he said hoarsely. "Not yet--not until you answer one question of my own."

"What question?" She was badly frightened now, her left hand clenched into a tight fist just above her munificent bosom.

"Does the name Miss Evelyn-Hyde mean anything to you?"

And suddenly she knew the reason for that terrible thundery feeling that had been inside her ever since Saturday night. Some part of her mind must already have had this gruesome thought and suppressed it, for she needed no explanation at all. Only the name of the unfortunate Miss Charlotte Evelyn-Hyde, late of Storping-on-Firkill, the village just to the west of Little Dunthorpe, was sufficient to bring a scream tearing from her.

"Oh, my saints! Oh, my dear Jesus! Has she been buried alive? Has she been buried alive? Has my darling Misery been buried alive?"

And now, before Geoffrey could even begin to answer, it was tough old Mrs. Ramage's turn to do something she had never done before that night and would never do again: she fainted dead away.

CHAPTER 5

Geoffrey had no time to look for smelling salts. He doubted if such a tough old soldier as Mrs. Ramage kept them around anyway. But beneath her sink he found a rag which smelled faintly of ammonia. He did not just pass this beneath her nose but pressed it briefly against her lower face. The possibility Colter had raised, however faint, was too hideous to merit much in the way of consideration.

She jerked, cried out, and opened her eyes. For a moment she looked at him with dazed, uncomprehending bewilderment. Then she sat up.

"No," she said. "No, Mr. Geoffrey, say ye don't mean it, say it isn't true--"

"I don't know if it's true or not," he said. "But we must satisfy ourselves immediately. Immediately, Mrs. Ramage. I can't do all the digging myself, if there's digging that must be done..." She was staring at him with horrified eyes, her hands pressed so tightly over her mouth that the nails were white. "Can you help me, if help is needed? There's really no one else."

"My Lord," she said numbly. "My Lord Mr. Ian--"

"--must know nothing of this until we know more!" he said. "If God is good, he need never know at all." He would not voice to her the unspoken hope at the back of his mind, a hope which seemed to him almost as monstrous as his fears. If God was very good, he would find out about this night's work...when his wife and only love was restored to him, her return from the dead almost as miraculous as that of Lazarus.

"Oh, this is terrible...terrible!" she said in a faint,

fluttery voice. Holding onto the table, she managed to pull herself to her feet. She stood, swaying, little straggles of hair hanging around her face among the muskrat-tails of her cap.

"Are you well enough?" he asked, more kindly. "If not, then I must try to carry on as best I can by myself."

She drew a deep, shuddering breath and let it out. The side-to-side sway stopped. She turned and walked toward the pantry. "There's a pair of spades in the shed out back," she said. "A pick as well, I think. Throw them in your trap. There's half a bottle of gin out here in the pantry. Been here untouched since Bill died five years ago, on Lammas-night. I'll have a bit and then join you, Mr. Geoffrey."

"You're a brave woman, Mrs. Ramage. Be quick."

"Aye, never fear me," she said, and grasped the bottle of gin with a hand that trembled only slightly. There was no dust on the bottle--not even the pantry was safe from the relentless dust-clout of Mrs. Ramage--but the label reading CLOUGH & POOR BOOZIERS was yellow. "Be quick yourself."

She had always hated spirits and her stomach wanted to sick the gin, with its nasty junipery smell and oily taste, back up. She made it stay down. Tonight she would need it.

CHAPTER 6

Under clouds that still raced east to west, blacker shapes against a black sky, and a moon that was now settling toward the horizon, the pony-trap sped toward the churchyard. It was now Mrs. Ramage who drove, cracking the whip over the bewildered Mary, who would have told them, if horses could talk, that this was all wrong--she was supposed to be dozing in her warm stall come this time of night. The spades and the pick chattered coldly one against the other, and Mrs. Ramage thought they would have given anyone who had seen them a proper fright--they must look like a pair of Mr. Dickens's resurrection men...or perhaps one resurrection man sitting in a pony-trap driven by a ghost. For she was all in white--had not even paused long enough to gather up her robe. Her nightgown fluttered around her stout, vein-puffed ankles, and the tails of her cap streamed wildly out behind her.

Here was the church. She turned Mary up the lane which ran beside it, shivering at the ghostly sound of the wind playing along the eaves. She had a moment to wonder why such a holy place as a church should seem so frightening after dark, and then realized it was not the church...it was the errand.

Her first thought upon coming out of her faint was

that My Lord must help them--hadn't he been there in all things, through thick and thin, never wavering? A moment later she had realized how mad the idea was. This was not a matter of My Lord's courage, but of his very sanity.

She hadn't needed Mr. Geoffrey to tell her so; the memory of Miss Evelyn-Hyde had done that.

She realized that neither Mr. Geoffrey nor My Lord had been in Little Dunthorpe when it had happened. This had been almost half a year ago, in the spring. Misery had entered the rosy summer of her pregnancy, morning sickness behind her, the final rising of her belly and its attendant discomfort still ahead, and she had cheerfully sent the two men off for a week of grouse-shooting and card-playing and footballing and heaven alone knew what other masculine foolishness at Oak Hall in Doncaster. My Lord had been a bit doubtful, but Misery assured him she would be fine, and nearly pushed him out the door. That Misery would be fine Mrs. Ramage had no doubt. But whenever My Lord and Mr. Geoffrey left for Doncaster, she wondered if one of them--or perhaps both--might not return on the back of a cart, toes up.

Oak Hall was the inheritance of Albert Fossington, a schoolmate of Geoffrey's and Ian's. Mrs. Ramage quite rightly believed that Bertie Fossington was mad. Some three years ago he had eaten his favorite polo pony after it had broken two legs and needed to be destroyed. It was a gesture of affection, he said. "Learned it from the fuzzy-wuzzies in Capetown," he said. "Griquas. Wonderful chaps. Put sticks and things in their smoochers, what? Some of 'em look like they could carry all twelve volumes of the Royal Navigation Charts on their lower lips, ha-ha! Taught me that each man must eat the thing he loves. Rather poetic in a grisly sort of way, what?"

In spite of such bizarre behavior, Mr. Geoffrey and My Lord retained a great affection for Bertie (I wonder if that means they'll have to eat him when he's dead? Mrs. Ramage had once wondered after a visit from Bertie during which he had tried to play croquet with one of the housecats, quite shattering its poor little head), and they had spent nearly ten days at Oak Hall this past spring.

Not more than a day or two after they left, Miss Charlotte Evelyn-Hyde of Storping-on-Firkill had been found dead on the back lawn of her home, Cove o' Birches. There had been a freshly picked bunch of flowers near one outstretched hand. The village doctor was a man named Billford--a capable man by all accounts. Nevertheless, he had called old Dr. Shinebone in to consult. Billford had diagnosed the fatal malady as a heart attack, although the girl was very young--only eighteen --and had seemed in the pink of health. Billford was puzzled.

Something seemed not at all right. Old Shinny had been clearly puzzled as well, but in the end he had concurred with the diagnosis. So did most of the village, for that matter--the girl's heart had not been properly made, that was all, such things were rare but everyone could recall such a sad case at one time or another. It was probably this universal concurrence that had saved Billford's practice--if not his head--following the ghastly _denouement_. Although everyone had agreed that the girl's death was puzzling, it had crossed no one's mind that she might not be dead at all.

Four days following the interment, an elderly woman named Mrs. Soames--Mrs. Ramage knew her slightly--had observed something white lying on the ground of the Congregational church's cemetery as she entered it to put flowers on the grave of her husband, who had died the previous winter. It was much too big to be a flower petal, and she thought it might be a dead bird of some sort. As she approached she became more and more sure that the white object was not just lyi g _on_ the ground, but protruding _from_ it. She came two or three hesitant steps closer yet, and observed a hand reaching from the earth of a fresh grave, the fingers frozen in a hideous gesture of supplication. Blood-streaked bones protruded from the ends of all the digits save the thumb.

Mrs. Soames ran shrieking from the cemetery, ran all

the way into Storping's high street--a run of nearly a mile and a quarter--and reported her news to the barber, who was also the local constable. Then she had collapsed in a dead faint. She took to her bed later that afternoon and did not arise from it for nearly a month. Nor did anyone in the village blame her in the least.

The body of the unfortunate Miss Evelyn-Hyde had been exhumed, of course, and as Geoffrey Alliburton drew Mary to a halt in front of the gate leading into Little Dunthorpe's C of E churchyard, Mrs. Ramage found herself wishing fervently that she had not listened to the tales of the exhumation. They had been dreadful.

Dr. Billford, shaken to within an inch of sanity himself, diagnosed catalepsy. The poor woman had apparently fallen into some sort of deathlike trance, much like the sort those Indian fakirs could voluntarily induce in themselves before allowing themselves to be buried alive or to have needles passed through their flesh. She had remained in this trance for perhaps forty-eight hours, perhaps sixty. Long enough, at any rate, to have awakened not to find herself on her back lawn where she had been picki g flowers, but buried alive in her own coffin.

She had fought grimly for her life, that girl, and Mrs. Ramage found now, following Geoffrey through the gates and into a thin mist that turned the leaning grave markers into islands, that what should have redeemed with nobility only made it seem all the more horrid.

The girl had been engaged to be married. In her left hand--not the one frozen above the soil like the hand of a drowned woman--had been her diamond engagement ring. With it she had slit the satin lining of her coffin and over God knew how many hours she had used it to claw away at the coffin's wooden lid. In the end, air running out, she had apparently used the ring with her left hand to cut and excavate and her right hand to dig. It had not been quite enough. Her complexion had been a deep purple from which her blood-rimmed eyes stared in a bulging expression of terminal horror.

The clock in the church tower began to chime the hour of twelve--the hour when, her mother had told her, the door between life and death sways open a bit and the dead may pass both ways--and it was all Mrs. Ramage could do to keep herself from shrieking and fleeing in a panic which would not abate but grow stronger with each step; if she began running, she knew, she would simply run until she fell down insensible.

Stupid, fearful woman! she berated herself, and then amended that to: *Stupid, fearful*, selfish *woman! It's My Lord ye want to be thinkin' of now, and not yer own fears!*

My Lord...and if there is even one chance that My Lady--

Ah, but no--it was madness to even think of such a thing. It had been too long, too long, too long.

Geoffrey had led her to Misery's tombstone, and the two of them stood looking down at it, as if mesmerized. LADY CALTHORPE, the stone read. Other than the dates of her birth and death, the only inscription was: LOVED BY MANY.

She looked at Geoffrey and said, like one awakening from a deep daze: "Ye've not brought the tools."

"No--not yet," he responded, and threw himself full-length on the ground and placed his ear against the earth, which had already begun to show the first tender shoots of new grass between the rather carelessly replaced sods.

For a moment the only expression she saw there by the lamp she carried was the one Geoffrey had worn since she had first opened her door to him--a look of agonized dread. Then a new expression began to surface. This new expression was one of utter horror mingled with an almost demented hope.

He looked up at Mrs. Ramage, eyes staring, mouth working. "I believe she lives," he whispered strengthlessly. "Oh, Mrs. Ramage--"

Suddenly he turned over onto his belly and screamed at the ground--under other circumstances it would have been comic. "Misery! MISERY! WE'RE HERE! WE KNOW! HOLD ON! HOLD ON, MY DARLING!"

He was on his feet a moment later, sprinting back toward the pony-trap, where the digging tools were, his slippered feet sending the placid groundmist into excited little roils.

Mrs. Ramage's knees unlocked and she buckled forward, near to swooning again. Of its own accord, seemingly, her head slipped to one side so her right ear was pressed against the ground--she had seen children in similar postures by the railway line, listening for trains.

And she heard it--low, painful scraping sounds in the earth--not the sounds of a burrowing animal, these; these were the sounds of fingers scraping helplessly on wood.

She drew in breath in one great convulsive gulp, re-starting her own heart, it seemed. She shrieked: "WE'RE COMING, MY LADY! PRAISE GOD AND PLEAD SWEET JESUS WE BE IN TIME--WE'RE COMING!"

She began to pull half-healed turves out of the ground with her trembling fingers, and although Geoffrey returned in almost no time, she had by then already clawed a hole some eight inches deep.

7

He was already nine pages into Chapter 7 – Geoffrey and Mrs Ramage had managed to get Misery out of her grave in the barest nick of time only to realize that the woman had no idea at all who they were, or who she herself was – when Annie came into the room. This time Paul heard her. He stopped typing, sorry to be out of the dream.

She held the first six chapters at the side of her skirt. It had taken her less than twenty minutes to read his first stab at it; it had been an hour since she had taken this sheaf of twenty-one pages. He looked at her steadily, observing with faint interest that Annie Wilkes was a bit pale.

'Well?' he asked. 'Is it fair?'

'Yes,' she said absently, as if this was a foregone conclusion – and Paul supposed it was. 'It's fair. And it's *good.* Exciting. But it's gruesome, too! It's not like *any* of the other *Misery* books. That poor woman who scraped the ends of her fingers off –' She shook her head and repeated: 'It's not like any of the other *Misery* books.'

The man who wrote these pages was in a rather gruesome frame of mind, my dear, Paul thought.

'Shall I go on?' he asked.

'I'll kill you if you don't!' she responded, smiling a little. Paul didn't smile back. This comment, which would once have struck him as in a league with such banalities as *You look so good I could just eat you up* now seemed not banal at all.

Yet something in her attitude as she stood in the doorway fascinated him. It was as if she was a little frightened to come any closer – as if she thought something in him might burn her. It wasn't the subject of premature burial that had done it, and he was wise enough to know it. No – it was the difference between his first try and this one. That first one had had all the life of an eighth-grader's 'How I Spent My Summer Vacation' theme. This one was different. The furnace was on. Oh, not that he had written particularly well – the story was hot, but the characters as stereotyped and predictable as ever – but this time he had been able to at least generate some power; this time there was heat baking out from between the lines.

Amused, he thought: *She felt the heat. I think she's afraid to get too close in case I might burn her.*

'Well,' he said mildly, 'you won't have to kill me, Annie. I want to go on. So why don't I get at it?'

'All right,' she said. She brought the pages to him, put them on the board, and then stepped back quickly.

'Would you like to read it as I go along?' he asked.

Annie smiled. 'Yes! It would be almost like the chapter-plays, when I was a kid!'

'Well, I can't promise a cliff-hanger at the end of *every* chapter,' he said. 'It just doesn't work that way.'

'It will for me,' she said fervently. 'I'd want to know what was going to happen in Chapter 18 even if 17 ended with Misery and Ian and Geoffrey sitting in armchairs on the porch, reading newspapers. I'm already wild to know what's going to happen next – don't tell me!' she added sharply, as if Paul had offered to do this.

'Well, I generally don't show my work until it's all done,' he said, and then smiled at her. 'But since this is a special situation, I'll be happy to let you read it chapter by chapter.' *And so began the thousand and one nights of Paul Sheldon,* he thought. 'But I wonder if you'd do something for me?'

'What?'

'Fill in these damned n's,' he said.

She smiled at him radiantly. 'It would be an honor. I'll leave you alone now.'

She went back to the door, hesitated there, and turned back. Then, with a deep and almost painful timidity, she offered the only editorial suggestion she ever made to him. 'Maybe it was a bee.'

He had already dropped his gaze to the sheet of paper in the typewriter; he was looking for the hole. He wanted to get Misery back to Mrs Ramage's cottage before he knocked off, and he looked back up at Annie with carefully disguised impatience. 'I beg pardon?'

'A bee,' she said, and he saw a blush creeping up her neck and over her cheeks. Soon even her ears were glowing 'One person in every dozen is allergic to bee-venom. I saw lots of cases of it before . . . before I retired from service as an R.N. The allergy can show in lots of different ways. Sometimes a sting can cause a comatose condition which is . . . is similar to what people used to call . . . uh . . . catalepsy.'

Now she was so red she was almost purple.

Paul held the idea up briefly in his mind and then tossed it on the scrap-heap. A bee could have been the cause of Miss Evelyn-Hyde's unfortunate live burial; it even made sense, since it had happened in mid-spring; in the garden, to boot. But he had already decided that credibility depended on the two live burials' being related somehow, and Misery had succumbed in her bedroom. The fact that late fall was hardly bee-season was not really the problem. The problem was the rarity of the cataleptic reaction. He thought Constant Reader would not swallow two unrelated women in neighboring townships being buried alive six months apart as a result of bee-stings.

Yet he could not tell Annie that, and not just because it might rile her up. He could not tell her because it would hurt her badly, and in spite of all the pain she had afforded him, he found he could not hurt her in that way. He had been hurt that way himself.

He fell back on that most common writers'-workshop euphemism: 'It's got possibilities, all right. I'll drop it into the hopper, Annie, but I've already got some ideas in mind. It may not fit.'

'Oh, I know that – you're the writer, not me. Just forget I said anything. I'm sorry.'

'Don't be s –'

But she was gone, her heavy tread almost running down the hallway to the parlor. He was looking at an empty space. His eyes dropped – then widened.

On either side of the doorway, about eight inches up from the floor, was a black mark – they had been left, he understood at once, by the hubs of the wheelchair when he forced it through. So far she hadn't noticed them. It had been almost a week, and her failure to notice was a small miracle. But soon – tomorrow, perhaps even this afternoon – she would be in to vacuum, and then she would.

She would.

Paul managed very little during the rest of the day.

The hole in the paper had disappeared.

8

The following morning Paul was sitting up in bed, propped on a pile of pillows, drinking a cup of coffee, and eyeing those marks on the sides of the door with the guilty eye of a murderer who has just seen some bloody item of clothing of which he somehow neglected to dispose. Suddenly Annie came rushing into the room, her eyes wide and bulging. She held a dustcloth in one hand. In the other, incredibly, she held a pair of handcuffs.

'What –'

It was all he had time for. She seized him with panicky strength and pulled him into an upright sitting position. Pain – the worst in days – bellowed through his legs, and he screamed. The coffee cup flew out of his hand and shattered on the floor. *Things keep breaking in here, he thought, and then: She saw the marks. Of course. Probably a long time ago.* That was the only way he could account for this bizarre behavior – she had seen the marks after all, and this was the beginning of some new and spectacular punishment.

'Shut up, stupid,' she hissed, and then his hands were pinned behind him, and just as he heard the click of the handcuffs, he also heard a car turning into the driveway.

He opened his mouth, meaning to speak or perhaps scream again, and she stuffed the rag into it before he could do either. There was some ghastly dead taste on the rag. Pledge, he supposed, or Endust, or something like that.

'Make no sound,' she said, leaning over him with one hand on either side of his head, strands of her hair tickling his cheeks and forehead. 'I warn you, Paul. If whoever that is hears something – or even if I hear something and *think* he might have heard something – I will kill him, or them, then you, then myself.'

She stood up. Her eyes were bulging. There was sweat on her face and dried egg-yolk on her lips.

'Remember, Paul.'

He was nodding but she didn't see. She was already running out.

An old but well-preserved Chevy Bel Air had pulled up behind Annie's Cherokee. Paul heard a door open somewhere off the parlor and then bang shut. It gave off the oddly interrogative squeak that told him it was the closet where she kept her outdoors stuff.

The man getting out of the car was as old and well preserved as the car itself – a Colorado Type if ever Paul had seen one. He looked sixty-five but might be eighty; he might be the senior partner of a law firm or the semi-retired patriarch of a construction company, but was more likely a rancher or a realtor. He would be a Republican of the sort who would no more put a bumper sticker on his car than he would put a pair of pointy-toed Italian shoes on his feet; he must also be some sort of town official, and here on town business, because it was only on town business that a man like this and a reclusive woman like Annie Wilkes would have occasion to meet.

Paul watched her hasten down the walk to the driveway, intent not on meeting but intercepting him. Here was something much like his earlier fantasy come true. Not a cop but someone IN AUTHORITY. AUTHORITY had arrived at Annie's, and its arrival here could do nothing but shorten his own life.

Why not invite him in, Annie? he thought, trying not to choke on the dusty rag. *Why not invite him in and show him your African bird?*

Oh, no. She would no more invite Mr Rocky Mountain Businessman in than she would drive Paul to Stapleton International and put a first-class ticket back to New York in his hand.

She was talking even before she reached him, the breath pluming out of her mouth in shapes like cartoon balloons with no words written inside them. He held out a hand dressed in a narrowly elegant black leather glove. She looked at it briefly, contemptuously, then began to shake a finger in his face, more of those empty white balloons puffing from her mouth. She finished struggling into her coat and stopped shaking her finger long enough to rake the zipper up.

He reached into the pocket of his topcoat and brought out a sheet of paper. He held it out to her almost apologetically. Although Paul had no way of knowing exactly what it was, he was sure that Annie had an adjective for it. *Cockadoodie,* maybe.

She led him along the driveway, still talking. They passed beyond his sightline. He could see their shadows lying like construction-paper cutouts on the snow, but that was all. She had done it on purpose, he realized dully. If he, Paul, couldn't see them, then there was no chance that Mr Rancho Grande might look in through the guest-room window and see *him.*

The shadows remained on the melting snowpack of Annie's driveway for about five minutes. Once Paul actually heard Annie's voice, raised in an angry, hectoring shout.

Those were a long five minutes for Paul. His shoulders ached. He found he couldn't move to ease the ache. After cuffing his hands together, she had somehow bound them to the bedstead.

But the dustcloth in his mouth was the worst. The stink of the furniture polish was making his head ache, and he was growing steadily more nauseated. He concentrated grimly on controlling it; he had no interest in choking to death, his windpipe full of vomit, while Annie argued with an elderly town official who got his hair trimmed once a week at the local tonsorial emporium and probably wore rubbers over his black oxfords all winter long.

Cold sick-sweat had broken on his forehead by the time they reappeared. Now Annie was holding the paper. She followed Mr Rancho Grande, shaking her finger at his back, those empty cartoon balloons issuing from her mouth. Mr Rancho Grande would not look around at her. His face was carefully blank. Only his lips, pressed together so tightly that they almost disappeared, gave away some inward emotion. Anger? Perhaps. Distaste? Yes. That was probably closer.

You think she's crazy. You and all your poker cronies – who probably control this whole minor-league ballpark of a town – probably played a hand of Lowball or something to see who got this shit detail. No one likes to bring bad news to crazy people. But oh, Mr Rancho Grande! If you knew just how crazy she really is, I don't think you'd turn your back on her like that!

He got into the Bel Air. He closed the door. Now she stood beside the car, shaking her finger at his closed window, and again Paul could dimly hear her voice: '– think you are so-so-so *smaa-aart!*'

The Bel Air began to back slowly down the driveway. Mr Rancho Grande was ostentatiously not looking at Annie, whose teeth were bared.

Louder still: *'You think you are such a great big wheel!'*

Suddenly she kicked the front bumper of Mr Rancho Grande's car, kicked it hard enough to knock packed chunks of snow out of the wheel-wells. The old guy had been looking over his right shoulder, guiding the car down the driveway.

Now he looked back at her, startled out of the careful neutrality he had maintained all through his visit.

'Well I'll tell you something, you dirty bird! *LITTLE DOGS GO TO THE BATHROOM ALL OVER BIG WHEELS!* What do you think of that? Hah?'

Whatever he thought of it, Mr Rancho Grande was not going to give Annie the satisfaction of seeing it – that neutral expression dropped over his face again like the visor on a suit of armor. He backed out of Paul's sight.

She stood there for a moment, hands fisted on hips, then stalked back toward the house. He heard the kitchen door open and explode shut.

Well, he's gone, Paul thought. *Mr Rancho Grande is gone but I'm here. Oh yes, I'm here.*

9

But this time she didn't take her anger out on him.

She came into his room, her coat still on but now unzipped. She began to pace rapidly back and forth, not even looking his way. The piece of paper was still in her hand, and every now and then she would shake it in front of her own nose as if in self-chastisement.

'Ten-percent tax increase, he says! In arrears, he says! Liens! Lawyers! Quarterly payment, he says! Overdue! *Cockadoodie! Kaka! Kaka-poopie-*

DOOPIE!'

He grunted into the rag, but she didn't look around. She was in a room by herself. She walked back and forth faster, cutting the air with her solid body. He kept thinking she would tear the paper to shreds, but it seemed she did not quite dare do this.

'Five hundred and six dollars!' she cried, this time brandishing the paper in front of his nose. She absently tore the rag that was choking him out of his mouth and threw it on the floor. He hung his head over to one side, dry-heaving. His arms felt as if they were slowly detaching themselves from their sockets. 'Five hundred and six dollars and *seventeen cents!* They *know* I don't want anyone out here! I told them, didn't I? And look! *Look!'*

He dry-heaved again, making a desperate burping sound.

'If you vomit I guess you'll just have to lie in it. Looks like I've got other fish to fry. He said something about a lien on my house. What's that?'

'Handcuffs . . .' he croaked.

'Yes, yes,' she said impatiently. 'Sometimes you're such a *baby.'* She pulled the key from her skirt pocket and pushed him even farther to the left, so that his nose pressed the sheets. He screamed, but she ignored him. There was a click, a rattle, and then his hands were free. He sat up, gasping, then slid slowly down against his pillows, mindful to push his legs straight ahead as he did. There were pale furrows in his thin wrists. As he watched they began to fill in red.

Annie stuffed the cuffs absently into her skirt pocket, as if police restraints were found in most decent houses, like Kleenex or coathangers.

'What's a lien?' she asked again. 'Does that mean they own my house? Is that what it means?'

'No,' he said. 'It means that you . . .' He cleared his throat and got another after-taste of that fumey dust-rag. His chest hitched as he dry-heaved again. She took no notice of that; simply stood impatiently staring at him until he could talk. After awhile he could. 'Just means you can't sell it.'

'Just? *Just?* You got a funny idea of just, Mr Paul Sheldon. But I suppose the troubles of a poor widow like me don't seem very important to a rich Mister Smart Guy like you.'

'On the contrary. I think of your troubles as my troubles, Annie. I just meant that a lien isn't much compared to what they *could* do if you got seriously in arrears. *Are* you?'

'Arrears. That means in the bucket, doesn't it?'

'In the bucket, in the hole, behind. Yes.'

'I'm no shanty-Irish moocher!' He saw the thin sheen of her teeth as her upper lip lifted. 'I pay my bills. I just . . . this time I just . . .'

You forgot, didn't you? You forgot, just the way you keep forgetting to change February on that damned calendar. Forgetting to make the quarterly property-tax payment is a hell of a lot more serious than forgetting to change the calendar page, and you're upset because this is the first time you forgot something that big. Fact is, you're getting worse, Annie, aren't you? A little worse every day. Psychotics can cope in the world – after a fashion – and sometimes, as I think you well know, they get away with some very nasty shit. But there's a borderline between lhe lands of manageable and unmanageable psychosis. You're getting closer to that line every day . . . and part of you knows it.

'I just hadn't got around to it yet,' Annie said sullenly. 'Having you here has kept me busier than a one-armed paperhanger.'

An idea occurred to him – a really fine one. The potential for brownie-points in this idea seemed almost unlimited. 'I know,' he said with quiet sincerity. 'I owe you my life and I haven't been anything but a pain in the tail to you. I've got about four hundred bucks in my wallet. I want you to pay your arrears with it.'

'Oh, Paul –' She was looking at him, both confused and pleased. 'I couldn't take your money –'

'It's not mine,' he said. He grinned at her, his number-one *Who loves ya, baby?* grin. And inside he thought: *What I want, Annie, is for you to do one of your forgetting acts when I've got access to one of your knives and I'm sure I can move well enough to use it. You'll be frying in hell ten seconds before you know you're dead.* 'It's yours. Call it a down-payment, if you want.' He paused, then took a calculated risk: 'If you don't think I know I'd be dead if it wasn't for you, you're crazy.'

'Paul . . . I don't know . . .'

'I'm serious.' He allowed his smile to melt into an expression of winning (or so he hoped – *please, God, let it be winning*) sincerity. 'You did more than save my life, you know. You saved two lives – because without you, Misery would still be lying in her grave.'

Now she was looking at him shiningly, the paper in her hand forgotten.

'And you showed me the error of my ways, got me back on track again. I owe you a lot more than four hundred bucks just for that. And if you don't take that money, you're going to make me feel bad.'

'Well, I . . . all right. I . . . thank you.'

'I should be thanking you. May I see that paper?'

She gave it to him with no protest at all. It was an overdue tax notice. The lien was little more than a formality. He scanned it quickly, then handed it back.

'Have you got money in the bank?'

Her eyes shifted away from his. 'I've got a little put aside, but not in the bank. I don't believe in banks.'

'This says they can't execute the lien on you unless the bill remains unpaid by March 25th. What's today?'

She frowned at the calendar. 'Goodness! That's wrong.'

She untacked it, and the boy on his sled disappeared – Paul watched this happen with an absurd pang of regret. March showed a white-water stream rushing pell-mell between snowy banks.

She peered myopically at the calendar for a moment and then said: '*Today is* March 25th.'

Christ, so late, so late, he thought.

'Sure – that's why he came out.' *He wasn't telling you they* had *slapped a lien on your house, Annie – he was telling you they would have to if you didn't cough up by the time the town offices closed tonight. Guy was actually trying to do you a favor.* 'But if you pay this five hundred and six dollars before –'

'And seventeen cents,' she put in fiercely. 'Don't forget the cockadoodie seventeen cents.'

'All right, and seventeen cents. If you pay it before they close the town offices this afternoon, no lien. If people in town really feel about you the way you say they do, Annie –'

'They hate me! They are all against me, Paul!'

'– then your taxes are one of the ways they'll try to pry you out. Hollering "lien" at someone who has missed one quarterly property-tax payment is pretty weird. It smells. Well – it stinks. If you missed a couple of quarterly payments, they might try to take your home – sell it at auction. It's a crazy idea, but I guess they'd technically be within their rights.'

She laughed, a harsh, barking sound. 'Let them try! I'd guthole a few of them! I'll tell you that much. Yes, sir! Yessiree *Bob!*'

'In the end they'd guthole you,' he said quietly. 'But that isn't the point.'

'Then what *is?*'

'Annie, there are probably people in Sidewinder who are two and three *years* behind on their taxes. No one is taking *their* homes or auctioning *their* furnishings down at the town hall. The worst that happens to people like that most of the time is that they lose their town water. The Roydmans, now.' He looked at her shrewdly. 'You think *they* pay their taxes on time?'

'*That* white trash?' she nearly shrieked. '*Hah!*'

'I think they are on the prod for you, Annie.' He did in fact believe this.

'I'll never go! I'll stay up here just to spite them! I'll stay up here and spit in their eye!'

'Can you come up with a hundred and six bucks to go with the four hundred in my wallet?'

'Yes.' She was beginning to look cautiously relieved.

'Good enough,' he said. 'Then I suggest you pay their crappy tax-bill today.' *And while you're gone, I'll see what I can do about those damned marks on the door. And when that's done, I believe I'll see if I can do anything about getting the fuck out of here, Annie. I'm a little tired of your hospitality.*

He managed a smile.

'I think there must be at least seventeen cents there in the night-table,' he said.

10

Annie Wilkes had her own interior set of rules; in her way she was strangely prim. She had made him drink water from a floor-bucket; had withheld his medication until he was in agony; had made him burn the only copy of his new novel; had handcuffed him and stuck a rag reeking of furniture polish in his mouth; but she would not take the money from his wallet. She brought it to him, the old scuffed Lord Buston he'd had since college, and put it in his hands.

All the ID had vanished. At *that* she had not scrupled. He did not ask her about it. It seemed wiser not to.

The ID was gone but the money was still there, the bills – mostly fifties – crisp and fresh. With a clarity that was both surprising and somehow ominous he saw himself pulling the Camaro up to the drive-in window of the Boulder Bank the day before he had finished *Fast Cars* and dropping his check for four hundred and fifty dollars, made out to cash and endorsed on the back, into the tray (perhaps even then the guys in the sweatshops had been talking vacation? – he thought it likely). The man who had done that had been free and healthy and feeling good, and had been without the wit to appreciate any of those fine things. The man who had done that had eyed the drive-up teller with a lively, interested eye – tall, blonde, wearing a purple dress that had cupped her curves with a lover's touch. And she had eyed him back . . . What would she think, he wondered, of that man as he looked now, forty pounds lighter and ten years older, his legs a pair of crooked useless horrors?

'Paul?'

He looked up at her, holding the money in one hand. There was four hundred and twenty, in all.

'Yes?'

She was looking at him with that disconcerting expression of maternal love and tenderness – disconcerting because of the total solid blackness underlying it.

'Are you crying, Paul?'

He brushed his cheek with his free hand and, yes, there was moisture there. He smiled and handed her the money. 'A little. I was thinking how good you've been to me. Oh, I suppose a lot of people wouldn't understand . . . but I think I know.'

Her own eyes glistened as she leaned forward and gently touched his lips. He smelled something on her breath, something from the dark and sour chambers inside her, something that smelled like dead fish. It was a thousand times worse than the taste/smell of the dust-rag. It brought back the memory of her sour breath

(!breathe goddammit BREATHE!)

blowing down his throat like a dirty wind from hell. His stomach clenched, but he smiled at her.

'I love you, dear,' she said.

'Would you put me in my chair before you go? I want to write.'

'Of course.' She hugged him. 'Of course, my dear.'

11

Her tenderness did not extend to leaving the bedroom door unlocked, but this presented no problem. He was not half-mad with pain and withdrawal symptoms this time. He had collected four of her bobby-pins as assiduously as a squirrel collects nuts for the winter, and had secreted them under his mattress along with the pills.

When he was sure she was really gone and not hanging around to see if he was going to 'get up to didoes' (another Wilkesism for his growing lexicon), he rolled the wheelchair over to the bed and got the pins, along with the pitcher of water and the box of Kleenex from the night-table. Rolling the wheelchair with the Royal perched on the board in front of him was not very difficult – his arms had gotten a lot stronger. Annie Wilkes might be surprised to know just how strong they were now – and he sincerely hoped that someday soon she would be.

The Royal typewriter made a shitty writing machine, but as an exercise tool it was great. He had begun lifting it and setting it down whenever he was penned in the chair behind it and she was out of the room. Five lifts of six inches or so had been the best he could manage at first. Now he could do eighteen or twenty without a pause. Not bad when you considered the bastard weighed at least fifty pounds.

He worked on the lock with one of the bobby-pins, holding two spares in his mouth like a seamstress hemming a dress. He thought that the piece of bobby-pin still somewhere inside the lock might screw him up, but it didn't. He caught the rocker almost at once and pushed it up, drawing the lock's tongue along with it. He had just a moment to wonder if she might not have put a bolt on the outside of the door as well – he had tried very hard to seem weaker and sicker than he now really felt, but the suspicions of the true paranoiac spread wide and ran deep. Then the door was open.

He felt the same nervous guilt, the urge to do this *fast.* Ears attuned for the sound of Old Bessie returning– although she had only been gone for forty-five minutes – he pulled a bunch of the Kleenex, dipped the wad in the pitcher, and bent awkwardly over to one side with the soppy mass in his hand. Gritting his teeth and ignoring the pain, he began to rub at the mark on the right-hand side of the door.

To his intense relief, it began to fade almost at once. The hubs of the wheelchair had not actually scored through the paint, as he had feared, but only scuffed it.

He reversed away from the door, turned the chair, and backed up so he could work on the other mark. When he had done all he could, he reversed again and looked at the door, trying to see it through Annie's exquisitely suspicious eyes. The marks were there – but faint, almost unnoticeable. He thought he would be okay.

He *hoped* he would be okay.

'Tornado cellars,' he said, licked his lips, and laughed dryly. 'What the fuck, friends and neighbors.'

He rolled back to the door and looked out at the corridor – but now that the marks were gone he felt no urge to go farther or dare more today. Another day, yes. He would know that day when it came around.

What he wanted to do now was to write.

He closed the door, and the click of the lock seemed very loud.

Africa.

That bird came from Africa.

But you musn't cry for that bird, Paulie, because after awhile it forgot about how the veldt smelled at noonday, and the sounds of the wildebeests at the waterhole, and the high acidic smell of the ieka-ieka trees in the great clearing north of the Big Road. After awhile it forgot the cerise color of the sun dying behind Kilimanjaro. After awhile it only knew the muddy, smogged-out sunsets of Boston, that was all it remembered and all it wanted to remember. After awhile it didn't want to go back anymore, and if someone took it back and set it free it would only crouch in one place, afraid and hurting and homesick in two unknown and terribly ineluctable directions, until something came along and killed it.

'Oh, Africa, oh, shit,' he said in a trembling voice.

Crying a little, he rolled the wheelchair over to his wastebasket and buried the wet wads of Kleenex under the wastepaper. He repositioned the wheelchair by the window and rolled a piece of paper into the Royal.

And by the way, Paulie, is the bumper of your car sticking out of the snow yet? Is it sticking out, twinkling cheerily in the sun, just waiting for someone to come along and see it while you sit here wasting what may be your last chance?

He looked doubtfully at the blank sheet of paper in the typewriter;

I won't be able to write now anyway. That spoiled it.

But nothing had ever spoiled it, somehow. It could be spoiled, he knew that, but in spite of the reputed fragility of the creative act, it had always been the single toughest thing, the most abiding thing, in his life – nothing had ever been able to pollute that crazy well of dreams: no drink, no drug, no pain. He fled to that well now, like a thirsty animal finding a waterhole at dusk, and he drank from it; which is to say he found the hole in the paper and fell thankfully through it. By the time Annie got back home at quarter of six, he had done almost five pages.

12

During the next three weeks, Paul Sheldon felt surrounded by a queer electric peacefulness. His mouth was always dry. Sounds seemed too loud. There were days when he felt he could bend spoons simply by looking at them. Other days he felt like weeping hysterically.

Outside this, separate of the atmosphere and apart from the deep, maddening itch of his healing legs, its own serene thing, the work continued. The stack of pages to the right of the Royal grew steadily taller. Before this strange experience, he had considered four pages a day to be his optimum output (on *Fast Cars* it had usually been three – and only two on many days – before the final finishing sprint). But during this electric three-week period, which came to an end with the rainstorm of April 15th, Paul averaged *twelve pages a day* – seven in the morning, five more in an evening session. If anyone in his previous life (for so he had come to think of it, without even realizing it) had suggested he could work at such a pace, Paul would have laughed. When the rain began to fall, he had two hundred and sixty-seven pages of *Misery's Return* – first-draft stuff, sure, but he had scanned through it and thought it amazingly clean for a first.

Part of the reason was that he was living an amazingly straight life. No long, muddled nights spent bar-hopping, followed by long, muddled days spent drinking coffee and orange juice and gobbling vitamin-B tablets (days when if his glance so much as happened upon his typewriter, he would turn away, shuddering). No more waking up next to a big blonde or redhead he had picked up somewhere the night before – a lass who usually looked like a queen at midnight and a goblin at ten the next morning. No more cigarettes. He had once asked for them in a timid and tentative voice, and she had given him a look of such utter darkness that he had told her at once to forget it. He was Mr Clean. No bad habits (except for his codeine jones, of course, still haven't done anything about that, have we, Paul?), no distractions. *Here I am,* he thought once, *the world's only monastic druggie.* Up at seven. Down two Novril with juice. At eight o'clock breakfast came, served at *monsieur's* bedside. A single egg, poached or scrambled, three days a week. High-fiber cereal the other four days. Then into the wheelchair. Over to the window. Find the hole in the paper. Fall into the nineteenth century, when men were men and women wore bustles. Lunch. Afternoon nap. Up again, sometimes to edit, sometimes just to read. She had everything Somerset Maugham had ever written (once Paul found himself wondering dourly if she had John Fowles's first novel on her shelves and decided it might be better not to ask), and Paul began to work his way through the twenty-odd volumes that comprised Maugham's *oeuvre,* fascinated by the man's canny grasp of story values. Over the years Paul had grown more and more resigned to the fact that he could not read stories as he had when he was a kid; by becoming a writer of them himself, he had condemned himself to a life of dissection. But Maugham first seduced him and then made him a child again, and that was wonderful. At five o'clock she would serve him a light supper, and at seven she would roll in the black-and-white television and they would watch *M*A*S*H** and *WKRP in Cincinnati.* When these were over, Paul would write. When he was done, he would roll the wheelchair slowly (he could have gone much faster, but it was just as well that Annie should not know that) over to the bed. She would hear, come in, and help him back into bed. More medication. Boom. Out like a light. And the next day would be just the same. And the next. And the next.

Being such a straight arrow was part of the reason for this amazing fecundity, but Annie herself was a bigger one. After all, it was her single hesitant suggestion about the bee-sting which had shaped the book and given it its urgency when Paul had firmly believed he could never feel urgent about Misery again.

He'd been sure of one thing from the start: there really *was* no *Misery's Return.* His attention had been focused only on finding a way to get the bitch out of her grave without cheating before Annie decided to inspire him by giving him an enema with a handful of Ginsu knives. Minor matters such as what the fucking book was supposed to be *about* would have to wait.

During the two days following Annie's trip to town to pay her tax-bill, Paul tried to forget his failure to take advantage of what could have been a golden opportunity to escape and concentrated on getting Misery back to Mrs Ramage's cottage instead. Taking her to Geoffrey's home was no good. The servants – most notably Geoffrey's gossipy butler, Tyler – would see and talk. Also, he needed to establish the total amnesia which had been caused by the shock of being buried alive. Amnesia? Shit, the chick could barely talk. Sort of a relief, given Misery's usual burblings.

So – what next? The bitch was out of her grave, now where was the fucking *story?* Should Geoffrey and Mrs Ramage tell Ian that Misery was still alive? Paul didn't think so but he wasn't sure – *not being sure of things,* he knew, was a charmless corner of purgatory reserved for writers who were driving fast with no idea at all where they were going.

Not Ian, he thought, looking out at the barn. *Not Ian, not yet. The doctor first. That old asshole with all the n's in his name, Shinebone.*

The thought of the doctor brought Annie's comment about bee-stings to mind, and not for the first time. It kept recurring at odd moments.

One person in every dozen . . .

But it just wouldn't play. Two unrelated women in neighboring townships, both allergic to stings in the same rare way?

Three days following the Great Annie Wilkes Tax Bail-out, Paul had been drowsing his way into his afternoon nap when the guys in the sweatshop weighed in, and weighed in heavy. This time it wasn't a flare; this time it was an H-bomb explosion.

He sat bolt upright in bed, ignoring the flare of pain which shot up hls legs.

'Annie!' he bawled. *'Annie, come in here!'*

He heard her thump down the stairs two at a time and then run down the hallway. Her eyes were wide and scared when she came in.

'Paul! What's wrong? Are you cramping? Are you –'

'No,' he said, but of course he was; his *mind* was cramping. 'No. Annie, I'm sorry if I scared you, but you gotta help me into the chair. Mighty fuck! I got it!' The dreaded effword was out before he could help it, but this time it didn't seem to matter – she was looking at him respectfully, and with not a little awe. Here was the secular version of the Pentecostal fire, burning before her very eyes.

'Of course, Paul.'

She got him into the chair as quickly as she could. She began to roll him toward the window and Paul shook his head impatiently. 'This won't take long,' he said, 'but it's very important.'

'Is it about the book?'

'It *is* the book. Be quiet. Don't talk to me.'

Ignoring the typewriter – he never used the typewriter to make notes – he seized one of the ballpoints and quickly covered a single sheet of paper with a scrawl that probably no one but himself could have read.

> They WERE related. It was bees and it affected them both the same way because they WERE related. Misery's an orph. And guess what? The Evelyn-Hyde babe was MISERY'S SISTER! Or maybe half-sister. That would probably work better. Who gets the first hint? Shinny? No. Shinny's a ninny. Mrs R. She can go to see Charl. E-H's mommy and

And now he was struck by an idea of such intense loveliness – in terms of the plot at least – that he looked up, mouth open, eyes wide.

'Paul?' Annie asked anxiously.

'She knew,' Paul whispered. 'Of *course* she did. At least strongly suspected. But –'

He bent to his notes again.

> she – Mrs R. – realizes at once that Mrs E-H has got to know M. is related to her daught. Same hair or something. Remember E-H's mom is starting to look like a maj. character. You'll need to work her up. Mrs R. starts to realize Mrs E-H MAY EVEN HAVE KNOWN MISERY WAS BURIED ALIVE!! SHIT ON A SHINGLE! LOVE IT! Suppose the ole lady guessed Misery was a leftover of her fuck-'em-and-leave-'em days and

He put the pen down, looked at the paper, then slowly picked the pen up again and scrawled a few more lines.

> Three necessary points.
>
> 1. How does Mrs E-H react to Mrs R's suspicions? She should be either

murderous or puke-up scared. I prefer scared but think A.W. would like murderous, so OK murd.

2. How does Ian get into this?

3. Misery's amnesia?

Oh, and here's one to grow on. Does Misery find out her mom lived with the possibility that not just one but two of her daughters had been buried alive rather than speak up?

Why not?

'You could help me back into bed now if you wanted,' Paul said. 'If I sounded mad, I'm sorry. I was just excited.'

'That's all right, Paul.' She still sounded awed.

Since then the work had driven on famously. Annie was right; the story was turning out to be a good deal more gruesome than the other *Misery* books – the first chapter had not been a fluke but a harbinger. But it was also more richly plotted than any *Misery* novel since the first, and the characters were more lively. The latter three *Misery* novels had been little more than straightforward adventure tales with a fair amount of piquantly described sex thrown in to please the ladies. This book, he began to understand, was a gothic novel, and thus was more dependent on plot than on situation. The challenges were constant. It was not just a question of Can You? to begin the book – for the first time in years, it was Can You? almost every day . . . and he was finding he *could.*

Then the rain came and things changed.

13

From the eighth of April until the fourteenth they enjoyed an unbroken run of fine weather. The sun beamed down from a cloudless sky and temperatures sometimes rose into the mid-sixties. Brown patches began to appear in the field behind Annie's neat red barn. Paul hid behind his work and tried not to think about his car, the discovery of which was already overdue. His work did not suffer, but his mood did; he felt more and more that he was living in a cloud chamber, breathing an atmosphere thick with uncoalesced electricity. Whenever the Camaro stole into his mind, he immediately called the Brain Police and had the thought led away in handcuffs and leg-irons. Trouble was, the nasty thing had a way of escaping and coming back time after time, in one form or another.

One night he dreamed that Mr Rancho Grande returned to Annie's place. He got out of his well-kept Chevrolet Bel Air, holding part of the Camaro's bumper in one hand and its steering wheel in the other. *Do these belong to you?* he asked Annie in this dream.

Paul had awakened in a less-than-cheery frame of mind.

Annie, on the other hand, had never been in better spirits than she was during that sunny early-spring week. She cleaned; she cooked ambitious meals (although everything she cooked came out tasting strangely industrial, as if years of eating in hospital cafeterias had somehow corrupted any culinary talent she might once have had); each afternoon she bundled Paul up in a huge blue blanket, jammed a green hunting cap on his head, and rolled him out onto the back porch.

On those occasions he would take Maugham along, but rarely read him – being outside again was too great an experience to allow much concentration on other things. Mostly he just sat, smelling sweet cool air instead of the bedroom's stale indoor smell, sly with sickroom undertones, listened to the drip of the icicles, and watched the cloud-shadows roll slowly and steadily across the melting field. That was somehow best of all.

Annie sang in her on-pitch but queerly tuneless voice. She giggled like a child at the jokes on *M*A*S*H** and *WKRP*, laughing especially hard at the jokes which were mildly off-color (which, in the case of *WKRP*, was most of them).

She filled in n's tirelessly as Paul finished Chapters 9 and 10.

The morning of the fifteenth dawned windy and dull with clouds, and Annie changed. Perhaps, Paul thought, it was the falling barometer. It was as good an explanation as any.

She did not show up with his medication until nine o'clock, and by then he needed it quite badly – so badly that he had been thinking of going to his stash. There was no breakfast. Just the pills. When she came in she was still in her pink quilted housecoat. He noted with deepening misgivings that there were red marks like weals on her cheeks and arms. He also saw gooey splatters of food on the housecoat, and she had only managed to get on one of her slippers. *Thud-slush,* went Annie's feet as she approached him. *Thud-slush, thud-slush, thud-slush.* Her hair hung around her face. Her eyes were dull.

'Here.' She threw the pills at him. Her hands were also covered with mixed streaks of goo. Red stuff, brown stuff, sticky white stuff. Paul had no idea what it was. He wasn't sure he wanted to know. The pills hit his chest and bounced into his lap. She turned to go. *Thud-slush, thud-slush, thud-slush.*

'Annie?'

She stopped, not turning around. She looked bigger that way, with her shoulders rounding the pink housecoat, her hair like some battered helmet. She looked like a Piltdown woman staring out of her cave.

'Annie, are you all right?'

'No,' she said indifferently, and turned around. She looked at him with that same dullard's expression as she pinched her lower lip between the thumb and first finger of her right hand. She pulled it out and then twisted it, pinching inward at the same time. Blood first welled between lip and gum, then gushed down her chin. She turned and left without speaking a word, before his stunned mind could persuade itself that he had really seén her do that. She closed the door . . . and locked it. He heard her *thud-slushing* her way down the hall to the parlor. He heard the creak of her favorite chair as she sat down. Nothing else. No TV. No singing. No *click-clink* of silver on crockery. No, she was just sitting there. Just sitting there being not all right.

Then there *was* a sound. It was not repeated, but it was utterly distinctive. It was a slap. A damned hard one. And since he was in here on one side of a locked door and she was out there on the other side of it, you didn't have to be Sherlock Holmes to figure out that she'd slapped herself. Good and hard, from the sound. He saw her pulling her lip out, digging her short nails into its sensitive pink meat.

He suddenly remembered a note on mental illness he had taken for the first *Misery* book, where much of the action had been set in London's Bedlam Hospital (Misery had been railroaded there by the madly jealous villainess). *When a manic-depressive personality begins to slide deeply into a depressive period, he had written, one symptom he or she may exhibit is acts of self-punishment: slapping, punching, pinching, burning one's self with cigarette butts, etc.*

He was suddenly very scared.

14

Paul remembered an essay by Edmund Wilson where Wilson had said, in typically grudging Wilson manner, that Wordsworth's criterion for the writing of good poetry – strong emotion recalled in a time of tranquility – would do well enough for most dramatic fiction as well. It was probably true. Paul had known writers who found it impossible to write after so much as a minor marital spat, and he himself usually found it impossible to write when upset. But there were times when a kind of reverse effect obtained– these were times when he had gone to the work not just because the work ought to be done but because it was a way to escape whatever was upsetting him. These were usually occasions when rectifying the source of the upset was beyond him.

This was one of those occasions. When she still hadn't returned to put him in his chair by eleven that morning, he determined to get into it himself. Getting the typewriter off the mantel would be beyond him, but he could write longhand. He was sure he could hoist himself into the chair, knew it was probably a bad idea to let Annie *know* he could, but he needed his other fix, goddammit, and he could not write lying here in bed.

He worked himself over to the edge of the bed, made sure the wheelchair brake was on, then grasped its arms and pulled himself slowly into the seat. Pulling his legs up onto the supports one at a time was the only part that hurt. He rolled himself over to the window and picked up his manuscript.

The key rattled in the lock. Annie was looking in at him, her eyes burned black holes in her face. Her right cheek was swelling up, and it looked like she was going to have a hell of a shiner in the morning. There was red stuff around her mouth and on her chin. For a moment Paul thought it was more blood from her torn lip and then he saw the seeds in it. It was raspberry jam or raspberry filling, not blood. She looked at him.

Paul looked back. Neither said anything for a time. Outside, the first drops of rain splatted against the wlndow.

'If you can get into that chair all by yourself, Paul,' she said at last, 'then I think you can fill in your own fucking n's.'

She then closed the door and locked it again. Paul sat looking at it for a long time, almost as if there were something to see. He was too flabbergasted to do anything else.

15

He didn't see her again until late afternoon. After her visit, work was impossible. He made a couple of futile tries, wadded up the paper, and gave up. It was a bust. He rolled himself back across the room. In the process of getting out of the chair and into bed, one of his hands slipped and he came within an ace of falling. He brought his left leg down, and although it took his weight and saved him the fall, the pain was excruciating – it felt as if a dozen bolts had suddenly been driven into the bone. He screamed, scrabbled for the headboard, and pulled himself safely over onto the bed, his throbbing left leg trailing behind the rest of him.

That will bring her, he thought incoherently. *She'll want to see if Sheldon really turned into Luciano Pavarotti, or if it just sounds that way.*

But she didn't come and there was no way he could bear the rotted ache in his left leg. He rolled clumsily onto his stomach, burrowed one arm deep under the mattress, and brought out one of the Novril sample cards. He dry-swallowed two, then drifted for awhile.

When he came back he thought at first he must still be dreaming. It was just too surreal, like the night when she had rolled the barbecue pot in here. Annie was sitting on the side of his bed. She had set a water glass filled with Novril capsules on his bed-table. In her other hand she had a Victor rat-trap. There was a rat in it, too – a large one with mottled gray-brown fur. The trap had broken the rat's back. Its rear feet hung over the sides of the trap's board, twitching randomly. There were beads of blood in its whiskers.

This was no dream. Just another day lost in the funhouse with Annie.

Her breath smelled like a corpse decomposing in rotted food.

'Annie?' He straightened up, eyes moving between her and the rat. Outside it was dusk – a strange blue dusk filled with rain. It sheeted against the window. Strong gusts of wind shook the house, making it creak.

Whatever had been wrong with her this morning was worse tonight. *Much* worse. He realized he was seeing her with all her masks put aside – this was the real Annie, the inside Annie. The flesh of her face, which had previously seemed so fearsomely solid, now hung like lifeless dough. Her eyes were blanks. She had dressed, but her skirt was on inside out. There were more weals on her flesh, more food splattered on her clothes. When she moved, they exhaled too many different aromas for Paul to count. Nearly one whole arm of her cardigan sweater was soaked with a half-dried substance that smelled like gravy.

She held up the trap. 'They come into the cellar when it rains.' The pinned rat squeaked feebly, and snapped at the air. Its black eyes, infinitely more lively than those of its captor, rolled. 'I put down traps. I have to. I smear the trip-plates with bacon grease. I always catch eight or nine. Sometimes I find others –'

She blanked then. Blanked for nearly three minutes, holding the rat in the air, a perfect case of waxy catatonia. Paul stared at her, stared at the rat as it squeaked and struggled, and realized that he had actually believed that things could get no worse. Untrue. Un-fucking true.

At last, as he had begun to think she had just sailed off into oblivion forever with no fuss or fanfare, she lowered the trap and went on as if she had never stopped speaking.

'– drowned in the corners. Poor things.'

She looked down at the rat and a tear fell onto its matted fur.

'Poor poor things.'

She closed one of her strong hands around the rat and pulled back the spring with the other. It lashed in her hand, head twisting as it tried to bite her. Its squeals were thin and terrible. Paul pressed the heel of a palm against his wincing mouth.

'How its heart beats! How it struggles to get away! As we do, Paul. As we do. We think we know so much, but we really don't know any more than a rat in a trap – a rat with a broken back that thinks it still wants to live.'

The hand holding the rat became a fist. Her eyes never lost that blank, distant cast. Paul wanted to look away and could not. Tendons began to stand out on her inner arm. Blood ran from the rat's mouth in an abrupt thin stream. Paul heard its bones break, and then the thick pads of her fingers punched into its body, disappearing up to the first knuckle. Blood pattered on the floor. The creature's dulling eyes bulged.

She tossed the body into the corner and wiped her hand indifferently on the sheet, leaving long red smears.

'Now it's at peace.' She shrugged, then laughed. 'I'll get my gun, Paul, shall I? Maybe the next world is better. For rats and people both – not that there's much difference between the two.'

'Not until I finish,' he said, trying to enunciate each word carefully. This was difficult, because he felt as if someone had shot his mouth full of Novocain. He had seen her low before, but he'd seen *nothing* like this; he wondered if she'd ever *had* a low as low as this before. This was how depressives got just before shooting all the members of their families, themselves last; it was the psychotic despair of the woman who dresses her children in their best, takes them out for ice-cream, walks them down to the nearest bridge, lifts one into the crook of each arm, and jumps over the side. Depressives kill themselves. Psychotics, rocked in the poison cradles of their own egos, want to do everyone handy a favor and take them along.

I'm closer to death than I've ever been in my life, he thought, *because she means it. The bitch means it.*

'Misery?' she asked, almost as if she had never heard the word before – but there had been a momentary fugitive sparkle in her eyes, hadn't there? He thought so.

'Misery, yes.' He thought desperately about how he should go on. Every possible approach seemed mined. 'I agree that the world is a pretty crappy place most of the time,' he said, and then added inanely: 'Especially when it rains.'

Oh, you idiot, stop babbling!

'I mean, I've been in a lot of pain these last few weeks, and –'

'Pain?' She looked at him with sallow, sunken contempt. 'You don't know what pain is. You don't have the slightest *idea,* Paul.'

'No . . . I suppose not. Not compared to you.'

'That's right.'

'But – I want to finish this book. I want to see how it all turns out.' He paused. 'And I'd like you to stick around and see, too. A person might as well not write a book at all, if there's no one around to read it. Do you get me?'

He lay there looking at that terrible stone face, heart thumping.

'Annie? Do you get me?'

'Yes . . .' She sighed. 'I *do* want to know how it comes out. That's the *only* thing left in the world that I still want, I suppose.' Slowly, apparently unaware of what she was doing, she began to suck the rat's blood from her fingers. Paul jammed his teeth together and grimly told himself he would *not* vomit, would *not,* would *not.* 'It's like waiting for the end of one of those chapter-plays.'

She looked around suddenly, the blood on her mouth like lipstick.

'Let me offer again, Paul. I can get my gun. I can end all of this for both of us. You are not a stupid man. You know I can never let you leave here. You've known that for some time, haven't you?'

Don't let your eyes waver. If she sees your eyes waver, she'll kill you right now.

'Yes. But it always ends, doesn't it, Annie? In the end we all swing.'

A ghost of a smile at the corners of her mouth; she touched his face briefly, with some affection.

'I suppose you think of escape. So does a rat in a trap, I'm sure, in its way. But you're not going to, Paul. You might if this was one of your stories, but it's not. I can't let you leave here . . . but I could go with you.'

And suddenly, for just a moment, he thought of saying: *All right, Annie – go ahead. Let's just call it off.* Then his need and will to live – and there was still quite a lot of each in him – rose up and clamored the momentary weakness away. Weakness was what it was. Weakness and cowardice. Fortunately or unfortunately, he did not have the crutch of mental illness to fall back on.

'Thank you,' he said, 'but I want to finish what I've started.'

She sighed and stood up. 'All right. I suppose I must have known you would, because I see I brought you some pills, although I don't remember doing it.' She laughed – a small crazy titter which seemed to come from that slack face as if by ventriloquism. 'I'll have to go away for awhile. If I don't, what you or I want won't matter. Because I do things. I have a place I go when I feel like this. A place in the hills. Did you ever read the Uncle Remus stories, Paul?'

He nodded.

'Do you remember Brer Rabbit telling Brer Fox about his Laughing Place?'

'Yes.'

'That's what I call my place upcountry. My Laughing Place. Remember how I said I was coming back from Sidewinder when I found you?'

He nodded.

'Well, that was a fib. I fibbed because I didn't know you well then. I was really coming back from my Laughing Place. It has a sign over the door that says that. ANNIE'S LAUGHING PLACE, it says. Sometimes I *do* laugh when I go there.

'But mostly I just scream.'

'How long will you be gone, Annie?'

She was drifting dreamily toward the door now. 'I can't tell. I've brought you pills. You'll be all right. Take two every six hours. Or six every four hours. Or all of them at once.'

But what will I eat? he wanted to ask her, and didn't. He didn't want her attention to return to him – not at all. He wanted her gone. Being here with her was like being with the Angel of Death.

He lay stiffly in his bed for a long time, listening to her movements, first upstairs, then on the stairs, then in the kitchen, fully expecting her to change her mind and come back with the gun after all. He did not even relax when he heard the side door slam and lock, followed by splashing steps outside. The gun could just as easily be in the Cherokee.

Old Bessie's motor whirred and caught. Annie gunned it fiercely. A fan of headlights came on, illuminating a shining silver curtain of rain. The lights began to retreat down the driveway. They swung around, dimming, and then Annie was gone. This time she was not heading downhill, toward Sidewinder, but up into the high country.

'Going to her Laughing Place,' Paul croaked, and began to laugh himself. She had hers; he was already in his. The wild gales of mirth ended when he looked at the mangled body of the rat in the corner.

A thought struck him.

'Who *said* she didn't leave me anything to eat?' he asked the room, and laughed even harder. In the empty house Paul Sheldon's Laughing Place sounded like the padded cell of a madman.

16

Two hours later, Paul jimmied the bedroom's lock again and for the second time forced the wheelchair through the doorway that was almost too small. For the last time, he hoped. He had a pair of blankets in his lap. All the pills he had cached under the mattress were wrapped in a Kleenex tucked into his underwear. He meant to get out if he could, rain or no rain; this was his chance and this time he meant to take it. Sidewinder was downhill and the road would be slippery in the rain and it was darker than a mineshaft; he meant to try it all the same. He hadn't lived the life of a hero or a saint, but he did not intend to die like an exotic bird in a zoo.

He vaguely remembered an evening he'd spent drinking Scotch with a gloomy playwright named Bernstein at the Lion's Head, down in the Village (and if he lived to see the Village again he would get down on whatever remained of his knees and kiss the grimy sidewalk of Christopher Street). At some point the conversation had turned to the Jews living in Germany during the uneasy four or five years before the *Wehrmacht* rolled into Poland and the festivities began in earnest. Paul remembered telling Bernstein, who had lost an aunt and a grandfather in the Holocaust, that he didn't understand why the Jews in Germany – hell, all over Europe but *especially* in Germany – hadn't gotten out while there was still time. They were not, by and large, stupid people, and many had had first-hand experience of such persecution. Surely they had seen what was coming. So why had they stayed?

Bernstein's answer had struck him as frivolous and cruel and incomprehensible: *Most of them had pianos. We Jews are very partial to the piano. When you own a piano, it's harder to think about moving.*

Now he understood. Yes. At first it was his broken legs and crushed pelvis. Then, God help him, the book had taken off. In a crazy way he was even having fun with it. It would be easy – too easy – to blame everything on his broken bones, or the dope, when in fact so much of it had been the *book.* That and the droning passage of days with their simple convalescent pattern. Those things – but mostly the stupid goddam *book* – had been his piano. What would she do if he was gone when she came back from her Laughing Place? Burn the manuscript?

'I don't give a fuck,' he said, and this was almost the truth. If he lived, he could write another book – re-create this one, even, if he wanted to. But a dead man couldn't write a book any more than he could buy a new piano.

He went into the parlor. It had been tidy before, but now there were dirty dishes stacked on every available surface; it looked to Paul as if every one in the house must be here. Annie apparently not only pinched and slapped herself when she was feeling depressed. It looked like she really chowed down as well, and never mind cleaning up after. He half-remembered the stinking wind that had blown down his throat during his time in the cloud and felt his stomach clench. Most of the remains were of sweet things. Ice-cream had dried or was drying in many of the bowls and soup-dishes. There were crumbs of cake and smears of pie on the plates. A mound of lime Jell-O covered with a crack-glaze of dried whipped cream stood on top of the TV next to a two-liter plastic bottle of Pepsi and a gravy-boat. The Pepsi bottle looked almost as big as the nosecone of a Titan-II rocket. Its surface was dull and smeary, almost opaque. He guessed she had drunk directly from it, and that her fingers had been covered with gravy or ice-cream when she did it. He had not heard the clink of silverware and that was not surprising because there was none here. Dishes and bowls and plate, but no cutlery. He saw drying drips and splashes – again, mostly of ice-cream – on the rug and couch.

That was what I saw on her housecoat. The stuff she was eating. And what was on her breath. His image of Annie as Piltdown woman recurred. He saw her sitting in here and scooping ice-cream into her mouth, or maybe handfuls of half-congealed chicken gravy with a Pepsi chaser, simply eating and drinking in a deep depressed daze.

The penguin sitting on his block of ice was still on the knick-knack table, but she had thrown many of the other ceramic pieces into the corner, where their littered remains were scattered – sharp little hooks and shards.

He kept seeing her fingers as they sank into the rat's body. The red smears of her fingers on the sheet. He kept seeing her licking the blood from her fingers, doing it as absently as she must have eaten the ice-cream and Jell-O and soft black jellyroll cake. These images were terrible, but they were a wonderful incentive to hurry.

The spray of dried flowers on the coffee-table had overturned; beneath the table, barely visible, lay a dish of crusted custard pudding and a large book. MEMORY LANE, it said. *Trips down Memory Lane when you're feeling depressed are never a very good idea, Annie – but I suppose you know that by this point in your life.*

He rolled across the room. Straight ahead was the kitchen. On the right a wide, short hallway went down to Annie's front door. Beside this hallway a flight of stairs went up to the second floor. Giving the stairs only a brief glance (there were drips of ice-cream on some of the carpeted stair levels and glazey smears of it on the banister), Paul rolled down to the door. He thought that if there was going to be a way out for him, tied to this chair as he was, it would be by way of the kitchen door – the one Annie used when she went out to feed the animals, the one she galloped from when Mr Rancho Grande showed up – but he ought to check this one. He might get a surprise.

He didn't.

The porch stairs were every bit as steep as he had feared, but even if there had been a wheelchair ramp (a possibility he never would have accepted in a spirited game of Can You?, even if a friend had suggested it), he couldn't have used it. There were three locks on the door. The police-bar he could have coped with. The other two – were Kreigs, the best locks in the whole world, according to his ex-cop friend Tom Twyford. And where were the keys? Umm . . . let me see. On their way to Annie's Laughing Place, maybe? *Yes-siree Bob! Give that man a cigar and a blowtorch to light it with!*

He reversed down the hall, fighting panic, reminding himself he hadn't expected much from the front door anyway. He pivoted the chair once he was in the parlor and rolled into the kitchen. This was an old-fashioned room with bright linoleum on the floor and a pressed-tin ceiling. The refrigerator was old but quiet. There were three or four magnets stuck to its door – not surprisingly, they all looked like candy: a piece of bubble-gum, a Hershey Bar, a Tootsie Roll. One of the cabinet doors was open and he could see shelves neatly covered with oilcloth. There were big windows over the sink and they would let in a lot of light even on cloudy days. It should have been a cheery kitchen but wasn't. The open garbage can overflowed onto the floor and emitted the warm reek of spoiling food, but that wasn't the only thing wrong, or the worst smell. There was another that seemed to exist mostly in his mind, but which was no less real for that. It was *parfum de Wilkes;* a psychic odor of obsession.

There were three doors in the room, two to the left and one straight ahead, between the refrigerator and the pantry alcove.

He went to those on the left first. One was the kitchen closet – he knew that even before he saw the coats, hats, scarves, and boots. The brief, yapping squeak of the hinges was enough to tell him. The other was the one Annie used to go out. And here was another police-bar and two more Kreigs. Roydmans, stay out. Paul, stay in.

He imagined her laughing.

'You fucking *bitch!*' He struck his fist against the side of the door. It hurt, and he pressed the side of his hand against his mouth. He hated the sting of tears, the momentary doubling of his vision when he blinked, but there was no way he could stop it. The panic was yammering more loudly now, asking what was he going to do, what was he going to do, for Christ's sake, this might be his last chance –

What I'm going to do first is a thorough job of checking this situation out, he told himself grimly. *If you can stay cool for just awhile longer, that is. Think you can do that, chickenshit?*

He wiped his eyes – crying was not going to get him out of this – and looked out through the window which made up the top half of the door. It wasn't really just one window but sixteen small panes. He could break the glass in each, but he would have to bust the lathes, too, and that might take hours without a saw – they looked strong. And what then? A kamikaze dive out onto the back porch? A great idea. Maybe he could break his back, and that would take his mind off his legs for awhile. And it wouldn't take long lying out there in the pelting rain before he died of exposure.

That would take care of the whole rotten business.

No way. No fucking way. Maybe I'm going to punch out, but I swear to God I'm not going to do it until I get a chance to show my number-one fan just how much I've enjoyed getting to know her. And that isn't just a promise – that's a sacred vow.

The idea of paying Annie back did more to still his panic than any amount of self-scolding had done. A little calmer, he flicked the switch beside the locked door. It turned on an outside light, which came in handy – the last of the daylight had drained away during the time since he had left his room. Annie's driveway was flooded, and her yard was a quagmire of mud, standing water, and gobbets of melting snow. By positioning his wheelchair all the way to the left of the door, he could for the first time see the road which ran by her place, although it was really no big deal – two-lane blacktop between decaying snowbanks, shiny as sealskin and awash with rainwater and snowmelt.

Maybe she locked the doors to keep the Roydmans out, but she sure didn't need to lock them to keep me in. If I got out there in this wheelchair, I'd be bogged to the hubcaps in five seconds. You're not going anywhere, Paul. Not tonight and probably not for weeks – they'll be a month into the baseball season before the ground firms up enough for you to get out to the road in this wheelchair. Unless you want to crash through a window and crawl.

No – he didn't want to do that. It was too easy to imagine how his shattered bones would feel after ten or fifteen minutes of wriggling through cold puddles and melting snow like a dying tadpole. And even supposing he could make it out to the road, what were his chances of flagging down a car? The only two he'd ever heard out here, other than Old Bessie, had been El Rancho Grande's Bel Air and the car which had scared the life out of him passing the house on the first occasion he had escaped his 'guest-room'.

He turned off the outside light and rolled across to the other door, the one between the refrigerator and the pantry. There were three locks on this one as well, and *it* didn't even open on the outside – or at least not directly. There was another light-switch beside this door. Paul flicked it and saw a neat shed addition which ran the length of the house on its windward side. At one end was a woodpile and a chopping block with an axe buried in it. At the other was a work-table and tools hung on pegs. To its left there was another door. The bulb out there wasn't terribly bright, but it was bright enough for him to see another police bolt and another two Kreig locks on that door as well.

The Roydmans . . . everybody . . . all out to get me . . .

'I don't know about *them,'* he said to the empty kitchen, 'but *I* sure am.'

Giving up on the doors, he rolled into the pantry. Before he looked at the food stored on the shelves, he looked at the matches. There were two cartons of paper book matches and at least two dozen boxes of Diamond Blue Tips, neatly stacked up.

For a moment he considered simply lighting the place on fire, began to reject the idea as the most ridiculous yet, and then saw something which made him reconsider it briefly.

In here was yet another door, and this one had no locks on it. He opened it and saw a set of steep, rickety stairs pitching and yawing their way into the cellar. An almost vicious smell of dampness and rotting vegetables rose from the dark. He heard low squeaking sounds and thought of her saying: *They come into the cellar when it rains. I put down traps. I have to.*

He slammed the door shut in a hurry. A drop of sweat trickled down from his temple and ran, stinging, into the corner of his right eye. He knuckled it away. Knowing that door must lead to the cellar and seeing that there were no locks on it had made the idea of torching the place seem momentarily more rational – he could maybe shelter there. But the stairs were too steep, the possibility of being burned alive if Annie's flaming house collapsed into the cellar-hole before the Sidewinder fire engines could get here was too real, and the rats down there . . . the sound of the rats was somehow the worst.

How its heart beats! How it struggles to get away! As we do, Paul. As we do.

'Africa,' Paul said, and didn't hear himself say it. He began to look at the cans and bags of food in the pantry, trying to assess what he could take with the least chance of raising her suspicions next time she came out here. Part of him understood exactly what this assessment meant: he had given up the idea of escape.

Only for the time being, his troubled mind protested.

No, a deeper voice responded implacably. *Forever, Paul. Forever.*

'I will never give up,' he whispered. 'Do you hear me? *Never.'*

Oh no? the voice of the cynic whispered sardonically. *Well . . . we'll see, won't we?*

Yes. They would see.

17

Annie's larder looked more like a survivalist's bomb shelter than a pantry. He guessed that some of this hoarding was a simple nod to the realities of her situation: she was a woman alone living in the high country, where a person must reasonably expect to spend a certain period – maybe only a day, but sometimes as long as a week or even two – cut off from the rest of the world. Probably even those cockadoodie Roydmans had a pantry that would make a homeowner from another part of the country raise his or her brows . . . but he doubted if the cockadoodie Roydmans or anyone else up here had anything which came close to what he was now looking at. This was no pantry; this was a goddam supermarket. He supposed there was a certain symbolism in Annie's pantry – the ranks of goods had something to say about the murkiness of the borderline between the Sovereign State of Reality and the People's Republic of Paranoia. In his current situation, however, such niceties hardly seemed worth examination. Fuck the symbolism. Go for the food.

Yes, but be careful. It wasn't just a matter of what she might miss. He must take no more than he could reasonably hope to hide if she came back suddenly . . . and how else did he *think* she would come? Her phone was dead and he somehow doubted if Annie would send him a telegram or Flowers by Wire. But in the end what she might miss in here or find in his room hardly mattered. After all, he had to eat. He was hooked on that, too.

Sardines. There were lots of sardines in those flat rectangular cans with the key under the paper. Good. He would have some of those. Tins of deviled ham. No keys, but he could open a couple of cans in her kitchen, and eat those first. Bury the empties deep in her own overflowing garbage. There was an open package of Sun-Maid raisins containing smaller boxes, which the ad-copy on the torn cellophane wrapper called 'mini-snacks'. Paul added four of the mini-snacks to the growing stash in his lap, plus single-serving boxes of Corn Flakes and Wheaties. He noted there were no single-serving boxes of pre-sweetened cereals. If there had been, Annie had chowed them down on her last binge.

On a higher shelf was a pile of Slim Jims, as neatly stacked as the kindling in Annie's shed. He took four, trying not to disturb the pyramidal structure of the pile, and ate one of them greedily, relishing the salty taste and the grease. He tucked the wrapping into his underwear for later disposal.

His legs were beginning to hurt. He decided that if he wasn't going to escape or burn the house down, he ought to go on back to his room. An anticlimax, but things could be worse. He could take a couple of pills and then write until he got drowsy. Then he could go to sleep. He doubted if she would be back tonight; far from abating, the storm was gaining strength. The idea of writing quietly and then sleeping with the knowledge that he was perfectly alone, that Annie was not going to burst in with some wild idea or even wilder demand, held great appeal, anticlimax or not.

He reversed out of the pantry, pausing to turn off the light, reminding himself that he must

(rinse)

put everything back in order as he made his retreat. If he ran out of food before she came back, he could always return for more

(like a hungry rat, right, Paulie?)

but he must not forget how careful he must be. It would not do to forget the simple fact that he was risking his life every time he left his room. Forgetting that would not do at all.

18

As he was rolling across the parlor, the scrapbook under the coffee table caught his eye again. MEMORY LANE. It was as big as a folio Shakespeare play and as thick as a family Bible.

Curious, he picked it up and opened it.

On the first page was a single column of newsprint, headed WILKES-BERRYMAN NUPTIALS. There was a picture of a pale gent with a narrow face and a woman with dark eyes and a pursy mouth. Paul glanced from the newspaper photo to the portrait over the mantel. No question. The woman identified in the clipping as Crysilda Berryman (*Now there's a name worthy of a* Misery *novel,* he thought) was Annie's mother. Neatly written in black ink below the clipping was: *Bakersfield Journal,* May 30th, 1938.

Page two was a birth announcement: Paul Emery Wilkes, born in Bakersfield Receiving Hospital, May 12th, 1939. Father, Carl Wilkes; mother, Crysilda Wilkes. The name of Annie's older brother gave him a start. He must have been the one with whom she had gone to the movies and seen the chapter-plays. Her brother had been Paul, too.

Page three announced the birth of Anne Marie Wilkes, d.o.b. April 1st, 1943. Which made Annie just past her forty-fourth birthday. The fact that she had been born on April Fools' Day did not escape Paul.

Outside, the wind gusted. Rain tore against the house.

Fascinated, his pain temporarily forgotten, Paul turned the page.

The next clipping was from page one of the *Bakersfield Journal.* The photo showed a fireman on a ladder, silhouetted against a background of flames billowing from the windows of a frame building.

FIVE DIE IN APARTMENT HOUSE FIRE

Five persons, four of them members of the same family, died in the early hours of Wednesday morning, victims of a smoky three-alarm fire in a Bakersfield apartment house on Watch Hill Avenue. Three of the dead were children – Paul Krenmitz, 8, Frederick Krenmitz, 6, and Alison Krenmitz, 3. The fourth was their father, Adrian Krenmitz, 41. Mr Krenmitz rescued the surviving Krenmitz child, Laurene Krenmitz, who is eighteen months old. According to Mrs Jessica Krenmitz, her husband put the youngest of their four children in her arms and told her, 'I'll be back with the others in a minute or two. Pray for us.' 'I never saw him again,' she said.

The fifth victim, Irving Thalman, 58, was a bachelor who lived on the top floor of the building. The third-floor apartment was vacant at the time of the fire. The Carl Wilkes family, at first listed as missing, left the building Tuesday night because of a water leak in the kitchen.

'I weep for Mrs Krenmitz and her loss,' Crysilda Wilkes told a *Journal* reporter, 'but I thank God for sparing my husband and my own two children.'

Centralia Fire Chief Michael O'Whunn said that the fire began in the apartment building's basement. When asked about the possibility of arson, he said: 'It's more likely that a wino crept into the basement, had a few drinks, and accidentally started the fire with a cigarette. He probably ran instead of trying to put the fire out, and five people died. I hope we catch up with the bum.' When asked about leads, O'Whunn said: 'The police have several, and they are following them up hard and fast, I can tell you.'

Same neat black ink below the clipping. *October 28th, 1954.*

Paul looked up. He was totally still, but a pulse beat rapidly in his throat. His bowels felt loose and hot.

Little brats.

Three of the dead were children.

Mrs Krenmitz's four brats downstairs.

Oh no, oh Christ, no.

I used to hate those little brats.

She was just a kid! Not even in the house!

She was eleven. Old enough and bright enough, maybe, to spill some kerosene around a cheap liquor bottle, then light a candle, and put the candle in the middle of the kerosene. Maybe she didn't even think it would work. Maybe she thought the kerosene would evaporate before the candle burned all the way down. Maybe she thought they'd get out alive . . . only wanted to scare them into moving. But she did it, Paul, she fucking did it, and you know it.

Yes, he supposed he did. And who would suspect her?

He turned the page.

Here was yet another *Bakersfield Journal* clipping, this one dated July 19th, 1957. It featured a picture of Carl Wilkes, looking slightly older. One thing was clear: it was as old as he was ever going to get. The clipping was his obituary.

BAKERSFIELD ACCOUNTANT DIES IN FREAK FALL

Carl Wilkes, a lifelong Bakersfield resident, died shortly after being admitted to Hernandez General Hospital last night. He apparently stumbled over a pile of loose clothing, which had been left on the stairs earlier, while on his way down to answer the phone. Dr Frank Canley, the admitting physician, said that Wilkes died of multiple skull fractures and a broken neck. He was 44.

Wilkes is survived by his wife, Crysilda, a son, Paul, 18, and a daughter, Anne, 14.

When Paul turned to the next page, he thought for a moment that

Annie had pasted in two copies of her father's obituary out of sentiment or by accident (he thought this latter the more likely possibility of the two). But this was a different accident, and the reason for the similarity was simplicity itself: neither had really been an accident at all.

He felt stark and simple terror steal into him.

The neat handwriting below this clipping read *Los Angeles Call, January 29th, 1962.*

USC STUDENT DIES IN FREAK FALL

Andrea Saint James, a USC nursing student, was pronounced dead on arrival at Mercy Hospital in North Los Angeles last night, the apparent victim of a bizarre accident.

Miss Saint James shared an off-campus apartment on Delorme Street with a sister nursing student, Anne Wilkes, of Bakersfield. Shortly before eleven P.M., Miss Wilkes heard a brief scream followed by 'terrible thudding sounds'. Miss Wilkes, who had been studying, rushed onto the third-floor landing and saw Miss Saint James lying on the landing below, 'sprawled in a very unnatural position'.

Miss Wilkes said that, in her effort to render aid, she almost fell herself. 'We had a cat named Peter Gunn,' she said, 'only we hadn't seen him for days and thought the pound must have gotten him because we kept forgetting to get him a tag. He was lying dead on the stairs. It was the cat she tripped over. I covered Andrea with my sweater and then called the hospital. I knew she was dead, but I didn't know who else to call.'

Miss Saint James, a native of Los Angeles, was 21.

'Jesus.'

Paul whispered it over and over. His hand was shaking badly as he turned the page. Here was a *Call* clipping which said that the stray cat the student nurses adopted had been poisoned.

Peter Gunn. Cute name for a cat, Paul thought.

The landlord had rats in his basement. Tenant complaints had resulted in a warning from building inspectors the year before. The landlord had caused a ruckus at a subsequent City Council meeting which had been lively enough to get coverage in the papers. Annie would have known. Faced with a stiff fine by councilmen who didn't like being called names, the landlord had sown the cellar with poisoned bait. Cat eats poison. Cat languishes in cellar for two days. Cat then crawls as close to his mistresses as possible before expiring – and killing one of said mistresses.

An irony worthy of Paul Harvey, Paul Sheldon thought, and laughed wildly. I bet it made his daily newscast, too.

Neat. Very neat.

Except we know that Annie picked up some of the poisoned bait in the cellar and hand-fed it to the cat, and if old Peter Gunn didn't want to eat it, she probably rammed it down his gullet with a stick. When he was dead she put him on the stairs and hoped it would work. Maybe she had a pretty good idea her roommate would come home tiddly. I wouldn't be a bit surprised . A dead cat, a heap of clothes. Same M.O., as Tom Twyford would say. But why, Annie? These clippings tell me everything but that. WHY?

In an act of self-preservation, part of his imagination had, over the last few weeks, actually *become* Annie, and it was now this Annie-part that spoke up in its dry and uncontradictable voice. And while what it said was perfectly mad, it also made perfect sense.

I killed her because she played her radio late at night.

I killed her because of the dumb name she gave the cat.

I killed her because I got tired of seeing her soul-kissing her boyfriend on the couch, him with his hand shoved so far up her skirt he looked like he was prospecting for gold.

I killed her because I caught her cheating.

I killed her because she *caught* me *cheating.*

The specifics don't matter, do they? I killed her because she was a cockadoodie brat, and that was reason enough.

'And maybe because she was a Missus Smart Guy,' Paul whispered. He threw back his head and donkeyed another shrill and frightened laugh. So this was Memory Lane, was it? Oh, what a variety of strange and poisonous flowers grew beside Annie's version of that quaint old path!

No one ever put those two freak falls together? First her father, then her roommate? Are you seriously telling me that?

Yes, he was seriously telling himself that. The accidents had happened almost five years apart, in two different towns. They had been reported by different papers in a populous state where people were probably always falling downstairs and breaking their necks.

And she was very, very clever.

Almost as clever as Satan himself, it seemed. Only now she was starting to lose it. It would be precious little consolation to him, however, if Annie were to be finally brought to bay for the murder of Paul Sheldon.

He turned the page and discovered another clipping from the *Bakersfield Journal* – the last, as it turned out. The headline read MISS WILKES IS NURSING SCHOOL GRADUATE. Home-town girl makes good. May 17th, 1966. The photo was of a younger, startlingly pretty Annie Wilkes, wearing a nurse's uniform and cap, smiling into the camera. It was a graduation photograph, of course. She had graduated with honors. *Only had to kill one roommate to do it, too,* Paul thought, and donkeyed his shrill, frightened laugh. The wind gusted around the side of the house as if in answer. Mom's picture chattered briefly on the wall.

The next cutting was from the Manchester, New Hampshire, *Union-Leader.* March 2nd, 1969. It was a simple obituary which seemed to have no connection with Annie Wilkes at all. Ernest Gonyar, age seventy-nine, had died in Saint Joseph's Hospital. No exact cause of death given. 'After a long illness,' the obit said. Survived by his wife, twelve children, and what looked like about four hundred grandchildren and great-grandchildren. There was nothing like the rhythm method for producing all descendants great and small, Paul thought, and donkeyed again.

She killed him. That's what happened to good old Ernie. Why else is his obituary here? This is Annie's Book of the Dead, isn't it?

Why, for God's sake? WHY?

With Annie Wilkes that is a question which has no sane answer. As you well know.

Another page, another *Union-Leader* obit. March 19th, 1969. The lady was identified as Hester 'Queenie' Beaulifant, eighty-four. In the picture she looked like something whose bones might have been exhumed from the La Brea Tar Pits. The same thing that had gotten Ernie had gotten 'Queenie' – seemed like that long-illness shit was going around. Like Ernie, she had expired at Saint Joe's. Viewings at 2:00 and 6:00 P.M. on March 20th at Foster's Funeral Home. Interment at Mary Cyr Cemetery on March 21st at 4:00 P.M

Ought to've had a special rendition of 'Annie, Won't You Come by Here', sung by the Mormon Tabersnackle Choir, Paul thought, and did the Donkey some more.

There were three more *Union-Leader* obits on the following pages. Two old men who had died of that perennial favorite, Long Illness. The third was a woman of forty-six named Paulette Simeaux. Paulette had died of that common runner-up, Short Illness. Although the picture accompanying the obit was even grainier and fuzzier than usual, Paul saw that Paulette Simeaux made 'Queenie' Beaulifant look like Thumbelina. He thought her illness might have been short indeed – a thunderclap coronary, say, followed by a trip to Saint Joe's, followed by . . . followed by what? Exactly what?

He really didn't want to think about the specifics . . . but all three obits identified Saint Joseph's as the place of expiration.

And if we looked at the nurses' register for March 1969, would we find the name WILKES? Friends, does a bear go cockadoodie in the woods?

This book, dear God, this book was so big.

No more, please. I don't want to look at any more. I've got the idea. I'm going to put this book down exactly where I found it. Then I am going into my room. I guess I don't want to write after all; I think I'll just take an extra pill and go to bed. Call it nightmare insurance. But no farther down Annie's Memory Lane, if you please. Please, if you please.

But his hands seemed to have a mind and a will of their own; they kept on turning the pages, faster and faster.

Two more brief death notices in the *Union-Leader,* one in late September of 1969, one in early October.

March 19th, 1970. This one was from the Harrisburg, Pennsylvania, *Herald.* A back page. NEW HOSPITAL STAFF ANNOUNCED. There was a photo of a balding, bespectacled man who looked to Paul like the type of fellow who might eat boogers in secret. The article noted that in addition to the new publicity director (the balding, bespectacled fellow), twenty others had joined the staff of Riverview Hospital: two doctors, eight R.N.'s, assorted kitchen staff, orderlies, and a janitor.

Annie was one of the R.N.'s.

On the next page, Paul thought, *I am going to see a brief death notice for an elderly man or woman who expired at Riverview Hospital in Harrisburg, Pennsylvania.*

Correct. An old duffer who had died of that all-time favorite, Long Illness.

Followed by an elderly man who had died of that perennial bridesmaid, Short Illness.

Followed by a child of three who had fallen down a well, sustained grievous head injuries, and been brought to Riverview in a coma.

Numbly, Paul continued to turn the pages while the wind and rain drove against the house. The pattern was inescapable. She got a job, killed some people, and moved on.

Suddenly an image came, one from a dream his conscious mind had already forgotten, which thus gained the delphic resonance of *déjà vu.* He saw Annie Wilkes in a long aproned dress, her hair covered with a mobcap, an Annie who looked like a nurse in London's Bedlam Hospital. She held a basket over one arm. She dipped into it. Brought out sand and flung it into the upturned faces she passed. This was not the soothing sand of sleep but poisoned sand. It was killing them. When it struck them their faces went white and the lines on the machines monitoring their precarious lives went flat.

Maybe she killed the Krenmitz kids because they were brats . . . and her roommate . . . maybe even her own father. But these others?

But he knew. The Annie in him knew. Old and sick. All of them had been old and sick except Mrs Simeaux, and she must have been nothing but a vegetable when she came in. Mrs Simeaux and the kid who had fallen down the well. Annie had killed them because –

'Because they were rats in a trap,' he whispered.

Poor things. Poor poor things.

Sure. That was it. In Annie's view all the people in the world were divided into three groups: brats, poor poor things . . . and Annie.

She had moved steadily westward. Harrisburg to Pittsburgh to Duluth to Fargo. Then, in 1978, to Denver. In each case the pattern was the same: a 'welcome aboard' article in which Annie's name was mentioned among others (she had missed the Manchester 'welcome aboard' probably because, Paul guessed, she hadn't known that local newspapers printed such things), then two or three unremarkable deaths. Following these, the cycle would start again.

Until Denver, that was.

At first, it seemed the same. There was the *NEW ARRIVALS* article, this time clipped from the in-house newspaper of Denver's Receiving Hospital, with Annie's name mentioned. The in-house paper was identified, in Annie's neat hand, as *The Gurney*. 'Great name for a hospital paper,' Paul told the empty room. 'Surprised no one thought of calling it *The Stool Sample.*' He donkeyed more terrified laughter, all unaware. Turned the page, and here was the first obit, cut from the Rocky Mountain *News*. Laura D. Rothberg. Long illness. September 21st, 1978. Denver Receiving Hospital.

Then the pattern broke wide open.

The next page announced a wedding instead of a funeral. The photo showed Annie, not in her uniform but in a white dress frothing with lace. Beside her, holding her hands in his, was a man named Ralph Dugan. Dugan was a physical therapist. DUGAN-WILKES NUPTIALS, the clipping was headed. Rocky Mountain *News,* January 2nd, 1979. Dugan was quite unremarkable save for one thing: he looked like Annie's father. Paul thought if you shaved off Dugan's singles-bar moustache – which she had probably gotten him to do as soon as the honeymoon was over – the resemblance would be just short of uncanny.

Paul thumbed the thickness of the remaining pages in Annie's book and thought Ralph Dugan should have checked his horoscope – whoops, make that *horrorscope* the day he proposed to Annie.

I think the chances are very good that somewhere up ahead in these unturned pages I am going to find a brief article about you. Some people have appointments in Samarra; I think you may well have had one with a pile of laundry or a dead cat on a flight of stairs. A dead cat with a cute name.

But he was wrong. The next clipping was a NEW ARRIVALS from the Nederland newspaper. Nederland was a small town just west of Boulder. Not all that far from here, Paul judged. For a moment he couldn't find Annie in the short, name-filled clipping, and then realized he was looking for the wrong name. She was here, but had become part of a socio-sexual corporation called 'Mr and Mrs Ralph Dugan'.

Paul's head snapped up. Was that a car coming? No . . . just the wind. Surely the wind. He looked back down at Annie's book.

Ralph Dugan had gone back to helping the lame, the halt, and the blind at Arapahoe County Hospital; presumably Annie went back to that time-honored nurse's job of giving aid and comfort to the grievously wounded.

Now the killing starts, he thought. The only real question is about Ralph: does he come at the beginning, in the middle, or at the end?

But he was wrong again. Instead of an obit, the next clipping showed a Xerox of a realtor's one-sheet. In the upper left corner of the ad was a photo of a house. Paul recognized it only by the attached barn – he had, after all, never seen the house itself from the outside.

Beneath, in Annie's neat firm hand: *Earnest money paid March 3rd, 1979. Papers passed March 18th, 1979.*

Retirement home? Paul doubted it. Summer place? No, they couldn't afford the luxury. So . . . ?

Well, maybe it was just a fantasy, but try this. Maybe she really loves old Ralph Dugan. Maybe a year has passed and she still can't smell cockadoodie on him. *Something* has sure changed; there have been no obituaries since –

He flicked back to see.

Since Laura Rothberg in September 1978. She stopped killing around the same time she met Ralph. But that was then and this is now; now the pressure is starting to build up again. The depressive interludes are coming back. She looks at the old people . . . the terminally ill . . . and she thinks about what poor poor things they are, and maybe she thinks, *It's this environment that's depressing me. The miles of tiled corridor and the smells and the squeak of crepe-soled shoes and the sounds of people in pain. If I could get out of this place I'd be all right.*

So Ralph and Annie had apparently gone back to the land.

He turned the page and blinked.

Slashed into the bottom of the page was AUG 43rd 1880 FUCK YOU!

The paper, thick as it was, had torn in several places under the fury of the hand which had driven the pen.

It was the DIVORCES GRANTED column from the Nederland paper, but he had to turn it over to make sure that Annie and Ralph were a part of it. She had pasted it in upside down.

Yes, here they were. Ralph and Anne Dugan. Grounds: mental cruelty.

'Divorced after a short illness,' Paul muttered, and again looked up, thinking he heard an approaching car. The wind, only the wind . . . Still, he'd better get back to the safety of his room. It wasn't just the worsening pain in his legs; he was edging toward a state of terminal freak-out.

But he bent over the book again. In a weird way it was just too good to put down. It was like a novel so disgusting you just have to finish it.

Annie's marriage had been dissolved in a much more legal fashion than Paul had anticipated. It seemed fair to say that the divorce really *had* been after a short illness – a year and a half of wedded bliss wasn't all that much.

They had bought a house in March, and that was not a step you took if you felt that your marriage was falling apart. What happened? Paul didn't know. He could have made up a story, but a story was all it would have been. Then, reading the clipping again, he noticed something suggestive: *Angela Ford from John Ford. Kirsten Frawley from Stanley Frawley. Danna McLaren from Lee McLaren.* And . . .

Ralph Dugan from Anne Dugan.

There's this American custom, right? No one talks about it much, but it's there. Men propose in the moonlight; women file in court. That's not always *how it works, but usually that's it. So what tale does this grammatical structure have to tell? Angela's saying 'Slip out the back, Jack!' Kirsten is saying 'Make a new plan, Stan!' Danna is saying 'Drop off the key, Lee!' And what was Ralph, the only man who's listed* first *in this column, saying? I think maybe he was saying 'Let me the hell out of here!'*

'Maybe he saw the dead cat on the stairs,' Paul said.

Next page. Another NEW ARRIVALS article. This one was from the Boulder, Colorado, *Camera.* There was a photograph of a dozen new staff members standing on the lawn of the Boulder Hospital. Annie was in the second row, her face a blank white circle under her cap with its black stripe. Another opening of another show. The date underneath was March 9th, 1981. She had re-taken her maiden name.

Boulder. That was where Annie really *had* gone crazy.

He turned the pages faster and faster, his horror mounting, and the two thoughts which kept repeating were *Why in God's name didn't they tip faster?* and *How in God's name did she slip through their fingers?*

May 10th, 1981 – long illness. May 14th, 1981 – long illness. May 23rd – long illness. June 9th – short illness. June 15th – short. June 16th – long.

Short. Long. Long. Short. Long. Long. Short.

The pages stuttered through his fingers. He could smell the faint odor of dried paper-paste.

'Christ, how many did she kill?'

If it was right to equate each obituary pasted in this book with a murder, then her score was more than thirty people by the end of 1981 . . . all without a single murmur from the authorities. Of course most of the victims were old, the rest badly hurt, but still . . . you would think . . .

In 1982 Annie had finally stumbled. The clipping from the January 14th *Camera* showed her blank, stonelike face rendered in newsprint dots below a headline which read: NEW HEAD MATERNITY WARD NURSE NAMED.

On January 29th the nursery deaths had begun.

Annie had chronicled the whole story in her meticulous way. Paul had no trouble following it. *If the people after your hide had found this book, Annie, you would have been in jail or some asylum – until the end of time.*

The first two infant deaths had not aroused suspicion – a story on one had mentioned severe birth defects. But babies, defective or not, weren't the same as old folks dying of renal failure or car-crash victims brought in still somehow alive in spite of heads which were only half there or steering-wheelsized holes in their guts. And then she had begun killing the healthy along with the damaged. He supposed that, in her deepening psychotic spiral, she had begun to see all of them as poor poor things.

By mid-March of 1982 there had been five nursery deaths in the Boulder Hospital. A full-scale investigation was launched. On March 24th the *Camera* named the probable culprit as 'tainted formula'. A 'reliable hospital source' was cited, and Paul wondered if perhaps the source had not been Annie Wilkes herself.

Another baby had died in April. Two in May.

Then, from the front page of the June 1st Denver *Post*:

HEAD MATERNITY NURSE QUESTIONED ON INFANT DEATHS

'No Charges Made As Yet,' Sheriff's Office Spokeswoman Says

By Michael Leith

Anne Wilkes, the thirty-nine-year-old head nurse of the maternity ward at Boulder Hospital is being questioned today about the deaths of eight infants – deaths which have taken place over a span of some months. All of the deaths took place following Miss Wilkes's appointment.

When asked if Miss Wilkes was under arrest, Sheriff's Office spokeswoman Tamara Kinsolving said she was not. When asked if Miss Wilkes had come in of her own free will to give information in the case, Ms. Kinsolving replied: 'I would have to say that was not the case. Things are a bit more serious than that.' Asked if Wilkes had been charged with any crime, Ms. Kinsolving replied: 'No. Not as yet.'

The rest of the article was a rehash of Annie's career. It was obvious that she had moved around a lot, but there was no hint that people in *all* of Annie's hospitals, not just the one in Boulder, had a way of croaking when she was around.

He looked at the accompanying photograph, fascinated.

Annie in custody. Dear God, Annie in custody; the idol not fallen but teetering . . . teetering . . .

She was mounting a set of stone steps in the company of a husky policewoman, her face dull, devoid of expression. She was wearing her nurse's uniform and white shoes.

Next page: WILKES RELEASED, MUM ON INTERROGATION.

She'd gotten away with it. Somehow, she'd gotten away with it. It was time for her to fade out and show up someplace else – Idaho, Utah, California, maybe. Instead, she went back to work. And instead of a NEW ARRIVALS column from somewhere farther west there was a huge headline from the Rocky Mountain *News* front page of July 2nd, 1982:

The Horror Continues:

THREE MORE INFANT DEATHS IN BOULDER HOSPITAL

Two days later the authorities arrested a Puerto Rican orderly, only to release him nine hours later. Then, on July 19th, both the Denver *Post* and the Rocky Mountain *News* announced Annie's arrest. There had been a short preliminary hearing in early August. On September 9th she went on trial for the murder of Girl Christopher, a female child one day of age. Behind Girl Christopher were seven other counts of first-degree murder. The article noted that some of Annie's alleged victims had even lived long enough to be given real names.

Interspersed among the accounts of the trial were Letters to the Editor printed in the Denver and Boulder newspapers. Paul understood that Annie had been driven to cull only the most hostile ones – those which reinforced her jaundiced view of mankind as *Homo brattus* – but they were vituperative by any standards. There seemed to be a consensus: hanging was too good for Annie Wilkes. One correspondent dubbed her the Dragon Lady, and the name stuck for the duration of the trial. Most seemed to feel that the Dragon Lady should be jabbed to death with hot forks, and most indicated they would be very willing to serve as a jabber.

Beside one such letter Annie had written in a shaky and somehow pathetic script entirely unlike her usual firm hand: *Sticks stones will break my bones words will never hurt me.*

It was apparent that Annie's biggest mistake had been not stopping when people finally realized *something* was going on. It was bad, but, unfortunately, not quite bad enough. The idol only tottered. The prosecution's case was entirely circumstantial, and in places thin enough to read a newspaper through. The district attorney had a hand-mark on Girl Christopher's face and throat which corresponded to the size of Annie's hand, complete with the mark of the amethyst ring she wore on the fourth finger of her right hand. The D.A. also had a pattern of observed entries and exits to the nursery which roughly corresponded to the infant deaths. But Annie was the head maternity nurse, after all, so she was *always* going in and out. Defense was able to show dozens of other occasions when Annie had entered the ward and *nothing* untoward had happened. Paul thought this was akin to proving that meteors never struck the earth by showing five days when not a single one had hit Farmer John's north field, but he could understand the weight the argument would have carried with the jury just the same.

The prosecution wove its net as well as it could, but the handprint with the mark of the ring was really the most damning bit of evidence it could come up with. The fact that the State of Colorado had elected to bring Annie to trial at all, given such a slight chance of conviction on the evidence, left Paul with one assumption and one certainty. The assumption was that Annie had said things during her original interrogation which were extremely suggestive, perhaps even damning; her attorney had managed to keep the transcript of that interrogation out of the trial record. The certainty was that Annie's decision to testify in her own behalf at the preliminary hearing had been extremely unwise. *That* testimony her attorney hadn't been able to keep out of the trial (although he had nearly ruptured himself trying), and while Annie had never confessed to anything in so many words during the three days in August she had spent 'up there – on the stand in Denver', he thought that she had really confessed to everything.

Excerpts from the clippings pasted in her book contained some real gems:

> Did they make me feel sad? Of course they made me feel sad, considering the world we live in.
>
> I have nothing to be ashamed of. I am never ashamed. What I do, that's final, I never look back on that type of thing.
>
> Did I attend the funerals of any of them? Of course not. I find funerals very grim and depressing. Also, I don't believe babies are ensouled.
>
> No, I never cried.
>
> Was I sorry? I guess that's a philosophical question, isn't it?
>
> Of *course* I understand the question. I understand all your questions. I know you're all out to get me.

If she had insisted on testifying in her own behalf at her trial, Paul thought, *her lawyer probably would have shot her to shut her up.*

The case went to the jury on December 13th, 1982. And here was a startling picture from the Rocky Mountain *News,* a photo of Annie sitting calmly in her holding cell and reading *Misery's Quest. IN MISERY?* the caption below asked. NOT THE DRAGON LADY. Annie reads calmly as she waits for the verdict.

And then, on December 16th, banner headlines: DRAGON LADY INNOCENT. In the body of the story a juror who asked not to be identified was quoted. 'I had very grave doubts as to her innocence, yes. Unfortunately, I had very reasonable doubts as to her guilt. I hope she will be tried again on one of the other counts. Perhaps the prosecution could make a stronger case on one of those.'

They all knew she did it but nobody could prove it. So she slipped through their fingers.

The case wound down over the next three or four pages. The D.A. said Annie surely would be tried on one of the other counts. Three weeks later, he said he never said that. In early February of 1983, the district attorney's office issued a statement saying that while the cases of infanticide at the Boulder Hospital were still very much alive, the case against Anne Wilkes was closed.

Slipped through their fingers.

Her husband never testified for either side. Why was that, I wonder?

There were more pages in the book, but he could tell by the snug way most lay against each other that he was almost done with Annie's history up to now. Thank God.

The next page was from the Sidewinder *Gazette,* November 19th, 1984. Hikers had found the mutilated and partly dismembered remains of a young man in the eastern section of Grider Wildlife Preserve. The following week's paper identified him as Andrew Pomeroy, age twenty-three, of Cold Stream Harbor, New York. Pomeroy had left New York for L.A. in September of the previous year, hitchhiking. His parents had last heard from him on October 15th. He had called them collect from Julesburg. The body had been found in a dry stream-bed. Police theorized that Pomeroy might actually have been killed near Highway 9 and washed into the Wildlife Preserve during the spring run-off. The coroner's report said the wounds had been inflicted with an axe.

Paul wondered, not quite idly, how far Grider Wildlife Preserve was from here.

He turned the page and looked at the last clipping – at least so far– and suddenly his breath was gone. It was as if, after wading grimly through the almost unbearable necrology in the foregoing pages, he had come face to face with his own obituary. It wasn't quite, but . . .

'But close enough for government work,' he said in a low, hoarse voice.

It was from *Newsweek.* The 'Transitions' column. Listed below the divorce of a TV actress and above the death of a Midwestern steel potentate was this item:

> REPORTED MISSING: *Paul Sheldon,* 42, novelist best known for his series of romances about sexy, bubbleheaded, unsinkable Misery Chastain; by his agent, Bryce Bell. 'I think he's fine,' Bell said, 'but I wish he'd get in touch and ease my mind. And his ex-wives wish he'd get in touch and ease their bank accounts.' Sheldon was last seen seven weeks ago in Boulder, Colorado, where he had gone to finish a new novel.

The clipping was two weeks old.

Reported missing, that's all. Just reported missing. I'm not dead, it's not like being dead.

But it was like being dead, and suddenly he needed his medication because it wasn't just his legs that hurt. *Everything* hurt. He put the book carefully back in its place and began rolling the wheelchair toward the guest-room.

Outside, the wind gusted more strongly than it had yet done, slapping cold rain against the house, and Paul shrank away from it, moaning and afraid, trying desperately hard to hold himself together and not burst into tears.

19

An hour later, full of dope and drifting off to sleep, the sound of the howling wind now soothing rather than frightening, he thought: I'm not going to escape. *No way. What is it Thomas Hardy says in* Jude the Obscure*? 'Someone could have come along and eased the boy's terror, but nobody did . . .*

because nobody does.' *Right. Correct. Your ship is not going to come in because there are no boats for nobody. The Lone Ranger is busy making breakfast-cereal commercials and Superman's making movies in Tinsel Town. You're on your own, Paulie. Dead flat on your own. But maybe that's okay. Because maybe you know what the answer is, after all, don't you?*

Yes, of course he did.

If he meant to get out of this, he would have to kill her.

Yes. That's the answer – the only one there is, I think. So it's that same old game again, isn't it? Paulie . . . Can You?

He answered with no hesitation at all. Yes, I can.

His eyes drifted closed. He slept.

20

The storm continued through the next day. The following night the clouds unravelled and blew away. At the same time the temperature plummeted from sixty degrees down to twenty-five. All the world outside froze solid. Sitting by the bedroom window and looking out at the ice-glittery morning world on that second full day alone, Paul could hear Misery the pig squealing in the barn and one of the cows bellowing.

He often heard the animals; they were as much a part of the general background as the chiming parlor-clock – but he had never heard the pig squeal so. He thought he had heard the cow bellow like that once before, but it had been an evil sound dimly heard in an evil dream, because then he had been full of his own pain. It had been when Annie had gone away that first time, leaving him with no pills. He had been raised in suburban Boston and had lived most of his life in New York City, but he thought he knew what those pained cow-bellows meant. One of the cows needed to be milked. The other apparently didn't, possibly because Annie's erratic milking habits had already dried her up.

And the pig?

Hungry. That was all. And that was enough.

They weren't going to get any relief today. He doubted if Annie would be able to make it back even if she had wanted to. This part of the world had turned into one big skating rink. He was a little surprised at the depth of sympathy he felt for the animals and the depth of his anger at Annie for how she had, in her unadmitting and arrogant egoism, left them to suffer in their pens.

If your animals could talk, Annie, they would tell you who the REAL dirty birdie around here is.

He himself was quite comfortable as those days passed. He ate from cans, drank water from the new pitcher, took his medication regularly, napped each afternoon. The tale of Misery and her amnesia and her previously unsuspected (and spectacularly rotten) blood kin marched steadily along toward Africa, which was to be the setting of the novel's second half. The irony was that the woman had coerced him into writing what was easily the best of the 'Misery' novels. Ian and Geoffrey were off in Southampton outfitting a schooner called the *Lorelei* for the run. It was on the Dark Continent that Misery, who kept slipping into cataleptic trances at the most inconvenient moments (and, of course, if she were to be stung by another bee – ever, in her entire life – she would die almost instantly), would either be killed or cured. For a hundred and fifty miles inland from Lawstown, a tiny British-Dutch settlement on the northernmost tip of the Barbary Coast's dangerous crescent, lived the Bourkas, Africa's most dangerous natives. The Bourkas were sometimes known as the Bee-People. Few of the whites who dared to venture into Bourka country had ever returned, but those who did had brought back fabulous tales of a woman's face jutting from the side of a tall, crumbling mesa, a merciless face with a gaping mouth and a huge ruby set in her stone forehead. There was another story – only a rumor, surely, but strangely persistent – that within the caves which honeycombed the stone behind the idol's jewelled forehead there lived a hive of giant albino bees, swarming protectively around their queen, a jellylike monstrosity of infinite poison . . . and infinite magic.

During the days he diverted himself with this pleasant foolishness. In the evenings he sat quietly, listening to the pig squeal and thinking about how he would kill the Dragon Lady.

Playing Can You? in real life was quite different from playing it in a cross-legged circle as a kid or doing it in front of a typewriter as a grown-up, he discovered. When it was just a game (and even if they gave you money for it, a game was still all it was), you could think up some pretty wild things and make them seem believable – the connection between Misery Chastain and Miss Charlotte Evelyn-Hyde, for instance (they had turned out to be half-sisters; Misery would later discover her father down there in Africa hanging out with the Bourka Bee-People). In real life, however, the arcane had a way of losing its power.

Not that Paul didn't try. There were all those drugs in the downstairs bathroom – surely there was some way he could use them to put her out of the way, wasn't there? Or to at least render her helpless long enough so he could do it? Take the Novril. Enough of that shit and he wouldn't even have to put her out of the way. She would float off on her own.

That's a very good idea, Paul. I tell you what to do. You just get a whole bunch of those capsules and stick them all through a pint of her ice-cream. She'll just think they're pistachio nuts and gobble them right down.

No, of course that wouldn't work. Nor could he pull a cutie like opening the capsules and mixing the powder into some pre-softened ice-cream. He had tasted it and knew. Novril in the raw was fabulously bitter. It was a taste she would recognize at once in the midst of the expected sweetness . . . *and then woe is you, Paulie. Woe to the max.*

In a story it would have been a pretty good idea. In real life, however, it simply did not make it. He wasn't sure he would have taken the chance even if the white powder inside the capsules had been almost or completely tasteless. It wasn't safe enough, it wasn't sure enough. This was no game; it was his life.

Other ideas passed through his mind and were rejected even more quickly. One was suspending something (the typewriter came immediately to mind) over the door so she would be killed or knocked unconscious when she came in. Another was running a tripwire across the stairway. But the problem was the same as the old Novril-in-the-ice-cream trick: in both cases neither was sure enough. He found himself literally unable to think of what might happen to him if he tried to assassinate her and failed.

As dark came down on that second night, Misery's squealing went on as monotonously as ever – the pig sounded like an unlatched door with rusty hinges squealing in the wind – but Bossie No. 1 abruptly fell silent. Paul wondered uneasily if perhaps the poor animal's udder had burst, resulting in death by exsanguination. For a moment his imagination

so vivid!

tried to present him with a picture of the cow lying dead in a puddle of mixed milk and blood, and he quickly willed it away. He told himself not to be such a numbnuts – cows didn't die that way. But the voice doing the telling lacked conviction. He had no idea if they did or not. And, besides, it wasn't the *cow* that was his problem, was it?

All your fancy ideas come down to one thing – you want to kill her by remote control, you don't want her blood on your hands. You're like a man who loves nothing better than a thick steak but wouldn't last an hour in a slaughterhouse. But listen, Paulie, and get it straight: you must face reality at this point in your life if at no other. Nothing fancy. No curlicues. Right?

Right.

He rolled back into the kitchen and opened drawers until he found the knives. He selected the longest butcher-knife and went back to his room, pausing to rub away the hubmarks on the sides of the doorway. The signs of his passage were nevertheless becoming clearer.

Doesn't matter. If she misses them one more time, she misses them for good.

He put the knife on the night-table, hoisted himself into bed, then slid it under the mattress. When Annie came back he was going to ask her for a nice cold glass of water, and when she leaned over to give it to him he was going to plunge the knife into her throat.

Nothing fancy.

Paul closed his eyes and dropped off to sleep, and when the Cherokee came whispering back into the driveway that morning at four o'clock with both its engine and its lights shut off, he did not stir. Until he felt the sting of the hypo sliding into his arm and woke to see her face leaning over his, he hadn't the slightest idea she was back.

21

At first he thought he was dreaming about his own book, that the dark was the dream-dark of the caves behind the huge stone head of the Bourka Bee-Goddess and the sting was that of a bee –

'Paul?'

He muttered something that meant nothing – something that meant only get out of here, dream voice, get gone.

'Paul.'

That was no dream voice; it was Annie's voice.

He forced his eyes open. Yes, it was her, and for a moment his panic grew even stronger. Then it simply seeped away, like fluid running down a partly clogged drain.

What the hell – ?

He was totally disoriented. She was standing there in the shadows as if she had never been away, wearing one of her woolly skirts and frumpy sweaters; he saw the needle in her hand and understood it hadn't been a sting but an injection. What the fuck – either way it was the same thing. He had been gotten by the goddess. But what had she – ?

That bright panic tried to come again, and once again it hit a dead circuit. All he could feel was a kind of academic surprise. That, and some intellectual curiosity about where she had come from, and why now. He tried to lift his hands and they came up a little . . . but only a little. It felt as if there were invisible weights dangling from them. They dropped back onto the sheet with little dull thumps.

Doesn't matter what she shot me up with. It's like what you write on the last page of a book. It's THE END.

The thought brought no fear. Instead he felt a kind of calm euphoria.

At least she's tried to make it kind . . . to make it . . .

'Ah, *there* you are!' Annie said, and added with lumbering coquettishness: 'I *see* you, Paul . . . those blue eyes. Did I ever tell you what lovely blue eyes you have? But I suppose other women have – women who were much prettier than I am, and much bolder about their affections, as well.'

Came back. Came creeping in the night and killed me, hypo or bee-sting, no difference, and so much for the knife under the bed. All I am now is the latest number in Annie's considerable body-count. And then, as the numbing euphoria of the injection began to spread, he thought almost with humor: *Some lousy Scheherazade* I *turned out to be.*

He thought that in a moment sleep would return – a more final sleep – but it did not. He saw her slip the hypo into the pocket of her skirt and then she sat down on the bed . . . not where she usually sat, however; she sat on its foot and for a moment he saw only her solid, impervious back as she bent over, as if to check on something. He heard a wooden *thunk*, a metallic *clunk*, and then a shaking sound he had heard some place before. After a moment he placed it. *Take the matches, Paul.*

Diamond Blue Tips. He didn't know what else she might have there at the foot of the bed, but one of them was a box of Diamond Blue Tip matches.

Annie turned to him and smiled again. Whatever else might have happened, her apocalyptic depression had passed. She brushed an errant lock of hair back behind her ear with a girlish gesture. It went oddly with the lock's dull dirty half-shine.

Dull dirty half-shine oh boy you gotta remember that one that one ain't half-bad oh boy I am stoned now, all the past was prologue to this shit hey baby this here is the mainline oh fuck I'm fucked but this is crystal top-end shit this is going out on a mile-high wave in a fucking Rolls this is –

'What do you want first, Paul?' she asked. 'The good news or the bad news?'

'Good news first.' He managed a big foolish grin. 'Guess the bad news is that this is THE END, huh? Guess you didn't like the book so great, huh? Too bad . . . I tried. It was even working. I was just starting to . . . you know . . . starting to drive on it.'

She looked at him reproachfully. 'I *love* the book, Paul. I told you that, and I never lie. I love it so much I don't want to read any more until the very end. I'm sorry to have to make you fill in the n's yourself, but . . . it's like peeking.'

His big foolish grin stretched even wider; he thought soon it would meet in the back, tie a lover's knot there, and most of his poor old bean would just topple off. Maybe it would land in the bedpan beside the bed. In some deep, dim part of his mind where the dope hadn't yet reached, alarm bells were going off. She loved the book, which meant she didn't mean to kill him. Whatever was going on, she didn't mean to kill him. And unless his assessment of Annie Wilkes was totally off the beam, that meant she had something even worse in store. Now the light in the room did not look dull; it looked marvelously pure, marvelously full of its own gray and eldritch charm; he could imagine cranes half-glimpsed in gunmetal mist standing in one-legged silence beside upland lakes in that light, could imagine the mica flecks in rocks jutting from spring grasses in upland meadows shining with the shaggy glow of glazed window-glass in that light, could imagine elves shucking their busy selves off to work in lines under the dew-soaked leaves of early ivy in that light . . .

Oh BOY are you stoned, Paul thought, and giggled faintly.

Annie smiled in return. 'The *good* news,' she said, 'is that your car is gone. I've been very worried about your car, Paul. I knew it would take a storm like this to get rid of it, and maybe even that wouldn't do the trick. The spring run-off got rid of that Pomeroy dirty bird, but a car is ever so much heavier than a man, isn't it? Even a man as full of cockadoodie as he was. But the storm and the run-off combined was enough to do the trick. Your car is gone. That's the *good* news.'

'What . . .' More faint alarm bells. Pomeroy . . . he knew that name, but couldn't think exactly how he knew it. Then it came to him. Pomeroy. The late great Andrew Pomeroy, twenty-three, of Cold Stream Harbor, New York. Found in the Grider Wildlife Preserve, wherever *that* was.

'Now Paul,' she said, in the prim voice he knew so well. 'No need to be coy. I know you know who Andy Pomeroy was, because I know you've read my book. I suppose that I sort of hoped you would read it, you know; otherwise, why would I have left it out? But I made sure, you know – I make sure of everything. And sure enough, the threads were broken.'

'The threads,' he said faintly.

'Oh yes. I read once about a way you're supposed to find out for sure if someone has been snooping around in your drawers. You tape a very fine thread across each one, and if you come back and find one broken, why you know, don't you? You know someone's been snooping. You see how easy it is?'

'Yes, Annie.' He was listening, but what he really wanted to do was trip out on the marvelous quality of the light.

Again she bent over to check whatever it was she had at the foot of the bed; again he heard a faint dull *clunk/clank,* wood thumping against some metallic object, and then she turned back, brushing absently at her hair again.

'I did that with my book – only I didn't really use threads, you know; I used hairs from my own head. I put them across the thickness of the book in three different places and when I came in this morning – very early, creeping like a little mousie so I wouldn't wake you up – all three threads were broken, so I *knew* you had been looking at my book.' She paused, and smiled. It was, for Annie, a very winning smile, yet it had an unpleasant quality he could not quite put his finger on. 'Not that I was surprised. I knew you had been out of the room. *That's* the bad news. I've known for a long, *long* time, Paul.'

He should feel angry and dismayed, he supposed. She had known, known almost from the start, it seemed . . . but he could only feel that dreamy, floating euphoria, and what she was saying did not seem nearly as important as the glorious quality of the strengthening light as the day hovered on the edge of becoming.

'But,' she said with the air of one returning to business, 'we were talking about your car. I have studded tires, Paul, and at my place in the hills I keep a set of IoX tire chains. Early yesterday afternoon I felt ever so much better – I spent most of my time up there on my knees, deep in prayer, and the answer came, as it often does, and it was quite simple, as it often is. What you take to the Lord in prayer, Paul, He giveth back a thousandfold. So I put the chains on and I crept back down here. It was not easy, and I knew I might well have an accident in spite of the studs and the chains. I also knew that there is rarely such a thing as a "minor accident" on those twisty upcountry roads. But I felt easy in my mind, because I felt safe in the will of the Lord.'

'That's very uplifting, Annie,' Paul croaked.

She gave him a look which was momentarily startled and narrowly suspicious . . . and then she relaxed and smiled. 'I've got a present for you, Paul,' she said softly, and before he could ask her what it was – he wasn't sure he wanted any sort of present from Annie – she went on: 'The roads *were* terribly icy. I almost went off twice . . . The second time, Old Bessie slid all the way around in a circle and kept right on going downhill while she did it!' Annie laughed cheerily. 'Then I got stuck in a snowbank – this was around midnight but a sanding-crew from the Eustice Public Works Department came along and helped me out.'

'Bully for the Eustice Public Works Department,' Paul said, but what came out was badly slurred – *Burry furdah Estice Pulleyqurks Deparrent.*

'The two miles in from the county highway, that was the last hard patch. The county highway is Route 9, you know. The road you were on when you had your wreck. They had sanded that one to a fare-thee-well. I stopped where you went off and looked for your car. And I knew what I would have to do if I saw it. Because there would be questions, and I'd be just about the first one they'd ask those questions to, for reasons I think you know.'

I'm way ahead of you, Annie, he thought. I examined this whole scenario three weeks ago.

'One of the reasons I brought you back was because it seemed like more than a coincidence . . . it seemed more like the hand of Providence.'

'What seemed like the hand of Providence, Annie?' he managed.

'Your car was wrecked in almost exactly the same spot where I got rid of that Pomeroy creep. The one who said he was an artist.' She slapped a hand in contempt, shifted her feet, and there was that wooden clunking sound as one of them brushed some of whatever it was she had down there on the floor.

'I picked him up on my way back from Estes Park. I was there at a ceramics show. I like little ceramic figurines.'

'I noticed,' Paul said. His voice seemed to come from light-years away. *Captain Kirk! There's a voice coming in over the sub-etheric,* he thought, and chuckled dimly. That deep part of him – the part the dope couldn't reach – tried to warn him to shut his mouth, just shut it, but what was the sense? She knew. *Of course she knows – the Bourka Bee-Goddess knows everything.* 'I particularly liked the penguin on the block of ice.'

'Thank you, Paul . . . he is cute, isn't he?'

'Pomeroy was hitchhiking. He had a pack on his back. He said he was an artist, although I found out later he was nothing but a hippie dope-fiend dirty bird who had been washing dishes in an Estes Park restaurant for the last couple of months. When I told him I had a place in Sidewinder, he said that was a real coincidence. He said *he* was going to Sidewinder. He said he'd gotten an assignment from a magazine in New York. He was going to go up to the old hotel and sketch the ruins. His pictures were going to be with an article they were doing. It was a famous old hotel called the Overlook. It burned down ten years ago. The caretaker burned it down. He was crazy. Everybody in town said so. But never mind; he's dead.

'I let Pomeroy stay here with me.

'We were lovers.'

She looked at him with her black eyes burning in her solid yet doughy white face and Paul thought: If *Andrew Pomeroy could get it up for you, Annie, he must have been as crazy as the caretaker that burned down the hotel.*

'Then I found out that he didn't really have an assignment to draw pictures of the hotel at all. He was just doing them on his own, hoping to sell them. He wasn't even sure the magazine was doing an article on the Overlook. I found that out pretty quick! After I did, I sneaked a look at his sketchpad. I felt I had a perfect right to do that. After all, he was eating my food and sleeping in my bed. There were only eight or nine pictures in the whole book and they were *terrible.*'

Her face wrinkled, and for a moment she looked as she had when she had imitated the sound the pig made.

'*I* could have made better pictures! He came in while I was looking and he got mad. He said I was snooping. I said I didn't call looking at things in my own house snooping. I said if he was an artist, I was Madame Curie. He started to laugh. He laughed at me. So I . . . I . . .'

'You killed him,' Paul said. His voice sounded dim and ancient.

She smiled uneasily at the wall. 'Well, I guess it was something like that. I don't remember very well. Just when he was dead. I remember that. I remember giving him a bath.'

He stared at her and felt a sick, soupy horror. The image came to him – Pomeroy's naked body floating in the downstairs tub like a piece of raw dough, head reclining aslant against the porcelain, open eyes staring up at the ceiling . . .

'I *had* to,' she said, lips drawing back a bit from her teeth. 'You probably don't know what the police can do with just one piece of thread, or dirt under someone's fingernails or even dust in a corpse's hair! You don't know but I worked in hospitals all my life and I *do* know! I *do* know! I know about *for-EN-sics!*

She was working herself into one of her patented Annie Wilkes frenzies and he knew he should try and say something which would at least temporarily defuse her, but his mouth seemed numb and useless.

'They're out to get me, all of them! Do you think they would have listened if I tried to tell them how it was? Do you? Do you? Oh no! They'd probably say something crazy like I made a pass at him and he laughed at me and so I killed him! They'd probably say something like that!'

And you know what, Annie? You know what? I think that just might be a little closer to the truth.

'The dirty birdies around here would say *anything* to get me in trouble or smear my name.'

She paused, not quite panting but breathing hard, looking at him hard, as if inviting him to just dare and tell her different. *Just you dare!*

Then she seemed to get herself under some kind of control and she went on in a calmer voice.

'I washed . . . well . . . what was left of him . . . and his clothes. I knew what to do. It was snowing outside, the first real snow of the year, and they said we'd have a foot by the next morning. I put his clothes in a plastic bag and wrapped the body in sheets and took everything out to that dry wash on Route 9 after dark. I walked about a mile farther down from where your car ended up. I walked until I was in the woods and just dumped everything. You probably think I hid him, but I didn't. I knew the snow would cover him up, and I thought the spring melt would carry him away if I left him in the stream-bed. And that was what happened, except I had no idea he would go so *far*. Why, they found his body a whole year after . . . after he died, and almost twenty-seven miles away. Actually, it would have been better if he hadn't gone as far as he did, because there are always hikers and bird-watchers in the Grider Preserve. The woods around here are much less traveled.'

She smiled.

'And that's where your car is now, Paul – somewhere between Route 9 and the Grider Wildlife Preserve, somewhere in the woods. It's far enough in so you can't see it from the road. I've got a spotlight on the side of Old Bessie, and it's plenty powerful, but the wash is empty all the way into the woods. I guess I'll go in on foot and check when the water goes down a little, but I'm almost positive it's safe. Some hunter will find it in two years or five years or seven years, all rusty and with chipmunks nesting in the seats, and by then you will have finished my book and will be back in New York or Los Angeles or wherever it is you decide to go, and I'll be living my quiet life out here. Maybe we will correspond sometimes.'

She smiled mistily – the smile of a woman who sees a lovely castle in the sky – and then the smile disappeared and she was all business again.

'So I came back here and on the way I did some hard thinking. I had to, because your car being gone meant that you could really stay, you could really finish my book. I wasn't always sure you'd be able to, you know, although I never said because I didn't want to upset you. Partly I didn't want to upset you because I knew you wouldn't write as well if I did, but that sounds ever so much colder than I really felt, my dear. You see, I began by loving only the part of you that makes such wonderful stories, because that's the only part I had – the rest of you I didn't know anything about, and I thought that part might really be quite unpleasant. I'm not a dummy, you know. I've read about some so-called "famous authors", and I know that often they *are* quite unpleasant. Why, F. Scott Fitzgerald and Ernest Hemingway and that redneck fellow from Mississippi – Faulkner or whatever it was – those fellows may have won National Pulitzer Book Awards and things, but they were nothing but cockadoodie drunken bums just the same. Other ones, too – when they weren't writing wonderful stories they were drinking and whoring and shooting dope and heaven knows what else.

'But you're not like that, and after awhile I came to know the rest of Paul Sheldon, and I hope you don't mind me saying it, but I have come to love the rest of him, too.'

'Thank you, Annie,' he said from atop his golden glistening wave, and he thought: *But you may have read me wrong, you know – I mean, the situations that lead men into temptation have been severely curtailed up here. It's sort of hard to go bar-hopping when you've got a couple of broken legs, Annie. As for shooting dope, I've got the Bourka Bee-Goddess to do* that *for me.*

'But would you *want* to stay?' she resumed. 'That was the question I had to ask myself, and as much as I may have wanted to pull the wool over my eyes, I knew the answer to *that* – I knew even before I saw the marks on the door over there.'

She pointed and Paul thought: *I'll bet she did know almost from the very first. Wool-pulling? Not you, Annie. Never you. But I was doing enough of that for both of us.*

'Do you remember the first time I went away? After we had that silly fight over the paper?'

'Yes, Annie.'

'That was when you went out the first time, wasn't it?'

'Yes.' There was no point in denying it.

'Of course. You wanted your pills. I should have known you'd do anything to get your pills, but when I get mad, I get . . . you know.' She giggled a little nervously. Paul did not join her, or even smile. The memory of that pain-racked, endless interlude with the phantom voice of the sportscaster doing the play-by-play was too strong still.

Yes, I know how you get, he thought. *You get oogy.*

'At first I wasn't completely sure. Oh, I saw that some of the figures on the little table in the parlor had been moved around, but I thought I might have done that myself – I have times when I'm really quite forgetful. It crossed my mind that you'd been out of your room, but then I thought, *No, that's impossible. He's so badly hurt, and besides, I locked the door.* I even checked to make sure the key was still in my skirt pocket, and it was. Then I remembered you were in your chair. So maybe . . .

'One of the things you learn when you've been an R.N. for ten years is that it's always wise to check your maybes. So I took a look at the things I keep in the downstairs bathroom – they're mostly samples I brought home off and on while I was working; you should see all the stuff that just goes rolling around in hospitals, Paul! And so every now and then I helped myself to a few . . . well . . . a few *extras* . . . and I wasn't the only one. But I knew enough not to take any of the morphine-based drugs. They lock those up. They count. They keep records. And if they get an idea that a nurse is, you know, chipping – that's what they call it – they watch that nurse until they're sure. Then, *bang!'* Annie chopped her hand down hard. 'Out they go, and most of them never put on the white cap again.

'I was smarter than that.

'Looking at those cartons was the same as looking at the figures on the little parlor table. I thought the stuff in them had been sort of stirred around, and I was pretty sure that one of the cartons that was on the bottom before was on top of some of the other cartons now, but I couldn't be *sure.* And I *could* have done it myself when I was . . . well . . . when I was preoccupied.

'Then, two days later, after I had just about decided to let it go, I came in to give you your afternoon medication. You were still having your nap. I tried to turn the doorknob, but for a few seconds it wouldn't turn – it was like the door was locked. Then it *did* turn, and I heard something rattle inside the lock. Then you started to stir around so I just gave you your pills like always. Like I didn't suspect. I'm very good at that, Paul. Then I helped you into your chair so you could write. And when I helped you into it that afternoon, I felt like Saint Paul on the road to Damascus. My eyes were opened. I saw how much of your color had come back. I saw that you were moving your legs. They were giving you pain, and you could only move them a little, but you *were* moving them. And your arms were getting stronger again, as well.

'I saw you were almost *healthy* again.

'That was when I started to realize I could have a problem with you even if no one from the outside suspected a thing. I looked at you and saw that I might not be the only one good at keeping secrets.

'That night I changed your medication for something a little stronger, and when I was sure you weren't going to wake up even if someone exploded a grenade under your bed, I got my little tool-kit from the cellar shelf and I took the keyplate off that door. And look what *I* found!'

She took something small and dark from one of the flap pockets of her mannish shirt. She put it in his numb hand. He brought it up close to his face and stared at it owlishly. It was a bent and twisted chunk of bobby-pin.

Paul began to giggle. He couldn't help it.

'What's so funny, Paul?'

'The day you went to pay your taxes. I needed to open the door again. The wheelchair – it was almost too big – it left black marks. I wanted to wipe them off if I could.'

'So I wouldn't see them.'

'Yes. But you already had, hadn't you?'

'After I found one of my bobby-pins in the lock?' She smiled herself. 'You bet your rooty-patooties I had.'

Paul nodded and laughed even harder. He was laughing so hard tears were squirting from his eyes. All his work . . . all his worry . . . all for nothing. It seemed deliciously funny.

He said, 'I was worried that piece of bobby-pin might mess me up . . . but it didn't. I never even heard it rattling around. And there was a good reason for that, wasn't there? It never rattled because you took it out. What a fooler you are, Annie.'

'Yes,' she said, and smiled thinly. 'What a fooler I am.'

She moved her feet. That muffled wooden thump from the foot of the bed came again.

22

'How many times were you out in all?'

The knife. Oh Christ, the knife.

'Twice. No – wait. I went out again yesterday afternoon around five o'clock. To fill up my water pitcher.' This was true; he *had* filled the pitcher. But he had omitted the real reason for his third trip. The real reason was under his mattress. The Princess and the Pea. Paulie and the Pig Sticker. 'Three times, counting the trip for the water.'

'Tell the truth, Paul.'

'Just three times, I swear. And never to get away. For Christ's sake I'm writing a book here, in case you didn't notice.'

'Don't use the Saviour's name in vain, Paul.'

'You quit using mine that way and maybe I will. The first time I was in so much pain that it felt like someone had put me into hell from the knees on down. And someone did. *You* did, Annie.'

'Shut up, Paul!'

'The second time I just wanted to get something to eat, and make sure I had some extra supplies in here in case you were gone a long time,' he went on, ignoring her. 'Then I got thirsty. That's all there is. No big conspiracy.'

'You didn't try the telephone either time, I suppose, or look at the locks – because you are just *such* a good little boy.'

'Sure I tried the phone. Sure I looked at the locks . . . not that I would have gotten very far in the mudbath out there even if your doors had been wide open.' The dope was coming in heavier and heavier waves, and now he just wished she would shut up and go away. She had already doped him enough to tell the truth – he was afraid he would have to pay the consequences in time. But first he wanted to sleep.

'How many times did you go out?'

'I told you –'

'How many times?' Her voice was rising. 'Tell the *truth!*'

'I am! Three times!'

'How many times, God damn it?'

In spite of the cruiser-load of dope she'd shot into him, Paul began to be frightened.

At least if she does something to me it can't hurt too much . . . and she wants me to finish the book . . . she said so.

'You're treating me like a fool.' He noticed how shiny her skin was, like some sort of polymer plastic stretched tightly over stone. There seemed to be no pores at all in that face.

'Annie, I swear –'

'Oh, liars can swear! Liars *love* to swear! Well, go ahead and treat me like a fool, if that's what you want. That's fine. Goody-goody for you. Treat a woman who isn't a fool as if she were, and that woman always comes out ahead. Let me tell you, Paul – I've stretched thread and strands of hair from my own head all *over* this house and have found many of them snapped later on. Snapped or entirely gone . . . just disappeared . . . poof! Not just on my scrapbook but in this hallway and across my dresser drawers upstairs . . . in the shed . . . *all over.*'

Annie, how could I possibly get out in the shed with all those locks on the kitchen door? he wanted to ask, but she gave him no time, only plunged on.

'Now you go right ahead and keep telling me it was only *three times,* Mister Smart Guy, and I'll tell you who the fool is.'

He stared at her, groggy but appalled. He didn't know how to answer her. It was so paranoid . . . so crazy. . .

My God, he thought, suddenly forgetting the shed, *upstairs? Did she say UPSTAIRS?*

'Annie, how in God's name could I get upstairs?'

'Oh, *RIGHT!*' she cried, her voice cracking. 'Oh, *SURE!* I came in here a few days ago and you'd managed to get into your wheelchair *all by yourself!* If you could do that, you could get upstairs! *You could crawl!*'

'Yes, on my broken legs and my shattered knee,' he said.

Again that black look of *crevasse;* the batty darkness under the meadow. Annie Wilkes was gone. The Bourka Bee-Goddess was here.

'You don't want to be smart to me, Paul,' she whispered.

'Well, Annie, one of us has to at least try, and you're not doing a very good job. If you'd just try to see how cr –

'How many times?'

'Three.'

'The first time to get medication.'

'Yes. Novril capsules.'

'And the second time to get food.'

'That's right.'

'The third time it was to fill up the pitcher.'

'Yes. Annie, I'm so dizzy –'

'You filled it in the bathroom up the hall.'

'Yes –'

'Once for medication, once for food, and once for water.'

'Yes, I told you!' He tried to yell, but what came out was a strengthless croak.

She reached into her skirt pocket again and brought out the butcher knife. Its keen blade glimmered in the brightening morning light. She suddenly twisted to the left and threw the knife. She threw it with the deadly, half-casual grace of a carnival performer. It stuck, quivering, in the plaster below the picture of the Arc de Triomphe.

'I investigated under your mattress a little before I gave you your pre-op shot. I expected to find capsules; the knife was a complete surprise. I almost cut myself. But *you* didn't put it there, did you?'

He didn't reply. His mind was spinning and diving like an out-of-control amusement-park ride. Pre-op shot? Was that what she had said? *Pre-op?* He was suddenly, utterly sure that she meant to pull the knife from the wall and castrate him with it.

'No, *you* didn't put it there. You went out once for medication, once for food, and once for water. This knife must have . . . why, it must have *floated* in here and slid under there all by itself. Yes, that's what must have happened!' Annie shrieked derisive laughter.

PRE-OP??? Dear God, is that what she said?

'Damn you!' she cried. *'God damn* you! *How many times?'*

'All right! All right! I got the knife when I went after the water! I confess! If you think that means I was out any number of times, go on and fill in the blank! If you want it to be five times, it was five. If you want it to be twenty, or fifty, or a hundred, that's what it was. I'll admit it. However many times you think, Annie, that's how many times I was out.'

For a moment, in his anger and dopey befuddlement, he had lost sight of the hazy, frightening concept inherent in that phrase *pre-op shot.* He wanted to tell her so much, wanted to tell her even though he knew that a ravening paranoid like Annie would reject what was so obvious. It had been damp; Scotch tape did not like the damp; in many cases her Ludlumesque little traps had undoubtedly just peeled off and floated away on some random draft. And the rats. With a lot of water in the cellar and the mistress of the manor gone, he had heard them in the walls. Of course. They had the run of the house – and they would be attracted by all the oogy stuff Annie had left around. The rats were probably the gremlins who had broken most of Annie's threads. But she would only push such ideas away. In her mind, he was almost ready to run the New York Marathon.

'Annie . . . Annie, what did you mean when you said you gave me a pre-op shot?'

But Annie was still fixated on the other matter. 'I say it was seven,' she said softly. 'At least seven. Was it seven?'

'If you want it to be seven, it was seven. What did you mean when you said –'

'I can see you mean to be stubborn,' she said. 'I guess fellows like you must get so used to lying for a living that you just can't stop doing it in real life. But that's all right, Paul. Because the *principle* doesn't change if you were out seven times, or seventy, or seventy times seven. The *principle* doesn't change, and neither does the *response.*'

He was floating, floating, floating away. He closed his eyes and heard her speak as if from a long distance away . . . like a supernatural voice from a cloud. *Goddess,* he thought.

'Have you ever read about the early days at the Kimberley diamond mines, Paul?'

'I wrote the book on that one,' he said for no reason at all, and laughed.

(pre-op? pre-op shot?)

'Sometimes, the native workers stole diamonds. They wrapped them in leaves and poked them up their rectums. If they got away from the Big Hole without being discovered, they would run. And do you know what the British did to them if they got caught before they could get over Oranjerivier and into Boer country?'

'Killed them, I suppose,' he said, eyes still closed.

'Oh, no! That would have been like junking an expensive car just because of a broken spring. If they caught them they made sure that they could go on working . . . but they *also* made sure they would never run again. The operation was called *hobbling,* Paul, and that is what I'm going to do to you. For my own safety . . . and yours as well. Believe me, you need to be protected from yourself. Just remember, a little pain and it will be over. Try to hold that thought.'

Terror sharp as a gust of wind filled with razor-blades blew through the dope and Paul's eyes flew open. She had risen and now drew the bed-clothes down, exposing his twisted legs and bare feet.

'No,' he said. 'No . . . Annie . . . whatever it is you've got on your mind, we can talk about it, can't we? . . . please . . .'

She bent over. When she straightened up she was holding the axe from the shed in one hand and a propane torch in the other. The blade of the axe gleamed. Written on the side of the propane torch was the word *Bernz-O-matiC.* She bent down again and this time came up with a dark bottle and the box of matches. There was a label on the dark bottle. Written on the label was the word *Betadine.*

He never forgot these things, these words, these names.

'Annie, no!' he screamed. *'Annie, I'll stay right here! I won't even get out of bed! Please! Oh God please don't cut me!'*

'It'll be all right,' she said, and her face now had that slack, unplugged look – that look of perplexed vacuity – and before his mind was completely consumed in a forest fire of panic he understood that when this was over, she would have only the vaguest memories of what she had done, as she had only the vaguest memories of killing the children and the old people and the terminal patients and Andrew Pomeroy. After all, this was the woman who, although she'd gotten her cap in 1966, had told him only minutes ago that she had been a nurse for ten years.

She killed Pomeroy with that same axe. I know she did.

He continued to shriek and plead, but his words had become inarticulate babble. He tried to turn over, turn away from her, and his legs cried out. He tried to draw them up, make them less vulnerable, less of a target, and his knee screamed.

'Only a minute more, Paul,' she said, and uncapped the Betadine. She poured a brownish-red muck over his left ankle. 'Only a minute more and it's over.' She tipped the blade of the axe flat, the tendons standing out in her strong right wrist, and he could see the wink of the amethyst ring she still wore on the pinkie finger of that hand. She poured Betadine on the blade. He could smell it, a doctor's office smell. That smell meant you were going to get a shot.

'Just a little pain, Paul. It won't be bad.' She turned the axe over and splashed the other side of the blade. He could see random flowers of rust blooming on this side before the goop covered it.

'Annie Annie oh Annie please please no please don't Annie I swear to you I'll be good I swear to God I'll be good please give me a chance to be good OH ANNIE PLEASE LET ME BE GOOD –'

'Just a little pain. Then this nasty business will be behind us for good, Paul.'

She tossed the open bottle of Betadine over her shoulder, her face blank and empty and yet so unarguably solid; she slid her right hand down the handle of the axe almost to the steel head. She gripped the handle farther up in her left hand and spread her legs like a logger.

'ANNIE OH PLEASE PLEASE DON'T HURT ME!'

Her eyes were mild and drifting. 'Don't worry,' she said. 'I'm a trained nurse.'

The axe came whistling down and buried itself in Paul Sheldon's left leg just above the ankle. Pain exploded up his body in a gigantic bolt. Dark-red blood splattered across her face like Indian war-paint. It splattered the wall. He heard the blade squeal against bone as she wrenched it free. He looked unbelievingly down at himself. The sheet was turning red. He saw his toes wriggling. Then he saw her raising the dripping axe again. Her hair had fallen free of its pins and hung around her blank face.

He tried to pull back in spite of the pain in his leg and knee and realized that his leg was moving but his foot wasn't. All he was doing was widening the axe-slash, making it open like a mouth. He had time enough to realize his foot was now only held on his leg by the meat of his calf before the blade came down again, directly into the gash, shearing through the rest of his leg and burying itself deep in the mattress. Springs boinked and squoinked.

Annie pulled the axe free and tossed it aside. She looked absently at the jetting stump for a moment and then picked up the box of matches. She lit one. Then she picked up the propane torch with the word *Bernz-O-matiC* on the side and twisted the valve on the side. The torch hissed. Blood poured from the place where he no longer was. Annie held the match delicately under the nozzle of the *Bernz-O-matiC*. There was a *floof!* sound. A long yellow flame appeared. Annie adjusted it to a hard blue line of fire.

'Can't suture,' she said. 'No time. Tourniquet's no good. No central pressure point. Got to

(rinse)

cauterize.'

She bent. Paul screamed as fire splashed over the raw and bleeding stump. Smoke drifted up. It smelled sweet. He and his first wife had honeymooned on Maui. There had been a luau. This smell reminded him of the smell of the pig when they brought it out of the pit where it had cooked all day. The pig had been on a stick, sagging, black, falling apart.

The pain was screaming. *He* was screaming.

'Almost over,' she said, and turned the valve, and now the ground sheet caught fire around the stump that was no longer bleeding, the stump that was as black as the pig's hide had been when they had brought it out of the luau pit – Eileen had turned away but Paul had watched, fascinated, as they pulled off the pig's crackling skin as easily as you might skim off a sweater after a football game.

'Almost over –'

She turned the torch off. His leg lay in a line of flames with his severed foot wavering beyond it. She bent and now came up with his old friend the yellow floor-bucket. She dumped it over the flames.

He was screaming, screaming. The pain! The goddess! The pain! O Africa!

She stood looking at him, at the darkening, bloody sheet, with vague consternation – her face was the face of a woman who hears on her radio that an earthquake has killed ten thousand people in Pakistan or Turkey.

'You'll be all right, Paul,' she said, but her voice was suddenly frightened. Her eyes began to dart aimlessly around as they had when it seemed that the fire of his burning book might get out of control. They suddenly fixed on something, almost with relief. 'I'll just get rid of the trash.'

She picked up his foot. Its toes were still spasming. She carried it across the room. By the time she got to the door they had stopped moving. He could see a scar on the instep and remembered how he had gotten that, how he had stepped on a piece of bottle when he was just a kid. Had that been at Revere Beach? Yes, he thought it had been. He remembered he had cried and his father had told him it was just a little cut. His father had told him to stop acting like someone had cut his goddam foot off. Annie paused at the door and looked back at Paul, who shrieked and writhed in the charred and blood-soaked bed, his face a deathly fading white.

'Now you're hobbled,' she said, 'and don't you blame me. It's your own fault.'

She went out.

So did Paul.

23

The cloud was back. Paul dived for it, not caring if the cloud meant death instead of unconsciousness this time. He almost hoped it did. Just . . . no pain, please. No memories, no pain, no horror, no Annie Wilkes.

He dived for the cloud, dived into the cloud, dimly hearing the sounds of his own shrieks and smelling his own cooked meat.

As his thoughts faded, he thought: Goddess! Kill you! Goddess! Kill you! Goddess!

Then there was nothing but nothing.

PART THREE

PAUL

It's no good. I've been trying to sleep for the last half-hour, and I can't. Writing here is a sort of drug. It's the only thing I look forward to. This afternoon I read what I wrote . . . And it seemed vivid. I know it seems vivid because my imagination fills in all the bits another person wouldn't understand. I mean, it's vanity. But it seems a sort of magic . . . And I just can't live in this present. I would go mad if I did.

JOHN FOWLES
The Collector

1

CHAPTER 32

"Oh blessed Jesus," Ia moa ed, a d made a co vul-sive moveme t forward. Geoffrey grasped his frie d's arm. The steady beat of the drums pulsed i his head like some-thi g heard i a killi g delirium. Bees dro ed arou d them, but o e paused; they simply flew past a d i to the cleari g as if draw by a mag et--which, Geoffrey hough sickly, hey

2

Paul picked up the typewriter and shook it. After a time, a small piece of steel fell out onto the board across the arms of the wheelchair. He picked it up and looked at it.

It was the letter t. The typewriter had just thrown its t.

He thought: *I am going to complain to the management. I am going to not just ask for a new typewriter but fucking demand one. She's got the money – I know she does. Maybe it's squirreled away in fruit-jars under the barn or maybe it's stuffed in the walls at her Laughing Place, but she's got the dough, and t, my God, the second-most-common letter in the English language – !*

Of course he would ask Annie for nothing, much less demand. Once there had been a man who would at least have *asked.* A man who had been in a great deal more pain, a man who had had nothing to hold onto, not even this shitty book. That man would have *asked.* Hurt or not, that man had had the guts to at least *try* to stand up to Annie Wilkes.

He had been that man, and he supposed he ought to be ashamed, but *that* man had had two big advantages over this one: *that* man had had two feet . . . and two thumbs.

Paul sat reflectively for a moment, re-read the last line (mentally filling in the omissions), and then simply went back to work.

Better that way.

Better not to ask.

Better not to provoke.

Outside his window, bees buzzed.

It was the first day of summer.

3

had been.

"Let me go!" Ian snarled, and turned on Geoffrey, his right hand curling into a fist. His eyes bulged madly from his livid face, and he seemed totally unaware of who was holding him back from his darling. Geoffrey realized with cold certainty that what they had seen when Hezekiah pulled the protective screen of bushes aside had come very close to driving Ian mad. He still tottered on the brink, and the slightest push would send him over. If that happened, he would take Misery with him.

"Ian --"

"Let me <u>go</u>, I say!" Ian pulled backward with furious strength, and Hezekiah moaned fearfully. "No boss, make dem bees crazy, dem sting Mis'wess--"

Ian seemed not to hear. Eyes wild and blank, he lashed out at Geoffrey, striking his old friend high on the cheekbone. Black stars rocketed through Geoffrey's head.

In spite of them, he saw Hezekiah beginning to swing the potentially deadly <u>gosha</u>--a sand-filled bag the Bourkas favored for close work--in time to hiss: "No! Let me handle this!"

Reluctantly, Hezekiah allowed the <u>gosha</u> to subside to the end of its leather string like a slowing pendulum.

Then Geoffrey's head was rocked back by a fresh blow. This one mashed his lips back against his teeth, and he felt the warm salt-sweet taste of blood begin to seep into his mouth. There was a rough purring sound as Ian's dress shirt, now sun-faded and already torn in a dozen places, began to come apart in Geoffrey's grasp. In another moment he would be free. Geoffrey realized with dazed wonder that it was the same shirt Ian had worn to the Baron and Baroness's dinner party three nights ago...of course it was. There had been no opportunity to change since then, not for Ian, not for any of them. Only three nights ago... but the shirt looked as if Ian had been wearing it for at least three years, and Geoffrey felt as if at least three hundred had passed since the party. Only three nights ago, he thought again with stupid wonder, and then Ian was raining blows into his face.

"Let me go, damn you!" Ian drove his bloody fist into Geoffrey's face again and again--his friend for whom, in his right mind, he would have died.

"Do you want to demonstrate your love for her by killing her?" Geoffrey asked quietly. "If you want to do that, then by all means, old boy, knock me senseless."

Ian's fist hesitated. Something at least approximating sense came back into his terrified, maddened gaze.

"I must go to her," he murmured like a man in a dream. "I'm sorry I hit you, Geoffrey--truly sorry, my dear old man, and I'm sure you know it--but I must... You see her..." He looked again, as if to confirm the dreadfulness of the sight, and again made as if to rush to where Misery had been tied to a post in a jungle clearing, her arms over her head. Glimmering on her wrists and fastening her to the lowest branch of the eucalyptus, which was the only tree in the clearing, was something the Bourkas had apparently taken a fancy to before sending Baron Heidzig into the mouth of the idol and to his undoubtedly terrible death: the Baron's blued steel handcuffs.

This time it was Hezekiah who grabbed Ian, but the bushes rustled again and Geoffrey looked into the clearing, his breath momentarily catching in his throat, as a bit of fabric may catch on a thorn--he felt like a man who must walk up a rocky hill with a load of decayed and dangerously volatile explosives in his arms. *One sting*, he thought. *Just one and it's all over for her.*

"No, boss, mussun'," Hezekiah was saying with a kind of terrified patience. "It like d'utha boss be sayin'...if you go out dere, de bees wake up from dey dream. And if de bees wake, it doan matter for her if she be dine of one sting or one-de-one t'ousan' sting. If de bees wake up from dey dream we all die, but she die firs' and de mos' 'orrible."

Little by little Ian relaxed between the two men, one of them black, the other white. His head turned toward the clearing with dreadful reluctance, as if he did not wish to look and yet could not forbear to.

"Then what are we to do? What are we to do for my poor darling?"

I don't know came to Geoffrey's lips, and in his

own state of terrible distress, he was barely able to bite them back. Not for the first time it occurred to him that Ian's possession of the woman Geoffrey loved just as dearly (if secretly) allowed Ian to indulge in an odd sort of selfishness and an almost womanly hysteria that Geoffrey himself must forgo; after all, to the rest of the world he was only Misery's friend.

Yes, just her friend, he thought with half-hysterical irony, and then his own eyes were drawn back to the clearing. To his <u>friend.</u>

Misery wore not a stitch of clothing, yet Geoffrey thought that even the most prudish church-thrice-a-week village biddy could not have faulted her for indecency. The hypothetical old prude might have run screaming from the sight of Misery, but her screams would have been caused by terror and revulsion rather than outraged propriety. Misery wore not a stitch of clothing, but she was far from naked.

She was dressed in bees. From the tips of her toes to the crown of her chestnut hair, she was dressed in bees. She seemed almost to be wearing some strange nun's habit--strange because it moved and undulated across the swells of her breasts and hips even though there was not even a ghost of a breeze. Likewise, her face seemed encased in a wimple of almost Mohammedan modesty--only her blue eyes peered out of the mask of bees which crawled sluggishly over her face, hiding mouth and nose and chin and brows. More bees, giant Africa browns, the most poisonous and bad-tempered bees in all the world, crawled back and forth over the Baron's steel bracelets before joining the living gloves on Misery's hands.

As Geoffrey watched, more and more bees flew into the clearing from all points of the compass--yet it was clear to him, even in his current distraction, that most of them were coming from the west, where the great dark stone face of the goddess loomed.

The drums pulsed their steady rhythm, in its way as much a soporific as the sleepy drone of the bees. But Geoffrey knew how deceptive that sleepiness was; he had seen what happened to he Baroness, and only thanked God that Ian had been spared that...and the sound of that sleepy hum suddenly rising to a furious buzz-saw squeal... a sound which had at first muffled and then drowned the woman's agonized dying screams. She had been a vain and foolish creature, dangerous as well--she had almost gotten them killed when she had freed Stringfellow's bushmaster--but silly or not, foolish or not, dangerous or not, no man or woman deserved to die like *that.*

In his mind Geoffrey echoed Ian's question:

<u>What are we to do? What are we to do for our poor darling?</u>

Hezekiah said: "Nothing can do now, boss--but she in n o danger. As long as de drums dey beat, de bees will sleep. And Mis'wess, she is goan sleep, too."

Now the bees covered her in a thick and moving blanket; her eyes, open but unseei g, seemed to be receding into a living cave of crawling, stumbling, droning bees.

"And if the drums stop?" Geoffrey asked in a low, almost strengthless voice, and just then , the drums did.

For a mom h hr of h m

4

Paul looked unbelievingly at the last line, then picked the Royal up – he had gone on lifting it like some weird barbell when she was out of the room, God knew why – and shook it again. The keys clittered, and then another chunk of metal fell out on the board which served as his desk.

Outside he could hear the roaring sound of Annie's bright-blue riding lawnmower – she was around front, giving the grass a good trim so those cockadoodie Roydmans wouldn't have anything to talk about in town.

He set the typewriter down, then rocked it up so he could fish out this new surprise. He looked at it in the strong late afternoon sunlight slanting in through the window. His expression of disbelief never altered.

Printed in raised and slightly ink-stained metal on the head of the key was:

E
e

Just to add to the fun, the old Royal had now thrown the most frequently used letter in the English language.

Paul looked at the calendar. The picture was of a flowered meadow and the month said May, but Paul kept his own dates now on a piece of scrap paper, and according to his home-made calendar it was June 21.

Roll out those lazy hazy crazy days of summer, he thought sourly, and threw the key-hammer in the general direction of the wastebasket.

Well, what do I do now? he thought, but of course he knew what came next. Longhand. That was what came next.

But not now. Although he had been tearing along like a house afire a few seconds ago, anxious to get Ian, Geoffrey, and the ever-amusing Hezekiah caught in the Bourkas' ambush so that the entire party could be transported to the caves behind the face of the idol for the rousing finale, he was suddenly tired. The hole in the paper had closed with an adamant bang.

Tomorrow.

He would go to longhand tomorrow.

Fuck longhand. Complain to the management, Paul.

But he would do no such thing. Annie had gotten too weird.

He listened to the monotonous snarl of the riding lawnmower, saw her shadow, and, as so often happened when he thought of how weird Annie was getting, his mind recalled the image of the axe rising, then falling; the image of her horrid impassive deadly face splattered with his blood. It was clear. Every word she had spoken, every word he had screamed, the squeal of the axe pulling away from the severed bone, the blood on the wall. All crystal-clear. And, as he *also* so often did, he tried to block this memory and found himself a second too late.

Because the crucial plot-twist of *Fast Cars* concerned Tony Bonasaro's near-fatal crack-up in his last desperate effort to escape the police (and this led to the epilogue, which consisted of the bruising interrogation conducted by the late Lieutenant Gray's partner in Tony's hospital room), Paul had interviewed a number of crash victims. He had heard the same thing time and time again. It came in different wrappers, but it always boiled down to the same thing: *I remember getting into the car, and I remember waking up here. Everything else is a blank.*

Why couldn't that have happened to *him?*

Because writers remember everything, Paul. Especially the hurts. Strip a writer to the buff, point to the scars, and he'll tell you the story of each small one. From the big ones you get novels, not amnesia. A little talent is a nice thing to have if you want to be a writer, but the only real requirement is that ability to remember the story of every scar.

Art consists of the persistence of memory.

Who had said that? Thomas Szasz? William Faulkner? Cyndi Lauper?

But that last name brought its own association, a painful and unhappy one under these circumstances: a memory of Cyndi Lauper hiccuping her way cheerfully through 'Girls Just Want to Have Fun' that was so clear it was almost auditory: *Oh daddy dear, you're still number one / But girls, they wanna have fuh-un / Oh when the workin day is done / Girls just wanna have fun.*

Suddenly he wanted a hit of rock and roll worse than he had ever wanted a cigarette. It didn't have to be Cyndi Lauper. Anyone would do. Jesus Christ, Ted Nugent would be just fine.

The axe coming down.

The whisper of the axe.

Don't think about it.

But that was stupid. He kept telling himself not to think about it, knowing all the while that it was there, like a bone in his throat. Was he going to let it stay there, or was he going to be a man and sick the fucking thing up?

Another memory came then; it seemed like this was an All Request Oldies day for Paul Sheldon. This one was of Oliver Reed as the mad but silkily persuasive scientist in David Cronenberg's movie, *The Brood.* Reed urging his patients at The Institute of Psychoplasmatics (a name Paul had found deliciously funny) to 'go through it! Go all the way through it!'

Well . . . maybe sometimes that wasn't such bad advice.

I went through it once. That was enough.

Bullshit was what that was. If going through things once was enough, he would have been a fucking vacuum-cleaner salesman, like his father.

Go through it, then. Go all the way through it, Paul. Start with Misery.

No.

Yes.

Fuck you.

Paul leaned back, put his hand over his eyes, and, like it or not, he began to go through it.

All the way through it.

5

He hadn't died, hadn't slept, but for awhile after Annie hobbled him the pain went away. He had only drifted, feeling untethered from his body, a balloon of pure thought rising away from its string.

Oh shit, why was he bothering? She had done it, and all the time between then and now had been pain and boredom and occasional bouts of work on his stupidly melodramatic book to escape the former two. The whole thing was meaningless.

Oh, but it's not – there is a theme here, Paul. It's the thread that runs through everything. The thread that runs so true. Can't you see it?

Misery, of course. That was the thread that ran through everything, but, true thread or false, it was so goddam silly.

As a common noun it meant pain, usually lengthy and often pointless; as a proper one it meant a character and a plot, the latter most assuredly lengthy and pointless, but one which would nonetheless end very soon. Misery ran through the last four (or maybe it was five) months of his life, all right, plenty of Misery, Misery day in and Misery day out, but surely that was too simple, surely –

Oh no, Paul. Nothing is simple about Misery. Except that you owe her your life, such as that may be . . . because you turned out to be Scheherazade after all, didn't you?

Again he tried to turn aside from these thoughts, but found himself unable. The persistence of memory and all that. Hacks just want to have fun. Then an unexpected idea came, a new one which opened a whole new avenue of thought.

What you keep overlooking, because it's so obvious, is that you were – are – also Scheherazade to yourself.

He blinked, lowering his head and staring stupidly out into the summer he had never expected he would see. Annie's shadow passed and then disappeared again.

Was that true?

Scheherazade to myself? he thought again. If so, then he was faced with an idiocy that was utterly colossal: he owed his survival to the fact that he wanted to finish the piece of shit Annie had coerced him into writing. He should have died . . . but couldn't. Not until he knew how it all came out.

Oh you're fucking crazy.

You sure?

No. He was no longer sure. Not about anything.

With one exception: his whole life had hinged and continued to hinge on Misery.

He let his mind drift.

The cloud, he thought. *Begin with the cloud.*

6

This time the cloud had been darker, denser, somehow smoother. There was a sensation not of floating but of sliding. Sometimes thoughts came, and sometimes there was pain, and sometimes, dimly, he heard Annie's voice, sounding the way it had when the burning manuscript in the barbecue had threatened to get out of control: 'Drink this, Paul . . . you've *got* to!'

Sliding?

No.

That was not quite the right verb. The right verb was *sinking.* He remembered a telephone call which had come at three in the morning – this was when he was in college. Sleepy fourth-floor dorm proctor hammering on his door, telling him to come on and answer the fucking phone. His mother. *Come home as quick as you can, Paulie. Your father has had a bad stroke. He's sinking.* And he *had* come as fast as he could, pushing his old Ford wagon to seventy in spite of the front-end shimmy that developed at speeds over fifty, but in the end it had all been for nothing. When he got there, his father was no longer sinking but sunk.

How close had he himself come to sinking on the night of the axe? He didn't know, but the fact that he had felt almost no pain during the week following the amputation was a pretty clear indicator of just how close, perhaps. That, and the panic in her voice.

He had lain in a semi-coma, barely breathing because of the respiratory-depressant side-effects of the medication, the glucose drips back in his arms again. And what brought him out of it was the beat of drums and the drone of bees.

Bourka drums.

Bourka bees.

Bourka *dreams.*

Color bleeding slowly and relentlessly into a land and a tribe that never were beyond the margins of the paper on which he wrote.

A dream of the goddess, the face of the goddess, looming black over the jungle green, brooding and eroded. Dark goddess, dark continent, a stone head full of bees. Overlying even all this was a picture, which grew clearer and clearer (as if a giant slide had been projected against the cloud in which he lay) as time passed. It was a picture of a clearing in which one old eucalyptus tree stood. Hanging from the lowest branch of this tree was an old-fashioned pair of blued steel handcuffs. Bees were crawling over them. The cuffs were empty. They were empty because Misery had –

– escaped? She had, hadn't she? Wasn't that how the story was supposed to go?

It *had* been – but now he wasn't so sure. *Was* that what those empty handcuffs meant? Or had she been taken away? Taken into the idol? Taken to the queen bee, the Big Babe of the Bourkas?

You were also Scheherazade to yourself.

Who are you telling this story for, *Paul? Who are you telling it to? To Annie?*

Of course not. He did not look through that hole in the paper to see Annie, or please Annie . . . he looked through it to get *away* from Annie.

The pain had started. And the itch. The cloud began to lighten again, and rift apart. He began to glimpse the room, which was bad, and Annie, which was even worse. Still, he had decided to live. Some part of him that was as addicted to the chapter-plays as Annie had been as a child had decided he could not die until he saw how it all came out.

Had she escaped, with the help of Ian and Geoffrey?

Or had she been taken into the head of the goddess?

It was ridiculous, but these stupid questions actually seemed to need answering.

7

She didn't want to let him go back to work – not at first. He could see in her skittery eyes how frightened she had been and still was. How close he had come. She was taking extravagant care of him, changing the bandages on his weeping stump every eight hours (and at first, she had informed him with the air of one who knows she will never get a medal for what she has done – although she deserves one – she had done it every four hours), giving him sponge baths and alcohol rubs – as if to deny what she had done. Work, she said, would hurt him. *It would put you back, Paul. I wouldn't say it if it weren't so – believe me. At least you know what's ahead – I'm dying to find out what happens next.* It turned out she had read everything he had written – all his pre-surgery work, you might say – while he lingered near death . . . better than three hundred manuscript pages. He hadn't filled in the n's in the last forty or so; Annie had done that. She showed him these with an uneasily defiant sort of pride. Her n's were textbook neat, a striking comparison with his own, which had degenerated into a humpbacked scrawl.

Although Annie never said so, he believed she had filled in the n's either as another evidence of her solicitude – *How can you say I was cruel to you, Paul, when you see all the n's I have filled in?* – or as an act of atonement, or possibly even as a quasi-superstitious rite: enough bandage-changes, enough sponge baths, enough n's filled in, and Paul would live. *Bourka bee-woman work pow'ful mojo-magic, Bwana, fill in all dese hoodaddy n's an' all be well again.*

That was how she had begun . . . but then *the gotta* set in. Paul knew all the symptoms. When she said she was dying to find out what happened next, she wasn't kidding.

Because you went on living *to find out what happened next, isn't that what you're really saying?*

Crazy as it was – shameful, even, in its absurdity – he thought it was.

The gotta.

It was something he had been irritated to find he could generate in the *Misery* books almost at will but in his mainstream fiction erratically or not at all. You didn't know exactly where to find *the gotta,* but you always knew when you did. It made the needle of some internal Geiger counter swing all the way over to the end of the dial. Even sitting in front of the typewriter slightly hung-over, drinking cups of black coffee and crunching a Rolaid or two every couple of hours (knowing he should give up the fucking cigarettes, at least in the morning, but unable to bring himself to the sticking point), months from finishing and light-years from publication, you knew *the gotta* when you got it. Having it always made him feel slightly ashamed – manipulative. But it also made him feel vindicated in his labor. Christ, days went by and the hole in the paper was small, the light was dim, the overheard conversations witless. You pushed on because that was all you could do. Confucius say if man want to grow one row of corn, first must shovel one ton of shit. And then one day the hole widened to VistaVision width and the light shone through like a sunray in a Cecil B. De Mille epic and you knew you had *the gotta,* alive and kicking.

The gotta, as in: 'I think I'll stay up another fifteen-twenty minutes, honey, I gotta see how this chapter comes out.' Even though the guy who says it spent the day at work thinking about getting laid and knows the odds are good his wife is going to be asleep when he finally gets up to the bedroom.

The gotta, as in: 'I know I should be starting supper now – he'll be mad if it's TV dinners again – but I gotta see how this ends.'

I gotta know will she live.

I gotta know will he catch the shitheel who killed his father.

I gotta know if she finds out her best friend's screwing her husband.

The gotta. Nasty as a hand-job in a sleazy bar, fine as a fuck from the world's most talented call-girl. Oh boy it was bad and oh boy it was good and oh boy in the end it didn't matter how rude it was or how crude it was because in the end it was just like the Jacksons said on that record – don't stop til you get enough.

8

You were also Scheherazade to yourself.

That was not an idea he was able to articulate or even understand, not then; he had been in too much pain. But he had known just the same, hadn't he?

Not you. The guys in the sweatshop. They *knew.*

Yes. That had the ring of the right.

The sound of the riding mower swelled louder. Annie came into view for a moment. She looked at him, saw him looking back, and raised a hand to him. He raised one of his own – the one with the thumb still on it – in return. She passed from sight again. Good deal.

He was finally able to convince her that returning to work would put him forward, not back . . . He was haunted by the specificity of those images which had lured him out of the cloud, and *haunted* was exactly the right word: until they were written down they were shades which would remain unlaid.

And while she hadn't believed him – not then – she had allowed him to go back to work just the same. Not because he had convinced her but because of *the gotta.*

At first he had been able to work only in painfully short bursts – fifteen minutes maybe half an hour if the story really demanded it of him. Even short bursts were agony. A shift in position caused the stump to come brightly alive, the way a smouldering brand will burst into flame when fanned by a breeze. It hurt furiously while he wrote, but that was not the worst – the worst was the hour or two afterward, when the healing stump would madden him with a droney itch, like swarming, sleepy bees.

He had been right, not her. He never became really well – probably could not do in such a situation – but his health did improve and some of his strength came back. He was aware that the horizons of his interest had shrunk, but he accepted this as the price of survival. It was a genuine wonder he had survived at all.

Sitting here in front of this typewriter with its increasingly bad teeth, looking back over a period which had consisted of work rather than events, Paul nodded. Yes, he supposed he had been his own Scheherazade, just as he was his own dream-woman when he grabbed hold of himself and jacked off to the feverish beat of his fantasies. He didn't need a psychiatrist to point out that writing had its autoerotic side – you beat a typewriter instead of your meat, but both acts depended largely on quick wits, fast hands, and a heartfelt commitment to the art of the farfetched.

But hadn't there also been some sort of fuck, even if of the driest variety? Because once he started again . . . well, she wouldn't interrupt him while he was working, but she would take each day's output as soon as he was done, ostensibly to fill in the missing letters, but actually – he knew this by now, just as sexually acute men know which dates will put out at the end of the evening and which ones will not – to get her fix. To get her *gotta.*

The chapter-plays. Yes. Back to that. Only for the last few months she's been going every day instead of just on Saturday afternoons, and the Paul who takes her is her pet writer instead of her older brother.

His stints at the typewriter grew gradually longer as the pain slowly receded and some of his endurance returned . . . but ultimately he wasn't able to write fast enough to satisfy her demands.

The gotta which had kept them both alive – and it had, for without it she surely would have murdered both him and herself long since – was also what had caused the loss of his thumb. It was horrible, but also sort of funny. *Have a little irony, Paul – it's good for your blood.*

And think how much worse it could have been.

It could have been his penis, for instance.

'And I only have one of those,' he said, and began to laugh wildly in the empty room in front of the hateful Royal with its gap-toothed grin. He laughed until his gut and stump both ached. Laughed until his *mind* ached. At some point the laughter turned to horrible dry sobs that awoke pain even in what remained of his left thumb, and when that happened he was finally able to stop. He wondered in a dull sort of way how close he was to going insane.

Not that it really mattered, he supposed.

9

One day not long before the thumbectomy – perhaps even less than a week – Annie had come in with two giant dishes of vanilla ice-cream, a can of Hershey's chocolate syrup, a pressure can of Reddi-Whip, and a jar in which maraschino cherries red as heart's blood floated like biology specimens.

'I thought I'd make us sundaes, Paul,' Annie said. Her tone was spuriously jolly. Paul didn't like it. Not her tone of voice, nor the uneasy look in her eyes. *I'm being a naughty girl,* that look said. It made him wary, put his wind up. It was too easy for him to imagine her looking exactly the same way when she put a heap of clothes on one set of stairs, a dead cat on another.

'Why, thank you, Annie,' he said, and watched as she poured the syrup and puffed two cumulus clouds of whipped cream out of the pressure can. She performed these chores with the practiced, heavy hand of the long-time sugar junkie.

'No need for thanks. You deserve it. You've been working so hard.'

She gave him his sundae. The sweetness became cloying after the third bite, but he kept on. It was wiser. One of the key rules to survival here on the scenic Western Slope was, to wit, *When Annie's treatin, you best be eatin.* There was silence for a while, and then Annie put her spoon down, wiped a mixture of chocolate syrup and melting ice-cream off her chin with the back of her hand, and said pleasantly: 'Tell me the rest.'

Paul put his own spoon down. 'I beg your pardon?'

'Tell me the rest of the story. I can't wait. I just can't.'

And hadn't he known this was coming? Yes. If someone had delivered all twenty reels of the new Rocket Man chapter-play to Annie's house, would she have waited, parceling out only one a week, or even one a day?

He looked at the half-demolished avalanche of her sundae, one cherry almost buried in whipped cream, another floating in chocolate syrup. He remembered the way the living room had looked, with sugar-glazed dishes everywhere.

No. Annie was not the waiting type. Annie would have watched all twenty episodes in one night, even if they gave her eyestrain and a splitting headache.

Because Annie loved sweet things.

'I can't do that,' he said.

Her face had darkened at once, but hadn't there been a shadowy relief there, as well? 'Oh? Why not?'

Because you wouldn't respect me in the morning, he thought of saying, and clamped down on that. Clamped down hard.

'Because I'm a rotten story-teller,' he answered instead.

She slurped up the remainder of her sundae in five huge spoonfuls that would have left Paul's throat gray with frostbite. Then she set her dish down and looked at him angrily, not as if he were the great Paul Sheldon but as if he were someone who had presumed to *criticize* the great Paul Sheldon.

'If you're such a rotten story-teller, how come you have best-sellers and millions of people love the books you write?'

'I didn't say I was a rotten story-*writer.* I actually happen to think I'm pretty good at *that.* But as a story-*teller,* I'm the pits.'

'You're just making up a big cockadoodie excuse.' Her face was darkening. Her hands were clenched into shiny fists on the heavy material of her skirt. Hurricane Annie was back in the room. Everything that went around came around. Except things no longer *had* been quite the same, had they? He was as scared of her as ever, but her hold over him had nonetheless diminished. His life no longer seemed like such a big deal, *gotta* or no *gotta.* He was only afraid she would hurt him.

'It's *not* an excuse,' he had replied. 'The two things are like apples and oranges, Annie. People who *tell* stories usually can't *write* stories. If you really think people who can write stories can talk worth a damn, you never watched some poor slob of a novelist fumbling his way through an interview on the *Today* show.'

'Well, I don't want to wait,' she sulked. 'I made you that nice sundae and the least you could do is tell me a *few* things. It doesn't have to exactly be the whole story, I guess, but . . . did the Baron kill Calthorpe?' Her eyes sparkled. 'That's one thing I *really* want to know. And what did he do with the body if he did? Is it all cut up in that trunk his wife won't let out of her sight? That's what *I* think.'

Paul shook his head – not to indicate she had it wrong but to indicate he would not tell.

She became even blacker. Yet her voice was soft. 'You're making me very angry – you know that, don't you, Paul?'

'Of course I know it. But I can't help it.'

'I could *make* you. I could *make* you help it. I could make you *tell.*' But she looked frustrated, as if knowing that she could not. She could make him say some things, but she could not make him tell.

'Annie, do you remember telling me what a little kid says to his mother when she catches him playing with the cleaning fluid under the sink and makes him stop? *Mommy, you're mean!* Isn't that what you're saying now? *Paul, you're mean!*'

'If you make me much madder, I don't promise to be responsible,' she said, but he sensed the crisis was already past – she was strangely vulnerable to these concepts of discipline and behavior.

'Well, I'll have to chance that,' he said, 'because I'm just like that mother – I'm not saying no to be mean, or to spite you – I'm saying no because I really want you to like the story . . . and if I give you what you want, you won't like it, and you won't want it anymore.' *And then what will happen to me, Annie?* he thought but did not say.

'At least tell me if that nigger Hezekiah *really* does know where Misery's father is! At least tell me that!'

'Do you want the novel, or do you want me to fill out a questionnaire?'

'Don't you take that sarcastic tone to me!'

'Then don't you pretend you don't understand what I'm saying!' he shouted back. She recoiled from him in surprise and unease, the last of that blackness going out of her face, and all that was left was that weird little-girl look, that I've-been-naughty look. 'You want to cut open the golden goose! That's what it comes down to! But when the farmer in the story finally did that, all he had was a dead goose and a bunch of worthless guts!'

'All right,' she said. 'All right, Paul. Are you going to finish your sundae?'

'I can't eat any more,' he said.

'I see. I've upset you. I'm sorry. I expect that you're right. I was wrong to ask.' She was perfectly calm again. He had half-expected another period of deep depression or rage to follow, but none had. They had simply gone back to the old routine, Paul writing, Annie reading each day's output, and enough time had passed between the argument and the thumbectomy that Paul had missed the connection. Until now.

I bitched about the typewriter, he thought, looking at it now and listening to the drone of the mower. It sounded fainter now, and he was marginally aware that wasn't because Annie was moving away but because *he* was. He was drowsing off. He did that a lot now, simply drowsed off like some old fart in a nursing home.

Not a lot; I only bitched about it that once. But once was enough, wasn't it? More than enough. That was – what? – a week after she brought those oogy sundaes? Just about that. Just one week and one bitch. About how the clunk of that dead key was driving me crazy. I didn't even suggest she get another used typewriter from Nancy Whoremonger or whoever that woman was, one with all its keys intact. I just said those clunks are driving me crazy, and then, in almost no time at all, presto chango, when it comes to Paul's left thumb, now you see it and now you don't. Except she didn't really do it because I bitched about the typewriter, did she? She did it because I told her no and she had to accept that. It was an act of rage. The rage was the result of realization. What realization? Why, that she didn't hold all the cards after all – that I had a certain passive hold over her. The power of the gotta. I turned out to be a pretty passable Scheherazade after all.

It was crazy. It was funny. It was also real. Millions might scoff, but only because they failed to realize how pervasive the influence of art – even of such a degenerate sort as popular fiction – could become. Housewives arranged their schedules around the afternoon soaps. If they went back into the workplace, they made buying a VCR a top priority so they could watch those same soap operas at night. When Arthur Conan Doyle killed Sherlock Holmes at Reichenbach Falls, all of Victorian England rose as one and demanded him back. The tone of their protests had been Annie's exactly – not bereavement but outrage. Doyle was berated by his own mother when he wrote and told her of his intention to do away with Holmes. Her indignant reply had come by return mail: 'Kill that nice Mr Holmes? Foolishness! *Don't you dare!*'

Or there was the case of his friend Gary Ruddman, who worked for the Boulder Public Library. When Paul had dropped over to see him one day, he had found Gary's shades drawn and a black crepe fluff on the door. Concerned, Paul had knocked hard until Gary answered. *Go away,* Gary had told him. *I'm feeling depressed today. Someone died. Someone important to me.* When Paul asked who, Gary had responded tiredly: *Van der Valk.* Paul had heard him walk away from the door, and although he knocked again, Gary had not come back. Van der Valk, it turned out, was a fictional detective created – and then uncreated – by a writer named Nicolas Freeling.

Paul had been convinced Gary's reaction had been more than false; he thought it had been pretentiously arty. In short, a pose. He continued to feel this way until 1983, when he read *The World According to Garp.* He made the mistake of reading the scene where Garp's younger son dies, impaled on a gearshift lever, shortly before bed. It was hours before he slept. The scene would not leave his mind. The thought that grieving for a fictional character was absurd did more than cross his mind during his tossings and turnings. For grieving was exactly what he was doing, of course. The realization had not helped, however, and this had caused him to wonder if perhaps Gary Ruddman hadn't been a lot more serious about Van der Valk than Paul had given him credit for at the time. And this had caused another memory to resurface: finishing William Golding's *Lord of the Flies* at the age of twelve on a hot summer day, going to the refrigerator for a cold glass of lemonade . . . and then suddenly changing direction and speeding up from an amble to an all-out bolt which had ended in the bathroom. There he had leaned over the toilet and vomited.

Paul suddenly remembered other examples of this odd mania: the way people had mobbed the Baltimore docks each month when the packet bearing the new installment of Mr Dickens's *Little Dorrit* or *Oliver Twist* was due (some had drowned, but this did not discourage the others); the old woman of a hundred and five who had declared she would live until Mr Galsworthy finished *The Forsyte Saga* – and who had died less than an hour after having the final page of the final volume read to her; the young mountain climber hospitalized with a supposedly fatal case of hypothermia whose friends had read *The Lord of the Rings* to him nonstop, around the clock, until he came out of his coma; hundreds of other such incidents.

Every 'best-selling' writer of fiction would, he supposed, have his own personal example or examples of radical reader involvement with the make-believe worlds the writer creates . . . *examples of the Scheherazade complex,* Paul thought now, half-dreaming as the sound of Annie's mower ebbed and flowed at some great echoing distance. He remembered getting two letters suggesting Misery theme parks, on the order of Disney World or Great Adventure. One of these letters had included a crude blueprint. But the blue-ribbon winner (at least until Annie Wilkes had entered his life) had been Mrs Roman D. Sandpiper III, of Ink Beach, Florida. Mrs Roman D. Sandpiper, whose given name was Virginia, had turned an upstairs room of her home into Misery's Parlor. She included Polaroids of Misery's Spinning Wheel, Misery's Escritoire (complete with a half-completed bread-and-butter note to Mr Faverey, saying she would be in attendance at the School Hall Recitation on 20th Nov. *inst.* – done in what Paul thought was an eerily apt hand for his heroine, not a round and flowing ladies' script but a half-feminine copperplate), Misery's Couch, Misery's Sampler *(Let Love Instruct You; Do Not Presume to Instruct Love)*, etc., etc. The furnishings, Mrs Roman D. ('Virginia') Sandpiper's letter said, were all genuine, not reproductions, and while Paul could not tell for sure, he guessed that it was the truth. If so, this expensive bit of make-believe must have cost Mrs Roman D. ('Virginia') Sandpiper thousands of dollars. Mrs Roman D. ('Virginia') Sandpiper hastened to assure him that she was not using his character to make money, nor did she have any plans in that direction – heaven forbid! – but she *did* want him to see the pictures, and to tell her what she had wrong (which, she was sure, must be a great deal). Mrs Roman D. ('Virginia') Sandpiper also hoped for his opinion. Looking at those pictures had given him a feeling which was strange yet eerily intangible – it had been like looking at photographs of his own imagination, and he knew that from that moment on, whenever he tried to imagine Misery's little combination parlor and study, Mrs Roman D. ('Virginia') Sandpiper's Polaroids would leap immediately into his mind, obscuring imagination with their cheery but one-dimensional concreteness. Tell *her* what was wrong? That was madness. From now on *he* would be the one to wonder about that. He had written back, a brief note of congratulations and admiration – a note which hinted not at all at certain questions concerning Mrs Roman D. ('Virginia') Sandpiper which had crossed his mind: how tightly wrapped was she? for instance – and had received another letter in return, with a fresh slew of Polaroids. Mrs Roman D. ('Virginia') Sandpiper's first communication had consisted of a two-page handwritten letter and seven Polaroids. This second consisted of a ten-page handwritten letter and *forty* Polaroids. The letter was an exhaustive (and ultimately exhausting) manual of where Mrs Roman D. ('Virginia') Sandpiper had found each piece, how much she had paid, and the restoration processes involved. Mrs Roman D. ('Virginia') Sandpiper told him that she had found a man named McKibbon who owned an old squirrel-rifle, and had gotten him to put the bullet-hole in the wall by the chair – while she could not swear to the historical accuracy of the gun, Mrs Roman D. ('Virginia') Sandpiper admitted, she knew the caliber was right. The pictures were mostly close detail shots. But for the handwritten captions on the backs, they could have been photos in one of those WHAT IS THIS PICTURE? features in puzzle magazines, where maxi-photography makes the straight-arm of a paper-clip look like a pylon and the pop-top of a beer-can like a Picasso sculpture. Paul had not answered this letter, but that had not deterred Mrs Roman D. ('Virginia') Sandpiper, who had sent five more (the first four with additional Polaroids) before finally lapsing into puzzled, slightly hurt silence.

The last letter had been simply, stiffly signed Mrs Roman D. Sandpiper. The invitation (however parenthetically made) to call her 'Virginia' had been withdrawn.

This woman's feelings, obsessed though they might have been, had never evolved into Annie's paranoid fixation, but Paul understood now that the wellspring had been the same. The Scheherazade complex. The deep and elemental drawing power of *the gotta.*

His floating deepened. He slept.

10

He dozed off these days as old men doze off, abruptly and sometimes at inappropriate times, and he slept as old men sleep – which is to say, only separated from the waking world by the thinnest of skins. He didn't stop hearing the riding mower, but its sound became deeper, rougher, choppier: the sound of the electric knife.

He had picked the wrong day to start complaining about the Royal and its missing n. And, of course, there was never a *right* day to say no to Annie Wilkes. Punishment might be deferred . . . but never escaped.

Well, if it bothers you so much, I'll just have to give you something to take your mind off that old n. He heard her rummaging around in the kitchen, throwing things, cursing in her strange Annie Wilkes language. Ten minutes later she came in with the syringe, the Betadine, and the electric knife. Paul began to scream at once. He was, in a way, like Pavlov's dogs. When Pavlov rang a bell, the dogs salivated. When Annie came into the guest bedroom with a hypo, a bottle of Betadine, and a sharp cutting object, Paul began to scream. She had plugged the knife into the outlet by his wheelchair and there had been more pleading and more screaming and more promises that he would be good. When he tried to thrash away from the hypo she told him to sit still and be good or what was going to happen would happen without the benefit of even light anesthesia. When he continued to pull away from the needle, mewling and pleading, Annie suggested that if that was really the way he felt, maybe she just ought to use the knife on his throat and be done with it.

Then he had been still and let her give him the injection and this time the Betadine had gone over his left thumb as well as the blade of the knife (when she turned it on and the blade began to saw rapidly back and forth in the air the Betadine flew in a spray of maroon droplets she seemed not to notice) and in the end of course there had been much redder droplets spraying into the air as well. Because when Annie decided on a course of action, she carried it through. Annie was not swayed by pleas. Annie was not swayed by screams. Annie had the courage of her convictions.

As the humming, vibrating blade sank into the soft web of flesh between the soon-to-be-defunct thumb and his first finger, she assured him again in her this-hurts-Mother-more-than-it-hurts-Paulie voice that she loved him.

Then, that night . . .

You're not dreaming, Paul. You're thinking about things you don't dare think about when you're awake. So wake up. For God's sake, WAKE UP!

He couldn't wake up.

She had cut his thumb off in the morning and that night she swept gaily into the room where he sat in a stupid daze of drugs and pain with his wrapped left hand held against his chest and she had a cake and she was bellowing 'Happy Birthday to You' in her on-key but tuneless voice although it was not his birthday and there were candles all over the cake and sitting in the exact center pushed into the frosting like an extra big candle had been his thumb his gray dead thumb the nail slightly ragged because he sometimes chewed it when he was stuck for a word and she told him *If you promise to be good Paul you can have a piece of birthday cake but you won't have to eat any of the special candle* so he promised to be good because he didn't want to be forced to eat any of the special candle but also because mostly because surely because Annie was great Annie was good let us thank her for our food including that we don't have to eat girls just wanna have fun but something wicked this way comes please don't make me eat my thumb Annie the mom Annie the goddess when Annie's around you better stay honest she knows when you've been sleeping she knows when you're awake she knows if you've been bad or good so be good for goddess' sake you better not cry you better not pout but most of all you better not scream don't scream don't scream don't scream don't

He hadn't.

And now, as he awoke, he did so with a jerk that hurt him all over, hardly aware that his lips were pressed tightly together to keep the scream inside, although the thumbectomy had happened over a month ago.

He was so preoccupied with not screaming that for a moment he didn't even see what was coming into the driveway, and when he *did* see it, he believed at first that it must be a mirage.

It was a Colorado State Police car.

11

Following the amputation of his thumb there had been a dim period when Paul's greatest single accomplishment, other than working on the novel, had been to keep track of the days. He had become pathological about it, sometimes spending as long as five minutes lost in a daze, counting back, making sure he hadn't somehow forgotten one.

I'm getting as bad as she is, he thought once.

His mind had returned wearily: *So what?*

He had done pretty well with the book following the loss of his foot – during what Annie so mincingly called his 'convalescent period'. No – *pretty well* was false modesty if ever there was such a thing. He had done *amazingly* well for a man who had once found it impossible to write if he was out of cigarettes or if he had a backache or a headache a degree or two above a low drone. It would be nice to believe he had performed heroically, but he supposed it was only that escape thing again, because the pain had been really dreadful. When the healing process finally did begin, he thought the 'phantom itch' of the foot which was no longer there was even worse than the pain. It was the arch of the missing foot which bothered him the most. He awoke time after time in the middle of the night using the big toe of his right foot to scratch thin air four inches below the place where, on that side, his body now ended.

But he had gone on working just the same.

It wasn't until after the thumbectomy, and that bizarre birthday cake like a left-over prop from *Whatever Happened to Baby Jane,* that the balls of crumpled-up paper had begun to proliferate in the wastebasket again. Lose a foot, almost die, go on working. Lose a thumb and run into some kind of weird trouble. Wasn't it supposed to be the other way around?

Well, there was the fever – he had spent a week in bed with that. But it was pretty minor-league stuff; the highest his temperature had ever gone was 100.7, and that wasn't exactly the stuff of which high melodrama was made. The fever had probably been caused more by his general rundown condition than any specific infection, and an oogy old fever was no problem for Annie; among her other souvenirs, Annie had Keflex and Ampicillin up the old kazoo. She dosed him and he got better . . . as better as it was possible to get under such bizarre circumstances, at any rate. But something was wrong. He seemed to have lost some vital ingredient, and the mix had become a lot less potent as a result. He tried to blame it on the missing n, but he'd had that to contend with before, and, really, what was a missing n compared to a missing foot and now, as an extra added attraction, a missing thumb?

Whatever the reason, something had disturbed the dream, something was whittling away the circumference of that hole in the paper through which he saw. Once – he would have sworn it was so! – that hole had been as big as the bore of the Lincoln Tunnel. Now it was no more than the size of a knothole which a sidewalk superintendent might stoop to snoop through on an interesting piece of building construction. You had to peer and crane to see anything at all, and more often than not the really important things happened outside your field of vision . . . not surprising, considering the field of vision was so small.

In practical terms, what had happened following the thumbectomy and ensuing bout of fever was obvious. The language of the book had grown florid and overblown again – it was not self-parody yet, not quite, but it was floating steadily in that direction and he seemed helpless to stop it. Continuity lapses had begun to proliferate with the stealth of rats breeding in cellar corners: for a space of thirty pages, the Baron had become the Viscount from *Misery's Quest.* He'd had to go back and tear that all out.

It doesn't matter, Paul, he told himself again and again in those last few days before the Royal coughed up first its t and then its e, *the damned thing is almost done.* So it was. Working on it was torture, and finishing it was going to mean the end of his life. That the latter had begun to look slightly more attractive than the former said all that probably needed to be said about the worsening state of his body, mind, and spirit. And the book moved on in spite of everything, seemingly independent of them. The continuity drops were annoying but minor. He was having more problems with the actual make-believe than he ever had before – the game of Can You? had become a labored exercise rather than simple good fun. Yet the book had continued to roll in spite of all the terrible things Annie had subjected him to, and he could bitch about how something – his guts, maybe – had run out of him along with the half-pint or so of blood he'd lost when she took his thumb, but it was still a goddam good yarn, the best *Misery* novel by far. The plot was melodramatic but well constructed, in its own modest way quite amusing. If it were ever to be published in something other than the severely limited (first printing: one copy) Annie

Wilkes Edition, he guessed it might sell like a mad bastard. Yeah, he supposed he would get through it, if the goddam typewriter held together.

You were supposed to be so tough, he had thought once, after one of his compulsive lifting exercises. His thin arms were trembling, the stump of his thumb aching feverishly, his forehead covered with a thin oil of sweat. *You were the tough young gunsel looking to make a rep off the tired old turd of a sheriff, right? Only you've already thrown one key and I see the way some of the others – the t, the e, and the g, for instance, are starting to look funny . . . sometimes leaning one way, sometimes leaning the other, sometimes riding a little high on the line, sometimes dipping a little low. I think maybe the tired old turd is going to win this one, my friend. I think maybe the tired old turd is going to beat you to death . . . and it could be that the bitch knew it. Could be that's why she took my* left *thumb. Like the old saying goes, she may be crazy but she sure ain't dumb.*

He had looked at the typewriter with tired intensity.

Go on. Go on and break. I'll finish anyway. If she wants to get me a replacement, I'll thank her kindly, but if she doesn't, I'll finish on my goddam legal pads.

The one thing I won't do is scream.

I won't scream.

I.

I won't.

12

I won't scream!

He sat at the window, totally awake now, totally aware that the police car he was seeing in Annie's driveway was as real as his left foot had once been.

Scream! Goddammit, scream!

He *wanted* to, but the dictum was too strong – just too strong. He couldn't even open his mouth. He tried and saw the brownish droplets of Betadine flying from the blade of the electric knife. He tried and heard the squeal of axe against bone, the soft *flump* as the match in her hand lit the Bernz-O-matiC.

He tried to open his mouth and couldn't.

Tried to raise his hands. Couldn't.

A horrible moaning sound passed between his closed lips and his hands made light, haphazard drumming sounds on either side of the Royal, but that was all he could do, all the control of his destiny he could seem to take. Nothing which had gone before – except perhaps for the moment when he had realized that, although his left leg was moving, his left foot was staying put – was as terrible as the hell of this immobility. In real time it did not last long; perhaps five seconds and surely no longer than ten. But inside Paul Sheldon's head it seemed to go on for years.

There, within plain sight, was salvation: all he had to do was break the window and the dog-lock the bitch had put on his tongue and scream *Help me, help me, save me from Annie! Save me from the goddess!*

At the same time another voice was screaming: *I'll be good, Annie! I won't scream! I'll be good, I'll be good for goddess' sake! I promise not to scream, just don't chop off any more of me!* Had he known, before this had he really *known* how badly she had cowed him, or how much of his essential self – the liver and lights of his spirit – she had scraped away? He knew how constantly he had been terrorized, but did he know how much of his own subjective reality, once so strong he had taken it for granted, had been erased?

He knew one thing with some certainty – a lot more was wrong with him than paralysis of the tongue, just as a lot more was wrong with what he had been writing than the missing key or the fever or continuity lapses or even a loss of guts. The truth of everything was so simple in its horridness; so dreadfully simple. He was dying by inches, but dying that way wasn't as bad as he'd already feared. But he was also *fading,* and that was an awful thing because it was moronic.

Don't scream! the panicky voice screamed just the same, as the cop opened the door of his cruiser and stepped out, adjusting his Smokey Bear hat as he did so. He was young, no more than twenty-two or -three, wearing sunglasses as black and liquid-looking as dollops of crude oil. He paused to adjust the creases of his khaki uniform pants and thirty yards away a man with blue eyes bulging from his white and whiskery old-man's face sat staring at him from behind a window, moaning through closed lips, hands rattling uselessly on a board laid across the arms of a wheelchair.

don't scream

(yes scream)

scream and it will be over scream and it can end

(never never going to end not until I'm dead that kid's no match for the goddess)

Paul oh Christ are you dead already? *Scream,* you chickenshit motherfucker! SCREAM YOUR FUCKING HEAD OFF!!!

His lips pulled apart with a minute tearing sound. He hitched air into his lungs and closed his eyes. He had no idea what was going to come out or if anything really was . . . until it came.

'AFRICA!' Paul screamed. Now his trembling hands flew up like startled birds and clapped against the sides of his head, as if to hold in his exploding brains. *'Africa! Africa. Help me! Help me! Africa!'*

13

His eyes snapped open. The cop was looking toward the house. Paul could not see the Smokey's eyes because of the sunglasses, but the tilt of his head expressed moderate puzzlement. He took a step closer, then stopped.

Paul looked down at the board. To the left of the typewriter was a heavy ceramic ashtray. Once upon a time it would have been filled with crushed butts; now it held nothing more hazardous to his health than paper-clips and a typewriter eraser. He seized it and threw it at the window. Glass shattered outward. To Paul it was the most liberating sound he had ever heard. *The walls came tumbling down,* he thought giddily, and screamed: *'Over here! Help me! Watch out for the woman! She's crazy!'*

The state cop stared at him. His mouth dropped open. He reached into his breast pocket and brought out something that could only be a picture. He consulted it and then advanced to the edge of the driveway. There he spoke the only four words Paul ever heard him say, the last four words anyone ever heard him say. Following them he would make a number of inarticulate sounds but no real words.

'Oh, shit!' the cop exclaimed. 'It's you!'

Paul's attention had been so fiercely focused on the trooper that he did not see Annie until it was too late. When he did see her, he was struck by a real superstitious horror. Annie had *become* a goddess, a thing that was half woman and half Lawnboy, a weird female centaur. Her baseball cap had fallen off. Her face was twisted in a frozen snarl. In one hand she held a wooden cross. It had marked the grave of the Bossie – Paul didn't remember if it was No. 1 or No. 2 – which had finally stopped bawling.

That Bossie had indeed died, and when spring had softened the ground enough, Paul had watched from his window, sometimes dumbstruck with awe and sometimes overcome with shrieking attacks of the giggles, as she first dug the grave (it had taken her most of the day) and then dragged Bossie (who had also softened considerably) out from behind the barn. She had used a chain attached to the Cherokee's trailer-hitch to do this. She had looped the other end of the chain around Bossie's middle. Paul made a mental bet with himself that Bossie would tear in half before Annie got her to the grave, but that one he lost. Annie tumbled Bossie in, then stolidly began refilling the hole, a job she hadn't finished until long after dark.

Paul had watched her plant the cross and then read the Bible over the grave by the light of a new-risen spring moon.

Now she was holding the cross like a spear, the dirt-darkened point of its vertical post pointed squarely at the trooper's back.

'Behind you! Look out!' Paul shrieked, knowing he was too late but shouting anyway.

With a thin warbling cry, Annie plunged Bossie's cross into the trooper's back.

'*AG!*' the cop said, and walked slowly onto the lawn, his pierced back arched and his gut sticking out. His face was the face of a man either trying to pass a kidney stone or having a terrible gas attack. The cross began to droop toward the ground as the trooper approached the window in which Paul sat, his gray invalid's face framed by jags of broken glass. The cop reached slowly over his shoulders with both hands. He looked to Paul like a man trying very hard to scratch that one itch you can never quite reach.

Annie had dismounted the Lawnboy and had been standing frozen, her tented fingers pressed against the peaks of her breasts. Now she lunged forward and snatched the cross out of the trooper's back.

He turned toward her, groping for his service pistol, and Annie drove the cross point-first into his belly.

'OG!' the cop said this time, and dropped to his knees, clutching his

stomach. As he bent over Paul could see the slit in his brown uniform shirt where the first blow had gone home.

Annie pulled the cross free again – its sharpened point had broken off, leaving a jagged, splintery stump – and drove it into his back between the shoulderblades. She looked like a woman trying to kill a vampire. The first two blows had perhaps not gone deep enough to do much damage, but this time the cross's support post went at least three inches into the kneeling trooper's back, driving him flat.

'THERE!' Annie cried, wrenching Bossie's memorial marker out of his back. *'HOW DO YOU LIKE THAT, YOU DIRTY OLD BIRD?'*

'Annie, stop it!' Paul shouted.

She looked up at him, her dark eyes momentarily as shiny as coins, her hair fungus-frowzy around her face, the corners of her mouth drawn up in the jolly grin of a lunatic who has, at least for the moment, cast aside all restraints. Then she looked back down at the state trooper.

'THERE!' she cried, and drove the cross into his back again. And his buttocks. And the upper thigh of one leg. And his neck. And his crotch. She stabbed him with it half a dozen times, screaming *'THERE!'* every time she brought it down again. Then the cross's upright split.

'There,' she said, almost conversationally, and walked away in the direction from which she had come running. Just before she passed from Paul's view she tossed the bloody cross aside as if it no longer interested her.

14

Paul put his hands on the wheels of the chair, not at all sure where he intended to go or what, if anything, he meant to do when he got there – to the kitchen for a knife, perhaps? Not to try to kill her with, oh no; she would take one look at the knife in his hand and step back into the shed for her .30.30. Not to kill her but to defend himself from her revenge by cutting his wrists open. He didn't know if that had been his intention or not, but it surely did seem like a hell of a good idea, because if there had ever been a time to *exeunt* stage left, this was it. He was tired of losing pieces of himself to her fury.

Then he saw something which froze him in place.

The cop.

The cop was still alive.

He raised his head. His sunglasses had fallen off. Now Paul could see his eyes. Now he could see how young the cop was, how young and hurt and scared. Blood ran down his face in streams. He managed to get to his hands and knees, fell forward, and then got painfully back up again. He began to crawl toward his cruiser.

He worked his way halfway down the mild slope of grass between the house and the driveway, then overbalanced and fell on his back. For a moment he lay there with his legs drawn up, looking as helpless as a turtle on its shell. Then he slowly rolled over on his side and began the terrible job of getting to his knees again. His uniform shirt and pants were darkening with blood – small patches were slowly spreading, meeting other patches, growing bigger still.

The Smokey reached the driveway.

Suddenly the noise of the riding lawnmower was louder.

'Look out!' Paul screamed. *'Look out, she's coming!'*

The cop turned his head. Groggy alarm surfaced on his face, and he grappled for his gun once more. He got it out – something big and black with a long barrel and brown woodgrips – and then Annie reappeared, sitting tall in the saddle and driving the Lawnboy as fast as it would go.

'SHOOT HER!' Paul screamed, and instead of shooting Annie Wilkes with his big old Dirty

(birdie)

Harry gun, he first fumbled, then dropped it.

He stretched out his hand for it. Annie swerved and ran over both his reaching hand and his forearm. Blood squirted from the Lawnboy's grass-exhaust in an amazing jet. The kid in the trooper uniform screamed. There was a sharp clang as the mower's whirling blade struck the pistol. Then Annie was swerving up the side lawn, using it to turn, and her gaze fell on Paul for one second and Paul felt sure he knew what that momentary gaze meant. First the Smokey, then him.

The kid was lying on his side again. When he saw the mower bearing down on him he rolled over on his back and dug frantically at the driveway dirt with his heels, trying to push himself under the cruiser where she couldn't get him.

He didn't even come close. Annie throttled the riding lawnmower up to a scream and drove it over his head.

Paul caught a last glimpse of horrified brown eyes, saw tatters of brown khaki uniform shirt hanging from an arm raised in a feeble effort at protection, and when the eyes were gone, Paul turned away.

The Lawnboy's engine suddenly lugged down and there was a series of fast, strangely liquid thudding sounds.

Paul vomited beside the chair with his eyes closed.

15

He only opened them when he heard the rattle of her key in the kitchen door. His own door was open; he watched her approach down the hall in her old brown cowboy boots and her blue-jeans with the keyring dangling from one of the belt-loops and her man's tee-shirt now spotted with blood. He cringed away from her. He wanted to say: *If you cut anything else off me, Annie, I'm going to die. It won't take the shock of another amputation, either. I'll die on purpose.* But no words came out – only terrified chuffing noises that disgusted him.

She gave him no time to speak anyway.

'I'll deal with you later,' she said, and pulled his door closed. One of her keys rattled in the lock – a new Kreig that would have defeated even Tom Twyford himself, Paul thought – and then she was striding down the hall again, the thud of her boot-heels mercifully diminishing.

He turned his head and looked dully out the window. He could see only part of the trooper's body. His head was still under the mower, which was, in turn, canted at a drunken angle against the cruiser. The riding mower was a small tractor-like vehicle meant for keeping larger-than-average lawns neat and clipped. It had not been designed to keep its balance as it passed over jutting rocks, fallen logs, or the heads of state troopers. If the cruiser hadn't been parked exactly where it was, and if the trooper hadn't gotten exactly as close to it as he had before Annie struck him, the mower would almost surely have tipped over, spilling her off. This might have caused her no harm at all, but it might have hurt her quite badly.

She has the luck of the devil himself, Paul thought drearily, and watched as she put the mower in neutral and then pushed it off the trooper with one hard shove. The side of the mower squalled along the side of the cruiser and took off some paint.

Now that he was dead, Paul could look at him. The cop looked like a big doll that has been badly treated by a gang of nasty children. Paul felt a terrible aching sympathy for this unnamed young man, but there was another emotion mixed with that. He examined it and was not much surprised to find it was envy. The trooper would never go home to his wife and kids, if he had had them, but on the other hand, he had escaped Annie Wilkes.

She grabbed a bloody hand and dragged him up the driveway and through the barn doors, which stood ajar on their tracks. When she came out, she pushed them along their tracks as far as they would go. Then she walked back down to the cruiser. She was moving with a calm that was almost serenity. She started the cruiser and drove it into the barn. When she came out again she closed the doors almost completely, leaving a gap just wide enough for her to slip in and out.

She walked halfway down the driveway and looked around, hands on her hips. Again Paul saw that remarkable expression of serenity.

The bottom of the mower was smeared with blood, particularly around the grass-exhaust, which was still dripping. Little scraps of khaki uniform lay in the driveway or fluttered in the freshly cut grass of the side lawn. There were daubs and splashes of blood everywhere. The trooper's gun, with a long slash of bright metal now scarring its barrel, lay in the dust. A square of stiff white paper had caught on the spines of a small cactus Annie had set out in May. Bossie's splintered cross lay in the driveway like a comment on the whole filthy mess.

She moved out of his field of vision, heading toward the kitchen again. When she came in he heard her singing. *'She'll be driving six white horses when she COMES! . . . she'll be driving six white horses when she COMES! She'll be driving six white HORSES, driving six white HORSES . . . she'll be driving six white HORSES when she COMES!*

When he saw her again, she had a big green garbage bag in her hands and three or four more sticking out of the back pockets of her jeans. Big sweatstains darkened her tee-shirt around her armpits and neck. When she turned, he saw a sweatstain that looked vaguely tree-like rising up her back.

That's a lot of bags for a few scraps of cloth, Paul thought, but he knew that she would have plenty to put in them before she was done.

She picked up the shreds of uniform and then the cross. She broke it into two pieces, and dropped it into the plastic bag. Incredibly, she genuflected after doing this. She picked up the gun, rolled the cylinder, dumped the slugs, put them in one hip pocket, snapped the cylinder back in with a practiced flick of her wrist, and then stuck the gun in the waistband of her jeans. She plucked the piece of paper off the saguaro and looked at it thoughtfully. She stuck it into the other hip pocket. She went to the barn, tossed the garbage bags inside the doors, then came back to the house.

She walked up the side lawn to the cellar bulkhead which was almost directly below Paul's window. Something else caught her eye. It was his ashtray. She picked it up and handed it politely to him through the broken window.

'Here, Paul.'

Numbly, he took it.

'I'll get the paper-clips later,' she said, as if this were a question which must already have occurred to him. For one moment he thought of bringing the heavy ceramic ashtray down on her head as she bent over, cleaving her skull with it, letting out the disease that passed for her brains.

Then he thought of what would happen to him – what *could* happen to him – if he only hurt her, and put the ashtray where it had been with his shaking thumbless hand.

She looked up at him. 'I didn't kill him, you know.'

'Annie –'

'*You* killed him. If you had kept your mouth shut, I would have sent him on his way. He'd be alive now and there would be none of this oogy mess to clean up.'

'Yes,' Paul said. 'Down the road he would have gone, and what about me, Annie?'

She was pulling her hose out of the bulkhead and looping it over her arm. 'I don't know what you mean.'

'Yes you do.' In the depth of his shock he had achieved his own serenity. 'He had my picture. It's in your pocket right now, isn't it?'

'Ask me no questions and I will tell you no lies.' There was a faucet bib on the side of the house to the left of his window. She began to screw the end of the hose onto it.

'A state cop with my picture means someone found my car. We both knew someone would. I'm only surprised it took so long. In a novel a car might be able to float right out of the story – I guess I could make people believe it if I had to – but in real life, no way. But we went on fooling ourselves just the same, didn't we, Annie? You because of the book, me because of my life, miserable as it has become to me.'

'I don't know what you're talking about.' She turned on the faucet. 'All I know is you killed that poor kid when you threw the ashtray through the window. You're getting what might happen to *you* mixed up with what already happened to him.' She grinned at him. There was craziness in that grin, but he saw something else in it as well, something that really frightened him. He saw conscious evil in it – a demon capering behind her eyes.

'You bitch,' he said.

'*Crazy* bitch, isn't that right?' she asked, still smiling.

'Oh yeah – you're crazy,' he said.

'Well, we'll have to talk about that, won't we? When I have more time. We'll have to talk about that a *lot.* But right now I'm very busy, as I think you can see.'

She unreeled the hose and turned it on. She spent nearly half an hour hosing blood off the mower and driveway and the side lawn, while interlinked rainbows glimmered in the spray.

Then she twisted the nozzle off and walked back along the hose's length, looping it over her arm. There was still plenty of light but her shadow trailed long behind her. It was now six o'clock.

She unscrewed the hose, opened the bulkhead, and dropped the green plastic snake inside. She closed the bulkhead, shot the bolt, and stood back, surveying the puddly driveway and the grass, which looked as though a heavy dew had fallen upon it. Annie walked back to the mower, got on, started it up, and drove it around back. Paul smiled a little. She had the luck of the devil, and when she was pressed she had *almost* the cleverness of the devil – but almost was the key word. She had slipped in Boulder and wriggled away mostly due to luck. Now she had slipped again. He had seen it. She had washed the blood off the mower but forgotten the blade underneath – the whole blade housing, for that matter. She might remember later, but Paul didn't think so. Things had a way of dropping out of Annie's mind once the immediate moment was past. It occurred to him that the mind and the mower had a lot in common – what you could see looked all right. But if you turned the thing over to take a look at the works, you saw a blood-slimed killing machine with a very sharp blade.

She returned to the kitchen door and let herself into the house again. She went upstairs and he heard her rummaging there for awhile. Then she came down again, more slowly, dragging something that sounded soft and heavy. After a moment's consideration, Paul rolled the wheelchair across to his door and leaned his ear against the wood.

Dim, diminishing footfalls – slightly hollow. And still that soft flumping sound of something being dragged. Immediately his mind lit up with panicky floodlights and his skin flushed with his terror.

Shed! She's gone to the shed to get the axe! It's the axe again!

But this was only a momentary atavism, and he pushed it roughly away. She hadn't gone into the shed; she was going down cellar. Dragging something down cellar.

He heard her come up again and he rolled back to the window. As her boot-heels approached his door, as the key slid into the lock again, he thought: *She's come to kill me.* And the only emotion this thought engendered was tired relief.

16

The door opened and Annie stood there, looking at him contemplatively. She had changed into a fresh white tee-shirt and a pair of chinos. A small khaki bag, too big to be a purse and not quite big enough to be a knapsack, was slung over one shoulder.

As she came in, he was surprised to find himself able to say it, and say it with a certain amount of dignity: 'Go ahead and kill me, Annie, if that's what you mean to do, but at least have the decency to make it quick. Don't cut anything more off me.'

'I'm not going to kill you, Paul.' She paused. 'At least, not if I have just a little luck. I *should* kill you – I know that – but I'm crazy, right? And crazy people often don't look after their best interests, do they?'

She went behind him and propelled him across the room, out the door, and down the hall. He could hear her bag slapping solidly against her side, and it occurred to him that he had never seen her carrying a bag like that before. If she went to town in a dress, she carried a big, clunky purse – the sort of purse maiden aunts tote to church jumble sales. If she went in pants, she went with a wallet stuck in her hip pocket, like a man.

The sunlight slanting into the kitchen was strong bright gold. Shadows from the legs of the kitchen table lay across the linoleum in horizontal stripes like the shadows of prison bars. It was quarter past six according to the clock over the range, and while there was no reason to believe she was any less sloppy about her clocks than her calendars (the one out here had actually made it to May), that seemed about right. He could hear the first evening crickets tuning up in Annie's field. He thought, *I heard that same sound as a small, unhurt boy,* and for a moment he nearly wept.

She pushed him into the pantry, where the door to the basement stood open. Yellow light staggered up the stairs and fell dead on the pantry floor. The smell of the late-winter rainstorm which had flooded it still lingered.

Spiders down there, he thought. *Mice down there.* Rats *down there.*

'Uh-uh,' he told her. 'Count me out.'

She looked at him with a level sort of impatience, and he realized that since killing the cop, she had seemed almost sane. Her face was the purposeful if slightly harried face of a woman making ready for a big dinner party.

'You're going down there,' she said. 'The only question is whether you're going down piggy-back or bum over teakettle. I'll give you five seconds to decide.'

'Piggy-back,' he said at once.

'Very wise.' She turned around so he could put his arms around her neck. 'Don't do anything stupid like trying to choke me, Paul. I took a karate class in Harrisburg. I was good at it. I'll flip you. The floor is dirt but very hard. You'll break your back.'

She hoisted him easily. His legs, now unsplinted but as crooked and ugly as something glimpsed through a rip in the canvas of a freak-show tent, hung down. The left, with the salt-dome where the knee had been, was fully four inches shorter than the right. He had tried standing on the right leg and had found he could, for short times, but doing so produced a low, primal agony that lasted for hours. The dope couldn't touch that pain, which was like a deep physical sobbing.

She carried him down and into a thickening smell of old stone and wood and flood and rotting vegetables. There were three naked light-bulbs. Old spiderwebs hung in rotting hammocks between bare beams.

The walls were rock, carelessly chinked – they looked like a child's drawing of rock walls. It was cool, but not a pleasant cool.

He had never been as close to her as he was then, as she carried him piggy-back down the steep stairs. He would only be as close once again. It was not a pleasant experience. He could smell the sweat of her recent exertions, and while he actually liked the smell of fresh perspiration – he associated it with work, hard effort, things he respected – this smell was secretive and nasty, like old sheets thick with dried come. And below the smell of sweat was a smell of very old dirt. Annie, he guessed, had gotten as casually catch-as-catch-can about showering as she had about changing her calendars. He could see dark-brown wax plugging one ear and wondered with faint disgust how the hell she could hear anything.

Here, by one of the rock walls, was the source of that flumping, dragging sound: a mattress. Beside it she had placed a collapsed TV tray. There were a few cans and bottles on it. She approached the mattress, turned around, and squatted.

'Get off, Paul.'

He released his hold cautiously and allowed himself to fall back on the mattress. He looked up at her warily as she stood and reached into the little khaki bag.

'No,' he said immediately when he saw the tired yellow cellar-light gleam on the hypodermic needle. 'No. No.'

17

'Oh boy,' she said. 'You must think Annie's in a real poopie-doopie mood today. I wish you'd relax, Paul.' She put the hypo on the TV tray. 'That's scopolamine, which is a morphine-based drug. You're lucky I have any morphine at all. I told you how closely they watch it in the hospital pharmacies. I'm leaving it because it's damp down here and your legs may ache quite badly before I get back.

'Just a minute.' She gave him a wink which had strangely unsettling undertones – a wink one conspirator might give another. 'You throw one cockadoodie ashtray and I'm as busy as a one-armed paperhanger. I'll be right back.'

She went upstairs and came back shortly with the cushions from the sofa in the parlor and the blankets from his bed. She arranged the cushions behind him so he could sit up without too much discomfort – but he could feel the sullen chill of the rocks even through the cushions, waiting to steal out and freeze him.

There were three bottles of Pepsi on the collapsed TV tray. She opened two of them, using the opener on her keyring, and handed him one. She upended her own and drank half of it without stopping; then she stifled a burp, ladylike, against her hand.

'We have to talk,' she said. 'Or, rather, I have to talk and you have to listen.'

'Annie, when I said you were crazy –'

'Hush! Not a word about that. Maybe we'll talk about that later. Not that

I would ever try to change your mind about anything you chose to think – a Mister Smart Guy like you who thinks for a living. All I ever did was pull you out of your wrecked car before you could freeze to death and splint your poor broken legs and give you medicine to ease your pain and take care of you and talk you out of a bad book you'd written and into the best one you *ever* wrote. And if that's crazy, take me to the loonybin.'

Oh, Annie, if only someone would, he thought, and before he could stop himself he had snapped: 'You also cut off my fucking foot!'

Her hand flickered out whip-quick and rocked his head over to one side with a thin spatting sound.

'Don't you use that effword around me,' Annie said. 'I was raised better even if you weren't. You're lucky I didn't cut off your man-gland. I thought of it, you know.'

He looked at her. His stomach felt like the inside of an ice-maker. 'I know you did, Annie,' he said softly. Her eyes widened, and for just a moment she looked both startled and guilty – Naughty Annie instead of Nasty Annie.

'Listen to me. Listen closely, Paul. We're going to be all right if it gets dark before anyone comes to check on that fellow. It'll be full dark in an hour and a half. If someone comes sooner –'

She reached into the khaki bag again and brought out the trooper's .44. The cellar lights shone on the zig-zagging lightning-bolt the Lawnboy's blade had chopped into the gun's barrel.

'If someone comes sooner there's this,' she said. 'For whoever comes, and then you, and then me.'

18

Once it was dark, she said, she was going to drive the police cruiser up to her Laughing Place. There was a lean-to beside the cabin where she could park it safely out of sight. She thought the only danger of being noticed would come on Route 9, but even there the risk would be small – she only had to drive four miles of it. Once she was off 9, the way into the hills was by little-traveled meadow-line roads, many fallen into casual disuse as grazing cattle this high up became a rarity. A few of these roads, she said, were still gated off – she and Ralph had obtained keys to them when they bought the property. They didn't have to ask; the owners of the land between the road and the cabin gave them the keys. This was called *neighboring,* she told Paul, managing to invest a pleasant word with unsuspected depths of nuance: suspicion, contempt, bitter amusement.

'I would take you with me just to keep an eye on you, now that you've shown how untrustworthy you can be, but it wouldn't work. I could get you up there in the back of the police-car, but getting you back down would be impossible. I'm going to have to ride Ralph's trail-bike. I'll probably fall off and break my cockadoodie *neck!*'

She laughed merrily to show what a joke on her *that* would be, but Paul did not join her.

'If that *did* happen, Annie, what would happen to *me*?'

'You'll be fine, Paul,' she said serenely. 'Gosh, you're such a worry-wart!' She walked over to one of the cellar windows and stood there a moment, looking out, measuring the fall of the day. Paul watched her moodily. If she fell off her husband's bike or drove off one of those unpaved ridge-roads, he did not actually believe he would be fine. What he actually believed was that he would die a dog's death down here, and when it was finally over he would make a meal for the rats which were even now undoubtedly watching these two unwelcome bipeds who had intruded upon their domain. There was a Kreig lock on the pantry door now, and a bolt on the bulkhead almost as thick as his wrist. The cellar windows, as if reflecting Annie's paranoia (and there was nothing strange about that, he thought; didn't all houses come, after awhile, to reflect the personalities of their inhabitants?), were not much more than dirty gun-slits, about twenty inches long by fourteen wide. He didn't think he could have wriggled through one of those even on his fittest day, which this wasn't. He might be able to break one and yell for help if someone showed up here before he starved to death, but that wasn't much comfort.

The first twinges of pain slipped down his legs like poisoned water. And the want. His body yelling for Novril. It was *the gotta,* wasn't it? Sure it was.

Annie came back and took the third bottle of Pepsi. 'I'll bring down another couple of these before I go,' she said. 'Right now I need the sugar. You don't mind, do you?'

'Absolutely not. My Pepsi is your Pepsi.'

She twisted the cap off the bottle and drank deeply. Paul thought: *Chug-a-lug, chug-a-lug, make ya want to holler hi-de-ho.* Who was that? Roger Miller, right? Funny, the stuff your mind coughed up.

Hilarious.

'I'm going to put him in his car and drive it up to my Laughing Place. I'm going to take all his things. I'll put the car in the shed up there and bury him and his . . . you know, his *scraps* . . . in the woods up there.'

He said nothing. He kept thinking about Bossie, bawling and bawling and bawling until she couldn't bawl anymore because she was dead, and another of those great axioms of Life on the Western Slope was just this: *Dead cows don't bawl.*

'I have a driveway chain. I'm going to use it. If the police come, it may raise suspicion, but I'd rather have them suspicious than have them drive up to the house and hear you making a big cockadoodie fuss. I thought of gagging you, but gags are dangerous, especially if you're taking drugs that affect respiration. Or you might vomit. Or your sinuses might close up because it's so damp down here. If your sinuses closed up tight and you couldn't breathe through your mouth . . .'

She looked away, unplugged, as silent as one of the stones in the cellar wall, as empty as the first bottle of Pepsi she had drunk. *Make ya want to holler hi-de-ho.* And had Annie hollered hi-de-ho today? Bet your ass. O brethren, Annie had yelled hi-de-ho until the whole yard was oogy. He laughed. She made no sign she had heard him.

Then, slowly, she began to come back.

She looked around at him, blinking.

'I'm going to stick a note through one of the links in the fence,' she said slowly, re-gathering her thoughts. 'There's a town about thirty-five miles from here. It's called Steamboat Heaven, isn't that a funny name for a town? They're having what they call The World's Biggest Flea Market this week. They have it every summer. There's always lots of people there who sell ceramics. I'll write in my note that I'm there, in Steamboat Heaven, looking at ceramics. I'll say I'm staying overnight. And if anyone asks me later where I stayed, so they can check the register, I'll say there were no good ceramics so I started back. Only I got tired. That's what I'll say. I'll say I pulled over to take a nap because I was afraid I might fall asleep behind the wheel. I'll say I only meant to take a short nap but I was so tired from working around the place that I slept all night.'

Paul was dismayed by the depth of this slyness. He suddenly realized that Annie was doing exactly what he could not: she was playing Can You? in real life. Maybe, he thought, *that's why she doesn't write books. She doesn't have to.*

'I'll get back just as soon as I can, because policemen *will* come here,' she said. The prospect did not seem to disturb Annie's weird serenity in the least, although Paul could not believe that, in some part of her mind, she did not realize how close to the end of the game they had now come. 'I don't think they'll come tonight – except maybe to cruise by – but they will come. As soon as they know for sure he's really missing. They'll go all along his route, looking for him and trying to find out where he stopped, you know, showing up. Don't you think so, Paul?'

'Yes.'

'I *should* be back before they come. If I start out on the bike at first light, I might even be able to make it back before noon. I should be able to beat them. Because if he started from Sidewinder, he would have stopped at lots of places before he got here.

'By the time they come, you should be back in your own room, snug as a bug in a rug. I'm not going to tie you up, or gag you, or anything like that, Paul. You can even peek when I go out to talk to them. Because it will be two next time, I think. At least two, don't you think so?'

Paul did.

She nodded, satisfied. 'But I can handle two, if I have to.' She patted the khaki purse. 'I want you to remember that kid's gun while you're peeking, Paul. I want you to remember that it's going to be in here all the time I'm talking to those police when they come tomorrow or the next day. The bag won't be zipped. It's all right for *you* to see *them,* but if they see you, Paul – either by accident or because you try something tomorrow like you did today – if that happens, I'm going to take the gun out of the bag and start shooting. You're already responsible for that kid's death.'

'Bullshit,' Paul said, knowing she would hurt him for it but not caring.

She didn't, though. She only smiled her serene, maternal smile.

'Oh, you know,' she said. 'I don't kid myself that you *care,* I don't kid myself about that at all, but you *know.* I don't kid myself that you'd care about getting another *two* people killed, if it would help you . . . but it wouldn't, Paul. Because if I have to do two, I'll do four. Them . . . and us. And do you know what? I think you still care about your own skin.'

'Not much,' he said. 'I'll tell you the truth, Annie – every day that passes, my skin feels more and more like something I want to get out of.'

She laughed.

'Oh, I've heard *that* one before. But let them see you put one hand on their oogy old respirators! Then it's a different story! Yes! When they see *that,* they yell and cry and turn into a bunch of real *brats!*'

Not that you ever let that stop you, right, Annie?

'Anyway,' she said, 'I just wanted you to know how things are. If you really don't care, yell your head off when they come. It's entirely up to you.'

Paul said nothing.

'When they come I'll stand right out there in the driveway and say yes, there was a state trooper that came by here. I'll say he came just when I was getting ready to leave for Steamboat Heaven to look at the ceramics. I'll say he showed me your picture. I'll say I hadn't seen you. Then one of them will ask me, "This was last winter, Miss Wilkes, how could you be so positive?" And I'll say, "If Elvis Presley was still alive and you saw him last winter, would *you* remember seeing him?" And he'll say yes, probably so, but what does that have to do with the price of coffee in Borneo, and I'll say Paul Sheldon is my favorite writer and I've seen his picture lots of times. I have to say that, Paul. Do you know why?'

He knew. Her slyness continued to astound him. He supposed it shouldn't, not anymore, but it did. He remembered the caption below the picture of Annie in her detainment cell, the picture taken in the *caesura* between the end of the trial and the return of the jury. He remembered it word for word. *IN MISERY? NOT THE DRAGON LADY. Annie reads calmly as she waits for the verdict.*

'So then,' she continued, 'I'll say the policeman wrote it all down in his book and thanked me. I'll say I asked him in for a cup of coffee even though I was in a hurry to be on my way and they'll ask me why. I'll say he probably knew about my trouble before, and I wanted to satisfy his mind that everything was on the up-and-up here. But he said no, he had to move along. So I asked if he'd like to take a cold Pepsi along with him because the day was so hot and he said yes, thanks, that was very kind.'

She drained her second Pepsi and held the empty plastic bottle between her and him. Seen through the plastic her eye was huge and wavering, the eye of a Cyclops. The side of her head took on a ripply, hydrocephalic bulge.

'I'm going to stop and put this bottle in the ditch about two miles up the road,' she said. 'But first I'll put his fingers on it, of course.'

She smiled at him – a dry, spitless smile.

'Fingerprints,' she said. 'They'll know he went past my house then. Or they'll *think* they do, and that's just as good, isn't it, Paul?'

His dismay deepened.

'So they'll go up the road and they won't find him. He'll just be gone. Like those swamis who toot their flutes until ropes come out of baskets and they climb the ropes and disappear. Poof!'

'Poof,' Paul said.

'It won't take them long to come back. I know that. After all, if they can't find any trace of him except that one bottle after here, they'll decide they better think some more about me. After all, I'm crazy, aren't I? All the papers said so. Nutty as a fruitcake!

'But they'll believe me at first. I don't think they'll actually want to come in and search the house – not at first. They'll look in other places and try to think of other things before they come back. We'll have some time. Maybe as much as a week.'

She looked at him levelly.

'You're going to have to write faster, Paul,' she said.

19

Dark fell and no police came. Annie did not spend the time before it did with Paul, however; she wanted to re-glaze his bedroom window, and pick up the paper-clips and broken glass scattered on the lawn. When the police come tomorrow looking for their missing lamb, she said, we don't want them to see anything out of the ordinary, do we, Paul?

Just let them look under the lawnmower, kiddo. Just let them look under there and they'll see plenty *out of the ordinary.*

But no matter how hard he tried to make his vivid imagination work, he could not make it come up with a scenario which would lead up to that.

'Do you wonder why I told you all of this, Paul?' she asked before going upstairs to see what she could do with the window. 'Why I went into my plans for dealing with this in such great detail?'

'No,' he said wanly.

'Partly because I wanted you to know exactly what the stakes are, and exactly what you'll have to do to stay alive. I also wanted you to know that I'd end it right now. Except for the book. I still care about the book.' She smiled. It was a smile which was both radiant and strangely wistful. 'It really *is* the best *Misery* story of them all, and I do so much want to know how it all comes out.'

'So do I, Annie,' he said.

She looked at him, startled. 'Why . . . you *know,* don't you?'

'When I start a book I always *think* I know how things will turn out, but I never actually had one end *exactly* that way. It isn't even that surprising, once you stop to think about it. Writing a book is a little like firing an ICBM . . . only it travels over time instead of space. The book-time the characters spend living in the story and the real time the novelist spends writing it all down. Having a novel end exactly the way you thought it would when you started out would be like shooting a Titan missile halfway around the world and having the payload drop through a basketball hoop. It looks good on paper, and there are people who build those things who'd tell you it was easy as pie – and even keep a straight face while they said it – but the odds are always against.'

'Yes,' Annie said. 'I see.'

'I must have a pretty good navigation system built into the equipment, because I usually get close, and if you have enough high explosive packed into the nosecone, close is good enough. Right now I see *two* possible endings to the book. One is very sad. The other, while not your standard Hollywood happy ending, at least holds out some hope for the future.'

Annie looked alarmed ... and suddenly thunderous. 'You're not thinking of killing her *again,* are you, Paul?'

He smiled a little. 'What would you do if I did, Annie? Kill me? That doesn't scare me a bit. I may not know what's going to happen to Misery, but I know what's going to happen to me . . . and you. I'll write THE END, and you'll read, and then *you'll* write THE END, won't you? The end of us. That's one I don't have to guess at. Truth really isn't stranger than fiction, no matter what they say. Most times you know *exactly* how things are going to turn out.'

'But –'

'I think I know which ending it's going to be. I'm about eighty percent sure. If it turns out that way, you'll like it. But even if it turns out the way I think, neither of us will know the actual details until I get them written down, will we?'

'No – I suppose not.'

'Do you remember what the old Greyhound Bus ads used to say? "Getting there is half the fun."'

'Either way, it's almost over, isn't it?'

'Yes,' Paul said. 'Almost over.'

20

Before she left she brought him another Pepsi, a box of Ritz crackers, sardines, cheese . . . and the bedpan.

'If you bring me my manuscript and one of those yellow legal pads, I'll work in longhand,' he said. 'It will pass the time.'

She considered, then shook her head regretfully. 'I wish you could, Paul. But that would mean leaving at least one light on, and I can't risk it.'

He thought of being left alone down here in the cellar and felt panic flush his skin again, but just for a moment. Then it went cold. He felt tiny hard goosebumps rising on his skin. He thought of the rats hiding in their holes and runs in the rock walls. Thought of them coming out when the cellar went dark. Thought of them smelling his helplessness, perhaps.

'Don't leave me in the dark, Annie. Please don't do that.'

'I have to. If someone noticed a light in my cellar, they might stop to investigate, driveway chain or no driveway chain, note or no note. If I gave you a flashlight, you might try to signal with it. If I gave you a candle, you might try to burn the house down with it. You see how well I know you?' He hardly dared mention the times he had gotten out of his room, because it always made her furious; now his fear of being left alone down here in the dark drove him to it. 'If I had wanted to burn the house down, Annie, I could have done it long before this.'

'Things were different then,' she said shortly. 'I'm sorry you don't like being left in the dark. I'm sorry you have to be. But it's your own fault, so quit being a brat. I've got to go. If you feel like you need that injection, stick it in your leg.'

She looked at him.

'Or stick it up your ass.'

She started for the stairs.

'Cover the windows, then!' he yelled after her. 'Use some pieces of sheet

. . . or . . . or . . . paint them black . . . or . . . Christ, Annie, the rats! The *rats!*'

She was on the third stair. She paused, looking at him from those dusty-dime eyes. 'I haven't time to do any of those things,' she said, 'and the rats won't bother you, anyway. They may even recognize you for one of their own, Paul. They may adopt you.'

Annie laughed. She climbed the stairs, laughing harder and harder. There was a click as the lights went out and Annie went on laughing and he told himself he wouldn't scream, wouldn't beg; that he was past all that. But the damp wildness of the shadows and the boom of her laughter were too much and he shrieked for her not to do this to him, not to leave him, but she only went on laughing and there was a click as the door was shut and her laughter was muted but her laughter was still there, her laughter was on the other side of the door, where there was light, and then the lock clicked, and then another door closed and her laughter was even more muted (but still there), and another lock clicked and a bolt slammed, and her laughter was going away, her laughter was outside, and even after she had started the cruiser up, backed out, put the chain across the driveway, and driven away, he thought he could still hear her. He thought he could still hear her laughing and laughing and laughing.

21

The furnace was a dim bulk in the middle of the room. It looked like an octopus. He thought he would have been able to hear the chiming of the parlor clock if the night had been still, but a strong summer wind had blown up, as it so often did these nights, and there was only time, spreading out forever. He could hear crickets singing just outside the house when the wind dropped . . . and then, sometime later, he heard the stealthy noises he had been afraid of: the low, momentary scuff-and-scurry of the rats.

Only it wasn't rats he was afraid of, was it? No. It was the trooper. His so-fucking-vivid imagination rarely gave him the horrors, but when it did, God help him. God help him once it was warmed up. It was not only warmed up now, it was hot and running on full choke. That there was no sense at all in what he was thinking made not a whit of difference in the dark. In the dark, rationality seemed stupid and logic a dream. In the dark he thought with his skin. He kept seeing the trooper coming back to life – *some* sort of life – out in the barn, sitting up, the loose hay with which Annie had covered him falling to either side of him and into his lap, his face plowed into bloody senselessness by the mower's blade. Saw him crawling out of the barn and down the driveway to the bulkhead, the torn streamers of his uniform swinging and fluttering. Saw him melting magically through the bulkhead and reintegrating his corpse's body down here. Saw him crawling across the packed dirt floor, and the little noises Paul heard weren't rats but the sounds of his approach, and there was but a single thought in the cooling clay of the trooper's dead brain: *You killed me. You opened your mouth and killed me. You threw an ashtray and killed me. You cockadoodie son of a bitch, you murdered my life.*

Once Paul felt the trooper's dead fingers slip, tickling, down his cheek, and he screamed loudly, jerking his legs and making them bellow. He brushed frantically at his face and knocked away not fingers but a large spider.

The movement ended the uneasy truce with the pain in his legs and the drug-need in his nerves, but it also diffused his terror a little. His night vision was coming on strong now, he could see better, and that was a help. Not that there was much to look at – the furnace, the remains of a coal-pile, a table with a bunch of shadowy cans and implements lying on it . . . and to his right, up a way from where he was propped . . . what was that shape? The one next to the shelves? He *knew* that shape. Something about it that made it a *bad* shape. It stood on three legs. Its top was rounded. It looked like one of Wells's death-machines in *The War of the Worlds,* only in miniature. Paul puzzled over this, dozed a little, woke, looked again, and thought: *Of course, I should have known from the first. It* is *a death-machine. And if anyone on Earth's a Martian, it's Annie-fucking-Wilkes. It's her barbecue pot. It's the crematorium where she made me burn* Fast Cars.

He shifted a little because his ass was going to sleep, and moaned. Pain in his legs – particularly in the bunched remains of his left knee – and pain in his pelvis as well. That probably meant he was in for a really bad night, because his pelvis had gotten pretty quiet over the last two months.

He felt for the hypo, picked it up, then put it back. A very light dose, she had said. Best to save it for later, then.

He heard a light shuffle-scuffle and looked quickly in the corner, expecting to see the trooper crawling toward him, one brown eye peering from the hash of his face. *If not for you I could be home watching TV now with my hand on my wife's leg.*

No cop. A dim shape which was maybe just imagination but was more likely a rat. Paul willed himself to relax.

Oh what a long night this was going to be.

22

He dozed a little and woke up slumped far over to the left with his head hung down like a drunk in an alley. He straightened up and his legs cursed him roundly. He used the bedpan and it hurt to piss and he realized with some dismay that a urinary infection was probably setting in. He was so vulnerable now. So fucking vulnerable to *everything.* He put the urinal aside and picked up the hypo again.

A light dose of scopolamine, she said – well, maybe so. Or maybe she loaded it with a hot shot of something. The sort of stuff she used on folks like Ernie Gonyar and 'Queenie' Beaulifant.

Then he smiled a little. Would that really be so bad? The answer was a resounding *HELL, NO!* It would be good. The pilings would disappear forever. No more low tide. Forever.

With that thought in mind he found the pulse in his left thigh, and though he had never injected himself in his life, he did it efficiently now, even eagerly.

23

He did not die and he did not sleep. The pain went away and he drifted, feeling almost untethered from his body, a balloon of thought drifting at the end of a long string.

You were also Scheherazade to yourself, he thought, and looked at the barbecue pot. He thought of Martian deathrays, burning London in fire.

He thought suddenly of a song, a disco tune, something by a group called the Trammps: *Burn, baby, burn, burn the mother down . . .*

Something flickered.

Some idea.

Burn the mother down . . .

Paul Sheldon slept.

24

When he woke up the cellar was filled with the ashy light of dawn. A very large rat sat on the tray Annie had left him, nibbling cheese with its tail neatly curled around its body.

Paul screamed, jerked, then screamed again as pain flowed up his legs. The rat fled.

She had left him some capsules. He knew that the Novril wouldn't take care of the pain, but it was better than nothing.

Besides, pain or no pain, it's time for the old morning fix, right, Paul?

He washed two of the caps down with Pepsi and then leaned back, feeling the dull throb in his kidneys. He was growing something down there, all right. Great.

Martians, he thought. Martian death-machines.

He looked toward the barbecue pot, expecting it to look like a barbecue pot in the morning light: a barbecue pot and nothing else. He was surprised to find it still looked to him like one of Wells's striding machines of destruction.

You had an idea – what was it?

The song came back, the one by the Trammps:

Burn, baby, burn, burn the mother down!

Yeah? And just what mother is that? She wouldn't even leave you a candle. You couldn't light a fart.

Up came a message from the boys in the sweatshop.

You don't need to burn anything now. Or here.

What the fuck are we talking about, guys? Could you let me in on –

Then it came, it came at once, the way all the really good ideas came, rounded and smooth and utterly persuasive in its baleful perfection.

Burn the mother down . . .

He looked at the barbecue pot, expecting the pain of what he had done – what she had *made* him do – to return. It did, but it was dull and faint;

the pain in his kidneys was worse. What had she said yesterday? *All I ever did was . . . talk you out of a bad book you'd written and into the best one you* ever *wrote . . .*

Maybe there was a queer sort of truth in that. Maybe he had wildly overestimated just how good *Fast Cars* had been.

That's just your mind trying to heal itself, part of him whispered. *If you ever get out of this, you'll work yourself around in much the same fashion to thinking you never needed your left foot anyway – hell, five less nails to clip. And they do wonders with prosthetics these days. No, Paul, one was a damned good book and the other was a damned good foot. Let's not kid ourselves.*

Yet a deeper part of him suspected that to think that way *was* kidding himself.

Not kidding yourself, Paul. Tell the goddam truth. Lying *to yourself. A guy who makes up stories, a guy like that is lying to everyone, so that guy can't ever lie to himself. It's funny, but it's also the truth. Once you start that shit, you might as well just cover up your typewriter and start studying for a broker's license or something, because you're down the toilet.*

So what was the truth? The truth, should you insist, was that the increasing dismissal of his work in the critical press as that of a 'popular writer' (which was, as he understood it, one step – a small one – above that of a 'hack') had hurt him quite badly. It didn't jibe with his self-image as a Serious Writer who was only churning out these shitty romances in order to subsidize his (flourish of trumpets, please!) REAL WORK! Had he hated Misery? Had he really? If so, why had it been so easy to slip back into her world? No, more than easy; blissful, like slipping into a warm bath with a good book by one hand and a cold beer by the other. Perhaps all he had hated was the fact that her face on the dust jackets had overshadowed his in his author photographs, not allowing the critics to see that they were dealing with a young Mailer or Cheever here – that they were dealing with a *heavyweight* here. As a result, hadn't his 'serious fiction' become steadily more self-conscious, a sort of scream? *Look at me! Look how good this is! Hey, guys! This stuff has got a sliding perspective! This stuff has got stream-of-consciousness interludes! This is my REAL WORK, you assholes! Don't you DARE turn away from me! Don't you DARE, you cockadoodie brats! Don't you DARE turn away from my REAL WORK! Don't you DARE, or I'll –*

What? What would he do? Cut off their feet? Saw off their thumbs?

Paul was seized by a sudden fit of shivering. He had to urinate. He grabbed the bedpan and finally managed, although it hurt worse than before. He moaned while he was pissing, and continued moaning for a long while after it was done.

Finally, mercifully, the Novril began to kick in – a little – and he drowsed.

He looked at the barbecue pot with heavy-lidded eyes.

How would you feel if she made you burn Misery's Return? the interior voice whispered, and he jumped a little. Drifting away, he realized that it would hurt, yes, it would hurt terribly, it would make the pain he had felt when *Fast Cars* went up in smoke look like the pain of this kidney infection compared with what he had felt when she brought the axe down, cutting off his foot, exercising editorial authority over his body.

He also realized that wasn't the real question.

The real question was how it would make *Annie* feel.

There was a table near the barbecue pot. There were maybe half a dozen jars and cans on it.

One was a can of charcoal lighter fluid.

What if Annie *was the one screaming in pain? Are you curious about how that might sound? Are you curious at all? The proverb says revenge is a dish best eaten cold, but Ronson Fast-Lite had yet to be invented when they made that one up.*

Paul thought: *Burn the mother down,* and fell asleep. There was a little smile on his pale and fading face.

25

When Annie arrived back at quarter of three that afternoon, her normally frizzy hair flattened around her head in the shape of the helmet she had been wearing, she was in a silent mood that seemed to indicate tiredness and reflection rather than depression. When Paul asked her if everything had gone all right, she nodded.

'Yes, I think so. I had some trouble starting the bike, or I would have been back an hour ago. The plugs were dirty. How are your legs, Paul? Do you want another shot before I take you upstairs?'

After almost twenty hours in the dampness, his legs felt as if someone had studded them with rusty nails. He wanted a shot very badly, but not down here. That would not do at all.

'I think I'm all right.'

She turned her back to him and squatted. 'All right, grab on. But remember what I said about choke-holds and things like that. I'm very tired, and I don't think I'd react very well to funny jokes.'

'I seem to be all out of jokes.'

'Good.'

She lifted him with a moist grunt, and Paul had to bite back a scream of agony. She walked across the floor toward the stairs, her head turned slightly, and he realized she was – or might be – looking at the can-littered table. Her glance was short, seemingly casual, but to Paul it seemed to go on for a very long time, and he was sure she would realize the can of lighter fluid was no longer there. It was stuffed down the back of his underpants instead. Long months after his earlier depredations, he had finally summoned up the courage to steal something else . . . and if her hands slipped up his legs as she climbed the stairs, she was going to grab more than a handful of his skinny ass.

Then she glanced away from the table with no change of expression, and his relief was so great that the thudding, shifting ascent up the stairs to the pantry was almost bearable. She kept up a very good poker face when she wanted to, but he thought – *hoped* – that he had fooled her.

That this time he had really fooled her.

26

'I guess I'd like that shot after all, Annie,' he said when she had him back in bed.

She studied his white, sweat-beaded face for a moment, then nodded and left the room.

As soon as she was gone, he slid the flat can out of his underwear and under the mattress. He had not put anything under there since the knife, and he did not intend to leave the lighter fluid there long, but it would have to stay there for the rest of the day. Tonight he intended to put it in another, safer place.

She came back and gave him an injection. Then she put a steno pad and some freshly sharpened pencils on the windowsill and rolled his wheelchair over so it was by the bed.

'There,' she said. 'I'm going to get some sleep. If a car comes in, I'll hear it. If we're left alone, I'll probably sleep right through until tomorrow morning. If you want to get up and work in longhand, here's your chair. Your manuscript is over there, on the floor. I frankly don't advise it until your legs start to warm up a little, though.'

'I couldn't right now, but I guess I'll probably soldier along awhile tonight. I understand what you meant about time being short now.'

'I'm glad you do, Paul. How long do you think you need?'

'Under ordinary circumstances, I'd say a month. The way I've been working just lately, two weeks. If I really go into overdrive, five days. Or maybe a week. It'll be ragged, but it'll be there.'

She sighed and looked down at her hands with dull concentration. 'I know it's going to be less than two weeks.'

'I wish you'd promise me something.'

She looked at him with no anger or suspicion, only faint curiosity. 'What?'

'Not to read any more until I'm done . . . or until I have to . . . you know . . .'

'Stop?'

'Yes. Or until I have to stop. That way you'll get the conclusion without a lot of fragmentation. It'll have a lot more punch.'

'It's going to be a good one, isn't it?'

'Yes.' Paul smiled. 'It's going to be very hot stuff.'

27

That night, around eight o'clock, he hoisted himself carefully into the wheelchair. He listened and heard nothing at all from upstairs. He had been hearing the same nothing ever since the squeak of the bedsprings announced her lying down at four o'clock in the afternoon. She really *must* have been tired.

Paul got the lighter fluid and rolled across to the spot by the window where his informal little writer's camp was pitched: here was the typewriter with the three missing teeth in its unpleasant grin, here the wastebasket, here the pencils and pads and typing paper and piles of scrap-rewrite, some of which he would use and some of which would go into the wastebasket.

Or would have, before.

Here, all unseen, was the door to another world. Here too, he thought, was his own ghost in a series of overlays, like still pictures which, when riffled rapidly, give the illusion of movement.

He wove the chair between the piles of paper and the casually stacked pads with the ease of long practice, listened once more, then reached down and pulled out a nine-inch section of the baseboard. He had discovered it was loose about a month ago, and he could see by the thin film of dust on it (*Next you'll be taping hairs across it yourself just to make sure,* he had thought) that Annie hadn't known this loose piece of board was here. Behind it was a narrow space empty save for dust and a plentiful scattering of mouse-turds.

He stowed the can of Fast-Lite in the space and pushed the board back into place. He had an anxious moment when he was afraid it would no longer fit flush against its mates (and God! her eyes were so *fucking* sharp!), and then it slipped neatly home.

Paul regarded this for a moment, then opened his pad, picked up a pencil, and found the hole in the paper.

He wrote undisturbed for the next four hours – until the points on all three of the pencils she had sharpened for him were written flat – and then he rolled himself back to the bed, got in, and went easily off to sleep.

28

CHAPTER 37

Geoffrey's arms were beginning to feel like white iron. He had been standing in the deep shadows outside the hut which belonged to M'Chibi "Beautiful

One" for the last five minutes, looking rather like a too-slim version of the circus strongman with the Baroness's trunk poised over his head.

Just as he came to believe that nothing Hezekiah could say would convince M'Chibi to leave his hut, he heard sounds of ~~rapid~~ movement. Geoffrey turned even farther, the muscles in his arms now twitching wildly. Chief M'Chibi "Beautiful One" was the Keeper of the Fire, and inside his hut were better than a hundred torches, the head of each coated with a thick, gummy resin. This resin oozed from the low trees of the area, and the Bourkas called it Fire-Oil or Fire-Blood-Oil. Like most essentially simple languages, that of the Bourkas could at times be oddly elusive. Whatever you called the stuff, however, there were enough torches in there to set this whole village afire — it would burn like a Guy Fawkes dummy, Geoffrey thought... *if*, that was, M'Chibi could be gotten out of the way.

Fear not to strike, Boss Ge'ffy, Hezekiah had said. M'Chibi, he come out firs' one, 'cause he the fire-man. Hezekiah, he be comin' out secon' one. So you don't be waitin' to see my gold toot' flash! You break that brat's head, damn quick!

But when he actually did hear them coming, Geoffrey felt a moment's doubt in spite of the agony in his arms. Suppose that, just this once, the o–

29

His pencil paused in mid-word at the sound of an approaching engine. He was surprised at how calm he felt – the strongest emotion in him right now was mild annoyance at being interrupted just when it was starting to float like a butterfly and sting like a bee. Annie's boot-heels rattled staccato down the hallway.

'Get out of sight.' Her face was tight and grim. The khaki bag, unzipped, was over her shoulder. 'Get out of s –'

She paused and saw that he had already rolled the wheelchair back from the window. She looked to make sure that none of his things were on the sill, then nodded.

'It's the State Police,' she said. She looked tense but in control. The shoulder-bag was within easy reach of her right hand. 'Are you going to be good, Paul?'

'Yes,' he said.

Her eyes searched his face.

'I'm going to trust you,' she said finally, and turned away, closing the door but not bothering to lock it.

The car turned into the driveway, the smooth, sleepy beat of that big 442 Plymouth engine almost like a trademark. He heard the kitchen screen door bang shut and eased the wheelchair close enough to the window so he could remain in an angle of shadow and still peek out. The cruiser pulled up to where Annie stood, and the engine died. The driver got out and stood almost exactly where the young trooper had been standing when he spoke his last four words . . . but there all resemblance ended. That trooper had been a weedy young man hardly out of his teens, a rookie cop pulling a shit detail, chasing the cold trail of some numbnuts writer who had wrecked up his car and then either staggered deeper into the woods to die or walked blithely away from the whole mess with his thumb cocked.

The cop currently unfolding himself from behind the cruiser's wheel was about forty, with shoulders seemingly as wide as a barnbeam. His face was a square of granite with a few narrow lines carved into it at the eyes and the corners of the mouth. Annie was a big woman, but this fellow made her look almost small.

There was another difference as well. The trooper Annie killed had been alone. Getting out of the shotgun seat of this cruiser was a small, slope-shouldered plainclothesman with lank blonde hair. *David and Goliath,* Paul thought. *Mutt and Jeff. Jesus.*

The plainclothesman did not so much walk around the cruiser as mince around it. His face looked old and tired, the face of a man who is half-asleep . . . except for his faded bluc eyes. The eyes were wide-awake, everywhere at once. Paul thought he would be quick.

They bookended Annie and she was saying something to them, first looking up to speak to Goliath, then half-turning and looking down to reply to David. Paul wondered what would happen if he broke the window again and screamed for help again. He thought the odds were maybe eight in ten that they would take her. Oh, she was quick, but the big cop looked as if he might be quicker in spite of his size, and strong enough to uproot middling-sized trees with his bare hands. The plainclothesman's self-conscious walk might be as deliberately deceptive as his sleepy look. He thought they would take her . . . except what surprised them wouldn't surprise her, and that gave her an outside chance, anyway.

The plainclothesman's coat. It was buttoned in spite of the glaring heat. If she shot Goliath first, she might very well be able to put a slug in David's face before he could get that oogy goddam coat unbuttoned and his gun out. More than anything else, that buttoned coat suggested that Annie had been right: so far, this was just a routine check-back.

So far.

I didn't kill him, you know. You killed him. If you had kept your mouth shut, I would have sent him on his way. He'd be alive now . . .

Did he believe that? No, of course not. But there was still that strong, hurtful moment of guilt – like a quick deep stab-wound. Was he going to keep his mouth shut because there were two chances in ten that she would off these two as well if he opened it?

The guilt stabbed quickly again and was gone. The answer to that was also no. It would be nice to credit himself with such selfless motives, but it wasn't the truth. The fact was simple: he wanted to take care of Annie Wilkes himself. *They could only put you in jail, bitch,* he thought. *I know how to hurt you.*

30

There was always the possibility, of course, that they would smell a rat. Rat-catching was, after all, their job, and they would know Annie's background. If that was the way things turned out, so be it . . . but he thought Annie might just be able to wriggle past the law this one last time.

Paul now knew as much of the story as he needed to know, he supposed. Annie had listened to the radio constantly since her long sleep, and the missing state cop, whose name was Duane Kushner, was big news. The fact that he had been searching for traces of a hotshot writer named Paul Sheldon was reported, but Kushner's disappearance had not been linked, even speculatively, with Paul's own. At least, not yet.

The spring runoff had sent his Camaro rolling and tumbling five miles down the wash. It might have lain undiscovered in the forest for another month or another year but for merest coincidence. A couple of National Guard chopper-jockeys sent out as part of a random drug-control sweep (looking for back-country pot-farmers, in other words) had seen a sunflash on what remained of the Camaro's windshield and set down in a nearby clearing for a closer look. The seriousness of the crash itself had been masked by the violent battering the Camaro had taken as it travelled to its final resting place. If the car had yielded traces of blood to forensic analysis (if, indeed, there had *been* a forensic analysis), the radio did not say so. Paul knew that even an exhaustive analysis would turn up precious few traces of blood – his car had spent most of the spring with snowmelt running through it at flood-speed.

And in Colorado, most of the attention and concern were focused on Trooper Duane Kushner – as he supposed these two visitors proved. So far all speculation centered on three illegal substances: moonshine, marijuana, and cocaine. It seemed possible that Kushner might have stumbled across the growing, distilling, or stockpiling of one of these substances quite by accident during his search for signs of the tenderfoot writer. And as hope of finding Kushner alive began to fade, questions about why he had been out there alone in the first place began to grow louder – and while Paul doubted if the State of Colorado had money enough to finance a buddy system for its vehicle police, they were obviously combing the area for Kushner in pairs. Taking no chances.

Goliath now gestured toward the house. Annie shrugged and shook her head. David said something. After a moment she nodded and led them up the path to the kitchen door. Paul heard the screen's hinges squeak, and then they were in. The sound of so many footfalls out there was frightening, almost a profanation.

'What time was it when he came by?' Goliath asked – it had to be Goliath. He had a rumbling Midwestern voice, roughened by cigarettes.

Around four, Annie said. Give or take. She had just finished mowing the grass and she didn't wear a watch. It had been devilish hot; she remembered that well enough.

'How long did he stay, Mrs Wilkes?' David asked.

'It's *Miss* Wilkes, if you don't mind.'

'Excuse me.'

Annie said she couldn't reckon on how long for sure, only it hadn't been long. Five minutes, maybe.

'He showed you a picture?'

Yes, Annie said, that was why he came. Paul marveled at how composed she sounded, how pleasant.

'And had you seen the man in the picture?'

Annie said certainly, he was Paul Sheldon, she knew that right away. 'I have all his books,' she said. 'I like them very much. That disappointed Officer Kushner. He said if that was the case, he guessed I probably knew what I was talking about. He looked very discouraged. He also looked very hot.'

'Yeah, it was a hot day, all right,' Goliath said, and Paul was alarmed by how much closer his voice was. In the parlor? Yes, almost certainly in the parlor. Big or not, the guy moved like a goddamned lynx. When Annie responded, her own voice was closer. The cops had moved into the parlor. She was following. She hadn't asked them, but they had gone in there anyway. Looking the place over.

Although her pet writer was now less than thirty-five feet away, Annie's voice remained composed. She had asked if he would like to come in for an iced coffee; he said he couldn't. So she had asked if he'd like to take along a cold bottle of –

'Please don't break that,' Annie interrupted herself, her voice sharpening. 'I like my things, and some of them are quite fragile.'

'Sorry, ma'am.' That had to be David, his voice low and whispery, both humble and a little startled. That tone coming from a cop would have been amusing under other circumstances, but these were not other circumstances and Paul was not amused. He sat stiffly, hearing the small sound of something being set carefully back down (the penguin on his block of ice, perhaps), his hands clasped tightly on the arms of the wheelchair. He imagined her fiddling with the shoulder-bag. He waited for one of the cops – Goliath, probably – to ask her just what the hell it was she had in there.

Then the shooting would start.

'What were you saying?' David asked.

'That I asked him if he'd like to take along a cold Pepsi from the fridge because it was such a hot day. I keep them right next to the freezer compartment, and that keeps them as cold as you can get them without freezing them. He said that would be very kind. He was a very polite boy. Why did they let such a young boy out alone, do you know?'

'Did he drink the soda here?' David asked, ignoring her question. His voice was closer still. He had crossed the parlor. Paul didn't have to close his eyes to imagine him standing there, looking down the short hall which passed the little downstairs bathroom and ended in the closed guest-room door. Paul sat tight and upright, a pulse beating rapidly in his scrawny throat.

'No,' Annie said, as composed as ever. 'He took it along. He said he had to keep rolling.'

'What's down there?' Goliath asked. There was a double thud of booted heels, the sound slightly hollow, as he stepped off the parlor carpet and onto the bare boards of the hallway.

'A bath and a spare bedroom. I sometimes sleep there when it's very hot. Have a look, if you like, but I promise you I don't have your trooper tied to the bed.'

'No, ma'am, I'm sure you don't,' David said, and, amazingly, their footfalls and voices began to fade toward the kitchen again. 'Did he seem excited about anything while he was here?'

'Not at all,' Annie said. 'Just hot and discouraged.' Paul was beginning to breathe again.

'Preoccupied about anything?'

'No.'

'Did he say where he was going next?'

Although the cops almost surely missed it, Paul's own practiced ear sensed the minutest of hesitations – there could be a trap here, a snare which might spring at once or after a short delay. No, she said at last, although he had headed west, so she assumed he must have gone toward Springer's Road and the few farms out that way.

'Thank you, ma'am, for your cooperation,' David said. 'We may have to check back with you.'

'All right,' Annie said. 'Feel free. I don't see much company these days.'

'Would you mind if we looked in your barn?' Goliath asked abruptly.

'Not at all. Just be sure to say howdy when you go in.'

'Howdy to who, ma'am?' David asked.

'Why, to Misery,' Annie said. 'My pig.'

31

She stood in the doorway looking at him fixedly – so fixedly that his face began to feel warm and he supposed he was blushing. The two cops had left fifteen minutes ago.

'You see something green?' he asked finally.

'Why didn't you holler?' Both cops had tipped their hats to her as they got in their cruiser, but neither had smiled, and there had been a look in their eyes Paul had been able to see even from the narrow angle afforded by the corner of his window. They knew who she was, all right. 'I kept expecting you to holler. They would have fallen on me like an avalanche.'

'Maybe. Maybe not.'

'But why didn't you?'

'Annie, if you spend your whole life thinking the worst thing you can imagine is going to happen, you have to be wrong some of the time.'

'Don't be smart with me!' He saw that beneath her assumed impassivity she was deeply confused. His silence did not fit well into her view of all existence as a sort of Big-Time Wrestling match: Honest Annie *vs.* that all-time, double ugly tag-team of The Cockadoodie Brats.

'Who's being smart? I told you I was going to keep my mouth shut and I did. I want to finish my book in relative peace. And I want to finish it for you.'

She looked at him uncertainly, wanting to believe, afraid to believe . . .

and ultimately believing anyway. And she was right to believe, because he was telling the truth.

'Get busy, then,' she said softly. 'Get busy right away. You saw the way they looked at me.'

32

For the next two days life went on just as it had before Duane Kushner; it was almost possible to believe Duane Kushner had never happened at all. Paul wrote almost constantly. He had given the typewriter up for the nonce. Annie put it on the mantel below the picture of the Arc de Triomphe without comment. He filled three legal pads in those two days. There was only one left. When he had filled that one, he would move on to the steno pads. She sharpened his half-dozen Berol Black Warrior pencils, he wrote them dull, and Annie sharpened them again. They shrank steadily as he sat in the sun by the window, bent over, sometimes scratching absently with the great toe of his right foot at the air where the sole of his left foot had been, looking through the hole in the paper. It had yawned wide open again, and the book rushed toward its climax the way the best ones did, as if on a rocket sled. He saw everything with perfect clarity – three groups all hellbent for Misery in the crenelated passages behind the idol's forehead, two wanting to kill her, the third – consisting of Ian, Geoffrey, and Hezekiah – trying to save her . . . while below, the village of the Bourkas burned and the survivors massed at the one point of egress – the idol's left ear – to massacre anyone who happened to stagger out alive.

This hypnotic state of absorption was rudely shaken but not broken when, on the third day after the visit of David and Goliath, a cream-colored Ford station wagon with *KTKA/Grand Junction* written on the side pulled into Annie's driveway. The back was full of video equipment.

'Oh God!' Paul said, frozen somewhere between humor, amazement, and horror. 'What's *this* fuck-a-row?'

The wagon had barely stopped before one of the rear doors flew open and a guy dressed in combat-fatigue pants and a Deadhead tee-shirt leaped out. There was something big and black pistol-gripped in one hand and for one wild moment Paul thought it was a tear-gas gun. Then he raised it to his shoulder, and swept it toward the house, and Paul saw it was a minicam. A pretty young woman was getting out of the front passenger seat, fluffing her blow-dried hair and pausing for one final appraising look at her makeup in the outside rear-view mirror before joining her cameraman.

The eye of the outside world, which had slipped away from the Dragon Lady these last few years, had now returned with a vengeance.

Paul rolled backward quickly, hoping he had been in time.

Well, if you want to know for sure, just check the six o'clock news, he thought, and then had to raise both hands to his mouth to plug up the giggles.

The screen door banged open and shut.

'Get the hell out of here!' Annie screamed. 'Get the hell off my land!'

Dimly: 'Ms Wilkes, if we could have just a few –'

'You can have a couple of loads of double-ought buck up your cockadoodie *bumhole* if you don't get out of here!'

'Ms Wilkes, I'm Glenna Roberts from KTKA –'

'I don't care if you're John O. Jesus Johnnycake Christ from the planet Mars! Get off my land or you're DEAD!'

'But –'

KAPOW!

Oh Annie oh my Jesus Annie killed that stupid broad –

He rolled back and peeked through the window. He had no choice – he had to see. Relief gusted through him. Annie had fired into the air. That seemed to have done quite well. Glenna Roberts was diving head-first into the KTKA newsmobile. The camera-man swung his lens toward Annie; Annie swung her shotgun toward the camera-man; the camera-man, deciding he wanted to live to see the Grateful Dead again more than he wanted to roll tape on the Dragon Lady, immediately dropped into the back seat again. The wagon was reversing down the driveway before he got his door all the way closed.

Annie stood watching them go, the rifle held in one hand, and then she came slowly back into the house. He heard the clack as she put the rifle on the table. She came down to Paul's room. She looked worse than he had ever seen her, her face haggard and pale, her eyes darting constantly.

'They're back,' she whispered.

'Take it easy.'

'I knew all those brats would come back. And now they have.'

'They're gone, Annie. You made them go.'

'They never go. Someone told them that cop was at the Dragon Lady's house before he disappeared. So here they are.'

'Annie –'

'You know what they want?' she demanded.

'Of course. I've dealt with the press. They want the same two things they always want – for you to fuck up while the tape's running and for someone else to buy the martinis when Happy Hour rolls around. But, Annie, you've got to settle d—'

'This is what they want,' she said, and raised one hooked hand to her forehead. She pulled down suddenly, sharply, opening four bloody furrows. Blood ran into her eyebrows, down her cheeks, along either side of her nose.

'Annie! Stop it!'

'And this!' She slapped herself across the left cheek with her left hand, hard enough to leave an imprint. 'And *this!*'

The right cheek, even harder, hard enough to make droplets of blood fly from the fingernail gouges.

'STOP it!' he screamed.

'It's what they want!' she screamed back. She raised her hands to her forehead and pressed them against the wounds, blotting them. She held her bloody palms out toward him for a moment. Then she plodded out of the room.

After a long, long time, Paul began to write again. It went slowly at first – the image of Annie pulling those furrows into her skin kept intruding – and he thought it was going to be no good, he had just better pack it in for the day, when the story caught him and he fell through the hole in the paper again.

As always these days, he went with a sense of blessed relief.

33

More police came the next day: local yokels this time. With them was a skinny man carrying a case which could only contain a steno machine. Annie stood in the driveway with them, listening, her face expressionless. Then she led them into the kitchen.

Paul sat quietly, a steno pad of his own on his lap (he had finished the last legal pad the previous evening), and listened to Annie's voice as she made a statement which consisted of all the things she had told David and Goliath four days ago. This, Paul thought, was nothing more than blatant harassment. He was amused and appalled to find himself feeling a little sorry for Annie Wilkes.

The Sidewinder cop who asked most of the questions began by telling Annie she could have a lawyer present if she wanted. Annie declined and simply re-told her story. Paul could detect no deviations.

They were in the kitchen for half an hour. Near the end one of them asked how she had come by the ugly-looking scratches on her forehead.

'I did it in the night,' she said. 'I had a bad dream.'

'What was that?' the cop asked.

'I dreamed that people remembered me after all this time and started coming out here again,' Annie said.

When they were gone, Annie came to his room. Her face was doughy and distant and ill.

'This place is turning into Grand Central,' Paul said.

She didn't smile. 'How much longer?'

He hesitated, looked at the pile of typescript with the ragged stack of handwritten pages on top, then back at Annie. 'Two days,' he said. 'Maybe three.'

'The next time they come they'll have the search warrant,' she said, and left before he could reply.

34

She came in that evening around quarter of twelve and said: 'You should have been in bed an hour ago, Paul.'

He looked up, startled out of the story's deep dream. Geoffrey – who had turned out to be very much the hero of this one – had just come face to face with the hideous queen bee, whom he would have to battle to the death for Misery's life.

'It doesn't matter,' he said. 'I'll turn in after awhile. Sometimes you get it down or it gets away.' He shook his hand, which was sore and throbbing. A large hard growth, half callus and half blister, had risen on the inside of his index finger, where the pencil pressed most firmly. He had pills, and they would take away the pain, but they would also blur his thoughts.

'You think it's good, don't you?' she asked softly. 'Really good. You're not doing it just for me anymore, are you?'

'Oh no,' he said. For a moment he trembled on the edge of saying something more – of saying, *It was never for you, Annie, or all the other people out there who sign their letters 'Your number-one fan.' The minute you start to write all those people are at the other end of the galaxy, or something. It was never for my ex-wives, or my mother, or for my father. The reason authors almost always put a dedication on a book, Annie, is because their selfishness even horrifies themselves in the end.*

But it would be unwise to say such a thing to her.

He wrote until dawn was coming up in the east and then fell into bed and slept for four hours. His dreams were confused and unpleasant. In one of them Annie's father was climbing a long flight of stairs. He had a basket of what appeared to be newspaper clippings in his arms. Paul tried to cry out to him, to warn him, but every time he opened his mouth nothing came out but a neatly reasoned paragraph of narration – although this paragraph was different each time he tried to scream, it always opened the same way: 'One day, about a week later . . .' And now came Annie Wilkes, screaming, rushing down the hall, hands outstretched to give her father the killing push . . . only her screams were becoming weird buzzing noises, and her body was rippling and humping and changing under her skirt and cardigan sweater, because Annie was changing into a bee.

35

No one official came by the following day, but lots of unofficial people showed up. Designated Gawkers. One of the cars was full of teen-agers. When they turned into the driveway to reverse direction, Annie rushed out and screamed at them to get off her land before she shot them for the dirty dogs they were.

'Fuck off, Dragon Lady!' one of them shouted.

'Where'd you bury him?' another yelled as the car backed out in a boil of dust.

A third threw a beer-bottle. As the car roared away, Paul could make out a bumper sticker pasted to the rear window. SUPPORT THE SIDEWINDER BLUE DEVILS, it read.

An hour later he saw Annie stalk grimly past his window, drawing on a pair of work-gloves as she headed for the barn. She came back some time later with the chain. She had taken the time to interlace its stout steel loops with barbed wire. When this prickly knitting was padlocked across the driveway, she reached into her breast pocket, and took out some red pieces of cloth. These she tied to several of the links to aid visibility.

'It won't keep the cops out,' she said when she finally came in, 'but it'll keep the rest of the brats away.'

'Yes.'

'Your hand . . . it looks swollen.'

'Yes.'

'I hate to be a cockadoodie pest, Paul, but . . .'

'Tomorrow,' he said.

'Tomorrow? Really?' She brightened at once.

'Yes, I think so. Probably around six.'

'Paul, that's wonderful! Shall I start reading now, or –'

'I'd prefer that you wait.'

'Then I will.' That tender, melting look had crept into her eyes again. He had come to hate her most of all when she looked that way. 'I love you, Paul. You know that, don't you?'

'Yes,' he said. 'I know.' And bent over his pad again.

36

That evening she brought him his Keflex pill – his urinary infection was improving, but very slowly – and a bucket of ice. She laid a neatly folded towel beside it and left without saying a word.

Paul put his pencil aside – he had to use the fingers of his left hand to unbend the fingers of his right – and slipped his hand into the ice. He left it there until it was almost completely numb. When he took it out, the swelling seemed to have gone down a little. He wrapped the towel around it and sat, looking out into the darkness, until it began to tingle. He put the towel aside, flexed the hand for awhile (the first few times made him grimace with pain, but then the hand began to limber up), and started to write again.

At dawn he rolled slowly over to his bed, lurched in, and was asleep at once. He dreamed he was lost in a snowstorm, only it wasn't snow; it was flying pages which filled the world, destroying direction, and each page was covered with typing, and all the n's and t's and e's were missing, and he understood that if he was still alive when the blizzard ended, he would have to fill them all in himself, by hand, deciphering words that were barely there.

37

He woke up around eleven, an almost as soon as Annie heard him stirring about, she came in with orange juice, his pills, and a bowl of hot chicken soup. She was glowing with excitement. 'It's a very special day, Paul, isn't it?'

'Yes.' He tried to pick up the spoon with his right hand and could not. It was puffy and red, so swollen the skin was shiny. When he tried to bend it into a fist, it felt as though long rods of metal had been pushed through it at random. The last few days, he thought, had been like some nightmare autographing session that just never ended.

'Oh, your poor *hand!*' she cried. 'I'll get you another pill! I'll do it right now!'

'No. This is the push. I want my head clear for it.'

'But you can't write with your hand like that!'

'No,' he agreed. 'My hand's shot. I'm going to finish this baby the way I started – with that Royal. Eight or ten pages should see it through. I guess I can fight my way through that many n's, t's, and e's.'

'I should have gotten you another machine,' she said. She looked honestly sorry; tears stood in her eyes. Paul thought that the occasional moments like this were the most ghastly of all, because in them he saw the woman she might have been if her upbringing had been right or the drugs squirted out by all the funny little glands inside her had been less wrong. Or both. 'I goofed. It's hard for me to admit that, but it's true. It was because I didn't want to admit that Dartmonger woman got the better of me. I'm sorry, Paul. Your poor hand.'

She raised it, gentle as Niobe at the pool, and kissed it.

'That's all right,' he said. 'We'll manage, Ducky Daddles and I. I hate *him*, but I've got a feeling he hates *me* as well, so I guess we're even.'

'Who are you talking about?'

'The Royal. I've nicknamed it after a cartoon character.'

'Oh . . .' She trailed away. Turned off. Came unplugged. He waited patiently for her to return, eating his soup as he did so, holding the spoon awkwardly between the first and second fingers of his left hand.

At last she did come back and looked at him, smiling radiantly like a woman just awakening and realizing it was going to be a beautiful day. 'Soup almost gone? I've got something very special, if it is.'

He showed her the bowl, empty except for a few noodles stuck to the bottom. 'See what a Do-Bee I am, Annie?' he said without even a trace of a smile.

'You're the most goodest Do-Bee there ever was, Paul, and you get a whole *row* of gold stars! In fact . . . wait! Wait till you see this!'

She left, leaving Paul to look first at the calendar and then at the Arc de Triomphe. He looked up at the ceiling and saw the interlinked W's waltzing drunkenly across the plaster. Last of all he looked across at the typewriter and the vast, untidy pile of manuscript. *Goodbye to all that*, he thought randomly, and then Annie was bustling back in with another tray.

On it were four dishes: wedges of lemon on one, grated egg on a second, toast points on a third. In the middle was a larger plate, and on this one was a vast

(oogy)

gooey pile of caviar.

'I don't know if you like this stuff or not,' she said shyly. 'I don't even know if I like it. I never had it.'

Paul began to laugh. It hurt his middle and it hurt his legs and it even hurt his hand; soon he would probably hurt even more, because Annie was paranoid enough to think that if someone was laughing it must be at her. But still he couldn't stop. He laughed until he was choking and coughing, his cheeks red, tears spurting from the corners of his eyes. The woman had cut off his foot with an axe and his thumb with an electric knife, and here she was with a pile of caviar big enough to choke a warthog. And for a wonder, that black look of *crevasse* did not dawn on her face. She began to laugh with him, instead.

38

Caviar was supposed to be one of those things you either loved or hated, but Paul had never felt either way. If he was flying first class and a stewardess stuck a plate of it in front of him, he ate it and then forgot there was such a thing as caviar until the next time a stewardess stuck a plate of it in front of him. But now he ate it hungrily, with all the trimmings, as if discovering the great principle of food for the first time in his life.

Annie didn't care for it at all. She nibbled at the one dainty teaspoonful she'd put on a toast point, wrinkled her face in disgust, and put it aside. Paul, however, plowed ahead with undimmed enthusiasm. In a space of fifteen minutes he had eaten half of Mount Beluga. He belched, covered his mouth, and looked guiltily at Annie, who went off into another gay gust of laughter.

I think I'm going to kill you, Annie, he thought, and smiled warmly at her. *I really do. I may go with you – probably will, in fact – but I am going to go with a by-God bellyful of caviar. Things could be worse.*

'That was great, but I can't eat any more,' he said.

'You'd probably throw up if you did,' she said. 'That stuff is very rich.' She smiled back. 'There's another surprise. I have a bottle of champagne. For later . . . when you finish the book. It's called Dom Pérignon. It cost seventy-five dollars! For *one bottle!* But Chuckie Yoder down at the liquor store says it's the best there is.'

'Chuckie Yoder is right,' Paul said, thinking that it was partly Dom's fault that he'd gotten himself into this hell in the first place. He paused a moment and then said: 'There's something else I'd like, as well. For when I finish.'

'Oh? What's that?'

'You said once you had all of my things.'

'I do.'

'Well . . . there was a carton of cigarettes in my suitcase. I'd like to have a smoke when I finish.'

Her smile had faded slowly. 'You know those things are no good for you, Paul. They cause cancer.'

'Annie, would you say that cancer is something I have to worry about just now?'

She didn't answer.

'I just want that one single cigarette. I've always leaned back and smoked one when I finished. It's the one that always tastes the best, believe me – even better than the one you have after a really fine meal. At least that's how it used to be. I suppose this time it'll make me feel dizzy and like puking, but I'd like that little link with the past. What do you say, Annie? Be a sport. *I* have been.'

'All right . . . but before the champagne. I'm not drinking a seventy-five-dollar bottle of fizzy beer in the same room where you've been blowing that poison around.'

'That's fine. If you bring it to me around noon, I'll put it on the windowsill where I can look at it once in awhile. I'll finish, and then I'll fill in the letters, and then I'll smoke it until I feel like I'm going to fall down unconscious, and then I'll butt it. Then I'll call you.'

'All right,' she said. 'But I'm still not happy about it. Even if you don't get lung cancer from just one, I'm still not happy about it. And do you know why, Paul?'

'No.'

'Because only Don't-Bees smoke,' she said, and began to gather up the dishes.

39

"Mistuh Boss Ian, is she--?"

"Shhhhh!" Ian hissed fiercely, and Hezekiah subsided. Geoffrey felt a pulse beating with wild rapidity in his throat. From outside came the steady soft creak of lines and rigging, the slow flap of the sails in the first faint breezes of the freshening trade winds, the occasional cry of a bird. Dimly, from the afterdeck, Geoffrey could hear a gang of men singing a shanty in bellowing, off-key voices. But in here all was silence as the three men, two white and one black, waited to see if Misery would live ...or--

Ian groaned hoarsely, and Hezekiah gripped his arm. Geoffrey merely tightened his already hysterically tight hold on himself. After all of this, could God really be cruel enough to let her die? Once he would have denied such a possibility confidently, and with humor rather than indignation. The idea that God could be cruel would in those days have struck him as absurd.

But his ideas about God--like his ideas about so many things, had changed. They had changed in Africa. In Africa he had discovered that there was not just one God but many, and some were more than cruel--they were insane, and that changed all. Cruelty, after all, was understandable. With insanity, however, there was no arguing.

If his Misery were truly dead, as he had come to fear, he intended to go up on the foredeck and throw himself over the rail. He had always known and accepted the fact that the gods were hard; he had no desire, however, to live in a world where the gods were insane.

These wretched musings were interrupted by a harsh, half-superstitious gasp from Hezekiah.

"Mist' Boss Ian! Mist' Boss Geoffrey! Look! She eyes! Look she eyes!"

Misery's eyes, that gorgeously delicate shade of cornflower blue, had fluttered open. They passed from Ian to Geoffrey and then back to Ian again. For a moment Geoffrey saw only puzzlement in those eyes...and then recognition dawned in them, and he felt gladness roar through his soul.

"Where am I?" she asked, yawning and stretching.

"Ian--Geoffrey--are we at sea? Why am I so hungry?"

Laughing, crying, Ian bent and hugged her, speaking her name over and over again.

Bewildered but pleased, she hugged him back--and because he knew she was all right, Geoffrey found he could abide their love, now and forever. He would live alone, could live alone, in perfect peace.

Perhaps the gods were not insane after all...at least, not all of them.

He touched Hezekiah on the shoulder. "I think we should leave them alone, old man, don' you?"

"I guess that be right, Mist' Boss Geoffrey," Hezekiah said. He grinned widely, flashing all seven of his gold teeth.

Geoffrey stole one last look at her, and for just a moment those cornflower eyes flashed his way, warming him, filling him. Fulfilling him.

I love you, my darling, he thought. Do you hear me?

Perhaps the answer which came back was only the wistful call of his own mind, but he thought not--it was too clear, too much her own voice.

I hear...and I love you, too.

Geoffrey closed the door and went up to the afterdeck. Instead of throwing himself over the rail, as he might have done, he lit his pipe and smoked a bowl of tobacco slowly, watching the sun go down behind that distant, disappearing cloud on the horizon--that cloud which was the coast of Africa.

And then, because he could not stand to do otherwise, Paul Sheldon rolled the last page out of the typewriter and scrawled the most loved and hated phrase in the writer's vocabulary with a pen:

THE END

40

His swollen right hand had not wanted to fill in the missing letters, but he had forced it through the work nonetheless. If he wasn't able to work at least some of the stiffness out of it, he was not going to be able to carry through with this.

When it was done, he put the pen aside. He regarded his work for a moment. He felt as he always did when he finished a book – queerly empty, let down, aware that for each little success he had paid a toll of absurdity.

It was always the same, always the same – like toiling uphill through jungle and breaking out to a clearing at the top after months of hell only to discover nothing more rewarding than a view of a freeway – with a few gas stations and bowling alleys thrown in for good behavior, or something.

Still, it was good to be done – always good to be done.

Good to have produced, to have caused a thing to be. In a numb sort of way he understood and appreciated the bravery of the act, of making little lives that weren't, creating the appearance of motion and the illusion of warmth. He understood – now, finally – that he was a bit of a dullard at doing this trick, but it was the only one he knew, and if he always ended up doing it ineptly, he at least never failed to do it with love. He touched the pile of manuscript and smiled a little bit.

His hand left the big pile of paper and stole to the single Marlboro she had put on the windowsill for him. Beside it was a ceramic ashtray with a paddlewheel excursion boat printed on the bottom encircled by the words, SOUVENIR OF HANNIBAL, MISSOURI – HOME OF AMERICA'S STORY TELLER!

In the ashtray was a book of matches, but there was only one match in it – all she had allowed him. One, however, should be enough.

He could hear her moving around upstairs. That was good. He would have plenty of time to make his few little preparations, plenty of warning if she decided to come down before he was quite ready for her.

Here comes the real *trick, Annie. Let's see if I can do it. Let's see – can I?*

He bent over, ignoring the pain in his legs, and began to work the loose section of baseboard out with his fingers.

41

He called for her five minutes later, and listened to her heavy, somehow toneless tread on the stairs. He had expected to feel terrified when things got to this point, and was relieved to find he felt quite calm. The room was filled with the reek of lighter fluid. It dripped steadily from one side of the board which lay across the arms of the wheelchair.

'Paul, are you *really* done?' she called down the length of hallway.

Paul looked at the pile of paper sitting on the board beside the hateful Royal typewriter. Lighter fluid soaked the stack. 'Well,' he called back, 'I did the best I could, Annie.'

'Wow! Oh, great! Gee, I can hardly believe it! After all this time! Just a minute! I'll get the champagne!'

'Fine!'

He heard her cross the kitchen linoleum, knowing where each squeak was going to come the instant before it did come. I *am hearing all these sounds for the last time,* he thought, and that brought a sense of wonder, and wonder broke the calm open like an egg. The fear was inside . . . but there was something else in there as well. He supposed it was the receding coast of Africa.

The refrigerator door was opened, then banged shut. Here she came across the kitchen again; here she came.

He had not smoked the cigarette, of course; it still lay on the windowsill. It had been the match he wanted. That one single match.

What if it doesn't light when you strike it?

But it was far too late for such considerations.

He reached over to the ashtray and picked up the matchbook. He tore out the single match. She was coming down the hallway now. Paul struck the match and, sure enough, it didn't light.

Easy! Easy does it!

He struck it again. Nothing.

Easy . . . easy . . .

He scratched it along the rough dark-brown strip on the back of the book a third time and a pale-yellow flame bloomed at the end of the paper stick.

42

'I just hope this –'

She stopped, the next word pulled back inside her as she sucked in breath. Paul sat in his wheelchair behind a barricade of heaped paper and ancient Royal stenomongery. He had purposely turned the top sheet around so she could read this:

MISERY'S RETURN

By Paul Sheldon

Above this sopping pile of paper Paul's swollen right hand hovered, and held between the thumb and first finger was a single burning match.

She stood in the doorway, holding a bottle of champagne wrapped in a strip of towelling. Her mouth dropped open. She closed it with a snap.

'Paul?' Cautiously. 'What are you doing?'

'It's done,' he said. 'And it's good, Annie. You were right. The best of the *Misery* books, and maybe the best thing I ever wrote, mongrel dog or not. Now I'm going to do a little trick with it. It's a good trick. I learned it from you.'

'Paul, no!' she screamed. Her voice was full of agony and understanding. Her hands flew out, the bottle of champagne dropping from them unheeded. It hit the floor and exploded like a torpedo. Curds of foam flew everywhere. *'No! No! PLEASE DON'T –'*

'Too bad you'll never read it,' Paul said, and smiled at her. It was his first real smile in months, radiant and genuine.

'False modesty aside, I've got to say it was better than good. It was *great,* Annie.'

The match was guttering, printing its small heat on the tips of his fingers. He dropped it. For one terrible moment he thought it had gone out, and then pale-blue fire uncoiled across the title page with an audible sound – *foomp!* It ran down the sides, tasted the fluid that had pooled along the outer edge of the paper-pile, and shot up yellow.

'OH GOD NO!' Annie shrieked. *'NOT MISERY! NOT MISERY! NOT HER! NO! NO!'*

Now her face had begun to shimmer on the far side of the flames. 'Want to make a wish, Annie?' he shouted at her. 'Want to make a *wish,* you fucking goblin?'

'OH MY GOD OH PAUL WHAT ARE YOU DOOOOOING?' She stumbled forward, arms outstretched. Now the pile of paper was not just burning; it was blazing. The gray side of the Royal had begun to turn black. Lighter fluid had pooled under it and now pale-blue tongues of flame shot up between the keys. Paul could feel his face baking, the skin tightening.

'NOT MISERY! she wailed. *'YOU CAN'T BURN MISERY, YOU COCKADOODIE BRAT, YOU CAN'T BURN MISERY!'*

And then she did exactly what he had almost known she would do. She seized the burning pile of paper and wheeled about, meaning to run to the bathroom with it, perhaps, and douse it in the tub.

When she turned Paul seized the Royal, unmindful of the blisters its hot right side was printing on his already swollen right hand. He lifted it over his head. Little blue firedrops still fell from its undercarriage. He paid them no more mind than he paid the flare of pain in his back as he strained something there. His face was an insane grimace of effort and concentration. He brought his arms forward and down, letting the typewriter fly out of his hands. It struck her squarely in the center of her wide solid back.

'HOO-OWWG!' It was not a scream but a vast, startled grunt. Annie was driven forward, onto the floor with the burning stack of paper under her.

Small bluish fires like spirit-lanterns dotted the surface of the board which had served as his desk. Gasping, each breath smooth hot iron in his throat, Paul knocked it aside. He pushed himself up and tottered erect on his right foot.

Annie was writhing and moaning. A lick of flame shot up through the gap between her left arm and the side of her body. She screamed. Paul could smell frying skin, burning fat.

She rolled over, struggling to her knees. Most of the paper was on the floor now, either still burning or hissing to ruin in puddles of champagne, but Annie still held some, and it was still burning. Her cardigan sweater was burning, too. He saw green hooks of glass in her forearms. A larger shard poked out of her right cheek like the blade of a tomahawk.

'I'm going to kill you, you lying cocksucker,' she said, and staggered toward him. She knee-walked three 'steps' toward him and then fell over the typewriter. She writhed and managed to turn over halfway. Then Paul fell on her. He felt the sharp angles of the typewriter beneath her even through her body. She screamed like a cat, writhed like a cat, and tried to claw out from under him like a cat.

The flames were going out around them but he could still feel savage heat coming off the twisting, heaving mound beneath him, and knew that at least some of her sweater and brassiere must be cooked onto her body. He felt no sympathy at all.

She tried to buck him off. He held on, and now he was lying squarely on top of her like a man who means to commit rape, his face almost on hers; his right hand groped, knowing exactly what it was looking for.

'Get off me!'

He found a handful of hot, charry paper.

'Get off me!'

He crumpled the paper, squeezing flames out between his fingers. He could smell her – cooked flesh, sweat, hate, madness.

'GET OFF ME!' she screamed, her mouth yawning wide, and he was suddenly looking into the dank red-lined pit of the goddess. *'GET OFF ME YOU COCKADOODIE BR –'*

He stuffed paper, white bond and black charred onion-skin, into that gaping, screaming mouth. Saw the blazing eyes suddenly widen even more, now with surprise and horror and fresh pain.

'Here's your book, Annie,' he panted, and his hand closed on more paper. This bunch was out, dripping wet, smelling sourly of spilt wine. She bucked and writhed under him. The salt-dome of his left knee whammed the floor and there was excruciating pain, but he stayed on top of her. I'm gonna rape you, all right, Annie. *I'm gonna rape you because all I can do is the worst I can do. So suck my book. Suck my book. Suck on it until you fucking CHOKE.* He crumpled the wet paper with a convulsive closing jerk of his fist and slammed it into her mouth, driving the half-charred first bunch farther down.

'Here it is, Annie, how do you like it? It's a genuine first, it's the Annie Wilkes Edition, how do you like it? Eat it, Annie, suck on it, go on and *eat* it, be a Do-Bee and eat your book *all* up.'

He slammed in a third wad, a fourth. The fifth was still burning; he put it out with the already blistered heel of his right hand as he stuffed it in.

Some weird muffled noise was coming out of her. She gave a tremendous jerk and this time Paul was thrown off. She struggled and flailed to her knees. Her hands clawed at her blackened throat, which had a hideously swelled look. Little was left of her sweater but the charred ring of the neck. The flesh of her belly and diaphragm bubbled with blisters. Champagne was dripping from the wad of paper which protruded from her mouth.

'Mumpf! Mark! Mark!' Annie croaked. She got to her feet somehow, still clawing at her throat. Paul pushed himself backward, legs sticking untidily out in front of him, watching her warily. *'Harkoo? Dorg? Mumpf!'*

She took one step toward him. Two. Then she tripped over the typewriter again. As she fell this time her head twisted at an angle and he saw her eyes looking at him with an expression that was questioning and somehow terrible:

What happened, Paul? I was bringing you champagne, wasn't I?

The left side of her head connected with the edge of the mantelpiece and she went down like a loose sack of bricks, striking the floor in a vast tumble that shook the house.

43

Annie had fallen on the bulk of the burning paper; her body had put it out. It was a smoking black lump in the middle of the floor. The puddles of champagne had put out most of the individual pages. But two or three had wafted against the wall to the left of the door while still burning brightly, and the wallpaper was alight in spots . . . but burning with no real enthusiasm.

Paul crawled over to his bed, pulling himself on his elbows, and got hold of the coverlet. Then he worked his way over to the wall, pushing the shards of broken bottle out of his way with the sides of his hands as he went. He had strained his back. He had burned his right hand badly. His head ached. His stomach roiled with the sick-sweet smell of burned meat.

But he was free. The goddess was dead and he was free.

He got his right knee under him, reached up clumsily with the coverlet (which was damp with champagne and striped with smeary black swaths of ash), and began to beat at the flames. When he let the coverlet fall into a smoking heap at the baseboard, there was a big smoking bald spot in the middle of the wall, but the paper was out. The bottom page of the calendar had curled up, but that was all.

He began to crawl back toward the wheelchair. He was halfway there when Annie opened her eyes.

44

Paul stared, unbelieving, as she got slowly to her knees. Paul himself was propped on his hands, legs trailing out behind him. He looked like a strange adult version of Popeye's nephew, Swee' Pea.

No . . . no, you're dead.

You are in error, Paul. You can't kill the goddess. The goddess is immortal. Now I must rinse.

Her eyes were staring, horrible. A huge wound, pink-red, glared through her hair on the left side of her head. Blood sheeted down her face.

'Durd!' Annie cried through her throatful of paper. She began to crawl toward him, hands outstretched, flexing. *'Ooo durd!'*

Paul pulled himself around in a half-circle and began to crawl for the door. He could hear her behind him. And then, as he entered the zone of broken glass, he felt her hand close around his left ankle and squeeze his stump excruciatingly. He screamed.

'DIRT!' Annie cried triumphantly.

He looked over his shoulder. Her face was turning slowly purple, and seemed to be swelling. He realized she actually was turning into the Bourkas' idol.

He yanked with all his might and his leg slithered footlessly out of her grasp, leaving her with nothing but the circlet of leather with which she had capped the stump.

He crawled on, beginning to cry, sweat pouring down his cheeks. He pulled himself along on his elbows like a soldier advancing beneath heavy machine-gun fire. He heard the thud of first one knee from behind him, then the other, then the first again. She was still coming. She was as solid as he had always feared. He had burned her broken her back stuffed her tubes full of paper and still still still she was coming.

'BIRT!' Annie screamed now. *'DIRT . . . BIRT!'*

One of his elbows came down on a hook of glass and it jabbed up into his arm. He crawled forward anyway with it sticking out of him like a push-pin.

Her hand closed over his left calf.

'AW! GAW . . .OOO OW . . . AW!'

He turned back again and yes, her face had gone black, a dusky rotted-plum black from which her bleeding eyes bulged wildly. Her pulsing throat had swelled up like an inner-tube, and her mouth was writhing. She was, he realized, trying to grin.

The door was just in reach. Paul stretched out and laid hold of the jamb in a death grip.

'GAW. . . OOO . . . OW!'

Her right hand on his right thigh.

Thud. One knee. *Thud.* The other.

Closer. Her shadow. Her shadow falling over him.

'No,' he whimpered. He felt her tugging, pulling. He held onto the jamb grimly, eyes now squeezed shut.

'GAW . . . OOO . . . AW!'

Over him. Thunder. Goddess-thunder.

Now her hands scuttled up his back like spiders and settled upon his neck.

GAW . . . OOO . . . DIRT . . . BIRT!'

His air was gone. He held the jamb. He held the jamb and felt her over him felt her hands sinking into his neck and he screamed *Die can't you die can't you ever die can't you –*

'GAW. . . G –'

The pressure slackened. For a moment he could breathe again. Then Annie collapsed on top of him, a mountain of slack flesh, and he couldn't breathe at all.

45

He worked his way out from under her like a man burrowing his way out of a snowslide. He did it with the last of his strength.

He crawled through the door, expecting her hand to settle around his ankle again at any moment, but that did not happen. Annie lay silent and face-down in blood and spilled champagne and fragments of green glass. Was she dead? She *must* be dead. Paul did not believe she was dead.

He slammed the door shut. The bolt she had put on looked like something halfway up a high cliff, but he clawed his way up to it, shot it, and then collapsed in a shuddery huddle at the door's foot.

He lay in a stupor for some unknown length of time. What roused him from it was a low, minute scratching sound. *The rats,* he thought. *It's the r –*

Then Annie's thick, blood-grimed fingers poked under the door and tugged mindlessly at his shirt.

He shrieked and jerked away from them, his left leg creaking with pain. He hammered at the fingers with his fist. Instead of pulling back, they jerked a little and lay still.

Let that be the end of her. Please God let that be the end of her.

In horrible pain now, Paul began to crawl slowly toward the bathroom. He got halfway there and looked back. Her fingers were still poking out from under the door. As bad as his pain was, he could not stand to look at that, or even think of that, and so he reversed direction, went back, and pushed them under. He had to nerve himself to do it; he was certain that the moment he touched them, they would clutch him.

He finally reached the bathroom, every part of him throbbing. He pulled himself inside and shut the door.

God, what if she's moved the dope?

But she hadn't. The untidy litter of boxes was still there, including the ones containing the sample packets of Novril. He took three dry, then crawled back to the door and lay down against it, blocking it with the weight of his body.

Paul slept.

46

When he woke up it was dark, and at first he didn't know where he was – how had his bedroom gotten so *small?* Then he remembered everything, and with his remembering a queer certainty came: she was not dead, even now not dead. She was standing right outside this door, she had the axe, and when he crawled out she would amputate his head. It would go rolling off down the hallway like a bowling ball while she laughed.

That is crazy, he told himself, and then he heard – or thought he did – a little rustling sound, the sound of a woman's starched skirt, perhaps, brushing lightly against the wall.

You just made it up. Your imagination . . . it's so vivid.

I didn't. I heard *it.*

He *hadn't.* He knew that. His hand reached for the doorknob, then fell uncertainly back. Yes, he knew he had heard nothing . . . but what if he *had?*

She could have gone out the window.

Paul, she's DEAD!

The return, implacable in its illogic: The goddess never dies.

He realized he was frantically biting his lips and made himself stop it. Was this what going crazy was like? Yes. He was close to that, and who had a better right? But if he gave in to it, if the cops finally returned tomorrow or the day after to find Annie dead in the guest-room and a blubbering ball of protoplasm in the downstairs bathroom, a blubbering ball of protoplasm who had once been a writer named Paul Sheldon, wouldn't that be Annie's victory?

You bet. And now, Paulie, you're going to be a good little Do–Bee and follow the scenario. Right?

Okay.

His hand reached for the knob again . . . and faltered again. He *couldn't* follow the original scenario. In it he had seen himself lighting the paper and her picking it up, and that had happened. Only he was to have bashed her *brains* in with the fucking typewriter instead of hitting her in the back with it. Then he had meant to work his way out into the parlor and light the house on fire. The scenario had called for him to effect his escape through one of the parlor windows. He would take a hell of a thump, but he had already seen how fastidious Annie was about locking her doors. Better thumped than crisped, as he believed John the Baptist had once said.

In a book, all would have gone according to plan . . . but life was so fucking untidy – what could you say for an existence where some of the most crucial conversations of your life took place when you needed to take a shit, or something? An existence where there weren't even any *chapters?*

'Very untidy,' Paul croaked. 'Good thing there's guys like me, just to keep things rinsed.' He cackled.

The champagne bottle hadn't been in the scenario, but that was minor compared with the woman's hideous vitality and his current painful uncertainty.

And until he knew whether or not she was dead, he couldn't burn the house down, making a beacon that would bring help on the run. Not because Annie might still be alive; he could roast her alive with no qualms at all.

It wasn't *Annie* that was holding him back; it was the manuscript. The *real* manuscript. What he had burned had been nothing more than an illusion with a title page on top – blank pages interspersed with written rejects and culls. The *actual* manuscript of *Misery's Return* had been safely deposited under the bed, and there it still was.

Unless she's still alive. If she's still alive, maybe she's in there reading it.

So what are you going to do?

Wait right in here, part of him advised. *Right in here, where it's nice and safe.*

But another, braver, part of him urged him to go through with the scenario – as much of it as he could, anyway. Get to the parlor, break the window, get out of this awful house. Work his way to the edge of the road and flag down a car. Under previous circumstances this might have meant waiting for days, but not anymore. Annie's house had become a drawing card.

Summoning all of his courage, he reached for the doorknob and turned it. The door swung slowly open on darkness, and yes, there was Annie, there was the goddess, standing there in the shadows, a white shape in a nurse's uniform –

He blinked his eyes tightly shut and then opened them. Shadows, yes. Annie, no. Except in the newspaper photographs, he had never seen her in her nurse's uniform. Only shadows. Shadows and

(so vivid)

imagination.

He crawled slowly into the hall and looked back down toward the guest-room. It was shut, blank, and he began to crawl toward the parlor.

It was a pit of shadows. Annie could be hidden in any of them; Annie could *be* any of them. And she could have the axe.

He crawled.

There was the overstuffed sofa, and Annie was behind it. There was the kitchen door, standing open, and Annie was behind *that.* The floorboards creaked in back of him . . . of course! Annie was *behind* him!

He turned, heart hammering, brains squeezing at his temples, and Annie was there, all right, the axe upraised, but only for a second. She blew apart into shadows. He crawled into the parlor and that was when he heard the drone of an approaching motor. A faint wash of headlights illuminated the window, brightened. He heard the tires skid in the dirt and understood they had seen the chain she had strung across the driveway.

A car door opened and shut.

'Shit! Look at this!'

He crawled faster, looked out, and saw a silhouette approaching the house. The shape of the silhouette's hat was unmistakable. It was a state cop.

Paul groped on the knick-knack table, knocking figurines over. Some fell to the floor and shattered. His hand`closed around one, and that at least was like a book; it held the roundness novels delivered precisely because life so rarely did.

It was the penguin sitting on his block of ice.

NOW MY TALE IS TOLD! the legend on the block read, and Paul thought: *Yes! Thank God!*

Propped on his left arm, he made his right hand close around the penguin. Blisters broke open, dribbling pus. He drew his arm back and heaved the penguin through the parlor window, just as he had thrown an ashtray through the window of the guest bedroom not so long ago.

'Here!' Paul Sheldon cried deliriously. *'Here, in here, please, I'm in here!'*

47

There was yet another novelistic roundness in this denouement: they were the same two cops who had come the other day to question Annie about Kushner, David and Goliath. Only tonight David's sport-coat was not only unbuttoned, his gun was out. David turned out to be Wicks. Goliath was McKnight. They had come with a search warrant. When they finally broke into the house in answer to the frenzied screams coming from the parlor, they found a man who looked like a nightmare sprung to life.

'There was a book I read when I was in high school,' Wicks told his wife early the next morning. *'Count of Monte Cristo,* I think, or maybe it was *The Prisoner of Zenda.* Anyway, there was a guy in that book who'd spent forty years in solitary confinement. He hadn't seen anybody in forty years. That's what *this* guy looked like.' Wicks paused for a moment, wanting to better express how it had been, the conflicting emotions he had felt – horror and pity and sorrow and disgust – most of all wonder that a man who looked this bad should still be alive. He could not find the words. 'When he saw us, he started to cry,' he said, and finally added: 'He kept calling me David. I don't know why.'

'Maybe you look like somebody he knew,' she said.

'Maybe so.'

48

Paul's skin was gray, his body rack-thin. He huddled by the occasional table, shivering all over, staring at them with rolling eyes.

'Who –' McKnight began.

'Goddess,' the scrawny man on the floor interrupted. He licked his lips. 'You have to watch out for her. Bedroom. That's where she kept me. Pet writer. Bedroom. She's there.'

'Annie Wilkes?' Wicks. 'In that bedroom?' He nodded toward the hall.

'Yes. Yes. Locked in. But of course. There's a window.'

'Who –' McKnight began a second time.

'Christ, can't you see?' Wicks asked. 'It's the guy Kushner was looking for. The writer. I can't remember his name, but it's him.'

'Thank God,' the scrawny man said.

'What?' Wicks bent toward him, frowning.

'Thank God you can't remember my name.'

'I'm not tracking you, buddy.'

'It's all right. Never mind. Just . . . you have to be careful. I think she's dead. But be careful. If she's still alive . . . dangerous . . . like a rattlesnake.' With tremendous effort he moved his twisted left leg directly into the beam of McKnight's flashlight. 'Cut off my foot. Axe.'

They stared at the place where his foot wasn't for long long seconds and then McKnight whispered:

'Good Christ.'

'Come on,' Wicks said. He drew his gun and the two of them started slowly down the hall to Paul's closed bedroom door.

'Watch out for her!' Paul shrieked in his cracked and broken voice. *'Be careful!'*

They unlocked the door and went in. Paul pulled himself against the wall and leaned his head back, eyes closed. He was cold. He couldn't stop shivering. They would scream or she would scream. There might be a scuffle. There might be shots. He tried to prepare his mind for either. Time passed, and it seemed to be a very long time indeed.

At last he heard booted feet coming back down the hall. He opened his eyes. It was Wicks.

'She *was* dead,' Paul said. 'I knew it – the *real* part of my mind did – but I can still hardly be–'

Wicks said: 'There's blood and broken glass and charred paper in there . . . but there's no one in that room at all.'

Paul Sheldon looked at Wicks, and then he began to scream. He was still screaming when he fainted.

PART FOUR

GODDESS

'You will be visited by a tall, dark stranger,' the gipsy woman told Misery, and Misery, startled, realized two things at once: this was no gipsy, and the two of them were no longer alone in the tent. She could smell Gwendolyn Chastain's perfume in the moment before the madwoman's hands closed around her throat.

'In fact,' the gipsy who was not a gipsy observed, 'I think she is here now.'

Misery tried to scream, but could no longer even breathe.

– *Misery's Child*

'It always look dat way, Boss Ian,' Hezekiah said. 'No matter how you look at her, she seem like she be lookin' at you. I doan know if it be true, but the Bourkas, dey say even when you get behin' her, the goddess, she seem to be lookin' at you.'

'But she is, after all, only a piece of stone,' Ian remonstrated.

'Yes, Boss Ian,' Hezekiah agreed. 'Dat what give her her powah.'

– *Misery's Return*

1

umber whunnnn
yernnnn umber whunnnn
fayunnnn
These sounds: even in the haze.

2

Now I must rinse she said, and this is how it rinses out:

3

Nine months after Wicks and McKnight carried him from Annie's house on a makeshift litter, Paul Sheldon was dividing his time between Doctors Hospital in Queens and a new apartment on the East Side of Manhattan. His legs had been re-broken. His left was still in a cast from the knee down. He would walk with a limp for the rest of his life, the doctors told him, but he would walk, and eventually he would walk without pain. His limp would have been deeper and more pronounced if he had been walking on his own foot instead of a custom-made prosthesis. In an ironic sort of way, Annie had done him a favor.

He was drinking too much and not writing at all. His dreams were bad.

When he got out of the elevator on the ninth floor one afternoon in May, he was for a change thinking not of Annie but of the bulky package tucked clumsily under his arm – it contained two bound galleys of *Misery's Return.* His publishers had put the book on a very fast track, and considering the world-wide headlines generated by the bizarre circumstances under which the novel had been written, that was hardly surprising. Hastings House had ordered an unprecedented first printing of a million copies. 'And that's only the beginning,' Charlie Merrill, his editor, had told him at lunch that day – the lunch from which Paul was now returning with his bound galleys. 'This book is going to outsell everything in the world, my friend. We all just ought to be down on our knees thanking God that the story *in* the book is almost as good as the story *behind* the book.'

Paul didn't know if that was true, and didn't really care anymore. He only wanted to get it behind him and find the *next* book . . . but as dry days became dry weeks became dry months, he had begun to wonder if there ever *would* be a next book.

Charlie was begging him for a nonfiction account of his ordeal. That book, he said, would outsell even *Misery's Return.* Would, in fact, outsell *Iacocca.* When Paul asked him, out of idle curiosity, what he thought the paperback rights for such a book might fetch, Charlie brushed his long hair away from his forehead, lit a Camel, and said: 'I believe we could set a floor at ten million dollars and then conduct one *hell* of an auction.' He did not bat an eye when he said it; after a moment or two Paul realized he either was serious or thought he was.

But there was no way he could write such a book, not yet, probably not ever. His job was writing novels. He *could* write the account Charlie wanted, but to do so would be tantamount to admitting to himself that he would never write another novel.

And the joke is, it would be a novel, he almost said to Charlie Merrill . . . and then held back at the last moment. The joke was, Charlie wouldn't care.

It would start out as fact, and then I'd begin to tart it up . . . just a little at first . . . then a little more . . . then a little more. Not to make myself look better (although I probably would) and not to make Annie look worse (she couldn't). Simply to create that roundness. I don't want to fictionalize myself. Writing may be masturbatory, but God forbid it should be an act of autocannibalism.

His apartment was 9-E, farthest from the elevator, and today the corridor looked two miles long. He began to stump his way grimly down to it, a t-shaped walking-stick in each hand. *Clack . . . clack . . . clack . . . clack.* God, he hated that sound.

His legs ached sickeningly and he yearned for Novril. Sometimes he thought it would be worth being back with Annie just to have the dope. The doctors had weaned him from it. The booze was his substitute, and when he got inside he was going to have a double bourbon.

Then he would look at the blank screen of his word processor for awhile. What fun. Paul Sheldon's fifteen thousand-dollar paperweight.

Clack . . . clack . . . clack . . . clack.

Now to get the key out of his pocket without dropping either the manila envelope containing the bound galleys or the sticks. He propped the sticks against the wall. While he was doing that, the galleys dropped out from under his arm and fell to the rug. The envelope split open.

'Shit!' he growled, and then the sticks fell over with a clatter, adding to the fun.

Paul closed his eyes, swaying unsteadily on his twisted, aching legs, waiting to see if he was going to get mad or cry. He hoped he would get mad. He didn't want to cry out here in the hall, but he might. He had. His legs hurt all the time and he wanted his dope, not the heavy-duty aspirin they gave him at the hospital dispensary. He wanted his *good* dope, his Annie-dope. And oh he was so tired all the time. What he needed to prop him up were not those shitty sticks but his make-believe games and stories. They were the good dope, the never-fail fix, but they had all fled. It seemed playtime was finally over.

This is what it's like after the end, he thought, opening the door and tottering into the apartment. *This is why no one ever writes it. It's too fucking dreary. She should have died after I stuffed her head full of blank paper and busted pages, and I should have died then, too. At that moment if at no other we really were like characters in one of Annie's chapter-plays – no grays, only blacks and whites, good and bad. I was Geoffrey and she was the Bourka Bee-Goddess. This . . . well, I've heard of denouement, but this is ridiculous. Never mind the mess back there on the floor. Drinky-poo first, pick-uppy-poo second. First be a Don't-Be and then be a –*

He stopped. He had time to realize the apartment was too dark. And there was a smell. He knew that smell, a deadly mixture of dirt and face-powder.

Annie rose up from behind the sofa like a white ghost, dressed in a nurse's uniform and cap. The axe was in her hand and she was screaming: *Time to rinse, Paul! Time to rinse!*

He shrieked, tried to turn on his bad legs. She leaped the sofa with clumsy strength, looking like an albino frog. Her starched uniform rustled briskly. The first sweep of the axe did no more than knock the wind from him – this was really what he thought until he landed on the carpet smelling his own blood. He looked down and saw he was cut nearly in half.

'Rinse!' she shrieked, and there went his right hand.

'Rinse!' she shrieked again, and his left was gone; he crawled toward the open door on the jetting stumps of his wrists, and incredibly the galleys

were still there, the bound galleys Charlie had given him at lunch in Mr Lee's, sliding the manila envelope to him across gleaming white napery while Muzak drifted down from overhead speakers.

'Annie you can read it now!' he tried to scream, but only got out *Annie you* before his head flew off and rolled to the wall. His last dimming glimpse of the world was his own collapsing body and Annie's white shoes standing astride it:

Goddess, he thought, and died.

4

Scenario: An outline or synopsis. A plot outline.
– *Webster's New Collegiate*
Writer: One who writes, esp. as an occupation.
– *Webster's New Collegiate*
Make-believe: Pretense or pretend.
– *Webster's New Collegiate*

5

Paulie, Can You?

6

Yes; of course he could. 'The *writer's scenario* was that Annie was still alive, although he understood this was only *make-believe.*'

7

He really did go to lunch with Charlie Merrill. All the conversation was the same. Only when he let himself into his apartment he knew it was the cleaning woman who had pulled the drapes, and although he fell down and had to smother a scream of fright when Annie rose up like Cain from behind the sofa, it was just the cat, a cross-eyed Siamese named Dumpster he had gotten last month at the pound.

There was no Annie because Annie had not been a goddess at all, only a crazy lady who had hurt Paul for reasons of her own. Annie had managed to pull most of the paper out of her mouth and throat and had gotten out through Paul's window while Paul was sleeping the sleep of drugs. She had gotten to the barn and had collapsed there. She was dead when Wicks and McKnight found her, but not of strangulation. She had actually died of the fractured skull she had received when she struck the mantel, and she had struck the mantel because she had tripped. So in a way she had been killed by the very typewriter Paul had hated so much.

But she'd had plans for him, all right. Not even the axe would suffice this time.

They had found her outside of Misery the pig's stall, with one hand wrapped around the handle of her chainsaw.

That was all in the past, though. Annie Wilkes was in her grave. But like Misery Chastain, she rested there uneasily. In his dreams and waking fantasies, he dug her up again and again. You couldn't kill the goddess. Temporarily dope her with bourbon, maybe, but that was all.

He went to the bar, looked at the bottle, then looked back at where his galleys and walking sticks lay. He gave the bottle a goodbye look and worked his way back to his stuff.

8

Rinse.

9

Half an hour later he was sitting in front of the blank screen, thinking he had to be a glutton for punishment. He had taken the aspirin instead of the drink, but that didn't change what was going to happen now; he was going to sit here for fifteen minutes or maybe half an hour, looking at nothing but a cursor flashing in darkness; then he was going to turn the machine off and have that drink.

Except . . .

Except he had seen something funny on the way home from lunch with Charlie, and it had given him an idea. Not a big one. Just a small one. After all, it had only been a small incident. Just a kid pushing a shopping cart up 48th Street, that was all, but there had been a cage in the cart, and in it had been a rather large furry animal which Paul at first thought was a cat. A closer look had shown him a wide white stripe up the cat's back.

'Sonny,' he said, 'is that a skunk?'

'Yeah,' the kid said, and pushed the shopping cart along a little faster. You didn't stop for long conversations with people in the city, especially weird-looking guys with bags the size of Samsonite two-suiters under their eyes who were lurching along on metal walking-sticks. The kid turned the corner and was gone.

Paul went on, wanting to take a cab, but he was supposed to walk at least a mile every day and this was his mile and it hurt like hell and to take his mind off the mile he started wondering where that kid had come from, where the shopping cart had come from, and most of all where the skunk had come from.

He heard a noise behind him and turned from the blank screen to see Annie coming out of the kitchen dressed in jeans and a red flannel logger's shirt, the chainsaw in her hands.

He closed his eyes, opened them, saw the same old nothing, and was suddenly angry. He turned back to the word processor and wrote fast, almost bludgeoning the keys:

-1-

The kid heard a sound in the back of the building and although the thought of rats crossed his mind, he turned the corner anyway--it was too early to go home because school didn't let out for another hour and a half and he had gone truant at lunch.

What he saw crouched back against the wall in a dusty shaft of sunlight was not a rat but a great big black cat with the bushiest tail he had ever seen.

10

He stopped, heart suddenly pounding.

Paulie, Can You?

This was a question which he did not dare answer. He bent over the keyboard again, and after a moment began to hit the keys . . . but more gently now.

11

It wasn't a cat. Eddie Desmond had lived in New York City all his life, but he had been to the Bronx Zoo, and Christ, there were picture-books, weren't there? He knew what that thing was, although he hadn't the slightest idea how such a thing could have gotten into this deserted East 105th Street tenement, but the long white stripe down its back was a dead give-away. It was a skunk.

Eddie started slowly toward it, feet gritting in the plaster dust

12

He could. He *could.*

So, in gratitude and in terror, he *did.* The hole opened and Paul stared through at what was there, unaware that his fingers were picking up speed, unaware that his aching legs were in the same city but fifty blocks away, unaware that he was weeping as he wrote.

Lovell, Maine: September 23rd 1984 / Bangor, Maine: October 7th 1986: *Now my tale is told.*